SCIONS OF THE BLACK LOTUS

THE COMPLETE TALES OF THE FLOATING WORLD

JC Kang

To Fans of Tian and Jie.

CONTENTS

MAPS

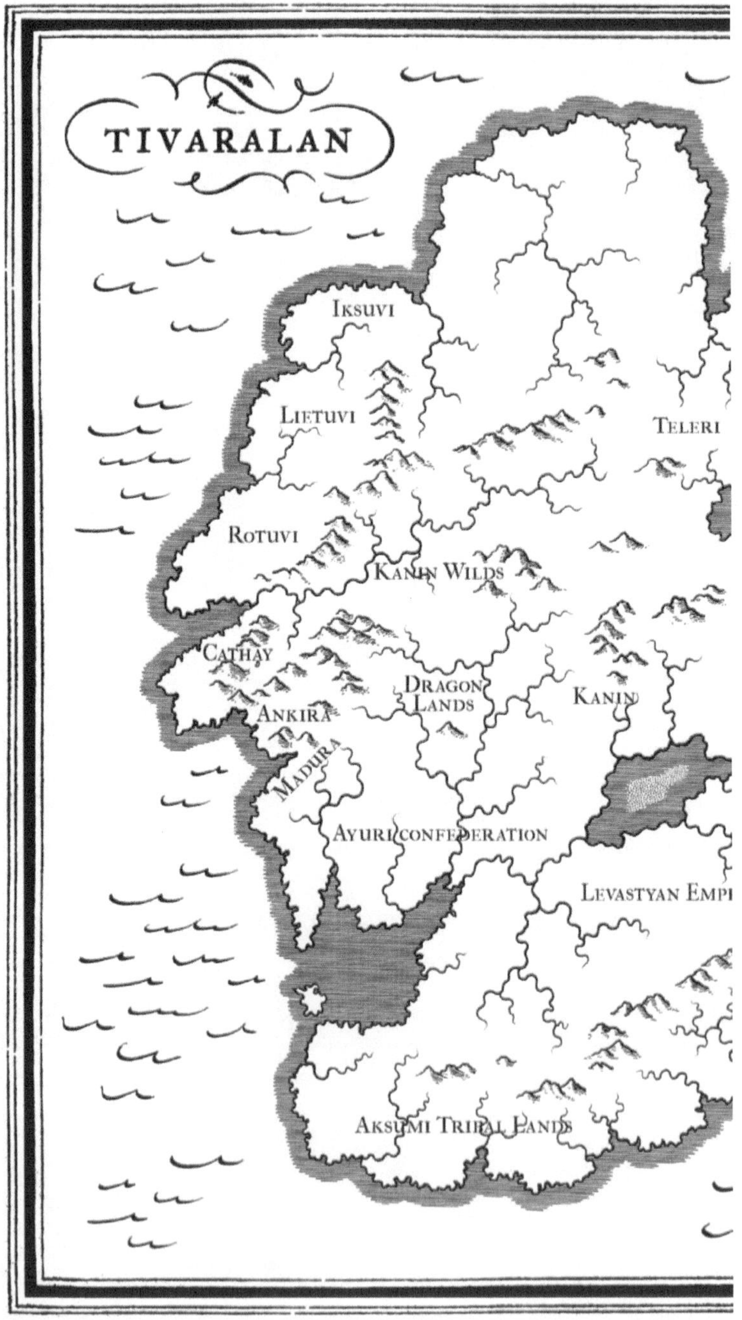
TIVARALAN
Iksuvi
Lietuvi
Teleri
Rotuvi
Kanin Wilds
Cathay
Dragon Lands
Kanin
Ankira
Madura
Ayuri Confederation
Levastyan Empi
Aksumi Tribal Lands

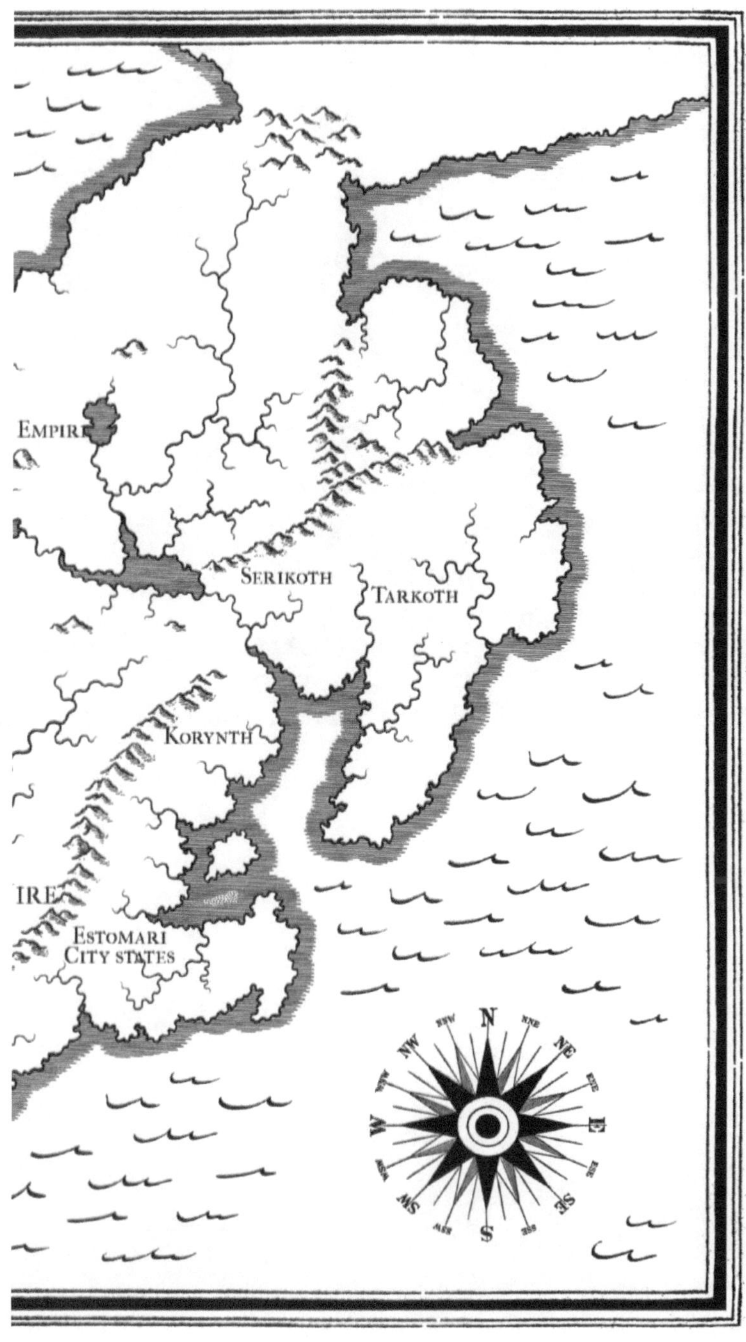
Serikoth
Tarkoth
Korynth
Estomari
City States
N
NE
E
SE
S
SW
W
NW

Cathay

Cloud Castle
Dongmen
Rotuvi
Honggang
Huajing
Jiangkou
Linshan
Zhenjing
Jiangzhou
Cathay
(Hua)
Fenggu
Ximen
Nanling
Yutou
Ankira
Madura

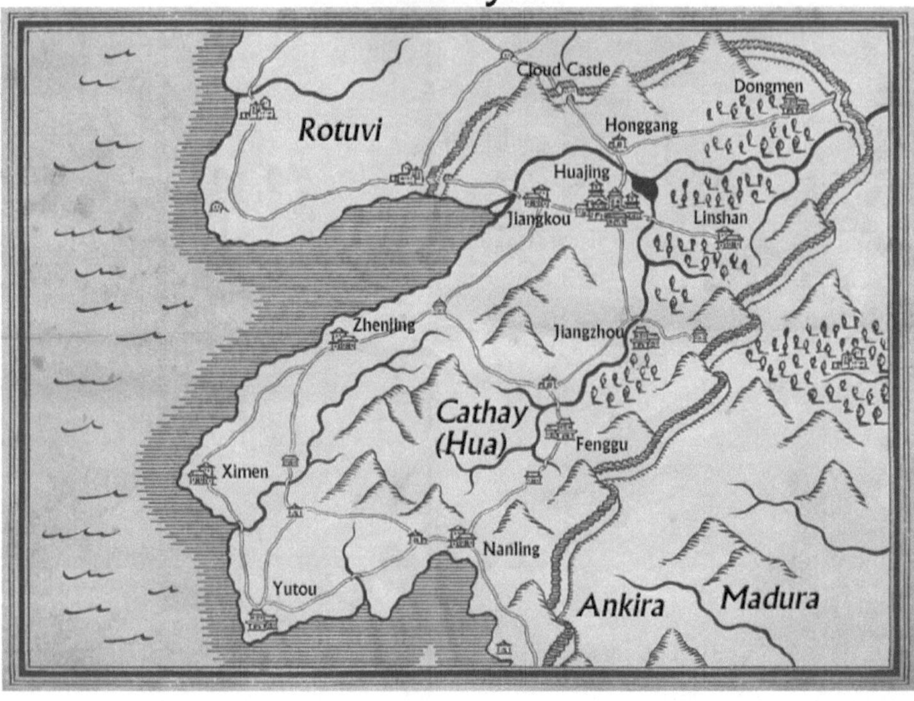

The Capital

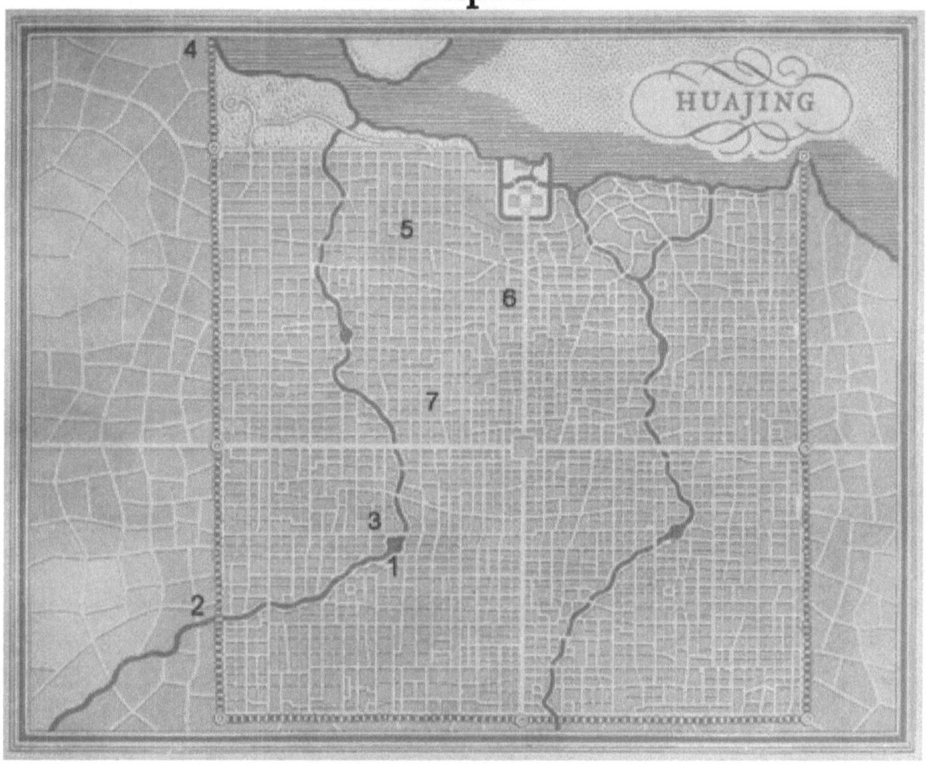

1. THE FLOATING WORLD
2. THE TRENCH
3. THE PROMENADE
4. SONGYUAN QUAYS.
5. LORD SHI'S HOUSE
6. YUSHAN JADE MARKET
7. CLOTHIERS DISTRICT

PRELUDE TO THORN OF THE NIGHT BLOSSOMS

When stealing keys from a traitor's robes, Jie found that distractions usually worked best.

Tonight, she was the distraction.

Well, she and Lilian, who lounged beside her on a Dragoncarved chaise.

After all, males were predictable: even in a spacious gallery filled with legendary works of magic-evoking art, Jie could count on drunken noblemen paying more attention to a pair of kissing courtesans.

Whatever she and Lilian normally did behind closed doors would bore a man, so they'd scripted this blatant display to titillate a male's taste.

Or lack thereof.

Lilian's lilac gown, an imitation of imperial court fashion, emphasized the curve of her neck and collarbones as she leaned in. Her honeysuckle scent intoxicating, she brushed soft lips from the tip of Jie's tapered ear, down her jawline.

Apparently, Jie was just as gullible as a man. The *Fluttering Butterfly* technique, meant to arouse anticipation with unpredictability, sent shudders up and down her spine. They'd have to try this again, in private.

Now though, Jie had to focus on the task at hand. She forced her eyes open, just in time to catch their clan sister's signal: Wen had lifted the moonstone key from their wealthy host's sash.

Lost in her exultation, Jie had almost missed it. Some cell leader she was, failing to execute her own scheme because she was enjoying herself. With a finger, she traced clan code across Lilian's nape. *Key retrieved, passed off.*

Lilian's lips lingered on Jie's neck before she pulled back, her gaze heavy and longing. They'd been best friends for most of their lives. Something more, yet unacknowledged, had blossomed between them in the past half year.

Heart squeezing, Jie felt like a snake beguiled by a foreign snake charmer. Perhaps this was how the Last Dragon, Avarax, had felt when he was sung to sleep with a Dragon Song.

"The only thing that could've made my chaise look better was the two of you on it." Mister Guan clapped, his gold rings clinking together. Careless whispers between the Floating World sheets suggested the wealthy merchant's involvement in a plot against the Emperor, and that the answers were tied to missing Dragon Arts.

Jie shifted her attention to the five other slobbering men surrounding them. There might be enough drool between them to relieve the drought in the central valley. They, like Guan, showed no sign of having witnessed Wen's sleight of hand.

Despite Jie's own near-misstep, the plan was on schedule. Next she had to extricate herself from the semi-circle and acquire the vault key. She tapped on Lilian's arm. *Now.*

Lilian let her outer gown slip off her shoulders and into the crooks of her elbows as she rose and bowed. "It's a beautiful collection, Mister Guan."

"I would like to add you to it." With Guan's eyes joining the others on Lilian's cleavage, it was the perfect time for Jie to escape.

Burying her disgust, Jie used Lilian as a screen and slipped out of the semi-circle. Her dark, modest dress, suited for a courtesan-in-training, allowed ease of movement and would help her blend into shadows. Its high collar mostly hid the mark Lilian's mouth had just left on her neck, even if she could still feel its echo. She'd have to cover it with concealer soon, lest one of these rakes think her fair game.

Of course, every lord and wealthy merchant who ever visited the Floating World had heard of her: the Chrysanthemum Pavilion's exotic half-elf, with a record bid on her virginity. Still, if one of these men didn't know any better, she'd have to stage an accident leading to a broken finger or three.

Cologne hung heavy in the air. The clashing mix of citrus, wood, spice, musk, and desperation made her head spin. Magic emanated from hanging scrolls, furnishings, and sculptures, but the clan had trained her to resist the enchantment bound in their intricate patterns.

She picked her way across the wood floors, keeping to men's backs as they squabbled over courtesans. Each of the Floating World's twelve great Houses had sent three full-fledged Blossoms, as well as a Floret like Jie. Ostensibly there for record-keeping, the latter were off limits, but would attract bids for their Plucking.

Jie, of course, was also here at the behest of the Emperor. Out of the forty-eight girls present, she located the six secret Black Lotus Clan sisters under her command.

Yangyang now had the key. She was sitting on a lord's lap, giggling at his bad joke, and slipped the round stone into Jie's palm as she passed.

Her fingers closed around the smooth edges. With her other hand covering Lilian's brand on her neck, she continued toward the atrium. Just a few more steps—

A large form stepped into her path. She looked up.

Unlike the lords and merchants in their colorful silk robes, this guest wore a black satin shirt with gold-embroidered cuffs and collar, and matching black pants with gold trim. Gold rings with squiggly engravings glittered on his fingers. Instead of silk slippers, he wore black leather boots. The dashing outfit suited the man himself, with his curly brown hair and large, light-blue eyes. His bow emphasized his foreignness, with one hand on his stomach and another extended to the side.

She squirrelled the moonstone into her sash as she set both hands in front of her and bowed low, the deliberate motion lacking the feminine grace expected of even a first-year Seedling in the Floating World. In the corner of her eye, she checked the time, glancing through the atrium windows. The Iridescent Moon hung in its permanent location in the sky, not far from the rising elliptic Blue and smaller White Moons. With it now waxing halfway to its third gibbous, she only had a quarter phase to cross the villa grounds and find the vault.

He set two fingers under her chin and drew her head up. His leer took her in. As a foreigner, he wouldn't know who she was, nor that it was forbidden to touch a Floret. When he spoke, his thick accent flowed like honey—not smooth and sweet, but as if it gummed up his mouth and he struggled to get the words out. "You are an exotic little whore."

Whore? He clearly didn't understand the difference between a common streetwalker and an esteemed Blossom of the

Floating World. Swallowing her irritation, she stepped back and dipped her chin. "Thank you, my Lord."

He followed, boxing her against the archway between the gallery and atrium. While his earthy cologne might've smothered his fermented milky smell to a human nose, Jie's wrinkled at the stench. That, combined with his looming body, overwhelmed her senses.

Perhaps not all of her fear was feigned as she planned to stage an accident. The way he leaned into the wall with his arm, the pressure point just past his elbow was exposed. She—

"My Lord." Lilian appeared at Jie's side, bowing with the grace of a weeping willow. "My Little Sister is only here to enjoy Mister Guan's beautiful collection."

Oh, how elegantly she moved! A mix of envy and appreciation coursed through Jie.

"Please forgive my foreign guest, Miss Jie." Guan shuffled over and claimed Lilian by resting a hand on her hip. "Master Adrian has an eye for beauty, but knows nothing of our customs."

Adrian withdrew and bowed again. "My humblest apologies, Miss Jyeh."

Though he mangled her name with his accent, Jie bobbed her head in acknowledgment. With time running out, she started to bid farewell.

"Since you are here," Guan continued, "allow me to introduce you. Master Adrian is a fellow art aficionado, hailing from Lykos."

"At your service," Adrian said, coming out of his outlandish bow.

"Lykos?" Lilian asked. "You have come a long way."

Jie nodded. Famed for its pikemen, Lykos was a free city in the faraway Sundered Empire. It wouldn't have been an easy trip.

"What can I say? I love beautiful things, and will go to great lengths to obtain them." Adrian gaze lingered on Jie for a moment before he gestured back toward the gallery. "I must thank my cousin for inviting me."

Cousin? The two men looked nothing alike. There was just enough time to satisfy Jie's curiosity. "If I may ask, how are you related?"

"Very distant cousins." All of Guan's straight, white teeth gleamed. "We are both descendants of the Last Imperator of Arkos."

Jie studied them. The Last Imperator was one of the greatest Runemasters who'd ever lived, reigning over the largest empire in history. After the Hellstorm shattered the world three centuries ago, the people rose up against the Runemasters, killing most and destroying all texts on their magic. With the imperator's blood in Adrian's veins, he might've been able to inscribe runes and evoke their magic, had all knowledge of the art not perished along with the Runemasters.

Guan, on the other hand, must've been harboring delusions. Historical records never mentioned the imperator ever coming this far southwest, and their host didn't look to have a drop of foreign blood in him.

"You're wondering how that could be." Guan's grin widened even more. "My ancestor was an ambassador to Arkos, and he married one of the imperator's grandnieces."

So, not a direct descendant. Jie suppressed a snort.

"As for me... Well, the imperator had a large harem." Adrian's eyes roved over her and Lilian. "How I envy him."

Jie wasn't sure how many baths she'd need to take to wash away the stains his leer left. She edged closer to Lilian, as if that would provide any protection from his hungry eyes.

Guan waved a dismissive hand. "In any case, Master Adrian came to our country a couple of months ago to have a work of Dragon Art appraised."

"How did he acquire it?" Lilian asked. "The imperial court is protective of our people's magic and hasn't allowed the export of Dragon Arts since the Hellstorm."

"This is sadly true." Adrian laughed, a grating sound reminiscent of a donkey's bray. "However, I am fortunate to own a war banner gifted by the last Yu Dynasty Emperor to the Last Imperator, before the Hellstorm."

Guan nodded. "It's emblazoned with a word by a renowned Dragonscribe. It evokes courage in its viewers."

Jie sucked on her lower lip. Something didn't sit right here. The Arkothi armies had used armor, weapons, and banners inscribed by their runemasters, which would bestow preternatural abilities on them. So why would they need Dragonscript on a banner, which would affect anyone who could see it, friend and foe alike?

Adrian clapped Guan on the back. "And since I was here, Mister Guan invited me to study your people's magic up close. What you see in the gallery is only a fraction of his magnificent collection."

Jie and Lilian exchanged subtle glances, no doubt thinking the same thing: maybe Adrian was using his visit to steal imperial arts.

Time, Lilian signed. *I'll distract them.*

She was right. Based on the phase of the Iridescent Moon, they only had another nine and a half minutes to reach the vault and unlock it. A clan sister was supposed to create a diversion for Lilian to slip away, but a glance into the gallery revealed they were otherwise engaged. If they missed this window of opportunity now, they'd have to wait until the same time tomorrow night, when they wouldn't have an excuse to be here.

"Oh!" Lilian placed a hand to her chest as one of her dull, non-lethal hairpins clattered to the floor. Even her gasp was adorable.

When both men bent over to retrieve it, Jie started toward the door.

"Oh, no!" Guan straightened, patting his sash where his moonstone should've been.

Shit. A betting half-elf would put money on Guan now sending several men to watch over the vault. That would make it even harder to sneak in. Time to improvise.

Lilian flashed a knowing glance before saying, "What's wrong?"

"I...I seem to be missing something."

Not having gone far, Jie knelt down and held up the moonstone. "It this what you're looking for? It just slipped from your robes and rolled over here."

His eyes locked on it, and relief washed over his expression. "Thank the Heavens." He reached over and plucked it from her palm.

"It's a moonstone key, isn't it?" Lilian asked. It was as if she'd read Jie's mind and was playing along.

Guan's eyes narrowed. "How would you know?"

Jie leaned in conspiratorially, and lied. "There's one for the Chrysanthemum Pavilion's safe, which can only be opened at noon."

His head rose and fell in slow nods.

"Oh, let me guess, you have more Dragon Art!" Clutching Guan's arm and pressing herself against him, Lilian squealed.

Jie's jaw clenched. It was just an act, she reminded herself. Wealthy men liked vapid girls. This wasn't really Lilian, just a necessary improvisation.

And it was working. If Guan's grin were any more wolfish, he'd have fleas. "Yes, and the moonstone will only open the safe for another few minutes. Would you like to see?"

Hook, line, and sinker. Lilian nodded with the enthusiasm of a seal. Perhaps not all of it was contrived, since this was even easier than the original plan. Though if Guan was inviting them to see his secret collection, the stolen works might not be there. Or perhaps he didn't think a Floating World Blossom would recognize them as imperial commissions, let alone know that they'd been pilfered. The theft wasn't common knowledge, after all.

Of course, it was highly probably his carnal urges were clouding his better judgement. It certainly wouldn't be the first or last time a man would do something stupid over a woman.

Now, it was time to see if Adrian just as lusty as Guan. After all, having two men in the vault would make it harder to search. Jie channeled her inner Lilian and batted her eyelashes at him. She gestured back toward the gallery. "I have yet to see all of the works displayed in the gallery. Would you show me your favorite piece?"

Adrian's leer broadened. "Come along, then."

"Please, take your time." Guan beckoned to his chamberlain. "See to it that all our guests find quarters in the pavilions tonight."

Toxin, Jie signed, slipping a glass vial out of a secret pocket on the inside of her sleeve. A mixture of herbs and *yinghua* flowers, the contact poison would make a male euphoric, pliant, and forgetful. Its effect had made many a rebellious lord forget spilling secrets during an epic night in the Floating World.

With a subtle acknowledgement, Lilian retrieved it as she clasped both of Jie's hands. "Be careful, Little Sister."

Taking his leave, Guan guided Lilian out into the courtyard.

Adrian reached for Jie's hand.

With no intention of actually exploring the gallery with the foreign lecher, she took a step back out of reach and bowed. "Please, lead the way."

Brow furrowed for a moment, he turned and headed back into the gallery.

Instead of following him, Jie used a *Ghost Echo* to throw her voice, to make it seem as if she was just a step behind. "These are my favorites," she said as he walked by a pair of hanging silk brocades.

He gestured straight ahead. "I am particularly intrigued by the calligraphy."

She turned and darted out the door. Chill air greeted her, sending her skin erupting into goosebumps. Up ahead, Lilian must've been even colder in her lighter dress.

Jie trailed after them, darting from trees boasting fall foliage to hedges with bright red berries, pausing by stone sculptures and in the shadows of white-stoned, green-tiled pavilions. They hadn't found the vault on the way in, though it would undoubtedly be a south-facing entrance for the moonstone to work.

A quick look at the Iridescent Moon indicated they only had four minutes left. Thankfully, Guan kept a brisk pace, slowed only by his palm on the inside of Lilian's inner gown, resting on her hip.

Jealousy twisted in Jie's gut. Though her own hands had spent plenty of time exploring Lilian's bare skin as a part of courtesan training, something had felt different in the past several months. Kissing practice would escalate to non-classical techniques with zero utility for a male client. In the aftermath, Jie didn't dare broach the subject for fear of ruining their lifelong friendship. Whenever she hinted at her growing affection, Lilian would always make a coy deflection.

Jie shook the thoughts out of her head to focus on the mission at hand. With only a few moments to spare, they rounded a corner into a smaller courtyard. The far building had a round steel door with an indentation the size of the moonstone key. Surprisingly, there were no guards. Had Jie been the one to implement security protocols, she would've assigned at least one person to watch over the vault during the hour it could be opened.

Maybe the moonstone lock had made Guan complacent. Jie closed the distance and stood right behind him in a technique a four-year-old clan initiate could execute. She peeked around him.

As with every dwarf-made vault, the rivets and seams between the door's metal plates blended into a single surface. It was simple, as far as dwarf security devices went; some also had combination locks and special keys made from rare metals.

He set the moonstone into the niche, then backed away. Jie took a quick step so he wouldn't run into her. When his shadow moved out of the way, the Iridescent Moon's light hit the moonstone.

A hiss emanated from the door as it opened on silent gears.

"After you, my lady." Guan extended his hand toward the portal. His other cupped Lilian's rear as he prodded her in, and she manufactured a convincing giggle.

Jie trailed him in, so close they were almost touching. She avoided making contact as he reached back and flipped a lever that caused the door to close.

A shuttered lamp shed a dim light over the eight wall shelves, filled with porcelains, rolled-up scrolls, wood carvings, jade sculptures, and more. In the middle were crates and Dragoncarved furniture.

"I have one of the largest collections of Dragon Arts in the realm, second only to the imperial family." Guan opened the lamp shutters, allowing the bright magical light to fill the room. For Jie, that meant altering her position so that her own shadow stayed within his.

"I've visited Sun-Moon Palace," Lilian said. "Do you have anything similar here?"

The circumstances of that visit knotted Jie's stomach, but she buried the memory and instead focused on Lilian's subtle probing.

"Only one." He led Lilian to a shelf and withdrew a vermillion silk bundle entitled *Cloud Rain*, a euphemism for relations between man and woman. "We're forbidden from owning genuine imperial arts, but this is a collection of erotic woodblock prints by Gao Liang. The Emperor gifted the original set to the Empress for their wedding." He unwound the braided cords and opened it to the first print.

Glimmering in vibrant colors, a man and woman were locked in an embrace with lifelike radiance. Their mutual affection spilled off the page. Of course, every House in the Floating World had similar works, and through both frequent viewing and clan training in resisting Dragon Arts, Jie barely felt the magic. It would arouse lust in the average person, however.

The way Guan looked sidelong at Lilian, he'd expected that effect. And indeed, Lilian claimed his lips. Clawing at his back, she backed him toward an embroidered cushioned chaise matching the one in the gallery. He worked her outer gown off, baring her shoulders.

Standing at his back, Jie was forced to retreat with him. She gritted her teeth. Lilian had never been as proficient in clan arts, and had succumbed to the Dragon Magic. If she—

Lilian flashed hand signals behind Guan's back. *Loop west. Search.*

Jie held in her sigh of relief. She looped west as Lilian turned Guan to his left and brought him down on her on the chaise.

The sound of cracking glass and the diffuse scent of *yinghua* flowers filled the air as the toxin vial shattered beneath Lilian. It would leak into her gown, and she'd only have a minute to guide his bare skin to that spot before it went inert.

In the meantime, with Guan's back to Jie, she had some time to search. If only they'd quiet down with their heavy breathing! It might only be an act on Lilian's part, but that didn't mean Jie had to like it. Forcing herself to focus on the mission, she made a quick scan of the shelf from which he'd pulled the prints.

Nothing resembled the stolen works commissioned by the Emperor. She sniffed around the shelves where Guan's natural woody scent was strongest, and therefore the most recent. There was just enough dust to suggest he hadn't come here in four to five days. With the robbery having occurred three days ago, these weren't them. Just to be sure, she used dexterous fingers to quietly unravel a scroll.

It wasn't one of the stolen works of Dragon Art.

Which left the crates.

From where Guan straddled Lilian on the chaise, back to Jie and hands roving who-knew-where, the boxes stood in his line of sight.

Jie sucked on her lower lip. The chances of the toxin working had fallen lower than Guan's trousers. From what she could see past Guan's form, it appeared as if Lilian was still mostly clothed for now. It wouldn't be long before he took it further.

Edging over to meet Lilian's gaze, Jie pointed behind the chaise. *The crates*, she mouthed.

Lilian hid a quick nod as she threw her head back in response to Guan's fondling. Only a man, secure in his own prowess, would believe such a contrived reaction. Gesturing Jie down and to the west, she hooked one of his legs with her heel, bucked her hips to the side, and rolled him over so that she now mounted him.

"Oh!" he gasped.

The flawless execution of Black Lotus grappling technique stirred Jie's heart even more than the magic woodblock prints.

And now, Lilian was blocking Guan's view. She glanced over her shoulder and winked. *Get back to work*, she mouthed.

Picking her jaw off the floor, Jie kept low and crept over to the crates on the other side of the chaise, where only Lilian could see her. A sour smell lingered amidst the scent of freshly-milled wood. She eased the top off one and looked.

Packed in rice paper, porcelain dishes with Dragonscribed blue dragons evoked a sense of joy. The five claws on each of their four feet indicated they were from the imperial kiln. She worked one out and held it up.

Lilian gave a subtle nod.

So Guan was the culprit. Forcing herself to ignore his hands on Lilian, Jie returned the dish to the crate and set the top back on. Another box contained Dragonwoven embroidery, also wrapped in rice paper. The scent was different with the third crate, sweet like rice, with traces of sourness.

Empty, save for fresh broken rice. Jie scooped some up on a finger.

Desiccant, Lilian mouthed.

If Guan wanted to keep the contents dry, the box had likely held the missing calligraphy and paintings. Jie sniffed the area again.

The sourness. It was stronger than Guan's smell around the box. She signed, *Adrian was here. Let's get out.*

It took no words between them. As Jie drew closer, Lilian brought her chest into Guan's face. She rose higher, leading his head high above the back of the chaise.

Jie crossed her arms around his now-exposed neck and squeezed. Lilian sunk her weight into him, burying his brief struggle.

Jie almost felt bad for him, but what lecher would mind passing out with his face in a beautiful woman's ample bosom? And he was a conspirator in stealing imperial art. They only had a few moments before he came to.

"These aren't the original crates." Lilian jumped up and retrieved her outer gown. "They'd use eldarwood, and it would be branded with the imperial sigil."

Jie unwound Guan's embroidered sash, catching the moonstone before it hit the floor. She modulated her voice using the clan's *Mockingbird's Deception* to imitate Adrian. "They must've transferred them to these crates, possibly as a shipment to Lykos."

"The accent is right, but your pitch is a little too low." Not needing to be told the plan, Lilian untied her own sash and blindfolded him. "Wouldn't the customs officials check them first?"

"A large enough bribe would get them to look the other way." Jie snorted.

Lilian gave a thumbs-up. "Perfect imitation of his voice."

Together, they pushed the chaise so that Guan's back was to the door, then came up behind him.

Jie patted him on the cheek and imitated Adrian's voice. "Wake up, sleepy head."

Groaning, he pulled at the bindings.

"Help!" Lilian whimpered, knowing Jie's plan without needing to ask. "Adrian tied me up."

Struggling against his sash, Guan craned his neck east, then west. "What...what happened?"

"I poured a mild toxin into your rice wine," Jie said in Adrian's voice.

"Why? What about our plan?"

What plan? Jie exchanged glances with Lilian. "What about it?"

"*The* plan." Guan tilted his head toward Lilian.

So he wasn't going to reveal more with Lilian in the room. Jie said, "I want more than just the art we stole from the Emperor. I want your entire collection."

"You bastard!" He jerked at his bonds again.

Jie imitated Adrian's annoying laugh. "You have to find me first."

"You think you can leave my villa without me allowing it?! I'll catch you, and nobody will care what happens to some foreigner."

"Only if you can find a way to untie yourself. Now, I shall take my leave. I'll take this pretty courtesan, too."

With Guan cursing every god under the sun, Lilian sobbed, even as she flipped the lever to the door. It slid open. Once they were out, Jie set the moonstone into the niche. If it worked like most of these vaults...

The door slid shut, cutting off Guan's voice. The Blue and White Moons had risen higher, and the Iridescent Moon now waxed past its third gibbous, indicating half an hour had passed.

"So Adrian is in this villa somewhere," Lilian said. "Can you track him? Of course you can." With an alluring smile, she tapped Jie's nose.

"Not if you overwhelm my poor nose." Jie pouted. "I know where that finger has been."

Batting her eyelashes, Lilian sucked on the finger.

Jie chuckled. Sniffing the night air, she kept to the shadows, Lilian a few steps behind as they headed back toward the gallery building. They paused at times to let a servant or an intoxicated lord with a Blossom on his arm pass by. Soon, though, Adrian's scent of earth mixed with sour milk grew stronger.

She followed it until they arrived at a pavilion deep inside the compound. Though made of white stone with steep, green-tiled eaves like the rest of the buildings in the villa, something about it felt off.

It was aesthetically imbalanced.

To the east of the main entrance, lights spilled through the decorative script carved into the first-floor window shutters. As they crept over, the smell of freshly milled and stained wood grew stronger. Dark flecks marred the shutters' finish.

They peered through. With bookshelves lining the wall, it looked to be a study. Adrian leaned over a long table, gold-handled brush sweeping over an unfurled scroll of calligraphy. Several more, rolled and unrolled, lay at the side, along with writing instruments made of bone, ivory, and precious metal. Could he even read a script so different from his native alphabet?

Imperial markings, Lilian traced code on Jie's back.

Jie nodded. Here were the missing scrolls. Guan had mentioned a plan he and Adrian were collaborating on. But... *Why is he defacing the art?*

Look at the way he's standing. Lilian pointed at his legs, visible beneath the table.

His knees were bent. Feet now bare, his toes curled, digging into the tiled floor.

Jie held in a gasp. It was just like... *Dragon Artists. They hold that stance to connect to the earth.*

That's what I was thinking. Lilian's head bobbed.

A foreign Dragonscribe... It shouldn't be possible. Though why was he altering a finished masterpiece? *Let's get word to the clan. The Emperor will send troops to raid this place. The—*

The building's aesthetic imbalance. She took three steps back and scanned the façade again. Though the characters carved into all the shutters matched, the ones by the study looked different. The wood was newer. The—

Adrian mumbled something unintelligible. The script in the shutters flashed. Lilian staggered back, bare arm covering her eyes, then started to collapse.

Jie started towards her.

The shutters swung open. Hands reached out of the window, seized Lilian, and dragged her in. The shutters closed as Jie reached them, and Adrian spoke again. Jie turned her head and jumped back. This time, however, there was no flash.

She looked back and saw a different set of characters glowing green. The open spaces were now filled with darkness, and no sound escaped. Rune magic! It was supposed to be lost, and here Adrian was, appropriating Dragon Arts. How was it even possible to mix two forms of sorcery? With a tentative hand, she reached for the shutter.

A jolt made her arm go limp.

She had to get to Lilian. Jie ran to the door and found it unsurprisingly locked. Checking to make sure there were no other scripts or sigils, she pulled lockpicks from her hair. She fumbled with the tumblers, but even with her numb fingers, it yielded.

Jie shouldered the door open and burst into a foyer with gleaming hardwood floors. A key slid into the lock of the study door. She sent a thrust kick at it, and it slammed into someone who made an Adrian-like grunt.

Drawing a bladed hairpin, she kept low as she swept in.

A rapier blade thrust into the space where her gut would've been had she been upright. She leaped into a forward roll, avoiding the downward slash, then sprang to her feet and took in the surroundings. His sword knocked the hairpin out of her hand.

Lilian lay near the window, unmoving. Just out of range, Adrian faced her, rapier in one hand, dagger in the other.

"You! You're more than just a whore, aren't you? Put your hands on your head." He flicked his sword upward.

She glanced at Lilian.

Her chest rose and fell, and it didn't look as if he'd done anything to harm her...yet.

Maybe there were a few seconds to trawl for information, to stroke his male ego. She put her hands on her head in surrender. "You know how to create and invoke runes. I thought all Runemasters were dead and your texts destroyed."

"Clearly no for the first, and mostly yes to the second." He smirked. "The mobs couldn't kill all of our ancestors, and there are many of us who don't even know they have the gift of inscribing runes. I was one of those, until I fell in with a cabal that knew the rudiments of patterns and materials."

This fit into what little the clan knew and taught about runes: that different ingredients and tools could affect the strength and longevity of their magic. Exploiting the male need to impress pretty girls, she said, "But you went beyond that."

"Yes. I noticed the Dragon Art war banner had a similar feeling to runes." His expression remained cautious. "When I came here, I learned to borrow Dragon Arts to create new forms of runes."

So that's why he'd come to Cathay. Compliments would only distract him for so long; it was time to antagonize, and thus unbalance him. "So you're not a Runemaster, just someone who corrupts our magic." She lowered her hands.

"Up!" Scowling, he jerked the rapier point up again.

She surged forward, closing the distance between them. He recovered quickly with rapid thrusts and slashes. With bobs and weaves, twists and turns, Jie avoided the barrage and got inside the reach of his sword. He stabbed with his dagger, but she spun out of the way.

In the same motion, she caught his wrist and wrenched it. His fingers slackened, and she plucked the weapon from his loose grip. She used it to cut at his palmar tendons, but he grunted out another sound. The gold embroidery in his clothes flashed. Her blade glided across his sleeve without shearing it or his flesh.

He jumped back. Rapier tip pointed at her, he again had the reach advantage. He shook out his left hand, glaring. "Tricky whore."

Jie flipped the dagger into an underhand grip. If his clothes were now as good as armor, she'd have to be surgical in attacking his exposed neck, head, and hands. He claimed the ground between them with zigzagging slashes, blocking each of her counters with his rune-protected arm. She backed into the table.

He'd expect her to move left or right, but not low. The glowing threads in his clothes started to dim, and her last slash had left a small tear. Could he reactivate the magic? She'd have to assume he could. Ready to feint left before diving for his feet, she watched for his next move.

It never came.

He muttered more guttural sounds.

Light glowed behind her. Invisible hands seized her arms and pulled her back. Her struggle proved futile, as some unseen force pulled her shoulders down to the table. To the top of the unfurled scroll. It felt as if an unseen net had tangled up her wrists and forearms. She struggled to keep the balls of her feet on the floor, with only Black Lotus training making her flexible enough to bear the sharp arch of her back.

"Guess what I learned a Runemaster could do with your people's Dragon Arts?" Laughing, he strolled over and slapped her wrist with the flat of his blade.

Pain flared. The dagger slipped from her fingers and clattered to the floor. Just what had entangled her? Magic from Dragonscript, twisted by a Runemaster's ink. It didn't even seem possible.

He leaned over, his face so close that his breath felt hot on her face when he spoke. "Now, who are you? Not just a whore, I'm sure."

"You!" Guan yelled from the door.

Adrian jerked back, straightened.

With her upper body immobilized, Jie strained to turn her head. Limber as she was, only an owl would be able to see the door. She could smell Guan, however, as well as more men. Three others, from the sound of their footsteps crowding in.

"Drop your weapon," Guan said.

Just how had he gotten out?

Adrian's eyes shifted east and west. Now, two of Guan's men scurried into Jie's peripheral vision. They anchored the repeating crossbow stocks to their hips, cocked them with the levers, and aimed at the foreigner, just as the runes in his clothes faded.

His expression twisted into confusion as he dropped the rapier. "Why the weapons, Mister Guan?"

"This is how we punish thieves!"

"What?" Adrian shook his head back and forth. "What are you talking about?"

"It's true," Lilian said, picking herself up.

At least Lilian was all right. Relief washed over Jie as she turned to see. The magic from the calligraphy loosened its hold, making it easier to move her upper body.

"He...he did awful things to me. With rune magic. And now he's going to do the same to Jie." Lilian hugged herself. While she might not have excelled at stealth or combat, she was an excellent actress.

Guan's face flushed even redder. "Shoot."

"No!" Adrian yelled.

Crossbow triggers clicked. Bolts streaked in from three directions and lodged into Adrian's chest and abdomen with sickening thuds.

Either he'd been too panicked to activate the runes in his clothes, or they only worked once. He crumpled to his knees just a few feet away from her, his breaths labored.

The crossbowmen marched over and set their weapons down. They seized Adrian by his head and either arm. Behind her, the remaining guard cranked his weapon.

Lilian rushed over to Jie's side. "Are you all right?"

Tugging against the magic binding her arms to the table, she gave a tentative nod.

With the third guard at his side, Guan stalked over and leaned in, face close to Adrian's. "You planned to leave me to die while you stole my collection. I'm going to make the rest of your short life very long."

"It...not me." Adrian's voice came out in rasps. He tried to shake his head, but the guards held fast. "Whores."

Guan froze.

Jie's heart raced, even as she tested the magic bonds again. They were easing up, but still strong enough to leave her hands useless if Guan decided to believe the foreigner. She exchanged glances with Lilian.

"*Whores.*" Guan looked over his shoulder, eyes narrowing. "In the vault, it was *courtesan*, a word I don't think our guest knows."

He'd figured it out. Searching with her foot, Jie found the dagger. She seized it in her toes. Twisting her body and kicking, she drove it into one of the guards' necks. He jerked back, taking her weapon with him. Blood spurted from his wound as he clawed at his throat.

The other guard released Adrian. He drew his knife and lunged at Jie.

She kicked up with both feet and caught his neck and knife arm in the crook of her left knee. She hooked her right knee around her left ankle, and pulled him to the side. His weapon thunked into the table.

Lilian spun in front of them, seized his knife before he recovered, and sank it into his kidney. Thrusting her hips, Jie sent him sprawling back into Adrian. With her feet finding the floor, her line of sight was now open.

As the guard and Adrian collapsed into a groaning heap, Lilian rounded on Guan. He stood out of Jie's reach, crossbow in hand, but Lilian would get there before he could aim—

He grunted out sounds similar to Adrian invoking the runes.

The script on a scroll to Jie's east flared. Even though Lilian couldn't have seen it, she stopped midstride. Maybe he truly was related to the Last Imperator, for him to use runes.

"Give me the knife." Guan held out his hand.

No! They'd both be at his mercy. Jie tugged against the invisible tethers, which loosened another tiny fraction.

Lilian flipped the blade and offered it to Guan hilt-first.

Shit.

"It works!" Refusing the weapon, Guan flashed a feral grin. "I'd hoped to save that scroll for the Emperor, but at least I can test if it can make someone go against their nature. Lilian, kill Jie."

Lilian turned around, eyes glazed, not really seeing Jie. She claimed the ground between them and raised her blade.

"No!" Jie's heart leaped into her throat. She pulled against the magical bindings, to no avail.

"Stop," Guan said.

Lilian froze.

Jie blew out a breath. Dying was not high on her to-do list; death at the hands of her best-friend-and-possible-lover even lower. And poor Lilian, beholden to fell magic…

"It would be such a waste." Guan chuckled. "Now, I have to say, you'd built up all that anticipation in the gallery, only to stop. Lilian, kiss Jie. On the lips, this time."

The lecher! No doubt this was prelude to some other depravity.

Gaze blank, Lilian set the knife down on the table. She leaned over and pressed her lips to Jie's. They'd kissed each other—and more—on countless occasions, but this time there was no affection, just rote motion.

Jie always longed to feel Lilian's lips, but not like this. Not when it wasn't by choice. Not to fulfill a pervert's fantasies.

Lilian loomed over her, eyes empty. If any part of her was still aware of the violation, she'd be mortified.

"Yes!" Guan approached, the hunger in his voice sending Jie's skin crawling.

Gulping, the surviving guard lowered his crossbow.

Lilian's mouth continued to explore Jie's, without a hint of need and desire. Jie's stomach twisted. Were they to be nothing more than unwilling entertainment?

"Deeper," Guan said.

Lilian's tongue pushed against Jie's lips. If any of her was cognizant, Jie had to let her know it wasn't her fault. They might not have chosen this now, and they'd always tip-toed around their mutual affection, but Jie was Lilian's, unconditionally. What happened next would be Jie's choice, not forced by corrupted Dragon Magic.

With the magical bonds still too strong for her to move her arms or lift her back off the table, Jie wrapped her legs around Lilian and drew her closer. She took a deep breath and let her neck and shoulders relax. Eyes closed, she parted her lips. Their tongues met.

The stiffness in Lilian's body melted away. One hand found Jie's hand while the other brushed over her ear. Jie opened her eyes to find Lilian's closed. She used her tongue to tap in clan code, *Are you back?*

Lilian's eyes fluttered open to reveal a focused gaze. With her finger on the top of Jie's head, she tapped, *I'm so sorry.*

Not your fault. He's right behind you. Jie unwrapped her legs.

Sweeping up the knife, Lilian straightened, spun around, and stabbed at Guan's chest.

He barked out guttural sounds, and the Dragonwoven designs in his robes lit up. The blade reverberated off the cloth, the force of the magic sending Lilian staggering toward Jie.

The remaining guard aimed the crossbow at them and squeezed the trigger.

Lilian coiled and jumped as she crashed into Jie. Understanding her intention, Jie kicked her legs up and back. Their combined momentum flipped the table onto its side, wood splintering as a bolt hit where they'd been. Lilian tucked into a forward roll.

Scrolls scattering, the table landed on its side with Jie still bound. The thud jarred her, though the magic slackened more. Blood rushed to her head as she dangled, inverted, from unseen tethers.

On the other side, the crossbow cocked again. It had looked like a standard magazine, holding twelve bolts, and three had been used.

For now, the table provided cover. Lilian pressed her back up against it.

It was disorienting, seeing her upside-down. "Are you all right?" Jie asked.

Nodding, Lilian scooted closer. "The scroll is stuck to the table, and you're hanging a few inches off of it. The script's glow is fading."

The crossbowman's footsteps came closer. Unless the magic faded soon, they'd be easy targets.

"The paper," Jie said. "Cut it, tear it, anything to damage the writing."

Lilian reached behind Jie. Paper sheared. The invisible bonds around Jie's arms disappeared, and she fell. She thrust her hands down and sprang back to her feet.

The crossbow barrel rammed into her chest. On the other side of the table, the guard snarled and squeezed the trigger. Twisting, she knocked the weapon off course, and the bolt flew harmlessly into the wall. She reached down, pulled Lilian's hairpin free, and lodged it between his third and fourth ribs.

He gawked at the wound as she wrested the crossbow from his trembling fingers. She cocked it and shot at Guan.

He muttered garbled sounds, and more threads of his robe lit up. His next movements blurred so inhumanly fast, it was nearly impossible to see what he'd done. It was just like stories of rune-inscribed armor. All Jie knew was that he was behind her, seizing her around the waist with his left arm and setting a blade to her throat with his right.

Lilian plucked the crossbow from her hands and cocked it. "Let her go!"

"What are you going to do?" Guan chortled. "There is Dragonscript in my clothes that make them impenetrable. With one word, I can make them cut through Jie's flesh and bone."

Jie looked sidelong at his sleeve. The Dragonscript, activated with rune magic, must've been how he'd gotten free of his bonds. Still, the cloth was flexible. There might be a chance. She flashed hand signals. *Circle west.* With a subtle nod, Lilian did as told.

"Don't move! I can activate the Dragonscripts in those scrolls." Guan pointed with the dagger at the bundles.

With his arm over her shoulder, Jie seized his wrist. She simultaneously smashed the back of her head into his jaw and yanked down. His elbow joint popped over her shoulder, and he screamed. She torqued her hips.

He tripped over her leg and slammed face-first into the floor. His body twitched, and he went silent.

"Are you all right?" Lilian ran up and wrapped Jie in an embrace.

"Better than Guan." Jie gestured toward the spreading circle of blood under his head. He must've fallen on his dagger. She reluctantly pushed out of Lilian's arms and heaved him over.

His eyes stared unseeing at the ceiling. In his attempt to hold onto the weapon while bracing his fall, he'd stabbed himself in the neck.

Lilian knelt down and unfurled a few of the scrolls on the floor. Jie looked over her shoulder. All were Dragonscript, though up close, like with the Dragoncarving in the shutters, there appeared to be motes of color adhering to the strokes and whorls of the script. Those must be the special inks for rune inscription.

Jie took Lilian's hand and leaned into her. Together, they'd uncovered not one, but two culprits of stolen art. Adrian, Guan, or perhaps both, had modified Dragonscribe work with those materials to co-opt the magic in their plot to control the Emperor. With both dead, their mixing of Rune and Artistic magic was lost. Maybe that was for the better.

What might not be for the better was their relationship, marred by Guan bringing his fantasies to life through coercive magic.

"About earlier, on the table," Jie said, searching Lilian's eyes. "When Guan was controlling you..."

Blinking innocently, Lilian pecked a chaste kiss on Jie's ear. "You must've stimulated the acupuncture points in my tongue, dispelling the magic." Her flippant tone belied the longing in her gaze as she pulled back, smiling.

Jie's heart fluttered. Whatever feelings hung between them looked to remain unacknowledged.... For now.

End of Prelude

PART 1:
THORN OF THE NIGHT BLOSSOMS

CHAPTER 1

The ongoing bid on Jie's virginity had already exceeded the highest recorded, in part because every other Night Blossom was claimed by sixteen. While seedy whorehouses in dingy back alleys dealt in whatever flesh a man with coin craved, and didn't necessarily keep accurate records, the Floating World's unwritten conventions stipulated that a Blossom remain unplucked before she flowered with Heaven's Dew. At twenty, Jie had extra years to catch the eye of wealthy men with her exotic features, and to her lament, had yet to bleed.

Unless she counted the cuts and scratches from her *other* training. She didn't, because even the stodgiest accountant in the Floating World would've needed an abacus to tally them all up.

Said grey-haired accountant happened to work as Florist for Jie's house, the Chrysanthemum Pavilion. Ju Wei now looked from the shopping list to her ledger on her office's rosewood desk, illuminated by the morning sun through an oval window. She gave an appreciative nod. "You bought ten bottles of rice wine for a silver *jiao*?"

Actually, Jie had haggled with the brewery for a dozen and gotten two copper *fen* in change. All it took was the right pout, and the man was paper ready to be folded by dexterous fingers. "Yes, Florist." She bowed, the motion still too awkward by a Night Blossom's standards.

Florist Wei laughed, bright and clear for her middling age. "The house might make more sending you shopping than attracting Hummingbirds. Now, run along. I mean, off you go. *No* running."

Jie bowed again. She turned and reached for the sliding door.

"Ahem." Wei's tone carried loving exasperation.

With a bow no better than the last, Jie knelt at the door and slid it open. Once she'd stood, passed through, and bowed, she knelt again and closed the door. It was such a tedious ritual, one which the full-fledged Blossoms didn't have to perform at this hour, after the guests had left the house. As a Floret, Jie was bound by the tedium.

She glided over the nightingale floors, not making a sound. In all the Floating World's reputable houses, the chirping floorboards allowed the Gardener to hear every coming and going, and help protect the Hummingbirds' anonymity. In a lord's castle, they were meant to deter spies.

Jie suppressed a laugh. All spies from the Black Lotus Clan learned to navigate the joists and joints as soon as they could walk. It required grace, though a different kind than that of the Night Blossoms of the Floating World. The only reason the lords of the realm thought nightingale floors worked was that no adept had ever been caught.

With her chores done, she headed to the only Blossom of the Chrysanthemum Pavilion not getting her beauty rest. As she moved down the hall, she kept her eyes set forward to avoid looking directly at the hanging scrolls of calligraphy and brush paintings. Created by Dragonscribes, their magic would cause an unsuspecting viewer to loosen their purse strings. Then again, most of the unsuspecting were usually too busy ogling the Blossoms to notice the art.

A full-fledged Night Blossom worked a very different kind of magic to achieve similar results, and few did better than the Chrysanthemum Pavilion's Corsage, Ju Lilian. How coincidental that the house nicknamed her *Beautiful Lotus*, never knowing her alter ego as the most beautiful Fist of the secret Black Lotus Clan.

Jie padded up the steps and crept down the hall to Lilian's room. Ear to the door, she listened, just to confirm that Beautiful Lotus' important patron had indeed left.

With Lilian's mastery of the *Viper's Skin*, her shallow breaths would've been inaudible even to most clan adepts. But not to Jie, with the tapered ears inherited from her worthless elf father; the same father whose blood slowed her aging and sped up her healing. It kept all but major lacerations from scarring, but also prevented Heaven's Dew from arriving.

Of course, Lilian didn't have to know whether anyone heard her or not. She lay in wait, suspended from the rafters on the other side of the door. As much fun as it would be to wait until her arms and legs got tired, an exhausted Fist endangered clan operations. Forgoing ceremony, Jie slid the door open and feigned unawareness as she stepped in....

...and spun out of the way, arcing a kick into the edge of the door in the same motion. Just enough force that it slid to a quiet shut.

Lilian landed right behind where Jie would've been, back exposed, without a sound on the plush wool carpet.

With equal silence, Jie swept a leg behind Lilian while wrapping an arm around her neck. She twisted her hips and sent the Blossom into a soundless heap on the ground. Rolling over, throwing her legs across Lilian's chest, she arched her back and locked Lilian in an armbar. Their silk gowns tangled in a flash of blues, yellows, and greens.

"Big Sister," Jie said in a loud voice. Although the thick walls and dense doors muted all but the loudest gasps and moans, Night Blossoms had a propensity for hearing things. Even with their reputation for discretion, the less they knew about the Black Fists in their midst, the better.

"Greetings, Little Floret." Lilian kept her voice even through gritted teeth. Any more leverage would dislocate her elbow.

Jie leaned back to apply a little more pressure. "I'm here for my lesson." If only it were true.

"You're late." Face red, Lilian surrendered with staccato taps on Jie's leg.

"My apologies, Big Sister." With a grin, Jie relented. She rolled backward into a crouch, fist to the ground, and stood.

"I appreciate your sincerity." Lilian's skirts billowed out as she twirled her legs like a windmill, vaulting herself upward feet-first and then landing. It was utterly immodest. Using clan hand signals, she signed, *You're not sorry at all, Big Sister.*

Not at all, Jie signaled back. She stood and placed her right fist in her left hand in a warrior's salute. "Please, teach me."

Lilian returned the gesture, adding a bow of her head. To the Chrysanthemum Pavilion, she was a full-fledged Blossom, the Corsage of the house; but she'd been an orphan of three when the Black Lotus Temple had adopted her, and six-year-old Jie had taken her under her wing.

She looked up from her bow.

What Lilian lacked in martial skill, she made up for in an elegance Jie hadn't deigned to master. Her thin, high-bridged nose accentuated large brown eyes. Glossy black hair, tousled first by entertaining an important guest the night before, and now by a more lethal form of grappling, framed her triangular face. At eighteen, she boasted ample curves.

A pit formed in Jie's throat. She'd been the Elder Sister, but still had a flat body, and was no closer to earning the clan her virgin price and leaving the Floating World. With a possible insurrection brewing in the North, the posturing and backstabbing of hereditary lords seemed much more interesting than the posturing and backstabbing of the entertainment district's great houses.

Lilian motioned toward the bed. "Come. We'll practice the *Jade Polishing* technique."

Jie's belly fluttered. *Jade Polishing*—a euphemism for some sex act, but for what? A Blossom had a plethora of techniques at her disposal, all which *looked* titillating, but the silly names had never been her priority. After all, she'd eventually return to the Black Lotus Temple to train new recruits in stealth, fighting, and poisons; or maybe even get sent on missions to eliminate threats to the realm.

Then again, she'd already been in the house four years longer than originally planned, and her body ached for release in more ways than one.

Whereas they'd taken care to keep their martial interaction silent, both relaxed as they walked across the room. Lilian looked paler than usual, and dark bags hung under her eyes. Usually the embodiment of grace, it seemed as if she were slogging through mud.

Are you all right? Jie's fingers danced out the signs.

Lilian perked up, smiling and nodding.

All contrived. Her guest last night, perhaps? All the great Houses of the Floating World knew of Lord Ting's penchant for a little rough play. There were certainly worse Hummingbirds, and the most recalcitrant men had earned a ban from the Floating World altogether. No amount of money in the empire could buy reentry.

Jie looked around for clues. At a casual glance, nothing looked out of place in the room. The landscape paintings—one imbued with magic to loosen a viewer's lips—hung in their usual places on the wall. A red lacquer platter with a porcelain decanter and matching eggshell cups sat on a low table to the side. From the scent, a sour plum had flavored the rice wine. Lilian's bedsheets were appropriately rumpled, and the rug had shifted a degree, but that came as no surprise given Lord Ting's vigor.

Gut twisting at the thought of having to share Lilian, Jie swallowed hard.

Lilian's honeysuckle fragrance clung the strongest in the center of the carpet and the west side of the bed, mingling with fresh incense and the dissipating odor of sour man-sweat. It didn't take much imagination to picture what Lord Ting had done, and where. Another scent lingered, hidden among the others: *yinghua* flowers, a contact toxin that made most males susceptible to questions, and left them with a forgetful hangover.

Did you find anything out from Lord Ting? Jie signed.

Nodding, Lilian knelt by the bed. She slid a hand between the futon and frame and withdrew a finger-length tube. "Lie down."

Excitement jolted up Jie's spine, and she settled back into the cool softness of thick blankets.

Full report here, Lilian signed as she plopped down beside her and passed the tube over. "Relax."

Something was wrong. Lilian's tone and posture lacked enthusiasm. Excitement melting away, Jie sat up. It didn't look like they'd be practicing *Jade Carving*, whatever it was. She took the tube and slid it into the hidden pocket sewn into her sleeve. *What's it say?*

Lords of the North are grumbling. "That's better. See?"

Jie let out a moan for anyone who might happen to be listening at the door, even as she imagined straddling Lilian.

Lord Ting plans to meet with them in secret, to calm them. She pointed with her chin to where the tube was stashed. "See, it's all in how you work your fingers."

Closing her eyes, Jie imagined Lilian's fingers walking up her belly, even as she considered Lord Ting. Known throughout the realm for his martial skill and bold leadership, he was staunchly faithful to the Emperor. The strategic location of his county helped keep the other lords around him in line, and the clan had taken keen interest in protecting him.

"Keep practicing." With a sigh, Lilian leaned in and rested her head on Jie's shoulder. Her delicate body shuddered.

What's wrong? Savoring the closeness, Jie tapped and slid her fingers in clan code on Lilian's wrist while draping her other arm over her shoulder. It was a strange occurrence in the Floating World, where an Elder Sister was supposed to comfort the house's Florets and Seedlings.

I'm tired. I don't want to do this anymore.

Jie searched Lilian's tear-filled eyes. *Why now?*

I never wanted to. Not past training and the virgin price.

Jie sucked on her lower lip. Using shell companies as bond holders, the clan sent many of its pretty girls to the Floating World. It usually lasted two years, not only so they could learn about pleasure, but also to hone other skills, and gather information about powerful men. Some, like Lilian, who lacked more than basic combat and stealth skills, were embedded in the prominent houses long-term.

A tear trickled down her cheek. *I wanted to be like the Beauty, not the Steel Orchids.*

Jie nodded. Three of the most celebrated adepts in recent memory, the Beauty and the Steel Orchids had entered the Floating World as apprentices at the same time. While the Steel Orchids had remained here, the Beauty joined the Surgeon and Architect to form a team that planned and carried out the most important clan operations throughout the continent. All three had died young, twenty-one years before, but every Black Lotus Fist and initiate still idolized them.

Instead, I'm used night in, night out. Lord Ting is the worst of them all. Lilian let out a despondent sigh, one that someone listening at the door might mistake as one of pleasure.

Setting bones and stitching lacerations came easy. Attending to emotional wounds... Well, clan training fell short. Jie patted her on the back.

Lilian's mask of cheerful Blossom slipped as the tears flowed freely now. Pain and disenchantment etched worry lines into the beautiful sculpting of her face. This, after just two years of receiving men.

This might be Jie's future, as well. Despite the constant, unfulfilled urges now, it would undoubtedly grow tiring, especially compared to all the more interesting places her skills would be of use. *I'll get you reassigned. Together.* As adopted daughter of the clan's grandmaster, she might actually be able to.

If she could come up with a good reason. Lilian's stealth, combat, observation, planning, and other skills lagged behind even clan members five years her junior. The Floating World really did make best use of her assets, and her connection to Lord Ting was invaluable to the realm.

And the posting would keep her safe. No Sister had been lost here since a deadly training accident twenty years ago.

Jie stared at the messenger tube, wondering what she should do.

CHAPTER 2

Heart heavy and mind racing, Jie returned to the Florets' and Seedlings' room. Large enough to house twenty, its austerity rivaled the barracks of Black Lotus initiates. Each girl had just enough space to sleep on the reed mats, and a chest for their few personal belongings. The sooner Jie could move into her own room, the better. Or better yet, out of the Floating World altogether. With Lilian.

At the mid-morning hour, all the bedrolls lay folded at the edge of the sunlit chamber. Not including her, thirteen pretty Seedlings and Florets, aged eight to fifteen, called this room home. While they'd all ultimately earn their keep with their bodies, life in the Floating World was far better than say, the Trench. There, prostitutes controlled by the Red Dragon Triads would service dozens of men a day. At this very moment, some young girl was being exploited, and it made Jie's blood boil.

At least here, though, most of the House sisters were currently out running errands, or taking poetry and music lessons in the district's theaters. Only thirteen-year-old Ai and twelve-year-old Yin remained, playing a game of chess.

"Big Sister." They both looked up and bowed, their motions the embodiment of grace even at such a young age. In this, they'd already surpassed Jie.

"How did your lesson with Lilian go?" Yin asked. Blessed with the exquisite features of the North, she'd suffered misfortune when her father had died in a mining accident. Scouts for the Floating World had pounced like carrion birds, buying her contract from a desperate mother with three other children to feed. She'd been with Chrysanthemum House for only a year, and any description of what happened behind closed doors—and sometimes open ones—would leave her mortified.

To spare her from fainting, Jie answered simply. "Well."

"It's such an honor to learn from the Corsage. What did she teach you?" Ai's face looked bright. Coming to the house as a Seedling of eight, she'd been here long enough that a graphic description of a sex act would affect her as much as basic bookkeeping. Which was to say, anyone could fake interest.

Jie looked from Ai to Yin. What was the name of the technique again? *Squeezing Jade*? No, it had to be something a little more elegant. *Jade Thrust*? Turning to shield her hands from Yin, Jie pantomimed a motion Lilian had taught years ago and hadn't reviewed since.

Yin covered her mouth and flushed an interesting shade of red.

Brows furrowed, Ai tapped her chin. "*Duel of the Phoenix and Dragon*?"

Ah, the poetic names for something so primal. Jie nodded. Now, what was the name Lilian had used?

"So lucky." Ai let out a wistful sigh. "The way she does it...mmmm."

If Yin's original shade of red had been interesting, their language had no word to describe the new one.

With a chuckle, Jie padded over to her own chest. Making sure Ai and Yin had returned to their game, she retrieved two throwing stars from the false bottom. She adjusted her hair, pinning it up in a popular style with a sharp hairpin.

Then, she closed her eyes and thought about Lilian's message. *Lord Ting meeting with disgruntled lords, Jade Teahouse, in two days.*

Here was a chance for her and Lilian to show they could do more than trawl for information from sated men. She'd added her own missive. *Lilian wants reassignment. Let her prove herself. A hit.*

"I'm going out." She waved with a smile, as the Florets were wont to do when the Blossoms, Gardener, or Florist weren't around.

Outside of the gaudy double doors, painted with half the emblem of a chrysanthemum on each side, Jie took a deep breath of the fresh air. The entrance faced south, an auspicious position, and up to the southwest, the Iridescent Moon hung in its reliable spot in the sky, waning toward a faint third crescent. Almost ten o'clock.

She crossed the courtyard and bowed to Master Deng at the front gate, albeit with less grace than any other girl who'd spent at least a year in the Floating World.

The guard returned her greeting with a nod. "Where are you off to?"

"I'm getting a dress altered." Jie smiled at him. Though Seedlings weren't allowed out by themselves, Florets who'd earned their houses' trust enjoyed freedom between chores and lessons. Jie's comings and goings might seem random to Deng, or any other casual observer, but coded poems known by every Black Lotus initiate and adept set a schedule of meeting times and locations.

The Floating World bustled at night with a myriad of colors and scents, but quieted by dawn, and turned into a ghost town by mid-morning. As she strolled down the narrow, stone-paved streets, a few men-at-arms nodded in greeting from the ornate brothel gates. A troupe manager stood under a theater's steeply pitched roofs and red banners and waved at her.

She returned each greeting with a polite bow appropriate for a Floret, even as her eyes assessed changes from the day before: what scent of incense burned in the Gold Orchid Shrine, the cost of opium in the dens, or the odds at the mahjong parlors.

All the buildings were packed in close, even tighter than before the fire ravaged most of the district twenty years ago. In the rush to rebuild and reap profits, nobody cared that it might happen again—save for the investors in the Chrysanthemum Pavilion and Peony Garden, who'd ensured there was plenty of space between the mansion and the walls.

Jie snorted. To think, somewhere over the years, no matter how much she'd wanted to leave, this tinder box had become home. The Floating World, named because it was where a man's dreams took flight, provided all kinds of entertainment at any budget. For Lilian, that meant letting wealthy men use her body. Maybe Jie would share the same fate, if the clan didn't deem her skilled enough for another assignment.

The heady scent of lotus incense beckoned. Turning down a secondary road, Jie paused at the Lotus Shrine, consecrated by Daoist priests long ago as a symbol for sexuality. Its lacquered black tiles, curving to give the squat, open structure the look of a lotus flower in bloom, looked dull in the morning sun. That meant a clan courier had not yet picked up messages and cleaned off a night's worth of smoke ash. A stele with a lantern at its crest rose up behind the flower, oftentimes mistaken as a symbol of male virility. Visible from anywhere in the Floating World, the lantern only lit up in a clan emergency.

With her back to Jie, a Floret in a blue dress stood with her head bowed before an ornate box which supposedly held the solid tear of the Blue Moon Goddess. She clapped once and wafted the incense smoke toward her face, in hopes of inviting the arrival of Heaven's Dew.

Jie suppressed a snort. While the rest of the realm recognized the Blue Moon as the Eye of Guanyin, Goddess of Fertility, the Daoists had their own ideas of immortality and sexuality. Tonight, lascivious men would visit and pray for an epic night in the Floating World. On occasion, Blossoms whose herbal contraception failed them would leave unwanted babies here, too, never knowing they would end up working for the Black Lotus Clan.

Finished with her prayer, the Floret turned around. She met Jie's gaze and bowed her head with well-trained grace.

Returning the bow with much less refinement, Jie approached the slat-top donation box. Using sleight of hand, she tossed one of her extra coppers and Lilian's message tube in. They clinked to the bottom, joining the coins and ingots that would help fund clan operations, as well as messages from clan sisters embedded in the other houses. She clapped her hands together and bowed her head. If anyone happened to pass by, they'd just assume they'd seen a Floret praying for her monthly cycles to begin, and not a mythical Black Lotus Fist delivering a message.

Satisfied, she continued on her way to the meeting of clan girls. She passed through a grove of cherry trees, where folded sheets of paper were tied into knots around branches, competing with the blooms for space. While most of the notes involved prayers for good health or a spectacular night, the one Jie snagged was folded in such a way that it would tear apart in untrained hands, and contained instructions from the clan. She stuffed it into her sleeve's inner pocket.

A few blocks later, a short, thin man in a gentleman's robe stumbled out of the Jade Teahouse. He hadn't enjoyed the establishment's renowned teas, if the reek of alcohol and his wobbling feet were any indication. The burly, scowling doorman with crossed arms added yet more evidence. What had a drunkard been doing in the teahouse, at this hour?

He shook his fist at the guard and shouted a few expletives at the closing door. With no response forthcoming, he turned around and looked up and down the street. His gaze fell on her.

Feigning demureness like a good Blossom, Jie shuffled along.

The weight of the man's stare fell on her back, as heavy as his approaching footsteps.

The hairs on the back of Jie's neck stood on end. Nobody ever attacked a Blossom in the Floating World. It just didn't happen. The district's enforcers, while well-dressed and polite, could inflict a lot of pain on a man who dared lay a finger on a nonconsenting employee. The unspoken threat of retribution made the Floating World the safest place in the capital, save for the Imperial Palace.

Woe be to this fool for targeting Jie, of all people. She stopped, turned, and bowed. "May I help you, kind sir?"

He leered at her, eyes drinking her up. It might've been threatening if he weren't so small, or if Jie didn't know a thousand different ways to defend herself. A feral grin contorted his lips.

From dusk to dawn, eyes watched from all over, and a member of the Floating World enjoyed the protection of community vigilance. From mid-morning to early afternoon, however, most denizens were asleep. A scream might bring people to her rescue, but by the time they got there, it would be too late.

Her cover would be blown, city authorities—who usually left the Floating World to its own devices, as long as the businesses paid taxes to the throne—would be called in, and she'd have to explain how a waif of a girl had incapacitated a man.

He'd have to be taken care of quietly, in a secluded place. Which happened to be her specialty.

Just choke him out, apply some *yinhua* flower essence, and he'd wake up never remembering he'd seen her. Though if he'd targeted her, he'd probably assault a defenseless Blossom in the future. Maybe it'd be better to get rid of him for good. That meant calling in a clan Cleaner to dispose of the body, however, before the aforementioned authorities investigated.

Feigning fear, Jie backed up. She modulated her voice into a tremble. "Please sir, I'm just a Floret. Please don't hurt me."

He advanced, claiming the ground between them.

Pretending her skirts slowed her down, she turned and ran just fast enough to stay ahead of him. After all, if he gave up the chase, he might harm a lone Floret or Seedling running errands.

With a glance over her shoulder, she put on a burst of speed and ducked into the narrow, south-north alley between the red-roofed shrine of the Money God and the orange-tiled shrine of the Fox Spirit. A few paces in, she pulled out her bladed hairpin and clenched it between her teeth. The narrow gap allowed her to pop-vault between the tall buildings that obscured the morning sun.

Stopping twelve feet up, she shot her arms and legs out and suspended herself horizontally between the two walls. No one ever looked up; now all she had to do was wait.

And wait.

Her arms and legs started to ache. Had he given up? Or lost her in his drunken haze? She took in the scents and sounds.

Quiet. Birds chirped.

His alcohol stench drifted in from the head of the alley. Surely he couldn't be so dense as to wait there: had she been running, she could have reached the other side. Then again, who knew what thoughts ran through an alcohol-muddled brain?

There were no man-shaped shadows at the intersection either, so he must be hiding around the corner of the western shrine's wall. Had he thought of that himself, or was it by chance? Though, unless he'd crossed the mouth of the alley when she started her ascent, she would've seen him. Her ears would've picked up his breathing.

Breaths! Shallow inhalations came from the far end of the alley. Then, a click.

She craned down and looked.

A crossbow bolt sped toward her.

She dropped as it zipped by, zigzagging between the walls, down to the pavestones. She landed in a crouch. A hooded man wearing the garb of a brothel enforcer stood at the far end of the alley, cocking a repeating crossbow. His steady stance spoke of fighting experience, likely in some foreign war where kings hired Hua mercenaries. Without aiming, he sprayed three bolts in tight arc.

The narrowness of the alley and near-impossible accuracy of the shots left no room to dodge more than one. She turned to present the side of her body, and the first brushed by her ear. She caught the second, then threw her back against the wall to avoid the third.

Why hadn't he shot another—

The drunkard—clearly not drunk—turned into the alley, a knife already coming down in a quick stab.

Crossbowman on one side, hired blade on the other. Jie ducked under the knife and slid feet-first between his legs. Spinning, she hooked his shin in the crook of her elbow and threaded her legs up and around his. Now inverted, she locked her ankles at his hip and arched back. His forward momentum dislocated his knee as he fell.

He screamed as his face hit the dirt.

Two seconds. She might have two seconds at most before the crossbowman came up and shot her in the face, point-blank, and she was still struggling with the first attacker.

Fighting through his pain, the knifeman somehow rolled over. She released him, lest he get the bright idea of slashing her Achilles tendon. Before she could get away, he was straddling her, his light weight still crushing the air out of her.

He stabbed down, but she caught his wrist in both hands. He leaned in, and her arms shook, already tired from laying her own ambush.

"Bitch." His lip curled into a sneer.

CHAPTER 3

Pinned beneath a man who'd tricked her into thinking he was a stupid drunkard looking for easy prey, Jie struggled to keep his knife out of her eye. Any second now, her trembling arms would—

His head snapped back. Blood sprayed. His muscles went slack, and Jie redirected his knife to the ground as he crumpled on top of her. His mass stifled her breath, and she struggled just to lift her head out from under him and spot the crossbowman a dozen paces away.

He looked from her to the space behind her. Though a mask hid his expression, his posture screamed of confusion. Had he shot his comrade? The crossbow trigger hadn't clicked again, had it? He turned and ran.

Closing her eyes and blowing out a breath, Jie let her head drop back down. The Floating World's twenty-year track record for clan Sister safety had almost come to an end...

"Are you all right, my sweet?" said a female voice.

Jie's eyes fluttered open, and she looked up at the source. Dressed in a simple green dress, Lilian knelt over her, her honeysuckle perfume heavy, familiar, and comforting.

What? Jie squirmed out from beneath her assailant. Her gaze flicked from Lilian to him.

A throwing spike was lodged in his eye, and he had bled all over her.

"You saved me." Jie nodded in appreciation. "That might be the best throw you've ever made."

Lilian gave a hesitant, utterly adorable bob of her head. "I never imagined you would need me to save you."

"How did you find me?"

"Coincidence." She smiled and extended a hand. "I was on my way to the gathering when I saw this man waiting on the street, with that knife."

Taking the proffered hand, Jie climbed to her feet and studied the body. Of course, there was nothing to identify him. Nothing clung under his nails, and his shoes showed no telltale clues. He'd spilled some strong rice wine onto his clothes and used it to rinse his mouth. Still, a trace of sesame-ginger marinade lingered there.

She looked up. "He knew who I was and where I would be."

"Impossible." Lilian shook her head. "The only ones who know our identities are other clan members."

Jie knelt down and checked him for other weapons. "He was waiting. He lulled me into complacency by acting like a drunk merely picking a target of opportunity."

Lilian's porcelain complexion blanched even more. "That means the crossbowman..."

"Knows about me, as well." Jie nodded. "And now also you, if they didn't already."

Still acting like a Night Blossom, Lilian covered her gasp with a delicate hand. With her other hand, though, she presented four crossbow bolts. "We need to track the crossbowman down."

"We also need to warn the others, and get word to the clan to bring a Cleaner to take care of this mess."

"I'll inform the clan." Lilian looked at the body and shuddered. Then she squared her shoulders and yanked her throwing spike from the man's face. She looked more like a Black Fist that way.

An intriguing mix of admiration and arousal shot up Jie's spine. She gave a satisfied nod. "Before you go, let me see what instructions they left for us." She withdrew the message she'd picked from the grove of trees and carefully unfolded it.

Coming up behind her, Lilian rested her chin on Jie's shoulder, her honeysuckle scent soothing after Jie's brush with death. Together, they read.

Chatter in the North of a hit on Lord Ting. He is key to stability to there. He must be protected.

Which meant that in all likelihood, the clan wouldn't reassign Lilian, Lord Ting's favorite. Jie looked over her shoulder.

Lilian's lips formed a tight line for a split second. "I didn't expect any other outcome."

"I'll think of something." Jie turned and leaned in so their foreheads touched. "Now, we need to hurry. I'll continue to the meeting. You go to the safehouse and bring more assets back to the silk market in an hour."

"As you command, Elder Sister." Lilian saluted with a fist in her palm, turned, and ran.

Jie strode to where the crossbowman had been and sniffed for any lingering smells. He'd eaten the same marinade as the dead man, and also washed his mouth out with alcohol. These men were real soldiers, and had specifically prepared to kill *her*.

It might be enough to go on. If only she could be in two places at once; then she would be able to track the crossbowman before the scent trail went cold. Still, the other girls' safety took priority, and Jie had already wasted enough time. She took off toward the meeting place, shuffling in a nominally ladylike fashion on the streets, and dashing through alleys.

A block away from the opera house, the site of today's gathering, she stopped and took in her surroundings. Like the rest of the Floating World at this hour, it was quiet, with only the three-story wooden structure's banners fluttering in the light breeze. Then again, if these assassins had been prepared for her, they might know how to breach the theater. An image of all the girls, captured or dead, appeared unbidden in her mind. She stepped into the lookout's line of sight, flashed a hand signal, and ducked back. She peeked around the corner.

A mirror flashed twice in the sun. *All clear.*

At least on the front end. Jie extended her hands and signed, *Extra vigilance. Possible security breach.*

The mirror blinked twice again in acknowledgement.

Somewhat relieved, Jie crept through another alley that came up behind the opera house. The lookout was hidden in the usual spot, and as in front, flashed the sign that everything was all right. With no other signs of abnormal activity, she slipped in through the service door. As always, a mess of costumes and make-up paints and brushes cluttered the hallways and dressing rooms. Several dresses hung from racks, all carrying the various familiar smells of Black Lotus sisters.

Voices and thumps grew louder as she approached the stage from the back. Still nothing out of the ordinary. She let out a breath and peeked in.

Twenty-six girls, ranging in age from eight to thirty-two, were practicing Black Fist techniques in black stealth suits. Some were engaged in knife duels, while others used blindfolds to maneuver through obstacles. One crossed a narrow wooden beam while dancing through a sword form. Even in the Floating World, they met to keep their weapons, stealth, and memory skills sharp.

She hadn't needed to worry about their safety: with their knowledge of the opera house's layout, and a predetermined emergency plan that made use of hiding places and bottlenecks, an attacker would be a fool to assail the location, even if they brought a thousand men.

The only danger would be if someone wanted to burn it down—but the flames would consume most of the Floating World, as the clan training accident had, twenty years ago. Today, only her own

Chrysanthemum Pavilion and the rival Peony Garden would survive, because of the space between the mansions and their walls.

That fire was never far from Jie's mind, since it had claimed all the clan's operatives in the entertainment district, including the legendary Steel Orchids. Renowned for their elegance and guile, they'd sniffed out conspiracies, rooted out traitors, and ended a rebellion before it started.

All the girls here now were heirs to that legacy, and Jie was their leader. Regardless of age or experience, they shared two things in common: pretty faces and Black Fist training. Full-fledged Blossoms brought Seedlings who were not yet allowed to leave their respective houses on their own. Jie's chest filled with pride as she watched. She'd taught many of them at the temple, and still coached them now.

Little Wen, a precocious sixteen-year-old from the Peony Garden, disarmed nineteen-year-old Meisha's knife. She disengaged and bowed. "Elder Sister Jie."

All training came to a stop. Twenty-six sets of fists went to palms, and heads bobbed. Though all were technically sisters in the clan, Jie's position as officially adopted daughter of Clan Master Yan made her de facto leader.

She returned their salute. "Sisters, we have an emergency. Two assassins, one armed with a Repeater, targeted me specifically on my way here."

Whispers erupted.

"Where's Elder Sister Lilian?" Yuna, Little Wen's fiery new apprentice asked, flipping a knife between her fingers. She was particularly gifted, excelling at many of the clan's techniques already. She'd just been working on the No-Shadow Cut, which only a few of the clan's blademasters could execute.

"She is bringing help from the safehouse." Jie searched their eyes. Certainly none of them could betray the clan. "In the meantime, have you noticed anything out of the ordinary? Has anyone suspicious been following you?"

Heads shook.

Jie sucked on her lower lip and let it go with a pop. All of these girls, even the youngest, knew how to spot and lose tails. They'd all been trained to notice such things. "We will err on the side of caution, and assume that whoever attacked me knows who all of us are. We are all targets."

More murmuring, even though hopefully that wasn't the case. Maybe Masked Crossbowman knew only about her, the half-elf. Still, for everyone's safety... "We will change our meetings to schedule pattern three. The attacker won't know our routines; at least not for a few days. Otherwise, maintain your regular activities."

"What about now?" Wen asked.

"Lilian is reporting back to the safehouse, and will hopefully bring more assets." Jie drew a finger in a circle. "We will assume our enemy knows we are gathering here, so we will disperse now. Those who can, reconvene at the silk market, infiltration mode."

Fists went into palms, and heads bowed. They changed back into their simple dresses. In staggered groups of two or three, they left the theater from the front and back doors.

Jie waited until last, relaying commands to the lookouts, and relieving the one in front while she changed and disappeared into the alleys. Satisfied everyone was clear of the theater, Jie set off toward the silk market.

Just outside of the giant lanterns hanging from the front gates to Floating World, the silk market was erroneously considered by the capital's denizens to be part of the entertainment district. While the latter quieted from mid-morning to mid-afternoon, the silk market bustled with activity from dawn until well past dark. It was one of the few places where other women would ever rub shoulders with a Blossom.

Rows upon rows of covered stalls lined the open square. They formed a maze of virtual streets, covered by a giant red tent. Hundreds of people milled about, chatting with friends or browsing. Others haggled with merchants over bolts of silk, cotton, and imported linen and satin, which came in all manner of designs and colors. Vendors hawked brocade shoes and the latest fashions in dresses, gowns, and robes.

Though women made up the vast majority of customers, the Floating World girls stood out with their beauty and graceful carriage, even in plain day dresses. Most servants paid them no mind, but groups of well-to-do housewives broke off in gossip, huddling together as they eyed Blossoms and Florets. The handful of noblewomen present might cast scathing glances at their husbands' possible paramours, and the reactions of their entourage of handmaidens and guards ranged from active avoidance to lecherous ogling.

While her clan sisters blended in with the crowds, Jie's tapered ears drew many eyes—just as planned, to keep the others safe. Hidden among the stares, the weight of a threatening gaze prickled the back of Jie's neck. Whether it was a run-of-the-mill serial killer, rapist, kidnapper, or an associate of the crossbowman, it was impossible to tell. If only she could find the source.

Maintain cover, she signaled while pretending to examine a godawful puce fabric. She continued on her way. Mirrors and other reflective surfaces failed to reveal her tail, and none of the other sisters indicated that they had made him, either.

There. The scent of that sesame-ginger marinade. Just a trace, but it was enough to suggest that Masked Crossbowman, or someone else who had eaten at the same place, was either nearby or had passed through within the hour.

She lifted a coin pouch off a noble's manservant on her way to one of her informants. While the slipper merchant and charm seller didn't have any worthwhile news, the jade bangle vendor did.

He flashed her a broad smile from across his table, where an array of sixty bracelets lay organized on a red silk tablecloth. He gestured to the cheapest one. "Miss Jie, I have some imperial green today."

"I was hoping you would." Jie set the stolen pouch on the table.

The vendor hefted it and nodded. "This particular piece hails from the Jinjing County. They've been trying to carve them into blossoms."

Jie picked up the bracelet as she pondered his message. Jinjing didn't have jade mines, and any reference to blossoms usually had to do with the Floating World. "The mine's owner? Or someone else?"

"The owner."

So, the Lord of Jinjing County was up to something in the Floating World. She gave a nod. "Thank you for this beautiful piece."

"Let me wrap it up for you." He plucked it from her hand, then wrapped it in a white cotton kerchief which was worth far more than the cheap stone, because of the handwritten poem on it. The writing seemed to extol spring blossoms, but was really a coded message. Back at the Chrysanthemum Pavilion she'd use the cipher to decode the poem in full, but at first glance it looked like the Lord of Jinjing was spending a lot of money in the Floating World.

With a bow of her head, she continued to check with her other sources. From the money she'd saved earlier that morning, she slipped a copper to a little pickpocket who always seemed to know the gossip. Another copper went to a beggar who had a good eye for which noble house bought what.

Little Wen and her apprentice Yuna, now both wearing pastel-pink day dresses and smelling of lavender, glided by. Wen's enviable grace made it easier to remember she was a full-fledged Blossom, despite her nickname. With a combination of hand signals and a few finger-taps on Jie's arm, she conveyed her message. *Lilian's back. No help coming.*

No help coming? Jie frowned. The message was percolating among the clan sisters, evident from the split-second looks of dismay. Not only that, the feeling of being watched disappeared.

A hush pregnant with expectation fell over the throng. People parted, opening a path.

Dan Lusha, the Corsage of the rival Peony Garden, glided through, chin held high, the epitome of elegance. Though she usually had her shiny black hair up in a style that set trends for the rest of the Floating World, today it cascaded down to her waist. She looked stunning in a plain pink day dress, even at an hour when most Blossoms were recovering from the previous night.

On one side, her Seedling wore a matching dress. No older than eight, the poor girl shivered like a cold puppy; certainly not from the temperature on this warm day. More likely it was because she had to uphold the standard of apprenticing to one of the most famous Blossoms in the Floating World—the one whose virgin price had held the previous record.

Though the guard at her other side wore the pastel-pink livery of the house, his gait exhibited competence. More importantly, he smelled of sesame-ginger marinade.

CHAPTER 4

While all eyes in the silk market lingered on the most celebrated Blossom, Jie evaluated her guard.

His stride, combined with eyes that roved for possible threats, spoke of competence. His height and build did not rule him out as Masked Crossbowman; although, unless he'd run off for a post-attack snack after trying to kill her, the sesame-ginger aroma was too heavy for him to be the same person.

Even so, they might be associates. Perhaps Masked Crossbowman worked for the Peony Garden, and their Gardener had specifically targeted her to maintain Lusha's record virgin price. It brought fame and honor to the House, after all.

If only Jie were so lucky. It would be better that way, since it would mean the clan sisters weren't in danger. It would also mean that just getting the whole deflowering thing over with would end the threat.

And, of course, there was also the possibility that the guard had just happened to eat at the same place as Masked Crossbowman, which would be helpful in tracking him down.

She slid between people and sidled up to Little Wen and Yuna. As a Blossom and Seedling of the Peony Garden, if anyone knew what management was thinking, it would be them. And clan fealty surpassed house loyalties. She tapped on her wrist. *What does your house say about my virgin price?*

Lusha hates you, and is constantly pouting about her record virgin price falling.

Would your Gardener act on it? While the Houses played a game of shifting alliances, betrayals, and backstabbing, Blossoms were tacitly off-limits to physical harm. Emotional harm was fair game, of course. Sending assassins was unheard of.

Ripples appeared on Wen's brow as she froze for a moment. *Maybe.*

What's she doing here?

Wen's lips quirked. *She's looking for a new dress for the weekend. A Tai-Ming Lord commissioned her for his son's first time.*

It was a great honor to be chosen by a First-Rank Lord's heir. *How much?*

An exorbitant amount.

Lusha was almost upon them now. Her eyes shifted to Jie for a split second before settling on Little Wen.

"Elder Sister." Wen bowed.

"Little Wen. Don't stand too close to mongrels, or you will get fleas." Lusha cast a scathing glance at Jie.

Mongrel. Clever. As if Jie hadn't heard that before.

Chatter erupted among the onlookers. Blossoms were known for duels of poetry or music, but Lusha's sharp tongue was the stuff of legends. They were about to witness an epic tongue-lashing.

Jie snorted. "You have nothing to worry about, Miss Lusha. My fleas have good taste."

A collective *ooooo* droned.

Sharp glare raking the crowd, silencing it, Lusha let out one of her famous little harrumphs. "Uncultured half-breed. Come to the Peony Garden tonight for a poetry duel, if you dare. There will be many guests on hand to celebrate Young Lord Peng Kai-Zhi's First Pollinating. His father has contracted me for ten thousand *yuan*."

Everyone in the Floating World knew about the celebration; as Corsage of the Chrysanthemum Pavilion, Lilian had received an invitation. Still, it was unusual to publicly announce a contract price, since rumors bred more interest than hard numbers. Then again, this was an ungodly amount, enough to buy a large villa in the capital. Predictably, the crowds murmured in excitement.

"And to think," Jie said, making a show of counting on her fingers, "my virginity is already worth over ten times his son's."

And more than Lusha's. The unspoken message was not lost on her, for she flushed, the ugly shade of red visible through her make-up.

Jie kept her expression innocent, as if the comment was unintentional. "As for your challenge... I'll be there."

With another huff, Lusha turned on her heel to leave. She looked over her shoulder. "See you tonight. After I'm done with you, they'll be rescinding their bids on your pock-ridden hole."

Jie feigned shock, even as her stomach churned. A poetry duel! The only rhymes Jie knew were those that clan initiates learned to memorize toxins.

Both Wen and Yuna turned and gaped.

Wen whispered, "What were you thinking? Lusha is a master poet. She'll savor making you look bad, especially if it ensures her record stands."

"It's my way in to the house to scout around, and also get a feel for your Gardener's intentions."

Pouting in the cutest way, Wen squeezed her hand. "I could've done that, without risking your virgin price."

Jie sucked on her lower lip. Wealthy men's obsession with virginity—their own and their partners'—just made them willing dupes over something whose value was based in perception. Her virgin price would fund clan operations for a year. And, if she had to admit it to herself, she was proud of it: utterly lacking in a Floating World Blossom's renowned grace, she still drew higher bids than the most celebrated Night Blossom of them all.

Right now, though, Wen's wounded expression took precedence. Jie smiled at her. "I need you to do something more important: her guard. Find out where he ate."

"Mister Meng?" Wen gave a perplexed rise of her eyebrow.

"His breath. It smelled the same as Masked Crossbowman. A sesame-ginger marinade. Lusha's breath didn't smell the same, so it isn't something she ate at your house."

Yuna's mouth formed a pretty circle. "Your nose never ceases to amaze me."

From what Jie could tell, full humans had poor vision and senses of smell. It was a wonder they'd lasted so long. "Can you find out?"

Wen gave an enthusiastic nod. "I'll ask him for a recommendation when he gets back to the house."

No sooner did Wen and Yuna head off then Meisha approached. The older Blossom tapped on Jie's wrist as she passed. *No Cleaner. No reinforcements.*

Jie's gut clenched. No Cleaner meant there was a dead body lying in an alley, waiting to be found. No reinforcements from the clan meant they were on their own. No doubt, this second message would be passed through taps and finger-brushes among all the sisters by now. She scanned the crowds, backtracking from Meisha to the other clan members.

Some of the younger ones' expressions were contorted in dismay, but by and large, they'd taken the bad news in stride. Hopefully, the assassin had been sent by the Peony Garden to specifically target Jie, and the others weren't at risk.

At the end of the message relay, she found Lilian, who gave her an apologetic nod.

Jie bowed as a junior should to a senior Blossom. "I couldn't find the color you wanted."

"Then we must hasten back for lessons." Lilian beckoned.

As she followed Lilian back toward the Floating World, Jie passed one last message to one of the sisters. *Resume regular activities. Maintain vigilance. Watch for light atop the Lotus Shrine.*

Hopefully, that would reassure them, even if Jie didn't feel much better.

Once they passed the gates and into the quiet of the late-morning Floating World, Jie whispered, "Why no clan support?"

Lilian sighed. "Only one brother was at the safe house. The Emperor stayed an extra day at the summer villa, so all extra hands are there to protect him. The only ones left in the city are in critical areas."

Jie's chest tightened. As if the Floating World wasn't the most important nexus of information, and the sisters gathering it weren't critical. "We need to dispose of the body before anyone finds it."

"We do?" Lilian's face turned an interesting shade of green. They'd all dissected cadavers as children, and if memory served, she'd nearly vomited every class. Apparently, little had changed. It might be that much harder to get her reassigned.

"Come on. It will cause quite the stir, and the local authorities won't know what to make of his fatal wound." Jie grinned. "It was a great throw."

"You already said so." Lilian flashed her crooked smile, which had enchanted many a wealthy patron. "But I don't mind you repeating it."

Stomach erupting in butterflies, Jie leaned in and rested her head on Lilian's shoulder. "It was a great shot."

Lilian squeezed her hand. To any prying eyes, it would look like the sisterly affection between Night Blossoms.

There was no activity around the opening to the alley; a good sign. Jie turned the corner.

And skidded to a stop.

The body was gone, along with all trace of the attack.

She turned to Lilian. "You said there was no Cleaner?"

Scanning the area, Lilian gave a tentative nod. "If not us, then who?"

"Masked Crossbowman or his friends." Jie knelt over the spot where the man had fallen and set her hand on the pavestones. They were a fraction warmer than those in the surrounding area, so it couldn't have been long. "He was quite dead, so he couldn't have walked off by himself. That means—"

"They didn't want his body found, either."

On second glance, though the pavestones looked clean, thin scuff marks from shoes and displaced grit suggested that whoever it was had dragged the body deeper into the alley. Jie followed the faint trail to where it stopped, about halfway down.

"What are you doing?" Lilian asked.

"A trail."

Lilian knelt and stared at the ground. "Where?"

Pointing, Jie sniffed the air. The coppery tang of blood still hung here, in minute traces. "They covered the wound; otherwise there'd be a blood trail, or a sign that they'd cleaned up afterwards."

Lilian looked up the shrine walls on either side, each rising nearly fifteen feet. "They somehow lifted him up and over?"

That would explain why the trail stopped there, with no body. Still, it would take a lot of effort to bring him up that high. Jie pop-vaulted to the top and looked over the side of each wall. Still no sign of the body. She came down and sniffed again. The scent of blood had thinned even more.

"Any clues?" Lilian asked.

Shaking her head, Jie sniffed around, but the scent didn't grow any stronger. "For now, our only lead is the guard at the Peony Garden."

Lilian's head rose and fell in slow bobs. "What do we do now?"

"I need your help with improvised poetry."

"Whatever for?" Lilian's brow furrowed.

Jie grinned. "I am going with you to the Peony Garden's soirée tonight. I accepted a poetry duel with Lusha."

"You did what?" Lilian blanched. "She's the most celebrated poet in the Floating World in a generation."

"Then you can't tell the Gardener or Florist that's why I'm going with you."

CHAPTER 5

"Absolutely not." Shaking her head so hard it might fall off, the Gardener stood up from her desk and slapped her palm on its shiny surface. Looking more like a Black Lotus trainer than a brothel owner, she glared from Jie to Lilian and back again.

Behind her stood Florist Wei, gaze sympathetic. She folded her hands into the long sleeves of her green dress.

Despite Jie's best efforts to keep her impromptu invitation to the Peony Garden secret, rumors in the Floating World sprouted faster than toxic mushrooms after a spring rain. Gardener Ju, a woman of middling years whose charm and talents—and supposedly an exceptionally limber body— still drew Hummingbirds to her bed, had summoned Jie and Lilian to her office just as the House's mid-afternoon preparations had begun.

Jie bowed her head. "Please, Gardener. I can't back down. I'd lose face."

"Not as much as when Lusha humiliates you." The Gardener's eyes sharpened like blades. "You've been here for six years, and still have less grace and propriety than a second-year Seedling."

Bowing low, Jie stewed. It wasn't as though she couldn't learn all the inane rituals. It just wasn't worth the effort. Not when she'd eventually leave the Floating World and make use of her real skills.

The Gardener rounded her desk, subtly limping from an old injury to her left leg. She harrumphed. "You'd be worthless, if not for your exotic face and pointed ears."

Behind her, the Florist gave a subtle shake of her head. How ironic that it was an accountant who had the most warmth among the seniors in this House.

The Gardener's ire shifted to Lilian. "And you: not only allowing her, but trying to hide it."

"I'm sorry." Lilian bowed low.

The Gardener turned back to Jie, teeth gritted. "Many wealthy patrons will be there tonight, including three of your highest bidders. If you lose badly, they'll be well within their rights to rescind their bids. That would be bad for our house, and bad for your contract holder."

Jie suppressed a smirk. The Gardener couldn't care less about her contract holder, supposedly a broker of orphan girls, but really a shell company for the Black Lotus Clan. Her concern was her cut of the virgin price, part of the payment for Jie's training. The clan, on the other hand... While it certainly stood to lose a pretty copper *fen*, the amount didn't begin to compare to the financial benefits of imperial patronage.

Still, every Floret cared about her virgin price, and Jie chastised her own vanity for feeling the same. She lowered her bow another several degrees. "I'm sorry, Gardener. I wasn't thinking of the consequences."

"It's time you learned." The Gardener searched her eyes. "Once you finish your afternoon chores, you will be confined to Lilian's room tonight, with a guard posted outside the door. His overtime pay will come from your bond."

Jie held her bow, if only to keep her smile hidden. No doubt, the Gardener assumed that with Lilian's room on the third floor, as far from the main entrance as possible, Jie had no way of sneaking out. Which she would, since the safety of her clan sisters preempted any concern about risks to her virgin price. "As you command, Gardener."

With a huff, the Gardener sat back down and returned to writing a letter.

The Florist cleared her throat. "Gardener, may they go?"

Not looking up, the Gardener waved a dismissive hand.

The Florist gave them a sympathetic look. "Off you go."

Coming out of her bow, Jie exchanged glances with Lilian and departed.

Lilian flashed hand signals. *Is there anything I can do to convince you not to go?*

Of course not. Jie grinned.

She followed Lilian back to her room. While Lilian freshened up for the soirée at the Peony Garden, Jie decoded the poem the jade vendor had given her, using a cipher made just for him. Since he'd written a poem, the message contained several ambiguities; but the gist was that the Lord of Jinjing had dropped an exorbitant amount of money in many of the houses over the last several months.

Not sure of what to make of it, other than his seed likely going dry, Jie went about her afternoon. Today it was her turn to clean and set up the spacious common room, which vaulted three stories up with mezzanines overlooking it. While most of the Seedlings and Florets despised the messy work, it was not all that different from processing a crime scene. Memories of which wealthy merchant or lord sat where, ate what, and saw whom, all formed a tapestry of information.

Last night, Lord Ting had sat in front of the right-hand side of the stage, his favorite spot, entertaining a minor lord. Perhaps trying to assuage his concerns about the empire? So dashing and formidable, he looked like a hero of old next to the other lord. Beloved by the imperial court. Adored by the populace. If only the common folk knew what he enjoyed behind closed doors.

Jie had served them, ostensibly to attract more bids on her virginity, but really to eavesdrop. They'd quieted as soon as she approached, despite the Floating World convention that anything that happened here, stayed here.

Nonetheless, Lilian had gathered significant damning information over the months: stockpiling of weapons, unapproved saltpeter mines, suspicious transactions. The Emperor had yet to order any action, hoping Lord Ting could solve the problem peaceably.

Now working where Lord Ting had sat, Jie looked up to the second-floor mezzanine. Lilian had stood there, beckoning him. His rosewood chair's angle in relation to the matching round table suggested he'd been in a hurry to leave. Apparently, a tumble between the sheets took precedence over talking an underling out of treason.

He wouldn't come calling tonight; not with Lilian at the Peony Garden.

Along with Jie, who'd find a way to slip the Gardener's watchful eye.

***

Jie studied the dwarf-made padlock, considering. Though the first-floor window shutters had simple hook locks, the second and third floors had none. The Gardener must've been quite concerned about Jie trying to escape to not only to lock this shutter, but also use an expensive device usually reserved for the most valuable treasures. It was almost flattering to be thought of as such.

Maybe it was meant as a warning; or perhaps punishment. Otherwise, it bordered on overkill. The Gardener didn't know Jie could scale the walls, after all. She also didn't know that elf ears could hear the tumblers in the lock.

Jie set to work, turning the combination at each click. Six turns and ten seconds later, it yielded with a snick.

She chuckled to herself. If the Chrysanthemum Pavilion had known about her true identity, the Gardener would've had Jie naked and chained. It certainly wouldn't be the first time that had happened to a Blossom in the House, though under very different circumstances.

Time to pick something out to wear. Lilian had numerous beautiful gowns, many gifts from Hummingbirds. Her pink dress with embroidered doves would suggest innocence, and possibly drive up bids. With a grin, Jie went to Lilian's closet and slid open the door.

Empty.

Her brow furrowed. The Gardener had taken beyond extraordinary precautions but she still underestimated Jie.

Channeling her Inner Steel Orchid, she lifted the carpet, revealing the floorboard door to a secret compartment. Inside, she found Lilian's stealth suit, a curved dagger, and several throwing spikes and stars. In a segmented compartment lay several vials of intoxicants, packed carelessly close to the three crossbow bolts retrieved from earlier today as evidence; unmistakable from Jie's own scent on the one she'd caught. Given Lord Ting's penchant for rough play, a jolt in the wrong place could crack the vials.

Jie banished the thought of Lilian taming Lord Ting with her body. She withdrew the stealth suit. The stretchy material would've been skin-tight but flexible on Lilian's larger frame, allowing freedom of motion without the risk of snagging a loose sleeve, or a droopy pant leg knocking something over. Even with Jie's smaller build, the clothes fit snugly. If the common folk believed that the Black Fists were more than boogiemen that stole disobedient children, the stealth suit embellished Lilian's curves so much that her patrons might want her to roleplay Naughty Assassin in it. *Seduce the Assassin Before She Kills You*, they'd call it.

Wearing Lilian's larger Black Fist shoes, with the big toe separated from the others, she tiptoed to the door and listened. The guard's breathing had slowed, perhaps to the point of dozing off. The sound of revelry carried on, though quieter than on most nights, given that everyone who was anyone would be attending the party at the Peony Garden. With free time on her hands, maybe the Gardener would check on her, maybe not. There was no way to prepare for that possibility.

Satisfied she could do no more to hide her tracks, Jie went to the window and looked. The chamber overlooked the capital's southeast reservoir, which reflected the red lanterns hanging above the Floating World's perimeter moat. It left the wall in darkness.

Yet another house guard patrolled the courtyard below. Maybe he was there to prevent intruders from climbing through a first-floor window, or attempting to go in through the door to the kitchens, but that wasn't standard procedure on a regular night.

And given that tonight would be slower than usual because of the festivities at the Peony Garden, it meant the Gardener had placed the guard there for her.

She turned to the last exit from the room: the fireplace. Only three rooms in the entire mansion had this rare architectural feature from the land of the fair-skinned: Lilian, as preeminent Blossom, had one; and right below, the Gardener's own room. On the first floor, the common room's hearth backed up to the kitchens' ovens. All four shared the same flue network, merging close to the roof.

With the ovens raging at full blast, those last three feet risked burns and smoke inhalation, and guaranteed soot and ash in every pore.

Still, it provided the easiest way out, and some ashes over her naturally pale complexion would help her move through the night. She took Lilian's pillow case and tore it to cover her hands, and her mouth and nose. It smelled like Lilian's hair, all honeysuckle and honey.

Then she started her climb. Past the wind shelf, the width of the first section of flue forced her to wriggle up, hands close to her body. At the flue junction, she reached up and tested the bricks.

Hot, but not scalding. She might have two seconds to clear this last section without burning her palms through the remains of Lilian's pillowcase. She took a deep breath, grabbed the hot ridge where the flues merged, and propelled herself up. Black smoke made it difficult to see. Her feet found purchase on the ridge, and she jumped, shooting her hands and feet out to suspend herself in the larger flue. The bricks heated her palms as she spider-climbed to the top. With a last burst of energy, she gripped the burning rim of the chimney, pulled herself out, and flipped over on to the tiles.

Her feet slipped on the steep pitch, the ash on the too-large shoes providing poor traction on slick tiles. She slid, much too fast, her body going over the eaves. At the last second, she shook off her improvised hand wraps and grabbed hold of the edge.

She'd almost become a splatter of half-elf in the courtyard below.

Heart racing, she blew out a breath and swung over to the closest window shutters. Her toes found the narrow ledge, and she reached under the eaves and pulled herself over. After the initial scare, the descent was child's play. She and Lilian had done this so many times that finding the hand and footholds in the planks, window sills, and awning tiles came easily.

Her feet landed on the pavestones without a sound. With her elf vision adjusting to the darkness and transforming the world into hues of grey-green, she dashed over to the compound walls, climbed over, and took shadowed back alleys to the Peony Garden. Chrysanthemum House's main rival in the Floating World, it lay just a block away. Their very layouts were similar, since they'd been designed by the same architect.

Which meant Jie might be able to get in and out without ever having to confront Lusha in a poetry duel.

CHAPTER 6

Jie stood toward the rear of the Peony Garden, a near-exact replica of the Chrysanthemum Pavilion. Given the hour and the festivities, there'd be no easy insertion points. The Florist's and Gardener's windows would certainly be locked from the inside, as would most of the other first-floor windows.

Yuna would be in the trainee room, but getting her attention risked waking the other Seedlings. Instead, Jie climbed over the walls, then up to the red-tiled awning on the second floor. There, she crept along, checking the other windows. Most stood unshuttered to let in the cool night air. In some rooms, Florets still fussed with their Blossoms' jewelry, hair, and make-up. From the giggling and grunting in a few others, some Blossoms had already left the party to bring impatient Hummingbirds back to their rooms.

Jie looked up at the third-floor windows. With her arms so exhausted, it wasn't worth the risk of finding yet more occupied rooms. She climbed down and proceeded to the kitchens.

As expected, the back door lay ajar and the kitchens buzzed with activity, like the Black Lotus Temple's training Hall of Darting Daggers. Chefs' apprentices prepped meats and vegetables, while higher-ups stir-fried, braised, and steamed delicacies fit for a great lord. Florets scurried to take small plates of snacks, only to transform into the embodiment of beauty as they passed through the doors to the common room.

Swallowing down a pit of jealousy, Jie entered. She threaded through the bustle, always using someone's back as cover, twisting or ducking to avoid the gaze of anyone who happened to look up from their work. She reached the open side door and slipped through into a side yard.

As in the Chrysanthemum Pavilion, the little courtyard provided easy servant access to the bathhouses. She kept to the shrubs lining the mansion, pausing behind each of the two cherry blossom trees before coming to the servants' door.

No sounds came from within, as would be expected at this hour. She opened the door and peeked in. Partially shuttered light-bauble lamps hung between three sliding doors on either side of the hall, shedding enough light for her vision to return to normal. The double doors at the far end muffled the festive sounds from the common room. If someone happened to open the door...

Jie zigzagged over the nightingale floors and came to the closest door. Confirming no one dallied inside, she slid it open and ducked in.

Warm, humid steam filled her lungs, percolating off a central wooden tub set into the wood floors. A polite half-elf would've scrubbed herself clean outside of the tub, using the basins on the floor and the towels in the cubbies. Time being of the essence, she stripped off the filthy stealth suit and slipped into the bath.

The tepid water nearly made her yelp. Though Black Lotus training included meditating under freezing waterfalls, many years had passed since Jie had done so. Heated by copper pipes which ran under the mansion from the central hearth, the baths had yet to reach optimal temperature.

A wave of ash and grit floated out from her sooty body, ruining the water for others. She rinsed out her hair and scrubbed her skin, all the while bemoaning her flat body. With very few half-elves mentioned in history to use an example, who knew when she'd fill out? Until then, she was cursed to remain in the Floating World, working as a Floret.

Satisfied she'd washed the evidence of her chimney escapades away, Jie climbed out, dried herself off, and donned one of the white silk bathrobes hanging from a hook above the cubbies. She tied her hair up and secured it with a bladed hairpin and lockpicks. To prevent some poor Seedling or Floret from receiving a browbeating for the dirty water, Jie unplugged the stopper—they came loose often during Hummingbirds' exuberant play.

She then removed the light baubles from the lamps and wrapped them in the stealth suit, which she in turn folded into the towel. With a quick look to see that the scene was otherwise undisturbed, she crept back into the hallway and out into the yard.

Slipping into Lilian's shoes, Jie glided around the outside of the bathhouse and into a wider courtyard. On the veranda off of the mansion, partially shuttered light baubles illuminated several distinguished-looking men cavorting with Blossoms. The ladies covered obligatory giggles at bad jokes with their dainty hands.

The white robe would make it difficult to sneak past them unseen, so Jie turned back. Fingers and toes finding handholds in the bathhouse's planks, she wormed her way up to the roof. Using the pitch of the roof to keep herself hidden from the veranda and balconies, she worked her way back to the central mansion.

A window overlooked the bathhouse roof, a line of light shining between the shutters. Testing the hinges to make sure they were well-oiled, Jie opened one of the leaves a crack and peeked in. No people or shadows moved, and the only the sounds came from the party below. She opened it just wide enough for her slight build and climbed in.

Rosewood chairs flanked a decorative table on a round wool carpet. A large bed with a matching rosewood frame occupied the east wall, while brush paintings hung on the walls. The lack of

Dragonscribe magic in them, and the spring motifs in the art, suggested the room belonged to a newer Blossom.

Jie crept over to the dressing niche and looked in a mirror standing on a make-up table. Indeed, compared to the celebrated Corsages of the Floating World, elf-blood made her exotic, unique: dark brown hair instead of black, a sharper nose, larger eyes, and those tapered ears. A clan elder had once said, *The wealthiest men in the realm will seek her out. Her virgin price alone will fund clan operations for a year, and even after, they'll line up for the chance to be next.*

She sighed. Like Lilian, she'd be stuck in the Floating World, gathering information and making money for the clan while lying on her back. Maybe it was time to practice the renowned grace of the Blossoms.

Shaking the thought out of her head, she turned her attention to the paper lodged into the mirror frames. The self-affirmations, notes on Hummingbird kinks, and a cosmetics shopping list indicated the room belonged to Namei, a pretty girl from the coast.

Jie's gaze settled on a bar where several gowns hung. All consisted of inner and outer gowns that embellished cleavage and exposed long legs—assets that the Heavens had yet to bless her with, and none suited a Floret trying to project innocence. Little Wen, however, might still have the perfect dress for the occasion.

Jie went to the door and slid it open enough to poke her head through. As in the Chrysanthemum Pavilion, the mezzanine overlooking the common room ran around the perimeter of the second floor, with doors to the Blossom's rooms. Music from the four-stringed *pipa* and eighteen-stringed *guzheng* percolated up from below.

This room lay up and to the right of the stage, and a tall man standing by the balcony blocked her from view. Wearing fine blue silk robes, he smelled of oiled steel. He held his thumbs and forefingers to form a rectangle, as if framing a picture. Maybe he was an artist? She followed his line of sight to the corner of the stage, where a Peony Garden Floret was serving drinks to a pair of wealthy-looking merchants while they ogled her.

If this man was an artist, he must've been influenced by the trends among the fair-skinned, since this particular scene was so...mundane. *Desperate Men*, she'd name it. If the opportunity presented itself, she'd be sure to get a look at his face.

She started to recede back to the wall, but paused. Lilian approached the two merchants in the corner and bowed with the grace of a phoenix. Jie remained transfixed. No matter how many times she'd watched Lilian at the Chrysanthemum Pavilion, her elegance never ceased to evoke both envy and arousal. With a hard swallow, she backed away.

Some Blossoms loitered with Hummingbirds along the mezzanine railing, giggling and pointing. With their backs to the doors, Jie stayed close to the wall and slunk behind them, turned a corner, and ducked into Little Wen's room.

The partially shuttered light-bauble lamp shed a dim light over a room furnished much like the other. Jie went to the bed and stashed Lilian's stealth suit and shoes underneath, then took one of the light baubles before going to the dressing niche. Deep within one of the drawers, she found the dress that had contributed to Wen's considerable virgin price, from a time when her build was similar to Jie's now.

Green silk with embroidered yellow and white flowers, the one-piece's neckline emphasized the nape, top of the shoulder blades, and collarbones. Hanging sleeves would slide into the crook of a bent elbow, embellishing willowy arms, and the single slit could expose just enough leg to tantalize. Jie slipped into it, then borrowed some of Wen's rouge to give her cheeks a pink tint. With a quick look in the mirror, Jie pinned her hair in a way that concealed her ears. She stashed the light bauble in her undergarments.

Now, it became a matter of sneaking down to the common room without being seen, in a dress that was meant to be seen; then finding an opportunity to investigate the Florist's and Gardener's offices for evidence of a plot against her or the clan.

Again using the Blossoms and guests along the railing as cover, Jie worked her way over to one of the stairwells and hurried down. It opened into a dimly lit hall between the common room and veranda, which also led to an office. Waiting for a drunk man on the arm of a Blossom to stumble past, she turned out of the stairwell. Not having time to find the joists in the nightingale floor, she stepped in time with the amorous couple in the opposite direction, and reached the office door.

A dwarf-made lock was set in the door, openable with the right key. The devices had flooded the market in the last ten years with increased trade with the East, but proved only a little harder to pick than the local padlocks. Not only that, a passerby wouldn't even notice it had been breached. It yielded to her lockpicks, and she slipped into the dark room.

Her elf vision took over, casting the office in hues of green and grey. With shelves of ledgers and an abacus, this had to be the Florist's office. While it was tempting to find out Lusha's actual virgin price, recent transactions would provide more insight into possible assassin hires. She pulled out the one with the most recent label. A folded sheet of paper slipped from between its pages, and Jie snatched it out of the air without a sound. Opening her mouth, she secured the light bauble between her teeth. She looked at the ledger's binding and found the subtle gap between pages where the sheet had slipped from.

She opened to that spot and found a record of the most current expenditures. Contracting a murder could cost upwards of a thousand gold *yuan*, so she looked first to the largest receivables. Three stood out, all listed as going toward Young Lord Peng's First Pollinating. Curiously, not all came from Lord Peng, though it was plausible the three companies who had paid the balance had received some favor in return. A quick skim over the past hundred days of transactions showed no totals that would add up to hiring an assassin.

Still, there was a familiar scent. She sniffed. The sesame-ginger marinade! She snuffled more, no doubt looking more like a pig searching for truffles than a Floret trying to attract bids. The minute traces came from...the folded sheet of paper.

She unfolded it and scanned. The script looked graceful and feminine.

The common room must be set up exactly like—

Laughing and chirping footsteps grew louder in the hall, coming to a stop at the door. The handle jiggled.

"It's unlocked," said a male voice.

CHAPTER 7

Standing by the desk in the Florist's office, Jie snatched up the ledger and returned it to its shelf, letter and all. She stashed the light bauble in her mouth and ducked under the table just as the door opened.

Two sets of legs staggered in, visible from under the writing table: one male in dark silk robes, the other the willowy limbs of a Night Blossom. They closed the door to a crack, allowing a blade of light in.

The couple approached, the male's feet pointed forward, the female's shuffling back as she giggled.

"I've always wanted to do it on a table," he said.

"We can't, my Lord." The voice was familiar: Meina, from the Peony Garden, a pretty but not-so-smart girl. "Not in the Florist's office. Come back to my room."

Yes, go back to your room. Jie gritted her teeth. The desk screeched on the floor as he pressed the girl into it, providing an up-close look at the middle of their thighs. As sturdy as it looked, the table probably wasn't built to support one person, let alone two in the throes of passion.

The woman squealed as her feet left the floor. She landed on the desk, which creaked in protest. His robe parted and his pants and undergarments dropped to his ankles. He grunted, and she gasped.

As part of her training, Jie had witnessed coupling more times than a child's abacus could calculate, from straightforward positions to those a yogi from the lands of the bronze-skinned would envy. It was neither titillating nor disgusting, just a means to an end. Right now, though, it might mean her end—either from a table collapsing on her, or their noise drawing someone in.

Angling herself to fit in the space between the table's legs and his, Jie slipped through. With the man preoccupied, she stayed low out of the Blossom's line of sight and darted through the space in the door. She gained her feet, smoothed the dress out, and hurried toward the common room.

She paused at the archway and looked.

Up on the balcony across from her, the artist was gone. In his place stood another man, peering at something on Jie's side of the room. She followed his gaze.

He was looking at the same corner by the stage, but this time several men wearing the livery of Lord Ting stood there. They gazed at Peony Garden Blossoms who were dancing sensually on stage to a quartet of stringed instruments. Her eyes shifted to the source of the music, a space in front of the stage. The famous Master Ding Meihui's fingers swam over her *pipa* strings, so mesmerizing that it was hard to tell if she created the music, or the music moved her fingers. Rumor had it she was close to rediscovering the lost magic of Dragon Songs, which had helped free mankind from the Tivari ages ago. Lord Peng must've paid a handsome sum; she usually performed for the Emperor himself, and supposedly even taught eight-year-old Princess Kaiya.

Jie's gaze shifted to the left of the musicians, where Dan Lusha sat in Young Lord Peng Kai-Zhi's lap, giggling like a girl ten years younger. Indeed, her heavy make-up almost accomplished that effect, even if the low cut of her white inner gown exposed far more than it hid, and the translucent outer gown left nothing it covered to the imagination. Peng Kai-Zhi was flushed red, whether from alcohol or embarrassment, it was hard to tell; but at just sixteen, he otherwise looked every part the heir to his province in his formal robes. Clan members embedded in the palace reported that his younger brother, Kai-Long, was adored by the Emperor—their maternal uncle—and that he helped keep an eye on Princess Kaiya.

Bowing lords and ministers all approached and toasted him, while prominent Blossoms of all the major houses introduced themselves with dainty bows. Lilian, dressed in a gown nearly as revealing as Lusha's, scanned the room as she mingled with the other Blossoms, her Black Fist-trained eyes taking in every detail without actually appearing to.

Jie sucked on her lower lip. This would be her future life—perhaps for decades, given the youthful effect of elf blood—if she didn't prove herself or get murdered over her virginity first. For now, though, she had to confirm she was the Peony Garden's only target.

The original plan had been to mingle with the guests, and perhaps eavesdrop on the Florist, until an opportunity presented itself to break away and investigate the offices. Now, with one office down, maybe there was a safer option: all she had to do was make it through the festivities and to the opposite hall without being noticed.

Checking to ensure her hair still covered the tips of her ears, she used a walking man as cover to cross a quarter of the room. She froze in a dead space, surrounded by backs. That sesame-ginger smell was emanating from somewhere in the room. Unfortunately, the same milling bodies that kept her hidden also prevented her from getting a good visual scan.

She swept up a porcelain tray with rice wine cups from a table and continued as if she were one of the house Florets, until she ducked behind yet another man in dark blue silk. The smell of oiled steel. The artist from the balcony.

Jie shot a glance up to the mezzanine corner. The man who'd been there moments before was gone, replaced by another man in crimson livery. What was it about that spot? That was a question for later, because here was a chance to see Artist's face. She angled the tray so that his face reflected in a cup of rice wine.

Given the position of the lights, a scar across his forehead was all that distinguished him. He started to turn.

Jie ducked away, continuing toward the opposite archway. It was too easy. The scent grew stronger. Just another few—

"You!" A middle-aged patron of the Chrysanthemum House waved at her from a table ahead to the left. Deputy Xun from the Ministry of War. "You're the half-elf Floret from the Chrysanthemum Pavilion! Jie, was it?"

Shit. Jie pretended she hadn't heard while continuing on her way. He reached for her as she passed, but she deftly avoided his hand by turning and setting the tray down on a nearby table. The sesame-ginger smell diffused.

And now, more eyes fell on her. Excited whispers broke out.

"It's Ju Jie!"

"I bid thirty thousand yuan on her virginity."

"She's almost too awkward for a Blossom, but that face!"

A large body stepped in front of her; easy enough to avoid, but doing so would raise questions.

Jie stopped and looked up.

Minister Li from the Imperial Treasury met her eye. Using his huge frame, he angled himself, boxing her against a wall. "So, you are the Chrysanthemum Pavilion's famous half-elf."

Men like this prowled the Floating World, using their size to project dominance over Blossoms and Florets alike. Every female, from Sprout to Gardener, had endured it. Despite their training to maintain calm while feigning demureness, most feared the experience.

Most, but not embedded Black Lotus Fists. Certainly not Jie. There were a dozen different ways to slip out of this trap, and even more to mete out pain or permanent injury. Still, clan training in keeping a clear head under duress melded perfectly with Floating

World skills in manipulating fragile male psyches. Jie cast her gaze down and trembled. "Yes, Master."

In an audacious move, he lifted her chin with a finger. His leer roved over her, making her feel dirtier than after the trip up the chimney. "What is your virgin price up to? I would like to make a bid."

"I'm sorry, only my Gardener and Florist know. You will have to speak with them."

"I'd like to speak to *you.*" His breath burned hot on her neck as he leaned in.

Her shudder this time might not have been entirely acting. Her arms and legs froze, and she couldn't form a coherent thought.

A hand clamped around hers.

Fighting reflexes took over, jolting Jie out of her fear. She turned her hand over and started twisting into a wrist lock.

Her captor's hand reacted smoothly, avoiding the technique with practiced skill. "Minister Li, thank you for finding my Little Sister."

Jie looked at the hand on hers. The dorsal side was delicate and smooth, belying the callouses on the palm and fingers. She followed a silk-clad arm up and met Lilian's stern gaze.

"Come along now, Little Jie." Lilian's voice sounded gentle, even as the swipes and taps of her finger on the back of Jie's hand said otherwise. Sometimes it was a good thing their clan's non-verbal communication didn't include expletives. *What are you doing here*?

"Thank you for your interest, Master." Jie bowed, while tapping back, *Scouting*.

Minister Li stared at the both of them, eyes wide and mouth moving, but no words coming out.

"Come, Little Jie." Lilian gave her a tug toward the entrance. *Too big a risk. We need to get you out before Lusha sees you.*

"Look what—I mean, *who* we have here!" Lusha's soft, melodious voice managed to boom over the throng. "I didn't see Little Ju Jie from the Chrysanthemum Pavilion. Lilian said you had later declined the invitation. Come, pay respects to Young Lord Peng."

Conversation quieted to a low murmur. Heads looked from the couple of honor to Jie, and the crowds parted to form an aisle between them.

Lusha beckoned with a graceful wave of her hand.

Jie sucked on her lower lip. Had everything gone perfectly, she would've been in and out without ever having to engage in a poetry duel.

"I'm sorry, Miss Lusha." Lilian bowed low. "My Little Sister is dizzy from all the guests. I was going to take her out for some fresh air."

The House Gardener, wearing a blue gown with a white inner dress, stepped into view. She beckoned to someone near the entrance. "Oh, it is much too cold outside. We don't want you freezing."

Never mind that it wasn't cold. House guards took up position at the entrance and the doors to the veranda. It wouldn't be hard to make it by them, but again, it would raise questions about how a Floret had such talents.

"I will assign one of our men to escort you to the conservatory. Plenty of fresh air, with all the open windows. Over here, Shixian."

Making it no warmer than outside, so temperature clearly wasn't the Gardener's concern. Her feral grin suggested ill intentions. She now hooked her hands into the crook of a handsome young man's elbow and pulled him into the aisle through the crowds.

Shixian was his name, apparently, and he was staring straight at her.

Then again, so was everyone else.

Shixian approached, the scent of rust growing stronger. His swishing robes didn't match the livery of the other house guards.

And he moved like a trained killer.

Like Masked Crossbowman.

CHAPTER 8

Jie took an involuntary step back as the Peony Garden guard, Shixian, approached. She tapped a message onto Lilian's arm as she pulled her back. *He's the one from this morning.*

Lilian looked down at her, brow creased. *Are you sure?* she mouthed.

Was she? Jie studied the tall man. It was hard to tell, since he wasn't advancing and retreating with a repeating crossbow in hand. He walked with purpose, though he didn't seem to have any weapons. Still, all it would take was deft sleight of hand to slip any number of poisons into Jie's drink. And of course, there were contact toxins.

Jie took a deep breath. It wouldn't be the first, and certainly not the last time someone tried to kill her. She still had Lilian, and...her eyes found Little Wen, the only other Black Lotus member among all the people present.

Lines of worry were etched into her pretty features. She signed, *Not a house guard. Get out.*

Brushing her hair behind her ears, Jie signaled with a combination of finger motions and eye expressions. *I will handle. Maintain line of sight.*

Shixian came closer. He had a strong jaw, and large eyes embellished by a high nose bridge and sculpted brow. Unlike most of the lechers in attendance, he was fresh, handsome. He beamed like a ray of sun stabbing through storm clouds.

Her pulse quickened against her better judgement.

He reached her and bowed. "Miss Jie."

"Mister Shixian." She returned his salute, deftly dodging his attempt to brush up against her.

His forehead scrunched up for a split second before he extended a hand toward the conservatory. As in the Chrysanthemum House, it lay through the archway to the other office. They passed through, crossed the hallway, and went under another arch. A cool—but not cold—breeze greeted her as they stepped into a long room lined with open windows. Empty save for a few rosewood chairs, it mirrored the veranda on the other side. Behind them, guards barred the way to any others. Lilian craned to keep an eye on them.

Well, if they wanted to kill Jie with no witnesses, they'd made a mistake: nobody would see what she could really do, either. Every muscle coiled, ready to react.

Using his body position, he corralled her out of Lilian's line of sight.

She sidestepped his attempt to touch her ear, and started to—

"You're a shy one, aren't you?" His tone was playful, his grin charming.

What? She gawked at him. That wasn't what an assassin would say. Where was he going with this? "Master Shixian, it wouldn't do to let a man touch me."

"But..." He pointed with that prominent jaw. "You have something in your hair."

She reached up, then scowled. "That's my ear!"

"You...you're an elf!" His mouth formed a perfect circle. "Heavens, forgive me."

"Half-elf." Surely he'd known well before. She searched his eyes.

There was nothing but sincerity. And now, even as close as he was, there was no smell of the sesame ginger, nor any toxin from the Black Lotus' sizeable lexicon. Maybe she'd been mistaken about the Peony Garden's intentions.

"I...I assumed you were half, but I thought you were half-Hua, half-Easterner. Not half-*elf*." He studied her, not like the lechers roving the Floating World, but with a childlike wonder. It was almost endearing. "I can see it now. There must be quite the story there."

She searched his eyes but found nothing but candid curiosity. The story wouldn't inspire the bards, though—she'd been a bawling babe left at the front gates of the Black Lotus Temple. Master Yan had raised her as his own, though he had lost the only hint of her identity. The letter pinned to her swaddling blanket spoke of a human mother who died giving birth and an elf father too busy to be burdened. Still, she stuck to the same cover story: "I assume I'm like all the few other instances of half-elves. A wanderlust-stricken mother left home, either fell in love or into a trap, and left me with humans."

His expression contorted into genuine concern, unlike any of the other prospective Hummingbirds, who'd just moved on to the next question. He seemed so earnest that it felt cruel to have lied. "Too bad for your mother," he said, "never knowing that her daughter grew into such a beauty."

Nothing but sincerity hung in his tone. Heat rose to the tips of her ears. Of all the handsome young men she'd lusted after, he was even more so. And warm. She would've given herself to him right there and then, if not for the issue of her record virgin price. "I am guessing you are not really one of the House guards. Who *are* you, Master Shi—"

"Lieutenant. Lieutenant Chen Shixian. I'm an officer of the Huayuan Provincial Cavalry." He bowed.

Goosebumps prickled on Jie's shoulders, and not from the breeze. While she and horses didn't get along, there was something dashing about a handsome soldier on a horse. "And how did you come to be here? A guest of Lord Peng?"

He shook his head, loosening his luxurious mane, then locked intense eyes on her. "I think you know why I'm here."

Her spine just about turned to jelly. All her pent-up desire felt like a raging torrent about to overrun a dam. If not for the matter of her virgin price, she'd take him there and then.

"You have something on your cheek." He reached into the fold of his robe and withdrew a kerchief. It unfurled, revealing intricate stitching, winding in a mesmerizing pattern. The Dragon Weaver magic woven into the cloth washed over her, making her...making her... Heat surged through her. She shook the haze out of her head.

"Are you all right?" Locking those gorgeous eyes on her, he dabbed the kerchief over her cheek. He pulled it back, revealing a dark smudge. He grinned again, so rakish and alluring. "It looks like ash."

Surely she'd cleaned it all off. But that didn't matter. What mattered was that he was now close.

And it didn't bother her.

On the contrary, his body heat and the masculine rust smell sent a jolt up her spine. Fire blossomed inside her.

Their eyes met, searching each other.

"You are so beautiful," he repeated.

Beautiful. Not exotic, or different. Virgin price be damned. Claiming what little space remained between them, Jie reached up and pulled his face to hers. She parted her lips, and welcomed his tongue.

He pressed against her, boxing her against the wall. His hands slid down her back to her waist, but she moved them lower, up under her skirts. So invited, his fingers brushed along the inside of her thighs, walking higher at a leisurely pace.

Too slow! Aching with heat and desire, she bucked her hips to meet his hand. He tore her undergarments off, lifted her legs up, and pushed into her.

***

"Sir!" Lilian barked from the archway. "Unhand my Little Sister."

Jie broke the kiss and looked over his shoulder.

At least a dozen people were there. Wide-eyed Blossoms covered their gaping mouths. Men muttered as their lips curled into sneers.

And Lilian. Confusion was scrawled over her face.

Jie pushed herself off Shixian as all heat drained from her. Her muddled head cleared. Heavens, what had she done?

The Peony Garden Gardener and Lusha pushed through the throng and passed to either side of Lilian. They exchanged knowing smirks.

"You've broken the rules of the Floating World, girl." The Gardener jabbed an accusatory finger at her. "A Blossom may not entertain a Hummingbird in another House without the Gardener's permission."

"I thought... I thought..." Brows furrowed, Shixian shook his head. "I wasn't a Hummingbird."

Jie nodded. "No. He...he wasn't. He was..." Oh, Heavens, no.

Holding up Jie's undergarment as if it were a scorpion, Lusha brought her hand to her chest. "Heavens, are you saying you gave in to passion?"

A different kind of heat flared in her cheeks. Was it? What was she thinking? No, there was no thought, just primal desire. For Shixian? He was handsome, for sure, but that alone wasn't enough for her to forget about the value of virginity. No, it had to be...the kerchief. It had Dragon Weaver magic imbued in it. She looked around, but there was no sign of it.

"So much for your virgin price." Lusha cast a cruel smile.

This had all been a set-up.

And it'd succeeded.

She'd walked right into it. No matter how much she'd wanted it, even before the magic, she wouldn't have. Not with her virgin price at stake. She glared at Shixian.

His eyes widened, and he waved his hand back and forth. "I am so sorry. I didn't know."

"Liar. You used a kerchief embroidered with Artistic Magic."

He shook his head so fast, his head might come off. He was a good actor, that was for sure; maybe not even a military man. "I know nothing about—"

"This?" The Gardener held up a kerchief. No waves of magic rolled off it. "It looks quite plain."

Had she swapped it? Or was it only single-use? No matter what, there was no proof of what Shixian had done.

The Peony Garden didn't want her killed, but deflowered. To keep Lusha's record virgin price safe.

And as horrible and underhanded and violating as it was, it left an even more sinister question: who'd tried to kill her this morning, and why?

CHAPTER 9

Though full-fledged Blossoms were allowed to take on lovers as long as it didn't interfere with house business, Florets had no such leeway. Even less so for Jie, whose virgin price would've fattened the house's coffers—and the clan's—beyond imagination. In their eyes, it was a dalliance that couldn't go unpunished.

Though technically her contract was held by a Black Lotus shell company, the Gardener had free rein to mete out judgement. She'd stormed over to the Peony Garden, guards in tow. They'd dragged Jie back to the Chrysanthemum House, and would've confined her to a long-unused cellar if it hadn't stunk like some animal had crawled in there and died. Instead, they locked her in a windowless storehouse, with a guard posted.

With nothing else to do, Jie had just wallowed in what had happened. Even though she'd wanted to give herself to Shixian, she wouldn't have. It was still rape, plain and simple, with Artistic Magic as the means. With the kerchief, they might be able to prove it and seek redress. Without it, there was no recourse. The Peony Garden would get away with the violation. She'd been tempted to open the high-proof bottles of White Lightning wine stored there to drown her sorrows, or perhaps light the surplus cases of New Year's firecrackers and just end it there and then.

Now, the morning after, as news of her *indiscretion* swirled throughout the Floating World, Jie knelt at the edge of the stage of the Chrysanthemum Pavilion's common room. Arms outstretched, she balanced trays laden with rice wine-filled cups. The entire House gathered below, a witness to her disgrace.

Still, no castigation in the Floating World could begin to compare with everyday Black Lotus training. In the Floating World, no girl, from Sprout to Blossom, was ever whipped, for fear of leaving scars. Kneeling on hardwood planks meant nothing to someone whose body was hardened to stone; and no amount of berating hurt more than Jie's own internal rebuke.

A trap, so obvious, and she'd fallen for it.

And Shixian. For all his charm, he was just manipulating her. Using magic, no less. Her chest clenched. That Turtle's Egg would pay for what he'd taken from her.

Her arms ached, though certainly not as much as anyone else's would in the same position. Definitely not as much as her heart right now.

Gardener Ju hobbled over and jabbed a finger into her chest, daring her to spill any of the rice wine. "I've sent word to the Golden Peacock Company to see what they want to do with you. You'll still fetch an ungodly amount, from all the Hummingbirds who've eyed you over the years."

That was the reality. Lilian's plight made more sense now. All the training as a spy and warrior meant nothing compared to her body's value to wanton men. Jie's heart knotted even more.

"Now, Lord Ting has reserved the entire house for him and Lilian tonight. He wants it empty, so the rest of you have the night off..."

He would've had to pay enough to cover the house's profits for the night. Thousands of *yuan*. It would've been far less expensive to take Lilian to his villa. What kind of depravity did he have in mind?

"...all except Jie. You will serve dinner to Lord Ting and Lilian tonight." The Gardener gestured to the corner of the stage.

Jie looked at the corner, the same one where Lord Ting had lounged two nights before. The same spot she'd cleaned yesterday.

"Maybe he will be your first Hummingbird."

"Gardener!" Lilian dropped to her knees and pressed her forehead to the floor. She looked up. "Little Sister Jie has not yet flowered with Heaven's Dew. She can't receive Hummingbirds yet."

"Gardener!" Speaking in unison, the other girls all dropped to their knees and bowed their heads. Even the Florist, stern but kind mother that she was, joined in.

The Gardener looked among them, lips tight.

Silence fell over the room, save for the soft weeping of Ai and Yin. Jie's heart wound so tight it might burst. Her House sisters, Sprout to Blossom, all supported her, and each other. Just like the Black Lotus Clan members embedded in the Floating World did.

The Gardener's chuff broke the quiet. "Little Jie has lived in the house long enough without earning her keep. Now that the blossom has been plucked, it doesn't matter. Youth is a commodity with diminishing returns, and the fact you've not blossomed with Heaven's Dew makes you even more unique for the Floating World. It will allow us to set an even higher contract price for your regular assignations, and schedule a few a day."

Anger churned in Jie's stomach. The adherence to this one convention had set the Floating World above every other seedy whorehouse in the land. Sure, she was already twenty, but if the Gardener was willing to make this exception now, who would she sacrifice in the future? "Gardener—"

"Silence! Who gave you permission to speak, selfish little slut?" The Gardener's glare shifted from Jie to the Florist. "Send out invitations to all who have bid on her."

The shuddering shoulders and sniffling among the girls intensified. Jie's heart broke more for them than for herself.

"Gardener," Lilian said, pressing her forehead to the ground again. "Please."

The Gardener slammed her hand down on the stage, making everyone wince. "Don't think that just because you are the Chrysanthemum House's Corsage I won't turn you out. I'll make sure no Floating World House will take you in. Golden Peacock Company will contract you to some back-alley whorehouse in the Trench, where you'll service fifty lowlifes a day."

The Gardener had no idea it was an empty threat, since the Black Lotus Clan would never do such a thing. Lilian knew it, too. She stood, scowling, and took a step forward, in what a trained eye would recognize as the start of an attack.

The room went silent, even as the tension wound tighter than a garrote. The Gardener cowered back, bumping up against the stage as her left leg wobbled.

"I'll do it, willingly," Jie said. Lilian might not have to worry about reprisals from the Gardener, and in fact, banishment from the Floating World was everything she wanted. But the other girls, if emboldened, did not have a clan of spies and assassins to go back to. Jie shot Lilian a warning glance, and would've used signals if her hands weren't full. *The other girls*, she mouthed.

Lilian met her gaze and sighed. Her shoulders slumped and fists unclenched, and she took two steps back and dropped to her knees. "I am sorry, Gardener."

"I'm glad that is settled." The Gardener regained her air of authority, even if her voice came out strained. She turned to Jie and pointed to the corner. "Tonight is an important night. For now, you are going to scrub his favorite table clean and polish every wood surface until I can see your pretty little reflection in them."

* * *

With the cleaning done, along with all her other chores, Jie lay on her side on Lilian's bed, arm supporting her head. Memories of the night before never strayed far from her thoughts. It was times like this that she needed to cuddle in the fluffy white fur of the dogs back at the clan's Black Lotus Monastary.

After repeated rebuffing, Lilian had finally given up trying to comfort her, and now sat at her make-up table in a plain dressing robe, lengthening her lashes. Late afternoon sun streamed in.

Jie finally broke the silence. "What were you thinking, challenging the Gardener?"

"Those are your first words?" Lilian lowered her brush. "I would ask you the same. Don't make this about me. Why did you even go last night? I told you it was dangerous. What if the Peony Garden really wanted to kill you? You never listen."

"I was worried that all our sisters were compromised. I had to hope it was just me."

Lilian's lips pursed. "You should have left it to Wen. She would have figured it out. You always take it upon yourself."

Jie sighed. It was true. Her own hubris, thinking that as senior and with superior senses, nobody could do a better job. But not just that... "I don't want anyone else to get hurt."

"At some point, you have to trust the rest of us."

Jie shook her head. How could she ask others to take risks? "I could never forgive myself if Wen had gotten caught."

"She wouldn't have. She's not as stealthy as you, but she's still good." Lilian glared at her. "Did you ever think that maybe you taking charge of everything has prevented the clan from seeing worth in the rest of us? Maybe that has kept many of us stuck spreading our legs in the Floating World."

Jie's heart sunk. The truths battered her confidence; her very sense of self. Tears threatened.

Lilian rose with enviable grace and glided over. She sat down in the curl formed by Jie's bent knees and body, and draped an arm over her. "Oh, my sweet. I'm so sorry."

Hot tears welled in Jie's eyes and ran down her cheeks.

Lilian climbed over her to the other side of the bed, then embraced Jie from behind. Her cheek pressed against hers. It was protective, comforting.

"I wanted to give myself to him," Jie said. Just saying it made it real. "But I wasn't going to. I couldn't, not with so much money at stake."

Lilian stroked her hair. "I know. Our bodies aren't our own. No matter how much it is drilled into us at the temple, and here in the house, a little piece of me dies every time."

So much sadness in her voice. Jie's stomach twisted. No matter what happened next, she had to convince the clan to reassign Lilian. For now, though, it was time to redirect the conversation. "Clearly, the Peony Garden had ill intentions, but they hadn't planned to go so far as to have me murdered."

"Which means someone else is targeting you." Lilian's nod rubbed against Jie's cheek.

"And maybe not just me."

Lilian's voice dropped lower than a whisper, as if voicing her words too loudly might make them true. "What if there's a traitor? A mole?"

"No." Jie closed her eyes. She'd trained every one of the clan sisters, knew their psychological profiles. "We're like the Steel Orchids. I trust each and every one of them with my life."

"You have a blind spot with us."

Jie started to shake her head, but stopped. She couldn't deny it. Though all clan brothers and sisters felt like family, the girls embedded in the Floating World forged even closer bonds. If one wanted to betray them, the rest wouldn't see it coming. "You're right. We need to contact the clan, to implement an objective evaluation."

"When?"

"Now." Jie started to rise.

Lilian held her down. "I'll go. There's still time before Lord Ting arrives."

"Masked Crossbowman saw you, too. It's too dangerous."

"Trust me. Trust my skill." The message was the same as just a few minutes earlier. Cupping Jie's cheeks, Lilian leaned in with a deep kiss.

Every nerve tingled, up and down her spine, to her toes and fingertips. Jie reached around to the small of Lilian's back and the nape of her neck, drawing her closer.

Lilian broke the kiss, and smiled. "I'll be all right."

Jie gave a tentative nod.

Stripping off her dressing robe, revealing her glorious figure, Lilian went to her secret floor compartment.

"I wore your stealth suit yesterday, and got it dirty going up the chimney. It's under Little Wen's bed in the Peony Garden."

"So that's how you got out." Lilian giggled, shaking her head. She went to her wardrobe and withdrew a dark shirt and pair of pants, and put them on. She twirled as if showing off a new dress. "How do I look?"

Stunning, even in plain clothes. A grin tugged at Jie's lips, unbidden. "Like a pig."

With a pig-like snort, Lilian opened her window shutters and climbed out.

A bad feeling twisted Jie's gut; the feeling that maybe that kiss would be her last memory of Lilian.

CHAPTER 10

Waiting in Lilian's dressing area, Jie applied make-up appropriate for a full-fledged Blossom, for what might her first assignation. With Lilian gone, Jie had cried until her tears ran dry, and now had dark rings under her eyes. Not even the powder foundation could hide them, so she applied paste concealer and kohl eyeliner. It was amazing she could keep a steady hand while worry tied her stomach in knots.

Dusk cast long shadows over the Floating World, and Lilian had yet to return.

All the girls had already left. From the sound of it, the kitchen staff had finished preparations and were getting ready to leave as well. Logs in the common room hearth crackled, the sound and heat carrying through the flues and into Lilian's room.

Hidden among the other noises were the sounds of hands and feet climbing up the wall.

Jie let out a sigh of relief and ran to the window, throwing open the shutters.

Little Wen's eyes widened. "Elder Sister! How did you hear me? Of course you heard me."

All her worries rushed back, cutting short her joy at seeing Wen. Jie helped her climb in. "What are you doing here?"

Wen brushed off her stealth suit, which embellished her curves even more than her gowns. "Lilian came to me. When I told her I'd found out where Masked Crossbowman ate, she decided to use herself as bait. She wants you to go there as backup."

Blood drained from Jie's head. Lilian wouldn't stand a chance. "Meet me outside the kitchen door."

Wen climbed back through the window; snatching up a high-collared, dark-blue gown, Jie rushed out to the balcony overlooking the common room. The Gardener and Florist were talking in Lord Ting's favorite corner, setting a feast at the round table and making a last check to make sure everything was perfect before they left for the night.

Zigzagging over the safe spots of the nightingale floors, Jie dashed to the stairwell, descended, and reached the room she shared with the Florets and Seedlings. She retrieved a dagger and throwing stars from her chest's false bottom, and put on her stealth suit. She threw the dark-blue outer gown on over it. Only a few minutes had passed by the time she returned to the hallway to the common room.

The Gardener and Florist were blocking the way to the kitchens, so she stayed low and crept over to the main door. Opening it just wide enough, she slipped out.

The vantage point gave her a good view of the main gates, where Lord Ting and his entourage of four men waited, their crimson livery ablaze even in the low light. He stood taller and broader than the rest, a man among boys. They were surrendering their swords and daggers to the gate guards, per the customs and conventions of the Floating World. For their part, the guards took longer than usual, no doubt instructed by the Gardener to stall until Lilian came down from her room—not knowing that Lilian was missing.

"You can keep that," the guard said, motioning to what looked like a wooden club, which one of Lord Ting's men presented.

The other's sash moved stiffly when he withdrew his scabbarded sword, as if a launderer had used too much starch. Jie stared at it for a moment, but Lilian's safety took priority. She tore her gaze away and ran along the side of the mansion to the rear, through the kitchen's side door and out the back.

Wen waited there, her expression scrunched up. She beckoned. "Come on. It's a stand outside Yue Heaven."

"No, you go light the lantern at the Black Lotus Shrine, then go to the safehouse." With a shake of her head, Jie took off down the alleys toward the Yue Heaven.

With the Floating World coming to life, she paused at intersections with major streets, and used the shadows cast by the red lanterns to move unseen and unheard. Laughing men filtered in for a night of adventure and debauchery, providing plenty of cover.

The scent of sesame-ginger grew stronger until she froze at the side of an opium den. Across the street stood the recently-opened Yue Heaven. Boasting euphoric properties, it came from a tree in the North, and the Imperial Court promoted it as a cheaper alternative to opium. Its only side-effects were increased libido and food cravings, which was probably why there was a stand beside it selling pork and vegetables on a skewer. The vendor, head wrapped in a kerchief, grilled the food behind a makeshift bar with six stools. Two men in guards' robes sat together, chatting. There was no sign of Lilian.

Maybe Masked Crossbowman and his comrades had already captured her, and Jie had arrived too late to help.

Heart racing, Jie checked both directions, gauging the way the crowds turned their heads. With the blind spots timed, she kept low and darted across the street, until she stood behind the vendor. The aroma of sesame and ginger drowned out all other smells.

Modulating her voice to a deeper timbre, she threw it with the clan's *Ghost Echo* technique to make it sound like it was coming from the two men. "That Ju Lilian of the Chrysanthemum Pavilion is a beauty!"

"She sure is," the vendor said, nodding as he turned over skewers, but thankfully not looking up.

"Wasn't she here earlier?" Jie asked.

"Haven't seen her recently." The vendor shook his head.

Jie sucked on her lower lip. Lilian had never even made it here. Maybe the conspirators had captured her.

"Huh?" One of the men turned away from his companion to look at the vendor.

"Didn't you ask about Ju Lilian?"

"Who's that?"

"The Corsage of the Chrysanthemum Pavilion," the vendor said. "Didn't you just mention her?"

The men exchanged glances, and with a coordinated snort, got up and left.

Something didn't add up, but there was still one shot in the dark. Or four shots in a shaded alley. Looking left and right to gauge interest in the stand, she went around to the front. "Excuse me."

The vendor looked up. "What would you like to order?"

Jie bowed, shaking her head when she straightened. "I'm looking for a Hummingbird."

His eyes roved over her. "Aren't you the Chrysanthemum Pavilion's half-elf?"

"Yes." She covered her mouth with a hand, an admittedly clunky gesture compared to other Blossoms. "I was supposed to meet a man with a Repeater here."

His brow furrowed. "A crossbow?"

She nodded.

"I have a regular who sometimes carries a crossbow around. He was here earlier with three, four friends. In fact, they were taking a repeating crossbow apart."

A standard military Repeater. Craftsmen specialized in making the individual components, while trained assemblers mass-produced them. Why would—Jie's blood ran colder than ice. "What were they wearing?"

"Crimson robes. Looked to be guards for a noble house."

"Did one have a scar?" Jie ran a finger across her forehead.

"Is that your Humm—"

Jie turned and raced back toward the Chrysanthemum Pavilion. It all made sense now. In the Peony Garden last night, the Artist wasn't framing a picture of desperate men, he was lining up a target. With the two houses being near-exact replicas, that target could be no other than Lord Ting, who would be sitting in his favorite corner right now. His own men had smuggled the Repeater parts past the house guards, where one would reassemble it inside. But why?

She skidded to a halt as the House guards stopped her at the gates, holding a light up to her face.

"Little Jie," one said. "The Gardener is looking all over for you. How did you get out?"

Pushing past them, she shed the gown as she bolted across the courtyard. She threw open the doors and ran into the common room.

Lord Ting sat in his favorite corner, sipping from a cup, a frown plastered to his face. "They said she had a surprise for me, but I've been waiting for an hour. Where is she?"

Standing at his side with a decanter of rice wine in hand, the Florist bowed low. "My apologies, my Lord."

Up and to the left, the head of a repeating crossbow peeked out from the shadows of the mezzanine.

"Get down!" Jie yelled, sprinting between tables and chairs.

Lord Ting turned to her, eyes wide. The Florist gawked, but stood transfixed. Four of his men flashed crimson in her peripheral vision, converging on her. One had a large scar on his forehead.

The crossbow clicked in rapid succession.

To Jie's eye, the two bolts flew in slow motion toward Lord Ting and the Florist, yet she ran even slower. She could only save one. A kind but stern mother figure? Or a loyal lord, who was instrumental to maintaining peace in the unsettled North?

A few feet away, one of his men reached out to grab Jie, but she turned to the side, just avoiding him. She leaped with an outstretched hand...

...and swiped the bolt out of the air.

The Florist's screams ceased, replaced by a gurgle.

Jie sprawled across the table, sliding face-first over and though succulent food, smashing porcelain dishes. With a slap of her hands, she popped herself into a flip and landed in a crouch between Lord Ting and the crossbowman. Any second now, more bolts would fly.

None came.

Jie's eyes blurred, and her balance swayed. A heady scent attacked her nose—deer musk, a key component of a clan contact toxin used on females—clung to the crossbow bolt in her hand. Meaning Lilian had been right about a traitor and Jie's blind spot. Whoever it was had even surmised Jie would catch the bolt.

But who? The Florist's ragged, dying breaths made it impossible to concentrate. Through the darkness encroaching on her vision, Jie squinted toward the balcony. A female form appeared at the edge of the shadows with the crossbow.

Little Wen? It was hard to see, but it made logical sense. She must've helped capture Lilian, then drawn Jie away so they could assassinate Lord Ting.

The crossbow clicked again, the sound echoing behind her. A bolt flew.

Jie swept a hand out.

It zipped past her.

Lord Ting grunted and slumped forward.

Jie collapsed back onto the table as all went black.

CHAPTER 11

The scent of ammonia assaulted Jie's senses, jolting her awake. Her head felt as if a dwarf had forged an axe on it. She was sitting in a chair, hands behind her back on either side of the chair's spindle. She went to stand, but rope bit into her wrists. Cord bound her feet together. She blinked several times to clear her vision, and the blurriness crystalized into focus.

Lord Ting sat slumped over in a chair by her side, with a crossbow bolt protruding from his back and a line of blood drying on the side of his mouth. Florist Wei, too, sat dead in another chair, head lolled to the left, unseeing gaze seemingly locked on Jie. One of Lord Ting's traitorous guards leered at her, eyes hungry, but then joined the others in walking to and from the kitchens, carrying crates of clinking bottles and setting them near the hearth. Another stacked bedding and linens near the main entrance. The scent of sesame-ginger mingled in with the coppery tang of blood.

Little Wen had made a mistake: she'd left Jie alive, with her feet bound but not immobilized. Once she escaped, she'd bring the wrath of the clan down on her. "Wen! What did you do with Lilian?"

A melodious laugh broke out behind her. "Nothing."

Jie's blood ran cold as she twisted to look over her shoulder. No, it couldn't be.

"Not Little Wen. She worships the ground you walk on." Lilian sashayed around to the front. Her loose, baggy pants allowed her to easily straddle Jie. Sighing, she cupped her cheek. "I told you you had a blind spot."

No, no, no. Tears flew as Jie shook her head. "Why? Why did you do this?"

"I told you," Lilian said. "I wanted out of this life. I'd held out hope that you'd be able to convince Master Yan to reassign me, but here's the truth: I played the Little Sister you adored for too long, and the clan thinks—thought— all I'm good for is sating Lord Ting's desires."

Jie's fault. All Jie's fault. "I can convince Master Yan. I swear."

Lilian shook her head. "This was my last chance to get out."

"The clan will hunt you down," Jie said, not with malice, but with an affection she couldn't deny, despite the betrayal.

"Not if they think I am dead." She gestured to a body near the hearth.

The man who'd posed as a drunkard. Jie gasped. "You stored him in that cellar. That's where the stench came from. You used a ruse, thinking I would kill him when he attacked."

"No. You were always a threat to the plan, and I'd originally planned on removing you altogether." With a sigh, she looked up at one of the men, whose gait marked him as Masked Crossbowman. "I couldn't bring myself to do it, and trusted your blind spot."

"She already killed one of your comrades," Jie yelled to Masked Crossbowman, hoping to drive a wedge between them. "What's to keep her from sacrificing you next?"

Masked Crossbowman paused, the bottles in his crate clinking. "Lin ran his mouth too much. We were going to kill him anyway. Less ways to split the reward."

Reward. Someone had ordered the hit on Lord Ting, enough for his men to turn on him. Jie turned back to Lilian. "How did you even get the body here?"

Lilian gestured toward the other men. "With help, of course, while you were warning the other girls."

"You never went to the safehouse to warn the clan."

"No. I needed the clan *not* to get further involved."

So all the failings were Jie's. She'd trusted Lilian implicitly. Now, she looked at the crates the men were stacking near the hearth. "The White Lightning and firecrackers. You are going to set the house on fire."

"Inspired by the training accident twenty years ago." There was no satisfaction in Lilian's voice, only sorrow. "I made sure all the girls and staff would be gone, and the distance from the mansion to the courtyard will keep the flames from spreading to the rest of the Floating World. The Gardener even agreed to douse the compound walls because I said they were too dirty for Lord Ting's visit."

She'd tried to minimize collateral damage; Lilian wasn't totally ruthless. Maybe there was still hope to turn her away from this path. Jie tilted her head toward the Florist. "What about her?"

Lilian shook her head. "An unfortunate casualty, but her body is more likely to be mistaken for mine than the other one."

Jie clenched her teeth. Anger welled inside her.

"I was worried you might figure it all out when the Gardener confined you to that specific storehouse."

"I was too busy crying over what that man did to me. Did you plan that, too?"

"No!" Lilian's eyes widened. "Of course not. I never wanted you going to the Peony Garden at all, because then you'd find out they had nothing to do with Masked Crossbowman. I even told the Gardener to keep a guard at the door and below the window, and used a dwarf lock, which you somehow picked."

The lock which hadn't been there when Lilian had left the house hours ago. Jie had overlooked it then, even though it was glaringly obvious now.

"I never imagined they would do that to you. Before I leave the Floating World forever, I will poison the Peony Garden's Gardener, ruin Lusha's face, and castrate your rapist."

Jie's chest swelled at the ferociousness in Lilian's voice. Conflicting emotions tore at her. Here was someone who loved her, but had also considered killing her. Who'd tried to arrange a hit on her, but then backed out. She shook her head. "Your plan was worthy of the Architect, except that you left me alive."

Lilian brushed her cheek, the softness of her curves and her honeysuckle scent intoxicating. She leaned in and whispered in her ear. "Don't you see? I never even wanted you here. When I left earlier, it was to trick Wen into getting you as far away as possible."

"So I wouldn't foil your assassination?"

"So I wouldn't have to make you choose between me and the clan."

"But you knew I'd come back. The crossbow bolt was meant for me to catch."

Lilian nodded. "A good plan always takes into account unlikely factors. Like this one. Join me. We can start our own clan. A sisterhood. The ones who contracted me to kill Lord Ting will pay well for our skills. Please."

"I can't just betray the clan that adopted me."

"You have thirty seconds to decide." Lilian squeezed tight. "Please."

"Are you sure this is what you want to do? No one will ever have to know you were involved in this plot."

Lilian shook her head violently. "Then I'll just be spreading my legs at some other House."

"I understand." Jie brought her heels up to the edge of the seat, sliding Lilian closer into her lap. Jie leaned into her.

The tension in Lilian's shoulders relaxed, and her smile looked so genuinely relieved.

Jie kicked back against the table. The force sent the chair tipping back. She thrust her legs to increase her speed, and yanked on her wrists as they crashed. The chair splintered under their weight, and

Jie's hands, while still bound, broke free from the remnants of the chair. She continued her backward roll, ending up on her tied feet, between Lilian's shins where she lay prone.

Turning onto her side, Lilian scissored her legs at the front of Jie's ankles and the back of her knees, but Jie leapt, drawing her knees to her chest and swinging her bound arms under her and to the front. Her feet hit the ground just as Lilian windmilled her legs up and flipped over into a crouch, one fist to the ground.

Lord Ting's men all paused mid-stride, gawking.

"You tricked me!" Lilian sprung up and surged forward with a barrage of punches.

Jie hopped back onto the table and snatched up a pottery shard. Spinning away from the attacks, she sawed through the bindings on her feet. She slid off, putting the table between them.

Lord Ting's men now set down the crates and stormed over with knives and cleavers from the kitchen. Two came around either side of the table, while Lilian leaped onto it with a dagger drawn.

Jie flipped the table up onto its side, throwing Lilian back, just as both men fell on her. One chopped down with a cleaver, but Jie lifted her bound wrists into its path. The blade nicked her forearm, but frayed the rope enough for her to pull her hands free.

Now entirely mobile, she spun out of the line of the other's stab. In the same motion, she pushed the table, sending its far legs slamming into the first man. He stumbled into the second, and Jie seized his wrist, twisted the knife around, and let him impale himself on the point. His eyes bulged, and she plucked his weapon away.

The survivor stared, dumbfounded at the turn of events. He lunged at her, but she slipped past him in the direction he'd come and pushed the table so that the leg clotheslined him. She yanked the crossbow bolt from Lord Ting's back and stabbed the man through his eye.

A musky scent stuck to her hand. Stupid half-elf! The toxin! With only a few more seconds of consciousness, she pulled the table down.

Lilian was gone, and given the way Jie'd spun the table right and left, blocking her view, Lilian could've used any of the exits, save for the kitchen.

The two surviving men, Scar Head and Masked Crossbowman—now unmasked—were running toward the main entrance. Torches in hand, they lit banners, paintings, and anything flammable along the way. Fire already raged in the two archways between the common room and the kitchens and conservatory. Meanwhile, a line of firepowder crackled and sizzled in a flash of light. It would ignite the improvised explosive before Jie could reach the makeshift fuse.

Thank the Heavens: the active ingredient of the toxin must've evaporated. Tucking the bolt away, she started toward the main entrance.

The men set the pile of bedding ablaze, blocking that route of escape.

With only seconds to escape the initial blast, she bolted to the hall, toward the veranda. She yanked on each set of double doors, only to find them barred from the outside.

An explosion erupted from the common room hearth. Timbers cracked and glass shattered. Firecrackers burst in a staccato beat. A fireball billowed toward her. She turned the corner and raced to the bathhouse. Crashing through the doors of the first room, she dove into the tub. Flames shot above her, filling the room with reds and oranges before receding.

Jie surfaced, but avoided taking a breath of the hot, choking air. The towels and robes were all burning, filling the room with smoke. She climbed out of the tub and, staying low, crawled to the hallway.

The moist wood hadn't caught, but it wouldn't be long before the fire from the rest of the mansion reached here. The servants' door had been blasted open. Jie scuttled through the hall and leaped through the exit.

She gulped in the cooler fresh air, and looked.

Flames raged from every window of the Chrysanthemum Pavilion's main mansion. Wood crackled, and ash floated on the smoke. From outside the compound walls, bells clanged and people shouted.

Finding out which way Lilian had escaped would take time, especially since the orange glow from the flames kept Jie's elf vision from kicking in and assessing the area around the mansion. The two surviving accomplices, however...

CHAPTER 12

First patting soot onto her face, Jie dashed around to the front of the burning mansion. The gate guards approached, running halfway between the main gate and the mansion.

Jie sprinted to meet them. "What happened to Lord Ting's men?"

Giving her a look from head to toe and back, the first guard pointed to the main gate. "They left to bring help."

Unlikely. "Did they claim their weapons?"

The guard nodded.

Bidding them farewell, Jie dashed out the front door to search. They couldn't be more than a few minutes ahead, though they had the advantage of knowing where they were going.

She sniffed. Hidden among the soot and ash smell, and the gathering crowds, was the sesame-ginger marinade. Using her nose, she followed the ever-stronger scent.

The neighborhood fire brigade ran by, laden with buckets, bamboo ladders, and poles, the colors of their blue uniforms flashing.

They passed, revealing the two men striding across the bridge out of the Floating World. One carried a Repeater, which the house guard had failed to mention.

Jie stuck to the shadows as she pursued them into the abandoned silk market. Inside, with the tent blotting out the moons and stars, her elf vision transformed the shadowed, empty stands into hues of green and grey. Though human eyes supposedly couldn't see as well in the dark, she still stayed low as she trailed them.

They paused at several stalls, looking back toward the entrance, and wagged their fingers. They were counting, trying to locate a specific stand.

"This is the one," one said.

"Are you sure? I'm counting three down, two over."

"That's what she said." The other threw his hands up.

"Just drop it off, then."

One knelt and stashed something under the table.

Jie sucked on her lower lip. Whatever else Lilian was, she was right about Jie's cavalier approach. She should've recruited clan sisters to help, because no matter her skills, she couldn't be in three places at once. Now, she had to choose: follow these men; wait for them to leave to see what they'd left behind, and who came to retrieve it; or track down Lilian.

"All right. Good job tonight. I'll see you tomorrow." One of the men saluted the other with a palm in his fist, head bowed.

The other returned the gesture.

If only there were four of her! She dashed up to them as they turned from each other, and pulled Masked Crossbowman's dagger from his sash. Reaching up and covering his mouth with a hand, she slashed his throat. She caught his crossbow before it clattered to the ground, then eased his body down.

She turned to chase after Scar Head. Just before he reached the edge of the tent, she caught up. She extended an arm—

He spun around, his broadsword sweeping from its scabbard.

Jie rolled backward under the weapon's arc, then backhand-sprung over his follow-up. She landed on one of the tables in a defensive crouch.

"You!" he said. "You just won't die."

"I'm like a cockroach." And in the dark, she had an advantage. Jie threw her voice to the side with *Ghost Echo*.

He chopped down toward the perceived source, his broadsword lodging into the table and sending a reverberation into Jie's feet. He yanked on the weapon to free it.

Jie darted over and slashed his palmar tendons.

He screamed as his fingers went slack about the hilt, but also whipped a dagger out with his other hand and stabbed.

She jumped to the other side of the table, then crawled under it. She threw her voice behind him. "Over here!"

When he turned his back to her, she severed his Achilles tendons. He buckled to his knees, but kept slashing back and forth with his dagger.

Jie came out behind him and cut through his triceps, locking his elbow in a bent position and rendering his weapon useless. She pulled his hair back, bringing him to the ground.

"Now," she said, stabbing the tip of her dagger into his cheek. "You will die tonight. Answer my questions, and it will be quick. Who hired you?"

"Your whore sister," he said through gritted teeth.

Jie dug deeper, eliciting a scream.

"I swear it. Our Lord has been her patron for a year—"

"*Had* been. You betrayed him. Now, go on."

"And she'd talk to us, all sweet." He sniffled. "She slept with us."

"Impossible. She'd never sleep with her patrons' guards, and you couldn't afford her."

"She loved us. It was true, genuine affection."

As any other Night Blossom except Jie could fake. She snorted. Lilian had set these men up.

"Well...." His face scrunched up, and he opened his mouth to speak, but then shut it.

Jie knew why. Her blind spot was obvious even to him. "Say it. I promise I won't hurt you more for the answer."

His eyes flitted to the blade. "Maybe you don't know her as well as you think."

Clearly not. "I've never seen you or the other three at the house."

He shook his head. "Only his most trusted guards went with him to the Floating World."

"And yet, he got stuck with a pack of traitors today, of all days."

"She had us poison their food. They were all sick today."

So Lilian had set herself up as the planner, fixer, recruiter, and operative. The clan had drastically underestimated her. Jie had drastically underestimated her. The blind spot. "So, you kill your lord, what then?"

"She said there'd be a reward and a new job, but never said where."

Jie looked over to the table where they'd dropped the package. "What did you leave under that table?"

"A message."

"Who is picking it up?"

"I don't know. She just told us to leave it there."

Jie sucked on her lower lip. If Lilian had wanted the message for herself, she would have gotten it from them at the Peony Garden. As was, she likely didn't want to be seen making contact with whoever planned to retrieve it.

Meanwhile, Masked Crossbowman seemed to be fading in and out of consciousness. In the bigger picture, he was just a pawn, and there was no point in making him suffer. His was a necessary death, lest rumors of real Black Fists get out. "As promised," she said, "I will make your death quick."

After slashing his throat, she went over to the table and retrieved the message. No seal, just a honeysuckle scent and Jie's own name written on it.

With trembling fingers, Jie unfolded the message and looked. It was a poem recounting the parting of lovers, written in Lilian's graceful hand. But she'd embellished certain words in a way that only a Black Lotus clan member would be able to decipher:

My Sweet. I am happy you found this, because it means that you survived. However, you also fell into my last trap. While you followed Ping's men, my trail has gotten colder. You were always too impulsive. Goodbye, my sweet. I've always loved you.

Jie's gut wrenched, twisted by conflicting emotions. She started to crumple the message up, but then stopped. This might be her last memento of Lilian. No matter how events had unfolded, she'd tried to keep Jie out of danger; and when that failed, attempted to turn her away from the clan. Even now, she would exact vengeance on the Peony Garden and—

Jie sucked in a breath. There was one last chance to track Lilian down.

CHAPTER 13

With the crowds gathering outside the conflagration of the Chrysanthemum Pavilion, the streets were nearly empty. Jie still kept to the back alleys, to avoid questions about why a half-elf in a stealth suit was running around. She paused only when she spotted a clan sister on her way to the shrine, and signed, *Come to the Peony Garden.*

Despite Jie's scandal the previous night, red banners hung from the Peony Garden's gates, in honor of Young Lord Peng Kai-Zhi's imminent First Pollinating. Two house guards stood at the main gate, but beyond, there was none of the usual chatter or sound of musical instruments coming from the mansion. Jie had seen the Peony Garden girls among the crowds outside the Chrysanthemum Pavilion.

She crept around to the back, and like the night before, entered through the empty kitchens. Even the hearth stood cold. Jie went over to it and listened, in case any whispers echoed through the shared flue system.

"I didn't know," moaned a disembodied male voice. Shixian's voice.

Jie's gut clenched, not with the pleasant butterflies from the night before, but with anger. He was upstairs, either in the Gardener's room or Lusha's.

"The Gardener told me she'd paid for it," he said. "That it was a gift. I didn't know about the virgin price. I swear. I—"

His scream cut short his words. A female shriek joined his.

Jie darted to the empty common room, leaped up to a tabletop, then pop-vaulted off a column to grab the floor of the mezzanine in front of the Gardener's room. She pulled herself up, flipped over the railing, and went to the door. No sound came from within, but Jie slid the door open and peeked inside.

The Gardener lay sprawled on the bed, sightless eyes open, blood flecking her lips. A cup rested on a table, but no steam wafted above it. Jie padded in and sniffed. Yue bark toxin, near imperceptible to a human's frail nose, and fatal in just a few minutes. The poor woman must've sipped the tea, started to feel light-headed, and then gone to lay down, never to wake up.

The Gardener deserved many things for what she'd done to Jie, but death?

Another scream echoed in the hearth, this time closer.

Jie ran out, climbed to the top of the mezzanine rail, and then jumped to catch the floor of the third-floor balcony. She pulled herself up, flipped over, and tried the door.

Locked.

Jie went through the next door, into another Blossom's room. She climbed through the window, shimmied over to Lusha's, and looked in.

In the area lit by a bauble lamp, ropes bound Shixian spread-eagled to the posts of Lusha's bed. Sweat beaded on his pale face, and he whimpered as he looked toward a bloodstain on his crotch. On the other side of the bed, cord suspended Lusha's tied hands to the rafters. Lines of blood trickled from multiple wounds on her face. A bloody cloth served as a gag.

Lilian had meted out all the vengeance Jie had sworn, when she'd knelt all alone in the storeroom the night before. From the sound of Lilian's soft sniffling to the side, she hadn't found it easy. Despite all she'd done, she was still sweet, gentle Lilian.

Jie's heart ached more at what she had to do now. She took a deep breath and bounded through the window, rolling over the carpet. A throwing star whirled at her head, and she handsprung out of its way. Twisting midair, she landed in a crouch, fist to the ground, dagger in her other hand.

Five paces away, Lilian presented her side, a noble's curved *dao* sword lifted over her shoulder with both hands. "How—?"

"Don't you remember? You told me you'd come here to punish them."

Lilian let out a cute laugh; the way her lips quirked stirred fond memories. "I guess you're not the only one with a blind spot."

"No." But maybe it had been meant to lull Jie into a mistake. She looked around for potential traps. "You planned everything so well, I'm surprised you didn't predict the possibility of a final confrontation."

"Who says I didn't?" Lilian raised an eyebrow.

"Because I suspect I would already be dead." Jie gauged possible lines of attack. Before tonight, she would never have considered the sword's longer reach to be an advantage, not in Lilian's hands. Now, though... She feinted with a stab.

The blade flashed into the space where she would've been, faster than Lilian had ever wielded it.

"You are full of surprises," Jie said.

Lilian snapped back into a ready stance. "I've always held back. Just like you taught me."

"You always let the other sisters win, then." Jie stayed at the edge of the sword's reach, ready to attack again. "To hide your true ability."

No, that wasn't it, judging by the way Lilian's lips pursed for a split second. She'd done it because she was a good person. She lowered her weapon. "I'm not going back."

"The clan wouldn't take you back, after what you've done. I have no choice but to bring you in for questioning."

"Or let me go."

"You know I can't do that." Jie lunged again, avoiding the chop, and stabbed.

Lilian slipped out of the first attack, then the follow-up, and riposted with an upward slash.

Jie dodged, but pain seared in her side. She looked down to see a split in the stealth suit, and the fine line of blood from a shallow wound. With a shorter blade and apparently equal skill, she was at a disadvantage. Jie jumped back and plucked the light bauble from the lamp.

She dropped it to the floor and crushed it underfoot. Her elf vision kicked in as the light winked out. She threw a grunt to Lilian's side with a *Ghost Echo.*

Turning her back on Jie, Lilian swept her sword through the spot.

Jie surged forward, seizing Lilian's wrist. She leaped up feet-first and wrapped them around Lilian's arm. The sword slipped out of her grasp, and its tip lodged into the floor. Jie leaned back to hyperextend Lilian's elbow, but she bent it, grabbing her wrist with the other hand. She thrust her shoulder down, slamming Jie into the hardwood floors.

The shock knocked the air from Jie's lungs, and her fingers went limp on Lilian's arm.

Lilian pulled her arm free, stood, and ran to the door. When she opened it, light from the common room flooded in.

Wheezing, Jie popped back onto her feet and staggered into pursuit.

Lilian threw herself over the mezzanine and dropped down so her feet landed on the railing below. She ran along it to the next column and slid down to the first floor. With a last look at Jie, she ran through the front door.

Jie gave chase, following the same route down to the first floor.

Lilian came back through the doors, then closed and barred them. She spun to face Jie, knife in hand. Her eyes spoke of fear.

"What is it?" Jie pointed her dagger at the doors.

"The clan sisters."

Jie closed her eyes and listened. Though their feet padded lightly, she could hear the daughters of the Black Lotus fanning out around the mansion. She opened her eyes. "They are spreading out to block every route of escape. You can't beat us all. Just tell me who hired you to kill Lord Ting, so the clan won't torture it out of you."

Lilian walked over, shaking her head. "Oh, Jie. I don't know. Whoever it was knew that Lord Ting was my patron, and left a message offering me enough money to buy out my contract. I went to the meeting place, only to find another message with a vial and instructions to poison Ting. It was a crude mixture, one which he would've noticed before he drank enough to kill him. I left a message saying as much, and told my new employer to leave it to me. We've been corresponding ever since."

"And you did all this? Not knowing who your employer was?" Jie looked around, gauging how close the other sisters were. They'd reach the common room in moments. "It could've been the clan, testing you!"

Lilian shrugged. "I decided months ago that I was through with the clan, one way or the other."

"Where are you exchanging messages?"

"I drop my messages off under the lucky cat figurine at the Jade Teahouse, and pick up messages from the same grove of trees the clan uses."

These clues might help in uncovering Lilian's employer, though no doubt he'd go to ground.

Black Lotus Sisters appeared on the mezzanine and archways in perfect synchronization. Jie would have felt pride if it weren't for the heaviness in her heart.

"What's happening?" Wen asked, expression contorted into confusion.

Yuna started to climb over the handrail.

Holding up a hand, Jie signaled them to hold back.

Lilian looked up at them and gave a wry smile. "Let this be our last dance."

Tears threatened to blur Jie's vision, but she blinked them away. "There has to be another way. The Viper's Rest, maybe." The dangerous technique would make someone appear dead, though it ran the risk of making them forget who they were.

Shaking her head, Lilian lunged with her knife. Their blades flashed as Jie backed up, ceding ground. It couldn't end. Not this way. There had to be some way to disarm and capture Lilian, and convince the clan to give her a second chance. Though practical, Master Yan wasn't coldhearted. Surely he'd understand the toll the Floating World took on the girls.

"Come on!" Lilian slashed in a zigzag, with deadly precision. No matter the affection between them, she gave no quarter. Around them, the girls all murmured.

"Jie!" Little Wen threw a shortsword over.

Lilian caught the scabbard, but Jie seized the hilt. She pulled the weapon free. With a blade in either hand, Jie renewed her half-hearted attacks.

"Dead." Lilian jabbed her in the chest with the scabbard, then bludgeoned her side with the backstroke. "Dead. Come on, honor me with a good fight. I'm not going to hold back anymore." Her eyes glinted with a deadly focus. She unleashed an onslaught of stabs with the knife and swings with the scabbard like never before, this time with intent to kill.

Jie's automatic reflexes kicked in. Slipping through the barrage, she cut Lilian's forearm, sending the knife clattering from her limp fingers, then sliced through the scabbard. The other end spun back, slashing Lilian across the cheek.

Blood flowed from the open wounds. Lilian staggered into Jie, knocking her down. The weight bore down on her.

Lilian lifted herself up. Her tear-filled eyes met Jie's before sweeping over the room. "They're all watching."

"It doesn't matter." Jie shook her head. If only she'd realized before she'd come to the Peony House. "These aren't fatal wounds." She started to throw the knife away.

Lilian caught her wrist. Blood flecked her lips. "Set me free."

Master Yan wasn't coldhearted, but he was practical. The clan could never truly set Lilian free, not after this betrayal. Tears blurred Jie's vision. If only she'd let her go before. Now, there really was no choice. She drove the knife through Lilian's neck.

The light went out of her eyes, and her body slumped. Jie scuttled up to her knees and rested Lilian's head in her lap.

Jie had done this. If her chest squeezed any harder, her heart would burst. She fought to take in a breath.

Around them, some clan sisters sniffled, while others openly sobbed.

Gaze dropping to her lap, Jie brushed matted hair out of Lilian's face. Her expression looked so...peaceful. If only things had turned out differently. Any number of decisions would have led to a different outcome. She could've broken off pursuit after killing the last two men. Or even before that, not returned to the Chrysanthemum House in a futile attempt to save Lord Ting.

Or even over the years, when her own blind spot had kept her from recognizing Lilian's skills, maybe trapping her in the Floating World.

One of Jie's tears plopped onto Lilian's cheek. She could have killed Jie on multiple occasions tonight, but had held back. In the end, it had been her decision to return here to punish the members of the Peony Garden, and her choice to sacrifice herself for Jie.

Wiping the tears from her eyes, Jie took a deep breath and cleared her throat. She straightened and fought to keep her voice steady. "Lilian was a traitor and deserved her fate."

They each sank to a knee, fist to the ground, head bowed. "Yes, Eldest Sister."

Jie nodded. "Little Wen, go to the safehouse and bring a Cleaner. The rest of you, start removing evidence. The Gardener is dead in her room, and the Corsage and her Hummingbird are witnesses on the third floor."

And there was still the matter of who'd turned Lilian. Jie would hunt him down and exact vengeance.

EPILOGUE

In the Peony Garden, the expert work of the Black Lotus Cleaners left no evidence of Lilian's rampage. Bound and drugged, Lusha and Shixian had been taken, along with the Gardener's body, to a Triad-infested neighborhood outside the city walls. Salacious rumors about unpaid debts circulated throughout the Floating World.

The fire at the Chrysanthemum Garden had been spun as an unfortunate kitchen accident. With it being a burnt-out husk of its former glory, its Blossoms, Seedlings, and Florets all found new homes at the other great houses of the Floating World.

All except Jie. After burying Lilian at the Black Lotus Temple's cemetery for adepts, she returned to the safehouse just outside of the Floating World. Evidence from that fateful night lay on the floor of one of the rooms: the murder weapon, crossbow bolts, ledgers and records from the Peony Garden, and everything recovered from the Chrysanthemum Pavilion. She spent sleepless days and nights poring through it all, and retracing the steps of Lilian's accomplices.

That was how her adopted father, Master Yan, found her a week after that fateful night. Though he usually managed to evade even her keen senses, he'd brought someone with him. A child, from the sound of the footsteps. Maybe some new girl, about to enter the Floating World as a Seedling.

The door opened, and she turned.

Even at middle age, Master Yan did not look young or old. His face was so plain, he could mingle into almost any crowd and never be remembered. So unlike her, the half-elf with exotic features.

"Greetings, my daughter."

She bowed her head. "Father."

"I'm sorry about everything that happened. Lilian was a kind girl. She was never meant for the life of a Black Fist."

Jie shook her head. "She hid so much from us. Her last plan was worthy of the Architect, the manipulation worthy of the Beauty, and the execution worthy of the Surgeon. It was only her affection for me that kept her from escaping after her successful assassination."

"Then you did the right thing in killing her. A renegade to the clan would be a dangerous asset for an ambitious lord."

The truth of his words didn't make it hurt less. Jie sucked on her lower lip.

"Speaking of which," he said, "have you made any headway into finding her employer?"

Jie's gaze raked over all the evidence. "I've tracked the men's families and pored through the records. My working theory is that it was one of the lords of the North."

"I've brought someone for you to train," Master Yan said, his face betraying no emotion.

"Another?" Jie glared at him for the first time in her life. Who was it this time? Little Fei? Little Mai? They'd all be reaching the age when they'd enter the Floating World as embedded Black Lotus sisters. "Father, we need to rethink our approach to the Floating World. How many girls are another Lilian, waiting to happen?"

"I will allow you to speak to the Elders." He gave her the same inscrutable look as always. "For now, though, I brought you an initiate with a preternatural ability to draw connections."

She cocked her head.

He stepped aside, revealing a quivering boy of no older than ten years. "This is Zheng Tian."

The boy's lips trembled, and he ducked behind Master Yan.

"He's a little shy." Master Yan gave a rare smile, then nudged the boy forward and pointed at the open ledgers. "Little Tian, what do you make of that?"

The boy's eyes darted to Jie before roving over the figures. He stammered as he said, in a tremulous voice, "These companies paid for the party for Lord Peng, who is from the South. They all operate in the North."

"How can you tell they operate in the North?" Master Yan asked.

"Jinjing Lumber Company—Jinjing is a county in the North. Luo Trading—it imports from the foreigners in the North."

Jie gawked. In just three seconds, the boy had deduced what had taken her days to research. He might not have all the answers now, but with more training, maybe he would.

And she could find out who had turned Lilian.

End of Part 1

PART 2:
WHITE SHEEP OF THE FAMILY

CHAPTER 1

Before yesterday, ten-year-old Zheng Tian had always believed Black Fists to be a fairy tale: mythical villains meant to scare children into good behavior. Today, he was an initiate of the Black Lotus Clan. Not kidnapped by their Fists, but saved from an imperial death sentence.

Maybe beheading would've been better than the humiliation. Now bruised and panting, he tried to lift his sword. His arms ached at the effort. He couldn't say he'd never been bested by a girl two years younger and a head shorter—only twenty-seven days had passed since the last instance—but this was the first time an opponent had worn a dress *and* blindfold, and made such short work of him.

His skinny opponent had him cornered in the small room, and the glare from the window made it hard to see as she darted in and stabbed. His foot slipped on the wood floor, and he couldn't raise his sword in time to parry. The blow landed with a dull thud on his padded armor. Pain flared in his ribs.

"Point, Yuna." Jie, the cruel half-elf judging the match, swept a red flag up with her left arm for the seventeenth time. "That's enough for today."

"You won." He hung his head and saluted with a fist in an open palm.

Yuna removed her blindfold and returned the gesture. "Thank you for letting me."

It was a victor's typical polite response, which never seemed to lessen the sting. It certainly didn't now.

"I'll need to work out the other arm to keep the muscles balanced." Jie rolled her left shoulder.

Tian frowned. His arms ached, too. After all, the practice sword weighed more than her flag.

"Yuna, you may go." Jie saluted, fist in palm. She didn't look much older than either Yuna or him, yet somehow she was in charge of his new world. "Your list for next time is, red, sword, wheel, dagger, green, stab, cloudy, spicy, crossbow, opera, bludgeon, slippery, sun, finger, six, two, zero, nine."

Was it a shopping list? Tian looked from the half-elf to the girl.

Closing her eyes, Yuna mouthed the words. Then, she bobbed her head in the cutest way, less like the swordswoman who'd thrashed him, more like Princess Kaiya.

Tian's stomach twisted. Four days. It'd been four days since he'd last seen the love of his life, the girl he'd promised to marry. The girl he'd never see again. Four days since his banishment from the capital.

Once Yuna left the small, sunlit room, Jie turned back to him. There was nothing cute about her, except maybe those pointed ears. Her gaze bore into him. "Zheng Tian, why did you lose?"

Why, indeed? He shouldn't have, given his opponent's stance and shorter reach. Maybe if there'd been more space. He stretched his arms out to the side, demonstrating the narrowness of the wood-floored chamber. "There was no room."

"If you get attacked in an alley, are you going to ask your assailant to take it out into the street?"

He started to respond, but closed his mouth. There was more than just the amount of space. He pointed to the window. "The sun was in my eyes."

It also cast Jie's hair in a unique shade of dark brown, unlike any other in a realm of black-haired people. "She was blindfolded."

That humiliation still stung, but there was more. His shoes' smooth soles had slipped more than once. "The floor was too slick."

The cruel half-elf rolled her eyes. "You fought on the same floor."

"She was barefooted!"

Jie shrugged. "Nobody said you had to wear shoes."

All the disadvantages, this one self-imposed. Still, despite him preempting Yuna's possible lines of attack and defense, she always landed a quick, decisive blow. His swordplay, in contrast, might've been as sluggish as a water buffalo. "Yuna was holding her weapon in stance six. But then, she used pattern two."

"And?"

"You are not supposed to mix the two. Every sword master says so."

"You're overanalyzing." Jie threw her hands up—the right higher than the left, proving her muscles were already balanced. "Swordplay isn't forensic accounting."

Whatever forensic meant, and what it had to do with counting, had to be better than getting beaten by an eight-year-old, blindfolded girl. He shook his head. "Her moves did not match her stance. It's not fair."

"Exactly!" The evil half-elf's lip quirked. "Had we been using real blades, you'd be dead twenty times over."

"Seventeen. Fifteen, because two were not fatal blows." He rubbed his ribs. Twice, her attempted finger jabs with her left hand had thrown off her sword attack.

Jie blew out a frustrated breath.

Tian's shoulders slumped. There was no denying the truth. "Yuna is better with a sword."

"I was waiting for that answer." Jie's smile looked less kindly, and more like the Lord of the Underworld bargaining for souls.

This had all been a lesson. These new teachers had to break him down before building him back—

"But no. You're the son of a hereditary lord. You've learned from great sword masters, and your technique is superior for your age. You have a longer reach and a size advantage. You might even be better than me." She chuckled. "Well, maybe not..."

Tian looked up. "The Founder wrote in the Art of War that knowing your enemy—"

"—will win you half your battles. Yes, yes." Jie held up a hand. "I'm glad you can recite the Founder. What did he say about choosing your battlefield?"

His mouth formed a circle of its own accord. It all made sense. "The narrow space limited what I could do. It neutralized my reach advantage. The slick floors slowed my reaction. Yuna kept the sunlight in my face to make up for the blindfold—"

Jie shook her head. "We will teach you to fight in the dark, using all your senses. But what you should get out of this is, forget everything you learned about duels. We don't fight fair. Do you remember how heavy your sword felt?"

"Yes."

"Yuna gave you the one with a lead core."

And when she did, she'd hefted it as if it were light. He made several slow nods. Really, he'd only lost his duels to Princess Kaiya because she didn't fight fair, either, and he let her get away with it. Out of love.

"But most importantly, don't analyze in the heat of the moment. Turn your brain off, and let your reflexes take over."

"I will try." Try to get used to this new world and new people.

When Jie smiled instead of smirked, it was like sunlight peeking out through the clouds on a rainy day. "There's hope for you yet."

***

There was no hope for the boy. In Yan Jie's twenty years with the Black Lotus Clan, the last six embedded in a brothel in the Floating World, she'd never seen such a hopeless initiate.

He might have exceptional swordsmanship for his age, a natural observational ability, and tenacious curiosity; but in every other aspect, he lagged well behind the others. They'd started training almost as soon as they could walk, after all. Yuna had even come close to landing the No Shadow Cut on him. Meanwhile, he could stand to lose some of his baby fat.

He was a handsome boy, at least, with a high-bridged nose and strong jawline. And those eyes. They took in everything, and gleamed with intelligence. Her adopted father, Master Yan, had saved him from beheading because of his brains, and that's what she needed now.

She led him back to another of the safe house's rooms. In the two days since Master Yan had brought him here, he'd rearranged all of the physical evidence regarding the murder of a great lord.

A murder she'd witnessed, perpetrated by a clan traitor.

A clan traitor she'd loved, and been forced to kill. Her chest clamped her heart. She took a deep breath and shook the thoughts out of her head so as to focus on the task at hand: With the loyal Lord Ting now dead, the treasonous lords who he'd kept in line were no doubt plotting their next move. Somewhere in the mess of information hid the identity of whoever ordered the hit. She looked to Tian.

The kid was studying her, but dropped his gaze as soon as her eyes fell on him. "I… I… look!" He pointed.

She followed his finger to the evidence she'd neatly organized before he'd come. After he'd gotten his hands on it, the ledgers, records, and weapons looked as if a drunken bull had gone for a romp in a pottery kiln. It made no sense, besides the chalked lines connecting them like a web spun by a spider high on yue.

"What?" she asked.

"The assa.. assassi... assassination!" Excitement grew in his tone as he found the word. He pointed to the mock-up of the crime scene she'd set up, using bangles and beads. It was the one thing he hadn't touched: the common room of her former home, the Chrysanthemum Pavilion. Once the preeminent brothel of the Floating World, it was now nothing more than a burnt-out husk. Destroyed by the explosion her love had rigged to fake her own death.

"What about it?" Jie asked.

"Are you sure this is where Lord Ting and the countant were sitting? And you were on this table?" He pointed to a fake jade bracelet which represented her.

Jie nodded, even as her heart squeezed. The memory haunted her, having to sacrifice the house Florist, who'd been like a stern but kind mother, and not even being able to save Lord Ting. "What about it?"

"There were two assass.. assassins."

The boy saw all kinds of connections, but this one... Jie shook her head. "I would remember if there were two."

"One just isn't possible. You said that Lord Ting was shot in the back?"

"Yes."

Tian pointed to the place where Lilian had shot the crossbow. "You were between the first assassin"—his face brightened—"and him. The countant was shot in the chest, him in the back."

She'd noted that at the time, but hadn't given it further thought in the chaos of the ensuing melee. Jie's gaze strayed to the repeating crossbow they'd recovered from the two of Lilian's accomplices who Jie'd killed. There'd been four in all, but Tian's observation suggested there was a fifth. If he were right, somewhere, out there, was another assassin, who might have answers. Still, "Where's the other crossbow?"

"With the killer?" He walked over and picked up the bolt which had killed Lord Ting and proffered it. "The shaft. It's a different wood from the others."

Jie took two steps back and looked. The shaft was made of a smooth, white wood; the others were eldarwood, now charred like the crossbow which fired it. During the assassination, she'd caught one of the former midflight, and it'd been coated with a contact toxin that'd knocked her unconscious. This one, too. Exposed to air for so long, the active ingredient had long since evaporated; but the musky scent still clung to the wood.

"What is wrong?" He pulled the bolt back.

"Smell it."

He brought it to his nose and sniffed like the fluffy white dogs at the Black Lotus Temple. He looked back at her and shrugged. "It smells like wood."

It never ceased to amaze her that full humans had lasted so long with such pitiful noses. "There's a poison on it—"

The boy dropped the bolt and scuttled back.

She buried a laugh. "Don't worry, even when it's fresh, it only works on females."

His lips rounded.

She pointed to a rack of vials on the far wall. "That's where we keep them. You'll have to learn all the poisons and toxins we use, and you're behind by six or seven years. Now tell me, what's so special about the wood?"

He eyed the bolt as if it were a spider before pinching it up by the fletching. "It is yue wood. It only grows in one place in the realm. Tieshan County."

A smile came to Jie's lips, unbidden. Amazing that he'd retain knowledge that most would consider trivial. Did he know yue sap was refined into a drug as euphoric as opium, but not as addictive? "How do you know of this tree from Tieshan?"

"My father took me there last year."

What would Lord Zheng, one of the eight highest-ranked lords of the realm, be doing in a county as insignificant as Tieshan? Jie raised an eyebrow. "Why?"

"To meet Lord Nan."

Lord Nan had often visited the Floating World with the murdered Lord Ting. His loyalty to the Throne had never come under scrutiny, but what if he'd provided the murder weapon? Still… "What did your father and Lord Nan talk about?"

His face flushed an interesting shade of red. "They… they wanted me to meet Lord Nan's daughter."

Jie suppressed a giggle, even as she considered the implications. A staunch ally to the Emperor, Lord Zheng was using his youngest son to join his family to Lord Nan's. Most likely to take the daughter hostage, to ensure Nan's loyalty to the throne; but what if Lord Zheng was scheming in the background? "Are you betrothed to her now?"

If his original blush had been red, his cheeks had since discovered an as-of-yet unnamed new shade. He sputtered. "I… I am supposed to marry someone else."

"Who's the lucky girl?"

"Princess Kaiya." His tone managed to combine defiance with pride.

Jie just about choked on her own spit. "Do you know what marriage means?"

"We get to hold hands any time. And maybe even—" His face turned redder than the hanging lanterns in the Floating World, and he lowered his voice to a whisper, "—kiss her."

It was too adorable. Rumor had it the princess didn't share her family's good looks, but the way he spoke about her, she might've been a once-in-three-generations beauty. Jie couldn't wipe the smile off her face. She, herself had practiced kissing many of the Blossoms and Florets in Chrysanthemum House, though Lilian was the only one who counted. That, and the man who… She shook the memory away. “Zheng Tian, is there anything else can you tell me about this murder?”

His expression brightened. “I would need to see the actual spot.”

Impossible, since it’d burned down. Though another brothel shared the exact same layout. And it was the place she’d killed Lilian. She swallowed hard. A new recruit never went into the field without a minimal level of proficiency. It was like asking an alchemy apprentice to mix fire powder correctly. Her better judgment screamed he wasn’t ready.

Still, she had to know. This might be the only lead to uncover whoever had turned Lilian. And with his sense of spatial relations, he might be the only one to solve this puzzle. And, it would be a simple in and out job, one that even he couldn’t mess up. “Zheng Tian, we’re going to the Floating World.”

“The Floating World?” All color drained from his face. “I cannot go there. I am not allowed. The Emperor banished me from the capital.”

“You’ve been in the capital this whole time. Don’t worry, it’s a big city, and the authorities rarely go into the Floating World. This will be your first lesson in blending in. Remember, the clan doesn’t exist. You aren’t its newest initiate.”

“But it does, and I am.” His eyebrows clashed together like dueling rams. “Right?”

It would’ve been cute, if it didn’t come with the risk of getting them killed.

CHAPTER 2

Tian lifted his face to the late afternoon sun and breathed in the fresh air. It was the first time the mean half-elf had let him outside. He looked up and down the paved street, noting his new home was one of several two-story wooden row houses. The signboards hanging above the first floors indicated a myriad of shops: a grocer, tanner, butcher; his brain took it all in, storing it away. His new house was apparently above an herbal pharmacy, which would explain the heady smell everywhere.

"Come on." Yuna beckoned with her free hand, the other clasping the hand of a pretty young woman.

It was the one Jie called Little Wen, even if *Little* Wen looked a few years older than Jie. Dressed in a beautiful blue gown, she turned with a willowy grace and beamed. "Little Tian! Elder Sister wants you to come with me."

Elder Sister... why so much deference to the half-elf? Tian tapped his chin. "Where is Jie? She was going to take me to... to... the Floating World."

"I'm taking you, and she'll be following." Little Wen—well, maybe not so little, since she stood a head taller—leaned in with another radiant smile. "If you spot her, I'll give you some candy."

Tian's lips twitched into a grin. Up to now, they'd fed him rice porridge with some chicken and leafy greens. Not nearly as delicious as the cooks in the Imperial Court, and not a single sweet among them. And, this was a challenge! He looked left and right, to see if he could find Jie among all the chattering townsfolk.

"Don't be so obvious." Little Wen poked him with a finger that looked delicate, but felt as if it were made of iron. "And don't trust your eyes, alone. You'll need all your senses."

They set off down the street. No matter how much Tian sniffed, listened, and looked, there was no sign of the mean half-elf.

"Do we have to walk so close to him?" Yuna, who'd been mothing the words on Jie's list, turned to Wen. "He looks like a dog trying to find its fleas."

Tian froze and looked.

Passersby were pointing and staring. So focused he'd been on finding Jie, he hadn't noticed everyone else around. Heat flooded into his cheeks.

Wen patted him on the head. "Wait until we get to the silk market, and I'll teach you a trick."

A trick! His heart picked up a beat. With a nod, Tian forced himself not to search for Jie.

Yuna tilted her head and brought the back of her wrist to her brow. "Now he looks like a walking corpse!"

"Just relax," Wen said, voice still gentle. "Imagine you're walking with Princess Kaiya."

Tian swallowed hard. How did Wen know about that? Neither she nor Yuna had been in the room when he let his secret slip.

"Elder Sister told me," Wen said, as if reading his mind.

"When? How?"

She took his hand and tapped on his wrist.

There was a clear pattern. Forehead tightening, he looked back at her.

Yuna sidled closer. "We have many ways of communicating. Tactile, visual."

Whatever tactile meant. Though this eight-year-old girl knew!

"I just used my finger to tell you that Jie told me by sign language."

Tian gawked. "How? When?"

"Just now. She's over there. Don't look."

He did, but saw only two elderly men arguing over the value of ginseng.

It was so overwhelming, the things these Black Lotus clan members did. And, Master Yan expected him to learn it all. All Tian wanted was to see Kaiya again. Well... and to find the assassin. And learn sign language. And—

"All right, here's the silk market."

They'd already walked two thousand, four hundred, seventy-one steps. Up ahead, an enormous red tent covered what looked to be an entire city block. He followed Yuna and Wen in. If the streets had been noisy and crowded, the silk market was deafening and stifling. People jostled each other in the narrow alleys formed by lines of stalls. Cloth, tailors, shoes, jewelry... anything and everything fashion related was for sale.

"Put this in your pocket." Wen handed him a *yuan*, the gold sparkling off the interior lamps. "And see if you still have it by the time we reach the other side."

Of course he would. Stashing the coin into his sash instead of his pocket, Tian snorted.

Yuna cupped a hand to his ear. Her breath tickled. "In a crowded place like this, a tail will get lazy. This is our best chance of making them."

Making tails? It was as if Yuna were speaking a different language.

Wen patted him on the head. "It means identifying someone trying to follow you. Oh, Yuna, give him back the coin."

Patting his sash, Tian gawked. "How..."

Yuna smirked as she stuffed the coin into his pocket. "I distracted you when I whispered in your ear."

"Oh." Tian stuffed his hand into his pocket and palmed the coin.

Wen shook her head. "You're just going to signal to any pickpockets that you have something worth taking."

Tian stuffed the coin into the lining of his undergarment.

Yuna's pretty nose scrunched up. "Well, you don't have to worry about me taking it now."

"Now, see all the reflective surfaces?" Wen pointed her delicate chin to a basin of water on a table, then mirrors in several stalls. "You won't catch a glimpse of Elder Sister though, not unless she lets you."

"Pretend like you are looking at wares," Yuna said. "But check the mirrors when you do."

It was fascinating really, and Tian did as instructed as they slipped through the crowds. Still, Jie never appeared.

At the far end, three hundred and twenty-one paces in total, they came out from under the tent. The chatter subsided to a low din. Up ahead lay a bridge over a moat. Large red lanterns hung from an arched gate on the other side. Smaller lanterns hung from rope all up and down the moat.

"Is this—?"

"The Floating World," Wen said.

He'd heard of it, of course. Father always went when they visited the capital, oftentimes with other lords. What they did there was never clear. "I had always imagined boats."

"Why?" Yuna gave him a curious stare.

Tian shrugged. "Why else would it be called the Floating World?"

"It's where men's dreams take flight." Wen's tone sounded not bitter, but more... what was the word? Mocking?

What was wrong with dreams? Tian could only ponder it as he followed them across the stone bridge and under the arch.

On the other side, the two-story wood buildings looked like any other street in the wealthy parts of the capital, save for all the red.

Red lamps hung on lines over the streets, suspended between restaurants and fortune tellers. Red banners emblazoned with flower emblems fluttered at entrances to mansions. Most of the very few people wandering the streets were girls a little older than Yuna, all dressed in simple, but pretty dresses. All bowed their heads as he passed.

Yuna bowed, and he started to return the greeting.

Wen shot her hand out, stopping him. "Don't bow back."

It seemed impolite. "Why not?"

Yuna bowed to a passing girl, who didn't bow back. "Florets. They are trained to be polite to all visitors and seniors. If you bow back, they'll bow again."

"But she didn't bow back to you."

Yuna shrugged. "I'm a Seedling."

"What about you?" Tian asked Wen.

"A Blossom."

Why the comparison to plants? It was all so confusing. Tian shook his head. "What does any of the Floating World have to do with Flowers?"

Wen exchanged glances with Yuna, before patting him on the head, *again*. She must've thought him a puppy. "Oh, my sweet, little boy. Don't you think Yuna is pretty? Like a flower?"

Tapping his chin, Tian studied the younger girl. She had an oval face with symmetrical features. Both of her eyes sat at pleasing angles, and her nose was high and thin. Her forehead—

"Stop." She glared back. "You're like a country bumpkin, evaluating his prize pig."

For someone younger than him, she used such big words. "But Wen asked—"

Wen squeezed his hand. "You need to learn subtlety."

Subtlety? He cocked his head. "What does that mean?"

"To see without looking. To notice without anyone realizing what you're doing. That is our way." Wen smiled. "So? Is Yuna pretty?"

"Yes, but not as pretty as Princess Kaiya."

Yuna's lips pursed.

Wen laughed. "Little Tian, you shouldn't be so blunt."

Everyone always said that, but she'd asked. Was he supposed to lie? "*You* are beautiful, Miss Wen." And she was, made even more so by every graceful motion.

She covered her lips with delicate fingers. "Like a flower?"

"It is a different kind of beautiful. And not all flowers are pretty."

She laughed again. "In the Floating World, the girls, from Yuna's age all the way to middle age, are supposed to be beautiful and elegant like flowers. Now, tell Yuna she is beautiful."

"But—"

Flicking her fingers, like she'd done in their duel, Yuna frowned. "Next time we duel, I'm going to hit you harder."

Wen snorted, a cute sound. "What about Elder Sister?"

That title! Jie couldn't be much older than him, and certainly younger than Wen. "Why does everyone listen to Jie?"

She covered a melodious laugh. "She's our senior."

Obvious... "But—"

Wen leaned in and whispered, "You should never ask a lady's age!"

How did she know he was going to ask? He frowned.

Yuna rolled her eyes."Her elf blood makes her look younger than she really is. And, she's Master Yan's adopted daughter."

With a chuckle, Wen turned into an alley between the walls of two shrines. Just wide enough for two of them to walk abreast, it didn't allow any sunlight in.

They were getting ready to test him. Tian clenched his fists, every muscle ready to fire.

Wen stepped back and gave him a curious glance. "What are you doing?"

"You're going to attack me, aren't you?" Tian held up his fists.

"Of course not. But look behind you."

A trick, no doubt. Tian held his ground, glaring.

The tap on his shoulder just about caused his soul to jump out of his body. He spun around.

The evil half-elf stood there, smirking. "Do you still have the coin?"

"Of course." He'd paid attention this time. Tian reached into his pants. His fingers closed around the now-warm metal, and withdrew the coin. Maybe they'd be nicer to him now. With a triumphant smile, he held it up for all to see. "Here it is!"

On the other side, Yuna pinched her nose and backed up three steps, her face twisted into horror.

Wen laughed. "Did you do that, Elder Sister?"

"Yes," Jie said, chuckling.

What was so funny? "Do what?"

Squinting, Yuna broke out into a girlish giggle.

Tian followed her gaze. In his fingers, he held not a gold *yuan*, but a silver *jiao*. "How?"

"I was hiding under the table of one of the stalls, and switched them out." Jie looked up to the others.

Wen patted him yet *again*. "Don't worry, you'll learn how not to get your pockets picked."

"And how to pick them," Yuna said.

With a smile, Wen opened her palm, revealing a coin. She picked it up with her other hand to show him. "See this?"

He nodded.

Beaming at him more warmly than anyone but Princess Kaiya ever did, she returned it to her hand and closed her fingers around it. "Is it still in my hand?"

Where else could it be? Tian smirked. "Of course."

She opened her hand, and it was gone.

Tian's jaw dropped. "Where is it?"

Reaching over, she pulled it from behind his ear.

Amazing! Tian clapped his hands.

"Easiest trick in the book." Snorting, Yuna showed how Wen had never returned the coin to her hand, and how she'd used her smile to distract him.

Tian's heart sunk. Had Wen's kindness up to now all been an act?

The mean half-elf's eyes shifted to Yuna. "Now that you've taught Tian a trick, recite the list."

"Six, two, zero, nine. Slippery, green wheel. Cloudy, sun." The girl wetted her lips. "Dagger, stab, finger. Red, sword, crossbow, bludgeon."

"Good job." Jie turned to Tian. "We teach you to create images in your head to remember details. What did you think of, Yuna?"

The girl beamed. "On a day when the sun peeks through the clouds, six thousand two hundred and nine slippery green wheels are arranged in a circle. Inside, there's a duel, one man with a dagger who stabs the other, who has a red sword in the finger. He retaliates by bludgeoning the first with a crossbow."

Jie gave a sharp nod and turned to Tian. "Yuna has exceptional experiential and visual memory, but average verbal memory. We use those strengths and limitations as a base, starting with small lists, and making them longer as an initiate's memory improves. I want you to practice that, starting with—"

"But she forgot the word, *spicy*."

Jie started to speak, but then closed her mouth and sucked on her lower lip.

"Your list," Tian said, "was Red, sword, wheel, dagger, green, stab, cloudy, spicy, crossbow, opera, bludgeon, slippery, sun, finger, six, two, zero, nine."

Yuna's lips rounded into a red circle. "In that order."

"How did you do that?" Wen's smile broadened.

How could he not? Tian shrugged. "I don't know. I just remembered."

The girls exchanged glances. Maybe they'd like him more now?

Jie let her lip go with a pop. "So...How much did you make?"

"Two golds, five silvers." Wen splayed two fingers with one hand, three with the other.

Yuna opened her hands, revealing a gold coin and seven silvers.

"That should be just enough." Jie sucked on her lower lip, a sign she was thinking, then locked her eyes on Tian.

"Enough for what?" Tian's stomach knotted. This couldn't be good.

CHAPTER 3

Tian might have an amazing memory, but he would be an old man before he gained a minimal proficiency in all the skills a Black Fist needed. At least, that's what Jie concluded after following the other clan members from the safe house to the Floating World. It would take more than memory and observation to succeed in their line of work. Now, with Yuna and Wen headed back to the Peony Garden, she took Tian to a theater.

At least he was practicing the coin trick in his pudgy fingers. Even more impressive, the boy's head turned left and right, drinking everything in while he practiced. If only he could do it more subtly, he might become a decent lookout during secret operations.

"The buildings are all made of wood. And so close together." He tapped his chin. "If a fire started..."

Jie nodded. "There was a fire twenty years ago, which burned the entire district down."

"They did not learn from it?"

She shook her head. "They made it worse. Nothing motivates men more than greed and uh, holding hands with women. Lots of wealthy investors bought up the land, and built connected buildings on narrower streets to take up less space."

He looked up and searched her eyes. "Did the clan buy land?"

Maybe the clan would've, but... "No. Here's a secret: the fire started when our members were training with firepowder. It killed all of them. Yuna has told you about the Steel Orchids?"

Tian's head bobbed. "Clan legends. Identical twins, pretending to be one."

And the clan had never found another set of identical twins since. "The initial blast killed them, and eighteen other clan sisters, before the ensuing fire claimed even more people. I will tell you more later, because we are here." She gestured.

Out front of the Red Boat Theater, one of the largest structures in the entertainment district, Old Feng hunched over a signboard, painting the playbill. In all likelihood, the rest of the troupe would be getting their beauty sleep somewhere in the city.

"Old Feng." Jie bowed, albeit with much less grace than a Blossom.

"Hey, Jie." Old Feng straightened, perhaps with more grace than her. "It's been a while. Glad to see you escaped the fire."

Jie suppressed a shudder. The explosion in the Chrysanthemum House had nearly blasted her to tiny half-elf bits. "I was lucky." Or skilled.

"I heard no house would take you after the, uh, incident. Incidents."

Tian looked from her to him and back again.

The clan had already decided to reassign her, but neither Old Feng nor Tian had to know. Jie cleared her throat. "I found work elsewhere. But that's why I'm here, I need your help."

"I am always pleased to be of service."

For the right price. Jie held out two gold coins.

The man's eyes locked on them. "I'm listening."

"I need to find out how much the Peony Garden contracts a Young Lord's First Pollinating." She gestured to Tian.

Tian's eyes widened, and he shook his head.

Old Feng's lips trembled before he broke out into a laugh. "He's a little young for that, isn't he?"

"Do you know what a First Pollinating is?" Jie asked.

Face red, Tian gave a slow nod. "My eldest brother Ming had his."

"What happened?"

"He held a girl's hand." He spoke in such a nervous, conspiratorial whisper, that maybe he knew what really went on during a First Pollinating.

Jie patted him on the head. "It's okay. We're just finding out the price, not arranging yours."

With a blatant expression of relief, Tian blew out a breath.

"You don't know what you're missing, kid," Old Feng said, his eyes straying to Jie's flat body.

Men. They were varying degrees of disgusting. She cleared her throat again. "I just need you to pose as a lord, or a wealthy merchant, or whatever, to get him in."

"You will need the best." Old Feng dipped into a flourishing bow. "You have come to the right place."

Jie rolled her eyes.

"But for a deception of such magnitude, I will require five *yuan*."

"Three," Jie said. "I will go to the Guardian Dragon Opera, if I need to."

"Don't send an acrobat to do an actor's job." Old Feng waved his hands back and forth. "There's also the cost of renting the right clothes for the disguise."

"You have them here!" Jie threw up her hands.

"Yes, but they will need to be cleaned when we're done. You know how the Houses smell."

"Better than your theater." Jie snorted. "Three *yuan*, five *jiao*."

"Come on, Four and a half. This is a rush job. I still need to set up before tonight's show."

Jie held up four fingers.

"Sold." Old Feng gestured toward Tian. "Come along, let's get you dressed. I might have something in your uh, larger size."

Jie pressed two gold coins into his open palm. "Two now. I'll leave Little Tian in your care, and meet you back here in an hour."

"An artist cannot be rushed," Old Feng said. "It'll take half an hour just to fold the robes at the right angle and apply makeup."

"An extra two *jiao* if you finish in half that time."

"Done."

With a bow, Jie headed toward the Peony Garden. Her gut twisted. Only six days had passed since she'd killed Lilian there, and the memories still felt like sorghum wine in raw wounds. How different things could have turned out, had Jie seen the signs of betrayal earlier, or had just let Lilian disappear.

The scent of lavender grew. The gates of the Peony Garden's white outer walls came into sight, along with two guards. The mansion rose three stories up, with red tile eaves pitching at graceful angles. Jie swallowed hard and snuck around to the back.

At this hour, the Seedlings would be cleaning the first floor, cleaning the house for guests tonight. The Florets would be in the upper chambers, helping Blossoms prepare to receive Hummingbirds. While sneaking Tian in to see the common room would've been impossible given the boy's limited skill set, it came second nature to Jie.

Leading to the kitchens, the back gate stood ajar. The sound of cleavers on chopping boards rapped out a soothing rhythm, and the smell of green onions and garlic percolated out. She approached the door, and seeing the chefs otherwise busy, slipped in. The noise provided easy cover for her to rush through to the side door.

Outside in the secluded courtyard between the kitchen and bathhouse, she leaned against the wall and heaved in air. Memories raced through her head, and her chest squeezed. She'd taken this exact same path the night before Lilian's betrayal. That night had led to her disgrace as a Floret.

She took a deep breath and settled her thoughts with the clan's *Pure Water* meditative technique. Better to learn from mistakes than dwell on them. It was all in the past. She headed over to the bathhouse, and, tying her skirts between her legs, scaled the wall to the sharply pitched roof.

Windows to the Blossoms' rooms were unshuttered, so she stayed low while traversing the bath wing's roof to the main mansion. With a quick look to ensure nobody was looking, she climbed into the same window she had on that fateful night.

The Blossom and her Floret prepared in a side dressing niche, and Jie tiptoed across the plush carpet, by the double bed, low table, and cushioned chairs to the sliding doors.

She slid it open, and finding the mezzanine overlooking the common room empty, darted to Little Wen's room. Save for the zigzagging over the joints and joists to keep the wooden planks from chirping like nightingales, it was the identical path from the last time, the only difference being that the House had hosted a major party that night, with a hundred people packing the downstairs and spilling up onto these balconies.

Now, the only activity consisted of Seedlings wiping down tables and chairs in the common room. Of the seven girls working, only Yuna looked up. She gave Jie a near-imperceptible nod before returning to her sweeping. Jie reached Wen's room without incident and slipped in.

The chamber might've been a twin to the one she'd passed through: a bed, two side chairs flanking a low table, and a thick woolen rug weaved in patterns of red and blue. From the location of the voices, Wen was in the dressing niche with her Floret. Jie snuck over, and using the window frame as a launching point, leaped to the ceiling. She squeezed herself between two rafters. Lilian had done the same in her many playful, and ultimately futile attempts to ambush Jie.

The position provided a direct view of Wen, wearing a white inner gown as she sat at a mirror, extending her lashes. Her Floret, a nine-year-old named Reina, fussed with her hair.

Jie cawed like a crow.

Without a pause in her makeup routine, Wen said, "Reina, I can finish the rest. Go help Eldest Sister Lusha."

Lusha, the former Corsage of the house... A sick feeling churned in Jie's stomach.

Reina froze. "But..."

"I'm sorry, I meant Elder Sister Yangyang."

Bowing, Reina scurried through the room, knelt at the door, and slid it open. She walked through, knelt on the other side, and slid it shut, all with the grace expected of a second-year Seedling.

Jie didn't miss that tedious ritual. She dropped down from the rafters, landing without a sound.

"Was the gold enough to secure Old Feng's services?" Wen asked without looking over.

"Yes." Jie came over and picked up where Reina had left off, brushing the tangles out of Wen's silky black tresses. "He should be here soon with Little Tian."

"I could've been your eyes and ears. Spare you the hurt."

"You're right. I'm sorry." Jie sucked on her lower lip. As de facto head of Black Lotus cell in the Floating World until a week ago, she'd failed to delegate duties, which in part had led to Lilian's betrayal. Old habits died hard, or perhaps didn't die at all.

Wen rose, forcing Jie to let go of her hair before making a mess. Wen turned around and wrapped Jie into an embrace. "I know it can't be easy coming back here."

"What's the news of Lusha?" Jie asked, thinking about the Blossom who'd arranged to have her deflowered, so as to protect her own record virgin price.

"Lilian was thorough with her bladework." Wen shuddered. "Lusha's face was so scarred, she'll never work as a Blossom in the

Floating World again. A Triad boss in the Trench bought her contract for coppers. Faceless Chang, I think."

Pushing away from Wen, Jie clenched her jaw. Whereas the Houses of the Floating World followed specific conventions, and the Blossoms even in the less exclusive Houses rarely saw more than a few Hummingbirds a night, the Trench was another story. Controlled by Triads like the Red Dragons and Fangs, the prostitutes there might service twenty or more men throughout the day, with very little rest. All while trying to avoid a serial killer who'd set up shop there in the last couple of months. Lillian's vengeance on Jie's behalf was far more brutal than the original offense.

The Peony Garden's Gardener Mu, who'd arranged the entire plot, had been poisoned; and to protect the secret of the Black Lotus Clan's existence, her body had been left in the Trench, the supposed victim of bad debts to the Triads. And then, of course... "What about Shixian?"

Wen's expression darkened even more. "He committed suicide. We suspect the loss of his manhood was too much to bear."

Jie blinked away a solitary tear. An up-and-coming cavalry officer, Shixian had been her first. It had been an exhilarating experience in the moment, but something she'd never have done without the influence of Dragonweaver magic. Not with her record virgin price on the line. For his part, he'd been an unwitting accomplice, tricked by the Gardener to deflower her.

All in this mansion.

And Lilian had castrated him.

Jie's ears twitched. The bells jingling at the front door tore her from the raw memories. She pushed out of Wen's embrace. "They're here."

Wen stared at her. "Your ears!"

Ignoring the compliment, Jie slipped out onto the mezzanine. Down in the common room, Old Feng wore the robes of a high government official. At his side, Tian looked cute in his own miniature gentleman's robes. He might fit in the one Floating World House which catered to a different taste—with Pistols and Stamens instead of Blossoms and Hummingbirds.

The Peony Garden's new Gardener glided out to greet them, though a slight hitch in her gait gave her away as...

Gardener Ju, the former owner of the Chrysanthemum Pavilion.

What was she doing here? She'd expected renown from the record virgin price that Jie never earned, and their parting words hadn't been pleasant. Heart sinking, Jie turned to Wen with a raised eyebrow.

She bought a majority share of the Peony Garden, Wen signed.

How was that even possible? Gardener Ju had undoubtedly made a huge fortune in her twenty years running the Chrysanthemum Pavilion, but most Houses didn't deal with banks, preferring to keep their money on site. She must've lost most of it in the fire. Though there had been a period of time, two years before, when she'd disappear from the House for hours on end. Could she have bene visiting a bank outside of the Floating World? Jie swallowed hard, and turned her attention to the common room.

The Gardener bowed low, with the grace Jie never bothered to master. Her supposed feats of flexibility still brought Hummingbirds to her bed, though she'd always been choosy about the ones she entertained. "Thank you for coming, Minister—?

Old Feng spoke with a dismissive tone, worthy of a high official. "Feng."

Easier to keep elements of the truth. Hopefully, Tian could play his role well.

CHAPTER 4

The mean half-elf's schematic didn't do the Peony Garden Justice. Though not as grand as some of the halls in the Imperial Palace, the mansion was nothing like any Tian had ever seen. The front double doors swung open into a large room, which vaulted three stories high. Banners hung from the mezzanines on the second and third floors, emblazoned with words for spring, flowers, clouds, and rain. At the far end rose a stage. Several young girls in pastel pink dresses wiped down the twenty-four tables and ninety-two chairs.

The room even had a stone-lined hole with a burning fire, like those he'd seen in paintings from the land of the fair-skinned… what was it called? A hearth?

"You honor my House." The woman was pretty in an aunty kind of way, with dyed black hair pinned up into a hairstyle which looked a like a beehive his friend Kai-Long had once tricked him into knocking over. Her eyes were dark brown, though one had yellow flecks in it. "I am embarrassed to say, I have never heard of you."

"I'm posted in Fenggu Province." Old Feng fanned his hand. "As I'm sure you know, there's nothing quite like the Floating World down there, and I want nothing but the best for my son's First Pollinating."

The woman's eyes studied Old Feng before falling on Tian. "He looks a little young for a First Pollinating. Tell me, young sir, how old are you."

Tian opened his mouth. "T—"

"Twelve," Old Feng said. "We caught him, uh, what's the term? Playing the Flute? So we know he's ready."

A flute was a girl's instrument. Mortified, Tian shook his head and looked up at the woman.

Her lower lip jutted out, like she'd just sucked a lemon for a split second. "*Polishing Jade*, you mean."

Polishing Jade? Forehead scrunching, Tian tapped his chin. He'd never played a flute or polished any jade.

The woman's expression softened, and she bowed. "It is nothing to be ashamed of, Young Sir."

If she knew he was the son of a Great Lord, she'd know just how shameful it was to play a woman's instrument, or do something as menial as polishing. He tried not to frown.

The aunty beckoned to a pretty serving girl, who glided over. She couldn't have been much older than Princess Kaiya, but wasn't nearly as beautiful. She bowed low first to them, then to the woman.

The woman whispered in her ear, and the younger disappeared through a side archway. She appeared on a stairwell a few seconds later, not far from where the first assassin shot the countant.

"She is pretty, isn't she?" The woman said.

Tian yanked his attention from the younger girl down to this aunty. "No."

Her eyes widened.

Old Feng jabbed Tian in the ribs. "Be more polite."

"But—"

"Not to worry." The aunty smiled. "Little Yaya will be back with some blossoms for the Young Sir to choose from."

Tian couldn't hold his frown any longer. First flutes, now flowers. They really must think him a girl.

Old Feng held up a hand. "Oh, we did not plan to pollinate now... unless you'd offer a doting father a sample." He grinned.

The woman's lips tightened into a thin line.

Old Feng coughed. "I mean, we just came to, uh, price out the flowers."

Her lips went from a thin line to an ugly frown. "Your Excellency, walking through these doors comes with many assumptions."

"Of course, of course. Let us see your blossoms. Would it be all right for my boy to look around the room?"

The woman bowed. "Of course."

Finally! Up to now, it'd felt like the assassin had been tickling Tian's ear with taunting whispers. Maybe now, he'd find some answers. Thus dismissed, he walked through the chairs and tables to the corner where the killing had taken place. There had to be some clue, and he had to find it. He sat in the chair and slumped over like the man who'd been murdered. If Jie's schematic were correct—unlikely, because the relative distances were all wrong—the second assassin would've been standing in plain sight. Any further back, beyond the archway, would be a near-impossible shot with a crossbow—maybe only the First Wang Emperor's consort could make it, if three hundred-year-old histories were true.

"Are you tired, Young Sir?" the woman called.

Excitement growing, Tian straightened and shook his head. "You cleaned up all the blood."

"Excuse me?" She looked as if the Orc Gods had returned on their flaming chariots. She took two steps back, with a slight limp.

"Isn't this where a good man was shot in the back?"

Gawking, the woman looked from him to Old Feng. "What is he talking about?"

How could she not know? Tian hopped up and down, waving a finger in a circle over his head. "Last week. And wasn't there a fire?"

All color drained from her face. "I think you need to leave now."

Wen appeared in the archway, and shuffled over, hips swaying like a kite in the wind. She looked even more beautiful than before, wearing a blue and white silk gown that bared her shoulders. She'd be able to jog the aunty's memory.

He clapped. "Wen!"

Old Feng's eyes widened, Wen's jaw dropped. Her eyes darted up to the mezzanine for a split second.

Tian, alone, followed her gaze, but saw nothing but shadows.

The aunty's eyebrows clashed together like two swords in a duel. "Wen, how do you know these gentlemen?"

Wen bowed. "I met Minister Feng and his son at the entrance to the Floating World. They asked me the best place for a young man's First Pollinating, and of course, I recommended the Peony Garden."

"I see." The older woman gave a slow nod.

"Tell them," Tian said. "About the good man dying here."

Wen waved a hand back and forth. "You are mistaken, Young Sir. A lord died in a fire at the Chrysanthemum Pavilion."

"But Jie said—"

"Jie?" Panic rose in the aunty's voice.

The door opened, revealing Lord Peng Xian, father of his friend Kai-Long. A great lord who knew about Tian's banishment from the capital.

***

As she stood in the shadows of the second-floor mezzanine, Jie's every nerve prickled. Despite her warning to him to stay quiet, Zheng Tian had turned what should have been a simple operation into an unmitigated disaster. Old Feng hadn't helped, using such vulgar language like *Playing the Flute*, but ultimately, it came down to the boy's obsessiveness overwhelming his common sense. No matter how observant, he'd never survive in the clan until he learned to temper his excitement.

All he'd had to do was look around, and see if he could determine the location of the second assassin from the Chrysanthemum Pavilion. He didn't even have to actually open his mouth. Wen had almost salvaged the situation, at least she had a good head on her shoulders.

Then, he had to mention Jie's name. It looked to have triggered bad memories for the Gardener, if her distraught expression were any indication.

Now though, the boy clung to the back of Wen's skirts like a frightened child. Jie followed his gaze to the front door.

Lord Peng Xian stood there with several of his men, all unarmed because of the conventions of the Floating World. His eldest son was to have had his First Pollinating with Lusha a couple of days ago, with an unprecedented contract price, possibly paid for by Lord Ting's enemies; but after Lusha's disappearance, the young man must've slept with someone else.

Oh, no. Her heart squeezed. As a great lord, Peng would know about Tian's banishment. That's why the boy was hiding.

Jie dashed down the steps, while keeping an ear toward the common room.

"Madame Dan." Lord Peng's voice echoed. "I have come to thank you for my son's First Pollinating. I'd like to arrange one for my second son, Kai-Long."

"I thank you for the great honor," the Gardener said. "Minister Feng, here, has also brought his son to arrange a First Pollinating."

Usually, such deals stayed anonymous and confidential in the Floating World, but if Jie'd learned anything about the Gardener from their years together at the Chrysanthemum Pavilion, it was that she had a uniquely shrewd mind to go along with her avarice.

No doubt, she'd play one off the other in a battle of face, to raise the contract price. She'd be sorely disappointed, given Feng's acting income.

Jie paused at the archway from the side hallway to the common room. When Wen met her gaze, Jie flashed hand signals. *Danger. Hide Tian. Escape on my mark.*

Wen made a nearly imperceptible nod, and angled herself to stay between Tian and Lord Peng.

"Since she is here, let me introduce Wen," the Gardener said.

Jie gritted her teeth. The moment Wen bowed low, like an appropriate Blossom, Lord Peng would see Tian. Unless he was busy staring at her chest, which wasn't out of the realm of possibility.

Making sure that no one was looking, Jie used the tables and chairs as cover and made for the front door. Halfway through the room, she flashed a signal.

Wen placed one hand over her mouth and another over her belly, and let out an adorable squeal. "My apologies, Gardener, Masters. I... I..." She bowed halfway, and backed toward the kitchens, Tian no doubt behind her.

"Are you all right?" Lord Peng took a step forward, hand extended.

Jie opened the front door, setting the wind chimes jingling.

All heads turned toward her.

"You!" The Gardener scowled. "You are not welcome here."

Jie grinned. "Madame Ju... I mean, Madame Dan, I am glad to see you survived the Chrysanthemum Pavilion's fire."

"Do not speak of it!"

Old Feng, Lord Peng, and all of Peng's men stared between the two.

Lord Peng cleared his throat. "If this is a bad time..."

"No, this filthy whore was just leaving." The Gardener gestured toward the door, the motion itself graceful.

"I was wondering," Jie said. "How could you possibly afford to buy this house after your old one burned down?"

Lord Peng's eyes darted back toward Wen. "Isn't that Lord Zheng's son? The one banished on pain of death?"

Oh, shit.

Eyes glinting with avarice, the Gardener motioned to a Seedling. "Go get the gate guards."

CHAPTER 5

Tian's mouth watered as Wen pulled him through the kitchens. After days of eating food that tasted like wet paper, he couldn't help but gaze longingly at the chefs as they prepared aromatic pastries. Their scrumptious smell rivaled the pastries served in the Imperial Palace. If he weren't the son of a Great Lord, he'd swipe some from the trays.

Wen stopped, leaned in, and whispered, "Go ahead, take one."

She always seemed to know what he was thinking. Tian shook his head. "Stealing is..."

"...is what we do. Now hurry and see if you can take one before the chefs see you."

Swallowing hard, Tian watched as the chefs turned this way and that, rolling dough, chopping it, then spinning around to deliver trays. Six in all, they fell into a beautiful rhythm like a dwarf-made clock. He swiped a pork bun and hid it in his sleeve, then looked around.

The cooks all continued their work, never breaking their intricate dance.

Laughing, Wen pulled him to the back door and saw him out. She pointed to an open door in the compound walls, twenty-two steps away. "Can you find your way back to the Red Boat Theater?"

He pouted. "You will not come with me?"

She gestured back toward the common room. "They're expecting me soon."

"All right." It shouldn't be that hard.

She flashed a pretty smile and started to turn around.

"Wait." He tugged back on her hand. "Why did the woman pretend not to know a man was shot here?"

"It wasn't here. There was another building, exactly the same, just a few blocks over." She waved to the east.

He followed her gesture, then turned back. "But her face. She knew about it."

"Wen!" the woman's voice yelled from the common room.

Wen nodded. "She owned the other house, before it burned down. Now, I have to go."

Burned down? As close as all the buildings were, it was a miracle that the fire hadn't claimed the entire Floating World, like Jie's story from twenty years ago. He watched as Wen hurried back through the kitchens.

Then, he took eight paces over the rear yard's pavestones and passed through the gates. Getting back to the theater would be easy, as long as he backtracked from the front gates; but the burned-down compound Wen had indicated was beckoning. That's where the answer was, and he *had* to know. He headed toward a single pole, which rose like a middle finger, from beyond the compound walls. It seemed to point at the Iridescent Moon, now waning to its second crescent. An hour to dusk.

Foot traffic had picked up since their arrival. Now, instead of young girls bustling through the streets, it was mostly loud men in fine clothes, pointing at the various buildings. Every now and then, he'd look back. With the Peony Garden's height and distinctive red tiles, it served as a perfect landmark to keep his bearings. The sloshing of lake water in the near distance indicated a proximity to the north edge of the Floating World.

"Are you lost, Young Sir?" a pretty woman approached, her feet wobbling. Unlike the gowns in the Peony Garden, which resembled Imperial Court fashions, this woman's dress looked like nothing he'd ever seen. The neckline plunged low, her breasts nearly spilling out, and the slit of her skirts rose up the side of her leg, revealing web-like undergarments. Her bloodshot eyes, however, stood out the most, even through her hooded lids.

Mouth dry, Tian backed up a step. "No, miss, I am going to the burned house."

"Whatever for? There's nothing there. Come with me to the Yue Heaven." She beckoned with fanning fingers and a crooked smile, but nearly tripped on her skirt.

Yue... made from the sap of the yue tree, some of the officials in the Imperial Palace smoked it, and the pungent smell stuck to everything. Shaking his head, Tian hurried on his way. Several dozen paces away, he looked back.

The woman was now talking with a group of three men in gentlemen's robes. If her breasts had been nearly spilling out before, she was now shrugging her shoulders in such a way that it showed just about everything. She'd adjusted her posture so that her leg jutted out from the slit in her skirts.

With a shudder, he continued at a brisker pace. He arrived at the spotless, white walls in a few minutes, along the eastern edge of the compound. It hadn't rained in a week, yet the walls were so clean, even after a fire. He ran his hand over the plaster as he worked his way around toward the south wall, which faced a main street.

Before he reached there, his fingers snagged on an indentation, and he paused. There were four identical marks, evenly spaced. A quick scan up and down revealed two more sets up, which would've been just out of reach from the first set; though the space between the set on the left side was closer than the right.

In the stories Mother used to tell, Black Fists used metal climbing claws to scale walls and sneak into naughty children's bedrooms at night. Before this week, it had all been cautionary tales to get him to behave; but now, he knew Black Fists were real. He'd have to ask the mean half-elf if climbing claws were real.

One thing was for sure, said mean half-elf was probably spry enough to run and jump and reach the top of the wall; so it wasn't her who'd used climbing claws—if indeed that's what they were, and not burrowing wasps with an excellent sense of space and distance. Testing the holes with a finger, he found they all had the same depth, tapering in a point.

He continued and rounded the corner to the main street. It was as if this one block were a ghost town. Across the empty street, the restaurants, a massage parlor, and a shrine all had *closed* signs on their doors. On the blocks to either side, life went on as usual.

Tapping his chin, Tian went to the compound's main gate. The doors, carved and painted with the logo of a chrysanthemum, hung ajar, the entrance blocked only by a warning sign.

He clenched his jaw. The sign, stamped with the official seal of the city watch strictly forbade entry, and a good boy would obey authority. He peered around it at the charred timbers. Up close, the single pole he'd seen from a distance turned out to be a brick chimney, rising three stories—just like in the Peony Garden.

Suspicion prickled at the back of his neck. A voice in his head that sounded like Princess Kaiya nudged him to enter. He *had* to see the spot. Looking left and right to make sure no one was watching, he ducked under the sign.

The white pavestones led through a lawn, lined by trees, the first several which had survived the fire. The ones closer to the building, however were nothing more than charred trunks, which still seemed to give off heat. The distance to the walls had probably saved the rest of the Floating World from burning down. Maybe the architect had had that foresight.

He went up the stone stairs and picked his way through the fallen timbers to the common room. The frame of the stage remained partially intact. Curiously, mangled copper pipes jutted from the enormous hearth. With a little imagination, he could see the banners and lanterns hanging from the mezzanines. Holding the image of Jie's schematic, he went over to where the man sat dead.

Surely he would've been sitting up, which meant the angle… he walked along the bolt's probable flight path to the archway between the common room to the veranda. If that one crossbow had survived the fire, and now lay with the other evidence in the clan safe house, the other would have, too. And if the clan hadn't recovered it, maybe it was just under the rubble.

His search had uncovered nothing by the time he reached the now non-existent archway. From here, the assassin had a clear line of sight on Lord Ting, but still would've been visible to Jie. Curiously, the spot lay almost directly between the climbing claw marks on the other side of the wall and Lord Ting's chair. That must've been how the assassin had come in and out.

If the assassin had needed climbing claws, they couldn't have possibly scaled the wall holding a repeating crossbow. Maybe strapped to their back, but Repeaters were heavy, and if the killer were in a hurry… No, in all likelihood, they would've left it behind. Or disassembled it and scattered the pieces.

But no, the telltale parts of an imperial Repeater were fire-resistant eldarwood, and even if they did burn, the metal components would've survived. Picking through the nearby rubble revealed nothing of interest. No wonder, given how thorough the clan had probably scoured the scene. He climbed through the remains of the veranda and walked toward where the claw marks would be on the opposite side of the wall.

In the grass near the wall, something glinted in the late afternoon sun. He hurried over and picked up a metal peg—part of the cranking mechanism of a repeating crossbow. He'd taken apart and reassembled dozens in his life, and all used standard parts.

While exactly the same length as a standard imperial issue part, this one was made of bronze instead of steel.

More connections to the North, home to many bronze foundries. If they could cast beautiful statues, it would be even easier to make a simple rod. All they had to do was make a mold from an imperial steel pin.

Now, why had the assassin been so careless as to drop it here, when everything else about the plan had been so exact? Tapping his chin, he looked at the wall and found the same climbing claw markings. He stuck his finger in the holes and found they went to the identical depth as the ones on the other side.

"Hey!" a gruff voice yelled from the entrance.

Heart leaping into his throat, Tian turned.

A scowling man in red robes drew a broadsword and pointed at him. "Come over here."

Tian swallowed hard. He wasn't even supposed to be in the capital. If this was an authority...

Wen had said this was an exact copy of the Peony Garden, which meant there was a back gate. Though this newcomer had longer legs, he would either have to run around the ruins, or pick his way through it, slowing him down.

Tian bolted toward the back.

"He's over here!" The man gave chase in long lopes, closing the distance to the burnt ruins faster than Tian covered the space between the side and rear yards.

At this rate, it would be close. Tian's heart hammered as he ran. The man rounded the side of the house just as Tian reached the back gate.

Charred timbers lay in a haphazard pile, but it looked like there'd be enough space for him to pick his way through. Chest heaving, Tian climbed over one beam and ducked under another. Pain bit into the back of his hand as he scraped it on something. The gate was right there.

He was on all fours, crawling toward the opening, when a hand clamped down on his pant leg.

Tian was halfway out from under the fallen timbers and into the alley. He yanked on his leg to no avail. The man's pull drew him inexorably closer, and the silk pants showed no sign of tearing. Capture in the capital, from which he'd been banished, meant a slow death.

"Stop struggling, Fatty!" the man bellowed.

What would a Black Fist do if their clothes snagged on something?

Gulping hard, Tian loosed the pants' drawstrings and lifted his knees. The pants ripped away, and he scuttled forth, out from under the debris.

"Come back, you little shit!"

Tian bolted down the alley, even as his stomach twisted. The man had yelled to some companions, which meant there could be more pursuers. Maybe they'd even round the wall ahead of him, cutting off the escape route.

He made it to the alley's intersection with a road. Looking both ways, he found he was close to the reservoir along the northern edge of the Floating World. To the south, a new man in pastel pink rounded the corner.

His eyes met Tian's. "There he is!"

Heart pounding, Tian dashed across the street into the next alley. The Peony Garden lay up ahead, where Jie could probably help him.

CHAPTER 6

Blocks away from the Peony Garden, Jie sniffed the air, picking up on Tian's red bean paste scent. It had grown more noticeable the further west she went. Which meant the kid had no sense of direction, if he'd followed Wen's instructions to meet at the Red Boat Theater.

Back at the Peony Garden, she'd stared down Gardener Ju, to create as much of a diversion as possible for Tian to escape. When the House guards had come to show her the exit, she'd dipped into a terse bow and left. Old Feng followed close on her heels, all acting skill forgotten. It was no wonder he only played minor parts in his troupe.

No doubt, the sharp Gardener had seen through his act. Which meant that her sending guards in search of Tian was not meant to reunite a lost son with a frantic father. No, she'd always been an avaricious woman. She never did anything if it didn't benefit her, and saw Tian as a bounty to be claimed.

No matter what, Jie had to find him first. If he had sense, he'd hide among all the men now milling about the Floating World.

Old Feng had cleared his throat. "I need to get back to the theater. So, about the balance of my fee..."

Jie peered at him. "I've seen shadow puppets with a better range of facial expression. You'll get paid when you help me find Tian."

He pursed his lips. "Fine. I'll go this way." He pointed in the direction of the theater.

That had been ten minutes ago. She looked up at the Iridescent Moon, now waning to half-crescent. Twelve minutes ago. With Tian's short legs and extra weight, he couldn't have gotten far.

Maybe he could hide? With the sun close to setting, the Floating World's red lanterns would cast the streets in a pink glow. He wouldn't know how to work the angled shadows. Following his scent, she worked her way west.

Tian's red bean paste aroma grew stronger, and her gut knotted as it mingled with the bitter scent of charred wood. The burnt husk of the Chrysanthemum Pavilion came into view, or at least, the chimney which had survived the fire.

She swallowed hard. She'd last been back several days ago, in the immediate aftermath of the explosion she'd barely escaped, to help collect evidence. If time healed all wounds, not enough of it had passed.

That was neither here nor there. Unsurprisingly, Tian had apparently figured out that the Chrysanthemum Pavilion was the actual site, and had gone to investigate. The boy had more intuition in his pinkie than most. It left little room for common sense. Squaring her shoulders, she broke into as fast a run as her dress would allow.

Several passersby's gazes fell on her. They whispered among themselves, but her elf ears picked up their furtive conversations:

"It's Jie."

"She's in a hurry."

"Which House does she belong to now?"

"I heard the Fangs in the Trench bought her contract."

"I had a bid on her virginity."

"Too bad, how that worked out."

"I'd still sell my mother off to pay for a night with a half-elf."

Having unique, exotic features made her instantly recognizable, one reason the clan felt she might be a liability on operations. Maybe they were right.

Ignoring the hushed excitement of pathetic men, she made it to the front gate of the Chrysanthemum Pavilion ruins.

Her heart squeezed. She'd spent six years of her life here, all with Lilian.

Something else was here now: a new smell, or rather several. The Peony Garden's lavender fragrance mingled with steel and minute traces of red bean paste. Tian had been here, and the Peony Garden's guards had followed him not long after. There was no sign of any of them now, though.

With a deep breath, she ducked under the city watch's rope line, and into the grounds. Tian's and the men's scents diverged, the different concentrations indicating they'd passed through the courtyard a quarter of an hour apart. She followed Tian's dissipating smell into the remains of the mansion's common room.

It'd been here that Lilian had assassinated Lord Ting, a devout vassal of the emperor who kept the North from rebelling. It had been an ingenious plan, one which Jie hadn't seen coming until it was too late to stop.

Lilian had spared Jie. Their mutual affection had been their weakness, and only one of them had survived.

If Tian was correct with his observation—and it made sense, given the angle at which the crossbow bolt hit Lord Ting—there'd been one more accomplice somewhere along the east side of the room. Jie picked her way through the rubble to the spot in front of the ruined stage. The area had been disturbed recently, given the scuffs in the charred floors. Tian must've looked around for a few minutes before the Peony Garden guards caught up with him.

She sniffed the air again. The red bean paste scent picked up the further east she went, through the ruins of the veranda and all the way to the compound's eastern edge. There, telltale signs of climbing claws dug into the walls. Which meant, someone trained in Black Lotus ways had used this point of insertion. Surely not

Lilian: she could jump and catch the top of the wall and climb. Someone else.

One of the other twenty-six clan sisters embedded in the Floating World? Before last week, it wouldn't have been imaginable. Usually, a Black Fist would fill the holes to hide evidence of their passing; so whoever it was had been in a hurry. They were also a little taller than Jie, given the distance between the marks.

The clan had missed this evidence a week ago. Of course, based on her own account of the murder, they had no reason to suspect a second shooter. Tian had somehow found this very spot. He might be out of shape and far behind in Black Lotus training, but he was proving his worth already.

She continued following his scent trail to the rear of the compound, where fallen timbers blocked the gate. Tian's pants draped over one of them, and fresh blood stained another. He'd been in a hurry to get out, and since he probably hadn't paused to relieve himself, his pursuers had snagged his pants. Likely the former, since the guard's smell was nearly as strong as Tian's here.

With a running jump, she grabbed the top of the wall and scrambled up. From the higher vantage point, she looked down the empty alley. No sign of a pants-less boy running around. No one—

Somewhere in the distance, excited shouts cut through the din of carousing men.

Jie hopped down and ran, using her ears and nose. Hopefully, she could reach Tian before the guards.

CHAPTER 7

Heaving for breath, Tian hunched over not far from the gates to the Peony Garden. Shorter than every other visitor to the Floating World, he'd zigged and zagged between the men. In the red glow, he'd lost the guards chasing him.

For the time being.

And, there was no sign of Jie.

Even now, his pursuers' loud voices demanded to know if anyone had seen a pants-less boy in a dark gentleman's robe.

His heart raced as he pictured the men in his mind. They'd all worn not the dark blue uniforms of the city watch, but the pastel pink livery of the Peony Garden. They'd drawn weapons, which meant they weren't simply trying to return him to Old Feng.

Whatever their intentions, they were looking for a pants-less boy. He needed to change clothes.

He ran into an alley between the Peony Garden and a fox shrine... and skidded to a stop.

A shadowed figure stood at the far end.

He started to back away, but back on the main street, his pursuers' voices grew louder.

"Tian." The figure hurried over.

Little Yuna's voice.

He blew out a bated breath and ran to meet her.

She'd since changed out of her simple dress, and now wore a robe and sash similar to the girls serving in the imperial palace. It exposed more of her neck.

Tian said, "I'm being—"

"Chased. Yes, I know. Eldest Sister told me." She flicked a finger at him. "Take off your clothes."

He gawked at her. He'd meant to change clothes, but... "What am I supposed to wear?"

"I wore a gown a little too large for me. It will be tight on you." She reached behind her and untied her sash, then opened the flap of her dress.

Oh, Heavens, this wasn't right. A gentleman shouldn't peek at a naked woman. And Yuna was only eight! Tian spun around. And he wouldn't be caught dead in girl's clothes.

"Don't be a baby. Just give me your robe."

He peeked over his shoulder.

Hand proffering the gown, she wore nothing but an undergarment over her groin, and her scowl showed zero sign of embarrassment. She yanked the cord binding his topknot, causing his hair to tumble down to his shoulders. "Turn around. Take it."

He turned around, but kept his gaze fixed on her forehead. His hand swatted empty air a few times before it found the proffered dress.

"Hurry up."

"What?"

"Your clothes! Give them to me."

Out on the street, the voices of his pursuers grew louder. With his other hand, he spun his finger in a circle. "Can you turn around?"

"You *are* a baby." She snorted. "You'll need to get used to seeing and being naked in the clan."

He swallowed hard. No sooner did he pull the gentleman's robe over his head than she snatched it and squirmed into it. It was much too big for her, but when she shook out her hair, then bound it in a boy's top knot, she might pass for him in the dim red lights of the Floating World.

She cleared her throat. When she spoke, her voice sounded suspiciously like his. "Hurry up and put it on."

"How did you do that? With your voice?"

"It's our clan's *Mockingbird's Deception.*" This time, her voice sounded even more like his, down to his broken sentences. "You'll learn it. If you're smart enough. Now put on the dress."

He swallowed hard again. If his robe were too large for her, her gown would make him look even more ridiculous. Thankfully, the hanging sleeves made it easy to slip his arms in, and though it squeezed his shoulder blades together, it was still manageable. The skirts, which would brush the floor on her, exposed his ankles, as well as his shoes—and there was no way he'd fit into Yuna's to complete the disguise. "I—"

"Shhh!" Finger over her lips, she cocked her head and turned an ear down the alley toward the street. He looked in that direction.

Three of his pursuers hurried past the opening to the alley, and their questioning voices faded in the distance.

She blew out a breath. "They wouldn't imagine you'd come back here. Was it good thinking, or just dumb luck that you did?"

"I—"

She held up a staying hand. With mesmerizingly deft fingers, she twisted, pulled, and braided his hair. A pouch, which appeared in her hands from out of nowhere, contained a brush, sticks, and powder. She attacked his face with the tools, and then stood back and looked.

"Well?" he ventured. "What do I look like?"

"It's hard to tell in the dark, but I'm good with quick makeup jobs."

He started to reach for his cheek, when she slapped his hand.

"Don't touch." Her eyes roved over him.

He covered his exposed neck.

"The dress makes you look fat." She snorted. "And let's face it, you probably had a few extra *jin* to begin with."

Heat rushed to his cheeks, which seemed even hotter for all the powdery stuff she'd applied to his face.

"Now, head back to the theater. Old Feng will keep you safe until Eldest Sister comes. Follow me to the end of the alley, and imitate the way I walk." She walked toward the back, small hips swaying a few degrees as she crossed one leg over the other. Her carriage remained upright, chin straight.

It looked elegant, but... "Wen walks better."

"She has hips, and has been doing it longer. Now, you try."

How hard could it be? He strutted toward the rear alley, crossing one leg over the other, just as Yuna had done, and turned around.

"You look like a pigeon who's just won a game of chess. This is hopeless." She threw her hands up. "But time is running out."

"What do we do?"

She pointed to the back alley. "Stick to the alleys. Return to the theater and stay with Old Feng. I'm going to draw your pursuers in the opposite direction." With a quick bob of her head, she headed toward the main street.

The layout of the Floating World, as if looking down on it from above, appeared in his imagination. He could stick to the northernmost alley for several blocks before turning south. He crept down the path, his mind's eye registering the back of shrines, gambling dens, and mansions. He paused at each intersection, waiting until the flow of people subsided, then channeled his inner Wen to cross with as much grace as possible. Given that the north-south roads dead-ended at the lake here, not many people passed, and everything had proceeded well up to the fifth intersection. One more block and he'd turn south along the moat.

"Look at that one!" a man dressed in gentleman's robes, standing down the street at the next intersection, pointed at Tian.

His equally wealthy-looking companion nudged him. "Quiet. It's just a Seedling. Mess with them, and every Floating World Enforcer will come and castrate you."

"Seedlings aren't out at this hour, and this one walks less like a Floating World Blossom, and more like a Trench Whore."

That word. Men used it, usually when saying mean things about girls. Tian's stomach twisted.

The man's stride lengthened as he approached. "They start young in the Trench, and I'm craving something plump tonight."

Tian's heart pounded. They'd mistaken him for a real girl, and nobody else was around.

The second hurried to catch up. "A whore from the Trench wouldn't come looking for business in the Floating World. Leave her alone."

The first brushed him off. "Hey little girl, aren't you too young to be out all alone at this hour?"

Tian avoided eye contact. They might be grown-ups, but they were still just merchants. As a Great Lord's son, he'd trained in fighting arts since as soon as he could walk, so he might be able to fight them off. Still, there was always the risk of injury, and Princess Kaiya never approved of violence. That left fleeing as the better option.

He gauged the distances. If he ran, he could reach the alley and then turn into a corridor between the buildings; but if they caught him there, no one else would be around. The other choice would be to run past them, and hope to get the attention of other revelers.

There'd been news of a murderer roaming the Trench preying on lone girls. The Floating World wasn't too far from the Trench, and right now, Tian looked like a lone girl. He ran toward the men, who froze with looks of surprise.

"What's she doing?" The first asked.

Tian dashed around him. He'd made it! He—

A yank on the dress sleeve bared his shoulder and jerked him back. His feet tangled up in the skirts, and he stumbled to the ground.

The first leered at him. "Where are you going, little girl?"

"Leave her alone, you're going to get us in trouble." The other's eyes darted back and forth.

"She just tripped. Right, little girl?"

The way he looked at Tian made him feel dirty and insignificant. He cast his eyes down.

Two arms hooked under his, hands lingering over his chest, and lifted him to his feet.

"There you go, all good," the first said. "Now, which House do you belong to? I can escort you there."

Tian started to speak, but then closed his mouth. His voice, while still not deep like his brothers, didn't sound like a girl's. Looking at the ground, he shook his head.

"So demure!" the man lifted Tian's chin.

"Wait." The second leaned in and scrutinized Tian's face. "He's a boy."

The first's hand jerked back. "What?"

"Look."

The first's eyes roved over him. His face puckered up like a dried date. "Disgusting." He shoved Tian to the ground, and pain flared in his butt as it hit the pavestones.

The man's companion pulled him back. "Calm down. He's probably a Pistil of the Snap Dragon."

Heat blazed in Tian's cheeks. To think, in his past life as a Great Lord's son, this merchant would never dare to be so bold. The girls—and boys—in the Floating World were nothing more than bugs to them. He aimed a quick kick at the first's shins.

The man howled. "You little shit, I'm going to—"

"Please, Kind Sir," a familiar voice said. "Please desist."

Head nodding, the second pulled back on the first. "I'm sorry."

Tian turned to the voice.

It was the woman in red, who'd earlier tried to sell him yue. She was bowing low, but she turned and winked at him, even as she addressed the men. "Won't you come to Yue Heaven? Smoking and women."

Tian looked back at the men as he scrambled to his feet.

Both's eyes were locked on the woman's breasts, fully exposed by her deep bow and plunging neckline. When she straightened, they exchanged glances.

"Yue's harmless fun," the first said.

"No, it's almost as bad as opium." The second shuddered.

The first waved a dismissive hand. "The Imperial Court makes it and controls its sale."

"Not the stuff in the Trench, I hear." The second pantomimed smoking a pipe. "Smoke it once, and you'll crave it for the rest of your life. Not worth the risk."

The first studied the woman. His eyes narrowed. "Yue Heaven's girls aren't really Blossoms, are they?" The way he said it came with the unspoken message: only House Blossoms were protected by the Enforcers.

The woman must've understood the meaning, the way she took two steps back and bowed again. "I was a Blossom at the Chrysanthemum Pavilion."

Just like Jie had been.

"It burned down." The first grinned as he claimed the distance between them. "Which means you're just a filthy whore. An unprotected, filthy whore."

That word again. It was one thing for them to bully him. To mistreat a woman, on the other hand... Tian stepped between the two.

The man's grin twisted into a snarl. He seized Tian's sleeve at the shoulder and started to yank him out of the way.

Tian gripped the man's hand, then twisted it, evoking a yelp as he buckled to his knees.

"You little turtle's egg!" The man leaned in and bit Tian's finger.

Tian jerked his hand back, and the man rose. Quivering with rage, he shoved Tian down again, and cocked a foot back.

"Stop!" the woman shrieked. "Yue Heaven is owned by the Red Dragons, and he is my little brother."

The man froze, his complexion paling. "Is that—?"

"Triads," the second whispered. "The Floating World Enforcers might kick you out, but the Triad goons will chop you into little pieces."

The first swallowed hard. "Let's get out of here."

Father had spoken about the Triads before. They'd taken over the Trench, but since they were outside the capital's walls, and apparently paid taxes, the Imperial Court left them alone. Still, their reputation was enough that the two merchants hurried off.

"That was very brave of you," the woman said, bending over to help Tian up.

Tian squared his shoulders. "A righteous man defends others."

"I didn't think righteous men wore dresses." She laughed. "I'm Naya. What's your name?"

"Tian."

"Are you hurt?"

Pain burned on Tian's elbows, where blood stained the dress sleeves. He pulled it up and looked. "Only a scrape."

"Come," she said. "I'll take you back to Yue Heaven to get cleaned up."

"Is it true, about the Triads?"

She laughed. "Yes, the Red Dragons own Yue Heaven. But I don't think they'd really care if some man killed me. They'd just replace me with another girl."

Tian frowned. People weren't repeating crossbow parts, cheap and replaceable.

"You don't know how to hide your feelings, do you? You're so adorable." She patted his head, yet another who thought him a puppy. "Even more so with the splendid make-up. I can see why they'd mistake you for a girl."

Yuna would've been pleased with the compliment on her makeup job, but... "I'm not a girl."

"No, you're a brave boy, who came to protect me." She took his hand. "Come, let's clean out your scrape."

"Where are we going?"

"To Yue Heaven."

CHAPTER 8

Following Tian's scent and the shouting of Peony Garden guards, Jie's nose and ears led her to the northeastern section of the Floating World. The number of voices suggested three men in pursuit, and they'd cornered Tian in an alley between the Gambling God's Shrine and the shadow puppet theater.

One stood at the alley's entrance, broadsword drawn, his back to her. Passersby paused to look down the alley, but invariably continued on their way.

Staying in the angled shadows cast by the red lanterns and rising White and Blue Moons, she withdrew a throwing spike from her hair. While the city authorities generally left the Floating World to govern itself, killing the man would bring them in to investigate. Whoever had turned Lilian and assassinated Lord Ting would likely go to ground.

Still, no telling what the guards and the Peony Garden had in store for Tian. She crept closer, mingling in with a group of men heading in the guard's direction.

Ten paces away. Just entering range for a fifty-fifty fatal shot. Eight paces. It had to be done. Just a few more steps and it would be a guaranteed kill.

Another guard emerged from the alley, sword in hand, shaking his head. "He's gone."

The first threw his hands up. "He was cornered!" He wouldn't have been so exasperated if he knew Tian getting away had saved his life.

"Don't believe me? Check for yourself." The second jerked a thumb behind him at the alley.

"Never mind. He couldn't have gotten far. You go that way." The first pointed west. "I'll go the other."

The two jogged off in opposite directions, and Jie headed into the alley. In the dark, her vision shifted to greys and greens. Combined with her sense of smell, she'd have an advantage over a full human.

She sniffed.

Tian's red bean paste scent faded the deeper she went, replaced by a lavender scent. She looked up.

Yuna sat atop a wall, dressed in the gentleman's robe Tian had been wearing. Grinning, she waved. "Six, two, zero, nine. Slippery, green wheel. Cloudy, sun." The girl wetted her lips. "Dagger, stab, finger. Red, sword, crossbow, bludgeon. Spicy."

"I didn't ask." Jie chuckled. "Next time, recite them in order, like Tian."

Yuna hopped down and landed lightly. "At least he has memory going for him."

"Don't get too enamored with him."

Yuna's cheeks darkened, no doubt blushing.

No, it wouldn't do to fall in love with another Black Lotus. It led to poor judgment, as proven by Lilian's deception. Jie cleared her throat. "That was a great idea, changing clothes and drawing the guards away."

The girl beamed for a split second before her expression returned to neutral. "What does the Gardener want with him?"

What, indeed. Jie shrugged. "Knowing Gardener Ju—no, Gardener *Dan*'s greed, she hoped to turn him in for a reward. Which is why we need to find him first."

With a nod, Yuna flicked her fingers to the west as if she were performing the No Shadow Cut. "I will need to get back to the Peony Garden soon. I'll lead the first guard back."

"All right. Where did you last see Tian?"

"I told him to go to the Red Boat Theater."

South and east of here. "I assume you put him in a dress."

"My green gown. It was a little tight." Yuna shook her head. "No, a lot tight."

The idea of Tian wearing that particular dress... Jie chuckled. With a quick salute, she returned to the main street and headed toward the theater. Just a block away, Tian's red bean paste scent grew stronger, standing out among the smell of drunken men, roasting meats, perfumes, and incense.

And a sesame-ginger marinade.

Her chest constricted tighter the stronger the scent grew. The henchmen Lilian had hired to help her with the hit on Lord Ting frequented the vendor who used that sauce. In a few moments, the stall came into view. Chicken crackled on the grill, its smoke curling in the dim red lights.

Like on the day of the assassination, the same two men in guards' robes now sat on the stools outside the stall. Only this time, instead of chatting and laughing, they muttered among themselves. Their heads were turned toward Yue Heaven.

Jie followed their gaze.

Between two burly gatekeepers, Tian was disappearing into the front door of the sprawling, single-story compound.

Smart. The Peony Garden guards would never think to look for him there.

Jie headed over, passing the stall.

"It's a disgrace," one of the patron's whispered.

The other nodded. "A child that young has no business smoking yue. Hope Big Brother Xi turns him away."

"Nah, he'd get his grandma hooked if it could make him money. Takes after Faceless Chang."

"I wouldn't have even let him in," the second said.

"Too bad for the kid your shift won't start for another half-hour, and Yang and Li are on duty."

Jie's head spun. Only the Triads used *Big Brother* as a form of address for an elder, and Faceless Chang was the mysterious head of the Red Dragons. They usually kept to the seedy neighborhoods outside the wall. Were they using Yue Heaven as a foothold in the Floating World?

And these two worked as guards at Yue Heaven. She brushed up against one, shifting his hanging sleeve enough to see the red swirls of a dragon tattoo on his forearm. The telltale mark of Triads.

The man swung around. "Watch where you're going!"

"Excuse me, kind sir." She bowed low, and looked up the sleeve of the other. He, too had Triad tattoos.

"Oh," the second said. "You're the half-elf from the Chrysanthemum Pavilion."

"Formerly." She bowed again, feigning demureness.

"What House do you belong to now?" asked the first.

"I don't."

"Just a streetwalker then." The first shook his head. "Such a waste of your beauty."

"Be careful," the second said. "If you don't belong to a House and try to proposition clients, the House Enforcers will break your leg."

Let one try. Jie feigned a shudder. "That's why I'm going to Yue Heaven. I hear a girl can use their back rooms for a cut of the profit."

The first's leer left an icky feeling that might take hours to wash off. "Well, come on, let me introduce you to Big Brother Xi."

"Big Brother?" For show, Jie cocked her head.

"Sorry, the manager."

Jie bowed again. "Please, take me to the manager."

The first hopped off the stool and beckoned. "Come with me." He looked up from her to the second man and grinned.

The second loomed behind her, his presence sending the hairs on the back of her neck standing. As they walked toward Yue Heaven, she cast a quick glance back. He, too, was smirking.

When they reached the gates, the first made a quick tilt of his head toward her, and the guard's eyes roved over her. With knowing smiles, they stepped aside. Whatever they thought was going to happen, they were sorely mistaken.

The heady aroma of yue sap hung in the air, growing more distinct as they crossed the small courtyard and came to a set of double doors. Just a couple years ago, this had been a tea house where scholars came to debate philosophy, while beauties served them tea. Now, instead of scholars, three silk-robed merchants with heavy-lidded eyes lounged on the veranda.

The first guard hustled her through the entrance into a large room. In Yue Heaven's two months of operation, she'd never been on the inside—Floating World girls had some level of independence, but they'd never risk their reputation in a yue den, especially if no one of importance ever visited. Nonetheless, it looked similar to the opium dens: the low light from mostly-shuttered lamps shone on bare wood.

There were no decorations. Twelve men lounged on rows of red cushioned chaises, puffing on imported glass pipes. A young woman dressed in what looked to be little more than ribbons was guiding a luridly-smiling man toward a back hall. Moans and grunts emanated from the doorway, leaving no doubt as to what was happening there.

Tian was nowhere to be seen, though his scent was stronger here than anywhere else in the last hour.

With the first guard taking the lead, the second prodded Jie in the same direction Ribbon Woman had gone. She might've resisted, except Tian's scent trail grew stronger that way. To keep the men at ease, she feigned naiveté. "Where are we going?"

Never breaking stride, the first looked over his shoulder. "Like I said, to meet Big Brother Xi."

This Xi might have an office in this back hallway, but with a burly guard standing by the exit to a side hall, a betting half-elf would guess a more direct route to the administrative offices lay that way. Still, she followed the man into the back so as to find Tian.

At the first open door, he grabbed her wrist and pulled her into a small, windowless room. Reeking of sour man sweat, it was just big enough for the creaky wooden bed and thin futon. It was nothing like the elegantly-decorated Blossom rooms in the great houses of the Floating World; it was just a dingy room for a man to rut and find his release. That must've been the first guard's plans as he closed the door behind him, leaving his comrade outside.

It was too easy, especially since she only had to face one at a time. To make him think he had complete control of the situation, she spoke with a tremulous voice. "Where's the manager?"

His eyes undressed her. "Before I introduce you to him, I have to test the wares. To see if you're worth the investment."

No surprise. Keeping up the act, Jie recoiled.

"Oh, I like that. Trained in the Great Houses to feign innocence, no matter how many men you've taken."

Which was only one, a mistake which had forfeited her record virgin price.

"Please, don't." Gaze averted, she crossed her arms over her chest and shook her head, even as she gauged position and distance.

"What's stopping me?" Leering, he closed the distance in a single stride.

She took a step back. "In the Floating World—"

"You're no longer a Blossom of the Floating World. You're just a filthy whore. The House Enforcers won't protect you. They'll maim you for daring to seek customers here." He reached for her.

Jie jabbed a series of phoenix eye fists into vital points on his arms and chest. His body went limp and he collapsed onto the bed. Removing a vial of *yinghua* toxin from an inner pocket, she uncorked the vial and dabbed some of the fluid on his neck.

His lips formed a stupid smile. "What are we going to do?"

She patted him on the cheek. "You're going to sleep. When you wake up tomorrow, you will only have a vague recollection of tonight. You might even believe we slept together. I am going to leave someone to warm your sheets, though."

His eyes fluttered a few times, and then his head lolled.

Satisfied he wasn't a threat, Jie went to the door and listened.

The second guard stood just outside, the quickening sound of his breathing indicating his back was to the door.

It was too easy. She opened the door.

"Done so soon?" He started to turn around.

Jie stepped into the back of his knee, then hooked her arms around his neck and pulled him into the room. Feet scuttling to find purchase, he clawed at her arms for a moment before his body went inert. His mass weighed on her arms, and she lowered him to the bed.

She wiped some of the toxin on his neck and stepped back to survey her handiwork. Goons like this, preying on vulnerable girls, deserved castration. It would raise too many questions, however, and the toxin would give them at least a vague recollection of her.

Instead, she pulled off their pants, rolled the second on top of the other, and arranged their faces and hands in compromising positions. With a last look at her handiwork, she crept out of the room and closed the door behind her.

From down the hall, wood cracked and a woman shrieked.

CHAPTER 9

Tian sat on a dirty bed, studying the cloth Naya had wrapped around his bleeding elbows as he waited for her to come back with boys' clothes. Besides Wen, no one had been as nice to him as Naya since he'd left the imperial palace.

He sighed. The Floating World might be where men's dreams took flight, but it seemed like they were using women as wings. Wen and Naya spent their nights holding hands with men, maybe even kissing them. Yuna would eventually grow into that life, and the cruel half-elf had apparently escaped it.

Naya's scream rent the air, muffled only slightly by the closed door.

Tian bolted to his feet. Dressed in a girl's dress or not, he had to do something. He opened the door and dashed out into the hall...

And would've careened into Jie if she hadn't pulled up short.

"There you are," she said. "Come on, let's get out of here."

Tian shook his head. "My friend is in trouble. I need to help her."

Another shriek rang out, clearer this time, along with a loud thump.

Jie's eyes searched his. "All right. You stay behind me."

She clasped his hand and jogged down the hall, passing four doors to either side. Naya's sobbing, as well as a male yelling Grown Up Words, intensified as they turned a corner.

At the far end of this new hall, two big men with scraggly beards and dressed in red vests flanked an open door. The shouting and screams came from within.

"After I took you in," a gruff, male voice said. "After all I've done for you, you worthless whore, you stole what belongs to me."

"Please, stop!" Naya pleaded.

Head forward, Tian lengthened his stride.

Jie barred his way with an outstretched arm. "Stay here until I take care of the guards."

The men had to be twice her size, if not three, and they held clubs in their hands. What could she possibly—

Jie darted toward them, and they stared at her, wide-eyed. By the time they registered what was happening, she was among them, each motion fast, efficient, and decidedly unfair. In two seconds, both lay groaning on the floor. She gestured for him, then went into the room.

Tian hurried as fast as the tight dress would allow, and picked his way between the prone guards. By the time he came to the doorway to a spacious room, Jie was pinning a groaning man face-down to a rosewood desk. Entangling his arms in her legs like twisted dough, she held a knife to his neck. She'd also positioned herself away from a window, whose lattice shutters provided a view of an alley. On one wall, a hanging scroll tilted at an angle that begged to be righted.

"That whore tried to steal my son's clothes," the man said.

Naya huddled in a corner, between a table and a chair, sobbing.

"Are you all right?" Tian ran over to her.

She blinked away her tears. "Tian, you came for me."

"You're welcome," Jie muttered.

Naya looked at the half-elf. "I never knew you were so..."

"Talented?" Jie shrugged. "Yes, there are many things the House sisters didn't know about me."

Tian looked from the half-elf to his new friend. They apparently knew each other. Helping Naya up, he shifted his gaze to the man. "Why did he hurt you?"

Face twisted in pain and rage, the man snarled. "The whore stole some clothes."

Naya sniffled. "I just wanted to get Tian some boy's clothes."

"You beat her, for that?" Jie twisted her hips, bending his arm into an awkward angle.

He bellowed. "Bitch! If I ever get my hands on you—"

Jie cranked more as she leaned in. "I'm sorry, I couldn't hear you over your screams. Now, I'm more interested in your ledgers here. Right, kid?"

Kid? Tian frowned and crossed his arms.

Jie's eyes shifted from him to the desk, her clashing brows leaving no doubt that she wanted him there, now.

He looked to Naya. "Are you all right for now?"

With a hesitant nod, she took Tian's hand and guided him to the desk.

The man snarled, and Tian flinched. He was safe though, since Jie had him well under control.

Tearing his gaze away, Tian looked down at the ledgers. Unlike facial expressions and body language, numbers made sense. Given the cost of yue, and the huge sums coming in and out of Yue Heaven, they were selling far more than their court-approved ration. Most of the transactions were with... "It looks like this place is a front of Jinjing Lumber."

Jie leaned over, eliciting a grunt from the boss. Her eyes zigzagged over the numbers. "How can you tell?"

It was so obvious, and yet no one else would ever understand. "It just is. See the repeating pattern of monies in and out between Yue Heaven, Jinjing Lumber, and Heavenly Yue?"

The half-elf gave a slow nod. "That's an astronomical amount."

Whatever astronomical meant. "More than yue is worth. And I overheard a customer. They are selling it cheaper than market prices."

Jie gave him a quizzical look. "Maybe they bought excess from other distributors."

"The ledgers don't suggest that." Tian swept a finger over the entries before looking at the mean man. "You're getting extra yue straight from Jinjing County, aren't you?"

The man's lips pursed and he turned his head to the side.

"Well?" Jie cranked his arm.

"Yes!" the man screamed.

"What is Heavenly Yue?" Jie let off some of the pressure.

Naya cleared her throat. "It's a Yue den run by the Red Dragons in the Trench."

All the same pack of bad men. Tian tapped his chin. "Where's your supply?"

The man went silent again, and though he yelped when Jie twisted his arm again, his lips remained sealed. "You're going to kill me, anyway."

"So why worry? There are many ways to die." Jie jerked his pinkie to an unnatural angle

He bellowed. "Filthy Cunt! Faceless Chang will kill my entire family if he finds out I betrayed him."

Jie grabbed the next finger. "See, Big Brother Xi? We will find out one way or another, and your dead body will ensure your family's safety."

"Can't you use that perfume?" Tian asked.

Jie shook her head. "I only have two male doses left, and I'd rather save it for the two guards instead of this scum who profits from others' misery. And he'd still have to explain to Faceless Chang why his inventory went missing."

"I will show you where they keep the supply," Naya said.

"Worthless whore!" Xi said. "You better hope I don't escape—"

"You won't." A knife flashed in Jie's hand. She pulled his head back and slashed his throat.

Naya's hands shot up to her mouth, but it did little to stifle her scream.

Blood poured out of the wound as the man's eyes went wide.

Bile rose in Tian's throat. He turned and emptied his stomach into a decorative planter beside the desk. It was one thing to learn about dealing death with a blade, and something else altogether seeing it done. Maybe one day, he'd have to do it himself.

Hold the dragonfly with care, Kaiya's voice resonated in his memories, quoting from one of her favorite songs about Dragon Singers. *For even their tiny lives have value.*

What was the value of a criminal's life? Or his death? Tian cleared the remaining vomit from his throat and mouth. "Why did you have to kill him?"

"It's better for his family if he's found dead." With a dispassionate expression, Jie collected the ledgers.

"Wouldn't it be better for them if he were still alive?"

"Maybe he is a bad father." Jie shrugged. "In any case, all the men I fought were witnesses. If I can't make them forget with the toxin, then I have to silence them in other ways."

Naya's hand shot to her mouth again. "What... What about me?"

Jie's expression softened. "I have a female-targeted toxin. You'll wake up somewhere in the Floating World with whatever money we can find here." She walked over to a wall and pulled a scroll painting down. It revealed a sixteen-inch by eight-inch safe door with a hanging padlock.

"How did you know that was there?" Tian gaped.

"It was hanging at an angle, and the scrapes on the wall line up with the scroll's anchor."

Fascinating! That's why it had looked wrong. Heart fluttering with excitement, Tian studied the scratches.

Jie hip-bumped him to the side and withdrew some wires from a strap on her thigh, and inserted them into the keyhole. With a few deft movements, the lock snicked. She tossed it to him. "We'll teach you how to pick locks."

Excitement tingled up and down his spine. If he'd known how to pick a lock, he might never have been banished.

She opened the door, revealing stacked silver ingots.

Naya gasped. "This is mine?"

"As much as you can carry," Jie said. "Now, where do they store their yue?"

"The dispensary is one door before this one. It has a cut-out to the smoking room."

Tian had noticed that on the way in. "There was a man handing out yue balls there. Please don't kill him."

"I won't, if I don't have to." Jie yanked the boss' shirt off and handed it to Tian. "Wrap that around your face."

Tian did as she instructed, winding it around his head so that only his eyes were exposed, just like the stories of the Black Fists. It smelled like sweat and wood.

"You've read too many fairy tales, if you think that's what we really look like." Jie snorted and adjusted the wrapping. "Keep it loose around your nose and mouth so you can breathe."

Thank the cloth for hiding his blush.

Jie turned to Naya. "You wait here."

Tian followed the scary half-elf out, stepping over the unconscious guards.

She came to the door to the dispensary and put her ear to it. "One man, just like Naya said," she whispered. "What do you suggest we do?"

"I'll draw him out, and you knock him out from behind."

Jie pointed at him, then curled her finger as she traced a hook in the air. "You draw him out."

Tian held up a hand, pointed at her, then wiggled two fingers. If he were right, that meant...

"Close." Jie's eyes widened. "Where did you learn that?"

"Wen used it in the market. She let you know when to pick my pocket."

She gave a slow nod. "You are perceptive to have noticed it. You just told me you'd be setting up an opening."

So Wen had distracted Tian at the moment Jie had swapped out the coins.

She now gave a subtle twitch of her thumb. "This assigns the attacker, non-lethal force."

"All right." Tian pointed at her and imitated her hand motion.

Smiling, she gave a single nod, and then flicked her pinkie. "That means, execute the plan."

Tian opened the door. "Hello? I need help."

"Hey!" The man in the same red tunic as the other gang members lowered himself from where he was leaning back in a chair. "You're not supposed to be back there."

Tian took two steps back into the hall. "I'm lost."

"You're going to be more than lost." The man rose and tromped toward him.

As soon as he cleared the door, Jie stepped into the back of his leg. He fell to his knees, and she wrapped her arms around his neck. Her own knee must've been pinned into his lower back, the way he arched back as he clawed at her arms. In just a few seconds, his eyes rolled back into his head, and his body went limp.

No sooner did he hit the floor than Jie burst into the room. Tian followed.

"Interesting," Jie said, studying the space under the counter.

Tian leaned in and looked over her shoulder.

A large window opened up onto the main room, where eight patrons—one more than when he came in with Naya—reclined on beds, eyes glazed over as they smoked.

A wooden counter ran along the lower edge of the cutout. Beneath it was two separate chests of waxy brown yue balls. The one marked *Official* contained fewer than the other. While the balls were exactly uniform in shape and size, the ones in the other container had a more yellowish tinge.

"They're different," Tian said.

Nodding Jie picked up two of each and wrapped them in separate silk kerchiefs. "And we're going to find out how."

CHAPTER 10

Jie stood in the clan's main apothecary, located in the back of an herbal pharmacy near the capital's center. Her trip here had two purposes: first, to find out why there were two different types of yue balls; and second, to get Cleaners sent to Yue Heaven.

With Tian's help, they'd already left Naya in a temple, rich and drugged with a musk toxin that would leave her with hazy memories of tonight. The Cleaners would stage the yue den to make it look like the Red Dragon's rivals, The Fangs, had raided it.

With a pair of tongs, the clan's local Poisoner held the different yue balls up under a light bauble, and studied them through a dwarf-made monocle. A wizened old operative with bushy white eyebrows that might've been caterpillars arching across his brow, he'd concocted toxins for the clan's legendary Architect, Surgeon, Beauty, and Steel Orchids.

He indicated the yellower ball that came from the non-official crate. "I won't know without further testing, but the lighter-colored ones match some of the others we've gotten ahold of. It's much-less refined, and for whatever reason, that makes it addictive."

"Oh?" Jie peered at the ball.

"Yes, Old Lu was investigating tax shortfalls in Honggang City, and found the populace's productivity had dropped because of yue addiction."

Jinjing Lumber—if Tian was to be believed—was behind this. It had sucked one city's economy dry, and was now looking for new markets for a controlled substance. And somehow, it was tied to the murder of Lord Ting, Lilian, and an unaccounted for assassin. Jie sucked on her lower lip. "Our new recruit says that these yellower ones aren't perfectly round."

"Really?" Squinting, the Poisoner looked from one to the other. He ran calipers over the illegal one. "Hmmm, that little lordling is right."

For all the boy's shortcomings, he noticed *everything*.

"The imperial alchemists use a dwarf-made machine to precisely refine the yue and give it a uniform shape. The fake is slightly oblong. I'll have to see if the other yellower ones share this inconsistency."

Had Lord Ting's assassination been over illegal yue, and not the opening salvo of a rebellion in the North? If she knew who was behind Jinjing Lumber, she'd have a better idea of their goals. Jie wrote a coded missive requesting an operative in the Imperial Treasury to find Jinjing Lumber's registration papers, and put it in the hands of a clan courier. Satisfied there was nothing else to do tonight, she returned to the safe house near the Floating World, expecting Tian to be fast asleep on a cot.

Instead, he was in the evidence room, still wearing Yuna's ill-fitting dress. He paced around, studying his chalk lines while subconsciously practicing the disappearing coin trick. And getting better at it.

"You should be asleep," she said.

He startled, his wide eyes shooting to her. "I... I didn't hear you come in."

"That's what it means to be a Black Fist. No one knows of our comings and goings, either because we move with silence, or we meld into the crowds."

He gave a slow nod. "Like Wen and Yuna in that mansion. They match all the other pretty girls."

Jie sucked on her lower lip. Just a week ago, she'd belonged to the Floating World, as well. The most talked-about Floret in living memory. Whose exotic looks had vaulted her virgin price to dizzying heights before it had been stolen away. "It's a little different in the Floating World. Our Sisters are meant to be seen and to stand out, so that they can attract the richest, most powerful men in the realm."

The boy tapped his chin. The quirk—a telltale giveaway that those dwarf gears were grinding in his head—was becoming quite endearing, really. "Is it good for our Sisters to kiss powerful men?"

"Men who've been, uh, kissed will sometimes tell secrets. Secrets that might be threats to the realm."

His mouth rounded for a split second. "But, why would they risk telling anyone?"

Jie leaned in closer. "Don't you have some secret you are dying to share, but you can't?"

If she'd blinked, she would've missed his expression brightening. He shoved his hands behind his back and hung his head.

She chuckled. "You see, sometimes a secret can be a burden, and you just have to tell someone. There's a saying, *What happens in the Floating World, stays in the Floating World.* Do you understand?"

He looked up from the floor. "It means that the Blossoms can keep secrets."

"Exactly."

He shook his head. "But that's... that's dishonorable. Our clan is breaking the rules."

Oh, he was just too adorable. "Remember your duel with Yuna? We don't play fair."

"But—"

"Because the *Tianzi's* enemies don't play fair."

He gave a tentative nod, then pointed down at her mock-up of the diagram. "I rearranged it. Your size was off."

Jie cocked her head. The mock-up didn't look any different from before.

"Had your dimensions of the common room been accurate, I could've told you that the second assassin shot from the opening to the veranda." He pointed at the chalk lines he'd used to represent the walls.

"Yes, you left a trail in the Chrysanthemum Pavilion ruins."

He flushed.

"I've thought about this." She pointed to the bracelet which marked herself, on a table near Lord Ting and the accountant, Wei, who'd been like a mother to her. "I would've seen or smelled the second shooter if they shot from the archway. Would the assassin have been able to hit Lord Ting at the correct angle, not from the archway, but from the edge of veranda?"

Tian tapped his chin, his eyes staring up for a moment. "I wondered, too. It would be very hard. Almost impossible, because of the archway's height."

Anywhere closer, and Jie would've smelled the second shooter; but there'd been anecdotes of such impossible shots. Three hundred-year-old historical records noted Wang Yuxiang, consort of the Wang Dynasty's Founder, making dozens of impossible shots with a bow, crossbow, and even a child's slingshot.

"You did a good job." She patted him on the head. "I found the climbing claw marks at the assassin's insertion point because of the trail you left."

"I have a new idea." Tian held out a small metal cylinder. "I found this at the Chrysanthemum Pavilion, near the insert... insertion point."

The color... "It's made of bronze."

"Yes!" His expression brightened. "And the best bronze foundries—"

"Are in Jinjing County." Jie nodded. There was a connection to Jinjing Lumber, but... "What is it?"

"A Repeater's cranking pin. I think the assassin took the crossbow apart and threw the wood parts into the fire."

Jie shook her head. "We would have found them. We found the other crossbow."

"Made of eldarwood. What if this one was made of yue, like the crossbow bolt which killed the nice man."

She suppressed a shudder. Lord Ting was hardly nice. His depravity had helped turn Lilian against the clan.

Tian motioned to said bolt. "The only thing I don't understand is why this one didn't burn. I've seen yue wood used to start fires."

"I retrieved it before the fire." She'd pulled it from Lord Ting's body and used it to stab one of Lilian's accomplices through the eye, but Tian didn't have to know the gory details.

He searched her eyes, mouth moving. Then he held his hand flat, about half a foot above his head. "Our second assassin was short. Enough to need climbing claws to scale the wall. He wasn't strong enough to carry the crossbow over the wall. So he destroyed it."

It was all coming together, thanks to an untrained boy. Still... "That could be a lot of different people."

"With the climbing claws, it was someone trained in Black Lotus Clan ways. A traitor, like the first assassin?"

Had Lillian recruited another clan member? In the aftermath of her betrayal, all clan sisters in the Floating World had been debriefed, their loyalty confirmed with the *Tiger Eye* technique. Maybe a member assigned outside the entertainment district? None in the immediate area were that short. Jie shook her head. "The clues might have been intentionally left there to throw us off. And, we're not the only ones who use climbing claws."

"Who else?"

Who else, indeed. "Thieves, assassins..."

Tian afforded her dubious look. "I... I... never mind."

Knowing what he was going to say, Jie sucked on her lower lip. Lilian had warned Jie of her blind spot. Maybe she was subconsciously exonerating clan members. Maybe she just didn't want to believe it possible. But no, it was more than that. Every Black Lotus who operated within striking distance was accounted for that night. "Nobody from the clan could have been the second shooter. All of the girls were questioned. Anyone else's whereabouts made it impossible."

Tian tapped his chin. "What about former members?"

"There's no such thing. We are Black Lotus for life."

"Nobody just... leaves?" His brow furrowed.

"We can't allow our secrets to leave the clan."

"What happens when someone is too old?"

Jie shrugged. "They will work making poisons, or planning, bookkeeping, or teaching initiates. There's always something to do."

The secret door between the herbal pharmacy and safe house whispered open, though Tian showed no sign of hearing with his human ears. Drawing a knife, Jie shuttered the bauble lamp. She corralled Tian into a corner, then crouched and waited.

Footsteps padded up the stairs, the visitor's breaths even despite his attempts at stealth.

Jie relaxed. It was just Old Qin, a tough clan Cleaner. Clan members always tried to sneak up on each other, though usually revealed themselves before anyone got hurt. As soon as he peeked into the room, she withdrew a light bauble.

Cursing, he shielded his eyes. "Was that necessary?"

"No." She grinned. "But it was fun."

Tian muttered something unintelligible, but his meaning was clear: these games didn't make sense to him. In time, if he survived, they would.

Qin surveyed Tian, eyes pausing on his dress, before turning to Jie. "I came to say the job is done. As you instructed, we were dressed as Fangs, and let Yue Heaven's guards escape. At least one headed to the Red Dragons' headquarters, and I'd expect more of the gang to come to investigate within the hour."

Jie looked out the window to where the Iridescent Moon waxed to its second crescent. "I am going to go stake out Yue Heaven to see who turns up."

"What about me?" Tian said.

With his lack of stealth skills, he was a liability in this case, and it was way past his bedtime. "You're going to change out of that dress and go to bed. You are dueling Yuna again tomorrow."

While he changed and went to bed, Jie donned her stealth suit, packed up Yuna's dress, and set out for Yue Heaven. At the late hour, festivities in the Floating World had gone indoors, leaving only a few men wandering the streets. That, and her stealth suit, made the trip fast and easy.

Lights shining through the windows of Yue Heaven, and flickering shadows, suggested some activity. Two of the burly men in the tunics of the Red Dragons from earlier flanked the gate, turning away the occasional straggler who considered a visit.

Had the Red Dragon enforcers already arrived? Jie looked up at the Iridescent Moon, now waxing halfway between its third and fourth crescents. The trip to the Trench should take almost an hour, assuming a brisk pace and taking into account the need to bribe the guards at the city wall to open the gates; Jie should've had a half-hour to spare. No, it had to be the other men she'd left alive.

She climbed to the sharply-pitched roof of the shrine across the street, and crouched low. While waiting, she considered Tian's assertions. Jinjing Lumber had made enormous purchases through the Floating World in the run-up to Lord Ting's assassination—including renting the Peony Garden to do a soft-run of the hit. Likely using the money they'd made through selling illegal yue.

Could it be, the plot had been all about profits, and had nothing to do with an attempt to seize power in the North?

Lilian, whose father had lost everything to an opium addiction, would've been mortified to have been involved.

The door to the den burst open, revealing a short figure. His heavy cloak and light behind him made it impossible to discern much about him; but limited clan intelligence revealed the leader of the Red Dragons was short. Faceless Chang had taken control of the Red Dragons in a power struggle six years ago. Rumor had it his face was so scarred, he always wore an opera mask which depicted Yanluo, God of Death. It would be odd that he was here without a cohort protecting him, though perhaps they were still in the den.

Faceless Chang stormed to the gate, his stride long for his stature. His voice came out gravelly. "Those fucking Fangs. They seized all our product and every tael. You're worthless." He backhanded both guards in a smooth motion.

"Sorry, Boss." Both recoiled and set their fists into their palms.

Faceless Chang looked up. As his gaze swept over the area, the lamplight from the streets glinted off the horns of a red mask with black-lined eyes. They froze on Jie's position.

She ducked beneath the ridge of the tiled roof. No, it couldn't be. A human shouldn't have been able to see her in the dark. She crawled laterally and peeked again.

Faceless Chang's gaze had shifted elsewhere, his body language not suggesting he was concerned by her presence—if he'd seen her. He gestured toward one of the guards. "Come with me."

The man bowed, and they disappeared back into the den.

Climbing down, Jie kept to the shadows as she darted to the narrow alley along Yue Heaven's east side. She stopped at the latticed shutters to the office and peeked in.

Faceless Chang stood with his back to her. He leaned down and studied Big Brother Xi's corpse, then looked up at the guard. He lowered his hood, revealing glossy black hair and the scent of lavender. "Tell me again what happened."

Jie's jaw dropped, her expression no doubt as surprised as the guard's.

Faceless Chang's voice belonged to a woman.

And not just any woman.

Head abuzz with racing thoughts, Jie thrust out a hand to brace herself against the wall. Yet another betrayal.

Little Wen.

CHAPTER 11

Reeling from the revelation of Faceless Chang's true identity, Jie fought the tears threatening to blur her vision. Of all the clan sisters, Wen. Lilian had been a lover, but Wen was like a little sister. She'd always displayed puppy-like admiration for Jie.

But it all made sense now. The veneration had all been an act. Lilian had even pointed out Wen's supposed admiration for Jie as a means of drawing suspicion away from the young Blossom. The two had been working together the whole time.

Jie closed her eyes, remembering. At the time of Lord Ting's assassination, she had sent Wen to light the Black Lotus Shrine's light, to summon all clan sisters; but it still would've left enough time for her to be the second shooter.

"—I don't remember," the guard was saying inside the office.

Jie forced her eyes open and peeked back in.

"You were caught with your pants down," Wen said. "Literally. Buggering one of your comrades. No wonder they were able to surprise you."

The guard shook his head. "It wasn't like that. We're not like that. It was a set-up."

A blade flashed in Wen's hand. She swept it across the table in a precise Black Lotus technique that caught the man's throat.

Blood sprayed. His eyes rounded as his hands shot to his neck, but then he crumpled onto the desk beside Xi.

Wen pulled the hood over her head and stormed out of the office.

Taking deep breaths, Jie leaned her forehead against the wood planks of the den. How had this happened? Why? Unlike Lilian, who'd expressed discouragement with working in the Floating World, Wen had always seemed to enjoy it. Though if she could conceal her betrayal from clan interrogators using the *Tiger's Eye*, no telling how talented she really was. It was just like Lilian, hiding her skills.

Now, though, Wen was alone, save for a couple of groggy guards. She'd gotten here so fast because she'd come from the Peony Garden, and not the Trench; and if Triad enforcers were coming from the Trench, there was a small window of opportunity to eliminate her.

Swallowing hard, Jie pulled the shutters open, careful that the hinges didn't squeak. She climbed in, and Wen's lavender scent greeted her. She padded to the door and peeked into the hallway.

Twenty feet away, Wen was turning the corner, into the hall where the prostitutes received clients.

Timing her own pace to Wen's tromping footsteps, Jie loped to the next door, the one to the dispensary. It stood ajar, and Jie stayed low as she slipped inside.

Popping up above the counter level, she made a quick scan of the main room. Beds were overturned, porcelain and glass pipe shards lay scattered across the floor. No people, dead or alive.

Wen's footsteps in the hall grew closer.

Clenching a dagger between her teeth, Jie palmed three throwing stars. Even if Wen avoided the barrage, it would distract her long enough for Jie to close the distance and stab her.

Wen would reach the room in three steps.

One.

Jie cocked back her arm, ready to throw the stars.

Two.

Her heart pounded. This was Wen. Her shadow preceded her into the main chamber.

Three.

Jie ducked back down. She couldn't do it. Not Wen.

Wen moved deeper into the room, muttering about Triad incompetence.

Jie took several deep breaths. She could do this. Had to do this.

The front door swooshed open and six sets of large footsteps hurried in. The window of opportunity had closed.

"Clear the den out," Wen said, now sounding male and gravelly. She was using the clan's *Mockingbird's Deception* to imitate voices. "Take anything of value. And hurry. The city watch will be crawling over the place like ants once they get wind of dead bodies."

Jie sucked on her lower lip. The city watch left the Floating World to its own devices, generally allowing the House Enforcers to rough up troublemakers. As long as the businesses paid taxes and nobody got killed, there was no reason to intervene. Now, though, there were at least two dead bodies, more if the clan Cleaners had decided to take matters into their own hands.

With nothing left to do for now, Jie crawled back through the open door, turned down the hall and into the office, then jumped through the window. She paused at the head of the alley. At the front of the den, another dozen Red Dragon Triads gathered.

Wen stormed out of the door, the lights now shining on the demon mask. She gestured toward the men. When she spoke, it was with the gravelly male voice. "Go help clean up."

"What about you, Boss?" one said.

"I need to work off some steam," Wen said. "And there's a whore at the Peony Garden who enjoys a little pain."

Jie grimaced. In her time at the Chrysanthemum Pavilion, some of the Blossoms tolerated that kind of play, but none enjoyed it. Though now, Wen was probably using it as an excuse to go home.

"But Boss, the Houses won't be taking customers this late."

"Oh, they'll take *me*." Wen waved a dismissive hand.

"Do you want us to accompany you for safety?"

Wen snorted. "This is the Floating World. Nobody ever gets attacked here."

"Um..." The Triad pointed back at Yue Heaven. "What if the Fangs did this, and now plan on ambushing you?"

Jie smirked. At least one of the henchmen wasn't stupid.

"I'll be fine," Wen said. "Now get to work."

The Triads saluted as they filed into Yue Heaven. Wen set off toward the Peony Garden. Sticking to the shadows, Jie followed.

The larger picture was coming into focus. Jinjing Lumber shipped illegal yue to the Red Dragons. Lord Ting must've found out. Wen, knowing Black Lotus procedures, had recruited Lilian.

Once Wen had walked a block, she broke into a hobbling jog. Had she injured herself? She hadn't shown signs of it earlier, though maybe she was hiding it from the Triads.

Just how long had she been Faceless Chang? Between her time at the Peony Garden and training martial skills, there was no way she could run a Triad operation...

Unless Faceless Chang was more than one person. With a mask, there could be any number of Faceless Changs. The only requirement would be a lack of height and the ability to mimic a gravelly voice.

The streets were deserted, providing another chance to attack. And it had to be now: they were just two blocks from the Peony Garden.

Jie took a deep breath. She could do this, Wen or not. Pausing at the corner of a building, she palmed three throwing stars and flung them in a tight spread at Wen's back.

Wen contorted like twisted dough, her body arching in a gravity-defying pose between the paths of the stars. Only her cloak was shredded.

How could this be? Wen had never shown such dodging ability. It was like legends of the great Black Lotus masters. And facing the other way, without even seeing the incoming barrage? That sounded like the aggrandizing official histories of Wang Yuxiang, the consort of the Wang Dynasty's Founder.

One of Wen's legs gave way, forcing her to thrust out an arm and flip into a one-handed cartwheel. She landed on one foot, in the clan's *Dipping Crane* stance. When she spoke, it was in the gravelly voice of Faceless Chang. "Cowardly Fangs, show yourselves."

Jie ducked back behind the building. She hazarded a glance around the corner.

"No? Well, you've declared war. The Trench will run red with your blood." Without any visible concern, Wen turned on her heel and headed back to the Peony Garden.

Dagger now in hand, Jie sucked on her lower lip. Like Lilian, Wen had hidden her true level of mastery. Unlike Lilian, her level far surpassed Jie's. It would be foolish to face her now, with no positional advantage.

She sheathed her weapon. Better to regroup. Maybe sleep a few hours.

Wen removed the mask a block away from the House gates. She lowered her hood, undid her topknot, and then tightened the cloak around her. At the gates, the guards gave a respectful bow and let her pass.

Jie found the Iridescent Moon in its reliable location. It now waxed just past its third crescent. A clan courier would pick up messages from the Black Lotus Shrine in three hours, then visit the safe house soon after.

Wen would be foolish to move against the clan, and it sounded like she was more interested in the Fangs. If some Triads killed each other, the world would be a better place, anyway. Right?

Despite niggling misgivings, Jie headed back to the safe house.

CHAPTER 12

Tian startled awake. His dreams sent a disturbing shiver down his spine: Princess Kaiya had been whispering a joke in his ear, and when he'd turned to her in shock, the princess had transformed into Wen. Eyes half-lidded, she leaned in closer, lips parted...

He shuddered again. It wasn't right. Princess Kaiya was his betrothed. They'd promised each other. They would find some way to get married, despite his disgrace and banishment... if she didn't hate him, after what had happened. So why had he dreamed about kissing Wen? She was a pretty woman, but one he'd just met.

Sunlight streamed in through the window, the angle indicating it was mid-morning. He'd overslept, and the evil half-elf hadn't woken him at dawn like the past few days. Pushing aside the covers, he rose from his bedroll. His neck and back ached. How he missed his fluffy bed. He shook out the numbness in his hand and scanned the little room.

Jie was curled into a ball, asleep on her own bedroll! It didn't seem possible for the slave driver *not* to wake at dawn. And now, her expression looked relaxed. Gone was the mischievous glint in her eyes and the naughty grin. She looked almost... angelic.

Well, no matter what, she wasn't supposed to sleep so late. The clan courier must've come and gone already. Tian knelt down to wake—

Jie seized him by the fold of his robe and pulled him down. Something cold pressed into his throat. Her sharp glare softened, and she released him. "Don't sneak up on me like that."

"I wasn't sneaking." Tian waved both hands back and forth. "I was just coming to wake you up. Wen and Yuna will be here soon."

Eyes widening, Jie bolted onto her feet. She was wearing the stealth suit from the night before, though it had a few new dust smudges. Her head darted left to right. "The courier?"

Tian shrugged. "He must've picked up the messages and left."

Jie sucked on her lower lip, as she tended to do when pondering something. Then she beckoned him.

He followed her back to the evidence room, where she stared at his layout of the Chrysanthemum Pavilion. "The second shooter... you're sure there's a remote possibility of her hitting Lord Ting from the edge of the veranda?"

"Her?"

Jie's expression turned serious. "I think I know who our mysterious assassin is, but I need you to confirm this."

Tian tapped his chin, creating a fused image of the Chrysanthemum Pavilion and the Peony Garden in his head. The shooter would have to arc the shot, and it would have to clear the top of the archway. With heavier eldarwood, even the Founder's Consort would need a touch of luck, but... "With a yue arrow, it's possible, but very difficult."

Taking a deep breath, Jie placed her hand on his shoulder. "Last night, I learned that Wen is head of the Red Dragons."

No. Not Wen. One of the few people who'd ever been nice to him. Tian shook his head. "It can't be. It's not possible."

She placed her other hand on his other shoulder. "It's true. I saw her, myself. The question is, could she have been the second shooter?"

Shaking his head, Tian plopped onto his butt. "Why would she?"

"To make money. To have power over men."

People weren't supposed to be like that. "But how? How could she lead Triads if she is in the Floating World?"

Jie nodded. "I thought the same thing. She was wearing a mask—"

"Then how can you be sure it is her?"

"It was her voice. She—"

Tian held up a hand. "Would Triads let a woman lead them?"

"Maybe that's why she wears a mask. She used our clan's *Mockingbird's Deception* technique to mimic a male's voice. Not only that, she smelled like the Peony Garden. She used Black Lotus techniques, and was even able to dodge a tight barrage of my throwing stars with her back turned."

That sounded near impossible. Jie had demonstrated her proficiency with throwing two days ago, and it had made him squirm. He gave a slow nod.

"And to top it off," she said, "the gate guards of the Peony Garden let her in. I suspect she might be a body double."

Tian's forehead crinkled. "What's that?"

"She takes the role of the Red Dragon's leader, Faceless Chang, when he can't be somewhere he needs to be."

"Like the Steel Orchids?" The Black Lotus girls all spoke of the legendary sisters in reverent tones, how they'd swapped places.

"Similar, except they were identical twins. They didn't need a mask. As for Wen—" Jie froze, ears twitching.

Tian looked around.

Jie put a finger to her lips, then made a series of hand signals, of which only *coming* was familiar. She then slunk without a sound to the open door.

Someone was coming. Wen? Tian didn't hear anything except the muffled conversations outside. His eyes strayed to the rack of toxins, organized in colored glass vials.

Jie relaxed, even before the newcomer's shadow crossed the threshold. "It's Yuna."

As if on cue, Yuna slunk in and saluted with a fist in her palm. "Elder Sister Jie, I'm here for our lesson. And here's a message from the courier. I was surprised you didn't retrieve it already." She held out a piece of paper, folded in an intricate pattern. She turned to Tian and gave him a slight nod.

"Where is Wen?" Jie asked, tone urgent. "The Gardener let you out without a Blossom?"

Yuna grinned. "I wouldn't say let me out. Elder Sister Wen had to speak with the Gardener, and sent me ahead so I wouldn't be late."

Tian swallowed hard. It was certainly suspicious. He exchanged glances with Jie.

She took the message and unfolded it, and her eyes roved over it. He snuck a glance, but it was all gibberish.

"What is it?" Tian asked.

Jie passed it over, as if he could read it. "Details about Jinjing Lumber. It's registered to a shell company, Jinjing Holdings."

Did they sell shells? Tian tapped his chin.

"Their taxes don't suggest massive windfalls from illegal yue."

It made sense now. "Because they are moving it to the Peony Garden ledgers."

"Laundering." With a nod, Jie turned to Yuna. "Yuna, have you ever seen an opera mask of Yan Luo in Wen's possession?"

The girl tilted her head. "I don't think so."

"What about a heavy red cloak?"

She shook her head.

Tian gave a satisfied nod. "See?"

"That doesn't mean she doesn't have them." Jie shook her head. "It might be hidden somewhere."

"What's going on?" Confusion scrawled across Yuna's pretty face.

Jie searched Yuna's eyes. "Are there times when you can't account for Wen?"

Yuna's brow furrowed. "When she's in the privy…"

Heat rose to Tian's face. He fought to keep an image of Princess Kaiya in the privy from surfacing.

"…and at night, after a Hummingbird has left, when she's sleeping."

"Which coincides with the time I might have seen her last night." Jie sucked on her lower lip and let it out with a pop. "Yuna, I suspect Wen might be a traitor."

Blood drained from Yuna's face as she shook her head. "It can't be."

Sniffling, Jie patted her on the head. "I know. I felt the same about Lilian's betrayal. We can't let it happen again."

"But…" Yuna's shoulders shuddered, and tears welled in her eyes.

Jie wrapped her in an embrace and stroked the back of her head.

Tian swallowed hard. All this closeness was so strange. He'd never hugged any of his three brothers before.

"What's the matter?" Wen's melodic voice came from the doorway.

Jie looked up, eyes widening. A blade flashed in her hand, which she thrust behind her back.

Tian followed her gaze.

Wearing grey pants and matching tunic, Wen walked into the room, slightly favoring her left leg. Though still pretty, her look was different without a dress and makeup.

Jie's gaze locked on Wen's legs. "Why are you limping?"

"I saw Secretary Geng, and then Lord Xun last night." Wen rolled her eyes. "They were both particularly vigorous."

Why would vigorous kissing make Wen limp? Tian shuffled on his feet.

"You entertained both in one night?" Jie asked. "That's not normal."

Wen shrugged. "It was chaos last night."

"That's strange." Jie looked to Yuna. "Between the Gardener and Florist, all Floating World Houses run like well-oiled dwarf gears. Especially the Peony Garden."

Tian tapped his chin. Reading people didn't come easily, but Wen's expression looked bewildered.

In a blink of an eye, Jie darted in and hooked the back of Wen's knees. With a tilt of her shoulder, she drove Wen to the ground and started to shimmy up so that she sat on Wen's stomach. Seizing Jie's arm, Wen bucked her hips and sent the half-elf tumbling to the side, then straddled her.

"Elder Sister!" Wen said. "What's going on?"

"You tell me." Jie clutched one of Wen's arms, then started to wrap her legs around it. Wen bent her elbow and rolled over so that the two girls were entangled. It looked like a wrestling match he'd once seen in a demonstration at the imperial court, between the ruddy-skinned horse riders from the northeast plains.

He looked over to Yuna, who, wide-eyed, covered her mouth with both hands.

"Please stop!" she shrieked.

The two flipped, with both securing each other's ankles in the crooks of their elbows. Both arched their backs, faces contorted.

There was an explanation for what had happened, though. He just had to get them to stop.

There, on a rack, was the musk-scented toxin that would make a woman euphoric before she passed out.

***

Jie's ankle burned as Wen cranked it, and she must've been feeling the same pain. It'd been years since they'd grappled, and Wen had improved. She'd recovered quickly from Jie's surprise attack, and neither had since gotten the upper hand. At this rate, they'd both end up with torn tendons.

For her part, Yuna was utterly useless, just standing there screaming. Tian, was now approaching though, what little good he could do with his lack of fighting skills. He'd probably only make things worse.

He touched her. The scent of musk hung around him. The little fool had used the female toxin on her!

Her vision narrowed and her head buzzed. Then all went black.

CHAPTER 13

Head feeling as if dwarves had forged an arsenal large enough to supply an army on it, Jie blinked several times to clear out the gunk. She was sitting, back to a wall, hands behind her back. How she'd ended up like this, she couldn't remember; but the haze over her mind felt as if someone had used the clan musk toxin on her.

A muffled conversation between a male and female carried on nearby.

What was her last memory? Tian, waking her up. Her, telling him about Wen's betrayal. No, Wen had come to the safe house, and they'd grappled. Had Wen prevailed?

Her vision cleared, only to reveal she was blindfolded. When she went to remove it, rope bit into her wrists. Her ankles were bound, as well. It felt eerily similar to when Lilian had captured her in the aftermath of Lord Ting's assassination. She listened.

From the breaths, there were two others here, at opposite ends of a large room. Small people. The lavender scent meant Yuna or Wen. Maybe both.

"Tian? Yuna?" Jie wiggled, trying to loosen her arms.

"I'm here." Yuna's voice came from her right. The way the sound echoed, they were in the room where Tian had rearranged all the evidence.

"I'm here, too." Tian said from her left. From the acoustics, it sounded like they were all sitting.

"What's going on?"

"We're all tied up," Yuna said.

"Where's Wen now?" After she'd defeated Jie, Yuna and Tian would've been easy targets.

"It wasn't Wen. I..." Tian's voice shook. "I used the toxin on you and her. I was afraid you were going to hurt each other."

From the ache in her ankle and heel, the toxin had taken effect before Wen had torn any tendons. And Wen would've been knocked out, too. So, how did they all end up restrained? "Why didn't you just use it on Wen?"

"She's not the second shooter."

So, how did they all end up restrained? "Then what happened?"

"Faceless Chang." Yuna said. "As soon as you both passed out, he came in through the window. Tian tried to get to the toxins, but crashed into them, instead. I couldn't handle him."

"Her," Tian said. "Faceless Chang is the Gardener of the Peony Garden. The second shooter."

Jie tried to focus through the cobwebs in her head. How was that possible?

Yuna sucked in a sharp breath. "Did you inform the clan?"

No, Jie had slept through the courier's check-in. "I—"

On the other side of the wall came a muffled yell, but now that the haze had started to lift from Jie's mind, the voice was obvious to her elf ears: Yuna. And the relative pitch and tone of the sounds suggested she'd said, *That wasn't me.*

Which meant whoever was in here wasn't Yuna. It was Gardener Ju, just like Tian had said. In the six years Jie had known her, how had she never guessed? Well, now was time to play along, to bide time and find out—

"It's not Yuna," Tian said. "It's Gardener Ju!"

No! The boy had all the smarts, none of the common sense.

From where Yuna had been sitting came a laugh. "Revealed. Yuna's a clever little girl, feigning unconsciousness. She had me fooled. And to think, she's close to mastering the No Shadow Cut." The voice was Gardener Ju's. She'd been there the whole time, mimicking Yuna's breathing patterns and voice.

The *Mockingbird's Deception* technique. And she knew about the No Shadow Cut. Which meant, she'd been trained in Black Lotus ways. Chances were, she'd imitated Yuna to find out how much had been shared with the clan. Just who—

"Right now, you are trying to figure out who I really am."

"One of the Steel Orchids," Tian said.

What? That wasn't possible. The Steel Orchids had died in an explosion along with all the other Black Lotus girls in the Floating World, nearly twenty years ago.

"The boy is smart. I was surprised he'd surmised not only that there was a second shooter, but that the second shooter was Gardener Ju. Tell me, Zheng Tian, how did you figure it out?"

"You fit Jie's description of Faceless Chang." Tian's tone grew more excited, like a child praised by a parent. "You're the same height and build as Wen. You favor your left leg. You smell like the Peony Garden, and their guards let you in late at night. The House was in chaos, because you weren't there to manage it."

"Impressive. How did you know I was the second shooter?"

Part of Jie wanted to tell him to shut up. The other part wanted to know, as well.

"The climbing claw marks on the Chrysanthemum Pavilion's walls," Tian said. "The spacing on the left side was narrower than the right. Because of your injury. Wen wouldn't even need the claws. She could jump and reach the top. Why did you imitate Wen?"

"Once I knew Jie was watching, I put on an act." Gardener Ju's tone sounded smug. "She's so impulsive, and now especially suspicious because of Lilian's betrayal, I knew I could trick her by pretending to be Wen. Turn the two on each other, and the cell would fall apart."

Jie had fallen for the trick, and it had almost succeeded.

"Now what impresses me the most," Gardener Ju continued, "is that you figured out I am one of the Steel Orchids."

This was indeed, impressive. How had Tian figured it out?

"You used clan techniques, but all clan members were accounted for. Unless, they'd faked their deaths. Like Lilian tried to do. Through an explosion."

Gardener Ju laughed. "I suspect that's where she got the inspiration."

Jie swallowed hard. Lilian had taken measures to make sure nobody else got hurt. This Steel Orchid had wiped out an entire cell, probably to leave no witnesses. Though if one Steel Orchid survived, she'd probably plotted the whole thing with her twin.

"You returned to the Floating World after enough time had passed," Tian said. "Anyone who knew you as a Blossom would've died in the fire. Or left the Floating World. Or forgotten who you were. And you're about the right age, too. Fifty-something."

"Maybe you're not that smart." Gardener Ju snorted. "A word of advice, Zheng Tian: if you live through today, always underestimate a lady's age to her face."

"I'm sorry," he said.

She laughed. "I jest."

"Why?" Jie asked. "Why did you desert the clan?"

"Same as your beloved Lilian. I was tired of spreading my legs for the Black Lotus. Master Yan had always promised me reassignment. When that didn't happen after The Beauty died, I knew it never would. I had to orchestrate my way out."

"Why did you kill your clan Sisters?"

Tian shuddered. "If she ever wanted to come back to the Floating World, she couldn't leave anyone who remembered her as Black Lotus."

"I even let my twin die, because she was too blinded by loyalty to the clan."

The nonchalance. A chill went up Jie's spine, even as a part of her died. She'd always assumed the clan Sisters embedded in the Floating World formed an even deeper bond than other clan members. "Why did you return to the Floating World at all, then?"

Gardener Ju laughed. "To make money, from other girls spreading their legs."

"And from selling yue," Tian said.

"Yes."

It was all about money. Jie snorted. "Why did you kill Lord Ting?"

"Oh, you will love this." Gardener Ju lowered her voice. "Lord Ting had a controlling stake in Jinjing Lumber. He was money behind the Fangs and the Red Dragons, and was getting quite rich off yue. But then, he made the mistake of siding with the Fangs."

"And you recruited Lilian to kill him."

"I'd identified both of you as clan assets almost as soon as you joined the Chrysanthemum Pavilion as Florets. I knew how to co-opt your communications, and I also knew she wanted out. I just gave her a path. It cost me the Chrysanthemum Pavilion, but the Floating World Houses pool money into a fund for such disasters—a lesson from my fire, oh so long ago. I'll be using that to rebuild a new House, complete with unpurified yue to keep the Hummingbirds coming back."

The self-satisfied tone. The hallmark of an enemy who knew they had the upper hand, and needed to gloat about their success. On the one hand, it meant Gardener Ju planned on killing them; on the other it could be used to stall.

"Now, Zheng Tian, I was going to turn you over to the Emperor and collect the reward. Now that I've seen how smart you are, that would be a waste. I'm going to find a way to keep you."

"I will help you, as long as you let Wen, Yuna, and Jie live."

In that order. Jie's snort was cut short by a cold blade pressed to her neck.

"Of course Wen and Yuna will live. They are too valuable to my House, and all it takes will be the *Tiger's Eye* and the musk toxin to make them believe whatever story I tell them."

Did she have the toxin? It was a secret formula that only the clan compounders knew, and any cache from when Gardener Ju had still been a clan member two decades ago would've lost its potency.

Jie sniffed. The saturation of the musk in the air suggested Tian had smashed most, if not all of the vials when he ran into it. Maybe that was for the better.

"As for Jie... If she tells me what I want to know, maybe."

There was no way Jie was leaving here alive. No doubt, Gardener Ju wanted to find out if the clan knew about her. Jie's best bet was to dissemble and stall. She feigned fear. "I... I'll tell you anything you want to know."

"I wonder." Gardener Ju wedged herself between Jie and the wall. The knife disappeared from her neck, while iron fingers clamped down on both her wrists over her pulse—another clan technique for detecting lies, and one which could be countered by controlling the heartbeat. "What is your name?"

"Yan Jie." Jie closed her eyes and concentrated on control of her pulse. The *Viper's Rest* technique could slow a heartbeat and breath so that all but the most skilled doctors would believe the person dead. It came with the nasty side effect of amnesia. Going a quarter of the way into the *Viper's Calm*, however, could help a Fist maintain composure under the most stressful situations.

"How long have you been in the clan?"

"Nineteen years." Actually twenty, her entire life, but the lie would throw off Gardener Ju's lie detection technique.

"When did you find out I was involved in the shooting?"

Time to mix in some of the truth. "Just now."

"So the clan doesn't know?"

"In my message to them, I told them Wen was Faceless Chang." Hopefully, her breathing technique disguised this lie.

"I can tell you are using the *Viper's Calm.*" Gardener Ju's hands left Jie's wrists. Her stealth suit rasped as its threads tore, exposing her back to the air. "Now, let's try again. Does the clan know about me?"

Pain seared in Jie's shoulder blade, yanking her out of the *Viper's Calm*. All coherent focus shattered into fragments of thoughts. Jerking forward, she screamed.

"What are you doing?" Panic rose in Tian's voice. "Leave her alone!"

"Oh, it's a very shallow cut, not even into the muscle. She's always been a fast healer, so this won't leave much of a mark. Now, little tramp, you who cost me your significant virgin price with your indiscretion: does the clan know about me?"

Skin peeled away from the incision, sending burning waves over her shoulder. Jie gritted her teeth and fought to regain concentration. "Thank you! The scar from this will keep me from ever being reassigned to the Floating World again."

"Had I known you enjoyed a little punishment, I would've let Lord Ting play with you, like he did with Lilian. Does the clan know about me?"

"The clan is all-knowing." Pain under control, Jie made her tone flippant. Another slow cut ran down the ridge of her spine. Despite her best efforts, she screamed again.

"Stop!" Tian's voice bubbled with tears.

The blindfold came off, and Gardener Ju's looming presence left. Jie squinted to allow her eyes to adjust to the light.

A blurry form gliding soundlessly across the room, albeit with a limp, crystallized into focus. Gardener Ju's stealth suit, an older version, clung a little too tightly to her plump figure. She moved behind Tian, blindfolded with hands bound in front of him. "If the half-elf won't talk, maybe you will."

Tian's lips trembled. Without clan training, he'd reveal that the clan knew nothing, and that would be Jie's death. Maybe his, too.

Jie's eyes darted to the shelf of toxins. The entire row of musk had been shattered. Shards of glass lay all over the floor. Not like she could reach it before Gardener Ju stopped her, anyway.

With a deft slash, Gardener Ju split open the back of Tian's robes, and he whimpered.

"Now, Little Tian, you will find out what it means to be a Black Lotus Fist. Enlighten me, what did Jie tell the clan?"

Tian's body went rigid. He was going to answer, and Jie'd be dead. She scooched forward with her bound hands and feet.

"Red, sword, wheel, dagger, green, stab, cloudy, spicy, crossbow, opera, bludgeon, slippery, sun, finger, six, two, zero, nine."

Brave boy. Jie had misjudged him.

Gardener Ju squinted, then looked to Jie. "What? Is this some kind of code?"

Jie shrugged. A stupid mistake, since pain from the wounds seared in her spine and shoulder. She yelped.

"There's one way to find out. Answer me." Gardener Ju ran the blade somewhere down Tian's back.

"Red, sword, wheel, dagger, green, stab, cloudy, spicy, crossbow, opera, bludgeon, slippery, sun, finger, six, two, zero, nine." His tone came out level, and his face contorted only a fraction.

How had a spoiled ten-year-old resisted, without training?

"How are you doing this, boy?" The traitor ripped off his blindfold.

He blinked several times, and his gaze met Jie's. His fists squeezed tight, and he thrust them between his legs, concealing them.

Gardener Ju's gaze locked on his hands. "Hmmm, you value your hands. Well, you don't need all your fingers to be useful to me."

She came around to the front of him and knelt. She seized his arm and pulled.

Head shaking back and forth, jaws clenched, he resisted.

Setting the blade between her teeth, she wrapped two hands around one of his arms. She leaned in—

Snick. Glass shattered. A musk scent filled the air.

Tian flung shards and liquid at her face.

The toxin! How had he hidden it from the Gardener? The coin trick, maybe.

"No! Clever little bastard." The blade slipped from Ju's teeth as she stumbled back a few steps, hands patting at her face. Her glare shifted from Tian to Jie. She retrieved the knife and then approached on wobbling legs. "Whatever happens, I'll make sure you won't live through this."

Nine steps. Jie might have nine steps before the toxin took effect, and the Gardener could cover the space between them in five. One, two, her knees buckled from the toxin coursing through her veins.

Three, she was within arms' reach.

Jie scuttled back to the wall, creating two extra steps. Tian rolled toward them, crushing or scattering all the evidence he'd painstakingly rearranged.

Four. If more toxin had splashed on her, the Gardener might have passed out already. Even now, her eyes were glassy. Five.

He bowled into the back of the Gardener's legs, sending her toppling toward Jie, blade pointed down.

Jie lurched to the side best she could with her ankles and wrists bound. Pain burned through her shoulders and spine. The knife tip passed within a hair of her cheek.

The Gardener collapsed with an oomph and a gurgle. Her body went limp. Her head lolled toward Jie, her glassed-over eyes managing a baleful glare. Blood leaked from the corner of her gawk.

With a little squirming, Jie flipped the Gardener onto her back.

The knife was lodged between her ribs, into her lung. The weapon must've turned on impact with the floor. If she died, the clan would lose the chance to interrogate her, to find out more about the Red Dragons, Lord Ting's murder, and Jinjing Lumber. More importantly, if the Gardener had trained any apprentices in Black Lotus ways.

Before Jie could do anything else, the hatred in the Gardener's eyes dimmed as her life winked out.

EPILOGUE

Tian studied his web of evidence, painstakingly rearranged in the two days since Gardener Ju's attack. Wen, Yuna, and Jie had scoured Gardener Ju's quarters in the Peony Garden, and added new items to the evidence room: the demon mask, red cloak, and climbing claws and other Black Fist weapons and tools. A porcelain vase containing ashes had a name inscribed on the bottom, confirmed by Master Yan to be the other Steel Orchid.

Most interesting to Tian were the ledgers and tax receipts to the imperial treasury. After a thorough investigation into every entity that had either paid or received monies from Gardener Ju, there was no evidence she'd ever invested money into training an apprentice in Black Lotus ways. Running a brothel, it was unlikely she ever had time, and perhaps no interest, either. If there was anything to be learned from her financial records, it was that the Lords of the North could be duped into paying twice as much for polished jade.

Gardener Ju's strangest expense, outlandish in that she never did anything that didn't benefit to her, had been payment to a midwife about two years ago. It *had* coincided with a period when Jie said she'd disappeared from the Floating World for hours at a time, but she'd never appeared to be pregnant. The clan had tracked down the midwife, who had record of the payment, but no memory of whose birth it had paid for. It was a mystery that might never be answered, yet one which kept him from sleeping.

In the end, everything added up. Lilian's betrayal and Lord Ting's murder had all been about money. Jie, now joining him at his side with Wen and Yuna, had been especially bitter at this conclusion.

Why, he wasn't sure. The clan knew, and they'd passed that information to the Emperor. Government soldiers had raided Jinjing Lumber, discovered the illegal yue production, and shut it down. Their ledgers and documents proved Gardener Ju's assertion that Lord Ting had been behind the company; and that after his death, Jinjing Holdings became the majority shareholder—and it was owned by yet another shell company. Gardener Ju's ledgers revealed her to be its sole owner.

Meanwhile, news out of the Trench was that the Red Dragons and Fangs, with no new yue on the way, were about to turn the area into a war zone. Tian let out a sigh.

Jie turned to him. "What?"

He tapped his chin. "Will the Emperor send troops to keep the peace in the Trench?"

"Only if tax revenues from the local magistrate's office decline significantly."

All the ideals Tian had had about a moral emperor ruling with the Mandate of Heaven were now evaporating. It was all about money.

Wen patted him on the head, while Yuna scoffed.

Jie's ears twitched, and Cleaner Qin entered with a salute.

"I'm here for the urn for the Steel Orchid," he said. "I am returning it, along with the ashes of Gardener Ju, to the Temple for burial."

"Do you still need it?" Jie asked Tian.

Shaking his head, he pointed to it.

Cleaner Qin picked it up. When he straightened, he reached into the folds of his robe and handed Jie a folded missive and a white sphere. About the size of a giant walnut, it was twenty-seven percent larger than the common light baubles.

"What is it?" Jie held it up to the light, revealing a brown circle.

That shade... Tian gasped. "That was Gardener Ju's eye."

Jie turned it over as she studied it. "A fake eye? How could she have possibly dodged my throwing stars without depth perception?"

"Or shot Lord Ting," Yuna said, craning in to examine it.

"It's masterfully done." Wen tilted her head as she looked. "Only Estomari glassmakers have this kind of skill."

Tian tapped his chin. Inhabiting the continent's east, Estomari were famed for their craftsmen, as well as their ability to Divine the future.

"There are tiny letters." Jie squinted at the glass eye. "It's too squiggly. The maker's signature, maybe?"

Wen pointed her pretty chin at the missive Qin had brought. "What does it say?"

Jie's fingers danced as they unfolded the message. Like before, it might as well have been gibberish, but all the girls' eyes roved over it.

Shoulders slumping, Wen pouted.

"What does it say," he asked.

"The clan bought the Peony Garden," Jie said. "After the death of two Gardeners in less than a week, the value dropped. They are making Wen the new cell leader of the Floating World."

Was that why she was pouting? Tian looked to Wen. "Isn't this good?"

"There's more," Wen said.

"I am being reassigned," Jie said. "I'll be teaching the younger initiates at the temple. I have four days to turn cell operations over to Wen before I take you there."

Four days! Tian shuddered. Going new places always made him sick to his stomach. He'd leave the capital for good, going farther and farther away from Princess Kaiya.

Jie gave him a wry smile. "But first, we are going to go into the Trench. If a Steel Orchid was a double for Faceless Chang, then he probably knows about the clan."

End of Part 2

INTERLUDE

In his former life as a Great Lord's son, ten-year-old Zheng Tian would've never imagined stealing. Then again, he'd never imagined killing a woman, either; and he'd just accidentally murdered a Steel Orchid, a female traitor to the Black Lotus clan.

Now, the stability of the realm depended on the clan retrieving her secret ledgers from a bank's vault. He stood with Yuna two-hundred and sixty one feet across the market square from the two-story stone block building, waiting for a gap in the crowds so they could pass unnoticed. Two guards in black robes embroidered with gold monkeys flanked the open double doors. Above them hung a red sign emblazoned with Gold Monkey Money Village in gold characters.

"See the way they walk and turn?" Wearing brown pants and shirt, Yuna pointed to a group of people between them and the bank. "A spot out of their line of sight will open in eight seconds. Follow me when you find an opening of your own." She started a casual stroll, never breaking pace as she crossed the square, and never in anyone's direct line of sight.

She was so amazing. Tapping his chin, Tian scanned the passersby. Eight coming from the east, six to the west, three approaching from the south, all at varying distances and walking speeds. Satisfied he'd identified an upcoming gap, he set off. And skidded to a halt in just two steps. So focused he'd been on activity up ahead that he hadn't seen the porter walking diagonally behind him, hunched by a rattan box.

In her spot to the east, with line of sight on the bank's entrance, Yuna rolled her eyes. Then, she flashed clan code. *Two guests, two agents, three guards. Hurry up.*

With a quick bob of his head, Tian hastened his pace to make up for the two-second delay, then continued it through the gauntlet. He came up to her side.

"About time," she hissed under her breath. She pointed with her chin at the bank.

Their position provided a view of forty-one percent of the interior, where a merchant stood by a central table, writing with brushes on rice paper.

"How do you know there are two agents and one more guest and guard?" he asked. They'd have to be on the eastern half of the building, hidden from their view by the walls.

"Our clan's *Eye of the Eagle* technique." She set her index fingers on her temples. "We'll teach you to see through solid surfaces."

How was that even possible? He gawked. "Really?"

She laughed. "No. Two agents and a guard by the vault is Golden Monkey's standard procedure, in every branch throughout the realm."

He nodded slowly. As a noble's son, he'd never concerned himself with money; but during the mission briefing, Yuna had explained how the banks helped fa-fa-facilitate business throughout the realm through lending money, insuring shipments, and transferring funds without actually having to haul silver ingots from one end of the empire to the other. Golden Monkey had a branch in every major city, and the clan had learned the Steel Orchid kept a safe deposit box there.

"There, one of the guests has left," Yuna said.

He watched as both of the merchants at the table disappeared from their line of sight while another emerged and left the building.

"Now remember what I taught you about using people as blinds and turning behind them as they turn." Yuna flashed a hand signal. "We're going to do that to get into the vault."

Tian made a single nod. "When Wen distracts them." He found Wen in the corner of his eye.

Beautiful in a modest dress, she was strolling across the square, making no attempt to avoid lines of sight. It would've been impossible, given the way men's heads turned to follow her. The same porter Tian had nearly careened into had set his load down, joining four similarly laden comrades in admiring the sashay of her hips. Her wide sleeves hung low, the right more than the left.

"Now." Yuna gave him a tug him into a walk.

Twenty-two steps later, they arrived at the bank's entrance a step behind Wen, and used her flowing skirts as a blind. The guards on the outside would see them, but that didn't matter for the plan.

"Welcome," one of the agents said. "How may we help?"

Both sat at a fifteen-foot-long table on the east, wearing the same black robes. Behind them was a door. According to the mission briefing, it was usually locked, and led to stairs going up to where records were stored. The merchant looked to have just finished his business.

So far, the operation, executed based on average transaction times, was going as planned.

"I'd like to make a deposit." Wen withdrew a pouch from her left sleeve. How odd that her right sleeve had hung lower.

He shook the silly observation out of his head to focus on the task at hand. With everyone's eyes on Wen, Yuna and Tian stayed low and darted under the table. He'd wondered about the particular shade of brown they wore, but it matched the floors. Nobody seemed to have noticed them, and their new location gave them a good view of everyone's legs.

Heart racing at what they were about to do, Tian looked over to the vault, to the sixteen feet away in the northeast corner of the room, where the last guard stood by a metal door. A large bulge protruded from his gut, like one of Father's vassals. Her-hernia, they'd called it.

Tian crouched lower to peek at their unfolding plan. If this didn't work, they'd have to escape, eight feet south to the entrance, before the guards closed in on them.

Wen glided toward the agent closest to the vault, while other looked crestfallen. The coin purse slipped from her hand.

Keeping low, Tian and Yuna darted toward the vault door. She flung a throwing star at the bell hanging from the upper east corner of the threshold.

Wen's pouch hit the floor, sending coins rolling just as the star's blades cut through the bell's twine.

The guard bent over to help Wen retrieve them, and Yuna swiped the key from one of his robe pockets. Tian swiped for the bell, but missed it. Heart leaping into his throat, he caught it with his other hand, half a foot from the floor. Heavens, he'd almost failed to silence the clapper. He set it on the floor, lest his trembling made it ring.

Half a breath later, Wen pretended to trip in her skirts and tumbled to the floor. With all the staff rushing to help her, Yuna unlocked the vault door, opened it just wide enough for them to pass, and slipped in.

Well, not wide enough for him, even after he'd lost an inch of waistline in his four days with the clan. Opening it finger-lengths wider, careful to avoid hitting the bell he'd left on the floor, he squeezed through, and closed it. All sound from in the main room went silent.

He blew out a breath and surveyed the room. Just as the mission briefing had described, hanging light baubles illuminated six corridors between banks of safes, which ran twelve feet from floor to ceiling. Somewhere among the four outer walls and ten walls between the rows was the Steel Orchid's box, labelled *jian-seven*. Now, they had three hundred seconds to retrieve the ledgers and get out. It was too short of time, and his heart sped up a beat.

Yuna pointed to the ceiling. "I'll disarm the gas trap, then check the east side. You search the west. If you find it, call me."

She spider-climbed between two walls of safes to a hole on the ceiling. From their pre-op briefing, he'd learned that any attempt to force a safe door open would result in a sleeping gas being released. There was a trigger outside the vault that would do the same.

Two-hundred and ninety-one seconds left. Doing as he was told, Tian studied the number-character combinations, which weren't sequential and didn't seem organized in any logical pattern. How the bank ever did business, it—

There. The numbers jumped according to a classic Yu-Dynasty poetic form, and the characters were from an old passage about wealth. Which would make *jian-seven...*

Two-hundred and fifty-six. He headed over three rows and one-third of the way in, he found a safe door about ten inches-square. "It's here!"

Yuna appeared at his side, eyes wide. "Wow, at two-hundred thirty seconds. That was fast. Really fast."

Praise from Yuna was rare. Tian's chest filled with pride. It wasn't worth telling her it'd been two-hundred and thirty-six seconds. "So now, you have to pick it."

She held up her hand. "I just jammed my thumb and index finger disarming the trap. You'll have to do it."

Him? Though they'd started teaching him the rudiments of lock picking over the last couple of days, it had been on simple mechanisms. This one here looked difficult. And just how did Yuna jam her fingers? "I don't know—"

She stuffed a set of lock picks into his palm. "Remember to check for traps, first."

Two-hundred and ten seconds. Why had they sent a new recruit for such a critical mission? Gulping, he shined a light bauble into the keyhole. "There's a coiled dart at the back. It looks like the key would prevent triggering it."

"You can spring it, and just stay out of the way."

"But—"

"Hurry, we only have one hundred and eighty-two seconds left."

One hundred and eighty-five, actually. At that time, Wen would create another distraction so they could slip out. Taking a deep breath, Tian chose two of the lock picks. His shoulder seared from where the Steel Orchid had flayed a strip of skin just yesterday, the movement pulling on Yuna's beautiful stitches.

He inserted the long pick at an angle where his hand wouldn't be in the path of the dart, and touched the spring.

Snick. The needle jabbed out.

He instinctively jerked his hand back, even though his precautions would have kept him safe, anyway.

"Come on, a hundred and fifty seconds left."

Holding the light bauble between his teeth, he squinted as he manipulated the tumblers. It was taking too long.

"Hurry. Ninety seconds."

"Shhhh." He continued struggling with the lock, yet it refused to yield. Time was slipping away. Why hadn't they sent Jie in here, instead of trusting him? She'd picked a lock in two seconds, and he'd already taken eighty-three.

"Thirty. We need to leave now."

"What about the Steel Orchid's ledgers?"

"*Jian-seven* is a pressure test. It's impossible to open. You did fine, not panicking." Yuna patted him on the shoulder. "The clan owns all the Golden Monkey Money Shops, and we run simulated missions. Most initiates never even locate the correct safe, and you broke the Architect's record by forty-three seconds."

Just a test? No wonder they had an unrealistically short period of time to accomplish the task. And he'd beaten the Architect, a legendary young master who'd died twenty-years ago. The tension in his shoulders melted away. "So I passed?"

"For now. The clan is always testing."

"What would happen if we were caught?"

She grinned. "All the staff and guards are former clan initiates who failed the training. The Cleaners would make them forget they even saw us."

How? Tian shuddered at the thought. "The clients, too?"

Yuna made a quick spider climb back to the gas trap and re-armed it. "No, they're real, and their patronage helps fund clan operations. We need to avoid them seeing us. Now let's get out."

So this had all been a test. No threat to the realm. No risk to himself. He buried a snort, and sidled up to Yuna at the side of the door. When the count reached three hundred, she pushed the door open and slipped out. Tian followed.

And froze.

Two feet away, the vault guard laid face up on the floor, his chest barely rising and falling, blood oozing from a wound to the gut. Two of the porters from before stood at the now-closed front doors, faces obscured by scarves, repeating crossbows raking back and forth. Two more stood on the east near the desk, repeaters aimed at the two employees.

"I told the bitch to be quiet." The fifth stood over Wen, who lay unconscious in front of the desk, a pool of blood spreading by her head. He turned to one of the bank staff. "Now, if you don't tell us where the vault key is, you'll be the first to die."

Thieves! What had started as a training heist had now become a real attempted robbery of clan assets. They'd already hurt Wen. Tian's pulse roared in his ears.

As of now, none seemed to have noticed the two children who'd just emerged. A knife flashed in Yuna's hand as she eyed the one by Wen.

What was Yuna thinking? She might be talented, but four men with repeaters would fill them with bolts in a matter of seconds. He tapped his limited clan code on her arm. *Five targets. Four crossbows. Danger.*

Wen in danger, she signed, her expression distraught.

Such loyalty! But she wouldn't be able to help with a dozen bolts protruding from her. Tian shook his head, even as a new option occurred to him.

Arm pressing Yuna back, he heaved the vault door open so that it obscured them from sight. As planned, it hit the bell he'd left on the floor.

"How did that happen?" the leader demanded, voice now projecting in Tian's direction.

"I... I don't know," the agent said.

"Do you have the keys to the safes?"

"Y-Yes."

"Well, come on now." The leader's long stride mixed with the agent's stuttered footsteps as they approached. The two crossbowmen near the desks sounded to be dragging the other employee toward the vault, as well.

Tian tapped on Yuna's wrist. *Two crossbow. Near entrance.* He pulled her down, then pantomimed a push. *Key.*

She looked at him, eyes wide. Did she understand his plan? She produced the vault key she'd stolen and set it in his hand.

She did understand! Tian held his breath as he waited until the three villains and two bankers went into the vault.

Staying low with the central table between him and the remaining lookouts, Tian ran and pushed on the vault door, slamming it shut. Yuna dashed forward to put herself edge of the central table. He shoved the key into the keyhole and locked it. Holding the key in place, he reached and flipped the lever to release the sleeping gas.

"What happened?" one of the lookouts said. "Closing the door wasn't part of the plan."

"I'll go check," said the other.

Now, the key twisted against his grip as someone inside the vault tried to unlock it. In the briefing, Jie said the gas would knock a victim out within a count of ten. He had to hold it just for a few more seconds.

The lookout's footsteps came closer, and he appeared at the side of the central table. He skidded to a hold as their gazes met. "What the—?

He let out a curse and tumbled backward to the floor as Yuna hooked the back of his ankle and drove her shoulder into his shin. The crossbow hit up against the table, discharging a bolt that brushed past Tian's ear and ricocheted off the metal door.

Yuna straddled the man, and tried to drive the knife into his throat; but he bucked his hips and ended up on top of her, pinning her wrist down and rendering her weapon useless.

Tian needed to do something, but if he let go of the key, the others would burst out.

The pressure on the key eased. Tian dashed over and swept up the fallen crossbow. A bolt from the lookout zipped by him, and he slammed the butt end into the closest man's temple. The motion pulled at his stitches with burning pain, but his victim crumpled on top of Yuna.

The lookout re-cocked the crossbow, and the trigger clicked. A bolt grazed Tian's shoulder. A dull pain throbbed there, but he was still able to cock the crossbow. He sidestepped so that the table provided some cover and leveled the weapon at the lookout. At his side, Yuna squirmed out from under the fallen man. She started to throw her knife.

"Hold," Wen said.

Yuna's arm froze, and she turned to the side. The lookout lowered his crossbow.

Wen? Wasn't she... Tian looked.

"I have to say, this is the most unique outcome to the *jian*-seven-double cross scenario I've ever heard of." Wen rose from where she'd been lying. "Though I think the Brothers won't be happy with getting knocked out."

Groaning, the attacker who'd tangled with Yuna sat up and rubbed his temple. "She almost stabbed me with a live blade!"

"What?" Lip trembling, Yuna stared at her. "What are you saying?"

Wen grinned. "The clan is always testing."

The lookout by the door pulled the scarf down, while the vault guard sat up, removing a bladder from the fake bolt wound.

"Don't ever do that again." Bursting into tears, Yuna ran over and wrapped her arms around Wen. "I thought... I thought you'd really been hurt."

"Not her blood." Tian gestured to the torn bladder, then caught sight of a crossbow bolt. "And blunted spongewood tips." No wonder the one that hit him hadn't hurt that much.

Wen stroked Yuna's hair. "It's all right, my pretty girl. More sweat in times of peace..."

"... means less blood in times of war," Yuna said through choking sobs.

"Yes." Wen's smile was radiant. "Now, let's get back to the safe house so you can get ready for your mission in the Trench."

End of Interlude

PART 3: WRETCHES OF THE TRENCH

PROLOGUE:

One Mother's Trash

As an abandoned orphan herself, fourteen-year-old Yan Jie's heart broke every time she saw a desperate parent sell a child. Now, as she knelt beside the beaming two-year-old girl, she felt only relief.

"You can't have my boys," the mother ways saying to the clan recruiter. "But Yuna's a stupid, worthless stain with diarrhea mouth."

"Diarrhea mouth?" The recruiter, disguised as a priest of the Black Lotus, took a half-step back. It *did* sound like a disease.

The mother looked sidelong at him. "You know, jabbering all the time."

In complete sentences, Jie signaled to him. Did this woman not realize how advanced that was for a two-year-old? Maybe she only cared about the twin baby boys strapped to her back. And whatever a stain was...

Still humming a unique but melodic tune, Yuna looked over her shoulder at her mother with a pout before returning her attention to the game of observation and coordination she and Jie were playing.

"But if you don't want a floater," the woman said, "The Red Dragons will pay three copper *fen* for her. They just took my sister's daughter."

Floater? Jie exchanged glances with the scout. *She's talented. Let's take her.*

Watching their hands, Yuna looked up and beamed. *I'm worth five.*

Had she already picked up the signs, just from watching? It wasn't possible. Not for someone so young. Not in such a short amount of time. The vast majority of people didn't even notice the clan's non-verbal communication, let alone learn to use them.

With an incredulous look at her, the scout turned to the mother and pressed a few coppers into her palm. He bowed. "For your trouble. We will take good care of her at the temple."

And train her to her full potential. If Yuna stayed here in the Trench, she'd probably end up a Triad prostitute. As an initiate in the Emperor's secret spy clan, she might one day save the realm.

CHAPTER 1

While nobody else remembered anything from before age three, eight-year-old Feng Yuna had vivid memories of Mama selling her. She'd berated Yuna for being a useless, babbling girl, before ultimately surrendering her for four copper *fen*. There'd been no contract, like with Seedlings indentured to the Floating World. Mama had just taken the Black Lotus clan recruiter at his word, that he was a priest picking up orphans.

Now, standing on the outskirts of the Trench, Yuna scanned the weathered wood buildings topped by equally worn tile roofs. Women in simple patched dresses sat outside doors, bouncing grimy children on their knees, while men in dirty shirts and pants laughed as they returned home from a grueling day's work. Many were covered in excrement—*shit diggers*, the locals called them.

Like the women, her hair now hung in a simple pony tail, and her own filthy dress matched theirs. The coarse fibers scratched, feeling so different from the weightless silk gowns she'd worn for the last season as a Seedling in the Floating World. This homecoming, after six years, was more likely to stir up feelings of trauma than nostalgia.

At her side, Elder Sister Yan Jie clasped her hand. She'd been there that day; posing as a half-elf orphan sent off to join the temple, but really there to test candidates for qualities that made good operatives. Now they were back, to assassinate a Triad boss who might know the truth about the Black Lotus Temple. Jie tapped and brushed the clan's coded language across the back of Yuna's hand. *How does it feel to be home?*

A strange feeling of guilt weighed on Yuna's shoulders. No, how could it possibly be guilt? It *should* be sadness. Or betrayal. No, it had to be the clothes. Still, vague recollections of suckling Mama's breast shifted to clearer images of first steps and words, before crystalizing into the birth of twin brothers. And Mama's doting on them, because a stupid daughter didn't deserve Mama's love.

Yuna shook the recollections out of her head to focus on the present. No matter how distinct the memories of hurt and loss, she didn't recall the air reeking so badly. She answered in subtle hand gestures, *It stinks.*

On the other side of her, the chubby ten-year-old new recruit, Tian, studied their motions. The wrinkling of his nose made his round, dirt-smudged face look like a piglet's. *It's the first thing I noticed*, he signed. "Why does it smell so bad?"

He'd only joined the clan four days ago, and picked up the sign language so fast! Up to now, she'd been the most promising young clan member, so much that they considered her the second coming of the Surgeon. The stealth, spying, and fighting skills that took most ten years to learn, she'd mastered in six. She'd also gained fluency in the three languages of the North. If the elders had all lauded her abilities, they'd anticipate molding his potential the way a starving man eyed an imperial feast. Jealousy knotted in her stomach.

Clothed in a tattered dress and a headscarf that covered her tapered ears, Jie gestured from the city walls to the stone-paved gash that ran like a scar through the district. "The capital's sewers empty into that ditch, and flow into the surrounding rice fields."

Thus, the name *the Trench.*

Her birthplace. Or as the locals said, where she'd been shat out.

If Tian's face had resembled a piglet's a moment ago, it now looked like an opera mask of the Surprised Sidekick. "You mean *baba* is mixed in with the rice?"

"Circle of life." Yuna snorted. As the son of a lord, he'd lived a life of clueless luxury up until his recent banishment. Most kids stopped saying *baba* by age six. "You eat the rice, it comes out as shit. Then the shit becomes rice."

Tian's mouth rounded so wide, it would have no problem accommodating an oiled jade pleasure ball. The thought was tempting to put into action once they got back to the Floating World.

"Come on." Jie started into the street. A half-elf with an exceptional sense of smell, it was a wonder she hadn't fainted from the overwhelming stench.

Tian shivered like a cold little dog. "Shouldn't we wait? The Blue Reaper starts to strike around dusk."

Yuna gave a bored shrug. Rumored to wear a blue hat and face scarf, the Blue Reaper had been terrorizing girls in the Trench for the last few months. Still, a simple serial killer wouldn't stand a chance against two Black Lotus members, even with Tian getting in the way.

"There's not enough time." Jie looked up to the Iridescent Moon, now waxing to its fifth crescent in its reliable seat in the heavens. "We only have three hours until we meet our informant."

Yuna followed, with Tian on her heels. Her ears perked up.

Up ahead, a dozen dust-covered laborers hopped out from an oxcart marked with the words *Zhang's Quarry* in faded paint. Two of the men approached, heedless of the three children in front of them. Despite the dirt masking their skin color, their large size, prominent noses, and heavy jowls marked them as foreigners, and they conversed in Nothori, one of the languages spoken by the pale-faced people from the North. Yuna was one of the few clan members who'd learned it.

The first man clapped the second on the back. "I made enough to buy a *yue* ball." He was just a few steps away, so engaged in conversation that the coin pouch stuffed in his sash would be easy pickings.

Edging her way past Tian, Yuna prepared to swipe the purse. Better that she have it, instead of the Triads selling yue.

"Don't you need the coin for your wife and little kid?" the second asked.

The first blew out a sigh. "You're right. Maybe I should wait until yue prices fall."

"Or just stop smoking that shit before you need to sell another daughter to the Red Dragons."

Fury and sadness twisted in Yuna's gut. She let them walk by without taking the addict's purse. Little did he know prices would keep rising, since the Imperial Court had raided the illegal supplier up North. In the coming weeks, the addicts going through withdrawal would turn the Trench into even more of a living hell. For now, though, the man's family would eat.

Tian and Jie came up on either side of her, and he beamed as he hefted the coin pouch. *I did it*, he signed.

Shaking her head, she gaped at him. *His family will starve.*

"You can speak their language?" If one pleasure ball could've fit in Tian's mouth with lubricant before, a dry one would now. "I didn't know. I'll return it." He started back.

"Sifters, are you?" a male voice called.

Yuna, Tian, and Jie all turned to the source.

Two wiry men in clean black tunics sauntered over as if they owned half the Trench. They probably did, since the imperial court didn't care what happened here, and the blue-and-green snake tattoos bared by the men's rolled-up sleeves marked them as members of the Fangs.

Triads. Tian gulped.

What's a sifter? Jie tapped on Yuna's back.

Pickpocket. Akin to the denizens who looked for treasures among the shit.

"I don't recognize you." The larger's eyes roved over them, a feral grin forming on his face.

The other laughed. "The boy has a little too much meat on him to be a Trencher."

Yuna started for her bladed hairpin, but Jie stayed her hand.

The half-elf bowed. "We're new here."

The smaller, who was still larger than the three of them combined, laughed. He nudged the first. "Then we'll have to forgive them this one time for not following the rules."

"Rules?" Jie asked.

"You can only sift from the foreigners, and half of your earnings go to the Fangs." The larger extended his hand.

"I was going to give it back," Tian said, gesturing toward the diminishing backs of the still-chattering foreigners. Whether it was naiveté, or skill worthy of a famous actor—no, it was Tian.

Definitely naiveté. Yuna rolled her eyes. "Sure you were." The larger laughed. "And my pa has tits."

"Really?" Tian's face scrunched up. "Maybe he drinks too much wine."

It would've been a perfectly-timed insult, if it hadn't been delivered with clueless sincerity. The two Triads exchanged confused glances.

"Are you shitting on my pa?" The big man loomed closer, hands clenching into fists.

Head cocked, Tian threw up his hands. "You were the one who said your father had breasts. I've noticed that when men drink too much wine, they—"

The man swung. He'd probably decked many a drunk with his sloppy haymaker, but Jie pulled Tian out of the way.

Yuna pushed forward and bowed low. "I'm sorry, sir. My brother drinks downstream." All the slang was coming back; in this case, the idiom for *stupid*. She proffered the purse, which she'd swept from Tian's grasp.

Harrumphing, the man snatched it up. "Since you made fun of my pa, I'm keeping all of it this time."

"Your pa's a crusty bucket," the second said.

Crazy, Yuna signed.

With the audacity of a lord, he took her chin between his thumb and forefinger and studied her. "You know, two pretty girls like you, I can give you a job that will make more than sifting the pockets of these pathetic foreigners. The boy's pretty enough, I could probably find a job for him, too."

Maintaining outer calm, Yuna seethed inside. The way his eyes roved over her left little doubt what kind of job he had in mind. In the Floating World, a girl would never lie with a man until she blossomed with Heaven's Dew. Apparently, such rules didn't apply in the Trench, and the idea that an eight-year-old, or even younger, might be used by a depraved...

Jie tugged Yuna back and bowed. "I'm sorry, kind sirs. We're just learning about the area."

The two men leaned in to each other and exchanged whispers.

The larger chuffed. "As long as you're on this side of the Trench, you belong to the Fangs. Don't cross to the other side."

Fangs on this side, Red Dragons—and the boss they needed to kill—on the other. Yuna shot a knowing look at Jie.

"Where are you staying?" the smaller asked.

"With family." Jie bowed again.

Though it was a lie, Yuna squirmed. Mama probably still lived somewhere near here.

"Well, if it gets too crowded in his house, we can find you lodgings and work. Go to our *Tang*, and ask for Big Brother Tu, and tell them Brother Zeng sent you." Leering, the smaller thumped his chest, then pointed at a white stone tower with rust-colored tiles in the distance, rising above the hovels. It looked like the other troop garrisons surrounding the city, but was apparently now home to the Fangs.

If the limited information the clan had gathered was correct, the aforementioned Big Brother Tu was one of the Boss' lieutenants. Yuna exchanged a glance with Jie.

The half-elf pulled her and Tian back, bowing to the men. "Thank you for your kind offer."

"And if any of the Flukes give you trouble, be sure to let us know." The smaller one cracked his knuckles before the two pushed past them and continued on their way.

Once they'd passed, Tian hefted the purse in his hand.

Grinning, Jie plucked it from his palm. She surreptitiously passed it to Yuna and motioned to the two foreign laborers in the distance. "Go return it. Tell the man he dropped it."

"What about our new friends?" Yuna tilted her head to the two Triads, who watched them from between two huts.

Jie nodded. "I'm sure they'll follow us. Lose your tail and meet up across the trench at the magistrate's office."

Where they'd connect with an informant who could arrange an introduction with Faceless Chang. He'd taken over the Red Dragons in a bloody coup six years before, possibly helped by a Black Lotus Clan traitor known as the Steel Orchid—who was so ruthless, she'd let her own twin sister die in a fire. Face scarred from decades of conflict, Faceless Chang now wore the opera mask of Yanluo, Lord of Hell. Since he probably knew about the clan, he had to die.

Yuna scanned the surroundings, and found the smaller of the Fangs peeking at them around the corner of a hovel. Squirreling away the purse, she took off after the two foreigners. She'd slip the money back onto the yue addict.

The weight and feel of it indicated four copper *fen*.

Four coppers. All a little girl was worth in the Trench.

Up ahead, a Hua man sat in an intersection, chained to a pole. A square board *canque* hung around his neck. The picture of penis painted on the wood displayed his crime against the Fangs.

It was there that the two Nothori laborers parted, one continuing and the yue addict turning down an alley between the ramshackle rowhouses. Yuna hurried to catch up. At the head of the alley, she froze.

"Andris Dukurs of Lietuvi?" spoke a slithery male voice in the Nothori tongue.

"Yes?" the yue addict said.

Clothes ruffled. Steel rasped, the short sound indicating a dagger being drawn. A smothered cry broke out, followed by gurgling.

Yuna covered her mouth. One of the men had just attacked the other. She listened.

Whoever had been stabbed now gasped in labored breaths, and heavy footsteps hurried deeper into the alley.

Taking a deep breath, she peeked around the corner.

Not far in, the yue addict was curled up, his lifeblood soaking into the packed dirt. A cloaked figure wearing a brimmed hat in the style of the fair-skinned neared the far end of the alley. He turned around, revealing a kerchief-covered nose and mouth. Though the rest of his face was shaded by his hat, a pair of white eyes found Yuna.

She ducked back, palming a throwing pin from her hair in one hand and snapping out a knife from a forearm strap with the other. He fit the description of the Blue Reaper, but didn't he only target girls? Why would he attack Andris Dukurs?

CHAPTER 2

Yan Jie's shoulder and spine burned from where the surviving Steel Orchid had flayed her skin off. Despite Yuna's superb stitching, and the fact that elf blood helped her heal faster and better than full humans, she'd probably end up with a scar.

That would be nothing, balanced against the emotional scars the denizens of the Trench must have. Living in a wealthy country getting richer off trade, it was hard to believe there was still so much poverty. While there were certainly less-affluent neighborhoods within the city walls, they didn't begin to compare with the ramshackle wood buildings here, and their cracking tile roofs. People in dirty, threadbare clothes roamed the hard-packed dirt streets. And the stench...

Then again, clan operatives stationed in the Nothori nations spoke of even more bitter conditions. Perhaps that's why so many citizens of those countries had come here. She'd never seen so many fair-skinned people in one place, though it was admittedly hard to discern their skin tone underneath the layers of dust and dirt. Some even had light-colored hair.

Though it begged the question: if Faceless Chang had enough money, why would he stay in such a ghetto?

To think, if Yuna had remained here, she might've ended up as a Triad prostitute, used by a couple of dozen men a day. Instead she'd become a high-class courtesan in the Floating World. With her quick mind and lethal training, the clan was grooming her to eventually lead the cell there.

By comparison, despite perhaps being even smarter, Tian was untrained and clueless. Now he stood at her side, gawking at the foreigners. In that moment, he looked less like the banished son of a great lord and more like a country bumpkin. He tugged on her sleeve. "Why do so many Nothori live here? And why are they so poor?"

"It's even poorer where they come from, thanks to civil wars and unrest," she said. "Now, their countries pay huge sums to an empire—"

"The Teleri." Tian's tone sounded self-satisfied.

Jie nodded. That nation, ruled by a race of large, aggressive men, had subjugated the Nothori nations two decade ago, turning them into impoverished vassal states. "Yes. I assume many of these people came here looking for a better life, and they work for less, doing jobs our own people don't want to do."

He tapped his chin. "What kind of work?"

"In the mines and quarries for the men. For the women, servants and uh, the same kind of work as in the Floating World." She looked over her shoulder.

Doing a poor job of trailing them was the large Fang from before. Even though he'd been whispering to his comrade before, her elf ears had picked up their conversation: find out where she and the others were staying, and then threaten the family into giving them up.

Well, the two goons would be sorely disappointed, since Jie didn't plan on spending the night. She pulled Tian through a gaggle of burly Nothori men, who chattered in their unintelligible language, and turned into an alley between the dilapidated rowhouses. Shoulder searing from her pulled stitches, she peeked out.

Their tail's head turned left and right as he pushed through the people. "Any of you Flukes seen two squirts? A girl and a boy?"

The men glared at him as he shoved them aside, but their expressions softened when their eyes fell on his black tunic and exposed tattoos. Several bowed.

"No see," one said with a heavy accent.

Another pointed in the opposite direction. "That way."

The man hurried off, and the foreigners shared a laugh. Clan reports out of the Trench had made only passing reference to foreigners, and had certainly not mentioned the tension with the local Hua that was playing out in front of them.

Still, the Nothori people leading the Fang astray had worked in their favor. Jie beckoned for Tian to follow.

They wound through the streets, where the lack of commerce was shocking. On the other side of the city walls—which were close enough to see soldiers patrolling along the battlements—stores lined every primary street, and most secondary streets. Here, there was nothing. However, the flow of women with baskets of vegetables hanging in the crooks of their elbows suggested there was a marketplace of some sort. Foreigners and locals alike deferred to passing Fangs.

Jie bowed to one of the Hua women. "Where's the bridge over the trench?"

The woman turned to her companions, who all shared a laugh. She pointed back the way she'd come.

Why was a bridge so funny? Bowing again, Jie led Tian against the growing tide of people. The Nothori and Hua people walked on opposite sides of the street, leaving a space to squeeze between. The din of voices grew louder, and the stench of shit heavier. Before long, they came to a market square.

People shouted back and forth as they bartered over produce that didn't look or smell fresh. While the apples and pears sold in the capital looked spherical, Jie couldn't quite describe the shape of some of their counterparts here.

At her side, Tian's lips pursed. "Nothing looks good."

A nearby Hua woman snorted. "Farmers sell their best produce in the city. We get the leftovers."

"And the Fangs sift a cut of the farmer's sales," added another.

As if on cue, one of the black-clad Fangs extorted a copper from the owner of a nearby vegetable cart, and another groped the rear of a young foreign woman. If the Nothori nations were really worse than this, Jie hoped she'd never have to go there.

They made their way to the bridge, and there was no wonder the women from before had laughed: maybe there'd been a real bridge in the past, but now it was just stone pilings with makeshift wooden planks spanning the twenty-foot gap. It lacked any kind of balustrade, but wasn't short of Triads armed with broadswords and daggers. With arms and necks baring tattoos, it was the Fangs, marked by green-and-blue snakes on one side, Red Dragons inked with their namesakes on the other. Goons at both ends fleeced the very few people teetering across, after checking bags and packs.

She looked down. The stone-lined slope was manageable, descending at a forty-five degree angle to the sewage eight feet down. Going that way meant slogging ten feet through the slow-flowing muck, and it was impossible to tell how deep it went. Rich and poor people's excrement looked and smelled the same, but while it ran underground within the city, here it was all out in the open.

"Are we going to cross here?" Tian looked up from the trench, his nose scrunched.

Crossing here meant getting checked. As if Triad hands roving over her wasn't bad enough, they might find her many concealed weapons, which would lead to questions. She shook her head.

Tian pointed back toward the city walls. "What if we go through the city, and up and around?"

Given the distance between the gates... "It would take several hours, and we have"—she looked up to the Iridescent Moon—"less than three."

Scanning the makeshift bridge, Tian tapped his chin. "The only people crossing are Hua. They are willing to pay a toll. Which means they must have a good reason to do so."

The boy had a point, and it was his sharp eye and deductive reasoning that would one day make him an invaluable clan asset. Jie tracked one of the men who'd just crossed as he picked his way through the crowds. He dropped off a bag of leafy greens at one of the carts, and collected several bunches of carrots from another.

She looked to the other side, where another marketplace sat. There were plenty of greens, but no carrots. Where there was need, enterprising people would find a way to make a profit. Even in the Trench.

"I bet there are other places to cross." Tian gestured upstream to down. "We can follow along."

And they needed to cross soon, if they wanted to meet their informant at the local magistrate's office.

* * *

Tian gritted his teeth, and not because of the cut the Steel Orchid had drawn across his shoulder the day before. As if this place wasn't already out of his worst nightmares, with the bad smell and rude people, there was also a murderer on the loose. It was like they'd stepped into a foreign country, especially with all the pale-skinned workers.

Of course, he'd seen important visitors like that at the imperial court, but never so many, and never so...ripe-smelling. Not only that, there appeared to be two distinct types: one group had heavier jowls, with the men sporting thick beards, while the other had finer features and thinner facial hair. Their style of clothing was similar, yet varied in button placement and necklines. Even the intonation and inflection of the words they exchanged in their harsh-sounding language fell into two different groups.

His curiosity was piqued; he had to know why. For now, though, he and Jie had to find a way to cross over to the other side. He wandered along the bank until he reached the edge of the marketplace. Here, hovels lined the trench, leaving only a narrow path formed by the stones of the spillway's lip. How awful it would be to live in one of these homes, so close to the sewage.

He squinted into the afternoon shadows. Deeper in...

"Jie!" He pointed down to a wooden plank that cleared the *baba* line by a couple of feet.

"Let's check it out." She took the lead and followed along the bank.

One foot in front of the other, he tottered after her.

When they reached the right spot, she looked down. "There are wooden boards nailed into the mortar between the pavestones. It's almost like stairs."

Tian gave them a dubious look. Maybe if someone had small elf feet, they were like stairs. For anyone else, they were a quick plunge into the sludge.

She skimmed sideways down the slope to the plank, arms not even outstretched for balance. Gliding across the span with effortless grace, she looked back and beckoned. "It's easy."

Easy for her, maybe. He gulped and wedged a foot onto the wood board. It felt firm enough, so he crouched low and continued. One step, then two. It wasn't that hard, it—

His foot slipped on the next rung. Hands flailing, he teetered the rest of the way down and onto the plank. Balance thrown off, he fell.

A hand clasped around his wrist, sending pain flaring in the stitches on his back and shoulder, but keeping him on the bridge.

Heart thumping, he looked up to find Jie. She'd somehow run back across the plank and caught him.

"Are you all right?"

"Yes." No. If the trench didn't have a flat bottom, he might have sunk in over his head into the *baba*. Squeezing her hand, he followed her across.

When they got to the other side, he bent over and grabbed the rungs as if they were a ladder, and crawl-climbed. Three-quarters of the way up, he just about head-butted Jie's rear.

She'd stopped, and now held both hands up.

He looked past to see three fair-skinned men in a third style of tunic at the top, pointing makeshift spears at them.

One barked something in their language, his inflection different from the other two versions in the marketplace.

Jie shook her head. "I don't speak your language."

"I think he said he wants money," Tian said. At least, the man had spoken the word used when money changed hands in the marketplace.

"You have to pay the toll," the man said in accented Hua.

One of his companions grinned. "Just a copper. Much less than the Fangs or Red Dragons charge."

"We don't have any money." Jie motioned to the non-existent purse at her waist.

"Then you'll have to keep sifting in the Fangs' territory." The third jabbed his spear in a threatening manner.

Tian flinched.

"I need to bring some medicine to my sick aunt," Jie said. "Please, let us up."

"I have a soft spot for sick aunts." The second flashed a wolfish grin. "I'll let you up if you suck my cock."

The first leered. "Mine, too."

"And mine!" The third laughed.

Scratching his head, Tian looked past them. There weren't any roosters around, and why they'd want their chickens sucked on didn't make much sense.

The second pointed at his crotch.

OH. Tian cringed and squeezed his knees together. Why would anyone want that? It sounded painful. And poor Jie, having to put her face so close to such a stinky place.

"All right." Jie held out her hands. "Help me up."

What? She was going to do it? Tian reached to stop her, but without even looking, she batted his hand away.

Grinning, the men lowered their spears. The second and third reached and took her hands.

And screamed. Their eyes went wide as Jie twisted their wrists. She released the second, then used both her hands to crank the third's wrist. He flipped head over heels and tumbled down the slope into the sewage. The splash would've hit Tian had he not leaned to the side, and nearly thrown himself off balance in the process.

"Why you..." The first leveled his spear and stabbed.

Jie caught it and yanked, sending him flailing down the stones to join his companion in the muck. The third's spear thrust out, but she turned her upper body out of the way, seized the shaft, and let him pull her back up. Spinning along the length of the haft, she caught hold of his hands, and leveraged the spear so that the butt end dug into his wrist.

He buckled to his knees, and with a shove, she sent him rolling down the slope.

She'd overcome three armed men, all larger than her, on uneven ground, in the blink of an eye. Tian could only gape as she lowered the butt end of the spear to him. "Take it."

He grasped it, and she dug in and helped pull him up. Again, his wound, so lovingly stitched by Yuna, pulled.

"Shit sucker!" one of the men yelled.

Tian looked down.

The three stood there, shaking their fists. More importantly, they were waist-high in the *baba*, indicating a flat bottom to the trench, and a total depth of twelve feet. An image of all the angles appeared in his head of its own accord.

"Don't let us catch you, we'll send you downstream!" The second wiped his face, but only succeeded in smearing more *baba* on it.

"Come on." Jie skipped up the path back toward the marketplace on this side.

As they got closer, the sound of shouting grew louder.

Tian squinted in the late afternoon sun that greeted them. "What's happening?"

"I don't know. Nobody is speaking in Hua." Her eyes locked on one of the entrances to the marketplace. "Wait, someone just said the Blue Reaper has reaped someone. Near the stocks."

Tian's heart squeezed. "That's where we were. I remember the *canque* at the stocks. He targets girls, and Yuna might still be there."

Jie started to turn back. Then her shoulders squared, and with a wince, she continued through the marketplace. "No, Yuna can take care of herself."

Could she? In the last couple of days, she'd proven good at fighting; Jie and Wen had whispered among themselves about how she'd almost executed a No-Shadow Cut, whatever that was. But would she stand a chance against an adult killer?

CHAPTER 3

Standing at the corner of the alley near the stocks, knife and throwing star ready, Yuna listened.

The cloaked man's footsteps grew fainter, nearly drowned out by his victim's heaving breaths.

With a quick look to ensure the attacker had left, she turned into the alley and knelt by the yue addict. Blood flowed from several precise arterial stabs, pooling around him and matting his dark hair.

"Please," he said in accented Hua, his frightened eyes meeting hers.

There was nothing short of divine intervention that could help this man. Still, even if he'd sold his own daughter like Mama had, nobody deserved to die alone. At the very least she could stay with him until he passed. It's what she'd want, herself. She clasped his clammy hand. "You'll be all right."

"You speak our language..." His eyes widened before he winced again. "Well enough to lie."

She buried a wry smile.

"Please. Find my wife and daughter." His hand squeezed tight around hers. "Promise me."

Yuna chewed on her lip. Jie and Tian were expecting her, and she was part of the distraction that would get Jie into the Red Dragons' *Tang* and assassinate Faceless Chang. A foreign peasant's murder wasn't her responsibility. Still, a small part of her hoped that Mama worried about a lost daughter, and daughters everywhere should be protected. She gave a nod. "Where do they live?"

He gave a single nod. "Cherry Blossom Avenue, number two seven six."

It was surprising they had actual street names and numbers here, considering the government left the area alone. No doubt she wouldn't be finding any cherry blossoms, nor would the street count as an avenue. "All right."

"Tell wife..." he said through labored pants. "Hide daughter."

Hide? "Why?"

"She has a gift." The light in his eyes winked out.

What kind of gift could this man's daughter have that he'd have to hide her? Brushing the man's lids closed, she rose and ran out of the alley.

"The Blue Reaper!" she screamed in both Hua and Nothori. She grabbed the arm of every person she passed, and pointed back to the alley. "Murder!"

Before long, she spotted the addict's companion. She caught up to him and grabbed his hand. "Your friend, Andris Dukurs, was killed."

He turned and looked down at her. "What?"

"A man in a cloak and hat stabbed him in that alley." She gestured toward the crime scene.

His mouth rounded. "The Blue Reaper. I warned Andris to be careful."

"The Blue Reaper?

"Yes, he's been stalking the Trench for months, sending people downstream."

Killing. "Doesn't he only target girls?"

He shook his head. "He's sending *our* people downstream."

His people. The Nothori. The rumors out of the Trench had mentioned the Blue Reaper, and that he killed starting around dusk and through the night; yet they said nothing about the victims being foreigners. Perhaps that's why the imperial court didn't bother to send an investigator. It would explain why he'd killed Andris. "He told me he lives on Cherry Blossom Avenue. Where is it?"

The man pointed back the way she'd come. "Two streets over. Andris was taking a shortcut."

This was taking even longer than expected, and Jie might already be scouting out the Red Dragons den or meeting with their informant. Still, Mama had always said to keep promises, and Yuna had made a promise to a dying man. She could always claim it had taken her longer to lose her tail. With a bob of her head, she took the next cross street over.

No signs marked the street names, and all the houses looked the same: one story, wood weathered grey, and connected to the next. Ribbons of smoke curled out from the backs.

She waved down the closest passerby. "Is this Cherry Blossom Avenue?"

The Nothori woman, in a homespun dress and cradling a child in her arms, gave her a wide-eyed nod.

"I'm looking for the house of Andris Dukurs."

The woman gestured down the street. "End of the next block."

Yuna ran in the indicated direction. Not only were there no cherry trees, there were no street signs or house numbers, either. How the local magistrate kept track of taxes was anyone's guess. Or maybe the government expected so little that they didn't bother to keep accurate records.

She went to the very end of the block and worked backwards. Nobody answered the first two doors, and the third was a Nothori man who reeked of some kind of liquor.

"I'm looking for Andris Dukurs' house."

He stared at her through bleary eyes, then pointed. "Second house. Tell that shit swimmer I want the two coppers I loaned him."

The drunkard wouldn't be collecting on his debt. Yuna dipped her chin into a bow and went up to the indicated home.

From inside Andris' house came a child's giggling. Yuna swallowed hard. It was hard enough to tell a wife she'd lost her husband; to tell a kid her father was gone...she'd been on the receiving end of that conversation, in a run-down building much like this one. She knocked.

A muffled voice spoke, and the giggling quieted. Footsteps approached the door.

Yuna took a deep breath.

A metal latch scraped as it was lifted from the inside. The door opened.

A Hua woman in her thirties stood there, a little girl on her hip. The child didn't look to be of mixed heritage at first glance, but on more careful inspection, her skin tone was indeed lighter than the natives, and her hair had a brown tinge to it. In some ways, she looked a little like Jie. Her mirthful eyes were larger and rounder, though certainly not as exotic as the half-elf's features. She was about the same age as Yuna had been when Mama gave her up. Even now, she was clutching a faded rag doll with dozens of beautiful stitches holding it together.

Heart squeezing, Yuna tore her gaze away and studied the mother.

Why did she look so familiar? Yuna remembered everyone she'd ever met, which made her a valuable asset to the clan, but she couldn't place this woman.

"May I help you?" the woman asked in an equally familiar voice.

Heavens, this was Mama's older sister. The one who'd run off with a foreigner. Andris Dukurs, apparently. Yuna had only met Auntie Luo once, when she'd come to Mama begging for money. Two-year-old Yuna had thought her beautiful at the time, but the intervening six years hadn't treated her well. Better to keep their familial ties secret for now. Trying not to gawk, Yuna found her voice. "Missus Luo Dukurs?"

"Yes?"

"I'm sorry to bring you this bad news." Yuna pointed in the general direction of the crime scene. "Your husband was murdered."

Auntie Luo's face blanched, and she reached out a trembling hand to support herself on the doorframe. "When?"

"Just now, by the Blue Reaper." Yuna stuffed Andris' coin purse into the fold of Luo's robe. "He wanted me to give this to you, and also to tell you to hide your daughter."

Shaking her head incredulously, Luo looked to the girl on her hip. "So it's true."

"What is?"

"The Blue Reaper." Tears welled in Luo's eyes. "I told Andris to be careful."

Her daughter, perhaps sensing something was wrong, began sniffling.

Yuna's chest tightened. "Why did the Blue Reaper kill Andris? Why would he want your daughter?"

Looking left and right, Luo beckoned her inside, and Yuna followed. The entirety of the dirt-floored house was smaller than a Blossom's spacious bedchambers in the great Houses of the Floating World. A single window opposite the door let in the day's last rays of sun. A clay platform *kang*, now used as a stove with the boiling pot on top, but which could double as a bed once the embers cooled, occupied most of this room. The bedding currently rested on two creaky-looking wood chairs. On a rickety low table sat some old ceramic teacups, one previously shattered but repaired so meticulously that it would've been impossible to tell at a casual glance. Hooks on the wall held the rest of their meager belongings.

"The Blue Reaper isn't hunting just anyone," Luo said in hushed tones.

"Yes, I've heard he only targets Nothori."

Luo shook her head. "Yes, but specifically those with the gift of magic."

Yuna could only stare at the child, with her puffy cheeks and cute round eyes. In her own experience at the brothel, magic could only be imbued by master artists: calligraphy which could trick a man into spending more money on a courtesan, or embroidery which could arouse a woman, so as to make entertaining a disgusting man tolerable. Before his gambling and an opium addiction had ruined the family, her own grandfather had supposedly been able to magically evoke emotion through his paintings.

Certainly this child couldn't draw anything more than stick figures. And... "Andris could use magic? Is that why the Blue Reaper killed him?"

Luo nodded.

Stomach unsettled, Yuna thought back to her education at the Black Lotus Temple. Besides her own people's Artistic Magic, the Paladins in the South could channel it into their fighting, and the dark-skinned Aksumi were masters of sorcery, who infused the baubles that lighted the world. In the North, though, the fair-skinned people had persecuted people who could use magic: the Arkothi had hunted down those who could imbue runes with demonic power, and the Nothori, like Andris...

"There weren't many Empaths to begin with," Luo said.

Empaths. Yuna chewed on the inside of her cheek. Legends spoke of how they could read minds, see and hear through others' eyes and ears, sense intention, and even take control of unwilling people. They'd helped free humanity from slavery under the orcs a thousand years before, and helped the Nothori people carve out great kingdoms...until they were blamed for the Hellstorm and persecuted. More recently...

"But when the Teleri Empire subjugated the Nothori Kingdoms, their schools were shut down, taken apart stone by stone. The masters were jailed or disappeared. Then the former students were sent to labor camps. Andris, even with his meager skills, fled back then."

"To here?" Yuna's chest squeezed of its own accord, something she usually only felt when sad. Why would she be sad about foreigners in a situation she had no control over?

Now crying and squeezing the ragdoll tighter, the girl wriggled in Luo's arms.

Tears also glistened in Luo's eyes. "All the building projects needed strong arms and backs, willing to work for less."

Yuna gave a slow nod. "But isn't the work they do just as bad here?"

"At least they aren't hunted down. At least they're free."

Working for almost nothing, and hated by the locals. Just because they had the spark of magic. Yuna gestured toward the child. "And she has the Gift of Empathy?"

Luo wiped tears with her sleeve and searched Yuna's eyes. "If she'd been born in Rotuvi before the schools shut down, she might've received the right training."

"What's her name?"

"Mikayla. *Mi*, in our language. Andris says...said...she's not nearly as gifted...gifted as..." Luo choked on her tears.

"As him?"

"Yes," she said almost too quickly. "She's not as gifted as him. But that doesn't matter to the Blue Reaper. He's killed the children of Empaths."

Mother and child were both sobbing now, but there was something she wasn't saying.

Of course. According to Andris' conversation with his friend, he'd sold a daughter to the Red Dragons. Yuna's cousin. If memory served, and it always did, her name was Rumei. At least, that's what Mama had called her. It would be the perfect excuse to visit the Red Dragon Tang.

"I know about Rumei. I can go warn her. Tell me where to find her."

Auntie Luo's expression blanked, before her eyes narrowed. "She's dead. Everyone knows."

So much for that. "Do you have somewhere to hide?"

"Nowhere. No family in the Trench. No family, I mean." The words came out forced.

A lie, maybe? For all Luo knew, Yuna could be working for the Blue Reaper. Or be the Blue Reaper, herself. And *no family in the Trench*? She was clearly protecting other Empaths, maybe Andris' kin.

It could also mean Mama was still alive somewhere, in this stinking cesspool. With Yuna's brothers.

A knock came at the door.

Luo's eyes shifted to it.

A pit formed in Yuna's stomach. "Are you expecting someone?"

Luo shook her head. She started to stand.

"Don't answer it." Yuna held up a staying hand. The hollow in her gut grew. How stupid! She might've led the Blue Reaper back here.

Mikayla broke out into a wail.

Once Yuna reached the door, she leaned in and peered through a gap in the wood.

The Blue Reaper stood there, hands behind his back.

CHAPTER 4

Tian stood at Jie's side, looking across the trench. The shouts grew louder, mostly in the language of the Northerners—with all three variations—but also in Hua. He tugged on Jie's sleeve. "I'm worried about Yuna. The Blue Reaper is an adult. He might be a trained assassin."

Jie's ears twitched, and she peered over the trench in the direction of the spreading news. "I'm hearing that the victim was Nothori. Yuna's smart enough to avoid trouble. Come on, we need to get to the magistrate's office."

Something gnawed at Tian's gut. Just because the victim wasn't Hua didn't make it any less a murder. And, smart or not, Yuna was just a little girl, alone in a strange place. Nothing kept the Blue Reaper from targeting her next. Despite these worries, there was nothing he could do. Feeling useless, he followed Jie as she worked her way through the south marketplace.

Vendors were packing up their wares and produce, occasionally stopping to make last-minute deals. Hua and Nothori bartered with each other, unlike on the other side of the Trench where they didn't interact. Curiously, while the two groups didn't mingle outside of trade, the disdain and resentment from his own people weren't as evident on this side. While a few children played, there were no girls among them.

One thing did remain the same, though: no city watch patrols, no government officials. The Triads looked to be in control. It was as if they were in another country altogether, where the Emperor's Mandate carried no weight. In that aspect only, it was a little like the Floating World, where Yuna was apprenticing to kiss men and hold their hands. Just like Jie had done before her.

Now, Jie was picking pockets. His eye was getting better at catching her deft timing: whenever the locals paused to bow to a passing Red Dragon Triad, she'd swipe the goons' coin purses and then plant them on a peasant. She turned to him. "How much further to the magistrate's office?"

Closing his eyes, he pictured the Trench's layout in his head. Then he pointed to a line of stone buildings that rose above the rest. "Near there. Not long now—"

Around them, the marketplace fell into silence, and Hua and Nothori alike bowed like a ripple crossing a pond. He craned his neck to find the source of the commotion.

On the opposite side of the market, a slim man wearing a horned, fanged red opera mask depicting Yanluo, Lord of the Underworld, rode above the crowds in a sedan chair. It was borne by four Red Dragons and surrounded by another eleven.

Faceless Chang.

Perhaps they'd finish their mission sooner than expected. Though finishing meant killing someone. A pit formed in his stomach as every muscle tensed.

At his side, Jie was reaching for one of her bladed hairpins. Her eyes were locked on the leader of the Red Dragons. Sitting high, with all the locals bowing low, he would be an easy target save for her own short height and the ring of Triad enforcers around him. Still, if anyone could do it, it would be the half-elf.

Above the crowds, Faceless Chang waved a hand. The locals came out of their bows and pushed past each other. More than one shoved Tian out of the way to get closer. They converged around Faceless Chang, stopping around the cordon of guard and extending their open palms.

The Triad boss flung handfuls of copper coins, sixty-seven in all, glinting in the setting sun. The people scrambled to get them, some shooting hands up to catch, others bending over to pick them up, and yet more jostling to get into a better position.

"Damn," Jie said, her eyes shifting left and right. She lowered her hand from her hair and lengthened her stride toward the Triads.

Tian followed, eyes locked on the man in the demon mask.

Reaching into his red silk robes, Faceless Chang started to toss another handful of coins, and then froze. His gaze raked toward them with sudden awareness, like the Black Lotus girls playing Hide and Go Stalk.

Jie pulled Tian behind a hulking Nothori man with a ripe smell, then peeked around him. Tian looked around the other side.

Faceless Chang jumped off the sedan chair with a lithe grace. The wall of guards provided only flashes of his short form as they continued walking. Had he seen them?

All readiness drained out of Jie's carriage. She tapped on his wrist. *We'll tail them.*

Once they cleared the marketplace, the flow of people subsided. He and Jie kept their distance, keeping close to the line of huts. It was the clan's stalking strategy, one which Yuna had tried to explain several times over. If done right, only someone trained to spot a tail would notice, and Jie'd said he was getting better. In fact, he—

Two Red Dragons in their twenties peeled off from the rear of the formation and marched back. Like the others, they carried daggers and broadswords on their sashes. Maybe it was a coincidence that their gazes were locked on him.

Or maybe not. One raised a halting hand. "You're fresh squirts here."

Fresh? Squirt? Tian looked to Jie, whose forehead crinkled.

"You're new kids," the man said.

Jie bowed. "We're from the city, coming to visit an uncle."

"Oh? Who?" asked the second.

"Old Chi." The answer came out glibly.

The two exchanged suspicious glances.

"Didn't he just float downstream?" asked the first.

Tian's stomach roiled. The idea of floating in the trench with all its *baba*... At his side, Jie shuffled on her feet.

"Died." The second said. "Old Chi just died."

Tian fidgeted. The cover story meant to make contact with the informant was falling apart. "Yes. We're here to pray for his, uh...peaceful rest."

"Repose." Jie patted him on the head.

The first grinned. "With a funerary donation, no doubt?"

It was no wonder everyone here was so poor. Tian started to speak, but Jie held out a stolen purse. It was almost poetic justice, that these Triads were getting paid with money stolen from their comrades.

The first took the pouch. He shook out the sixteen copper *fen* into his palm, counted out eight, which he returned to the purse, and handed it back. "You're lucky we found you. Sixteen coins. One and Six. Very bad luck. Eight is a lucky number."

Wouldn't two eights be twice as lucky? Tian started to speak.

"Thank you for your advice and guidance, Big Brother." Jie bowed, and prodded Tian to do the same.

The first waved them away. "Well, off you go. If you need any help, come to the Red Dragons' *Tang*. We are always here to help."

Help lighten their purse, maybe. Tian tried not to frown. If any more Red Dragons stopped them, they'd end up with nothing.

The second one leaned in. "Look out for the Blue Reaper. He's sent several squirts downstream."

Tian shuddered as he watched them stride away in opposite directions. Beyond them, Faceless Chang and his retinue had disappeared.

"Back to the original plan." Jie smirked.

Tian hung his head. "I'm sorry, they must have seen me."

"We should be so lucky for it to be that easy." She patted him on the head, yet *again*. "If we have to stop for every Red Dragon, our informant will have left the magistrate's office. The back alleys will be faster."

"What about the Blue Reaper?"

"He just killed someone on the other side of the Trench. If he does cross over..." a blade danced in her hand for a split second before disappearing back into its forearm sheath "...we won't be reaped as easily as these poor folks."

Such confidence, but she had proven deadly. Tian gave a hesitant nod, and followed the half-elf into an alley that ran in the direction of the taller rowhouses. Smoke drifting out from side vents filled the air, at least partially dulling the *baba* stink.

The wood hovels that backed onto the path were connected. Most had a single window. All were shuttered, despite the pleasant temperature, with flickering blades of light coming from between the seams. Which meant two things: the residents were too poor to even afford a light bauble; and if the Blue Reaper did attack him and Jie, people would hear, but not see.

Gulping hard, he hurried to keep up with Jie. "How did the Triads take control of the Trench, and why does the imperial court not do anything about it?"

Not breaking stride, she shrugged. "If the Emperor cared, the clan would've planted an operative in their ranks. For now, all we know is that the district pays its taxes."

"What about the informant?"

"He's not a clan member. Just an old man who works in the local magistrate's office, who keeps an eye on things and makes connections for us, in exchange for some extra pay."

They crossed a street and entered another alley, when the hairs on the back of Tian's neck prickled.

CHAPTER 5

With the Blue Reaper reaching for the door, Yuna stood to the side, knife in hand. At the other end of the room, Auntie Luo had just finished laying blankets across the hot *kang* platform to create an insulated path to the window. Little Mikayla was slung on her back. How insane was this, trying to stall a skilled assassin? Yuna was supposed to be assisting Jie on a mission, not saving a two people of no consequence to the realm.

Then again, they were family. Not, not family. The clan was family. But they were blood. Mama's blood. Using the clan's *Mockingbird's Deception* technique, Yuna mimicked Luo's voice. "I'll be there in a moment. I just need to—"

A red line of molten metal formed on the metal latch. The door crashed open.

Heart leaping into her throat, Yuna prepared to stab the Blue Reaper. If he didn't know she was there, she'd try the No Shadow Cut.

He didn't enter.

Yuna shot a glance to the window, where Aunty Luo now had one leg outside. She looked back, and—

A dagger broke the threshold and spun through the air toward the frightened woman, who was now looking back, eyes wide with horror. The blade lodged into the side of her stomach. She cried out and tumbled back onto the *kang*. Mikayla lay pinned beneath her, bawling.

The Blue Reaper strode in, his cloaked form breezing by. Yuna waited for him to pass, watching that spot at the base of his neck where a stab would paralyze him. It was a little out of her reach, so she leaped up and thrust. The blade turned on something hard, wringing her hand.

He spun around. Between the brim of the hat and the scarf over the rest of his face, his eyes locked on hers. When he spoke, it was in heavily accented Hua. "You, again!"

He'd left his flank open. It was the perfect opportunity. With a snapping twist of her wrist, Yuna slashed at him with the zigzagging No Shadow Cut, but he jumped out of range.

Yuna silently cursed herself. Master Yan could execute the technique so fast, the blade didn't even cast a shadow. In practice, she'd nearly pulled it off against Tian with a training knife, but Tian was Tian.

The Blue Reaper was something else altogether. He drew a dagger with a gloved hand, probably the same with which he'd gutted Andris. She darted in with three quick cuts, but he evaded and countered. Pain seared in her forearm. She'd barely seen his attack, and it was more luck than skill that he hadn't severed anything important. She disengaged and looked.

Left-handed with a left lead, he had a greater reach with his longer blade and arm. She'd usually take a defensive approach, but now she also had to defend the others. In the corner of her eye, Luo's blood was soaking into the blankets as she struggled to turn and let wailing Mikayla out from the hot blanket. For her part, the girl was clawing for that old ragdoll.

Angling to his flank, Yuna feinted with a stab. The Blue Reaper's sidestep put his back to the door, and Yuna interposed herself between assassin and prey. At least that had worked. She yelled over her shoulder, "Get out!"

Eyes blooming with understanding, the Blue Reaper advanced with a frenzy of stabs and slashes.

Yuna leaped back onto the *kang*, one foot landing on the insulating blanket, the other stomping down on his hand, pinning it to the hot surface.

He roared and yanked back. Smoke wafted off his glove as he shook it and glared. "Little cunt. You're going to die slowly."

"You'll have to catch me first." Yuna kicked the pot, sending simmering stew at him.

He spun and swept his cape out, shielding himself from a scalding splash.

Turning around, Yuna scooped up little Mikayla in her sling and jumped through the window, into a smoke-filled, narrow alley between the back of the rowhouses. She was heavy in Yuna's arms, and the landing sent a flare of pain through her ankle. Behind her, Luo was screaming. Mikayla went deathly silent. Had she been stabbed? No, she was all right.

"Where did your daughter go?" the Blue Reaper was asking in a husky voice.

Preoccupied with deflecting the stew, he must not have seen them escape. Yuna had to keep Mikayla quiet. She wrapped the sling to keep the child pressed to her chest, and patted her on the back. After a few hobbling steps, she fought through the pain and broke into a jog. Emerging onto a side street, she looked around.

A handful of workers straggled home, laughing and chattering. All the rumors of the Blue Reaper spoke of him attacking lone people, either in back alleys or in homes. Out here in the open, she and the child with Empath potential might be safe. Limping out into the middle of the road, she sat down, cut a strip of cloth from her dress, and wrapped her ankle. Mikayla whimpered. Passersby walked around her, with only a few affording her a curious glance, and none offering to help.

When she stood, she tested her weight on the injured ankle. The pain had eased, and her gait improved as she trailed a group of Hua men.

"The Blue Reaper reaped another one of the Flukes," one said to his friend.

Flukes...they were the little white worms that crawled through shit. It wasn't a term she remembered from her infancy, but these men were comparing Nothori people to them. Her fists clenched of their own accord.

"One less parasite." The other laughed. "If the Emperor won't expel them—"

A third snarled. "The Emperor only cares about money. The companies bribe the court with silver, because they pay the Flukes coppers."

"And the Triads are just as useless," said the first. "They were supposed to chase the Flukes off. Instead, they just sift them."

Yuna's stomach twisted. It just wasn't fair. The companies reaped profits off cheap labor, and instead of blaming the companies, the locals blamed the Nothori. As if that weren't enough, the Triads exploited them as well.

She looked up to the Iridescent Moon. Waxing to half; she had to cross over the trench and meet up with Jie.

What to do with the now-sleeping Mikayla? Even now, the weight of a stare fell on Yuna's back. Had the Blue Reaper reacquired her? Waiting to catch her alone? She took a surreptitious scan of the area, but saw no sign of him.

For the time being, she stuck to the middle of this major thoroughfare, walking against the flow of people toward what looked to be a marketplace. Maybe she'd see Mama.

Maybe it would be better not to. Not with Yuna's mission to protect the clan. The people who really cared about her. Her real family.

With the sun about to set, vendors were already forming a caravan out of the square, protected from covetous locals by Fang enforcers in their black tunics. Shoulders aching, she moved the sleeping child to her back.

She reached the marketplace, where dirty Hua boys and girls ran about, kicking a ball. No Nothori kids were to be found, either excluded or just too scared with the Blue Reaper targeting them. A bridge lay at the far end. She hurried as fast as she could with her injured ankle and Mikayla's weight, shifting the child back and forth, from front to back, as her own spine tired.

A Fang stood guard, tattoos exposed, yelling across the trench. "You wouldn't dare come across. We'd send you downstream so fast..."

Yuna looked to the other side.

A Red Dragon flashed an obscene gesture. "The last time we crossed, we shat over half your territory!"

"Hardly half. You got two houses, for a couple of hours." The Fang's back was to her, his coin pouch out for everyone to see.

If the men were stationed there to keep each other out of their respective territory, they probably wouldn't care if she crossed. She slipped by the Fang, swiping his purse along the way. She tucked it behind her, between her back and Mikayla in the sling.

The bridge, which had looked like stone at a distance, was actually little more than several planks of wood nailed together. Lacking any kind of guard rails, it rested on footings that rose out of the trench. It held firm under Yuna's and Mikayla's combined weight.

"Hey, you little shit! You didn't pay the toll!" The Fang's hand breezed past her ponytail, catching only air as she took several quick steps toward the middle. He followed after them, his weight causing the wood to bow. Looking over her shoulder, she timed his next step...

And jumped just as his weight shifted. Coiling, she thrust her legs into the plank. Her ankle protested, but the reverberation sent his arms flailing. Timing the vibration, she sunk her weight again. The resulting crest threw him off the side and into the muck below.

Chortling, the Red Dragon on the far side pointed. "The shit is drinking downstream!"

The Fang surfaced, covered in sewage. He shook his fist at her. "Shit-sucker, I'm going to hunt you down, fuck you raw, and then slash your throat and send you downstream. Then I'll do the same thing to your little friend."

Yuna shuddered. How could life be so cruel?

The Red Dragon laughed, this time even more mockingly. "Come on across and find her."

She reached the other side, where the Red Dragon held out an arm, barring her way. Thin wisps of fuzz covered his upper lip, and his disheveled mop of black hair gave him a boyish look.

"You made the right choice," he said, "coming over to this side. Now you'll have to pay the toll."

She held out her open hands. "I don't have anything."

"That's what they all say." His hands roved over her, lingering in areas a gentleman's wouldn't on any woman, and certainly not on an eight-year-old girl.

Though Black Lotus training sometimes involved getting undressed in front of others to desensitize initiates and eliminate all sense of modesty, anger still surged into her face. When he spun her around, she switched the Fang's purse and her knife to the front fold of her robe. "I told you, I don't have anything. I'm new here. Looking for the magistrate's office."

"You really don't have anything." Shaking his head, he squeezed her rear with one hand while pointing with the other. His voice sounded almost sympathetic. "So many squirts like you. Orphans, who need to feed a little brother or sister. I have a sister, too."

So that's what he thought of her and Mikayla. Siblings. Something which could be used in the future. She nodded.

"Don't worry. We'll register you with the local magistrate. See that line of rooftops?"

Her gaze followed his finger. Indeed, a row of several stone buildings capped with red tiles rose two stories above the wooden hovels surrounding it. Compared to the Fangs' single tower, it was almost magnificent. Setting Mikayla down to ease her aching back and shoulders, she nodded.

The little girl's knees wobbled. She clutched the ragdoll to her chest with one hand, and clung to Yuna's hand with the other.

"That all belongs to us. Actually, everything, everyone, on this side of the Trench belongs to us." He laughed, then took her hand. "Come, we'll take care of you."

They'd take care of her, as long as she did what they wanted. And this particular goon probably wanted child's flesh. Yuna suppressed a shudder and resisted his pull. She pointed to the bridge, where the Blue Reaper would cross if there was no guard to stop him. "Don't you need to stand guard?"

"Nobody will cross at night. Too easy to slip and fall."

Or he just wanted to be the one to force himself on her, and maybe even on Mikayla, in some dark alley. Without little Mikayla to care for, he'd be easy to lose. "My Da told me never to trust a stranger."

"My name is Lin Gu." He bowed his head. "Now we're not strangers. What's your name?"

Using her real name might help, if Mikayla's older sister Rumei remembered a cousin. Maybe he even knew Mama. She bowed back. "My name is Feng Yuna."

His expression showed no sign of recognition, remaining as expectant as before.

She started to speak, but froze.

Further upstream, if the sludge could be considered a stream, came the sound of wood striking stone. Yuna peered into the shaded valley formed by hovels on either side of the trench. A dark figure was midway through a pole-vault from the Fang to Red Dragon side.

Her pulse jolted. Given the size, no doubt it was the Blue Reaper. Lin Gu undoubtedly had ill intentions, but with a Red Dragon escort, she'd have a little protection from a more dangerous threat. Or at least someone she could push into harm's way.

And in the meantime, she could probe him for information about Faceless Chang and Mikayla's sister, Rumei. Or maybe even Mama.

CHAPTER 6

Jie's every nerve tingled as she and Tian moved deeper into the alley. She held up a staying hand.

Tian froze. "What is it?"

"Shhhh." Jie's nose wrinkled and her ears twitched. Hiding among all the other foul smells hung a new scent. Water trickled in the distance, just above the din of conversations muffled behind closed shutters.

Wringing his hands, Tian sniffed like one of the White Temple dogs. No doubt his poor human nose wouldn't pick out much beyond the Trench's persistent stench.

She tapped and drew across his wrist. *Man urinating ahead.* He was picking up the code pretty quickly, so maybe he understood.

His face contorted, and he peered down the alley.

He might not see it, but indeed, someone in a tunic was pulling their pants up. He turned toward them. A local? The houses weren't large enough for a privy, so perhaps he was just out there to relieve himself.

Turn back? Tian tapped on Jie's forearm.

She shook her head. *No time. Let's go. Maybe local.*

His head bobbled back and forth, and he scrawled a pattern on her palm. *Long way to urinate.*

Long way. Yes, given the length of the alley, he would've had to walk a long distance to relieve himself. Unless he'd climbed out of the window. But why climb out, when he could just piss out of the window?

I know, she tapped. She moved his hand to the small of her back, where she clasped a knife. "That's what this is for."

"Oi! Who are you?" Given the man's confident tone and lengthening saunter, he was probably a Red Dragon.

"Just taking a short cut to our uncle's," Jie called.

"What do we have here?" The man came up to them, a broadsword slapping up against his thigh. Though the color was hard to discern in the low light, his tunic looked just like the other Triads', and he wasn't wearing the Blue Reaper's signature hat and face scarf. "It's not safe back here. I could've been the Blue Reaper, coming to reap a couple of squirts."

Jie bowed. "We'll be more careful."

Up close, the man had several scars on his beefy forearms. "I'm headed the same way. I'll take you."

"That's very kind of you," she said. Though up to now, none of the Triads had been kind or helpful without some other motive.

"The Red Dragons are here to protect you." He grinned. "But I can only take you one at a time. Boy, you stay here."

Expression contorting, Tian tapped his chin. He grabbed Jie's arm with both of his hands and pulled her back. "I'm scared. I need my sister."

The kid might be getting better at many of the clan skills, but acting wasn't one of them. No doubt he was worried about her, and for good reason. The Triad's muscled frame made him two and a half times her size, and his weapon and long arms gave him significant reach advantage.

Pushing Tian behind her, Jie took a few steps back. Enough was enough. These Triads were growing tiresome. How onerous life must be for the locals, especially the women and girls, to have to put up with them on a daily basis.

Despite his bulk, this one moved with the grace of a trained fighter. A former soldier maybe; but instead of seeking out work as a caravan guard or a mercenary in a foreign army, he'd come home to prey on the weak as a Triad.

"I can't leave my brother alone. He—"

"I told him to stay here." He seized her wrist and yanked her away from Tian. Pain seared in her back as the stitches on her spine and shoulder pulled. Her knife slipped from her fingers and fell into the dirt. With a kick from his huge foot, he sent Tian flying down the alley and into the side of a house. He pulled her down the path as if she were a little dog, and her shorter legs stumbled along.

She wouldn't stand a chance if she couldn't reestablish her footing. Despite decades of Black Lotus training to remain calm under pressure, her heart raced.

Shutters cracked open, sending lights dancing through the alley before they quickly shut again. Scooping up her knife, Tian jumped to his feet and ran after them. With his stumpy legs, he might not catch up; and lacking short blade training, maybe that was for the better.

Feet unable to find purchase, stitches searing, Jie staggered as the huge Triad dragged her. He'd probably done this to several girls already. How terrified they must've been in their last moments.

She took a deep breath. She wasn't a helpless little girl. Sooner or later, he'd come to a stop, to do whatever he intended. And then—

"Stop!" Tian yelled. Despite his extra weight, poor conditioning, and shorter legs, he was gaining ground.

"Persistent little shit." The Triad looked over his shoulder. With a snarl, he came to a halt.

Jie lunged feet-first into him. Locking his knees with one leg and his ankles with the other, she turned her weight over and squeezed him with a scissoring motion.

His grasp on her wrist loosened as he fell to his knees. The momentum sent him face-first into the dirt.

If she'd timed it wrong and he'd been prepared for the initial attack, he might've been strong enough to resist the scissor-kick. As it was, she drew his dagger and rolled on top of him. His body coiled, but went flaccid when she set the weapon to his carotid artery.

"Let me guess," she said, "you are the Blue Reaper."

"Of course not." His hands clenched and unclenched. "I'm not wearing a blue hat and face scarf."

"Stay still, or I'll slash your throat." Jie nicked him.

He grunted and went rigid. "You do, and you'll bring the Red Dragons on you and your family. Faceless Chang will make sure you don't die slowly, either."

"So many witnesses." Jie laughed, gesturing down the empty alley. "Which is why you bring helpless girls back here to do Heavens knows what."

He turned his head, trying to see her. "See all those windows? The neighborhood is watching."

Indeed, the shutters all up and down the alley were cracking open again. Tian came to a halt and hunched over. Hands on his knees, he heaved for breath. "Are you all right?"

"Yes." She motioned to the Red Dragon's broadsword.

Nodding, he pulled the blade, scabbard and all, from the brute's sash.

"Now," she said. "I don't think the neighborhood will care if a Red Dragon turns up dead. One less bully extorting money."

"You don't get it. Everyone on this side of the Trench is a Red Dragon."

Tian's eyes widened. "What do you mean?"

"The Red Dragons wouldn't exist if the neighborhood didn't support us. We find them jobs. Keep order. The money we collect goes to widows, cripples, and the elderly."

After Faceless Chang took his cut, no doubt. Jie raised her voice. "Does anyone mind if a predator of young girls goes missing?"

A chorus of *No*s echoed down the alley.

Beneath her, the Red Dragon went rigid again.

"Looks like you won't be missed." Jie made a shallow cut down the back of his neck. "But I'll let you live, if you answer some questions for me."

Tian gawked at her. He started to open his mouth, but she silenced him with a shake of her head.

The Triad's hands were again opening and closing. "What do you want to know?"

"I've heard Faceless Chang can be in more than one place at a time."

"He's like a Black Fist." The man cut his laugh short. "Except he doesn't steal naughty children at night."

The reference couldn't just be a coincidence. Jie exchanged glances with Tian. "So he's a Black Fist?"

The man chortled again. "Do you seriously believe in Black Fists? They're just a fairy tale."

"Enough with the games." Jie nicked him again. "How does he do it?"

"It's just part of his legend! He can't really be in two places at once."

So this Red Dragon, at least, didn't know about the Steel Orchid who served as Faceless Chang's body double. Or had, before Tian killed her. "All right then, what about the yue?"

"Just who are you?" He squirmed. "I know a kid your age won't smoke yue."

"You do realize I am the one asking the questions?" Jie dug the tip deeper, taking care not to puncture his artery. It was a shame the dagger was so dull compared to clan blades.

Nonetheless, he stilled. "We got the yue from up North, but the supply started to dry up a few weeks ago."

Jie sucked on her lower lip. Greedy Lord Ting was in charge of illegal yue production, and had decided to support the Fangs over the Red Dragons. It had resulted in his death at the hands of Lilian, Jie's lover; and led Jie first to uncover the identity of the surviving Steel Orchid twin. Which had now brought them to the Trench. This Triad probably didn't know it would dry up completely, now that imperial forces had shut down their suppliers. She looked to Tian. "Anything you want to ask him?"

Tian scowled. "How many little girls have you— "

Jie shut him up with a glare of her own. "Any relevant questions?"

Demurring, he tapped his chin. "Does Faceless Chang see any visitors from outside the Trench?"

Good question. Jie gave the boy an appreciative nod.

"I'm not his steward. I don't keep his schedule."

"Then you've never seen an outsider visit him?" she asked.

"No."

She turned to Tian. "Anything else?"

He shook his head.

"Now about those little girls you raped and murdered." Seizing the brute's hair, Jie jabbed the dagger into his eye.

He screamed. Tian gasped.

The Red Dragon bucked. If this was what it was like to ride a horse, then may she never need to do so. Still, with years of grappling practice, it was easy to adjust to his romping. She yanked his head back and stabbed his other eye.

Shrieking, he pushed up to his knees, and Jie hopped off. His hands shot to his ruined eye sockets. She moved around to his back and used his dagger to stab him in the groin. As he keeled over, she raked the blade through the tendons in the back of one of his knees. With the reverse motion, she sliced off one of his ears.

"Now," she said, coming around to his remaining ear, "you'll have a hard time terrorizing little girls. And maybe your Tang will take care of you like they do widows, cripples, and the elderly."

Tian's hand was on his mouth, and the brittle light from the hovels cast his face in a shade of green. He turned to the side and vomited. With the rest of his life committed to the clan, the boy would have to get used to gore.

The Red Dragon rolled onto his back, screaming. Jie's fingers darted into his open mouth, and with a smooth motion, she pulled his tongue out and slashed it off.

Tian's eyes rounded even more, and he swallowed hard.

Withdrawing a vial of flower toxin, she dabbed some it on the Triad's neck. In a few seconds, he slumped down, rolled onto his side and into unconsciousness. The poison would leave him with only hazy memories of the night, just in case they were still in the Trench tomorrow. Even if he could no longer talk, the less he remembered, the better.

"Look!" Tian pointed at the brute's inert form.

A dash of blue peeked out from the fold of the man's tunic.

Jie gave it a tug, revealing a blue scarf. Further searching uncovered a rumpled blue hat, and a pouch of silver and copper coins which she tossed to Tian.

She blew out a breath. Could it be? The timing from the last murder to their encounter just now was right. They'd inadvertently rid the area of the serial killer. She looked up, thankful that the alley ran in a direction that provided a view of the Iridescent Moon. Now waxing just past half, they had two hours to meet the informant.

"The Blue Reaper!" she screamed. "He's attacked a Red Dragon!"

Then she beckoned Tian along.

CHAPTER 7

Though Lin Gu's offer to take Yuna to the magistrate was likely a ruse for his undoubtedly ill intentions, she agreed to follow him as protection against the Blue Reaper. She scooped up Mikayla and slung her on her back.

"Such a good sister. Come on." Lin Gu flashed a grin, showing straight teeth.

With her ankle pain subsiding, she followed, keeping her ears and eyes open for the Blue Reaper. Like on the other side of the sewage ditch, people and merchants were clearing the marketplace. Curiously, though the Hua and Nothori didn't mingle beyond a few last-minute transactions, the Hua here didn't express such obvious contempt as those on the other side. All paused and bowed to Lin Gu as he sauntered by. As a Red Dragon, no doubt he was God on Earth to them, at least until a higher-ranking Triad came along.

The Blue Reaper was certainly following, either clinging to the shadows or perhaps removing his hat and face scarf and mixing in with the people. Her short stature and the lack of reflective surfaces made it impossible to spot him.

Though now his gaze no longer weighed on her. Had he broken off pursuit? Surely he wouldn't? Despite clan training in maintaining calm in the face of the unknown, her chest squeezed.

"What's wrong?" Lin Gu asked.

Heavens, was she that obvious? "I'm scared."

"You're under my protection." He thumped his chest. "No one will dare touch you."

"What about the Blue Reaper?" Or Lin Gu himself?

He broke out into a laugh. "You're right to worry. He's going after girl squirts. But I'd send him downstream if he tried."

Little girls? Not Nothori, like Aunty Luo had said? Or was Lin Gu trying to scare her into staying with him? She gave a tentative nod. "I'm looking for my cousin. I hear she joined the Red Dragons six years ago."

"Girls don't join the Triads." He gave a lurid grin. "At least, not like we men do."

Of course, Feng Rumei had been sold off to be a prostitute, and Lin Gu probably had similar ideas for Yuna. She held back a snort. "She would've been sixteen at the time. Maybe you know her?"

"I wasn't in the Tang back then." He shrugged. "And most girls don't last more than a couple of years."

An involuntary shudder ran through her. In the Floating World, a Blossom could receive men for twenty, even thirty years, though most had paid off their bond and saved enough to start a new life within ten. What happened to these Trench girls? Cast back out into the streets once they'd been used up? Murdered? "Her name is Rumei."

"Rumei." He scratched his head. "There's nobody by that name now, but most of the girls go by a nickname, anyway. Maybe one of the Older Brothers might remember who she is."

Hopefully Aunty Luo had lied, and Rumei was still alive. Maybe she'd take Mikayla in.

They continued along the dirt roads. The dwindling passersby, now all adult males, stopped and bowed to him. He dismissed them with a dip of a chin and continued on. Before long, the trickle of men slowed to a stop.

She looked over toward the row of buildings that served as the Red Dragons' Tang. "Big Brother Lin, we are farther from the Tang now."

"Yes, the direct route is dangerous." He licked his upper lip, the telltale sign of a lie. They way he'd groped her before left little doubt as to his intentions now.

Deserted area, fewer people... "You said I would be safe as long as I stayed with you."

"Of course you are. Come on." He beckoned her toward an alley.

Shaking her head, she froze in place. "I'd rather stay here."

His boyish features, which had looked friendly before, now contorted. "Don't be a pants-shitter. Come on."

Mikayla, awake again, whimpered. Maybe as an Empath, she could sense his ill intentions.

Without the threat of the Blue Reaper nearby, and Lin Gu taking her farther from the Red Dragons' Tang, he'd outlived his usefulness. Yuna feigned fear as she nodded. "All right."

He prodded her forward, and she pretended to stumble into the alley formed by the backs of rowhouses. It was narrow, and all the windows were shuttered. Wavering candlelight flickered between the cracks of wood.

To think, Mama grew up in a hovel like this, living in constant fear of being taken as a plaything for the Triads. Muscles coiled, every nerve ready to fire, she walked deeper in, Lin's presence hovering behind her. Soon, she'd end him.

Up ahead shutters were open, filling the alley with light. From beyond came low, pained moans, pitching above the chatter of the residents.

"Hurry," Lin Gu said, concern growing in his voice. He nudged her on.

Lying on his side in a pool of blood in the middle of the alley was a large man, his red tunic marking him as a Red Dragon. Both eyes had been gouged out, and an ear had been cut off.

Pushing past her, Lin Gu sucked in a sharp breath. "Big Brother Ni!"

The injured man moaned again.

"Shits!" Lin Gu knelt beside him. "What happened? Who did this?"

Only garbled sounds came out of his mouth.

Yuna's eyes shifted to a tongue lying on the ground, which explained why Big Brother Ni couldn't speak. Given the precision of the wounds, it was probably either Jie or the Blue Reaper who'd attacked him. Though given that Ni preyed on young girls, he was probably someone unfortunate enough to try and waylay the half-elf.

Or could he be the Blue Reaper himself? She scanned the area and found a blue scarf and rumpled blue hat. Of course. It would explain why the Blue Reaper had stopped pursuing her earlier.

"Did anyone see what happened?" Lin Gu's voice rose.

The alley faded back into darkness as windows closed. If there'd been any witnesses, they weren't going to be talking.

In any case, with Lin Gu now preoccupied with his Triad friend, it was a good time to give him the slip, without having to injure him. Yuna looked up to the Iridescent Moon, which now waxed half a phase toward its first gibbous. The informant would leave the magistrate's office in an hour and a half, and by now Jie had probably met with him. She was probably waiting for her at this very moment. Yuna backed away.

Mikayla let out a sniffled cry.

Lin Gu looked up and over his shoulder at her.

She froze.

From the way his forehead scrunched, any number of thoughts were bouncing around in his head. At last, his expression softened in what looked like relief. He stood, and when he spoke, his tone sounded resigned. "Come on, let me get you to the Tang. I need to tell the higher-ups about this."

Yuna's own brow furrowed. Just a moment ago, it seemed like Lin Gu had planned to take her into this quiet alley and do who knew what. Now he looked and sounded as if a burden had been lifted from his shoulders. She gave a tentative nod.

He took her hand, gently this time, and headed back the way they'd come.

There was a deeper story here. "You were working with Ni, weren't you?"

"What?" He skidded to a halt, jerking her to a stop.

"You were so excited before. That all changed when you saw Ni. Now, we're doubling back, away from the route you said was safe."

"Yes. Ni is the Blue Reaper." Lin Gu's shoulders slumped. "He likes squirts your age, and he'd been eyeing my sister. I begged him not to send her downstream, and he said he would leave her alone, as long as I brought him other girls."

Apparently the Blue Reaper had other interests, besides killing Empaths and their children. Yuna swallowed hard, considering: Lin Gu had planned on sacrificing her. Stuck in the same circumstances, she might consider doing equally evil things herself, if it could protect the ones she loved. How horrible the Trench was, where mothers sold daughters, and brothers would do horrible things to protect their sisters.

Mikayla was whimpering again. Had she lost that ragdoll? It was so worn, probably older than the girl.

"I'm sorry," he said.

"It's all right." Even if it wasn't. "You did what you had to do."

"No." Straightening, Lin Gu lunged and took Yuna's neck in both hands. "Sorry for what I'm going to do."

The pressure around her throat increased, preventing her from taking a breath.

He shoved her toward the wall of a shack. "I'm sorry. Really, I am. You know too much, and the Tang will send me downstream for it. But I'll make sure the Red Dragons take care of your sister. I swear."

There were only a few feet left before she'd be pinned to the wall. Pulse pounding in her temples, Yuna shrugged the sling off, letting Mikayla slip to the ground. Then she dipped her chin, creating enough space for a tiny breath. She seized one of his wrists and jumped. Twisting midair, she wrapped one leg over his neck and the other over his chest, trapping his arm between her knees. An arch of her back loosened his grip, allowing cool air into her lungs.

He grunted as his arm strained to bend against her leverage. He lifted her and started to slam her down, but she threw her weight into another twist, sending them both face-first into the ground. The packed gravel hurt, but not as much as it would hurt him. His elbow made a satisfying pop. He screamed.

Yuna climbed to her feet just as he was rolling over. She drove a heel into his head, and his body went still.

She took a few heaving breaths and drew her knife.

CHAPTER 8

Eyes puffy from having thrown up, Tian trailed after Jie. Unlike his own brothers, she hadn't made fun of him for weakness. If anything, she'd been understanding of his horror.

He cast one last look over his shoulder and sighed. The mean man had deserved it, and he wouldn't be able to hurt any more little girls. Still, to see such a maiming, executed with such coldblooded efficiency, was stomach-churning. Despite being stuffed in a cute little package, Jie was scary.

Picking up his pace, he caught up to her and whispered, "I'm glad you did that."

"Clan business," she whispered back. "It wasn't personal."

Crippling the man didn't seem to benefit the clan, though. Maybe she really did care about people. Their mission wasn't to eliminate the Blue Reaper, but to assassinate Faceless Chang because he might know about the true purpose of the Black Lotus Temple. Which meant... "If it turns out the Red Dragons don't know anything about the clan, aren't we now leaving evidence?"

She shrugged. "If what he said about the Red Dragons really caring about the denizens of the Trench is true, I don't think they would turn a blind eye to his extra activities if they knew. So maybe they'll assume it was the Blue Reaper who did it."

"Doesn't he only prey on girls?"

"Up to now. If we're lucky, maybe it will scare the Triads. Even though the serial killer has nothing to do with our mission, we can still help people. And people not living in fear can better serve the Empire."

The logic made sense, but it really sounded like she was trying to justify her actions as clan interest. Maybe it was better to keep quiet about it.

They continued in silence, sticking to alleys until they finally reached the magistrate's office, which lay at the end of a deserted street not far from a long row of tall stone buildings. Though not as ramshackle as all the peasant hovels in the Trench, in the light of the three moons, it still looked rundown compared to all the many other government offices he'd seen in his life. Moss and stains covered patches of the brick walls. The window shutters were faded and warped, as was the signboard over the double doors. In violation of procedure, no imperial soldier stood guard.

Jie swept a hand along the side of the doorway.

How fascinating! Tian leaned closer. "A key?"

"No; our informant leaves messages in the space between the bricks and doorframe. A clan courier comes by weekly to pick them up. No new messages since his last visit."

Tian looked up to the Iridescent Moon, now waxing to its first gibbous. They'd made it, with an hour to spare. Still... "The office is closed."

"Our contact works until the second gibbous."

"So we just knock?"

Jie shook her head as she ran a hand over the window shutters. "He won't answer."

Tian stared at her. "Then how do we contact him?"

"I'll go in and find him." Jie flashed a grin. "Come on."

Why didn't she just pick the lock? Tian followed as she went around to the side, which was shaded from the moon.

Jie sniffed. "Yuna hasn't arrived yet."

Yuna smelled like lavender, though he had to be close to detect it. She'd shoved him away when he tried to sniff her hair. On the other hand, the half-elf's sense of smell was nothing short of mindboggling. Now, she was looking up at the second-floor window.

He peered at the first-floor window right below. "Why the second floor and not this one?"

"Locked."

"And the second floor isn't?" Tian tapped his chin.

"There's always one unlocked window on the top floor of every government office."

Tian tapped his chin. "Why?"

"By imperial order, so that clan members can get in and out if they need to. Of course, only one person in each office knows to leave it unlocked every night."

"How can you tell which window?"

"It's marked in the shutter decorations." She pointed. "See the lotus flower?"

He peered through the night. Nothing except plain scrollwork. He shook his head.

"Once you know what to look for, you'll see it on every government office. Now go around to the front." She hopped up to the first-floor window's shutters and, using the wood as a foothold, proceeded upwards. Though the surface looked flat, her little fingers and toes found spaces between the bricks. Reaching the second-floor windowsill, she wiggled her dagger into the gap between the shutters. With a flick, they popped open, and she somehow managed not to get knocked back. She disappeared into the building.

He blew out a breath and pinched the flesh on the side of his waist. If the clan ever thought he would one day be able to do that, they'd be sorely disappointed.

His palms dripped as he headed around front. After their scary evening, there was no telling if more Triads or murderers would pass by while he stood there, alone. His heart thumped as he rounded the corner and came to the entrance.

In a few minutes, the doors swung open a crack. A hand grabbed his arm and pulled him in.

While every other magistrate's office boasted two-story entryways that flaunted the power of the imperial court, this one screamed of inattention. Illuminated by a light bauble hanging from the vaulted ceiling, the room had simple wooden benches on the side walls and a desk at the back. No hanging scrolls, no portrait of the Emperor, no carpet on the stone floor. An archway behind the desk was the only exit, save for the two windows in the front on both the first and second floors. The sound of a broom brushing across the floor emanated from beyond.

"That's our contact," Jie said, pitching her voice to carry. "I didn't see him on my way down."

The sweeping stopped. A man's crackling voice rang out, "Who's there?"

The tone was so gruff, Tian would've cowered behind Jie if she were any larger.

A wizened face appeared in the archway, eyebrows clashing together, followed by the rest of a body clothed in the robes of a government worker. The stooped man held a broom over his shoulder as if it were a cudgel. "Get out! The office is closed."

"Old Zeng, we're looking for Uncle Chi." Jie bowed her head and presented a small jade plaque in two hands. Wherever she'd been hiding that, all the Triads patting her down throughout the afternoon hadn't uncovered it.

"Heavens." The old man's brows relaxed, and his cracked lips rounded. He bowed low. "I never thought I'd see an actual agent. I didn't think they'd send children. How may I serve the Emperor?"

Tian craned his neck to get a better view of the jade plaque. Whatever it was had changed this Old Zeng's attitude in the span of a heartbeat.

"We need you to arrange a meeting with Faceless Chang," Jie said.

His eyes went wide as teacups. "Whatever for?"

"Imperial business." Jie held the plaque up.

The old man bowed to the plaque again. "It's not that easy. When he's inside the Tang, you'd have to pass an introduction with their entire senior hierarchy to meet with him."

"We saw him outside the Tang," Tian said.

"Then you probably saw him surrounded by his toughest guards. Did they let you get near?" Old Zeng sounded smug.

Tian shook his head. They'd kept everyone well beyond arm's length.

"So you see, you have no chance of meeting with Faceless Chang."

"Surely you have contacts inside the Tang?" Jie asked.

The man shuffled on his feet.

She harrumphed. "Then what does the Emperor pay you for?"

"I do, but..." His lip quivered.

"Have you been inside the Tang?" Tian asked. "Can you tell us what it looks like?"

Old Zeng studied him, then turned the broom upside down and traced lines on the floor. "It's eight buildings, with passages connecting them all on all three levels."

Jie held up a staying hand. "They're only two stories high."

Tian shook his head. From the height of the building... "There's an underground level."

"Smart boy." The old man grinned. "That was originally the storage level."

"Storage? For what?" Jie asked.

Tian jumped up and down as the histories came back to him. "They are part of the city's outer walls!"

"You know your history." The man beamed. "Go on."

Excitement built in his chest. "The Founder's Consort, as Queen Regent. She had them built to store arms and supplies. When she died at the great old age of one hundred twenty-four, the land was at peace. They'd only just started construction of the outer walls. Her heir thought it was a waste of funds, so they stopped."

"Right," Old Zeng said. "Anyway, Faceless Chang's office and residence is on the eastern side of the second floor. The only way to get there is by going to the steps on the western side of the first floor. All the first-floor windows are boarded up, and the only way in is from the first-floor doors on the eastern side."

The image burned in Tian's head. To get to Faceless Chang, they'd have to wind up and around, and go through who knew how many Triad guards. "What is on each floor?"

"First floor is gambling tables and a bar. Second floor is space for the Triads: barracks, offices, and the like."

Tian swallowed hard, not wanting to know the answer to his next question. "And the lower level?"

"Yue, opium, and prostitutes."

Tian shuddered. Down below, the stuffy air would smell of yue smoke and kissing women. How—

The front door creaked open.

Heart leaping into his throat, Tian spun around.

Yuna slid in between the two doors, and her eyes fell on them.

Relief washed over him; he smiled in spite of himself.

For the first time, she returned his smile.

"Get out!" the old man said. "We're closed."

"She is with us," Jie said, moving past Yuna and shutting the doors.

"The Emperor sent three children?"

Eyes shifting to Old Zeng, Yuna walked in, moving more slowly than before. Was she injured? Tian moved to help her, but then she unslung a weight from her back and eased it to the floor. It looked like...

CHAPTER 9

Yuna's shoulders ached from running with little Mikayla on her back. She'd let Lin Gu live, leaving him unconscious in the alley. With the Blue Reaper incapacitated, she'd been able to hurry over here without worrying about being followed. And for whatever reason, despite Tian's overall incompetence, there was something endearing about his genuine smile.

"She sure likes her doll." Tian leaned over the sleeping girl and inspected the ragdoll.

"It brings her comfort," Yuna said.

"It's really old." Brow furrowing, Tian drew a finger over the stitches.

The half-elf's stern expression showed she didn't care much for the doll. "A toddler? Why?"

Yuna licked her lips. "The Blue Reaper was going to kill her."

"The Blue Reaper can't hurt anyone anymore," Tian said. "Jie crippled him."

Yuna nodded. "He was tailing me for a while. He was very skilled. I couldn't shake him until he broke off pursuit."

"And attacked us." Jie nodded. "He had me worried for a moment, too. But what are we supposed to do with a toddler?"

Yuna licked her lips. To tell the truth meant revealing that she'd put blood ahead of the clan, and even now, that decision didn't make sense to her. Still, Jie was good at sniffing out lies. "She's my cousin."

Tian's lips rounded. "How?"

"Her mother is my mama's older sister."

"You went to visit family?" Jie raised an incredulous eyebrow.

Yuna swallowed hard. "Not on purpose. The foreign man we saw when we came into the Trench, Andris Dukurs, was her father."

"Was?" Jie asked.

"The Blue Reaper murdered him. With his dying breath, he made me promise to warn his wife that his daughter was in danger. I didn't know they would be my family."

Tian leaned over the sleeping girl again. "She doesn't look like she has foreign blood. At least, not as much as Jie."

"Jie is part elf," Yuna said. "So maybe that makes a difference. And Mikayla is still a very young child, so maybe her features will change as she matures."

"You shouldn't have brought her." Jie's gaze was so heavy with reprimand, it might've been a dwarf anvil.

It took all of Yuna's discipline not to squirm. After all, the clan came first. They were more family than her real family. "The Blue Reaper killed her mother, too."

"I understand why you'd want to help a girl. I would too, especially a cousin." Jie looked sidelong at the man, Old Zeng. "But we have pressing matters to attend to."

"Wait," Tian said. "I thought the Blue Reaper killed girls. Why would he kill the daddy?"

His comment allowed for a better excuse. "What we heard was wrong: in addition to girls, the Blue Reaper targeted Nothori Empaths. Andris was an Empath. So is his daughter." Yuna gestured to Mikayla, betting Jie would see the benefit to the clan.

"An orphan." Understanding bloomed on Jie's face.

"Even if we can't take her in, she's an excuse to visit the Red Dragons. They take care of orphans, and her late sister was once one of their prostitutes."

The old man *tsk*ed. "It's a shame. Too many girls, claimed too early."

"The Red Dragon said they registered people with the magistrate," Yuna said. "Maybe you would've heard of her?"

"What was your cousin's name?"

"Feng Rumei."

"Feng Rumei?" The man's gawked.

"You know her?" Tian asked.

"Everyone from back then knows *about* her. I might be the only one who knows her by that name, because I registered her household. Half-Nothori, Half-Hua. A real beauty. The Triads nicknamed her Ivory. And she was no prostitute. She caused the upheaval in the Red Dragons that led to Faceless Chang's rise."

"How is that?" Jie asked.

Old Zeng scratched his thinning hair. "If memory serves, Faceless Chang joined the Red Dragons twenty years ago. He was just a mid-level Triad around the time of his coup. He'd eyed Rumei for a while. Demanded that Andris Dukurs hand her over."

Yuna cocked her head. It didn't mesh with what Andris' friend had said about him selling his daughter to the Red Dragons, a story repeated by Aunty Luo years ago. Then again, stories had a way of changing over time...though usually to make the teller look better, not worse.

"Andris finally relented, and Faceless Chang claimed her. However, both the Red Dragon boss and his right-hand man coveted her."

Men. Stories throughout history told how they did stupid things because of a woman. "And Faceless Chang won?"

The man nodded. "Faceless Chang used Rumei to drive a wedge between the boss and his right-hand man. While they were busy scheming against each other, Faceless Chang built up his own supporters in secret, and was able to take over."

It was similar to a story from the Warring States Period, when the Hua people were emerging as a free people from the War of Ancient Gods. A warlord had sent his concubine, Lady Lanyu, to a rival king, ostensibly to seal an alliance. Really, it had been to break his enemy's focus as he became besotted with the girl. Yuna swallowed hard. In the end, Lanyu died. "What happened to Rumei? Her mother said she died."

The man's sigh was pregnant with emotion. "Because the Tang had fractured, and many of its senior hierarchy all wanted Rumei for themselves, Faceless Chang killed her."

"How horrible." Tian covered his mouth.

"Yes, a girl's life isn't worth a dragonfly's to the Triads." The old man shook his head.

Yuna's stomach churned. She'd never met her cousin, but the idea that anyone would be killed so callously, just for being a beautiful distraction, made her chest squeeze. Now, she had taken responsibility for another cousin. One she'd have to get out of the Trench, lest she share a similar fate.

Looking at her, Tian tapped his chin in the cutest way. "Why are they even called Triads?"

"It's from classic texts," Old Zeng said. "The Union of Heaven and Earth, through the Man in between."

Jie snorted. "It sounds like a righteous name for such horrible people."

For now, Tian's deflection to the Triads had made Jie forget about Mikayla. Yuna stifled her sigh of relief. "What can you tell us about them?"

"They were founded with the noblest intentions." The man let out a nostalgic sigh. "The current magistrate's predecessor was at wits' end. This area has always been poor, because nobody with money wanted to live near the exposed sewer. Desperate people do desperate things."

Yuna nodded. That's what had prompted Mama to sell her for four lousy coppers.

"The government demanded taxes, but provided no support. It was twenty-two years ago that the last troops were withdrawn from the barracks. So the magistrate organized young men under the banner Union of Heaven Earth, implying they worked with the Emperor's blessing. The ministries provided weapons and gave them the mandate to keep the peace and collect taxes—in exchange for them keeping a cut."

In theory, it didn't sound so bad. Still, without regulations and oversight...

"But then they started investing in prostitution and opium. Those brought in men and gold from the city. If it were just that, maybe things wouldn't have gotten so bad. But then the light-skinned refugees flooded in. Lietuvi and Iksuvi on the north side, and the Rotuvi on the south. They were desperate and worked thankless jobs for much less than we would. The locals went to the magistrate to demand the foreigners be expelled. He went to the Imperial Court, but the Ministry of Public Works had been bribed by the companies who hired the foreigners. So the locals turned to the Triads. Whatever influence the magistrate had, he lost."

Yuna's gaze raked over the foyer, whose size matched the grandeur of other government offices, but whose furnishings and overall cleanliness left much to be desired. "Why would anyone take this post?"

"Oh, with his salary, he still lives like a prince in the city. The Triads still pay him bribes and ensure the tax revenues meet the quota—that keeps the imperials out, leaving the Triads in charge."

Yuna held in a sigh. It couldn't go on like this, with the Triads bullying the Nothori and squeezing the locals for what little they had. Maybe they'd be better off eliminating more than just Faceless Chang. "Elder Sister, here's a new idea that can help us bypass the

Red Dragon hierarchy. Mikayla is Feng Rumei's sister. I can bring her to the Tang as an excuse to meet with Faceless Chang."

Old Zeng shook his head. "Even if he were interested, you would still end up meeting with a low-level Red Dragon first."

"And from our interactions with the Triads up to now," Jie said, "we'd probably have to sleep with every underling before we even had a chance to talk with someone high up enough to get us close to Faceless Chang." She turned to Old Zeng. "Who is your highest-level connection in the Red Dragons?"

Old Zeng shuffled on his feet, lips tight.

"If you don't tell me," Jie said, "I'm going to recommend the Emperor find a new contact."

Old Zeng paled. "Black Hand Jing. He's mid-tier, and he is sympathetic to the magistrate's office. He could help you bypass the lower levels, maybe even get you into the main building...with the right bribe."

So Black Hand Jing's sympathy only went as far as money could buy. Yuna turned to Jie, and signed, *Easier to stake out the Tang and kill when he comes out.*

He might not come out until tomorrow. We need to finish tonight. Jie gave a slight shake of her head and turned to Old Zang. "How do we make contact with Black Hand Jing?"

"He has a black hand and arm to cover old tattoos. He's usually around the brothel entrance at night." Old Zeng fished in the sleeves of his robe and withdrew a metal disk with characters inscribed on it. "Give this to him, tell him what you want, and he'll tell you how much it will cost."

Yuna looked to Jie, who was sucking her lower lip. She was no doubt scheming multiple ways of getting close to Faceless Chang.

Something didn't sit right in Yuna's gut. As it was, Old Zeng didn't know their mission, but there was no way to understand the potentialities without asking. "What would happen if Faceless Chang were removed from the picture?"

Old Zeng didn't look the least surprised by the question. "He's better than any of his predecessors. The locals might not like the Rotuvi refugees, but he's ensured they aren't treated badly."

"I'm surprised a Triad would even care," Jie said.

"Most don't. There was a time about two years ago when Faceless Chang would disappear for days on end, and the Red Dragons acted more like the Fangs in terrorizing the residents of their turf."

"Where did he go?" Tian tapped his chin.

"He was going into the city to spend time in the Floating World." Old Zeng opened his mouth, but then closed it.

Yuna had still been training at the temple, and hadn't been living in the Floating World back then. She looked to Jie and signed, *Wouldn't we know if a small man with a scarred face was frequenting the Houses?*

Jie gave a subtle nod of agreement.

"Setting up Yue Heaven?" Tian asked.

Yuna chewed on her inner cheek. The web of connections was too convoluted: Yue Heaven had been the den selling a highly-addictive variant of yue. The partnership between Lord Ting—whom Lilian, Jie's lover, had assassinated—and the Red Dragons, had led to the revelation that one of the Steel Orchids had survived the Floating World fire decades before.

"Maybe." Jie prodded Old Zeng. "Go on, you were going to add something."

"One of his lieutenants, Du, had introduced him to an alluring Blossom. I thought Du was trying to take over the Tang while Faceless Chang dallied in the Floating World." Rubbing his hands, Old Zeng leaned in and grinned. "Rumor has it that Du got to his position by being Faceless Chang's Peach Bottom."

Tian's forehead crinkled up. He hadn't shown signs of knowing the dance between men and women, which meant he probably had no idea about men who enjoyed each other's' company. Yuna, on the other hand, shared a nod with Jie. There was a House in the Floating World that catered to that type of entertainment, and its boys were quite charming.

"Regardless of salacious rumors," Old Zeng said, "Faceless Chang knows that less conflict is good for business. City folk looking for cheap opium and prostitutes are more likely to visit this side of the Trench than the Fang's side. Same with farmers selling leftover produce. When he came back for good, things were right again."

Yuna turned to Jie and signed, *If we kill him, the locals will suffer.*

Jie shook her head. *Clan anonymity comes first.*

If only there were a way to remove Faceless Chang without throwing the Trench into turmoil.

CHAPTER 10

With little Mikayla weighing her down, Yuna stood in the shadows of the closest hovel. Tian hunched over, hands on his knees, tired from having carried the kid for a block, and Jie was busy scanning the row of two-story rowhouses that served as the Tang for the Red Dragons. Yuna followed the half-elf's lead and studied the buildings.

Made of brick with pitched tile roofs, the structure didn't look much like unfinished city walls. How had Tian noticed that detail before? As Old Zeng had described, the first-floor shutters had boards nailed across them, but the second-floor windows were all open. An eight-foot diagonal bamboo grid fenced in the rowhouses, forming something of a compound. Guards patrolled the perimeter.

Red lanterns, whose script revealed they'd been salvaged or stolen from the Floating World, hung from posts on either side of the gateway. They shined on men filing in, all better dressed than the denizens of the Trench, but certainly far below the affluent patrons of the Floating World's elite Houses. Young women and girls stood by the doors, all wearing clothes that revealed more than they hid, beckoning towards potential clients.

Some weren't much older than Yuna. Stomach twisting, she swung her cousin around and patted her on the back to keep her from crying. Jie had agreed: if the little girl were truly an Empath—or at least had the potential to become one—she was almost too valuable to bring here. It'd been tempting to tell Tian to remain with the child at the magistrate's office and stay out of the way, but as Yuna pointed out, Feng Rumei's little sister was the easiest way for one of them to get in.

Jie turned to her. "You take Mikayla to Black Hand Jing, and see if he'll introduce you to Faceless Chang. We are going to go around back, and I'll climb to the second floor and see if I can locate Faceless Chang myself."

Yuna nodded. It was the plan Tian had outlined, and they'd filled in. "When one of us can get into a position for the kill, first come to any of the second-floor back windows and signal Tian."

"And then I'll make a loud sound." Tian tapped his chin. "What kind of sound?"

Jie patted him on the head. "Screech like a peacock. If you see anything out of the ordinary, caw like a crow."

"I can't make those sounds. And what counts as *anything out of the ordinary*?"

Yuna chuckled. He was almost cute in his uselessness.

"Use your best judgement," Jie said.

Which up to now hadn't necessarily been reliable. Still, taking him into the compound was a liability, and he *was* observant. Yuna gave him a pat which was probably too fond, since they'd only known each other for less than a week.

"Once we hear Tian's peacock screech, whoever isn't close to Faceless Chang will draw guards away. The other will wait a few minutes and move in for the kill."

Drawing a circle with her finger, Jie led Tian toward the back. Hefting Mikayla higher on her back, Yuna set off toward the line of men. As she passed them on the way to the front, several whistled and heckled.

"I'll take that new one." A somewhat nicely-dressed man pointed at her.

His companion smacked him on the head. "I'll pay double, if she's a virgin."

"Of course she is!"

"You never know in the Trench."

Yuna kept her head down. The Floating World Hummingbirds might ogle her, but none would be so blatantly rude as these dredges. They might've worn nicer clothes than the locals, but their souls were dirty.

Out of the corner of her eye, she found the prostitutes near the entrance. Behind their seductive smiles and suggestive body language hid fear and desperation.

Her gut roiled. By the time she reached the front of the queue, a sour taste stuck to the back of her throat. Despite the years of clan training, her stomach heaved, and she had to bend over and cover her mouth. The line quieted. Several of the waiting patrons jumped back, looks of horror on their face.

Good. If they were disgusted, they were less likely to harass her. She looked up and met the glare of a stocky Triad gatekeeper.

He poked her. "Handouts are in the morning...wait. Big Brother Du." He beckoned a wiry, dour-looking comrade from inside the fence.

Yuna held her breath. Could this be the same Du who'd tried to take control of the Tang from Faceless Chang two years ago? And had been his Peach Bottom, if Old Zeng was right?

"What is it?" Big Brother Du approached, hand on a broadsword.

"I don't recognize this one. Do you?"

Du's eyes fell on her, and his hand left his sword. He held up a lantern to her face and leaned in. With her stomach already in rebellion, the smell of sausage and garlic on his breath when he spoke nearly made her vomit. "She's not from this side of the Trench."

Yuna bowed her head. "Kind sirs, Black Face Jing told me to bring this child to him."

"What's so special about it?" The second shifted the light over to Mikayla, who shielded her eyes and burst into tears. His sleeve sank into the crook of his elbow, revealing a lean forearm with a tattooed dragon coiling around it.

"*She* is the sister of Feng Rumei."

"Rumei?" Du stepped back. "*The* Rumei?"

"Who's that?" The first cocked his head.

"You're too young to remember. Real beauty, that one. Such a shame Faceless Chang made an example of her." He leaned in closer. "But if this girl is her sister..."

Exposing Mikayla to these goons had been a horrible idea. Yuna pulled the girl closer to her. "Blackface Jing—"

"That bastard wants the credit for dredging the kid up himself!" Du looked to the girl first, then reached for Yuna. "Come with me."

Yuna shrank back. This would get her close to Faceless Chang, but if she failed, it would condemn Little Mikayla to a life of being a Triad plaything. "But Blackface Jing—"

The second's hand clamped down on her shoulder, but she twisted a fraction, leaving him with a handful of her dress. She could break free, but to what end? Several of the clientele had crowded in behind her, making escape all the more difficult, and she needed to either locate Faceless Chang or create a diversion, anyway. She relaxed, and let the Triad guide her in through the front door.

The din of people chattering, clattering tiles, and clinking coins greeted her. Smoke hung around the ceilings, filtering the light from bauble lamps and cloying the air with the heady smell of yue. Men, some with scantily clad women on their laps, sat at tables, gambling at Cover Coins or Mahjong. More half-naked women roved around, some carrying spicy-smelling alcohol, others looking for a client for a quick tumble. Archways to either side led out of the room to equally loud spaces.

Visitors looked upon Du with fearful eyes and made way as he pulled her through the crowds to the west side arch. It felt different from the locals earlier in the day, who treated the Triads with respectful awe. As they got closer to the exit, a pack of boys in red tunics marched through, ranging in age from six to ten. They all bowed their heads and saluted Du with fists in their palms.

Du stopped. "Have any of you seen Black Hand Jing?"

"He's managing the fucking rooms." One of the younger boys gestured to the opposite arch.

Such vulgar language for kids so young. Yuna looked from him to the handsome boy beside him. They looked so similar, not so much like cherry pairs, but more like a snap pea pod and snow pea pod. They had to be brothers. Had to be...twins. She couldn't help but stare. They looked like her, too.

"What are you looking at, whore?" the thinner one said.

The other boys laughed. It made her feel so small and dirty, despite the fact that she really was training to be a courtesan.

"Shut up, Feng Qi." Du clapped him on the head and turned to her. "This is our honored guest. Right...what's your name?"

Yuna was never at a loss for words, but now she could only gawk. Feng Qi was indeed her younger brother. Which meant the other was Feng Tan. And they were involved with the Red Dragons at the tender age of six.

"What, can't find your tongue?" Du slapped her in the shoulder and laughed.

Did Mama ever tell them about her? There was one sure way to find out. "Feng Yuna," she said, studying their reactions.

She could've said *Zhang Li*, the most common girl's name in the Empire, for all the interest they showed. Maybe Mama had never told them about an older sister? Maybe she had just never told them her name?

Why did her knees feel like gelatin? It's not like Mama had ever cared for her, beyond the four coppers she'd made. The clan did care, though. Gritting her teeth, Yuna turned to Du. "Boys are gross. Can we continue?"

"You better get used to them. Come along." Du laughed and led her toward the next room.

The boys dispersed behind her, and she resolved not to look back at her twin brothers ever again.

"Out of my way!" A woman's shrill voice rose from the entrance, above the din.

That voice! A shiver ran up Yuna's spine. She kept her eyes forward.

"Feng Qi, Feng Tan! What did I tell you about coming here?"

Against her better judgment, Yuna looked over her shoulder toward the door.

The burly doorman was holding a woman back, though he was surprisingly gentle. Many of the gamblers had paused to watch. Feng Qi and Feng Tan were now ducking behind larger patrons.

"I see you, you little good-for-nothings!" Mama jabbed a finger in their direction. She'd filled out, no longer a fresh-faced seventeen-year-old, but worn by another six years living in the Trench.

Yuna froze in place. To think, Mama had been only fifteen when Yuna was born. Younger than some of the clan sisters who had yet to flower with Heaven's Dew.

"Never mind that crusty bucket." Du gave Yuna a tug. "Doesn't know what's good for her."

It was true. She didn't. With a nod, Yuna took a decisive step toward the next room. A step away from a miserable past and toward—

"Had I known you shits would turn into little thugs, I would've never given up your sister!"

CHAPTER 11

Jie watched Yuna head toward the Red Dragon Tang before readying herself for the more challenging insertion. Sending Mikayla, a potential future asset, into possible danger wasn't the brightest idea, but it would certainly provide a distraction.

With one last emphatic nod to freeze Tian in place, she tied her skirts into a knot between her knees, and worked her way to the back of the compound. She dashed to the fence, placing herself in the dark gap between the patrols' light bauble lamps. Sneaking along in the same direction they circled, she evaluated the fencing. Lashed together with cord, the bamboo posts were enough to support her weight, and the space in between wide enough for her to pass through. Clearly, it was meant to keep adult male intruders out. She jumped through—

Her hair snagged in the joint between two bamboo posts, dislodging one of her bladed hairpins. It fell into the dirt on the other side, the crunch in the dirt loud in her elf ears. The next guard was so close, maybe he'd heard it too. With the light approaching, there wasn't any time to get it, and he probably wouldn't see it on the other side, anyway. She ran over to the boarded window of the closest building.

The muffled sounds of rolling dice, clinking coins, and laughing men proved Old Zeng's description correct: the first floor served as a gambling den. No matter what purpose these buildings had served in the past, they were likely connected through interior passages—either in their original design, or through Triad renovations later.

The next patch of light shifted across the wall toward her as a guard followed his path along the wall. Running on tiptoes to stay ahead of it, Jie leaped and grabbed one of the horizontal boards nailed across the shutters of the next window. She swung, caught the top of the shutters and pulled herself up, then reached to the sill of the lit second-floor window. She raised her body into a horizontal position—

The light passed over the lower half of her body and paused.

Had the guard seen? Fingers aching from holding herself up, she gritted her teeth and looked. Dressed in the same red tunic as his fellow goons, he tilted his head left and right, gaze raking across her current position. Her body was out of the light now, but if he came closer and raised it—

He started toward the building.

Feet first, she arched herself up and in.

"Intruder!" the man yelled.

Now inside, the windows on the opposite side provided a view of the city walls. With a quick scan revealing sturdy wood doors on either side, the west one unbarred with a key in the lock, Jie ascertained this spacious room was some kind of antechamber to the one on the east. The finely-carved bloodwood chairs and low table all showed signs of repair. They sat on a thick wool carpet, which was made from sewn-together scraps of differing designs. Along with the patched brush paintings and decorative bauble lamps, the contents of this room alone, even repaired and refurbished, would've been worth more than the rest of the Trench combined.

Based on Old Zeng's layout, this room would be close to Faceless Chang's office and bedchambers. Why would it be empty? She tilted her head to listen to the door to the east. A woman's muted moans barely made it through, but left little doubt what was going on. She turned to listen to the opposite door.

"Intruder! Second floor!" the man's voice came from outside, almost directly below.

Heavy footsteps stuttered over creaky floors on the other side of the door to the west. Jie dashed over to its side, just as it burst open. She put her hands out to slow it to a stop, to prevent the brackets for the bar from impaling her, and also using it as cover from the newcomer.

If the guard warned Faceless Chang of an intruder, all hope of catching him unawares would dry up like a drop of rain in the desert. Jie withdrew her knife and peeked around the door that was hiding her.

Across the room, a burly Triad held his ear to the door.

She eased her door shut. Tiptoeing over, Jie worked her way towards his back.

The man started to knock.

She flung the knife. It whirled through the air and lodged in his nape. He let out a squelch as he clawed at the back of his neck, then started to collapse toward the door.

Bounding over, Jie eased him to the ground before he crashed. Knee to his chest, covering his mouth with a hand, she put her ear to the door and listened. The moaning continued, so the amorous couple either hadn't heard the guard's death cry, or just didn't care. She applied pressure, but when the door didn't budge, she inspected the locking mechanism. Dwarf-made; it wouldn't be too hard to pick, but Faceless Chang might detect the snick.

Several sets of footsteps rattled up a flight of wooden steps to the west, in the same direction the guard had come from. She dashed back across the room, and closed the door. After turning the key, she lowered the bar onto the brackets. Still, it wouldn't be long before the reinforcements raised a ruckus as they tried to barge through.

With all this running, maybe she should take the safer job as clan courier. Though that might involve horses. She hurried over to the window closest to Faceless Chang's office and looked out.

The window to the office was too far away to reach with a jump, and would probably make too much noise. Instead, she climbed through the window, then went up onto her tiptoes and reached up to test the roof tiles. They felt sturdy and well-attached, so she pulled herself up to the roof. With little time before the reinforcements arrived, she shimmied stomach-down along the edge of the eaves. The sharp slope made it a challenge, but when she made it to the spot above the first window, she kicked off one shoe and caught it, and then used her bare toes to pull off the second shoe. She reached back and grabbed it, then stuffed both into her sash.

The moaning grew louder here. From her years training to be a courtesan in one of the most famous Houses of the Floating World, it sounded as if Faceless Chang was either close to bringing the woman to climax, or she wasn't bad at faking it.

Twisting while clasping the end of the tiles, Jie lowered herself headfirst until she dangled by her waist. She gripped the arched tiles higher up with her toes and withdrew a mirror. Stretching out, she angled it to provide a view of the office.

If the antechamber had been luxurious, the office might've been a room in the imperial palace. A wool rug in the red-and-blue medallion design of the Ayuri South covered most of the floor, though it had been stitched so the geometric shapes didn't line up. Exotic flowers bloomed in porcelain planters, which in turn were decorated with the five-clawed dragon reserved for the Emperor himself. Intricately carved bloodwood chairs with plush blue cushions faced a huge matching desk which would dwarf an ogre. Another door lay directly behind it.

Angled diagonally from the window, someone was sitting on the edge of the desk, leaning back with their fingers gripping the sides with white knuckles. The horns of his demon mask marked him as Faceless Chang. His back was arched and his head bent back. His hiked-up red silk robes bared smooth bent legs, the space in between occupied by the head of a kneeling woman in a pink gown. Its elegant cut was more suited to a courtesan of the Floating World than a Trench streetwalker. The slurps of a lashing tongue left little doubt what she was doing.

Or did it?

Jie's brow furrowed. Something was wrong with the position, and it didn't take an apprenticeship in the Floating World to tell what: the way Faceless Chang's legs were spread, knees and ankles up. The woman's head wasn't moving in the right direction, and really wasn't in the right place for...what was it called in the Floating World? *Polishing Jade*?

Faceless Chang's scream of ecstasy left no doubt at all.

She was a woman.

The prostitute lifted her head, revealing the side profile of a pretty face marred by multiple cuts. Stitched in the Black Lotus Clan's standard pattern.

It took all of Jie's control not to gasp.

It was Lusha, once the most celebrated Blossom of the Peony Garden—its Corsage. She'd tricked Jie into an encounter which had forfeited her record virgin price, and Lilian had ruined Lusha's face for it.

Now she was here. No wonder her pink dress had looked so familiar.

It all made sense now. When they'd first seen Faceless Chang in the marketplace, it seemed as if he'd spotted them. Just like when the surviving Steel Orchid, Gardener Ju, had spotted her a few nights before, inside the Floating World. Gardner Ju and Faceless Chang had the same build, moved in a similar fashion. And he'd joined the Red Dragons twenty years ago, right when the Floating

World burned as cover for at least one of the Steel Orchids to escape the clan. Maybe the identical twin hadn't really died in the blaze.

CHAPTER 12

Tian wrung his hands as he peered through the darkness at the scrambling guards. They'd seen Jie, and sounded the alarm. Patrons had already started trickling out with the Triads' not-so gentle prodding, a handful coming up the side streets. What was he supposed to do now?

Probably nothing, really. They hadn't really needed a lookout. After all, he couldn't even imitate a peacock screech, and they had several ways of contacting each other. It was all an excuse. They just didn't want him to get in the way. He folded his arms in front of his chest. If that's—

A dark shape darted from the far side of the street to the fence.

Tian squinted. If only he could see in the dark like Jie.

As it was, the dark blob barely stood out from the rest of the sea of blackness. Like the half-elf, it crept halfway between the lights of the patrols. In quick succession, two thin lines of red light, like burning embers, flared in one of the horizontal pickets, two feet apart. When Tian blinked, the shape was standing on the other side.

How was that even possible? He had to know. He started forward, when a voice that sounded suspiciously like Jie's reminded him to stay put. Maybe that's what she'd said, but he was supposed to be a lookout, and surely she'd want to know about this new intruder. Even now, it worked its way toward the rowhouses.

The guard walking ahead of it froze, the lamplight stopping with him. The intruder walked right into it.

It wore a brimmed hat and blue scarf around its face.

The Blue Reaper! He stepped back into the darkness, even as the light from the next guard approached.

How could this be? Unless…though this Blue Reaper was stocky, he wasn't as large as the man he and Jie had encountered. And Yuna had said the Blue Reaper targeted Nothori Empaths. The man they'd faced had gone after Jie; and while girls were still out playing on the other side of the Trench, they'd all cleared out of the marketplace on this side.

There were two Blue Reapers. Or, one Blue Reaper and someone taking advantage of the Blue Reaper's notoriety. Now why would the real one be here?

To finish the job he'd started with Andris, in all likelihood.

Neither of the Triads seemed to have taken note of him, and for Tian, it had been hard to keep track of him when he stepped into the light, then back into the dark.

The second guard stopped where the Blue Reaper had entered and studied the fence. "This is strange."

"So is this." The first one knelt down, reached through the fence, and picked something up. It was the spot Jie had entered. Maybe she'd dropped something? "A long, thin blade. Maybe it belongs to our intruder. What do you see over there?"

Tian gritted his teeth. Jie'd dropped evidence of the clan. He peered into the line of dark between the two lamps, and again, thin, vertical lines of light, like burning embers, appeared in the wall of the building.

"A straight burn line in the bamboo." The guard shrugged. "Maybe I just never noticed it before."

Now the two lights converged as the second guard met the first.

The Blue Reaper had disappeared from the last spot he'd been in.

"Men!" called a voice from above.

Tian looked up.

Another Triad stood in the same second-floor window that Jie had entered, beckoning. "Guard the side entrances!"

The two men on the ground saluted, and ran off to opposite sides of the building.

Tian tapped his chin. He was supposed to stay here, but those red lines of embers called to him. And the Blue Reaper. None of their plans had taken him into account. With a quick check to ensure no one was around, he hurried over to the Blue Reaper's—what did Jie call it?—insertion point. It was too dark to see, and using a light would alert anyone nearby to his presence, so he felt the burn lines with his finger. They felt smooth, no different from— Pain flared in his finger and he jerked his hand back.

One of the spots had a sharp edge. He pushed on the bar, and it slid free. In the dim light, it looked like the edge was a perfect cut, like a *dao* sheering through rolled reed mats. He walked through, and then reset the wood into the fence, where it glided into place perfectly.

Too perfectly. A saw would've left a gap.

Maybe this was a bad idea. Gulping hard, he crept over to the spot by the building where the Blue Reaper had last been. Muffled sounds came from inside. Two horizontal boards were nailed across the wood shutters. In the darkness, the burn lines were just barely visible in the seam between the shutters and the outer edge. He gave the shutter a light pull, and it swung open, faster than he could control it.

He ducked down.

When nobody came to investigate, he rose and peeked in.

The stink of yue assaulted his nose, which scrunched up of its own accord. Eighteen square tables, each with four chairs, fanned out from the center of the room in a disturbingly haphazard fashion. Mahjong and other game tiles lay scattered across the tabletops. The Red Dragons were hustling many of the patrons out, though some games continued, with men casting quick glances over their shoulders at the guards. For now, none were looking at him.

"Hurry," a gambler said at a nearby table, motioning to a game where they were removing four coins from a rotating platter.

Which way would the Blue Reaper have gone? The departing patrons would've seen him if he'd headed in that direction, so the other?

He swallowed hard. This could get him in big trouble, but he needed to warn Yuna and Jie about the Blue Reaper. He set his hands on the windowsill, bent his knees, and jumped.

And didn't reach high enough to straighten his arms. He landed back on the ground. Maybe Yuna was right about him needing to lose some weight. He tried again, this time using his toes to scramble up the side of the wall. The dirt layer on it didn't make the climb easy. Arms straightening, he leaned forward. His weight listed, and he tumbled headfirst into the room.

This would be a quick end to his misadventure. He looked around...

...only to find no one was paying attention. Rising, he brushed himself off and started toward the left.

He skidded to a stop near a table where the dealer had just dumped a pile of coins onto the rotating platter. The four patrons leaned forward, eyes roving. He looked. Twenty-three coins in all; the dealer started removing four coins at a time until only three remained.

"Number three wins." The dealer tossed a clinking bag of coins on the table in front of one of men.

This had to be Cover Coins, a game of pure chance. Father sometimes played it with other nobles, bidding favorite pieces of jewelry and other trinkets. The dealer poured another mass of coins, thirty-five this time.

Tian pointed to the previous winner. "You win again!"

Five sets of wide eyes shifted him to a split second, with all but the dealer's returning to the pile of coins on the platter. The dealer turned and beckoned to a guard.

A stupid mistake! Time to get out of here. Tian started toward the next room, when a familiar voice cried out in the one behind him.

"Mama," Yuna was saying. "I'm a good girl now."

He froze. Yuna always spoke like a grown-up, using big words. Now, she sounded her real age; like Princess Kaiya, even. He crept back with the flow of patrons.

In the next room, Yuna looked different. She'd always carried herself with elegance as a Seedling in the Floating World, and played a convincing role of downtrodden child of the Trench. Now, though, her expression looked desperate in a different kind of way.

"Yuna?" asked a grown-up woman. The blood was draining from her face with each of her rapid breaths.

"Yes." Yuna started forward, arms outstretched.

"Yuna? You know her?" An even younger boy in the red tunic of a Red Dragon pushed forward.

"Uh, no." The woman swallowed hard. "I... I just overheard them say her name."

Anger flared in Tian's cheeks. If this was really Yuna's mother, how could she just deny it?

"Then why did she call you Mama?" Another boy joined the first. Standing together, they had to be brothers. And their faces looked like Yuna's.

Yuna's slumped shoulders straightened. "Because she is my mother. I am your sister."

Still clutching the old doll with the intricate stitches, Little Mikayla burst into tears.

"Is it true?" the first boy said.

"Yes." The woman's expression hardened. She pointed at Mikayla. "Did the priests knock you up? Or did you come back and start hooking? You're just as bad as your brothers."

Tian clenched his fists. A voice that sounded suspiciously like Princess Kaiya's in his head urged him to go to Yuna's defense. Another voice, which was undoubtedly Jie's, told him to stay hidden.

Yuna's cheeks flushed as she shook her head. "Heaven's Dew hasn't even arrived."

"Dew? What the hell is that?"

Tian wondered, too. The clan members in the Floating World had talked about it. How Heaven could have dew didn't make any sense.

Yuna looked from the twin boys, to the stragglers among the crowd of departing visitors, to the Triads. Her face glowed brighter than the Floating World lanterns. "This is Aunty Luo's daughter, Mikayla."

The mother's brow furrowed. "Mi-what?"

"Feng Mi is her name in our language."

The woman's head tilted. "She had another child?"

"I don't get it." The second boy jabbed an accusing finger at her mother. "You said our sister died after you gave her away!"

"You'll all be dead if you don't shut up." An older, lanky Triad snapped his fingers at a group of Triads. "Come on, we're taking them to Faceless Chang."

One of the men grabbed Yuna's wrist and yanked her along. Little Mikayla's beloved ragdoll fell to the floor, and she burst out crying. The other Triads prodded Yuna's mother, and her brothers followed.

Screams erupted from below.

"The Blue Reaper!" a man yelled, voice muffled by the floorboards.

Tian scooped up Mikayla's doll and hurried after Yuna.

CHAPTER 13

Head reeling from the revelation that Faceless Chang might be the remaining Steel Orchid, Jie pulled herself back up to the rooftop. Discretion was the better part of valor, and it would be better to take this information back to the clan, formulate a foolproof plan, and strike with twenty operatives.

After all, the identical twin that she and Tian had killed two days before had proven skilled in combat, able to avoid a tight barrage of throwing stars thrown at her back. This one might be equally talented, if all the old stories about them were true. And the Triads were aware of an intruder. She'd know about her twin's death, and be prepared for a possible Black Lotus strike.

Her languid moans, however, suggested she hadn't given the possibility of imminent death much thought. At this moment, she was alone and vulnerable, and by the time the clan was ready she might've already gone to ground.

The time to strike was now.

And soon, because the flurry of activity in the other rooms indicated the Triads were coming in force to warn Faceless Chang. The door she'd locked and barred probably wouldn't hold them for long, and the ruckus they'd raise trying to ram it open would be just as good a warning as any verbal alert. It was time to get Tian to try his best rendition of a peacock, so that Yuna could create a distraction.

He would be scanning the windows, not the roofline, so Jie would need to lower herself one more time to allow the light from the window to silhouette her. She looked to the corner where Tian was hiding...

...and had to suppress a curse.

He wasn't there!

This had to be done now. Jie crept across the rooftop to the easternmost of the rowhouses, and lowered herself at the closest of the two windows. Like all the others on the second floor, its shutters were open. Partially-closed bauble lamps cast the room in a dim light. A large canopy bed made of bloodwood sat at the far end, and a matching armoire lay between two windows opposite her. The porcelain wares all shared the same imperial motif as the antechamber and office, and brush paintings decorated the walls. For a Steel Orchid, famed for their unparalleled feminine wiles in their heyday, Faceless Chang had an austere, masculine taste in décor. Or at least, kept up the appearance of masculinity.

Listening for any signs of life, Jie grabbed the top of the window, twisted, and swung in. The thick wool rug, which covered almost the entire floor, made her landing silent. A quick scan revealed no weapons, but as a former Black Lotus operative, Faceless Chang would've hidden throwing stars, knives, poisons, and who knew what else in the floorboards, rafters above, or who knew what else. There might also be booby traps.

With no time for searching the room, Jie crept toward the door. She opened it slowly, finding it well oiled; if Faceless Chang had abided by her training, the door would open silently to the point she could slip out. Jie continued opening it until the crack provided a view of the desk. The line of sight was almost perpendicular to her original position from the window, exposing Faceless Chang's back.

Her head was tilted back, enough to reveal her closed eyes through the slits in the demon mask. She was screaming in the throes of ecstasy, brought there as only a Blossom of the Floating World could accomplish.

Heart fluttering, Jie buried memories of Lilian. Drawing a throwing star, she waited for Faceless Chang to straighten and provide a clear shot at her back.

Bucking forward under Lusha's skillful ministrations, Faceless Chang exposed her back. Jie threw open the door and flung the star.

Faceless Chang dropped back-first to the desk. The star whirled through the space she'd just been, and passed just over Lusha's head. It lodged into the opposite wall with a thunk.

It was just like the other Steel Orchid, who'd avoided a sure shot at her back! Jie drew her knife and surged in.

Faceless Chang tilted her head back, hypnotic brown eyes peering through the demon mask to meet Jie's. Without breaking her gaze, she rolled over onto her stomach, hands flat on the desk, ready to spring up. "Ju Jie. I've been waiting for you."

Of course she had. There was probably some kind of trap. Still, Jie's head spun. Faceless Chang had used Jie's fake surname, Ju, from when she'd been a Floret at the Peony Garden, so maybe she didn't know everything about her.

"Ju Jie?" Lusha now stared as well, eyes gleaming with baleful hate. "It really is you."

"But your surname really isn't Ju, is it?" Faceless Chang said, more statement than question.

Maybe she *did* know. Almost tangible suspicions niggled in the back of Jie's mind.

"Oh, yes. Gardener Ju told me quite a bit about you." Faceless Chang's purr had a lulling quality to it.

Jie sucked on her lower lip. Faceless Chang knew about the Black Lotus. She had to die. Didn't she?

"Oh, and we have other guests," Faceless Chang said. "Be a good girl, my pretty Blossom, and open the door."

Glare never leaving Jie, Lusha wiped her mouth and glided across the carpet. Even with her ruined face, she moved with the willowy grace of the Floating World. She even knelt when she unlocked the door and opened it.

The muffled sounds from the other side crystalized into focus as twelve—no, thirteen—sets of footsteps of varying weight crossed the middle of the antechamber.

Eight Triads hustled in a young woman, and two boys who looked so similar they had to be twins. In fact, they looked a lot like Yuna, who now emerged from among them, still holding whimpering little Mikayla on her hip.

* * *

Knife in hand, Tian hid outside the door to Faceless Chang's office. To reach this point unseen, his stealth skills must've improved, at least enough to hide his footsteps among the heavier boots of the Triads and the rambling of Yuna's brothers.

The huddle of Triads and Yuna's family didn't give Tian a clear line of sight, but he could see enough: Faceless Chang sat atop his desk, which like everything else in this antechamber and that office, was repaired. Jie stood in the door of the next room, knife in hand; while the wiry lieutenant, Du, moved to interpose himself between them.

As bad as killing someone was, the window of opportunity for a clear shot was disappearing by the second. Why wasn't Jie taking it?

The woman with a stitched-up face, who'd opened the door, glided back toward Faceless Chang's desk.

Draping one arm over her shoulder, Faceless Chang held up a hand. When he spoke, his voice came out gravelly. "Now, as you know, I'm in need of a new enforcer. Why don't you join me, Yan Jie?"

"Me?" Jie lowered her weapon, effectively ending any chance of a quick kill.

How could she even consider it? Tian squeezed the hilt of his own blade, counting. To get a clear shot of his own, around all the Triads, he'd have to go six and a half steps into the room.

"Yes." Laughing, Faceless Chang brushed a small hand over a porcelain bowl on his desk. "I like broken things. And you, Yan Jie, are broken since Lilian's betrayal."

Broken things.

Broken things!

While Jie's expression twisted, Tian was now seeing the connection, like the web of repairs in the ceramics: white with the cobalt five-clawed dragon reserved for Princess Kaiya's family, the planter by the door probably came from the imperial kilns—where any imperfect wares unfit for the Emperor were smashed instead of letting them fall in the hands of commoners.

He squinted at the stitch pattern in the woman's scarred face. It wasn't like the stitches Yuna had sewn in Jie's, and presumably his, wounds. No, it was more like—

The door into the antechamber opened, revealing the Blue Reaper, knife in hand. His gaze looked past Tian, into the office.

"Now, Jie," Faceless Chang said. "Kill the girl's mother."

Tian swallowed hard as possible outcomes warred in his head. If Jie attacked Yuna's mother, and the Blue Reaper tried to kill Mikayla... There were just too many sources of chaos. Tian ran into the room, shut the door, and lowered the bar.

Around him, the room erupted into chaos. Jie's eyes were locked on Yuna's mother. While the Triads opened a path for her, Yuna stood in the way, still holding the screaming Mikayla close.

Wait. Yan. Faceless Chang had used Jie's real surname. Tian reached into robe and pulled out Mikayla's old ragdoll. The stitch pattern was the same as the woman's face. He raised the bar and opened the door to let the Blue Reaper in.

* * *

It was so quiet, Yuna could hear her heart pounding in her ears. What was Jie doing, acquiescing to Faceless Chang? And Tian! He could be adorable with his naiveté, but now, he'd just made a stupid mistake. The Blue Reaper appeared at the door, coming to kill Mikayla.

Mama or Mikayla.

There was no way to save both.

And right now, trembling Mama was between her and Jie, with the half-elf closing fast.

Yuna looked over her shoulder, where Tian stepped out of the way and let the Blue Reaper through without a fight.

"Get out of the way!" Tian gestured her to the side. "The Blue Reaper is coming for Feng Rumei."

Feng Rumei? That didn't make sense.

"Rumei is controlling Jie. If the Blue Reaper kills her, maybe Jie will stop."

It sounded impossible, but if it were true... Yuna dropped Mikayla, shouldered past Mama, and lunged toward Jie. The half-elf spun away, allowing Yuna to recover and block the path to Mama. Behind her, the Blue Reaper swept past.

"Attack the Blue Reaper!" Faceless Chang yelled.

If the room had been shocked into still silence a moment ago, it now erupted into chaos. Broadswords rasped from scabbards. As one of the Triads dashed by Jie, she swiped a knife from his belt.

Her gaze remain locked on Mama with a determined focus, akin to the clan's *Tiger's Eye* technique.

Heart racing, Yuna pressed her back to Mama. She circled as Jie tried to move into a flanking position. The new vantage point provided a view of the Blue Reaper moving like a blur through the Triads, dispatching them with precise stabs. Mikayla sat on the floor screaming as bodies fell around her.

Jie advanced with zigzagging slashes, forcing Yuna to back up and push Mama with her. Even with a weapon, facing the clan master's daughter would be suicide.

With no weapon, no fighting skill, Lusha moved in between Feng Rumei and the Blue Reaper, but he raked a blade across her throat. Blood spurted as the once-celebrated Corsage of Yuna's own Peony Garden collapsed to the floor.

Yuna and Mama were just about backed up to the wall as Jie claimed the ground between them.

Faceless Chang disappeared behind the Blue Reaper's broad form, and she screamed a very female scream.

With a quick feint that caught Yuna out of position, Jie jabbed a deadly thrust toward Mama.

Yuna jumped knock the weapon away; but caught flat-footed, she'd left herself open. The blade came toward her flank, seemingly in slow motion.

Jie lurched to the side as Tian tackled her. The stab which would have dealt a mortal wound to Yuna's liver instead glanced off a rib. Pain blossomed in the spot.

"Stop it, crazy half-elf!" Tian yelled.

At Faceless Chang's desk, the Blue Reaper froze, then turned around. His gaze locked on Jie, and he stalked over. Behind him, a groaning Faceless Chang covered a stab wound to her stomach.

Tian threw his knife hilt-first to Yuna, and she caught it. Jie pushed him off and took a step toward Mama. Yuna sank back down into a defensive stance.

With her single-minded focus on Mama, and her back to the Blue Reaper, Jie didn't see him about to slash at her. Yuna dove into Jie's legs, sending them both to the floor.

The Blue Reaper loomed above them. He aimed a kick at Jie's exposed ribs, but the half-elf rolled out of the way and kip-upped to her feet. The cold, determined look had disappeared. She counter-attacked with a flurry of stabs and slashes that had the Blue Reaper in retreat.

She turned to Yuna. "Pattern seven. Before Rumei takes control of me again."

Yuna gasped. With pattern seven, Jie would put herself in a vulnerable position to allow Yuna to flank. It was tantamount to self-sacrifice. Before Yuna could object, Jie shifted her position, leaving her side undefended.

The Blue Reaper lunged at the opening. She grunted as his blade slashed across her arm. His motion exposed his flank, and Yuna snapped the knife with a twisting stab that slid into the space between his ribs. The No Shadow Cut, she'd done it! Hot, black blood washed over her hand, and she lost her handle on the weapon as he jerked to the side. Ignoring the wound, which would surely kill him, he followed up with what would be a fatal blow to Jie's unprotected kidneys.

Yuna threw herself into the path of the strike. The Blue Reaper's blade plunged deep into her flank. Unbearable pain seared through her, and she sank to her knees. White flashes clouded her vision.

* * *

No, no, no, not Yuna! Jie's heart pounded in her ears. She reversed the grip of her knife as the Blue Reaper pulled his own from the girl who'd just sacrificed herself. Yuna's blade still protruded from between his ribs, so deep it had to have penetrated into his lungs. Even still, he stood firm, ready to—

Tian seized the killer's ankle and drove his shoulder into the back of his knee. It would've worked better from the front, but the Blue Reaper still sank to a knee. Jie raked her blade across his carotid artery, spraying a mist of black blood. Probing at this newest wound, he fell face-first onto the floor. His brimmed hat plopped off, exposing the back of his head, and she slid the knife into the space between his skull and the top of his spinal column.

The room went silent, save for Mikayla's cries, Faceless Chang's groans, and Yuna's heaves.

"Yuna!" Tian said.

"Yuna!" Her mother, cowering in the corner with her twin sons, covered her mouth.

Jie ran over and knelt by the girl, so pretty and precocious. A stream of blood trickled from the side of her mouth, and her beautiful eyes were dimming with each of her labored breaths. The Blue Reaper's blade had bit deep into her liver, and it was a wonder she was still alive, let alone conscious. She'd taken the death blow that should've been Jie's, and not even the clan's *Viper's Rest*, a self-induced coma which Yuna had yet to master anyway, could save her from such a devastating injury.

"Go sit with her." Tian pulled at the mother's arm. In the week Jie had known him, his voice had never sounded angry. Now it carried enough acerbity for the both of them.

Her mother's first tentative steps lengthened into a determined stride. She knelt down and rested Yuna's head in her lap. She brushed her hair out of her face. "You saved Mama. You're a good girl. Come, Feng Qi, Feng Tan. Tell your big sister how proud you are."

The two boys came and knelt around her.

Tears ran from the corner of Yuna's glassed eyes, down her temples, mirroring the ones blurring Jie's vision and drawing rivulets down Tian's cheeks.

She'd found her family. Her real family. Jie pulled Tian away. No matter how the Black Lotus emphasized clan loyalty over blood, Yuna had always held on to the latter. It was better to let her die with—

"Jie." Yuna's voice came out a whisper as she pulled her hand from her brother's and reached out. "Tian."

Tian was at her side in a blink of an eye, and Jie not long after. They each took one of her hands, cold and clammy.

"Say...goodbye...to Wen...for me." The light went out of Yuna's eyes, her gaze frozen on the beyond.

CHAPTER 14

Rising from where Yuna's family surrounded her, Jie stood and picked her way through the dead Triads. She paused to look at Lusha, who lay motionless at the foot of the desk.

Faceless Chang—Feng Rumei—slumped in her chair, hands pressed against the stomach wound. She wouldn't last the hour, and the Black Lotus would need that hour to answer some last questions.

"You are going to die," Jie said. "But I can either make your death even more painful, or very fast. I need you to answer me."

Feng Rumei let out a sneering sound, and no doubt her lip curled beneath her mask. Well, if she wanted to play that way...

"Wait." Tian shuffled up, Little Mikayla in his arms.

She was quiet now, clasping that same ragdoll to her chest.

"Mikayla is your daughter, isn't she?" Tian asked.

Daughter? Gawking, Jie stared at the boy.

Feng Rumei coughed as she fumbled to remove the mask, and Jie helped her loosen the straps on the back. When the visage of the demon fell away, it revealed a girl, exotic in her mixed heritage, beautiful despite her pallor and the blood running down her chin. She finger-combed her matted brown hair. Her gaze found a cracked mirror, and she clawed for the mask. "Please, don't let Feng Mi see me like this."

Moving the mask out of Feng Rumei's reach, Jie dabbed the sweat and blood from her face, arranged her hair the best she could, and gestured toward Yuna's inert form in her mother's lap. "Your daughter won't care what her mother looks like."

"What did you want to know?" With a nod, Feng Rumei stretched out her arms, and Tian hefted Mikayla into them. The girl quieted.

"You used one of the Steel Orchids as a body double," Jie said. "Where's the other one?"

"Dead. She was the original Faceless Chang. After I helped her take over the Red Dragons, I had to kill her."

It wasn't exactly what Jie had suspected. "How?"

"With Empathy. I made the clan believe she was Feng Rumei, and ordered them to kill her. I kept her frozen so she couldn't defend herself."

"Wait," Tian said. "Didn't she and Gardener Ju switch out on occasion? How did she accept you as her twin?"

"Again, Empathy. I made her believe I was her twin."

"And she trained you in our ways?" Jie asked. "You were able to avoid my throwing star."

Every shake of Feng Rumei's head looked painful. "Empathy. I could sense your intention."

If true, that would be a relief. "Does anyone else know about the Black Lotus Clan?"

"No. The fewer people who knew, the more the legend of Faceless Chang grew."

Unless she was protecting someone, there was no reason to lie. It looked as if the secret of the Black Fists was safe. Jie let out a sigh.

"Please, grant my last request." Feng Rumei bowed her head. "Please take care of Feng Mi. If I can't keep an eye on her..."

"What about her father?" Tian asked.

She lifted her chin to the wiry Triad, dead by the Blue Reaper's hand. "Du was her father, but I made sure he never knew."

Tian nodded. "Right. The months you supposedly wasted in the Floating World with a Blossom, you were pregnant."

"And that coincided with when Gardener Ju was often absent," Jie said.

"Yes." Feng Rumei let out a long sigh. "I could never let the Triads know I was a girl, and Gardener Ju filled in for me at times."

Tian shuddered. "Why did you bring Feng Mi back to the Trench?"

"I'd hoped my father could teach her the rudiments of Empathy. And I wanted her close. Sadly, she has no talent for it."

Jie looked over her shoulder at Yuna. Mothers came in all forms, apparently, though Yuna, Mikayla, and Jie were the same in that they barely knew theirs, if at all.

Feng Rumei coughed a few times. When she spoke again, her voice was even weaker than before. "Tell Feng Mi...tell her that Mama took down the leadership of the Red Dragons, and made the Trench a better place."

"I will."

"Do you promise?"

Jie nodded.

Feng Rumei's voice came out as a barely audible whisper. "There's more to Lilian's story. Fixer Zhang has the answers..." Her eyes rolled up and her body went limp.

EPILOGUE

Jie bounced Mikayla on her hip in the safehouse room that Tian had co-opted for his web of evidence, watching as he pored through Gardener Ju's ledgers. Whether or not she had Empathic power, she was a pretty girl; and if she was half as clever as her cousin Yuna, she'd become a valuable asset to the clan.

Still, Little Feng Mi would never fill the hole in Jie's heart left by Yuna's death.

Wen joined several clan sisters kneeling at the far end of the room. Tears streaked her cheeks as they washed Yuna's body before the Cleaners came. They'd take her back to Temple and cremate her, and lay her ashes to rest with the thousands of others who'd lived and died for the Black Lotus.

In order to protect the clan's anonymity, they'd used the last of the safehouse's supply of musk and flower toxins on Yuna's mother and brothers. It would leave them with, at best, hazy recollections of the night's events. How easy it would be for her mother, to assume her daughter was still alive somewhere; and for her brothers, who would continue to believe their older sister had died long ago.

It was not so easy for Jie, Wen, and all the clan sisters who'd loved Yuna. The girl looked peaceful in death.

The same could not be said about the Blue Reaper, who turned out to truly be blue. He wasn't even human. Tusks rose from his lower jaw. With his black blood, he could only be an Altivorc, though unlike his hideous brethren, he was quite handsome. His blue scarf proved to be magic of some sort; no amount of pulling, cutting, stabbing, or burning could affect it. In addition to his knife, they'd recovered a finger-length metal cylinder. They couldn't figure out what it was, or what it was used for. Jie had written a message to Master Yan, suggesting they should seek out Arkothi Runemasters or Aksumi Mystics to study the strange artifacts. Why he'd targeted Nothori Empaths, there was no way of knowing. While Tian did not like coming to conclusions without plenty of evidence, he conjectured that in this case, it had to do with the First Empath's role in liberating mankind from the shackles of orc slavery a thousand years ago.

These things weren't her concern. More daunting was the Trench. Feng Rumei had made half of it a better place. Now, with the Red Dragons' leadership dead and the yue supply about to dry up, it was a firepowder keg, ready to ignite. She would send word to Master Yan, requesting the clan send someone in to become the new Faceless Chang.

It might be an easy solution, but more perplexing were Feng Rumei's last words. There was more to Lilian's story, and perhaps that meant the murder of Lord Ting and the machinations of the Steel Orchids were yet to be fully resolved. Which meant Jie's part in that story was unfinished also.

There were three days before Jie was to take Tian to the Black Lotus Temple to start his training. Three days to figure out who Fixer Zhang was, and then learn Lilian's secret.

Jie would do this.

For Yuna.

For Lilian.

End of Part 3

PART 4: TEMPTRESS OF FATES

PROLOGUE

Yan Jie avoided the knife slash and countered with a twisting No-Shadow Cut. The wooden practice blade would've left an oil mark on Wen's white padded armor, had Lilian not slipped by and tried to seize Jie's wrist. The sloppy technique would've bruised Lilian's ribs if Jie hadn't pulled up short.

As adopted daughter of the Black Lotus Clan's grandmaster, she felt the weight of responsibility for her juniors on her fourteen-year-old shoulders. It was getting harder, now that ten-year-old Wen and eleven-year-old Lilian—both of whom she'd taken under her wing when they came to the temple—had outgrown her. She followed up with a stab slow enough that Lilian could evade.

"Break!" the master yelled. His gruff voice echoed off the walls of the Hall of Blades, the cushioned reed mats doing little to soften the sound.

With the precision of the antique dwarf clock in the Hall of Time, Jie and Wen disengaged and looked back to the wizened old man. Lilian stepped back a second late. With a knowing nod between them, Jie and Wen waited so all three could salute in unison, palms into fists. They had to take care of each other, after all.

"As usual, Yan Jie's armor is clean." How he could tell, with his supposed nearsightedness? It was the talk among all the students, from initiates to apprentices. "As usual, Lilian has more stripes than a tiger and more spots than a leopard. What went wrong?"

Jie sucked on her lower lip. Poor Lilian always bore the brunt of criticism.

She bowed her head and saluted again. "Eldest Sister would've dealt Little Wen a fatal blow, so—"

"So you sacrificed yourself." The master shrugged. "Perhaps if your team had to ensure Wen returned from a mission, that would make sense. Was that your intention?"

Lilian shuffled on her feet. "No. I was trying to disarm Jie."

"Your failure would've cost you your life. A dead operative means more work for the Cleaners."

Bowing her head, Wen took a step forward. "Master, my initial attack was poorly timed. It was my fault."

"No, it was mine." Jie advanced, palm in fist. "I—"

"Your fault was in not finishing your attack. That might've been the third time you successfully executed a No-Shadow Cut, had you not pulled up short."

Heat flared to the tips of Jie's ears. She'd been the youngest clan member to ever succeed at it, though only twice in the hundreds of times she'd tried.

The knife master waved toward the hall's double doors. "Now, the grandmaster is waiting for you in the Audience Hall."

"Yes, Master," they all replied in unison.

Jie exchanged glances with her friends. They must be in store for more reprimands. Dismissed, they filed out of the Hall of Blades in silence, and out into the whirrs and buzzes of insects in the Shadow Grove. The shade from the eldarwood trees did little to cool the stifling summer heat as they headed toward the Audience Hall.

Along the way, they passed by the Hall of Knowledge. A twin to the Hall of Blades, the vaulting wood building was crowned with a steeply pitched, green-tiled roof. The open double doors provided a view of the long table where kneeling young initiates were learning to read and write. Two-year-old Yuna, who Jie had just rescued from the Trench, jumped up and ran over. The precocious little girl had clung to Wen like a wet leaf ever since she'd arrived.

She did a front roll off the veranda, landed on the path, and wrapped her arms around Wen's legs. "Jie, Wen," she said, her pronunciation perfect for someone so young. "Where are you going?"

It never ceased to amaze Jie how well she could already speak. She knelt down. "We're meeting with Master Yan. Now go back to your studies."

Pouting, Yuna climbed back up, shuffled back to her place at the desk and knelt.

Jie couldn't help but smile. She turned to Lilian and Wen. "I remember when you two were here, trying to write your names. Yuna is already much smarter than you."

"But I'm cuter." Wen batted her eyelashes. As the daughter of a celebrated Floating World Blossom, abandoned as a baby at the Black Lotus Shrine there, she was one of the clan's prettiest girls.

Jie looked sidelong at Lilian as they continued on their way. If anyone was the most beautiful, it was her, though her origins were a mystery. She'd been abandoned in the neighboring town as a three-year-old, starved to not much more than skin and bones. She'd almost died, and was so traumatized she barely remembered her own name. The only clue they had to her identity was her Northern high-bridged nose, mixed with crude mannerisms and diction, and a central valley accent. Most likely, she was like many other abandoned children: born to impoverished families, sold to bondsmen. No doubt her birth and bond were registered at one of the thousands of magistrate offices in the central valley. Master Yan had challenged Lilian to one day track down those documents, infiltrate the office, and steal them.

Jie shook the memories out of her head as they arrived in the Audience Hall to find six more apprentices kneeling in a row on the floor—five girls and one boy, all dressed in training robes. Five of the clan elders formed a semi-circle at the head. Master Yan sat cross-legged in the middle, while to his right knelt a woman in her late twenties, who Jie had only seen a few times in the past.

Her eyes studied them as they walked in, like the village farmers evaluating prize pigs.

Jie dropped to her knees to the west of the others. She realized that all the summoned students were close in age, all among the best-looking. Of course. Master Yin came once a year, and usually a handful of newly minted adepts left with her on assignment. Which meant...

"You nine have mastered the basics of our clan," Master Yan said, "and are now ready for your first deployment. Master Yin?"

The woman had a hard beauty to her, which echoed in her tone of command. "Stand."

Jie rose in perfect synchronicity with the rest of the students, save for Lilian just to her east, who as usual was half a beat behind.

Master Yin rose with the grace of a willow's branches swaying in a breeze and glided over to the west side of the line. Her eyes studied Wen and, with a nod, came to Jie. She looked back to Master Yan. "Your daughter is older than the rest. Has she flowered with Heaven's Dew?"

"No." Master Yan shook his head. "Given her age, and the doctor's reading of her pulse, we think it will be within the year."

Master Yin scrutinized Jie, and her laugh sounded like a chorus of nightingales. "My predecessor said Jie's virgin price would fund clan operations for the year. With such an exotic face, I don't doubt it."

Jie fought the urge to squirm. Adepts who'd left with Master Yin in past years always moved more gracefully when they came back for visits. The girls mentioned lying with men to collect information, *and* getting paid to do so, the most when they did it for the painful first time.

Of course. Master Yin's predecessor had died in the fire which had killed an entire cell in the capital's Floating World. It had claimed the famous twins, the Steel Orchids.

"But," Master Yin continued, "I also hear her fighting and stealth skills already equal seasoned operatives. Are you sure this won't be a waste of her talents?"

"Yes," Master Yan said. "She can sharpen the rest of the cell."

With a nod, Master Yin continued to Lilian. "She is the most beautiful of this group. Given what else I've heard, the Floating World suits her the most of any other assignment."

Jie's stomach knotted. Everyone knew Lilian would be a fair operative at best. At least maybe in the Floating World she could serve the clan well. And they could be together.

Master Yin reached the end of the line, where the twelve-year-old boy, Dun Lai knelt. He was a pretty young man, his looks ruined by the way he bullied the younger kids, and especially Lilian.

Master Yin studied him, she returned to the head of the room. "You are all proficient in fighting and spying. Starting now, I'm going to teach you a very different kind of skill."

CHAPTER 1

Amid chatter of a threat to the Emperor, the Black Lotus Clan had assigned Jie to retrieve the contents of a lord's safe. Instead, she was sitting on a stone fountain in the northwest of the capital. Yuna's death the night before, and the revelation that there might be more to Lilian's betrayal, felt like a vise on her heart. Her chest squeezed so tight it was hard to draw in a breath.

It had been ten minutes since she'd made contact with the mysterious Fixer Zhang's contact, an old male temple sweeper with a bushy beard and eyebrows. He'd told her to come to this paved square and set a copper *fen* on the fountain beside her. Surrounded by well-kept, two-story wooden rowhouses with ordinary shops on the first floor, and residences on the second, it was typical of many neighborhoods in the city. Incense hung in the balmy air, mingling with the scent of fresh fruits.

Wen had stayed back to surveil the sweeper, and now Jie watched middle-class residents go about their morning chores. Perhaps Fixer Yang was among them, but nobody made eye contact. Her pulse pounded like horse hooves on pavement, and the scarf covering her elf ears made her head sweat. The stitches on her shoulder itched.

Light footsteps approached, belonging to someone no more than fifty *jin*, and it took all her discipline not to sneak a glance.

Someone sat down behind her and spoke in a flitting female voice. "Don't turn around."

A woman? It shouldn't have been a surprise, since the last three villains Jie had faced were female. She gave a nod, but took in the newcomer's gardenia scent.

"Fixer Zhang?" Jie asked.

"Maybe. What do you want?"

"I'm told you have information about Ju Lilian, a Blossom who recently perished in the Floating World fire." Or rather, Jie had had to kill her—her own lover—for betraying the clan.

"Usually, people want hitmen, uniforms, or forged documents. This will take a little longer."

Longer? Jie shifted. In the corner of her eye, the pool reflected a flash of brown.

"Wait here for five minutes. If you follow me, you will not get your information. If you turn around, you will not get your information. Do I make myself clear?"

There were ways of drawing answers out of people, and the painless option was off the table, since Tian had destroyed the supply in order to trick another clan traitor who'd been presumed dead for two decades. Still, this woman might not be Fixer Zhang after all.

Jie nodded, and the woman got up and headed north. Without her turning around, reflective surfaces didn't provide a better look at the woman. Before long, her footsteps and scent mixed in with everyone else's.

Waiting. The anticipation made each minute feel like an eternity; she was so close to answers she wouldn't have thought to ask the questions for. On the count of three hundred seconds, someone new approached, with heavier footsteps and the scent of fermented soybeans, and sat down behind her. His deep breaths suggested a man with a barrel chest. Thank the Heavens she hadn't followed her impulse and captured the first woman.

"The famous Floating World half-elf, Ju Jie," he said, voice croaking.

"Tell me something I don't know." If this was Fixer Zhang, he knew her given name and assigned surname. Of course, there was only one half-elf around, and almost everyone in the capital knew of the most promising Floret in the Floating World, whose virgin price would've been a new record had she not been tricked into forfeiting the bid.

"There are many things I know that you don't, but I am told you want specific information. About Lilian."

"Well?" Jie tapped her toe.

He laughed. "Information comes at a price."

"Name it."

"The Lord of Jinjing has a safe in the bedroom of his home in the capital. Bring me the contents."

Jie hid her shock. Fixer Zhang wanted the same thing the clan did. And it was all coming together: over a week ago, a jade vendor in the Silk Market had mentioned something about the Lord of Jinjing wanting to carve jade into blossoms, and a lumber company in Jinjing County had been processing yue sap into an addictive form for illegal sales.

It had been those ill-gotten profits that had put a target on Lord Ting's back, the Steel Orchid who hit that target with a crossbow, and Lilian who'd orchestrated it all. Was it a coincidence that the ruler of Jinjing was Lord Shi, one of Lilian's regular Hummingbirds?

"Yes, you are putting it all together. Really, you wouldn't believe what I will tell you without one of the items you'll find in that safe."

Was Zhang only a Triad fixer? Or did he know about her real identity as an operative of the Black Lotus Clan? It was time to probe. "What makes you think I can open it?"

He let out a fake yawn. "You're a pretty girl. Use your imagination. I sure am." Even though they were back-to-back, his tone might as well have been leering.

It always came down to *that*. "There are a lot of pretty girls who could have done this for you."

"But of all the pretty girls, Lord Shi of Jinjing only made a bid on *you*. And, you now have extra motivation to open his safe."

Was he referring to her need to find out about Lilian, or the clan wanting the contents, too? Something didn't sit well in Jie's gut. Why would Fixer Zhang want the same thing as the Emperor? And if he worked not just with the Triads, but also with the peers of the realm, just how had he evaded clan scrutiny?

Heavens, she was thinking of going against the clan. Master Yan, her adopted father. But what if this was really the clan, testing her loyalty?

"Lucky for you, Lord Shi and his key just came back into town last night for his audience with the imperial court tomorrow."

Jie sucked on her lower lip. In all likelihood, the contents of the safe were related to Lord Shi's audience with the Emperor. Now, Fixer Zhang wanted it; but why? "So I am supposed to bed him, and when he's fast asleep, find his key, unlock the safe, remove its contents, and then get out?"

"Something like that."

"Who is in his house?"

"His fourteen-year-old son lives there year-round, with one guard, a steward, and a servant. A maid comes twice a week to help with cleaning and sewing."

Not that many at all, but... "How many guards is he travelling with?"

"Two hundred, but only four are usually in the house when he is there. The rest will be quartered nearby. You're a smart girl to consider this."

Two hundred. According to rules established by the Founder, who didn't want sizeable groups of potential enemies around him, it was the maximum number allowed in the capital. It was large enough that they might not all know each other. A plan formulated in her head. "You're a Fixer. In order to succeed, I am going to need a set of their ceremonial robes, for someone a little taller and wider than me."

"I don't think Lord Shi is into playing dress-up. Lord Tong, maybe..."

Lord Tong was among the Emperor's favorites, along with Lord Shi, Lord Yang, and the deceased Lord Ting. They were the key to keeping the rest of the North loyal. Perhaps not so coincidentally, the latter three had frequented Lilian's bed. Lord Tong, however, had been banned from the House. She said, "I need some way to get out of the house, with the safe's contents concealed."

"You're good at this. Maybe you should consider working for me when this is done. Imagine, a prostitute who could glean information or steal from important lords."

It didn't take much imagination, since that's what the Black Lotus Clan's cell in the Floating World did. The cell Jie was still the head of for three more days. "So, can you get me that robe?"

"Two hours. Meet me at the Yushan Jade Market."

"I look forward to it." Fixer Zhang rose and shuffled off. Jie looked for reflective surfaces, just in case a vain woman happened to be walking by looking in a mirror, but like before, she had no such luck.

Now she had two hours to work out the details of her real plan for getting into the safe. While many of the clan assets around the capital moved to the palace to counteract the potential threat to the Emperor, she'd have to use the Floating World cell...and lie to them about her true intentions.

CHAPTER 2

With Yuna's death weighing heavily on ten-year-old Zheng Tian's shoulders, he trudged to his assigned spot inside of the Yushan Jade Market. Located in what was once a vaulting brick warehouse, eighty-seven vendors hawked all qualities of jade, in everything from bracelets to carvings, necklaces to statuettes. At this mid-morning hour, there were ninety-three customers milling about the stalls, admiring the wares, haggling with the merchants, and buying trinkets.

He pulled at his blue gentleman's robes, which the cell believed suited his current acting abilities, and looked around without being obvious. The motion caused the stitches in his shoulder to pull, though they hurt less each day. That wasn't important now; somewhere among the crowds was the mysterious Fixer Zhang.

From what they'd learned from questioning Triads before leaving the Trench, he was their go-to for information, smuggled goods, people with special talents, and who knew what else. Jie had surmised from her earlier interaction that he probably also had his tentacles reaching into the nobility. The potential connections had Tian's brain dancing with possibilities. Combined with sadness over Yuna, it was a distraction from the task at hand.

As she'd taught, he constantly checked reflective surfaces as he worked his way through the market, yet always kept an eye on Jie. She kept her ears covered with a red headscarf. Despite the bright color, it was still hard to keep track of her, given how short she was compared to the people around her.

A boy about Tian's age brushed by him.

Tian seized the urchin's wrist and held it up.

The boy gave a sheepish grin and dropped Tian's coin purse.

Tian swept it out of the air. Not that there was much more than rocks in the pouch, anyway, to give the appearance of fullness and complete his disguise. Tian released the kid, and watched as he ran off. His pickpocketing skill was so poor, he would more likely get caught than score a purse. He turned back to Jie.

She was gone.

No, there she was, a flash of her green dress moving through the forest of people. She flashed subtle clan hand signals. *Swap is on. All eyes on girl in grey. Continue exchange.*

Girl in grey? There were six in the market! Still, the swap was on, so Tian went along his assigned route, scanning for—there, Little Aina in plain pink, a Seedling from the Lily Pond, had a package bound in brown silk. She passed it off to Little Duoduo from the Orchid Palace, wearing a matching dress and hair pinned up in the same fashion. Only two of the six girls in grey were on the move, one headed this way. Just twenty-seven paces away, the package switched to Meisha, skinny Blossom of the Orchid Palace, who cradled it with nonchalant grace. He was up next to receive it.

The girl in grey passed. Instead of continuing his leg of the relay, he turned and trailed her out of one of the market's many entrances.

When no one was around, he ran and caught up to her, grabbing her dress at the shoulder. "Hey!"

She spun around, eyes wide, and struggled to break free. "I didn't steal anything, I swear!"

His eyes landed on a coin purse in her hand.

"I didn't steal it." She clutched it to her chest.

This couldn't possibly be Fixer Zhang. Could it? Maybe? After all, the clan traitor's and Faceless Chang's identities had both been surprises. "Where did you get the brown silk package?"

"A man gave it to me, and told me to give it to the girl with the red headscarf."

Most likely she was...what was the term? A horse? Still, Jie was wearing a different-colored headscarf from when she'd met her informant—possibly Fixer Zhang—earlier, for the very purpose of making Fixer Zhang come in person to identify her. Tian tapped his chin. "What did he look like?"

She held a hand above well above her head. "This tall, hair in a ponytail. He was wearing a brown tunic."

That could describe at least four people who'd passed through the market. Tian put two fingers to his eyes. "How far apart were his eyes? What shape was his nose?"

"I don't remember."

"Where did it happen?"

She pointed to the centermost entrance on the east.

The sun would've been at the man's back, making it impossible for anyone inside to make out his features. He also would've had line of sight on Jie. Fixer Chang knew what he was doing.

"She's just a mule," Jie said.

Tian's heart just about jumped into his throat. The half-elf delighted in sneaking up on him! He swung on her.

Gone was her usual mischievous grin, replaced by a downcast expression. "You can let her go."

Tian released the girl, and she scampered off, still clutching her purse.

"We have the package," Jie said, "and if Fixer Zhang had eyes on me, he shouldn't know where it ended up. We can't let him know our real plan."

The real plan. Jie had said the clan wanted the contents of a safe, and they had to beat Fixer Zhang to it. He nodded.

"Now come on, we're going to call on an old friend."

* * *

Tian hid in an alley with Jie at his side, watching Lord Shi of Jinjing County taking tea with his son, Shi Han, on the patio of a teahouse. Located in the northwest, it was near a district with many courtyard homes of minor nobility.

He'd often seen the forty-one-year-old Lord Shi at court—the Emperor favored him, to the point where they travelled together—but fourteen-year-old Shi Han only came occasionally. He'd always kept his distance from the younger children, but sometimes conversed with Tian's good friend, Peng Kai-Long.

Both father and son carried a little too much weight in their cheeks and torsos, and their brown robes did little to hide it. The *wen* insignia on their shoulders depicted a black flower with four petals on a white field. Two identically dressed guards stood watch nearby, broadswords hanging on their hips, as opposed to the fine *dao* blades tucked into their masters' sashes.

Tian rubbed a hand over his own stomach. In just a week of exertion and no sweets—well, he had snatched a red bean paste bun from the Peony Garden a few days before—he'd lost plenty of weight.

"The diet and activity are doing you good," Jie whispered without looking at him. She'd been so focused since their return from the Trench.

His chest filled with pride, though it didn't feel that good, considering his slowness might've cost Yuna her life.

Jie pointed her chin at the pair. "See the way Young Lord Shi waves his hand at the servant?"

Tian nodded. It was a dismissive gesture, bordering on rudeness.

"And see Lord Shi scowl? I would guess he is disappointed in his son."

It was a sentiment Tian knew too well. He'd never lived up to Father's expectations, and now he'd even been banished from the capital. Of course, he was still here, and getting caught by the authorities would mean a slow death.

"Here he comes," Jie said.

Tian turned to the flash of swishing blue robes.

Old Feng, a second-rate actor from the Floating World's Red Boat Opera, sauntered toward Lord Shi's table. He waved a hand. "Lord Shi!"

The two guards sidestepped together, hands on their weapons, barring his way.

Holding up two hands, Old Feng took a step back. "I'm an old business associate, here with a proposal."

Lord Shi's bored expression brightened, and he beckoned. "Let him through."

After several groveling bows, Old Feng straightened and pushed through the guards as if they were ants, coming to the table. He bowed again.

In this, his acting was much better than when he'd nearly gotten Tian captured a few days before.

"Please." Lord Shi beckoned to the seat between him and his son.

With a broad smile, Old Feng plopped into the chair. "Thank you, my Lord."

Young Lord Shi Han looked up at the Iridescent Moon. The way he fidgeted...

"Yes, he wants to be somewhere else, soon." Jie's whisper tickled Tian's ear.

"How may I help you?" Lord Shi asked.

Old Feng dipped into a surprisingly grand bow for someone sitting. "I am glad you asked. I hear you are reporting to the Emperor tomorrow."

Lord Shi sat up straight. "You are well-informed."

Only because Jie told him as much. Tian snorted.

"In my line of business, I need to be." Old Feng rubbed his hands together.

"And what line of work is that?" Shi Han asked.

Lord Shi hissed. "Quiet, boy. Adults are talking."

Lips tightening into a hard line, the boy hung his head.

"Ahhhh..." Old Feng looked from father to son and back to father again. "I'm Feng of Feng Trading. Your steward bought some red wheat liquor from me many years ago."

Tian snorted. Of course, Old Feng only knew about there being a steward from Jie's report on Lord Shi's local household. And of course, Lord Shi's blank expression showed he knew nothing about this fictional transaction. Which meant he probably let the steward run his house in the capital.

"So." Old Feng cleared his throat. "I want a permit to import red wheat from Rotuvi, so I can distill it into wine here. Maybe you could bring it up to the Emperor."

Not that the Emperor cared about such mundane matters; some ministry was likely in charge. Lord Shi, however, smiled. "I will consider it..."

The trailing tone suggested he was waiting for a bribe. Sadly, Old Feng was poorer than dirt, thanks to a gambling and alcohol habit. If he really imported red wheat liquor, he'd probably drink it all himself.

"Get to it," Jie muttered under her breath.

Old Feng motioned to the west. As planned, Wen strutted by in a white-and-yellow gown, whose neckline dipped low. One foot crossing in front of the other, each step revealed a shapely leg. Still, something was off about it. Her usual nonchalant grace was gone, replaced by forced elegance.

Tian tapped his chin. Yesterday had been Wen's seventeenth birthday, and the only gift she'd received was the news of Yuna's death. She'd taken it particularly hard, since Yuna was her Big Sister both in the clan and in the Peony Garden, and now she had to live a lie told to her House: that Yuna's bond had been bought out, and she'd returned home.

Whether Wen looked more awkward or not, Lord Shi probably couldn't tell from the way he was gawking. Shi Han's eyes followed her as well, though not with such obvious hunger.

"There's nothing more beautiful than a Floating World Blossom," Old Feng said. "My Lord, I confess, this is no chance meeting."

"Oh?" Lord Shi didn't look back at Old Feng, head instead rocking with the sway of Wen's hips.

"I noted that Young Lord Shi must be close to his First Pollination. That Blossom's House is the premier location for all the realms' great lords. The great Lord Peng's two sons both chose her for their first."

Lord Shi licked his lips. "I can see why."

"I've taken the liberty of contracting her House, the Peony Garden, for Young Lord Shi."

If Shi Han was excited in the least, it didn't show.

And they needed him to be excited, if Jie's plan for getting the contents of the safe for the clan was to work.

CHAPTER 3

With the loss of two dear friends in less than a week, Dan Wen found it hard to fake an alluring smile at the pudgy lordling. Still, clan business came first: the Emperor needed the contents of Lord Shi's safe, and getting Young Lord Shi Han to choose her for his First Pollination was all part of Jie's plan to crack it.

It shouldn't be this hard: after all, Old Feng had specifically pointed her out. Still, Shi Han leaned back in a chair in the Peony Garden's common room, manicured finger on his chin. His brown robes did little to hide his bulk. With all the vigor of a fourteen-year-old youth, his eyes roved over the seven other Blossoms, who wore titillating gowns and held even more suggestive poses.

Her heart juddered. He hadn't once even considered her, his eyes sliding past to an older House sister.

Sitting at his side, his even bulkier father's eyes never left her. The ruler of Jinjing County, Lord Shi Mu had frequented Lilian's bed, and she'd mentioned his inferiority complex. Among the nobility, he was thought to be one of the Emperor's most loyal vassals. So why did the clan want the Floating World cell to investigate his safe?

Wen tried to focus on the task at hand. If only she could be like Elder Sister Jie. She'd met with Fixer Zhang's representative this morning to find out more about the conspiracy that had led to

Lilian's and Yuna's deaths. Putting whatever she'd learned to the side, she'd pivoted to the clan mission with renewed focus.

It was time for Wen to do the same. There was still one way to tilt this back in her favor: manipulate men's fragile egos. She, Jie, and Tian had spent an hour observing Lord Shi and his son, learning their timbres and intonations when speaking, and their body language. More for Tian's sake, but it was time for her to put that information to use.

Wen modulated her voice with the clan's *Mockingbird's Deception* to mimic Elder Lord Shi's, and used a *Ghost Echo* to throw it. "Which one did Lord Peng choose for his two sons' First Pollination?"

No. Grief was messing with her concentration. Had her voice come out raspy enough?

Lord Shi sat up straight, brows furrowed. That was to be expected, especially if she'd done it correctly, since he'd wonder why he'd heard his own voice when he hadn't even spoken. He opened his mouth—

"Brilliant question, my Lord." Florist Qin, acting as interim Gardener for the House, gestured toward Wen. "That would be Wen. She is especially skilled at first times."

Lord Shi's lips snapped shut, and he leaned back. Of course, no vain minor lord would turn down a compliment about his taste. Just as he had an hour before, his eyes undressed her. It was a daily occurrence, but today, it made her feel dirty.

Still, her tactic had yielded the desired result: young Shi Han's gaze came back to her.

Tilting over to expose more of her cleavage, Wen forced a smile. The movement came off awkward, the smile blunt. She was so useless today, unable to perform the most elementary suggestive body language. She suppressed a sigh.

Tearing his eyes from her chest, he waved a dismissive hand and turned to the Florist. "She's beautiful, but why's she so sad?"

Heavens, this was an unmitigated debacle.

"My Young Lord," the Florist said, with a lilting giggle. "Only a virile young lord like yourself can bring a smile to her lips."

His own lips twitched into a grin, making the thin wisps of peach fuzz dance. How satisfying it would be to smack it right off his face.

Lord Shi cleared his throat. "She is the one."

"But Father—"

Lord Shi scowled. "She is much prettier than the maids you grope back home."

Wen's smile, fake as it was, slipped for a split second. After three years of spending her days gratifying entitled men, it shouldn't have come as a surprise that this little brat took advantage of girls whose livelihood relied on enduring his unwanted advances.

"Fine." The boy waved another dismissive hand. "Do I get a party, too, like Young Lord Peng?"

Maybe the father paled, or maybe it was just Wen's imagination. "There's no time to plan such a grand event."

Or most likely, Lord Shi couldn't afford the king's ransom that a party of that magnitude would cost. Wen fiddled with her pinkie. Young Lord Peng's party, a once-in-a-generation event, had been a way for Gardener Ju of the Chrysanthemum Pavilion and Lord Ting to launder illegal drug sales. Ironically, Gardener Ju had also used the party as a dry run for Lilian's successful assassination of Lord Ting. Gardener Dan had used it in a plot to preserve House Corsage Lusha's record virgin price.

Tears threatened to blur her vision, but she blinked several times to make it look like innocence. As a result of that one party, Jie had been violated and lost the astronomical bid on her virgin price, Lilian had killed Gardener Dan, and Jie had been forced to kill Lilian. On top of that, it had turned out that Gardener Ju had once been one of the clan's most celebrated operatives: the Steel Orchid twin who'd burned down the Floating World to stage her own death. Tian had killed her to save Jie.

"Fine. Shall we begin?" Shi Han was saying. He rose out of his chair, his eyes locked on her chest.

Wen bowed low, allowing him an even better view. The House sisters bowed as well, staying genuflected as she straightened. There'd never been any shame in giving herself to men. It was for the clan that raised her, and really, she had power over the Hummingbirds who thought they controlled the Blossoms. If only Lilian had seen it that way, maybe she wouldn't have betrayed the clan, and died for it.

Now, though, Wen's heart squeezed. This was the first male she would receive since learning of Yuna's death last night. She'd just cleaned her apprentice's body earlier today, preparing it for cremation. Tonight, after their mission was accomplished, she'd dress Yuna for her final journey.

That was later. All that mattered now was this moment. Wen held out her hand. "This way, Young Lord."

His expression remained sour as he took her hand and, fingers limp, allowed himself to be guided through the common room to the stairs. Never before had a young lord seemed so unmotivated. Maybe he'd wanted someone else? Even if she really wasn't in the mood for this, it still hurt not to be wanted. Behind them, one of the giggling House sisters settled in Lord Shi's lap. It was surprising she had enough of a perch, given how much space his belly took. The rest of the girls dispersed, returning to their preparation for the night.

Shi Han's eyes bulged as he took in the surroundings. Though from a noble family, he wouldn't have ever seen the delicate beauty of the Floating World. The hanging scrolls, rendered by Dragonscribes, would ease anyone's spending inhibitions if they didn't prepare themselves before looking—which very few visitors to the Floating World did. Whatever misgivings he'd had before, the paintings must've eased them: his hand fumbled for her hip, and it took all her discipline not to wince.

By the time they made it to the third floor, the boy was panting. She led him along the mezzanine overlooking the common room. Each footfall on the bare wooden floors chirped like a nightingale, a feature that allowed Blossoms to know when someone was in the halls. Down below, Lord Shi sat back in his chair. He watched her with hunger in his eyes, ignoring the two Blossoms vying for his attention.

Wen dragged out the walk to her room—the room of the Corsage, the House's most celebrated Blossom—yet it seemed they arrived too soon. It'd only been a week since she'd moved to this room, after Lilian had ruined Lusha's face in revenge for her role in Jie's violation. Just that fact made it feel haunted.

She knelt by the heavy door, bowed, and slid it open.

Young Lord Shi's gaze weighed on her as he passed, and the tremble in his body showed that the supposed lack of interest he'd shown before had all but disappeared. If virgin boys had one thing in common, it was their pent-up frustrations. His hand ran through her hair as he entered.

She rose, followed him in, and knelt again. No sooner did she slide the door shut than his hands hooked under her arms and pulled her to her feet. No doubt, the Dragonscribed magic in her room's decorations fueled his excitement. He spun her around, buried his face into the side of her neck, and slavered kisses on it.

This script had played out on more than a dozen occasions, and it was one which she could normally follow. Still, things needed to slow down if she was to keep Young Lord Shi occupied long enough for Tian to crack Lord Shi's safe.

Her moan sounded more like a dying cow in her ears. Usually, it was easy to fake arousal, but today...

"Yes, that's it, feels good, right?" He pulled back and searched her eyes.

With practiced ease, she tilted her head shyly, and returned his gaze through half-lidded eyes. "Please, more. I need you."

It sounded so contrived to her, but pulling her toward the bed, he leaned in. "I have a secret: this isn't my first time. I've been fucking the maid, and I can make her scream for hours. She says I'm the best she's had. Better than Father."

Good, if he had that kind of stamina, then it would give Tian plenty of time. Even better, because doing a convincing job for a typical First Pollination would be near-impossible with the heaviness in her heart today. All she had to do was lie on her back and act as if he were the God of Virility. The latter, she did on a nightly basis.

Leaning into him, she reached for the knotted clasps across the chest of his robe, but he brushed her hands away. He loosened the drawstrings of his pants and let them drop to his ankles. The outline of his manhood bulged beneath the robe, standing at attention as only that of a young man in his prime could.

There was no art, no grace, no seduction as would be expected with a regular Hummingbird. He pulled her clothes off with no appreciation for their design, lowered her to the bed, and entered. What he'd said about sleeping with the maid was likely true: unlike most virgins who eschewed a Blossom's guidance, he found the right orifice.

She let out a few obligatory moans—Heavens, they sounded so fake, an eavesdropper would be laughing. She thrust her hips to meet him and dug her nails into his back, all rote motions that allowed her to ponder Fixer Zhang, and what he might know about the deaths of Lilian and Yuna. It was just a name; he could be anybody. Probably someone they all knew. The answer was so close, yet they had to put that to the side, because the clan needed the contents of that s—

Like most virgin boys who eschewed a Blossom's guidance, it ended in not much more than half a minute.

So much for his boasts. He collapsed with a groan on top of her. A hard cylinder on his chest, beneath his robe, bit into her cheek, though not enough to hurt.

Her aching heart thanked the Heavens it was over. The logical part of her brain reminded her that she needed to keep him here. If he left the Floating World now, Lord Shi would make it back to the villa before Tian could even find out where the safe was. Their mission would be doomed, the cell and its sisters shamed.

"Well, that was nice." He rose, and reached down to pull his pants back up.

CHAPTER 4

Having never worn platform shoes before, Tian worried he was going to fall on his face. A voice that sounded suspiciously like Yuna's spoke in his mind, reminding him to take deep breaths to calm his nerves. They'd known each other for less than a week, and she hadn't been nice to him for most of that time. Yet her loss left his stomach feeling hollow.

He dabbed sweat from his brow. Whether that came from the afternoon sun on the brown gentleman's robes Fixer Zhang had provided, or from nerves, it was hard to tell. Heart pounding as he navigated the *hutong* warrens of courtyard houses, he approached the gate of Lord Shi's home. Two stone lions, each his height, flanked the entrance, ready to ward off evil spirits; a gate guard was also stationed there to ward off interlopers.

It should be Jie doing this, since she could just climb the walls, sneak around inside, and pick the safe's lock. After all, he'd been banished from the capital on pain of death. Although he'd actually never left the city in the two weeks following his punishment, he also hadn't gone so close to the imperial palace. However, she was certain Fixer Zhang had set a tail or three on her; so, while she was out following Lord Shi, pretending to work up the nerves to approach him and then back off, it was up to him now.

Located in an auspicious corner, the grey brick compound was part of a row of homes belonging to minor lords and officials. Though spacious, with the main building at the far end rising two stories above the walls and topped with gracefully sloping green-tiled eaves, it would fit inside Father's capital villa eight and two-thirds times over.

The gate guard bowed. "Young Lord, back so soon?"

Young Lord. That had been the way everyone addressed Tian in the past, but no one had used that title in nearly two weeks. Of course, the chamberlain thought he was seeing Shi Han, a testament to Wen's incredible use of cosmetics.

Plus, you're pudgy, just like him, Yuna would say, even though he'd lost much of his baby fat. *Now, keep your head at an angle that shades your face so he can't get a good look.*

Just like she'd taught him. She'd also started showing him the *Mockingbird's Deception*, which he now used to imitate Shi Han's voice. "I forgot something."

"Ah, nerves." The guard leaned in, and whispered, "A first time can make a lad nervous. Here's a secret: all your friends didn't perform nearly as well as they told you."

Whatever was he talking about? Tian waved a dismissive hand, a motion he'd picked up when he, Jie, and Wen were studying Shi Han interacting with his father at tea. Bowing, the guard let him pass.

Tian blew out a breath and looked over his shoulder. The guard continued his vigil, none the wiser. Tian climbed up the three steps, continued on his way through the corridor between the outer gate and the front gate, then turned into the small courtyard. A single plum tree bedecked with white blooms rose in the center, and a well stood in the southeast corner.

At Father's villa, he'd be challenged by at least two more guards and greeted by the chamberlain by now. But Fixer Zhang had said Lord Shi kept a skeleton staff here: just a steward, two maids, and a guard. Of his family, only his eldest son lived here this year; Lord Shi himself had just arrived the evening before to report to the Emperor. After the next Spring Festival, he, his wife, and their remaining children would be expected to take up residence for the year.

After just two weeks with the Black Lotus Clan, things were becoming clearer. Whatever lord's family member lived in the capital, they were virtual hostage to the Emperor. Tian himself had been a permanent fixture in Father's capital villa, and like other children of the great hereditary lords, had spent most of his time in the Imperial Palace itself—to guarantee Father's good behavior. The revelation that he, the youngest, had been essentially sacrificed would've felt depressing, had his time in the capital not been spent with Princess Kaiya. She and Yuna were the same age...

He shook the thought out of his head as he ambled across the courtyard, trying to imitate Shi Han's leisurely gait. The platform shoes made that difficult, too, but the only one he had to trick was the ancient servant with bad eyes. The younger maid only came once a week, and today she was at Lord Yang's villa several blocks away. By now, Jie had broken off Lord Shi, and was keeping the steward busy.

Walking around the tree and passing between the east and west wings—mirror buildings with white bricks and green-tiled eaves—he came to their Big Brother, the main residence. So far, so good. He pulled on the door—

"Young Lord," a creaky voice said. "You must be hungry after your big day."

Tian froze and looked over his shoulder.

A silver-haired woman, bent over with age, smiled at him. Reports said that Lord Shi's mother was back in Jinjing County, so this had to be the servant. One who didn't have a good sense of time, if she thought Shi Han could take a rickshaw to the Floating World, hold hands with Wen, and make it back by now.

He modulated his voice to sound like Shi Han's, hopefully well enough that her old ears wouldn't tell the difference. "I didn't get far. I just forgot something, and came back."

"Young Lord, you won't need *that.*" The old woman creaked out a laugh as she clapped her hands together. "Floating World Blossoms take many herbs, so they are very safe. And you won't accidentally plant a seed. And they're skilled in the ways of making sure the encounter lasts. Why, I still remember when your Father..."

She babbled on, none of her words making sense. How could a Blossom be dangerous? And why worry about planting seeds too quickly? Did Blossoms hold hands *and* farm? If the servant kept him here much longer, the real Shi Han would get back.

"I'll be right out." Tian waved the young lord's dismissive hand at her, then went in and closed the door behind him.

A set of stairs wrapped around the two-story foyer. Doors lay to the east, west, and north on both levels; though the north room would be too small to be Lord Shi's bedchambers. No, Father had commissioned a Feng Shui geomancer to lay out their villa, and the wizened man had said something about the northwest corner bringing fortune. Tian slid out of the platform shoes, ran up the steps, and then to the northwest door. Unsurprisingly, it was a standard key lock, which yielded in seconds to his improving lockpicking skills. Hopefully, the safe would be as easy.

He opened the door and peered in. It was sparsely decorated as only an austere Northerner would keep it. The window shutters were open, letting in the early afternoon sun. The Iridescent Moon sat just off-center of the south window. The asymmetry, and the lack of what would've been minimal effort to center the moon in the window, pricked at Tian's nerves. To the west, under the window, sat two plain chairs and a side table. In the north, the bedframe was made of unadorned rosewood. The blankets lay askew, and the pillow held the indent of someone's head. Lord Shi, who'd arrived just last night, must've slept here, and the old servant had yet to tidy up.

The walls were unadorned, save for the scroll painting of the Great Wall above the bed's headboard. It hung askew by a degree, enough that Tian had to fight the urge to right it. Not only that, but it was off-center over the bed by half a finger-length. He padded over and studied the wall it hung on. Scuff marks.

He lifted the painting, revealing the door to a safe. Easy! He was ahead of schedule, he...

Froze. It was unlike any he'd ever seen, a fact which would've been more impressive if he'd seen more than six safes in his lifetime. Still, it was beautiful in its intricacy: two keyholes, vertically aligned, with one combination lock in between. Above them on the line was a clear, round stone the size of his fist, which swirled with colors like a soap bubble.

Lockpicking had been one of the most interesting skills the clan had taught him so far. Studying the top keyhole, he withdrew a light bauble and his first set of picks from a hidden pocket in the inside of his robe. With the bauble between his teeth shining light into the hole, he probed the interior, discovering twenty-one—twenty-one!—tumblers of different thickness and depths.

He didn't even have enough picks to manipulate them, let alone start working on the lower lock. He might not even be able to actually unlock the first, even if he did have enough picks. No, this was a job for Jie. But at least he could learn more about the locks to save her time.

Putting his ear to the combination lock, he twisted the dial. The rhythmic clicking of the discs against the cam was almost hypnotic. And it was also impossible to hear the open spot that indicated when to turn the dial back the other way. In this, Jie's elf ears would have to suffice.

He went on to the second keyhole, and—hah! A spring-loaded poison dart was hidden in the depths. Yuna had told him to look out for them.

Yuna.

He let out a sigh, and, careful to avoid the trigger, started to test the tumb—

Snick!

He jerked his hand back.

With several deep breaths, he evaluated himself. No pain in his finger; maybe it hadn't hit him? He didn't feel lightheaded, cold, or drunk.

All right, maybe it had missed him. He used one of his lockpicks to wipe the needle tip. With a sample, the clan poisoner could probably figure out what it was. He held his breath and used other picks to work the needle back, so as not to leave evidence of his tampering. It locked back with a click.

He blew out a breath. He was way in over his head. And what if they didn't get another chance? It'd taken a significant bribe to get Old Feng to recommend Wen and the Peony Garden to Lord Shi for Shi Han's First Pollination, and a First Pollination only happened once. This might be their only opportunity to crack the safe, and the clan might get mad at Jie.

Maybe the keys were hidden somewhere. He turned around and searched the places where he'd hide sweets in his room: beneath the bed, behind a bauble lamp, in a side table drawer...nothing.

Voices spoke in the courtyard—a woman. A splash of green and yellow flashed in the south window.

He dropped to the floor and listened.

"Miss Tang," the old servant said. "This isn't your day to come."

"Oh," a melodious voice answered. "Young Lord Shi asked me to help him hem in his new robe. I was coming to pick it up."

It had to be the second maid.

"Oh, he's just got back to the main residence, and should be out any minute. He has an, uh, appointment."

Oh, no. Tian rose enough so that he could peek out the window.

Miss Tang wore a simple but nice yellow dress with green embroidery and knotted buttons. With the high-bridged nose, large eyes, and full lips of a Northerner, she was almost as pretty as Wen, though certainly not as beautiful as Princess Kaiya. Her eyes shifted up toward the window.

He ducked back down.

Had she seen him? His disguise might work against a nearsighted old woman, but a young maid...

"Well, I don't want to slow him down," Miss Tang said. "I'll just fetch a thread and needle. Don't even tell him I'm here, or else he'll..."

The old woman let out her creaky laugh. "Yes, yes. He has very grabby hands. Don't worry, I think he will be in a rush for *this* appointment."

Grabby. It was a good word to describe so many of the men Tian had seen over the last week in the Floating World and the Trench. He shook the thought out of his head. There was a window of opportunity for him to get out while Miss Tang was retrieving her sewing supplies. He peeked out the window again, just in time to see her disappear into the east wing, and the old servant stomp off to the west wing.

He returned the room back to the way it had been, locked it, then ran down the steps to the door. He skidded to a stop and turned back: he'd almost forgotten those annoying shoes. Slipping them on, he squared his shoulders and tried to imitate Shi Han's gait as well as the platform shoes would allow.

Hurrying through the courtyard, he shot a glance to the east wing.

A splash of yellow disappeared behind the doorway.

The real Shi Han must be a monster for poor Miss Tang to want to avoid him. Lengthening his stride, he headed to the inner gate.

The clattering of rickshaw wheels over pavestones came to a stop outside. The outer gate creaked.

Someone was coming home.

Had Jie failed to delay the chamberlain? Or had Wen not kept Shi Han busy?

CHAPTER 5

Despite training for years to become a courtesan in the Floating World, Yan Jie had never quite mastered feminine grace. Mostly for lack of trying. It was always assumed she would only spend a year or so at the Chrysanthemum Pavilion attracting bids for her virgin price, then be plucked once Heaven's Dew arrived. Six years later, she'd yet to start her monthly cycles. Why bother to learn to be a Blossom when her exotic looks alone had sent her virgin price to the Blue Moon, and her true interest lay in using her other skills?

How she regretted that now, because her unique facial features had yet to catch the eye of Lord Shi's steward as he went shopping in the capital's sprawling open-air herb market. Or maybe the high-collared one-piece dress' slit rode so high on her leg, it made her look even flatter than she really was.

That didn't stop people, men and women alike, from lingering on her, and one gentleman even recognized her from her time at the Chrysanthemum Pavilion before it had burned down. Or rather, before her former lover, Lilian, had burned it down in an attempt to fake her own death and escape the clan. A knot formed in Jie's throat, but she swallowed it.

Was there really more to Lilian's betrayal and subsequent death at Jie's own hands? Whether she gave the contents of the safe to Fixer Zhang to find out, or surrendered it to the clan, she needed to make sure the steward didn't make it back to the house while Tian was still cracking it.

The steward was a good-looking man in his thirties, with smooth skin, a strong chin, and a prominent brow. Dressed in a brown silk robe which did little to hide his brawny physique, he was now working his way through the rows of stalls. Roots of varying sizes and scents lay in neat lines in some bins, while dried leaves of differing colors and shapes sprawled haphazardly in others. Twigs, barks, dried fruits, and more were interspersed in boxes. An auctioneer's voice on the central stage boomed above the din of hawkers and buyers, inviting bids on the latest shipment of myrrh and frankincense from Ayuri lands.

Keeping her tapered ears exposed, she'd brushed by him three times already. It was enough that she could have swiped his purse, returned it, and swiped it again, but he still hadn't taken notice of her. At least she'd been able to sneak a glance at his shopping list. He'd picked up goat weed and steamed red ginseng, both aphrodisiacs, and was looking for a third, morinda. Perhaps Lord Shi had trouble getting aroused, or maybe he'd planned a particularly amorous night with a lover in the capital. Either way, the realm's economy seemed to run on men's urges and women's vanity.

She sucked on her lower lip as she planned her next approach. If the steward finished shopping in the next few minutes, he'd make it back in time to find Tian, and the boy's budding disguise skills wouldn't be enough to deceive someone who saw Young Lord Shi Han on a daily basis. It looked as if the steward wasn't going to take notice of her, so it was time to initiate contact. He was now leaning over a bin of morinda, picking up individual pieces of the long, flat grey root, placing some on a sheet of paper and throwing most back.

Here was her in, to play the role of the ditsy girl that men loved to help. All she had to do was ask him about the herb, and they'd waste ten minutes while he showed off his knowledge. She started toward him.

"It's top-quality morinda," the vendor said. "From the mountains of Nanling Province. I just got it in this morning."

Shit. The chance meeting would have to wait, for it to be plausible that she hadn't heard.

With a dismissive snort, the steward handed the vendor the herbs, who weighed them out on a hand scale. He then looked up. "Two silver *jiao*."

The steward lifted his left arm, revealing a string of coins in his hanging sleeves. Some people carried money this way, mistakenly believing that cutpurses and pickpockets wouldn't be able to steal it as easily as a coin purse. There were surprisingly few coins—mostly silver and copper—for the steward of a heredity lord. Yet that didn't catch her eye as much as a cylindrical key which looked to be made of a bluish metal, strapped to his forearm with a common thong. Readily available, clan members used them to quickly flick hidden daggers out. Maybe it was her imagination, but the key seemed to vibrate almost imperceptibly.

When the transaction was done, Jie sidled up to him, brushing against the pressure points in his left arm. It would slightly desensitize the limb for several hours, hopefully enough for him to not notice when she snagged the key. "Excuse me kind sir, this is morinda, right?"

"That's what the bin says," he said in a deep, annoyed voice. He didn't even bother to turn away from stringing his change.

Jie bowed her head, to make sure her ear appeared in his peripheral vision. "Thank you, I was looking for it. Can you tell me how to choose the best quality?"

"Look, miss," he started, turning his head and looking down at her.

She brushed a lock of hair over her ear, and tilted her head in a demure manner. Lilian had been an expert at this coy look. Jie, on the other hand...

His eyes widened, and he put his hand on his chest. "Oh, my. You're the Floating World half-elf."

"My notoriety precedes me, I see." She flashed a smile, waiting for him to expose his arm again.

He smiled and waved his hands back and forth. "No, no. My lord placed an early bid to uh, pluck your blossom."

The way he said it bordered on distaste, as if she'd been a common streetwalker, and not a budding courtesan of one of the greatest Houses. She bowed, the motion lacking a Blossom's grace. "It's nothing to be ashamed of. It's an honor to receive any bid."

"Oh, I meant no disrespect. I...I am going to shut my mouth before it gets me in more trouble." He put a hand over his mouth in the cutest manner.

She let out a girlish giggle. It looked like her plan to stall him would not only work, it might also be a way of trawling for information. "If I may ask, who is your lord?"

"I'm not at liberty to..."

She drew a light finger over the four-petal *wen* emblem on a white patch stitched to his shoulder, desensitizing him even more. "Lord Shi of Jinjing County."

"You know your *wen*." His shiver at her touch said she had him where she wanted.

"He was a patron of my sister, Lilian." With a conspiratorial smile, she leaned in and pointed at his herb list. "I see you've chosen aphrodisiacs. Does your lord have difficulties saluting the moon? Or does he have a big night planned?"

"Saluting the—?" His brow furrowed before his lips rounded. "Oh. Oh, my. I am sorry, I am not at liberty to say."

His prim and proper attitude did not fit his stature or his warrior's build, the mismatch being rather endearing. It might even be arousing, if Yuna's death didn't weigh so heavily on her now. She shook fond memories out of her head, lest they cloud her focus for the mission. He'd taken the bait; now it was time to reel him in. She pressed up against him and whispered in his ear, "Would you like to taste what your lord could not?"

He took several steps back, eyes large like a shocked doe. He looked up to the Iridescent Moon. "I must be getting back."

No, no, she'd been too aggressive. What would Lilian have done in this situation? Jie jutted out her lower lip and hung her head. "Am I not pretty?"

"It's not that. I'd love to find out how you keep your skin so clear. Asking for his lordship's lady." He gave an apologetic smile. "I just don't have the coin."

She swept a finger over his thumb, a trick that always worked for Lilian. "I didn't ask for it. I would like you to recommend me to your lord."

He pulled his hand back. "Well, I can do that."

How was this not working? Even if she'd never really practiced the art of seduction, what man would turn down a tumble between the sheets with the realm's only known half-elf, and a pretty one, at that? She scuffed her toe in a circle on the ground. She kept her voice low and wounded, and maybe some of that tone wasn't contrived. "You don't want to have a taste yourself?"

"I'm afraid that would not be appropriate. I really must be going." He pulled away, bowed, and scurried off.

Somewhere on the ground, Jie would have to find her ego. Just not now, because the Iridescent Moon now waxed to its third crescent. The steward would make it home in a quarter of a phase, and Tian would most likely still be there.

The steward paused, gaze shifting to the ass of a young man bent over a bin of herbs. A smile flickered across his face.

That might be the reason he'd shown little interest in her. Still, he continued on his way. If he were taking the fastest path, he'd cut through an alley.

There, she could use a different skill set, a reliable one she'd hoped not to resort to.

CHAPTER 6:

Wen rubbed her face from where something hard on Young Lord Shi Han's chest, beneath his robe, had dug into her cheek. Tian had estimated she needed to keep the young lord occupied for an hour, in order for him to crack Lord Shi's safe and leave the plausible scenario that Shi Han had stopped by home before going to the Floating World. Now, six minutes from the time she'd brought him to the room, the kid was already pulling his pants back up.

Well, if there was one reliable thing about teenage lords, besides their oversized egos and quickness to anger when that was challenged, it was that it didn't take long for them to recover from spilling their seed. Actually, there were many more reliable things about teenage lords, all things Wen had planned to teach Yuna.

That was neither here nor there. What mattered was the clan mission. Up to now, the niggling question of who had set all the things in motion that had led to Lilian's and Yuna's deaths had distracted Wen from the goal at hand, and she'd failed at the most elementary of tasks.

Shaking all those thoughts of her head, she sat up and folded her knees beneath her. She crossed her hands over her chest, leaving a hint of her cleavage visible. She made a point of studying the Dragonscribed painting on the wall. "Young Lord."

Shi Han's eyes followed hers. Then his fingers froze on his drawstrings, and his gaze fell on her.

Baited. Using her most breathy voice, she said, "You are the most well-endowed Hummingbird I've ever been with."

A grin twitched at his lips. "That's what Tang Li said."

Almost hooked. She cast her eyes down, but then looked up through her lashes. "I was so close to reaching Heaven."

"Oh?" His smile slipped. "I thought you did."

She fiddled with her pinkie. Oh, the poor boy. What had Lord Shi's maid done to misinform him so? Perhaps she'd just wanted him to get it over with, and faked it to the point where he couldn't read her body language. Wen beckoned him closer. "You are so large, and I was so close." She held her thumb and index finger at a distance where a sheet of paper could barely slide between them. Never mind that he was of average size, and that the largest men were the most artless of the lot, thinking that length and girth with a few good thrusts were all it took.

Shi Han took a tentative step closer.

She took his hand, then drew him knees-first onto the bed. She leaned in and whispered, "To tell you the truth, I've never reached the Heavens with a man."

His eyes went wide as a kite taking in the wind. "You have with a woman?"

"And what if I did?" She let out her most titillating laugh.

Eyes glazing over, Shi Han gulped. As expected, his member bulged through his pants and robe, as he no doubt let his imagination run. Of course, no matter how much he adored this Tang Li, he was imagining several Blossoms entertaining him at the same time, as many wealthy Hummingbirds requested.

Let him believe that, and not the truth that as early as Florets, they'd explored each other to learn about pleasure; and as Blossoms, receiving selfish men day in, day out, it wasn't uncommon to find comfort in another Blossom's arms. Maybe, just maybe, Jie and Lilian had found that in each other. A twinge of jealousy, mixed with sadness, pulled at her heart. She still smiled and bowed her head. "Young Lord, may I?"

He looked at her, like a doe staring down a hunter's bow. "May you...?"

She pulled one of his shoulders while pushing the other, the torque thrusting him back-first onto the bed in a technique that, in the Floating World, only the embedded Black Lotus sisters knew. His pants drawstrings weren't yet tied, so it was easy to lower them to his knees. His breath came in labored pants. Maybe he'd crest the wave again, right now.

She reached beneath his robes, but he pushed her hands away. "Don't look at it."

Oh, the poor boy. Had this Tang Li said something to him? "What's wrong?"

His lip trembled, and the way his eyes glassed over, it looked like he was about to burst into tears. "My father. He called it...called it... Have you fucked him before?"

"Yes," she lied. If pressed, she could always make up details based on what Lilian had told her. "Have you heard the adage, 'What happens in the Floating World, stays in the Floating World?'"

He cocked his head.

"It means that whatever happens here is a secret. A Blossom will never repeat what they've seen or heard." A Black Lotus sister, however...

"And?"

"I'm going to break that rule now." She leaned in closer. "You have to promise you will never tell anyone I did this, or else I might be punished."

His eyes searched hers. "All right, I promise."

"Your father is a selfish lover." At least, that's what Lilian had said. Whether it was true or not really didn't matter, as long as the words manipulated his son. "He doesn't know how to please a woman."

Shi Han's eyes brightened. "That's what Tang Li said, too!"

"So you have nothing to worry about." Wen flashed a smile.

His hands shot down to his manhood. "Well, don't look at it."

What had the boy's father said to traumatize him so much? What could possibly be wrong? Was it small? Misshapen? It hadn't *felt* that different from any of the others she'd taken. Maybe a disease? She suppressed a shudder—the herbal medicines they drank, and washed with before and after receiving a Hummingbird, prevented most sicknesses.

She'd respect the poor boy's wishes. At least while he was paying attention, so that he'd never know she'd seen whatever he was so ashamed about. After all, a Black Lotus' thirst for knowledge was never sated.

Holding his gaze, Wen took hold of him and pushed his robe to the side. Straddling his hips, she guided him inside of her. His eyes widened and mouth rounded. Unless his true first, Tang Li, was trained as a Blossom, she wouldn't know how to evoke the look of wonder that so many lordlings got with their first encounter with a woman. More likely he'd done the work, without any idea of the art of lovemaking.

Unlike the first time, when she was dwelling on Yuna, she concentrated on Shi Han's reactions. Keeping her fabricated moans light, she rocked gently most of the time to avoid overstimulating him, and paused whenever he appeared to come close to cresting.

Time trickled on, and Shi Han was coming close to the point of no return. Wen glanced at the dwarf-made water clock. Just a little longer. Arching her back, she threw her head back and let out a well-practiced scream. She pitched forward, letting him slip out of her, and panted as she lay on his chest, her hand between them and right over whatever had stabbed her when their roles were reversed.

It was cylindrical with nubs, and the way it had felt on her cheek suggested it was metal. A key. Maybe the one that opened Lord Shi's safe, which poor Tian was probably trying to pick at this very second.

She turned and rested her ear against his heart. It pattered as his breast rose and fell, and she chose that moment to sneak a glance at his manhood.

A black birthmark, shaped like a worm, marred the shaft. The poor boy, to be taunted by his own father. She looked up and met his eyes. "Thank you for taking me to Heaven, my Lord."

He patted her on the back; such a gentle motion, unlike every other Hummingbird. "I can make Tang Li crest many times."

Wen buried her laugh. No matter how much credit she wanted to give the boy, he always said something to ruin it. In the corner of her eye, she found the water clock. An hour had passed, and she could send him on his way now.

Still, with such an awful father, maybe he'd enjoy a good memory. He was still hard, so she took him to Heaven. At least someone should reach there today.

He collapsed back, arms splayed out. Frowning.

She propped her head up on one elbow and drew circles on his chest with a finger. "What's wrong, my Lord?"

"Father made me come here today. He's got some kind of rivalry with Lord Peng, and we're going to see him at Lord Wu's moons-viewing reception tonight."

With that kind of Father, the kid might grow into a monster himself. Wen leaned on his shoulder. "He made you come... Am I not beautiful?"

"Yes! You are! But...but... I love Tang Li."

Heavens, the passion of young men. She let out a sigh. "You are a young lord. You're expected to buzz from flower to flower."

His face scrunched up, as if he were tasting a strange fruit and deciding if he liked it. "But I love her."

Ah, the poor boy. Of course, he'd never be allowed to marry a simple maid. She sat up and held out her hand to help him up. "Come, let's take you down so you can go back to your Tang Li."

He gave a quick, enthusiastic nod.

She'd held up her end; now it was a matter of waiting and seeing if Jie had been able to delay the chamberlain, giving Tian enough time to crack the safe.

To give him just a little more time to complete the clan's mission, she took her time dressing. No matter his professed love for this maid, Shi Han's gaze weighed on her naked form from where he sat on her bed. She flashed a sultry look over her shoulder, teasing him with a last glance at her rear.

When she was done, she took the young man's hand and guided him out of her room. On the mezzanine, she looked down into the common room.

Lord Shi was gone.

CHAPTER 7:

With someone entering the front gate to Lord Shi's courtyard home, Tian set his back to the courtyard tree. Realizing he was too broad for the trunk to conceal him, he turned to his side and peeked around.

Lord Shi. He was pulling his scabbarded *dao* from his sash.

Tian's chest squeezed. Maybe a near-sighted old woman would mistake him for young Shi Han; but his own father? It wasn't very likely. Not only that, but Lord Shi would've been with his son at the Peony Garden. If he saw Tian now, he'd wonder when his son had either learned to run fast, or travel back in time.

"Steward Zhu!" Lord Shi's voice boomed across the courtyard.

Guilt twanged in Tian's stomach. Jie delaying the poor steward meant he'd probably be punished. Then again, Tian was trespassing, and Lord Shi wouldn't recognize him as a great lord's son. And maybe that was better, because Tian wasn't supposed to be in the capital anyway.

The man's boots echoed across the pavestones. "Steward Zhu!"

He was close now, only three paces away. Hands sweating, Tian drew a knife. Not like that would have much of a chance against a *dao*. He circled the trunk, keeping it between him and the lord. Still, the chance of him catching sight of his robe—

"Lord Shi," Miss Tang's voice rang out from the east wing. "Welcome home."

"Little Li." The lord's tone softened.

Tian would've blown out a breath, but that would've given him away. He focused instead on the tone of Lord Shi's voice: happy. And hers, lilting, like the way Wen spoke to her men. Did these two hold hands? Had they arranged to meet while Shi Han was away?

"What are you doing here?" Lord Shi asked, disproving that theory.

"I came to hem in Young Lord Shi's robe. He's grown so fast, and needs to look presentable during your audience with the Emperor."

"Yes, yes." He blew out a sigh. "That's a very good idea. Sadly, that prodigal son will find a way to ruin my plans with his stupidity. I'm sure of it."

What did *prodigal* mean? And what kind of plans would Lord Shi have? Was that why the clan wanted the safe opened?

"Please, my Lord," she said, voice louder. "Give him more credit. He has more potential than you think."

Lord Shi snorted.

"Come, my Lord. Let me show you my new underwear."

"I'm glad you came, then." Lord Shi laughed.

Heavens. She *did* hold hands with Lord Shi.

His footsteps clopped up the three steps to the east wing.

Tian peeked around the tree.

Miss Tang Li was guiding him along. Just as they stepped over the threshold, she looked over her shoulder, past Lord Shi, and right at Tian.

Tian ducked back. Had she seen him?

"I oiled the hinges of this door." Miss Tang spoke even louder than before. "You won't hear them when it shuts."

Was she informing Lord Shi? Or telling Tian that she was creating an opening for him? After all, she knew from the old servant that Shi Han—well, Tian—was here. With a last look, Tian pulled off the platform shoes and ran the rest of the way across the courtyard, through the inner gate.

On the other side, in the corridor between the inner and outer gates, he leaned back against a wall and blew out his breath. That had been close, and he might've been caught if not for Miss Tang.

With his luck, he'd run into the servant, or the chamberlain would come home right as he was leaving; but somehow his luck held up and he cleared the outer gate without incident. He cast one last glance at the house, then continued on his way back to the Peony Garden.

He cut through an alley. On the other side, he made a hard turn to the north...

...and careened into someone.

Whoever it was, they were as sturdy as the Great Wall, and knocked Tian back on his feet. He looked up.

Lord Shi's steward.

And Tian was dressed just like Shi Han, with the emblem of Jinjing County on both shoulders. The white patches stood out on the brown robes like a light bauble in the middle of the night. He held his breath.

Steward Zhu started to look d—

"Steward Zhu!" Lord Shi called from behind the big man.

The steward turned around.

In that moment, Tian scrambled to his feet, covered his shoulders with his hands and, using a trick Yuna had taught him, twisted behind Steward Zhu as he turned back around. He'd have to deal with Lord Shi, but...

...but Lord Shi was back at his home holding hands with Miss Tang. Up ahead, from where the voice had come, was nothing but a wall.

"Watch where you're going, dunderhead!" Steward Zhu yelled at Tian's back.

Without turning around, stopping, or uncovering his hands from his shoulders, Tian bobbed his head several times. Behind him, Steward Zhu harrumphed before his footsteps faded into the alley.

Tian dropped his hands and blew out his biggest sigh since...ten minutes ago in Lord Shi's courtyard.

He began to hurry along when a hand tugged him into a new alley. Drawing a knife, he sunk into a defensive position and found his assailant in his peripheral vision. He spun, blade at the ready.

"It's me, Tian." Jie stood there just out of reach, hands up.

All tension melted out of his shoulders. "Heavens. I almost stabbed you."

"You would've missed." Jie grinned. "Did you open the safe?"

He shook his head. "Too complicated."

Her expression fell for a moment. "Well, at least you saved the steward from a nasty headache. Now come on. We need to rendezvous with Wen."

On their brisk walk back to the Peony Garden, he practiced the clan's subtle sign language, recounting Lord Shi's return, Miss Tang, and the safe—though he'd not yet learned the terms for *combination dial*, *poison dart*, or *clear gemstone*. All the while, he kept his eye out for tails and anything out of the ordinary. They ducked into the silk market to avoid Young Lord Shi Han as he crossed over the bridge from the Floating World, then merged with the crowds starting to enter for a night of carousing.

They crept around to the rear of the Peony Garden, to the back entrance near the kitchens. He followed Jie at a distance through the busy kitchens. Though it teamed with chefs, he used the techniques Yuna had taught him about finding dead spaces between lines of sight and behind moving and turning people. He slipped through the door into the common room, then stayed at the backs of Seedlings as they wiped down tables and chairs, straightened banners and paintings, and swept the floors. It was getting easier and easier.

Finally he rounded into the hallway, just as Jie disappeared into the Gardener's office—their new temporary base of operations—at the end and closed the door behind her. With footsteps coming down the steps to this hall, he ran on tiptoes to the door and pulled on the handle.

Locked.

The footsteps grew louder. Stuck at the end of the hall, he was cornered, with no means of escape and nowhere to hide. If he couldn't pick the lock and get in before whoever was coming down the steps came in, it could expose their new hideout.

CHAPTER 8

About to be discovered in the Peony Garden, Tian internally shouted Big Person Words at Jie for locking the door. Looking back to the stairwell and gauging the speed at which the shadow of a Blossom approached, he probably had five seconds to pick the lock. He withdrew his picks. With a few quick twists, it yielded in his best time yet. Chest filling with pride, he opened the door, slipped in, and started to close it behind him.

"Wait," Wen's voice hissed behind him.

Tian's shoulders slumped. His personal best lockpicking time wouldn't have mattered anyway. He held the door open.

Wen glided down the hallways, elegant as always, even in a simple blue robe. If anyone could rival Princess Kaiya's grace and beauty...well, no one could, but Wen would be a distant second. She flashed the same big smile that she had the day they met, yet something was missing. Yuna's death had hurt her most of all. She patted him on the head as she entered, and took a seat in a cushioned bloodwood chair across from Jie at the huge matching desk.

He closed the door and plopped down beside Wen, but then looked to the open window. If they were going to discuss Lord Shi and his safe, it would be better to shutter it on the off chance someone passed by. He started to speak.

Jie held up her hand. "Two more sisters are almost here."

With the Houses coming alive at this hour, which clan sister would be able to join them right now? The Seedlings would all be going to bed, the Florets serving food and drink, and the Blossoms...well, soon, they'd be holding hands with Hummingbirds. Tian looked back to the door.

Wen let out her cute giggle, the first time she'd laughed since learning of Yuna. She took Tian's head and turned it to the window.

A pair of hands appeared on the window sill. A blur of greyish-black shot through the window and landed without a sound on the thick wool carpet. She looked up, revealing Big Sister Meisha in a stealth suit which clung to her slender form. A nineteen-year-old Blossom from the Orchid Palace, she had a husky voice that didn't match her thinness. A second later, another woman popped in, dressed identically, though she was more filled out. At twenty-four, Yangyang of the Lily Pond was one of the oldest clan sisters embedded in the Floating World. Both set a fist into a palm in salute, then slid into chairs around the desk.

Pointing at the window, Tian turned to Jie. "Why didn't we come in that way?"

Jie stood and closed the shutters. "You won't get better at stealth, lockpicking, and keeping a clear head under pressure if you take the easy way."

Full lips twisted into a grin, Yangyang nodded, and Meisha chuckled. Wen patted him on the head, yet again. They all thought him a pet.

Still, it made sense. What didn't, was... "How come Elder Sisters Meisha and Yangyang aren't at their Houses tonight?"

The ladies all exchanged glances, and whatever silent signal passed between them, Tian had yet to learn.

Yangyang's lilting voice carried like a songbird's. "Blossoms get three nights off when their best friend comes each month."

That sounded so sweet, and so considerate of friends. Tian nodded in complete understanding. What he would do to see his best friend, Princess Kaiya, again.

"So," Jie said, returning to her seat. "Tian was not able to crack the safe, because it was a giraffe lock?"

Giraffe? Tian flashed the hand signal for *multiple*.

Wen bent his pinkie. "Multiple."

Nodding, Tian leaned over the desk, dabbed a brush on the inkstone, and drew the safe on a sheet of paper. He frowned that the combination lock wasn't in the exact spot between the two keyholes, and that the round stone's size was off by a hair. He was about to crumple it up and start over.

"That's pretty amazing detail." Wen stayed his hand. "Maybe you should've been a Dragonscribe."

"It's a complicated set-up," Meisha said, her voice deep and sultry.

Tian pointed to the lower keyhole. "There was a dart trap here."

Jie peered at his work. "Are you sure this is it?"

He nodded.

"What is it?" Wen ran a finger from the bottom lock up, through the combination, to the second keyhole, and then around the stone.

It left a smudge. Tian scowled and reached for the paper again.

Jie pulled it out of his reach. "It comes from the Blackhammer dwarf clan in Thironar. They only made a dozen or so."

"Or so?" Tian frowned. "Thirteen? Fourteen?"

"I'll ask a dwarf next time I see one." Jie snorted. "In any case, it was five, maybe six years ago."

The lack of specifics was grating. "Five or s—"

"Five years, six months, seven days." Jie counted on her fingers.

Tian brightened. "Really?"

"Will it shut you up if I say yes?"

"Yes."

"Then yes." Jie grinned. "Now, as I was saying, they are the pinnacle of Dwarven ingenuity. They're impervious to blows. Flameproof and waterproof, they can protect its contents from heat, cold, and moisture for six hours. The keys are made from a unique metal, found only on Ayudra Island, and which only the Blackhammer clan can work."

Tian leaned forward in his chair, fascinated. The capital of the sprawling Ayuri Empire, Ayudra lay in the shadow of one of the world's great pyramids. When the Hellstorm rained fire from the heavens three centuries before, it destroyed the city and its levees, allowing the ocean to claim vast swaths of the Ayuri heartland. Once a coastal city, Ayudra was now an island of ruins. The Order of Paladins, who could supposedly fight with superhuman speed, had since established a school for their trainees there. Not that Tian would ever have the chance to meet a Paladin, let alone visit the island. But for now, he could enjoy the stories. "Go on."

"Some people believe the stones are Dragonstones, but they are actually moonstones."

"Oh!" Tian clapped his hands together, startling Meisha and making Yangyang glower. Dragons supposedly chased flaming stones around, but the one he saw... "It swirled with color, like the Iridescent Moon."

"I've heard of these safes," Wen said. "There's a gear in the combination lock whose clicks mask the disk's clicks."

"If you're a human," Jie said. "The clan has one of these combination locks on one of its safes, and I can hear when to switch directions. However, Lord Shi's safe is more complicated. After the combination is correctly entered, both keys have to be turned simultaneously."

"Is that all?" Meisha laughed, deep like her voice.

"No." Jie shook her head. "The moonstone being there means it can only be opened during a one-hour window. It's—"

"Lined up with the Iridescent Moon." It was all Tian could do not to jump up and down. The window and safe had been lined up in Lord Shi's room, which explained why both hadn't been perfectly centered with the furniture. At least it hadn't been laziness.

"It's such an impressive lock," Yangyang said. "How come there are only a dozen?"

Such a lack of specificity! Tian grit his teeth.

Jie smirked at him. "They were custom-built for our lords. They were very popular at first, until they ran into a problem: if you needed something from the safe, you had to wait until the right time to open it. Also, the keys are unique, because only the Blackhammer Clan knows how to forge that metal. So if you lost it, you could never open the safe again. I've heard there are three or four—" she shot a glance at Tian— "that are permanently locked. After so many complaints, nobody ordered any more. However, it turns out that being near the keys helps Dragonscribes and Dragonweavers make their magic, so they are highly prized. You can find counterfeits in the Northwest Promenade."

"Those won't help us," Meisha said. "How can we open the safe?"

Jie's expression lit up. "Lord Shi's steward has one of the keys. He keeps it on his wrist."

"About this long?" Wen held her fingers four and a half *cun* apart.

Jie nodded.

"Then I think Lord Shi's son has the other." Wen touched her cheek. "I felt something that size and shape hanging from his neck.

"That still doesn't help us with the time," Yangyang said.

"We might be able to find out from Steward Zhu," Wen said. "Or the old servant, or the maid, Tang Li."

"Tang Li." Jie stood up straight. "She was an older Blossom, almost thirty, at the Chrysanthemum Pavilion. Very pretty, but not the sharpest *dao* in the armory."

Wen's pretty lips rounded. "I thought the name sounded familiar."

"It *is* a common name," Yangyang said.

Jie nodded. "If it's the same Tang Li, Lord Yang was one of her regulars."

"And Lilian's," Wen said.

Jie frowned. "In any case, he bought out her contract a couple of years ago."

"A couple?" Tian asked.

"Two years, three months, four days," Jie said.

"Really?"

"Will it shut you up if I say yes?" Jie asked.

He nodded.

"Then yes." Jie snorted.

Meisha blinked innocently. "Lord Yang has rarely left the capital since. He's probably been bedding her every night."

"While ingratiating himself with the Emperor during the day," Yangyang said. "The whispers between the sheets say Lord Yang might receive the late Lord Ting's county."

Tian tapped his chin. Father had always said that Northerners were a rugged people, prone to discontent with the imperial court. Would Lord Yang be able to maintain control of so much land?

"Surely Tang Li must've earned out her bond by now," Meisha said. "I'm surprised she'd work as a maid instead of joining a Floating World House as an independent Blossom."

Jie chuckled. "As I said, she wasn't very bright."

Or maybe she didn't like to hold hands with men. Tian frowned.

"Young Lord Shi is utterly besotted by Tang Li." Wen let out a sigh, which could only be described as wistful.

"Young love." Though Yangyang's tone was almost as wistful as Wen's, she rolled her eyes.

With the clan sisters waxing poetic about Shi Han's devotion to Tang Li, Tian felt he needed to remind them: "Lord Shi is reporting to the imperial court tomorrow. The Emperor wants to know what's in that safe beforehand. What if Lord Shi is tied up in the threat on the Emperor?"

The table went silent.

Yangyang shook her head. "Lord Shi has always been in the Emperor's good graces. They travel together often. Other lords joke and say Lord Shi and Lord Yang fight to sit on the Emperor's lap."

"We can't be too careful," Tian said. How come he was the only one seeing plots and conspiracies?

"Tian is right." Jie nodded to him. "Back to the safe. What are our assets?"

Tian tapped his chin. There were twenty-six sisters left in the cell, plus him. "Light the spire of the Black Lotus Shrine." Visible from almost everywhere in the Floating World, it would bring all of the members to the safehouse outside the district.

Jie shook her head. "It would take a long time before everyone saw it at this hour. Many of the Blossoms are already receiving Hummingbirds."

"Florets will be serving in the common rooms, with no line of sight," Yangyang added.

Wen gave a single bob of her head. "Seedlings will be headed to bed, and they might see it. But they're so young, I don't think we should risk them."

"I agree," Jie said. "By the time everyone saw it and convened at the safehouse, we would have wasted too much time."

Tian tapped his chin. "Then one of us goes to each of the houses—"

"It would take too long," Wen said, "and we'd lose one person until the job was done."

"What if we split up and went to the houses?"

"We'd still lose time, and it could be for nothing." Jie shook her head. "If Lord Shi tried to act against the Emperor in Sun-Moon Palace—and remember, he will only be allowed to have his dagger— the clan's best operatives are there to protect him. No matter what, the clan wants us to find out what's in that safe, and I think we have all the womanpower we need."

Tian coughed. Apparently, they were forgetting about him. Even if he couldn't unlock the safe, he could play a role.

Yangyang pulled at the sleeve of her stealth suit. "How much of the musk and flower toxins do we have?"

"Tian smashed most of the flower toxin when he incapacitated Gardener Ju." Wen patted him on the head.

There was no blame in her voice, but Tian's shoulders slumped of their own accord all the same.

"And I used most of our supply of the musk in Yue Heaven and the Trench," Jie said. "Some of our Blossoms might have a little, but if they are receiving Hummingbirds in their rooms, it will be almost impossible to get ahold of."

"A party." Wen clapped her hands together. "Young Lord Shi Han wanted a party, but Lord Shi didn't have the coin for it. How about if we take the party to him?"

Yangyang shook her head, sending her ponytail wagging. "How would you justify it? A Blossom wouldn't do it for free."

"Old Feng," Tian said. The actor had done well this morning, after all. "We bribed him to recommend Wen for Shi Han's First Pollination. What if we get him to come with us? It would be a gift."

"Wait," Wen said. "I just remembered, they won't be there. Shi Han mentioned that he and his father will be at Lord Wu's reception tonight. Lord Shi planned to boast to Lord Peng that Shi Han had his First Pollination with me."

"It's going to be at a new luxury river barge, straight out of his shipyards." Meisha traced a boat-like shape in the air with her slender finger.

Jie raised an eyebrow. "How do you know?"

"Everyone has been talking about it," Yangyang said. "Most of the Blossoms from my House are going. It will take off from Songyuan Quays at the second waxing gibbous. The Emperor would have been there, had it not been for the possible threat. Of course, I had to decline, because of my best friend."

Tian smiled. It was so sweet that Yangyang would turn down an event for a friend.

Jie looked to Wen. "How come we hadn't heard about it?"

"Maybe Gardener Ju would've told us, had she survived."

Tian shuddered. Though he hadn't killed Gardener Ju, his actions had led directly to it. It was the first time he'd been responsible for someone's death.

"Are any of our sisters going?" Yangyang asked.

"Not that I know of," Jie said. "I'm sure they would've reported it."

Wen turned to Meisha. "So you were you invited. If you showed up with some pretty friends, would they let you aboard?"

Yangyang and Meisha exchanged grins, and nodded in unison.

Meisha winked. "Lord Wu likes to make sure his receptions are memorable."

"That will get you three in," Jie said.

Wen batted her eyelashes. "I'll get the key from Young Lord Shi Han."

"We'll need it to swap it out with a fake so he doesn't realize it's gone," Jie said. "We can find a duplicate in the Northwest Promenade on the way."

Meisha leaned into Yangyang. "We can relay the real key off the barge."

"You're doing the swimming, if it comes to that," Yangyang said.

"You should." Meisha pinched Yangyang's cheek. "You're much more insulated than I am."

"How do we get it to the courtyard house?" Jie asked. "That's an hour's palanquin ride from the quays. Three-quarters that time by rickshaw."

"There should be horses. I can uh, borrow one." Tian gulped hard. The map appeared in his head. "At full gallop, my father's best charger would take a count of three-hundred ninety-seven to reach the main streets' intersection with the *hutong* warrens. We'd have to slow down inside the alleys. I'm sorry I can't tell you about horses I don't know."

Gawking, Wen shook her head. "If you're caught violating your banishment..."

"None of us can ride a horse," Jie said. "We don't have any other choice. To save time, I'll be at the courtyard house."

Wen laughed her refreshing laugh. "Where you can use your charms to get the key from the steward."

"Maybe not." Jie held up a hand. "I think he prefers thorns over blossoms."

Tian tapped his chin. What did that mean?

Jie met his gaze. "It means he likes to hold hands with boys instead of girls."

Tian's finger froze. These clan sisters—now *his* sisters—would hold hands with these lords without a second thought. In little over a week, they'd become even more like family than his own, accepting him when nobody else did. Only Princess Kaiya and Peng Kai-Long had ever been as nice to him. For once in his life, he belonged. He owed it to them. "Then I'll do it."

CHAPTER 9

"Absolutely not," Wen and Eldest Sister Jie said in unison.

If Wen shook her head any harder, her brains might leak out. Heavens knew that after crying all night and into the morning, it didn't feel there was much fluid left in her head. But Tian—sweet, refreshingly innocent Little Tian. He'd been so endearing with his confused expressions when the girls spoke of the dance between dragon and phoenix, and so clearly he didn't understand what he was volunteering for.

"Why not?" Yangyang was scowling.

"He's the same age as a Seedling," Meisha said, "who we wouldn't put in harm's way."

Tian's forehead scrunched up in the most adorable way. "Harm's way?"

Yangyang chuffed. "He's of the age where other clan brothers would."

"I can do it." Tian puffed out his chest.

"Oh, my sweet boy." Wen patted him on the head. "You wouldn't really be holding his hand. You'd be Polishing his Jade or letting him Pit your Peach."

Tian shrugged. "Those are simple tasks that a servant does, but I'll do it for the clan. And peaches aren't in season."

Meisha and Yangyang giggled, and the poor child didn't know they were laughing at his expense.

Sighing, Wen took Tian's hand. It was time to disabuse him of all his innocent notions, and perhaps ruin everything that was so adorable about him. "*Polishing Jade* is poetic way of describing your mouth on a man's penis. *Playing the Flute*, the term that the actor, Old Feng used when he brought you to this very House to spy, is a more vulgar way."

His eyes widened as he looked from her to Yangyang, from Meisha to Jie. "You mean, when you hold hands with a man..."

Jie took his hands in hers. "We are doing much more than holding hands, and we are usually undressed."

His mouth open and closed, but no words came out.

"Oh, my sweet boy." Wen rested her forehead to his.

"Do you know the difference between boys and girls?" Meisha asked.

He broke contact and gave a hard nod. "Of course. Boys *niaoniao* standing up. Girls squat. Girls put their hair up all pretty, and wear nice dresses. When they're young, their chests are like Jie's. But when they grow up..." His gaze swept from Meisha's small breasts to Yangyang's fuller cleavage, and finally fixed on Wen's for a moment before turning away.

None of them so much as flinched, having had all modesty trained out of them. Of course, he hadn't grown up in the clan—probably hadn't ever seen a woman's naked body—and still held on to social mores.

He'd have to come to understand some stark realities. Wen stood, and his eyes returned to hers. Then she loosened her sash and opened the folds of her gown. She untied the laces to her bust binder, which floated to the ground; and then those of her underpants, which slipped down to her ankles. She was bared, save for the throwing stars strapped to her thigh and the knife attached by a thong to her forearm.

His eyes lowered to her breasts, in the most analytical, objective way, then down to between her legs. His brow furrowed. Even with these truths revealed, he was still adorable. When he spoke, his tone sounded awestruck. "You are perfect. Like a painting."

The wonder in his voice stood in stark contrast to Shi Han's reaction. Heat flared in her cheeks, something which rarely happened anymore, at least not involuntarily. She tightened the gown around her. "To serve the clan and the Emperor, we let men, and sometimes women, enter us. But for you, since you don't have the same parts, you'd have to let Steward Zhu Pit your Peach."

For a moment, the poor boy looked as if he were about to faint. Then his expression crystalized into an intense focus, puckering up like a dried date. The way he tapped his chin in deep thought, he was probably calculating the airspeed of an Eldaeri messenger bird.

"If that's what it takes to get the key, I'll do it."

"Absolutely not," Jie and Wen again said together.

Wen cupped his cheek. "You're too young to do this. You don't know men the way we do."

"At the very least, we can use him as bait," Yangyang said.

Meisha nodded. "Or a distraction."

Like they'd used Yuna in the Trench. While that hadn't led directly to her death, it had been a contributing factor: had she not entered the Red Dragon Tang as a distraction, she wouldn't have run into her long-lost mother. Wen shook her head.

Jie, however, nodded.

"At least let me do that," Tian said.

Something churned in Wen's stomach. They'd only met less than a week ago, but to lose him too, so close to Lilian and Yuna...her heart would burst.

Meisha looked at the water clock. "We only have two hours to get ready, get in a rickshaw, find and buy a fake key, and then make it to Songyuan Quays. We need to start now."

"We'll have to borrow some of your gowns." Yangyang looked to Wen.

Tian's eyes studied the three as he tapped his chin. "Meisha is taller and skinnier, and Yangyang is shorter and fatter. Will you fit?"

If a stare could kill, Yangyang's glare would have surely slain Tian. Meisha gaped, while Jie buried a snort.

Wen covered her own chortle. His lack of subtlety just added to his adorableness. "Little Tian, never call a woman fat."

"Or old," Meisha said, then pointed her chin at Yangyang. "Even if they are."

"Enough fun," Jie said. "Tian will go ahead to the Northwest Promenade to find a duplicate key. He'll meet you at the quays and give it to you, while I scout out Lord Shi's courtyard home."

This time, Jie let Tian depart through the window. Wen led the way through the hall, up the stairwell, and to the second-floor mezzanine, while Meisha and Yangyang zigzagged over the joists and joints of the House's nightingale floors. She paused at times to shield them from the eyes of the scurrying Florets. She was almost to her room when—

"Wen," the Florist called from down in the common room.

Shit. Wen went to the balustrade. "Yes, Florist?"

"You will need to work tonight after all."

"But Florist, after Young Lord Shi's First Pollination..." It hadn't been particularly vigorous, but Wen had requested the night off for this mission, and let the Florist's imagination do the rest.

"A courier from Lord Peng just arrived with a palanquin. He would like you to join him for a moons-viewing reception on Lord Wu's river barge tonight."

Well, that was a fortunate coincidence. Wen fiddled with her pinkie. No doubt Lord Peng had gotten wind of Shi Han's First Pollination with her, and now had to flaunt her on his own lap. While this would mean a convenient ride to the quay, it also meant either Meisha or Yangyang would have to seduce Shi Han and coax the key off his neck. She bowed to the Florist. "I'll be down after I prepare."

She continued to her room, slid the door open, and went in.

Rummaging through her rack of gowns and wardrobe, now wearing only simple loincloths for their periods in lieu of lacy underpants, were Yangyang and Meisha. Wen sighed and closed the door behind her.

"Where's your gold-and-red satin?" Yangyang asked.

Wen snorted. "As if you'd fit in that."

"Since you will be fawning on Lord Peng or his sons or all three, we decided I would be the one to work Shi Han." Yangyang squeezed her breasts between her arms. "I'm better suited than Twiggy here."

Holding up the coveted gold dress, Meisha used her free hand to flap the skirts. "You're so short, you'd be tripping over the hem."

Wen suppressed a chuckle. As Tian had pointed out, her wardrobe would not be a good match for either the taller Meisha's waifish physique, or the shorter Yangyang's voluptuous curves. With both fastidious about their image, it might've been faster had they returned to their respective Houses and used their own clothes. "Your best friend is here, though," she said.

"I have other ways to entertain a teenage boy." Yangyang batted her eyelashes at Meisha.

Meisha pantomimed vomiting.

After all the losses, it was good to have a good laugh. Wen reached for a blue silk outer gown.

Meisha pulled a lilac-colored dress from a rack and held it up next to her in the mirror.

"No," Wen yelled, a pit in her stomach. While many of her gowns and dresses had been gifts from patrons, this one she'd chosen herself, the first one she'd bought with patron gratuities. She snatched it away.

Releasing the garment as if it were a snake, Meisha backed up several steps.

"I'm sorry." Wen clutched it to her chest. It was only by timing and circumstance that she still had it in her room. "Yuna adored it. I was going to gift it to her for her Plucking." Instead, she'd dress her body in it. Yuna would return to ash beautiful.

"No, *I* am sorry." Meisha sank to her knees, hands in her lap, and pressed her forehead to the ground, the elegant obeisance the mark of a Blossom and not a Black Lotus Fist.

Tears threatened. "Please stand. You didn't know."

They dressed in somber silence. Both Yangyang and Meisha chose translucent shawls, bust binders, and leg wraps. The ensembles could be loosened or tightened to suit their figures.

With little time to spare, they applied light make-up and glided down to the front doors. Seedlings all bowed low without question as they passed; it was not uncommon for Blossoms from other Houses to call on friends on their nights off.

Outside, light from the White and Blue Moons shone on an ornate palanquin sitting in the courtyard. Large enough for two lords to sit across from each other, it would be a tight fit for three. Eight bearers, the courier, and four guards, all dressed in Lord Peng's blue livery, were impatiently fidgeting, but now stopped and slavered. They bowed in a disorganized fashion, no doubt dazzled by the beauty and grace that only Floating World Blossoms could project.

The courier straightened. "Miss Wen, you honor our lord."

"The honor is mine." Wen bowed and straightened. "Would it be too much of an imposition if two of my friends joined?"

If one thing was more reliable than the Iridescent Moon's seat in the heavens, it was men and their urges. To a man, the guards and bearers wore silly grins. The courier opened and closed his mouth before finally nodding and gesturing for them to alight.

"We will need to hurry," he said, "if we are to make it in time."

Yangyang pointed with her chin. "The palanquin bears the insignia of Phoenix Trading."

Wen silently reprimanded herself for missing it. Yuna's death was affecting her attention to detail.

The courier looked, and turned back. "Oh, yes. Lord Peng was using his own. Phoenix Trading owes him many favors, and graciously allowed him to borrow this one for your comfort."

Wen exchanged glances with Yangyang and Meisha, who nodded.

One of the bearers kneeling by the doors on the palanquin side bowed his head and slid them open.

As the invited guest, Wen ducked in first, followed by Yangyang, the senior, and finally Meisha, who sidled up against Wen. Despite earlier concerns of size, three Blossoms took up not much more space kneeling on the fluffy cushions than two cross-legged warriors. It was still a tight fit, with Meisha's slender hips pressing against her own.

When the door closed, Yangyang and Meisha sprawled their legs out and lounged. With a quiet laugh, Wen did the same. In private, comfort took priority over propriety and grace.

The palanquin lifted into the air, and they set off. The gates to the Peony Gardens opened, where the guards received their broadswords. The bearers picked up the pace, jostling them.

"The moons will be beautiful tonight," Yangyang said, while signing, *These bearers have to be new team. They're awful.*

It's like we're already on a boat, but in a storm. Meisha squirmed. "On the river, I bet the reflection will be magnificent."

"I've never been to one of Lord Wu's receptions; I hear they are legendary," Wen said. *If there are a lot of guests coming by palanquin, the lords probably ran out of liveried servants, and had to hire extra.*

"His parties are the thing of epic tales, at least if you're a male." Meisha laughed. *I didn't recognize any of the bearers or soldiers.*

Heart squeezing, Wen pressed her ear to the wall to better hear the men's muffled conversation.

"We're just supposed to make her late," the courier said, breathless.

Wen's eyes widened, and she signed, *Possible trap.*

Yangyang and Meisha shifted.

The palanquin came to a stop.

CHAPTER 10

It wasn't the first, and probably wouldn't be the last time Jie was being followed.

Unlike previous occasions, however, her current stalker was doing a decent job of avoiding detection. Whenever she'd almost caught a direct glimpse of him in a reflective surface, he'd duck behind a store signboard, or the handful of city folk headed home for the day. The skill hinted at Black Lotus trailing techniques, and after a run-in with a supposedly dead former member, it was impossible to rule it out.

Most likely, though, it was another street urchin, following her at the behest of the mysterious Fixer Zhang. No matter how omniscient Fixer Zhang wanted to portray himself, he hadn't known about Lord Shi's invitation to Lord Wu's moons-viewing party. So, let her tail believe she was just following the original plan, to meet Lord Shi at his home. The less accurate the information he reported back to Fixer Zhang, the better leverage Jie would have for finding out the rest of Lilian's story.

There, she'd admitted it to herself. She was putting her own need to know ahead of the clan's mission. Worse, she was using cell assets. She hadn't even told them. And the guilt was pricking at her.

With a sigh, she turned the corner into the warren of courtyard homes. The paved streets were wide enough for ten people to walk abreast, though now, only a couple of people remained outside. All the houses were nice, but not extravagant, probably belonging to mid-level government officials or very minor lords. Really, it was well below the level of wealth expected for the hereditary ruler of a county.

Then again, the North was the poorest region in the realm, which might've been why Lord Ting had resorted to selling illegal yue, and why the Triads in the Trench had gotten Lilian to kill him.

With fewer hiding places, Jie's stalker fell back, occasionally poking his head out from beyond a corner in the distance. He probably didn't realize how elf vision could pick out his shape in the dark.

Up ahead, at the front gate of a house, metal whispered across stone as a knife sharpener worked behind a pushcart. A light bauble hanging from its frame formed a bubble of illumination around him, and also shined on a male servant at the threshold. The craftsman handed a cleaver back, and received a few coins, which he slipped into a pouch. The servant disappeared back behind the gates.

Black Lotus training taught to maintain distance from sharp objects, so Jie gave the sharpener a wide berth.

He turned to her and held out a small package wrapped in grey cloth. She froze, and he grunted and extended it again.

"What is it?" No doubt, it was a gift from Fixer Zhang.

"I don't know," he said in a gruff voice, throwing up his hands. "I was just told to give it to a girl in a grey dress."

So the mule had seen her departure from the Peony Garden, or at least heard it from her tail. She took it, the weight light in her hands. Paper crinkled inside. "Who told you? When did it happen?"

"The time it takes to sharpen a knife. It was some street kid. It was too dark, and he was too dirty to make out any features."

So about five minutes or so prior. It likely wasn't her tail, because they would've made contact and just given it to her; but the tail would've had time to pass it on to someone else. Whatever else could be said about Fixer Zhang, he enjoyed his anonymity. Most likely, neither the woman nor big man she'd met at the fountain were him, but they might be an asset, like the cell used Old Feng.

Jie bobbed her head, and continued on her way. Two turns later, she arrived near Lord Shi's corner home. The road was empty, though the din of muted conversations carried over from the courtyards all up and down the block. She ducked into an alley between two, where there was just enough light from the full White Moon to read.

Unwrapping the cloth, she found a dwarf key. What? Had Fixer Zhang already acquired one? She unfolded the paper and read.

Top key here. Steward has other. No need to go to Lord Wu's reception.

So Fixer Zhang now knew about the reception, but hadn't when they'd met this morning. Though by the time Wen was stalling Shi Han, who had the second key, Lord Shi had already decided to go. Tian had spotted Lord Shi here at the time. Somewhere in between, Fixer Zhang had acquired the second key from Shi Han, and also learned about the change in plans. Of course, this also meant that Wen, Meisha, and Yangyang wouldn't find the key on the boat, and Tian would be waiting at the quays, and wouldn't be able to be used as a distraction for Steward Zhu.

Jie hefted the key. She was on her own, but with one in hand, and the other not hard to acquire with a little violence, all she needed was to be able to hear the clicks in the combination lock, and know the time the safe would open.

* * *

Tian jogged through the streets of the capital, keeping his head low in case someone who knew him from his previous life as a noble's son saw him. To think, in that previous life, he'd be heaving for air after this much running.

At last he arrived at the Northwest Promenade. An open-air market, it was located on the north bank of the reservoir, directly across from the Floating World. With the onset of dusk, shoppers filed out from between the rows of stalls. Most vendors were packing up their wares, while many tables were already closed. Aksumi baubles on tables or being wrapped up created a dance of light and shadows.

Somewhere, there had to be one of these fake dwarf keys to swap out with Young Lord Shi Han's.

But first, he needed money. As naughty as it was, he swiped a few purses as he scanned the merchants closing down shop. Five minutes and six purses later, he ducked into an abandoned stall, to combine his ill-gotten wealth into a single purse. In all, two gold *yuan*, eleven silver *jiao*, and twenty-three copper *fen*.

Was it enough? Never having bargained, or even shopped for anything before, it was impossible to tell.

Up ahead, a merchant specializing in timepieces was haggling with a military officer. The metal rings, with twelve curved grills though the middle, allowed time to be measured by looking through them at the Iridescent Moon. Some included magnifying glasses and more grills, likely to measure time more accurately. Maybe it could be used to...

This would be awful, but with no telling how expensive a dwarf key would be, there was no other alternative. Tian whisked by and snapped up one of the timepieces. He held his breath as he maintained the same pace. Hopefully, neither the customer nor the vendor had noticed. He'd return it when he was done with it.

Sixteen steps later, he blew out that breath.

And skidded to a halt.

Right beside him, an elderly merchant was wrapping up silver bracelets in red cloth. Wrinkles streaked along his papery skin as he reached for what looked to be a dwarf key. He'd been so focused on getting away from the timepiece stall, he'd almost missed it.

He hopped over. "I want that key."

"This one?" Scooping it up, the old man squinted at him. "It's a rarity. Will make a Dragonweaver's—"

"It will make a Dragonweaver's magic stronger." Tian reached out for it.

The man pulled it back. "Then you know how valuable it is. I'll part with it for ten *yuan*."

Hiring Old Feng for an acting job had cost two gold coins. It sounded reasonable enough. However... "I don't have that much."

"Ah, I was waiting for the bargaining to begin!" A long smile caused more wrinkles to erupt across his face.

Tian emptied the contents of the purse on the table. "This is all I have."

The old man leaned in, eyes searching among the coins, then looked up. "You're either trying to cheat me, or you're really poor and bad at bargaining."

"Please, I really need that key."

"Are you a Dragonweaver? Weave me something to make me young, and it's yours."

Could Dragonweavers even do such a thing? Tian wasn't one, and apparently, two *yuan*, eleven *jiao*, and twenty-three *fen* wouldn't be enough. Maybe there would be another key somewhere in the market, but its owner might demand even more. He didn't need to use his new timepiece to see time was running out.

Heavens, forgive him for what he was about to do. He reached out, seized the old man's hand, and twisted it.

The merchant let out a yelp, but his fingers loosened on the key, and Tian plucked it away.

"Thief!" the merchant yelled.

Tian raked his gaze across the market. Everyone had frozen, and all eyes were locked on him. Including those of two of the city watch.

Oh, *baba*. He broke into a run.

A chorus of "Thief!" erupted around him.

It didn't hurt nearly as bad as the reprimanding voice in his head, which sounded suspiciously like Father's.

The things he would do for the Black Lotus.

The two city watch ran, their longer legs gaining ground.

CHAPTER 11

Wen hadn't been paying attention to the distance they'd covered, or the number of streets the palanquin had turned down, but now they'd come to a stop.

She signed to the others, *Where are we*?

Lips pursing, Meisha shook her head.

Near the clothier's district, Yangyang gestured.

At least someone hadn't forgotten their training. This was strictly a commercial district, which meant the back alleys would be nearly deserted. Wen slid the palanquin window open enough to make the voices less muffled.

"Well," said the front left bearer, "We're all tired of jogging, and if she just needs to be delayed, we don't have to go all the way."

"If we're going to be out of breath," added one of the guards, in a rich voice, "I know what I'd rather be doing. When else would you, or any of us, have a chance to fuck a Blossom?"

Weapons? Wen signed. Of course, they all had bladed hairpins, and she'd strapped three throwing stars to one leg, and a knife to her wrist.

Meisha patted her thigh. *Knife. Hairpin.*

I expected to lose my skirt tonight, Yangyang signed. *Hairpin only. And a flashpowder packet.*

"It's wrong," the courier said.

"They're whores," said Rich Voice.

The sentiment echoed all around them.

If there was anything reliable about males, it was that they were governed by base desires. Wen's heart squeezed.

Meisha and Yangyang exchanged knowing, nervous glances.

Hiking up her skirts, Wen acquired her knife with a flick of her wrist. She retrieved the throwing stars with her other hand, and passed them to Yangyang.

At her side, Meisha squirmed and drew her own knife.

The palanquin lowered to the ground.

"Why are we stopping?" Wen slid the window all the way open. Not much larger than two hands, the field of vision provided wasn't wide enough to see the bearers. Two of the guards moved around either side, entering the blind spots.

On the other side, Meisha opened her window and pressed her face up against it. Then jerked back.

The doors slid open, revealing several of the men, crowding together, bending over. All their faces were now covered, save for the courier, who stood to the side with his arms crossed.

Nothing good would come of this.

"Get out," said Rich Voice. One of the soldiers, he was standing at the middle, in front of the others. Though only of medium build, he was larger than any of them. He patted his broadsword hilt.

"We're here already?" Wen crawled over Meisha and put herself in the middle of the opening. All thirteen men were now in her field of vision, deployed in an arc that cut off any lines of escape.

She and her friends were outnumbered by larger, stronger men, four with weapons. Behind her back, she flashed hand signals. *Two soldiers left, one center, one right. If we fight, we can't leave witnesses.*

"We're taking a break. We figured you'd want to...stretch your legs." He looked over either of his shoulders, and the men broke out into laughs.

Yangyang made a show of clutching Wen's arm, but ran her finger in swirls and taps. *I have line of sight on the two to the left. If we let them use us, we'll be late for the reception. And, to remind you, I'm menstruating.*

Heaven forbid we're late. On the other side, Meisha sidled up and rested her chin on Wen's shoulder. With one hand, she took Wen's third throwing star; with the other, she signed on her back, *I have the one on the right.*

I have no intention of being used like a public bathhouse, Wen signed behind her back. *Deserted area.*

Thirteen less rapists, Yangyang tapped. *The world won't miss them.*

Wen gave a slight nod, and signed behind her back, *Deadly force. Neutralize armed men first. I have leader.* She feigned fear, recoiling back. "You don't understand, we don't just...just do *that.* In the Floating World—"

"We aren't in the Floating World." Rich Voice stepped forward and grabbed for Wen's wrist.

She let him seize it and yank her out of the palanquin. Stumbling into his arms, she buried her knife in his gut. She pushed herself off him before his blood could splash on her gown, drawing his sword in the same motion.

Three whirling stars crossed behind her in quick succession. Eyes widening, the two soldiers on the left and the one on the right clutched their throats and sank to their knees. The courier and remaining bearers gawked.

Knife flashing, Meisha darted out to the left, Yangyang to the right, hair now out of place since she'd pulled her hairpin. Wen flung her knife at the courier with the bauble lantern, it hit him in the gut, and he dropped the light.

The bauble shattered. The alley blinked into darkness. With the advantage of weapons and *Seeing Ears*, against eight unarmed men, the question was not if they would win, but how quickly and quietly. The sisters were in and among the palanquin bearers, and men's muffled cries rang out.

By the time Wen's eyes adjusted to the moonlight, only she, Meisha, and Yangyang were standing.

"Clear," she whispered.

"Clear," the others said in unison.

"Check your clothes for blood." Wen crept over to the bearer, whose breaths came out staggered. She knelt down to inspect his injuries.

His gut wound wouldn't kill him tonight, but he wouldn't last much longer than that. The poor man hadn't condoned the attempted gang rape.

Then again, he hadn't done anything to try and stop it. Wen drew the sword over his fingertip. He flinched, and would've brushed her with his bloody finger had she not redirected his hand to the side.

"Who...who *are* you?" he said through gritted teeth.

"You are going to die from that stomach wound," she said. "I can make your remaining time in this world very painful, or I can end it quickly. Who hired you?"

"Fixer Zhang."

How had Fixer Zhang known they were planning on going to the reception? And if he was trying to stop them, did he know about their clan mission to crack Lord Shi's safe? She cut another one of his fingers. "You're lying."

"I'm not!"

"Then you work for him?"

He shook his head. "We do jobs for him, and other people, too."

Maybe he was part of a gang. "So it wasn't really Lord Peng behind this?"

He shook his head. "Fixer Zhang provided the uniforms and the palanquin."

"They have tattoos," Meisha said.

Typical of gangsters. Wen pulled the man's high collar to the side, revealing snake tattoos on his neck. "Which gang do you belong to?"

"The Fangs."

"From the Trench?" Wen looked over her shoulder at the others. The Fangs had been involved in the illegal yue trade, and had the backing of Lord Ting, who Lilian had killed.

He nodded.

"What was your job tonight?"

"We were just supposed to make you late for the moons-viewing party."

"If we don't hurry," Yangyang said, "they'll accomplish that goal."

Wen hushed her. "Why did he want us to be late?"

"He didn't say. We just did the job."

Wen brushed the man's matted hair out of his face. "I'm sorry this had to happen. It wouldn't have, if your brothers had just done their job. Are you ready?"

He gave a nod.

She ran the blade across his throat, careful to avoid the spray. She turned to the others. "We need a Cleaner. Where's our closest safehouse?"

"The one near the Floating World, probably." Yangyang said.

Meisha shook her head. "No time, and most of clan assets are in and around the palace because of the threat on the Emperor."

Wen nodded to Yangyang. "You said you have a flashpowder packet. Will it light the palanquin's cushions?"

"We can try."

Wen checked herself for blood. "Do it." *And quickly scan to see if Fixer Zhang had someone following us.*

With no sign of a tail, they retrieved their weapons, lit the palanquin, and were off in search of a rickshaw.

CHAPTER 12

As if stealing wasn't bad enough, now Tian was a fugitive from the law two times over. He ran, the sound of his pursuer's footsteps getting closer. He looked over his shoulder.

Two of the city watch sprinted in pursuit, their strides long in comparison to his. The first would catch him in seventy-two feet, and the second in seventy-four. If he were lucky, they'd give him a beating; but if they took him to a magistrate's office, and they identified him, it would mean death.

"Sorry!" he yelled as he yanked a tablecloth of trinkets into the path behind him. The vendor shook a fist and screamed expletives.

"Regrets!" He upturned a table as he passed. Amid the dance of light and shadows, he ducked under the next one to cut over to the parallel row.

Other passersby startled at his sudden appearance, but continued on their way.

Perhaps this kind of resourcefulness would make him a good member of the clan; but then, an operative wouldn't have gotten caught in the first place.

"Where did he go?" one of the guards yelled from two rows over.

Tian slowed his pace to a quick walk and took the closest lane out of the promenade. Based on the number of paces and turns, he was on the avenue that ran along the east side of the market. For now, he was safe.

Moving one block to the east into the warrens of courtyard homes, he jogged north, then turned back west. A few people were trickling out of their homes, headed toward the great park on the northwest edge of the city, their chatter suggesting they wanted a better view of the moons.

The rest of the trip was uneventful, save for a few times he ducked his head as members of the city watch strolled by. Soon, he was catching up to the parade of palanquins and armed entourages. From the sigils on the banners and livery, they were likely many of the great lords on their way to Lord Wu's moons-viewing party.

Citizens all moved to the side of the road, though up ahead, as they neared the city gates, many bowed low. Dressed in commoners' garb, he'd mix in with everyone else. Still, he kept behind the first line of spectators, staying low as he reached the bowing people, just in case one of the nobles recognized—

A familiar voice was singing a familiar song.

Tian's heart soared...that voice. It couldn't be. Lord Wu's reception was for men. And with chatter of a threat to the Emperor, he'd be sequestered behind the walls of Sun-Moon Castle. Tian turned to find the source.

The imperial flags with the five-clawed dragon fluttered above a line of blue-robed imperial guards with their Dragonscribe-etched breastplates. The awe-inspiring magic infused within sent a chill up his spine. No wonder all the people were bowing. The largest palanquin in the formation, borne by twenty and wide enough to seat six, had its narrow window open. Though it was impossible to see who was inside, the voice and song were unmistakable. Princess Kaiya was there, singing *Yanyan's Lament.* A ballad about the legendary Dragon Charmer, who'd sung the Last Dragon Avarax to sleep, they sang it together when she was scared or sad.

Princess Kaiya. Oh, to look into her eyes again! But no. To do so would mean death, and the failure of his mission. Heart racing, he swallowed hard and dropped to his knees, behind a pair of bowing women.

The notes floated out, riding on the wind so thick, he might be able to actually touch them. His pulse quickened. Around them, people looked up from their bows, faces filled with wonder.

When she came to the refrain, Tian joined in, as he always did. Together, they would raise each other's spirits.

The singing stopped.

Tian covered his mouth. Heavens. He'd just revealed himself to her.

"Halt," Princess Kaiya said.

What had he just done?

Her large, beautiful eyes appeared in the window slowly. She was looking in his general direction, irises roving, but not finding him.

Tian's stomach clenched as the procession ground to a stop. The princess' palanquin door slid open before the runner could open it himself. The princess stumbled out, and her legs uncharacteristically wobbled as she stood. She looked abnormally pale, and sweat clung to her brow.

Was she sick? Every instinct screamed to go to her side, but in that second, everyone pressed their forehead to the ground.

Tian followed suit, but there'd been a split second where he'd been looking up, dumbfounded. Maybe she'd seen him.

* * *

Alone, without Tian to help entice Steward Zhu, Jie decided to get more information before coming up with a plan of action. Listening through the evening chatter, picking out scents hiding among the aromas of cooking food, she crept to the courtyard home directly across from the Lord Shi's. With no sign of a tail, she tied her skirts between her knees. She scaled the rear building, which formed the outer wall of the compound.

Making it to the top, she kept low on the tile roof, leaped over the eight-foot gap, and seized the sill of a dark second-floor window on the main building. She pulled herself up, then continued the climb to the roof. The new vantage point gave a good view of the back half of Lord Shi's courtyard home.

Light baubles shone in the windows of the east wing, and the smoke curling off the side of it suggested it held the kitchens. And likely the old servant, cooking for the steward and remaining guard. There didn't look to be—

"Miss Li." Though unseen from this angle, the gate guard spoke in an echoing voice.

The steward hustled out of the east wing, headed south, and disappeared behind the front building.

Jie closed her eyes and listened.

The mid gate swung open, followed by the front gate.

"Miss Li, the lord told us to expect you. Come in, come in. We're just getting ready to eat."

The lord? Had he stayed back, turning down the honor of attending Lord Wu's moons-viewing reception in favor of a tumble between the sheets? Though if he were here, surely the bauble lamps in the main building would be unshuttered?

Steward Zhu reappeared, this time with Tang Li a few steps behind. For now, their path only provided a view of her back; but in the two years since she'd left the Chrysanthemum House, her hair still looked black and glossy in the moons' light as ever.

It was time to formulate a plan. One guard, the old servant, the steward, and Tang Li. The guard was on the outside, and wouldn't be an issue if she didn't use the front gate. The servant, steward, and Tang Li could be moving around, but Jie would likely be able to hear them, and slide out a window or under furniture if they were close to discovering her. It was a matter of luring the steward into a secluded area, choking him out, and taking his key. If only Tian had acquired a fake key and brought it to her, she could swap it out, and the steward might never know. As it was, she might have ten to fifteen minutes to unlock the safe...and she still didn't know what time.

She climbed down from the roof and alighted on the outside of the compound. Listening and sniffing for possible tails, she worked her way around to the alley behind Lord Shi's home. Again, she climbed the outer wall and worked her way across the rear building, listening, sniffing, and watching the main residence for signs of life. Satisfied it was empty, she jumped to a second-floor windowsill. This time, instead of continuing to the roof, she slipped in through the window.

It appeared to be a private study, with a tidy writing desk by the window and bookshelves on two of the walls. A door lay directly ahead. As was to be expected with austere and practical Northerners, the room lacked paintings, rugs, or any other kind of decoration.

Careful not to disturb the desk, Jie leaped over it and landed without a sound on the wood floors. She turned back and studied the desk. A letter organizer was built into the top, and there appeared to be plenty of correspondence. Lord Yang Ken, Lord Tong Baxian, and the deceased Lord Ting had all written poetry. Unless they were involved in some epic poetry duel, it had to be some coded language.

All four were long-time confidantes of the Emperor, helping to keep order among the dozen fiercely independent Northern lords. They'd even travelled with him all over the country. Just what secrets could Lord Shi be keeping in his safe?

Jie padded over to the bookshelf. The books were arranged in an orderly fashion, with none showing signs of having been pulled more recently than the others. From the titles, Lord Shi looked to be well-read in history, strategy, and agriculture. Strange, in that

Jinjing County, like much of the North, was known more for its mountainous terrain and wispy trees than for farmland.

The door to the study was locked. Listening to make sure no one had come into the main building, Jie turned the bolt. The door creaked as she opened it, making her wince. She slipped out and into the hall, then used her lockpicks to relock it.

Tian had said the halls didn't have nightingale floors, so she tiptoed over to the northwest door. The lock was so simple, it was a wonder anyone had even bothered to install one. It yielded to her lockpicking skills in a few seconds, and she darted in.

The room was just as Tian described, with sparse decorations. At the moment, only the muted light from the Iridescent Moon peeked in through the south window. She went over to that window and hazarded a glance out.

Unlike the neighbor's rooftop, which provided only line of sight on the rear half of Lord Shi's compound, this window had a commanding view of the entire courtyard, the east and west wings, and the front inner wall and front building.

The old servant, Steward Zhu, and Tang Li all sat at a simple table, chopsticks in hand as they picked food from shared plates and shoveled rice from plain porcelain bowls. The angle provided a side profile of Tang Li and her high-bridged nose and smooth skin. She hadn't been the most beautiful of the Blossoms when she'd lived in the Chrysanthemum Pavilion—that honor belonged to Lilian, the Corsage—but she was pleasant on the eyes, even two years later. She sat up straight compared to the others, as a Blossom would.

Jie sucked on her lower lip. Something had been niggling at her, and now it hit her: even for a Northerner, Lord Shi bought the humblest of things. With the exception of Tang Li herself, everything was so plain.

Squirreling away the observation to the back of her brain, Jie headed over to the hanging scroll and the safe behind it. Though her mind's eye wasn't as exacting as Tian's, the lopsided painting angle he'd described looked to be the same here. Lord Shi had not opened the safe since the afternoon—perhaps he couldn't, with the Iridescent Moon out of phase with the moonstone.

Her heart started to race. Soon, very soon, she'd find out more of Lilian's story. She shifted the painting to the side, revealing the safe, framed by the brittle light from the Iridescent Moon. The moonstone lit up, its colors shifting and swirling.

The key didn't fit in the top hole, so she tried the second.

It didn't fit either.

She sucked on her lower lip. One hour.

They had a one-hour window to open the safe, and they didn't even know when.

CHAPTER 13

Though they certainly had the stamina to jog the rest of the way, Wen and the others found rickshaws and rode. Their dresses weren't meant for running, and it wouldn't do to arrive at the moons-viewing party to seduce lords all sweaty. Without money, she offered a jade bracelet as payment; the drivers accepted kisses instead.

Located where the Jade River emerged from Sun-Moon Lake, the Songyuan Quays were the main freight docks for transporting goods between the capital and the seaport of Jiangkou. Now, instead of dockworkers loading and unloading freight, there were guards and porters milling around palanquins, sedan chairs, and horses. Wen wrinkled her nose. Even with all the pomp, the area still smelled of hard labor.

While one would normally find cargo boats docked here, Wen noted not one, but two enormous barges. Long and flat, with one-level sterncastles taking up a third of their sterns, both had banks of oars below the main deck. One flew a blue flag with a white ship, marking it as the property of Lord Wu's Zhenjing Province; the other boasted a white five-clawed dragon on a blue field, the mark of the Emperor himself.

Wen exchanged glances with Meisha. "You said Lord Wu was holding a reception. If the imperial barge is here, wouldn't the Emperor be the host?"

"I don't know." Shaking her head, Meisha scanned the docks. "If the Emperor, or any of the Imperial Family is here, our brothers and sisters should be, too. There."

Wen followed the tilt of Meisha's head to the deck of the imperial barge, where Elder Brother Kun Dai was disguised as a deckhand in imperial livery.

"He's so handsome," Yangyang said. "I hear he's good between the sheets."

Wen's face scrunched up. Kun Dai had a symmetrical face with large eyes and strong chin. However, he knew how handsome he was, and flaunted it. She scanned the head of the dock, where Elder Brothers Chong Xiang, Zu, and Li were similarly dressed, checking lords' families as they boarded.

"Look," Yangyang said, pointing to the other barge. "Lord Shi and his son are already aboard."

Whereas the imperial barge was full of women and children, with a handful of the most powerful hereditary lords, there were a couple dozen minor lords and their older sons lounging around the other. Most of the women mingling with them were Blossoms from the Floating World Houses. Lord Shi was chatting with Lord Yang of neighboring Chengfu County—both close confidantes of the Emperor—while his son hung in their shadows.

Grinning, Meisha adjusted her clothes. "Shall we?"

"We need to wait for Tian," Wen said. Without a fake key, they wouldn't be able to swap it out with Shi Han so that he wouldn't realize it was missing.

"Where is he?" Yangyang asked. "Are those fake dwarf keys that hard to find?"

"Look." Meisha gestured to the city walls. "The imperial procession."

Three palanquins surrounded by two dozen imperial guards passed through the walls. One was larger than the others, likely bearing the Emperor and Empress. Elder Brothers Zhang, Shun, and

Ling blended in among the palanquin bearers. The guards, porters, and servants already at the docks all bowed low as the procession arrived.

Wen tugged at her pinkie. It was madness for the Emperor to come out from the impregnable gates of Sun-Moon Castle with a potential threat; but perhaps it was meant to project confidence to the lords.

She let out a sigh of relief as Tian appeared, trotting along the edge of the light cast by multiple light baubles. He'd lost his excess weight so fast, and though he looked winded by the time he reached them, he wasn't hands-on-knees, heaving for air.

"Did you acquire a key?" she asked.

He held one out. "I overheard the imperials talking. It turns out Lord Wu gifted a barge to the Emperor. A surprise."

"And His Eminence came out for its maiden voyage?" Yangyang asked.

"No. Just the two princes and..." He shuffled on his feet. "And Princess Kaiya."

The way he said her name carried a fondness. Had he known the princess well? Rumor had it she didn't share her family's good looks, but possessed an exceptional singing voice. She took the key and patted him on his head. "Why the larger palanquin, then?"

He shrugged. "It's only her inside."

It was strange for anyone other than the Emperor himself to ride in that palanquin. A daughter by herself, no less...

"All right," Yangyang said. "We need to board now. If we can swap the key before they push off, it will be all the easier to get it to Tian."

"I'll wait over there." Tian gestured to the horses.

Getting aboard proved easy. After passing a few signals to a clan brother at the head of the dock for the imperial barge, confirming he couldn't reassign assets to their mission, they came to Lord Wu's barge. A pair of porters in Lord Shi's brown livery trudged ahead of them, lugging a keg labeled *wheat wine, Jinjing County*. The grains and whorls in the white wood indicated it was made of yue.

"What is this?" a page asked.

"Red wheat wine, a gift from Lord Shi," said one, voice straining.

The page looked up from a scroll. "I don't see it on the list."

The porter tilted his head toward the other barge. "It's good enough for the Emperor."

With a harrumph, the page gestured them across the gangplank, then froze as Wen approached. His eyes predictably settled on her chest. "May I help you?"

"We were invited by Lord Wu to come entertain. I am Dan Wen from the Peony Garden. This is Bai Yangyang from the Lily Pond, and Lan Meisha from the Orchid Palace."

"Uh..." The man fumbled to another scroll. His gaze roved over the names on the guest list before lifting to meet hers. "I don't see you on the list."

"We received a late invitation." Wen looked up through her lashes, while Yangyang and Meisha slipped their arms into the crook of her elbows and pressed their own breasts against her.

He swallowed hard, making no attempt to hide the fact he was ogling their bodies. "I..."

You have him, Yangyang tapped. "Would you look again?"

Locking her gaze on him, Wen claimed the space between them and brushed a finger over his hand as she touched the list. "Oh, there we are."

"Yes," he droned without looking down, "there you are."

He's aroused, Meisha swept a finger into the small of Wen's back. *If he hasn't already wet himself.*

Whether he had or not, it was impossible to tell because of the way the scroll dangled in front of him. He stepped to the side. "Welcome aboard."

"Thank you." Wen batted her eyelashes a few times before leading the other two over the gangplank. His gaze weighed on the sashay of her hips as they boarded.

About twenty feet wide, the deck itself must've stretched several dozen paces to the sterncastle, its smooth eldarwood planks freshly stained. The heady wood scent hung in the air.

At least thirty county lords lounged on cushioned chaises, with cups in hand and Blossoms in laps. Male servants in Lord Wu's blue livery moved about with decanters, pouring wine. And there, near the—bow, did they call it?—were Lord Shi and Lord Yang on their own seats, chatting with each other. Along with Lord Ting, both had been Lilian's frequent patrons at the Chrysanthemum Pavilion. Now, their sons stood behind them, sharing dour looks.

"Look at them," Yang was saying, gesturing to a group of lords closer to the sterncastle. "Faking loyalty and kissing up to Young Lord Wu."

Wen followed the motion and studied the men. Some were familiar, all lords of the North who frequented the Floating World. Most were descended from loyalists of the previous Yu Dynasty, their ancestors too powerful for the Founder to execute and incite uprisings; but fearful enough that they accepted the loss of their bountiful fiefs in return for lordship over the counties in the North. Instead of being incorporated into its own province, it remained under the direct administration of the capital, and a vein of resentment still ran through those weakened noble families. Wearing fake smiles now, they were bobbing their heads like pigeons at Lord Wu's eldest son.

Lord Shi chuffed. "All the while complaining about how the rest of the empire exploits them. Lord Ting kept them in line, but now..."

"Nobody can replace Lord Ting." Lord Yang bowed his head.

"May he rest with his ancestors," Shi said, then looked over his shoulder at his son. "Do you hear this, Little Han? It's now up to us to keep the North loyal."

If Shi Han looked any more bored, moss might grow on him. He gave an unenthusiastic nod. "Yes, Father. You say it all the time, how you will one day rule the—"

"Shut it," Lord Shi hissed.

"Oh, we all know. Lord Tong is trying hard enough." Lord Yang waved a hand in the direction of the lords.

"One of us has to," Lord Shi said, with maybe a little too much ambition in his voice.

Wen found Lord Tong among the group. With his flat, round face and pudgy nose, the forty-four-year-old looked more like a Southerner than a Northerner; and he had a reputation in the Floating World for enjoying rough pleasures. Luckily for the Blossoms, he very rarely visited. Despite this, his loyalty, along with Yang's, Shi's, and the late Ting's, was unquestioned. If Lord Ting had been the bedrock on which the North was built, the other three were the pillars.

With Yangyang and Meisha following her lead, Wen sashayed up to them and bowed low. "Thank you, Lord Shi, for honoring me this afternoon."

"Rise," Lord Shi said.

Her friends straightened with her. Wen bowed her head to Shi Han, though not before making out the outline of the key beneath his high-collared gentleman's robe. "And to you, Young Lord Shi, for the amazing experience."

"Oh?" Lord Shi looked sidelong at his son.

Wen turned her head at an angle and raised a hand in front of her cheek, as if hiding a blush. At the same time, she looked to the line of guests by the gangplank. How much time did they have before they shoved off? "Young Lord Shi was absolutely toe-curling."

Guffawing, Lord Yang turned and clapped a hand on Shi Han's back. "Well done, Little Han. I'm sure Yang Lin here did a fine job during his First Pollination, but I don't remember the Blossom complimenting him."

Shi Han's mouth opened and closed, but no words came out. With the Blue Moon fully open and casting its cerulean light, it was hard to tell what shade he was blushing.

"This is Bai Yangyang of the Lily Pond, and Lan Meisha of the Orchid Palace." Wen gestured to her friends.

The two bowed with the grace of the Floating World. "We are pleased to serve."

"Heavens, forgive my rudeness." Wen covered her mouth and bowed low again. "I just realized we are blocking your view of the moon."

"Oh, this view is quite nice." Lord Shi's eyes never moved from her chest. He extended his hand. "But perhaps we can enjoy the view together."

Behind him, Shi Han was frowning. The unspoken friction between them would make it easier to get Shi Han alone. Wen took the father's hand, and he tugged her into his lap. He lifted her leg and brought it up and over so that she straddled him. With a contrived gasp, she placed a hand on his shoulders to keep him from pulling her closer.

"I'm jealous." Lord Yang beckoned to Yangyang and Meisha as if he owned them. Of course, he would assume Lord Wu had paid for their services tonight.

Giggling, Meisha obeyed. No sooner did she slide sidesaddle into his lap, than his hand crept up her skirts. As disgusting as entitled men were, it was also their weakness; one which the Black Lotus sisters would exploit tonight.

Yangyang made a cute wave of her hand at the sons. "I want to experience just how good Young Lord Shi is, too."

"Woooo," Lord Yang said over his shoulder. "Yang Lin, do you hear that? You must bring honor to our family name, and not let Young Shi Han outdo you."

Though watching as Yangyang moved between the two sons, Wen found Lord Shi in the corner of her vision. He was staring at his son, frowning.

If Shi Han was bothered by the glare, it didn't show. He was grinning ear-to-ear—no, he knew exactly what he was doing, the way he shot glances at his father.

Get his key, Wen signed.

Yangyang gave a slight nod, and started massaging Shi Han's shoulders. Nibbling his ear, she pressed her bosom against his back. He let out a light groan, and she guided one of his hands to the back of her head, then the other to her thigh.

Not to be outdone, Yang Lin came up behind her, nuzzling her neck while his hands explored under her skirts, and she let out a gasp worthy of a celebrated stage actress. A wide grin spread across Yang Lin's face, and he looked to his father for approval.

So amateur, but to be expected of a young buck. And Lord Yang was too busy fondling Meisha to notice. No doubt, he'd done that and more to Lilian in the past.

Now, it was only Lord Shi, the elder, paying attention to Yangyang and her ample bosom. Wen cupped his head and turned him to face her. "Lord Shi, I imagine you taught your son everything he knows?"

"I've held back many secrets." Attention now fully on her, he grinned.

Wen rested her hands on the back of his neck, and leaned in so that his face was in her breasts. Behind him, Yangyang had already loosened Shi Han's collar, while Shi Han rocked back and forth.

Eyes closed, Wen signed. Maybe he was imagining Tang Li, but either way, he was totally unaware of Yangyang slipping the necklace with the key over his head and passing it to Wen.

Fingers moving quickly, ignoring Lord Shi's lips on her chest, she loosened the key from the thin chain and attached the fake.

Young Lord Yang started to look up from behind Yangyang's neck.

Block his view, Wen signed, closing her fist around the keys. Part of the chain still dangled.

Yangyang let out a decadent sigh and leaned her head back into Yang Lin's face. With one hand, she guided Shi Han's hand deeper into her skirts. Letting out another moan, she reached out. Wen passed both keys to her. Yangyang slipped the real key into her cleavage while setting the fake back around his neck.

Got it, she mouthed. Letting out a gasp, she bucked her hips and pulled Young Lord Shi's hands out from under her skirt. The mortification in her voice would win the praise of the stodgiest opera troupe director—who would happen to be Old Feng. "Oh, Heavens!"

Lord Shi pulled back and looked over his shoulder. Lord Yang craned around. Both sons looked up, eyes wide at the red staining Shi Han's fingers.

"Heavens," Meisha said, sliding off of Lord Yang's lap and putting an arm around Yangyang. "Are you all right?"

Covering her mouth, Yangyang made a swift exit toward the gangplank.

"I'm sorry!" Shi Han called after her. He turned back and met Wen's gaze. "What just happened?"

Wen rose, then bowed low. "Please. Please forget this happened. It's a Blossom's worst nightmare." Well, not true, since abusive patrons were the worst, as Lilian's story proved.

"I don't understand," Shi Han said, shaking his head.

Wen lowered her voice to a whisper. "It's her Best Friend."

"Her what?" Confusion scrawled over his face.

At the exit, Yangyang disembarked, and Meisha flashed a *clear* signal.

In the meantime, for the third time in a day, it looked as if Wen would have to teach a young man about female bodies. She looked up to the Iridescent Moon, now waxing to its second gibbous. What time could the safe be opened?

CHAPTER 14

Today was the day Tian truly became a thief. First he'd stolen a time piece, and then, just minutes later, a key. Now he was making off with a horse. Well, the horse belonged to his family, but Father would still say it was stealing.

He looked over his shoulder toward the imperial barge. Father and Mother were both on board, enjoying the moons-viewing party with other great lords.

He'd been so close. How nice it would've been, to hug Mother and reassure her that he was all right. That new people cared for him.

And, of course, there was Princess Kaiya. She'd almost seen him near the city walls, but with him being prone and having lost weight, combined with the imperial guards urging her back into the palanquin, he'd escaped undetected. Part of him wished she'd seen him, even if it meant death.

Now, though, he had a mission. Yangyang had hurried off the barge, looking so distraught he'd wondered if something had gone wrong. Yet she flashed him a grin as she walked past, slipping the key into his hand.

Ignoring the hails of the guards at the city gates, he rode hard down the street. It was slower going than in an open field, especially with all the commoners flocking to parks and open spaces for the moons viewing.

They might have a one-hour window to succeed, and he might have a way to make that longer—as long as they had both keys in and the combination deciphered before midnight. He looked up at the moon, to see it waxing to its second gibbous.

Three phases to go.

Three phases to get this key to Jie, and then help her get the second key from the steward.

He reached the road leading to the warren where Lord Shi's home was located in seven hundred and sixty-three seconds—three hundred and sixty-six seconds slower than Father's charger could run in perfect conditions. He guided the horse in, and through some twists and turns. People heading out to the main street made way—he was on a large horse, after all, bearing the livery of Dongmen Province.

About a block from Lord Shi's courtyard home, a light flashed twice from the roof of the main building. Squint as he may, even in the light of the full White Moon and fully open Blue Moon, all he saw was a dark shape.

It was Jie, no doubt, so he flashed a hand signal. *Have key. Meet at central well.*

He led the horse to a small square, occupied by a circular pool fed by a hand pump. He dismounted and loosened the horse's cinch. She was a docile mare, so he removed the tack and let her drink more easily. He splashed water on her, then checked her hooves. Passersby muttered, some about how a horse was getting the water dirty, others about how thankful they were to have their own well. Still, none dared to challenge what looked to be a lord's courier.

Lord's courier! That would be a way into Lord Shi's courtyard home. He leaned in, scooped up some mud from the bottom of the pool, and filled the timepiece with it.

"It took you long enough," Jie said from behind.

Tian's soul just about jumped out of his body. He'd expected the surprise, and she'd still snuck up on him. He turned.

She wasn't there.

"Over here," she said from across the pool.

She was kneeling there, no doubt smug at throwing her voice with a *Ghost Echo* to trick him.

Maybe he'd be able to do it one day, as well. He held the key up.

Grinning, she walked around the pool and took it. "Now, we need to get the other key from Steward Zhu. I was thinking—"

"I can get in, claiming to be a courier for my father, with a message."

She studied him. "You look more like a very young horse thief than a courier."

He tapped his chin. Maybe he should've borrowed livery, as well. "Then we can just go up and beg?"

"Tang Li is there, and she would recognize me. Steward Zhu would be suspicious, since he saw me this morning. We'll stick with your courier plan. It only has to work for a split second, and the horse is convincing. It has to be you. But I have an idea." She started brushing the dust and dirt off of him, then pointed at the pool. "Go rinse your face."

"But people drink from that."

"So do horses, apparently."

He frowned.

"Anyway, you will need to look clean."

"Do I have to hold the Steward's hand?"

"Yes, but not *that* way. Let me tell you about sympathetic movement."

"What's that?"

"Hold out your right hand."

He did, and she grabbed it, and then leaned back hard. His grip tightened around her hand to keep her from falling. When he pulled her straight, she pointed to his left forearm. A leather strap with a key was attached.

"How?" he asked.

"When you tense your muscles on your right arm, your left arm tenses, too, and it is easy for you to ignore sensation there. This morning I brushed up against Steward Zhu's pressure points, and hopefully he will still be even less sensitive on his key arm."

It was just too fascinating. He hung on to her every word, and nodded.

"Now, let's practice. Slip the key onto my arm." She held out her right hand.

He caught it as he leaned back, and as she pulled him up, he slid the strap around her arm.

She shook her head. "Too obvious."

They repeated the process several times, while she explained her plan. To passersby peering through the bright moonlight, it looked like they were playing a game along the rim of the pool. Most muttered complaints. It was only the mare who didn't seem to care about their practice.

"You're almost there," Jie said. "One more time."

She put out her hand. When he reached for it, she pulled back, and he missed. Hands flailing for balance, he splashed into the pool.

He sat up, spluttering water out of his mouth. "Why did you do that?"

"Besides it being fun?" Jie grinned. "We are playing up to Steward Zhu's interest in young men. He's more likely to help a shivering young lad than me. Now let's go."

Frowning, Tian climbed out of the pool and handed her the timepiece. He tightened the horse's cinch, set the bridle, and then climbed into the saddle. He spurred the mare on, going as fast as possible through the narrow streets before pulling up short in front of Lord Shi's home. He swung out of the saddle, then dropped to one knee, fist to the ground. His teeth chattered; whether it was a total act, or the chill from riding in wet clothes at night, he wasn't sure.

"What is it?" the guard asked.

Tian held the lines he'd rehearsed in his mind. "An urgent message for Steward Shu from Lord Shi, courtesy of Lord Zheng."

The guard bowed. Turning around, he climbed the three steps, opened the gate, and passed through.

Jie peeked out from the stone lion to the left of the door. She gave him a quick nod, then ducked back as footsteps approached.

"Good evening." Steward Zhu appeared at the door, the guard behind him.

Tian rose and, teeth chattering, started climbing the steps. His heart raced. Hopefully he wouldn't mess this up. Hopefully, the steward wouldn't let him fall and crack his head. "I have an urgent message from—" Falling toward the left, he flailed his arms and reached for the steward's right hand.

The steward reached out and caught Tian, his other hand grabbing the stone lion for support. Jie's little hands reached into his sleeve. Tian pulled himself up and reached for the steward's left hand. The second he released the lion, Jie cut the key off, and when he reached to help Tian, Tian slid the fake key on.

"Are you all right?" the steward asked.

Tian nodded. "Yes. Thank you. As I said, urgent message. Lord Shi needs your help at the quays."

"What happened?"

Tian leaned in and whispered, "Clothes. He soiled his clothes."

The steward covered his mouth, looking very much like the clan sisters around Hummingbirds. He beckoned Tian in. "Come in, come in. While I'm getting some clothes for the lord, I'll get you some, too. Otherwise you'll freeze."

Going into the compound was never part of the plan, but he could be a distraction, to make sure no one walked in on Jie. He handed the reins to the guard, who just stared at them, dumbfounded.

* * *

Standing on Lord Shi's bed, heart galloping like a horse's hooves, Jie studied the safe. She had all she needed to unlock it: both keys, her ears for the combination, and Tian's solution for bypassing the moonstone's time constraints. Soon, very soon, she'd learn more about Lilian's betrayal. It wouldn't make her death or Yuna's any less painful, but at least she'd know why. She'd figure out what to do about the clan's orders later.

After swiping the steward's key, she'd gone back up along the back and returned to the room. Tian, too, was down by the east wing, waiting for the steward to bring him a set of dry robes; though maybe he had other intentions as well. Hopefully his rush to bring clean clothes to his master would keep Tian safe in that regard. The half of her that needed to protect Tian warred with the half that needed to know about Lilian.

Her selfish half, no doubt inherited from a worthless elf father, won out. She had to take several deep breaths to calm the pounding of her heart in her ears. Ear to the safe door, she twisted and turned the dial. The clicks from the extra gear harmonized with those of the combination disk, creating a louder sound in the disk's notch; it was probably enough to trick pathetic human ears, but not half-elf ears. Twelve turns later, the safe door emitted a clunking sound.

Her grin formed of its own accord. One step closer to finding out more of Lilian's story.

Down below, Tang Li's chirpy laugh rang out. "Little Tian, you're so adorable. Where did Lord Zheng find you?"

"I'm from his province," Tian answered. The girls had tried to teach him to lie, but he just wasn't good at doing it convincingly, when he did it all. This, though, was the truth, if not the whole truth.

"He *is* adorable." The steward's voice was just a little too friendly. "These robes are a touch too big for him, but they should do. Go in, change out of those wet clothes."

Jie's gut clenched. She really should create a diversion. But the safe...

If the stories about the dwarf lock were true, the keys wouldn't actually turn until the moon was at the right phase—but Tian's idea should work, at least until midnight, when the Iridescent Moon waxed to full. It was worth testing their fit now.

Below, the door to the east wing opened and closed, while the steward and Tang Li chattered outside. Tian was safe, at least for the time being.

Here, the key from the steward slid easily into the bottom hole. Her heart was fluttering so fast, her head felt woozy. She inserted the one stolen from Shi Han into the top.

It jammed a quarter of the way in.

No, no, no, there had to be a mistake. She swapped positions, with even less success: the steward's key didn't fit into the top at all, and Shi Han's again went one quarter of the way in. Not only that, as soon as she pulled the steward's key, the safe's dial whirred, more clicks and clunks sounding in a symphony inside.

Shit.

If her heart was racing before, now it was clenching. She closed her eyes. Shi Han carried a decoy. Fixer Zhang's key was also a fake. Where was the real one?

A near-imperceptible hum buzzed in her ears. She opened her eyes.

It was coming from the steward's key. Just like this morning.

Shi Han's key, however, was silent.

She held the steward's key up to the moonlight.

It glowed a faint blue, like the Paladin swords forged by the Blackhammer clan.

The other key only reflected the moons' light, but didn't actually glow. Shoulders slumping, she let out a quiet sigh.

She went to the window and looked to the east wing. Tian was emerging, now dressed in the brown livery of Jinjing Province. It was a little too large, but the way the steward looked at him wasn't much different from the way Hummingbirds ogled Blossoms in the Floating World.

She'd been derelict in her duty to protect him. Even in death, Lilian was still Jie's blind spot. Skin crawling, she let out a peacock caw, a clan signal.

Tian himself might sound like a dying crow when trying to make the sound, but he'd still recognize it. He looked up.

Jie darted her hands out of the window and signed, *Wrong key. Right key glows blue in moonlight*. Hopefully he'd see and understand.

"Let me bring the lord's clothes to the guard, so he can take them to Lord Shi." If the steward's voice were any sweeter, they could use it in desert recipes. "I'll be right back."

Tian took the clothes with a deft swipe of his hand. "I will take them to Lord Shi," Tian said. "I will be faster on the horse."

Smart boy. It might leave her here with the steward still in the compound, but it would get him away faster.

"But..." The steward's mouth opened and closed, until he finally bowed his hand. "Very well. But do come back. You went to all the trouble, and we have extra sweets."

Jie cringed again. She really should've ensured Tian was safe around the steward earlier, instead of pursuing her own selfish goals. She flashed hand signals. *Don't come back, unless you happen to find the key on Lord Shi.*

Hopefully, Wen, Yangyang, and Meisha were still working that angle.

CHAPTER 15

With their mission accomplished, Wen was no longer in the mood for using feminine wiles on these pathetic lords. Acting usually came easy, but Yuna's death was still too fresh, too raw. She let out a sigh. *Her* Seedling. *Her* responsibility.

Leaning over the railing of the aft upper deck, she looked up at the moons. The fully-open Eye of Guanyin only coincided with the full White Moon once every eleven years. Separated by about ten degrees, they stared back at her. At this moment, they formed a triangle with the Iridescent Moon, now waxing to its third gibbous. Three more hours until it reached full.

The barges had set off a phase earlier, and were now anchored about a *li* offshore, at the mouth of Sun-Moon Lake. Had Yuna lived just one more day, she could've enjoyed this view as well. Wen's heart squeezed tight.

Meisha's long fingers intertwined with hers on the rail. "You're thinking about Yuna, aren't you?"

With a nod, Wen rested her head on Meisha's shoulder. "I should've protested. Never have let her go into the Trench."

"You couldn't know what would happen." Meisha tilted her head on Wen's. "She was already a full-fledged Fist. She went in with all the skills she needed. She was close to the No-Shadow Cut, which neither of us can do. It was her choice to sacrifice herself."

It was true, but that didn't make it hurt any less. Wen would miss Yuna's sharp tongue and playful giggles. She would've eventually become leader of the clan's Floating World cell; and with her exceptional intelligence and talent, she could've become as storied as the Steel Orchids or the Beauty.

"Ladies!" Lord Shi called out from behind. "I wondered where you'd disappeared to."

Wen's heart squeezed. Of course, being stuck on this boat for the next two hours or more meant having to entertain this wolf if he came calling. She and Meisha turned around. Meisha's arm draped over her shoulder, and she wrapped her own around Meisha's waist.

"Lord Shi." She set her smile to look blatantly uninterested. There was no way out of this, except to make herself as unattractive as possible. If she resisted his advances and he complained to Lord Wu, they'd find out she hadn't been invited. A commoner might be executed for deigning to stowaway on a lord's ship and attend his party; as a Blossom, she might still face some consequence.

His eyes shifted from her to Meisha. "I was beginning to think you used Yangyang's departure as an excuse to avoid me."

"Of course not," Wen said a tone that conveyed, *Of course.*

"My, my seeing the two of you like this is so...enticing." The way he closed the distance between them, it didn't look as if he cared how uninterested she was. Of course he wouldn't.

She pressed her hand against his chest to stall.

And found something cylindrical and hard.

A key.

Similar in size and shape to the one worn by Shi Han.

She brushed signals along Meisha's waist. *Another key.*

Meisha turned to her, eyes wide.

If it was one of the real keys, that meant the one Shi Han had was a fake. And that would make total sense, to both make the son feel important and to trick potential thieves. Wen tapped out more signs. *Find Shi Han. Get the fake key.*

Bowing, Meisha twisted away. "I'll give you some privacy."

"Oh?" Lord Shi snorted like a pig. "I'd hoped to be like a barbecued pork bun, enveloped by two beauties."

Wen conjured up an obligatory giggle. Whereas she'd wanted to make herself as unappealing as possible just a moment ago, she needed to get that key now. Nothing better to make an entitled lord feel desirable than to laugh at his bad jokes.

Meisha hurried off before he could say anything more. He turned back to her and grinned. "No matter, you're the one I wanted to *talk* to. So tell me, what did my son do with that pocked cock of his that was so toe-curling?"

He was dwelling on that, was he? Of course he was. He was a man, after all, not to be shown up by his own son.

Loosening his collar, she leaned in and whispered, "He was gentle." A chain link necklace, like Shi Han's, ran along the back of his neck.

He pulled back and laughed. "Was it *his* first time, or *yours*?"

She giggled, and this time it wasn't completely fabricated. She took two steps back, crossing one foot behind the other to let her hips sway, until she was up against the rail. "A little variety sets the mood. Young Shi Han was perfect for that moment."

He followed, like a predator stalking prey, not knowing that he was the real quarry. "What do you crave right now?"

"Your bare chest against mine." They might not be the most believable words she'd ever made up, but selling lies was the heart of being a Blossom. She raked a glance over the upper deck and what she could see of the lower. Neither Meisha nor Shi Han were around. No doubt a lord wouldn't want to bare himself in front of his peers, so wherever they went, she needed to leave a trail for Meisha to follow.

His expression soured for a split second as he looked over his shoulder. He pressed up against her again, gripping the rail on either side, and ground his arousal against her.

It certainly wasn't the first, or the hundredth time that had happened. Easy enough to escape, if need be. It wouldn't be hard to send him for a swim if he presented any real danger. Feigning urgency, she unhooked the knot buttons that ran the left breast of his brown gentleman's robe.

He caught her hand. "Not here."

What was it about the Shis and their need to keep covered? She ran her palm over the rail. "I wonder what it would be like to have my wrist chained to this."

His eyes lit up, and he swallowed hard. He took her hand. "Come with me."

He took long, fast strides as he just about yanked her to the stairs down to the main deck. At times, she scuffed her shoe against the fresh varnish to leave a trail for Meisha. He opened the door to the sterncastle and guided her in.

The spacious room spanned a third of the barge's deck, with a few cabins to both the port and starboard. Servants lounging at a makeshift bar with food and drink snapped to attention.

"How can we help you, my Lord?" A middle-aged man in Zhenjing blue livery bowed.

"See that I'm not disturbed." Snarling, he took her to the open door to one of the small cabins.

A porthole across from the door illuminated the room in soft moonlight. Four cushioned bunks were built into the bow and stern walls, the rumpled covers looking as if they'd been recently used. Some servants' livery hung from hooks.

It would be harder to pull off a switch here. Wen shook her head and, taking the lead, pulled him to the next room.

It had a porthole overlooking the waters, but was otherwise empty save for what looked to be two barrels of wine. Coils of ropes hung from hooks on the walls, while bars hung from the ceiling. They would have to do.

She kicked the door shut. Lavishing kisses on his neck, she pulled him toward one of the hooks, until her back was against an interior wall.

He pulled her outer gown off, baring her shoulders, while she finished unbuttoning the front flap of his robe. His fingers worked swiftly. Her inner gown dropped and pooled at her ankles, leaving her only in lace underwear.

She crossed her arms over her chest. “Now you, my Lord.”

A frown twitched across his lips for a second, but his eyes roved over her. It was so different from when Tian had studied her with a clinical eye, or even Shi Han, when he’d gazed at her with wonder. This was the stare of a lecherous wolf, pure and simple.

“I just want to feel your bare chest on mine.” It didn’t sound any more genuine in her own ears the second time around, but lust filled his eyes. Of course a lord would believe in his own virility. She reached for the flap of his robe, and his eyes locked on her now-exposed breasts. She pulled his robe open, revealing a splotchy birthmark that stretched across his sagging pectorals, from nipple to nipple.

And right between them, the dwarf key.

Ignoring both it and the birthmark, she wiggled the robe down over his arms. It reached to around his elbows now. How easy it would be to bind him up in his own robe and just take the key! No, the job was to swap his key, without him ever knowing. If only she had musk toxin to knock him out and make him forget about the night. She continued until his robe dropped to the deck, leaving him only in his pants.

Now he crossed his arms over his chest, his expression sheepish. Had she lingered too long on the key, making him think she was staring at his birthmark?

The poor man! Then again, he’d bullied his own son, making him want to cover up as well.

A light series of taps rapped across the door. *Here*, it said.

Meisha. Hopefully with the key.

"The lord doesn't want to be disturbed," said a muffled voice out in the central cabin.

Meisha was smart; she'd find a way in. There was nothing Wen could do about it right now. She brushed both index fingers from his shoulders down his arms, and to his hands. She intertwined their fingers. Gently, she pried his arms open, then lifted them up above her head. She looked up at their joined hands, then released his as she crossed her wrists over the hook. "Chain me."

Grinning, he reached for the rope.

She shook her head. "Chain. I want to feel the metal bite into my wrists." Heavens, had those words just come out of her mouth? Would he really believe that?

His head raked back and forth around the room.

"There are no others." With a giggle, she raised her leg, stretching up to pinch the key between her toes. "This."

"You are flexible." His hand shot to her ankle, keeping her from lifting the chain over his head. Then his eyes strayed to the apex of her thighs, bared, vulnerable, and tantalizing as planned. Licking his lips, he took the necklace, key and all, and wrapped it around her wrists above the hook. It wasn't even tangled or tied.

Which made it easy to steal. Now, she needed Meisha to sneak in and swap the keys while Lord Shi was otherwise occupied.

And occupied he was. He clawed at the ribbons holding her lace underwear up, then the drawstrings of his own pants. They dropped to his knees. "Oh, I've been waiting all night for this."

So had she, though not for the same reasons. Taking hold of the hook, she lifted her other leg and would've draped it over his hip, if his paunch hadn't made it impossible. Instead, with the control of a dancer, she held it there. He hooked his arms under her knees and pushed in.

Hopefully he'd last longer than his son. Although the way he was grunting, it was doubtful. She let out a stuttered moan, imitating the taps of their code. *Now.*

Meisha's head appeared inverted in the porthole. Her eyes scanned the room, then met Wen's. Exchanging nods, she slipped in. Gone was the makeshift skirt, leaving her lower body covered only with her plain white loincloth, her upper body in the bust binder. The shawl, too, was missing.

Both articles of Wen's clothing, maybe lost, or claimed by some depraved lord as a trophy. Wen's lips twisted of their own accord.

Lord Shi didn't appear to notice her frown as he continued thrusting. Her poor back would be rubbed raw against the wall if this kept up much longer. With the deliberate pace of a contortionist, Meisha swung bar to bar, lean muscle cording up on her thin frame. She ended up right behind him, and looped her knees through the bar.

He started to lean back. Without the pressure between him and the wall holding Wen up, she started to slip. Meisha froze.

Clamping the hook between her wrists and locking her ankles together behind the small of his back, she reeled him in. His body pressed her against the wall again.

Meisha resumed, unwrapping the key in silent but tortuously slow circles.

If only she'd hurry. Lord Shi's hips bucked and his body went rigid. Wen wrapped her arms behind his head and pulled his face to her neck as she let out scream after manufactured scream, again in code. *Hurry.*

Using Wen's moans as cover, Meisha wound the fake key around Wen's wrists in quick circles. Real key between her teeth, she swung from bar to bar to the porthole. The key glinted as it caught the reflection of the Blue Moon, just as she paused by the opening. *Are you alright?* she signed.

Wen blinked twice, *Yes.*

With a bob of her head, Meisha dove out.

If Lord Shi heard the splash over Wen's timed moans, he didn't show any sign of it. Tension fled his body, and he slumped against her.

Hopefully, Meisha was strong enough a swimmer to make it to shore.

CHAPTER 16

The ride back to the Songyuan Quays took just a few counts longer than the inbound trip, and nobody bothered to stop a boy in Jinjing livery riding a horse bedecked in Dongmen colors. He dismounted where dozens of others were hitched, and taking care to avoid Father's servants, led his mare to a groom wearing the livery of Lord Peng's Nanling Province. After two gallops with little rest, she'd need the care of someone who knew what he was doing.

"This isn't one of ours." The groom pointed to where the Dongmen Province horses were hitched. "This one goes over there."

Ignoring him, Tian put the reins in the boy's hands. He kept his head low and crept toward the docks. There had to be a way to get back on Lord Wu's barge and tell Wen about the missing key.

"Are you deaf?" the groom called after him. Grumbling, he stomped off, hopefully to bring the horse to her rightful owners.

Tian reached the docks and scanned the waters.

Both barges were well out in the water, where the river emerged from Sun-Moon Lake. Though lights shone through some of the sterncastle windows, both barges' decks were shrouded in darkness, the shapes of people barely discernable in the light of the moons. Maybe he could swim out, but how would he get aboard? And then he wouldn't have the energy to swim back.

Perhaps Yangyang was around, and could come up with a good idea. If not... He searched the docks, looking for a small boat he could uh, borrow. There were several tied to one of the far quays. Coming from an inland province, he'd never rowed before, but how hard could it be?

Out in the water, a rhythmic sloshing grew louder. A boat? Maybe Tian could trade some nice brown robes for a ride out to the barges. He peered through the darkness. In the reflection of the moons' light on the water, a shape approached.

A swimmer!

Wen had said something about swimming back, if need be. Staying low, he worked his way to intercept them. He had to pick his way back among the various guards, porters, and servants, but eventually arrived at a narrow strip of sand by the seawall which divided the lake from the river.

The swimmer came ashore close by. He crept over, squinting to try to make them out.

Whoever it was, she was naked. It was definitely a she, and it was the second naked woman he'd seen in his life—both times within four hours. Well, she wasn't completely naked. She wore a loincloth which sagged with water, but seemed not the least bit concerned about being in a state of undress. Taller and thinner than Wen, her wet hair stuck in tangled knots. Her head turned his way.

"Tian?" It was Meisha's voice.

Heart soaring, he ran over and threw his arms around her.

She laughed and patted him on the head. "Why so affectionate?"

Because she was family. "I'm glad you're safe." Like a proper gentleman, he averted his eyes and proffered Lord Shi's clean robe.

Laughing again, she took it. "You should know by now that we don't mind being seen naked. If we act shy, it's only that: an act."

He stared at the ground. Maybe one day, he could be so brave as to be naked in front of someone; but not today.

She took his hand and pressed a key in it. "This came from Lord Shi. Please get it to Elder Sister. Once I find Yangyang, we'll head your way."

"What about Wen?" he asked. Hopefully, she hadn't tried to swim too?

"Back on the barge. She's fine. Now off you go."

Making it back to Lord Shi's home was no more difficult than the first time. He borrowed another one of his father's horses and sped through the city gates, down the main avenues, and eventually turned into the warrens.

He returned to the central pool. Jie would surely see, hear, or smell his arrival, and would think to meet him there. This horse was not as friendly as the last, so while Tian did loosen his cinch, he left the bit and bridle in place.

"Do you have the key?" Jie's voice came from the other end of the pool, on the other side of the now-drinking horse.

Tian turned around to the opposite direction.

Jie stood there, big eyes even bigger. "You learn fast."

His heart swelled. Besides Princess Kaiya and Mother, nobody had ever complimented him. He held out the key. "Meisha got it from Lord Shi."

Taking it, Jie patted him on the head. "We'll make a Black Lotus of you yet. Now, go back to the house and keep the steward and the rest of the staff occupied, and away from the main residence."

Tian put his fist in his palm in salute, swung back up onto the horse, and trotted to Lord Shi's home. The guard still stood outside. Tian dismounted and handed him the reins. "The steward wanted me to report."

The guard nodded and opened the door.

That was easy. Tian bobbed his head and went through, his third time entering in the same day. He paused at the inner gate and scanned the courtyard. The old servant was cleaning up the dishes. Lights in the east wing were unshuttered, where the maid, Tang Li, hummed to herself. Steward Zhu was unaccounted for. The only other building with light spilling from the windows was the first floor of the main residence.

A shadow flitted across the unshuttered window. Large in size, it could only be the steward, unless someone else had come while he was gone. Either way, Jie would be inside soon.

Tian strode across the courtyard as fast as his legs could take him without actually breaking into a jog. The old servant continued with cleaning up, never turning in his direction. In the east wing window, Tang Li looked up from her work, but showed no sign of seeing him.

He came to the door to the main house and eased it open. He peeked in.

Climbing the steps to the second floor, the steward was holding a pile of folded clothes. If Jie had already reached the bedroom, he'd walk in on her.

Which meant Tian would've failed with his part of his mission. Failed his new family.

Steward Zhu was nearing the second floor now.

Tian pushed the door all the way open and stepped in. "Steward Zhu!"

The steward halted. "Little Tian. You're back."

"Yes." Nodding, Tian shuffled to the center of the foyer. "You said you had some sweets."

The steward turned and came down the stairs. The grin he wore looked the same as those of the Hummingbirds looking to hold hands with the Blossoms.

Tian's stomach twisted. He touched his lips. "I'm thirsty."

"Well, I'll go get you some wine." Smiling, the steward set the clothes down on a chair by the door, and left.

That might buy a few minutes; less, if the steward was in a hurry. Blowing out a breath, Tian raced up the stairs.

The door to the middle room opened, revealing Jie, knife in hand and murder in her eyes. "Quick thinking. You just saved his life."

Tian swallowed hard. *Hold the dragonfly with care*, Princess Kaiya's voice sang in his head, *for even their little lives have value.* Was recovering the contents of the safe for the clan worth killing for?

Jie darted across the mezzanine to Lord Shi's rooms, picked the lock as if it were a toy, and darted in.

He should stay here, stall the steward, but every nerve ending tingled with excitement. Tian followed.

By the time he got there, Jie was already standing on the bed, holding up both keys. They glowed in the light of the moons.

It was a beautiful shade of blue. Tian's lips rounded of their own accord.

Focused on her task, Jie didn't even acknowledge his presence.

* * *

Like the first time at the safe, Jie's heart pounded. The keys glowed, but what if Lord Shi's didn't fit? What if it did fit, but one or the other didn't turn?

Ear to the safe door, she twisted the dial back and forth, the sound of the clicks oddly comforting. When it made a clunking sound like the first time, she inserted the steward's key in the bottom. Then, she took a deep breath and tried the second key.

It fit.

She blew out that breath. Everything needed to open the lock was here.

Except an extra set of hands. She'd need Tian's help. She turned—

And there he was. *Not* standing lookout. A reprimand died on her lips as she beckoned him.

He hurried over.

Looking out the window to see the Iridescent Moon nearing full, she handed him the timepiece. "Let's see if your trick works."

Nodding, he received the timepiece and held it in front of the moonstone, adjusting the distance so that its shadow covered it. "Are you ready?"

"Yes." No. Her heart was racing so fast, her fingers trembled. Well, she didn't need a steady hand to turn a pair of keys.

He poked out the mud caked in the first grill, allowing light from the Iridescent Moon to trickle through and shine on the moonstone, as if it were fifth waxing crescent.

Moment of truth. Jie turned both keys.

They didn't budge.

Out in the courtyard, glass smashed, and something hit the ground.

Tian turned his head to the window, but then tore his attention away from the courtyard and cleared out the next grill, with the same result on the lock. He hurriedly poked the mud from the next.

Jie turned the keys.

The safe clicked.

Her heart swelled. Finally! Tian's timepiece trick worked. The safe would unlock during the third waxing crescent.

They were so close to discovering Lilian's secret, Jie could taste it. She pulled the safe door open.

A cloud of powder puffed out, hitting Jie square in the face. Shit. She might have a second of consciousness. She spun to shove Tian away.

Before she reached him, everything went black.

CHAPTER 17

Pulse pounding in her ears, Tang Li ran up the steps. Lord Shi's safe would be open and unguarded. At long last, she could finish this job for her employer. Far beyond her meager lockpicking skills, she'd had to trick the half-elf into doing it for her.

How Tang Li knew the half-elf could it, and why this was more than a job, she wasn't sure. Though not prone to curiosity—a trait which made her perfect for her line of work—she'd developed an inexplicable urge to see what was in the safe. Ever since she'd taken tea with Lilian a couple of weeks ago. What had been a long game became urgent.

Now, she could satisfy that niggle and leave this pitiful house. The safe was the only reason she'd been here, having to tolerate sharing both the miserly lord's and the young lord's beds for nearly a year, playing them off one another in an attempt to figure out which key was the real one. Then again, fucking them wasn't much different from her former life as a Blossom in the Chrysanthemum Pavilion, where she'd been keeping a close eye on Gardener Ju until Lord Yang had bought out her contract.

This was just one job out of the many she'd taken on since, though rarely did she get her own hands dirty like today. Violence was never her preferred option, but smashing a vase over Steward Zhu's head had been quick and expedient. Old Yi was too nearsighted to be a threat; and the poof of air indicated the half-elf must've triggered the safe's last trap.

She tiptoed up to the door, though some of the boards did creak beneath her. It wasn't like the Floating World, where all the floorboards chirped, but if the half-elf and her friend from earlier in the day were still awake...

Withdrawing the key to Lord Shi's room, she unlocked the door and peered in.

The safe was open.

The half-elf and boy lay sprawled out on the bed, the gentle rise and fall of their chests indicating the poison hadn't killed them. Thank the heavens. Better that no one had to die for the contents of the safe; and as long as they never figured out who'd tricked them, they might be resources to use for a future job.

Covering her nose and mouth with a cloth, just in case, she climbed up onto the bed and picked her way past them. It was a hard surface, which Lord Shi claimed helped his back pain; but it always left her sore when they'd fucked on it.

Heart racing, she looked inside the safe. Some things, she'd expected: stock certificates in Jinjing Holdings, held in trust by the late Gardener Ju. A ball of yue, most likely the illegal, addictive forgery made by Jinjing Lumber.

Two things she didn't know what to make of: a raw gold nugget. Then, there were the rumpled sheets embossed with a five-star dragon, marred with a blood stain. From as assignation in her former life as a Blossom, she recognized the other patterns in the sheets: it was bedding from an inn in Yanhu, a scenic town on the shores of Teardrop Lake, which was supposedly formed when the Goddess Guanyin's tear fell to Earth.

Of course. Lord Ting, Lord Yang, Lord Shi, and Lord Tong had all travelled to Yanhu with the Emperor many years ago. Heavens knew Lord Shi would never let anyone forget about it. He was saving this bedsheet for leverage, for when he made his power play.

She pulled the sheets further out, and something clinked out onto the floor. She looked—

Her knees buckled. Bony arms wrapped around her neck. She clawed at them, but to no avail. Disjointed thoughts raced through her mind as lightheadedness took over. Darkness encroached from the edge of her vision, and her arms and legs went limp. Then, nothing.

* * *

No, no, no. *Hold the dragonfly with care....* Tian released the rear naked choke on Tang Li, hoping he hadn't accidentally killed her. He eased her down to the bed. Setting his ear to her mouth, he stared at her chest.

It rose and fell, and the warmth of her breath tickled his ear.

He blew out his own breath. Thank the heavens.

Scooching over to Jie, he studied her. Asleep, she looked even more fae-like, like a being descended from heaven, instead of some spirit trickster.

Though maybe he was the real trickster.

Throughout the evening, he'd been trying to figure out how Jie had gotten the key, and how Fixer Zhang had known about Lord Shi's decision to go to Lord Wu's moons-viewing party. Riding back and forth between the quays and Lord Shi's house, it started coming to him.

One of the few people who knew about Shi Han's First Pollination was Old Feng. The only one able to get Lord Shi's fake key was Tang Li, who'd distracted the lord to help Tian escape the house earlier in the day. Maybe it wasn't because she mistook him for Shi Han, but because she knew he was helping Jie.

With access and knowledge, Steward Zhu had been the other option; but when Tian had seen Tang Li smash a vase over his head...

He looked down at her now. Fixer Zhang. She wasn't skilled in stealth, and she hadn't noticed Tian playing dead. Thank the heavens, Jie, even unconscious, had been able to shove him clear of the dust cloud.

Once the half-elf came to, they'd be able to question Tang Li and finally get some answers.

CHAPTER 18

Mission accomplished, Wen bowed low, her back burning from where it had been rubbed up against the wall.

Hands on his knees, Lord Shi leaned over, breaths heaving. Now that he was sated, she'd find a corner to hole up in, away from men who might want her.

"Thank you, my Lord," she said. Thanking him for his part in helping the cell accomplish their mission. She held out her wrists, still bound by his—or rather, his son's—necklace.

Grinning, he straightened. "Oh, I'm not done yet."

No? It shouldn't be a surprise, based on Lilian's stories about his quick bursts. Wen tried to hide the disappointment and disgust welling in her chest.

Not that he cared what she thought. He ogled her. "I'll take you to Heaven and back a dozen times over. If you think my son was good, prepare yourself for a real man."

Young Shi Han had been almost tender at the end. It was doubtful his father would even consider it. Still, there was no way to extricate herself from this. Maybe faking a few climaxes would get it over with sooner.

He grabbed her hips, spun her around and prodded her to one of the barrels. He bent her over it.

She suppressed a sigh. Despite his age, he was like a boy on the cusp of manhood, rebounding quickly, taking her from behind. Now, her chest and belly would be as rubbed as raw as her back.

The position provided a view of the keg, and she focused on the grain pattern. It was a familiar-looking barrel. Something about the lines and whorls. It was hard to focus on the design of nature's hand on the wood, as she heaved back and forth over it. Its contents swished like sand, and something else rattled.

Rattled.

It was the barrel from Lord Shi the porters had brought in. Supposedly wheat wine.

Which shouldn't be rattling. Nor should it smell like someone pissed on a burnt log. Nose crinkling, she twisted to look at the side.

Wine. Jinjing County.

It was the barrel from when they'd boarded, which hadn't been on the list of gifts.

The porters had suggested an identical one had been brought aboard the imperial barge. Which meant...

She screamed, an ear-splitting shriek which would never be mistaken as one of pleasure.

Gasping, Lord Shi backed away. His eyes went wide. "What's the matter? Are you all right?"

Wen screamed again, picking up her clothes with her still-bound hands and pulling them to her chest. The act would make her words more believable.

His expression twisted into genuine concern.

Maybe he wasn't so awful a person, but he was still a traitor. She screamed again.

"What's wrong? Please, tell me."

She huddled back into the corner, bringing her knees to her chest as if terrified. Let whoever came in think that.

The doors burst open, revealing a pair of armed guards in Zhenjing Province's blue livery. "What's the matter here?" one said.

Lord Shi swept up his robe and clutched it to his chest with one hand, while gesturing to her with another. "I don't know. She won't stop screaming."

Of course, nobody would take a Blossom's word over a great lord's. Unless there was physical proof. She pointed a shaking finger at the barrel. "It's a firepowder trap."

"What?" Lord Shi took several steps back.

The guards drew their swords.

More importantly… Wen raised the back of her wrist to the forehead. "I overheard the porters talking. There's another one aboard the imperial barge."

One of the guards dashed out, while the other set his blade to Lord Shi's throat.

"I don't know what's going on." Head shaking, Lord Shi raised his hands.

Was he telling the truth? Or acting? Wen studied him.

The fear in his eyes wasn't a giveaway; he'd be afraid whether he was a conspirator or not. But there was apparently something in his safe that Fixer Zhang wanted, and which supposedly tied Lilian to more than just the assassination of Lord Ting.

Young Lord Wu stormed in, more guards in tow. A young man, he had the strong chin and high cheekbones of Hua's middle coast. His hair was pinned back. "Lord Shi, explain yourself."

"I don't know. I don't know." Bowing low, Lord Shi babbled, barely coherent. "It's not from me. It's not mine."

"The Emperor's investigators will have to determine that. Take him." Lord Wu jerked his head to the side, and the guards hurried to follow his orders.

Wen looked to Lord Shi with sympathetic eyes. Besides the official investigators, the clan would also take part. Sometimes, pain was involved.

Young Lord Wu looked to her, his eyes less leering, more kind. "Are you all right?"

Wen bowed low, still keeping herself covered as if she really were modest. “Yes, my Lord.”

“Men, come. Let’s give the young woman some privacy. We’re going back to the docks.” With a bob of his head, he turned on his heel and left.

The guards led Lord Shi out after him, but then he spun around and reached for her. “The key. Give me my key.”

The guards restrained him and dragged him out to the main cabin. Young Shi Han was already there, hands on his head, surrounded by guards. The poor boy. Surely he couldn’t have known about his father’s treachery?

EPILOGUE

A loud groan jolted Tang Li into consciousness. Her body ached, and her head felt as if it had been crushed in an Arkothi wine press. She hadn't been so miserable since a patron had forced her to drink enough rice wine to drown a small village. She started to rise, only to find her wrists and ankles bound and secured to something, as they'd been when she'd had the misfortune of receiving Lord Tong a few years ago. She opened her eyes.

Darkness. Because of a blindfold.

Her heart leaped into her throat. Was this one of Lord Tong's games? No, that was years ago, and after she'd earned out her bond she'd only fucked men of her choosing; usually to establish connections. Thankfully, she'd never had to endure the sick games Lord Tong enjoyed. So where was she now?

She'd just pulled the contents out of Lord Shi's safe, that's it. She'd been so close to satisfying a need to open it. Then, someone had choked her.

And they'd let her live.

She listened.

She was alone, and this was Lord Shi's hard bed. Where were—

"You're awake," the half-elf said, her pained tone sounding as if she'd been choked out as well. Right, she'd breathed in the toxin, which should've kept her knocked out for a few hours.

Tang Li gasped. Had she been out that long? Unless whoever had choked her had revived the half-elf. "What do you want?"

"Many things, but mainly I want to know about Lilian."

Lilian... "We had tea last week."

"What did you talk about?" Excitement rose in Jie's voice.

What had they talked about? Tang Li's appointment book showed they'd sat for two hours, but she only recalled greeting each other, then leaving. "I don't remember."

Silence.

Then the blindfold came off.

Tang Li craned her neck and turned her head. The half-elf stood there, holding the side of her head. Directly ahead, the Iridescent Moon shone in the south window. It was now waxing toward its fourth gibbous. She'd been out for only a few minutes.

"Tell me again," Jie said. "What did you and Lilian talk about?"

"I don't remember."

Jie sucked on her lower lip. "What can you tell me about the contents of the safe? Stock certificates, a yue ball, a gold nugget, and some bloody sheets."

"My employer wanted them, not me," she said.

"Who's your employer?"

Tang Li's mouth clamped shut. In the last two years, she'd worked hard to make connections, and to betray an employer would be a blow to her reputation.

And this particular employer was particularly ruthless: knowing that Lord Shi had planned to expose his involvement in the illegal yue trade, he'd plotted to frame Lord Shi for attempting to sink Lord Wu's ship.

It'd been a dud—she knew, because she'd procured it. Had she been able to prevent Wen, Meisha, and Yangyang from reaching the barge, her contact onboard would've conveniently discovered it just after the fifth waxing gibbous.

Which meant… "We need to leave here, soon. Imperial soldiers will be swarming here before the full moon." And if they caught her here, it'd mean torture. Still, something drew her to the safe. "Wait, there was something else in the safe."

"I heard it," a new voice chirped. The boy.

"Shhh," Jie hissed.

More shuffling about the room. Tang Li tilted her head and found the boy. He must've been hiding out of her line of sight earlier.

Jie sucked in a sharp breath. Then she held up a hairpin, shaped like a lotus. "Was this what you were looking for?"

Tang Li's eyes went wide as memories of her meeting with Lilian came flooding back, as if a shuttered light bauble was suddenly open. They'd talked about Lord Ting and the North. And then, Lilian had waved her hands and wiggled her fingers. It was then Tang Li had forgotten the conversation and developed the urge to open the safe. Now, though, one detail came back, and it would keep her alive for the time being. "Lilian was the daughter of the late Lord Yu Qian, the last prince of the Yu Dynasty. She was the last heir of the North."

And there was more, a poem repeating over and over in her head.

She spoke it out loud: "When three eyes open. More truths shall be revealed. Hero or traitor."

End of Part 4

PART 5:
LAST HEIR OF THE NORTH

PROLOGUE:

One Mother's Treasure

Mama told three-year-old Yu Mei to stay quiet. She was a good girl, so she did. It was hard, because they were playing hide-and-go-seek in the root cellar, and she was afraid of the dark. It smelled so dirty and moldy.

The shouts and screams outside got louder.

"Be brave," Mama whispered.

Brave? For a game?

Maybe this wasn't a game. Mama never had time to play during the day. Mei put a hand on Mama's big tummy. She was going to be a big sister soon. Big sisters had to be brave. Just like Big Brother Ken. He was up above, keeping the Seekers from finding them.

The door to the root cellar flung open. Bright, afternoon sunlight streamed in. Mei's eyes hurt. She put a hand on her forehead to see better, and blinked several times.

"Get out," said a man with a Big Voice.

The Seekers had found them! That meant they'd have to find a new hiding place. The game would start again.

No. Something was wrong. Mama was sniffling. She took Mei's hand and rose to her feet. Her voice sounded scratchy. "Come on."

"Hurry," the mean man said.

On wobbling feet, Mei climbed up the steps. Mama's hand felt cold and wet.

It was so bright outside. But it smelled different. The chrysanthemum smell was there. But it was also smoky, like when the cooks burned the pig. And people were crying. The sobbing was even louder than the stream of water that fell from the mountain and into the pool.

Mei blinked away the orange in her eyes.

Daddy's friends lay on the stones, near the wall with iron logs. They were bleeding. So much blood. And armored men with blue banners surrounded them, pointing bows.

Mei's heart hurt. She grabbed Mama's leg.

Maybe the dark cellar would be better.

Big Brother Ken was on his knees, hands on his head.

Mama patted her on the head. "It's all right, my Beautiful Lotus. Be a good girl."

"Young Lord Yu Ken." A man with a pig face walked over to Big Brother. His armor jingled.

Big Brother bowed his head. "Lord Tong."

"Your father has been inciting unrest in Chengfu County, using your descent from the last Yu emperor as a claim to legitimacy."

Those were all big words. What did they mean?

"It's not true!" Big Brother shook his head. "My father is loyal to the Emperor. He went to the court to turn over the Yu Dynasty Seal."

"Lord Yang." Lord Tong beckoned to someone behind all the other men.

A skinny man strode forth, a round basket in hand. He withdrew a green cube from his robe.

"No," Big Brother said. "You were Father's most trusted advisor."

Sobbing, Mama pulled Mei's head into her fat tummy. "Don't look, my Beautiful Lotus."

"Your father never made it to the court," Pig-faced Tong said.

Around them Daddy's men gasped. Mama pulled her closer. What was going on?

"You are a traitor to the North." Big Brother was using his Big Voice, now. "A running dog to the Emperor."

"You had promise, Young Lord Yu," Pig Face said. "Too much."

Metal flashed. Big Brother let out a strange sound.

Mama shrieked.

Heart thumping, Mei pulled away and turned her head.

Big Brother lay on the stones. Blood gushed from his neck. His eyes were looking at her. But he wasn't seeing. Pig Face stood over him. He held a bloody knife.

Behind him, Skinny Man was holding...

Daddy's head.

Mei screamed. It was just too much. She couldn't be a good girl. She turned her head back into Mama's big tummy.

Hands grabbed her, pulling her away. Mei looked up to see Daddy's gardener. She never liked him. His skin was so tight on his head, he looked scary.

"Little Sister." Pig Face drew closer to Mama, and gestured first to Skinny Man, then to a fat man. "You should've married Lord Yang or Lord Shi, and joined our families. Then, the North would've been stronger. We might've been able to stand against the Emperor."

"You're all vile. I won't marry him. Not then, not now. May Yanluo drag you down to Hell."

Mama never used such mean words. She was always nice. Gentle.

"Sadly," Pig Face said, "you don't have a choice."

"I refuse." Mama shook her head.

"Oh, you misunderstand me. You carry Lord Yu's heir."

Mama always had a pretty color. Now, her face was white. One hand was on her tummy. She backed away. "It's a girl. The doctor said it was just a girl."

A girl? Was Mei going to have a sister?

"It's a boy," Daddy's gardener said.

How did he know? Tears ran down Mei's face. Something bad was going to—

"I'm sorry, Little Sister." Pig Face grabbed Mama, and put a knife into her chest.

Mama's eyes grew big. She sank to her knees.

Screaming, Mei pulled free of the gardener and ran over.

Mama fell onto her side.

Tears blurred Mei's vision. She pulled and pulled. If Mama didn't get up now, she might never. She needed Mei's help.

"My Beautiful Lotus," Mama whispered. Blood ran from the side of her mouth. Her next words were almost too soft to hear. Her hand wrapped around Mei's. Something bit into her palm. Cold and hard. "Remember, you are the last princess of the Yu Dynasty."

Mei wiped the blood with her sleeve. She shook Mama. "Mama. Get up. Please get up."

Bony fingers pulled her off. She shrieked and kicked.

A hand clapped into her cheek. It burned, and she quieted.

Pig Face's face filled her world. His breath smelled like garlic when he spoke. "Niece, you would have grown up to be a pawn, married to form an alliance. We can't have that, not even now."

Pawn? Daddy and Big Brother played a game with those little pieces. She wasn't one of those. Mei opened her palm. Mama's favorite hairpin. Silver. Shaped like a lotus.

"What will you do with her, my Lord?" the gardener asked.

"She has to die." Pig Face leaned over and pulled the knife out of Mama.

Mei looked from Mama to Big Brother. Her tummy twisted into knots. Her mouth tasted sour. Tears made everything look strange.

"Please," the gardener said. "I've always wanted a daughter. After I've trained her, and a few years go by, she won't even remember today. And, a decade from now, if your dreams come closer to reality, I can bring her back: the long-lost descendant of the Yu Dynasty, whose husband can claim the North."

Pig Face's jaw wobbled back and forth. He looked like more like a cow now.

He looked over his shoulder. "What say you, my Lords?"

A fat man in brown exchanged glances with Skinny Man, then both nodded.

Pig Face looked even more gross when he smiled. "We will seed the rumor that she survived, to give the North hope."

The gardener's smile looked strange. He gave Mei's hand a tug. "Come."

Sobbing, she pulled and pulled, trying to get back to Mama. "Mama. I want Mama."

"Your mother is going somewhere you can't follow," the gardener said. "Not yet. Now come."

He was wrong. Mama was just asleep. She'd get up.

Something soft and wet touched her neck. It smelled like flowers.

Her head felt strange. Her eyelids were heavy. And all went black.

* * *

Many weeks had passed since the gardener had taken Mei away from home.

She had to be big.

Because Mama told her to be big.

Most of the time, she rode on Boney Face's back. He wanted her to call him *Father.*

He wasn't her father.

Her daddy was Lord Yu Qiang.

And Mama. She wanted to see Mama.

The gardener made her watch his fingers dance. He made her act and talk different.

Mama wouldn't like the way she acted and talked.

He wanted her to eat.

But food tasted like wet paper.

And every day, her arms, legs, and head felt heavier. It was almost impossible to stand.

"You're a bad girl," he said one day, when she refused to eat. "You'll die."

Die. That's what Mama said when Mei had once stomped on a worm. The worm was gone forever.

Just like Mama.

And the baby in her tummy.

She wasn't going to be a big sister. She didn't need to be a big girl anymore.

Mei's eyes wanted to cry, but nothing came out.

And he still made her watch his fingers.

Eventually, they came to place with big walls and lots of houses. Inside this place was a bridge over some water, and a big red lantern.

All the houses had pretty red flags and lanterns, with even prettier women walking around. But none were as pretty as Mama. And Mama didn't like those lanterns. She didn't like the pretty women in those red lantern houses.

Boney Face took her to a nice room in one of the biggest houses. Two women with the same face were there, though one wore a scary mask at first. It only had eyes. Like a ghost.

"I can't raise her," Boney Face said. "She won't eat. Raise her as a Seedling. Train her in our ways."

The first woman shook her head. "You've messed her up with the Tiger's Eye. It's beyond anything a doctor can fix. She's going to die."

Die.

Mei wanted to.

Boney Face threw his hands up. "What should I do?"

"I know only one person who can fix your fuck-up." The second had the same voice as the first.

"Wait. If we are going to do that, we can undo the clan." The first pulled the others together. They tapped their fingers on each other's arms. Were they talking, too?

Mei could barely lift her head. She couldn't hear, no matter how hard she tried.

Boney Face came over. He moved his fingers in front of her. Just like before. Mei followed the motion, and her head got heavier and heavier.

"Forget," he said.

Grey at the sides of her vision darkened to black.

* * *

She opened her eyes.

"She's awake!" a voice that chirped like a bird said. A beautiful girl appeared over her. She had pretty pointed ears and big eyes. Maybe she was a faerie. A messenger from the gods. "You're awake. What's your name?"

Name... What was her name? Who was she? Where had she come from, and how did she get... "Where am I?"

The faerie held up a hairpin, shaped like a lotus. "This is yours. Does it look familiar?"

A lotus. It did look familiar. Her heart beat fast. It was a name. *Her* name. "Lotus. My name is Beautiful Lotus." Wasn't it?

The faerie sucked on her lower lip. "Beautiful Lotus... Lilian. Hello Lilian, I'm Jie. You are at the Black Lotus Temple. We are going to be sisters from today."

CHAPTER 1

The Present

While the Black Lotus Clan wanted to learn about Tang Li's interest in Lord Shi's safe, Jie needed to find out what the Triad fixer knew about Lilian. If Tian hadn't destroyed their supply of *yinghua* toxin, this would be so much easier. Then again, if he hadn't, the Steel Orchid might have succeeded in killing them a few days ago.

With all the citizens milling through the streets, awaiting a rare celestial event, she and Tian had been unable to move Tang Li from Lord Shi's courtyard home to a more secure location. Instead, Yangyang and Meisha had come to them, scaling the compound's rear wall and jumping over to one of the rooms in the main building. Wen remained unaccounted for, probably still on Lord Wu's barge for his full moons viewing party; she would run ahead of Lord Shi back to the house, giving them forewarning of his arrival.

Less predictable was if and when the clan would send Cleaners or Enforcers to check on Jie's progress in cracking the safe. They'd seize the contents of the safe, and likely make Fixer Zhang disappear. For her own peace of mind, Jie needed to extract answers before that happened.

Still wearing the simple maid's dress they'd captured her in, Tang Li—who was probably Fixer Zhang—was tied to a chair. Even if her claim that Lilian was the last heir of the rebellious North had only been a ploy to stay alive, it was working.

Burying a frustrated snarl, Jie felt Fixer Zhang's pulse and studied her expressions, looking for telltale signs of a lie. The method didn't work if the subject was trained to resist, however, or was just a pathological liar.

"Do you know who I am?" Jie asked. An easy question, one which would set the baseline.

"Of course. Jie. We were at the Chrysanthemum Pavilion together for four years." Tang Li's pulse remained steady, her gaze focused. Whether she knew about their true identities as Black Lotus Fists, they'd soon find out.

"Did you like Gardener Ju?" The now-deceased owner of the Chrysanthemum Pavilion, and later the Peony Garden, had been the aforementioned Steel Orchid.

"Yes." Tang Li's pulse stuttered a few beats, and her lips pursed. A sign of a lie, but one trained to resist this detection could fake those by thinking of something else. "Not all the time. She was fair, but greedy."

All true enough. "Did you know she was a Steel Orchid?"

Tang Li's erratic heartbeat punctuated the silence that hung between them, but that could be the result of not wanting to answer the question.

"Maybe we should report back," Yangyang said. "We could get a team to help extract her to a secure location."

Waving off Yangyang's suggestion without breaking eye contact with Tang Li, Jie spun a knife between her fingers. "Answer me, or I will have to resort to less friendly measures." Ones that had been proven not to work, but at least the threat would usually cause a change in the pulse.

"I've never heard of a Steel Orchid until just now." Tang Li's heartbeat remained steady. A truth. So what had she tried to hide up to now?

"Are you really Fixer Zhang?" If so, she could reveal more answers about Lilian...if Faceless Chang had told the truth with her dying breaths.

"Yes." She spoke in an even tone, nothing in her pulse or expression indicating a lie. Of course, there was also the possibility that she was one of the less than one in a thousand people who could dissemble without any physiological response. It would probably be good trait in a fixer.

The next answer, though, could be verified. "When I met your contact, what did they tell me about Lord Shi's safe?"

"That its contents would reveal answers about Lilian."

Since this was true, it verified that Tang Li either was or worked for Fixer Zhang. Jie held up Lilian's lotus hairpin again. "What is it about this trinket that made you recall that Lilian was the last heir of the North?"

Tang Li's brows furrowed. "I don't know. I saw it, and remembered my last conversation with her."

"Go on then," Jie said. Sometimes a scent or sight could stir a memory. "Tell us more about Lilian."

"I wish I could."

Jie bit back a snarl. There had been no sign of a lie. She pointed the knife. "Then you are of no use to me...to us."

"Wait." Tang Li shook her head. "Let me tell you a story."

Jie had heard many of them, and this one would no doubt run in circles and waste time. If only there were flaying tools on hand. Not because they worked in exacting the truth, which they generally didn't, but because the frustration grew unbearable. "I'm listening."

Tang Li's lips quivered. "When we were at the Chrysanthemum Pavilion, Lilian came to me often for counsel."

Jie sucked on her lower lip. Though they'd all lived in the same House in the Floating World, it wasn't as if they spent every phase of the Iridescent Moon together. Especially after Lilian had started receiving Hummingbirds. After that, they'd grown closer in some ways; in others...

"We enjoyed a lot of time together. Brushing each other's hair, helping each other with make-up, mending clothes, painting..." Her voice sounded wistful.

Jealousy pitted in Jie's gut. She and Lilian had grown up together in the clan. She was the one Lilian came to, not Tang Li. Tang Li was just a Blossom, trained in the art of acting. This had to be a lie.

"And we'd chat. About mundane things, like gossip and dreams." Tang Li looked up from her reverie. "But there are parts where I remember what we were doing, but not what we were talking about."

Jie snorted. "Maybe you have a bad memory."

"It's more like blank spots. Holes in my memory." Tang Li's eyes searched Jie's, almost pleading.

Blank spots? Holes? As a Blossom, it was possible Tang Li had hit her head against a headboard one too many times, or had to drink with a Hummingbird until the point of blacking out.

But there was something more here.

It was time to retake the initiative. Pretending to care, Jie adopted a concerned tone. "What is your first recollection of her?"

"When you both came to the Chrysanthemum Pavilion. You walked in like you already owned the place, while she hung back a few steps, and clung to you like a wet leaf."

Jie sucked on her lower lip. That's the way Lilian had been, ever since she came to the temple.

* * *

Thirteen Years Ago

Seven-year-old Jie sat on the veranda of the Hall of Scribes. The sharply-pitched green roof provided shade in the afternoon heat. The buzz and whirr of insects was pleasant, especially after heraldry class. After having to memorize the colors and sigils of the rebellious lords of the North, and listening to Master Pan ramble about the lost Yu imperial seal, it was nice to clear her mind.

Preceded by her honeysuckle scent, Lillian skipped out of the double doors like a rabbit. She was just four, after all. Her eyes met Jie's, and a big smile flashed across her face. "Big Sister!"

"I hate reading." Lavender wafted on the air, and Wen's shoulders drooped as she trudged out. Of course, every three-year-old hated reading. Lucky for them, kids their age only spent a quarter of a phase on it each day. Jie's own writing class was twice as long, and more painful than her age group's torture resistance training.

Jie chuckled. "Well, no more reading. It's break time now."

"What are we going to play?" Lilian hopped up and down. Though her accent and mannerisms had once marked her as coming from the central valley, she now spoke and acted like a child from the capital.

"You'll see." Grinning, Jie took their hands and pulled them toward the playground.

Not six steps later, Doudou barred their way out of the courtyard, his hackles raised. His teeth, white as his fluffy fur and sharp as the shape and keenness of his ears, bared in a snarl.

Jie's own spine went rigid for a split second. Wen and Lilian both clutched her arms. Even though the temple dogs knew the children and wouldn't bite them, they were still scary.

They were also a test.

Taking a deep breath, Jie melted the tension in her body. She met Doudou's gaze, and let out a short hiss.

The dog's posture relaxed. He sat, his expression changing from mean to dopey.

Though both calmed a little, Lilian and Wen angled behind her. Jie guided them along, petting his head as they passed.

Wen reached out with a tentative hand to do the same, but Jie pulled it back. "Only with confidence."

Up ahead, Yun and Nan jumped from one wobbly wood pillar to another, and ran across a narrow beam as they raced toward the Hall of Spears. Both girls were Jie's age. It would've been fun to join them, but Lilian still needed help getting used to life at the temple.

Even after a year.

Yun and Nan had almost reached the climbing wall, where the boys in their training group were playing Dodge Blades. No one could hit Jie, unless she let them. She did, sometimes, because it made them like her more, and the dulled practice knives and throwing stars hurt but didn't cut.

Little Kong crouched behind the climbing wall. He was probably one of the Targets in a game of Hide-and-Go-Stalk. Though no one could see him, the way he breathed and smelled gave him away.

At least, to Jie. She excelled at this game, and not just as the Stalker. As a Target, she could squeeze into the tightest, strangest places.

"Worthless." Lai, the Stalker, hurled a rock at Lilian.

It would've slammed into her back had Jie not reached over and caught it. She flung it back, hitting Lai in the shoulder.

He flinched. "She's not worth your time."

That Turtle's Egg always bullied Lilian because she learned fighting and stealth so slowly. Now, she hung her head and pressed up against Jie. Flashing a big-person gesture at Lai, Jie pulled her companions along.

To the west side of the playground, past the swinging spears, kids in Wen's and Lillian's age group milled about blindfolded, their distinct smells mingling together.

Digging in with her heels, Lilian shook her head. "I don't want play Pin the Knife in the Traitor."

Neither did Jie. She might be able to see well in the dark, but the full humans were better than her blindfolded as they tried to identify the Traitor and poke them with a blunt knife. In her age group, they used the basics for a more complex game, Root Out the Mole.

"Don't worry," Jie said. "We're going to play Chameleon Skin. Just the three of us."

Lilian clapped her hands together. It was her favorite game, after all. Since she could never remember her past, it was easy for her to make up stories and convince herself they were true. More importantly, she could convince others. She walked up behind one of the jumping stones. Taking on a pleasant, welcoming expression, she said, "Welcome to Lilian Bakery. What would you like?"

Jie smiled. This game was fun. Instead of a being an abandoned half-breed, whose elf father had given her up so that he could continue his adventures unburdened by a baby, she could become, at least for half an hour, a dressmaker, warrior, or princess. She turned to Wen. "If Lilian is the baker, then you're the farmer's daughter. The one with the hurt left leg."

Wen's head cocked.

"You played her in the spring." And would have to remember every detail she'd dreamt up back then. Jie grinned.

"That's not fair!" Wen's face flushed.

Snorting, Jie pointed to Lilian's fingers. "You don't have any burn scars. You can't be a baker."

"I don't work at the ovens." Lilian shrugged. Of course, she showed no sign of a lie, since kids her age were only allowed in the temple kitchens to practice cutting meats and vegetables. Mixing truths with lies, they were taught, made a story more believable.

Jie shushed her and took Lilian's hands. "Your hands have too many callouses to be a baker."

"We work our dough until it is the softest in the realm." While certainly a lie, her tone was no more proud than the owners of the real bakery in nearby Lianjing Town.

Jie suppressed a smile. So far Lilian wasn't good at weapons or sneaking, but she was a good liar when she needed to be.

* * *

The Present

Jie stared out the window of Lord Shi's bedroom, lost in her memories. Even from the beginning, Lilian had been better than they thought at just about everything.

"Eldest Sister," Yangyang said. "We should inform the clan that we have accomplished our mission, and we need help extracting Fixer Zhang to a secure location."

"I heard you the first time." Jie scowled.

Yangyang and Meisha exchanged nervous glances. For now, Jie commanded their loyalty, especially if they believed they were following clan orders. But if their seeds of doubt sprouted, she might have even less time to learn the answers to the questions that had twisted her heart for the last several days.

CHAPTER 2

The Present

Lord Wu's moons-viewing party had come to a sudden end with Wen's discovery of the firepowder bomb aboard the barge. They'd docked, and though imperial soldiers had escorted Lord Shi and his son Shi Han away, no one else had been allowed to disembark.

Of course, a few imperials wouldn't stop a Black Lotus Fist. While they herded the guests onto the main deck, Wen slipped into a cabin where she'd seen servants' livery. It was right next door to the room with Lord Shi's firepowder bomb.

Despite her misgivings about being blown to pieces, she wanted to see it. She changed into livery that fit, then squeezed out through the porthole. Creeping along the decorative ridge that ran along the hull, she peeked into the cabin with the bomb.

No one was there. From the sound of it, someone stood guard outside the cabin.

Wen snorted. Had the Black Lotus led the investigation, they'd be studying the weapon now. And as the only Fist still on board, it was up to her.

Taking a deep breath, she slipped in through porthole and tiptoed to the barrel, now sitting upright instead of on its side. The glued, ironbound wood slats were a design from the lands of the fair-skinned barbarians to the north. Though still rare in Cathay, Wen had seen enough of these barrels in the Floating World. Their smoky flavor diffused into the wines, and patrons considered them exotic.

As a bomb, how would it work? There were no holes for fuses, nor any place marked to tap, to possibly create a spark and ignite it. Also, the contents hadn't been tightly p—

Footsteps stomped toward the door.

"Let me see the device," a muffled voice said.

If discovered, they might think she was the saboteur: even though she'd been the one to reveal it to authorities, she was now a woman in provincial livery. Wen dashed back and pushed through the porthole. She worked her way along the ridge toward the dock side. Waiting for a blind spot in the flow of bustling guards and servants on the quays, she dropped down and followed a soldier off.

There was no sign of Meisha or Yangyang. They'd probably met up with Tian and Jie back at Lord Shi's home by now. It was up to her to relay the news of his treasonous plot. She looked up at the Iridescent Moon, now waxing halfway between its fourth and fifth crescent. It would wax to full in an hour and a half; imperial troops would raid Lord Shi's and disturb any material evidence of his plot against the Emperor well before then.

Once she cleared the commotion, she broke into a run. While the city was usually asleep at this hour, citizens milled about the streets, slowing her down. Soon, for the first time in eleven years, the Blue, White, and Iridescent Moons would all be full in the sky at the same time.

She turned into an entrance to the *hutong* warrens, where hundreds of courtyard homes formed a network of narrow roads, and stirred a memory from years ago.

* * *

Eleven Years Ago

With the sun beating down and the air so humid, today was a miserable day for a training mission. Holding hands with Jie, and with Lilian on the half-elf's other side, Wen skipped across the footbridge over the stream that separated Lianjing Township from the Black Lotus Temple. The oppressive heat made Wen's hand sticky, and she fought the urge to let go of Jie's.

"Look, it's the Triplets," the middle-aged confectioner said to his new wife, who beckoned from the window of the store.

Wen rolled her eyes. Although elf blood made Jie look younger than her actual nine years, she still looked older than six-year-old Lilian and Wen's own five years. It didn't stop the locals from affectionately using the nickname. Never mind that they looked nothing alike, either.

Of course, half the townsfolk were literally feebleminded.

Jie led them down the paved highway between the three-story rowhouses. Made of white bricks, they had shops on the first floor and residences on the upper levels. Master Yan said this was rare in towns this size, but typical of the realm's major cities.

Lianjing Town was special.

"Here you go, a sample for pretty girls." Shopkeeper Chen held out three doughy *tangyuan* on a white porcelain plate.

Wen and Lilian released Jie's hands and reached for the mouth-sized, spherical sweets.

Jie managed to swipe one before Shopkeeper Chen pulled the tray back. "What do you say?" he asked.

"Please!" all three said in unison. In the three years since her arrival at the temple, Lilian had changed the way she spoke. She no longer sounded funny; or maybe Wen had simply grown used to it.

Grinning stupidly, the vendor held the plate out again, and they snapped them up.

"Remember, tell everyone how yummy they are!" His cheery young wife waved.

They all waved back as they skipped along.

"Should we eat it?" Wen whispered, studying hers. If the shopkeeper had put something like dreamflower pollen in it, the sweet would amplify drowsiness, while its strong scent would hide the pollen's telltale smell.

Wen wouldn't have been able to tell for sure, but Jie looked sidelong at them, confirming the candies were indeed laced with some kind of poison.

Lilian started to pop her treat into her mouth.

"No!" Jie slapped Lilian's hand up, sending the *tangyuan* flying. For her to do that meant her keen nose had sniffed out a toxin, and if they were to beat the other teams, all three of them needed to stay sharp.

Wen swiped it out of the air.

"Hey!" Lilian reached with *Darting Hands.*

Wen turned enough that Lilian came up empty-handed. "Stop, people might see you." Revealing even this basic technique would lead to gossip. If one person in Lianjing Town knew, within a few days just about everyone would know.

"What do you think? Is the confectioner a Plant or a Cousin?" Jie held up the three *tangyuan*. "I'm guessing if he's trying to poison us..."

Wen gasped. Jie had swiped both of the sweets from her. Of course, that was nothing new. As to whether the shopkeeper was trying to poison them or not... "Maybe it wasn't the shopkeeper. For all we know, Master Zhan might've slipped the ingredients in the night before."

Lilian's forehead scrunched up. It was quite cute, though it might very well be an act. Maybe she already knew the shopkeeper's wife was one of the feebleminded Cousins, something

Wen had figured out the last time they were in town, two weeks ago.

With a sigh, Jie drew them closer. "The real plant is the new wife. I'd bet she's the one who added the poison to the *tangyuan*."

Wen drew back and searched Jie's eyes. It was against the rules to tell others.

Then again, breaking the rules without getting caught was encouraged. And the three of them always helped each other. A smile tugged at Wen's lips, unbidden.

Grinning as well, Jie looked to Wen. "We might be able to use those *tangyuan* later."

Up ahead, Wen caught sight of the three boys of Viper Team heading toward the pick-up point. Already, they'd lost the spring in their step. They'd eaten the sweets. Jie pulled Lilian and Wen to the side of the street, so they could pass around a caravan of eight covered wagons, their cargo marked as cloth from the central valley.

"This is it," Jie whispered. "A shipment from the imperial kilns, bound for Sun-Moon Palace."

Wen nodded.

"It says cloth." Lilian stared at the wagons. "The guards look like mercenaries, not imperial soldiers. How can you tell it's from the imperial kilns?"

It was a good question, since dozens of caravans passed along the highway each day. Wen tilted her head at each detail: "They're sitting too low to be textiles. Guards are riding imperial stallions, and the pommels of their swords indicate they are imperial issue. And they're riding in unison. It's too heavily guarded for cloth."

"Our target, then." Lilian gave a nod. "Which one?"

Jie motioned up ahead, to where the Viper, Wasp, and Tiger Teams were walking past the other wagons, looking for their specific target. Like them, each team was made up of two children in Lilian's and Wen's age group, and an older leader from Jie's age group. Jie, in turn, was part of a trio led by Yangyang, which ran more difficult training missions.

Dun Lai, the ten-year-old leader of the Wasps, met Jie's gaze and sneered.

Such a Turtle's Egg. He delighted in tormenting Lilian—hiding her training knives, tripping her, or stealing her food. Wen's stomach clenched of its own accord.

"There's ours," Jie said.

Four wagons up, theirs was marked with a sigil carved into its side. Wen fiddled with her pinkie. With each wagon flanked by a guard, slipping through their line of sight would be near impossible without...

"A distraction," Lilian said. "We need to work with the other teams."

Jie nodded, and up ahead, based on the way the other teams were passing signals, it looked as if they had come to the same conclusion. *One person each team, meet up front.*

"You go." Jie nodded to Lilian.

Wen nodded. The half-elf would always take the greatest risk, and do her best to protect Lilian. After all, she was the most likely candidate among their group to end up as a Cousin, her memories of the temple blocked by Master Yan's *Tiger's Eye* technique.

With a bob of her head, Lillian skipped off to the front.

Jie turned to Wen. "I need you to distract the guard and driver of the wagon behind ours, in the event Lilian's acting doesn't work. Both when I get in, and again after a count of a hundred, when I am ready to get out."

Wen gave a short nod, even as a commotion broke out near the front of the column.

"Out of the way, urchins!" yelled a gruff voice. "This is no place to play."

Horses nickered, and men cursed. Black Lotus children, with Lilian at their head, darted in between the wagons in a mock game of tag. The guards on the flanks held their formation.

Wen ran under their wagon, and kept low.

"Hey, get out from under there!" the driver yelled, craning to look down. "You'll get trampled or run over!"

The guard jumped down off his horse, his boots thudding on the pavestones. His legs tromped over, and he bent down, his eyebrows clashing together. "You! Get out from under there!"

In the corner of Wen's vision, Jie's little feet hopped up into the wagon.

Starting her count to a hundred, Wen darted out the back, then looped around to the store-side of the street. "You can't catch me!"

The guard spun around, just as Wen dashed past him. His hand caught hold of her ponytail. "I got you!"

Up ahead, Lilian yelped. The wagon at their side lurched to a stop.

"You'll get yourself killed!" the driver yelled. "Stop playing!"

Wen and the guard both froze, then looked toward the front.

Stumbling up from where she'd fallen, Lilian scuttled to the other side. Lai from the Wasps appeared behind her, sneering. Among the most talented in Jie's age group, he boasted of being the reincarnation of the Surgeon.

The guard looked back down at her. "Your little friend almost got run over. No playing around here."

The count had reached seventy-three. She'd have to keep him occupied just a little longer, so she stuck her tongue out.

Scowling, he cuffed her on the cheek.

Pain flared in her face, and she hung her head and let fake tears roll. "I'm sorry."

"You better be. Now go." He released her and gave her a shove.

Wen flashed a quick glance toward the other teams. While the Viper and Tiger Teams were still milling about their wagons, the Wasps were now running down the side streets. Lai smirked at her.

Lilian came up, limping from a scrape on her knee. "He tripped me. Made me fall right in front of the driver. He's either trying to kill me, or get me *Tiger Eyed.*"

Kneeling, Wen examined the wound. It was shallow. "No broken bones, no torn tendons, you'll be all right."

"Where's Jie?" Lilian asked.

"Here." Jie slipped out of the shadows, missive in hand, folded in the clan style so that it would shred in the hands of someone who didn't know how to open it. "It was in one of the vases. Now come on, before the Tigers beat us."

They ran up a side street, crossing over a broad avenue which could've been a street in the capital, and then two middle-sized streets which were a mix of residences and shops. The next two turns put them on a smaller street, where red lanterns hung from doors and pretty women beckoned men over; another turn brought them to a market square where craftsmen hawked their wares. Finally, they turned into the *hutong* warrens.

Unlike the capital, which had sprawling neighborhoods of courtyard homes, Lianjing Town only had a few dozen. *Microcosm*, was the word Master Yan used. Built with imperial gold, Lianjing had a little of everything.

The perfect training grounds for Black Lotus initiates and novices, and a repository of all the Cousins who'd failed to meet expectations in training. It was a place for Fists to do dry runs of missions, and where the honored old and disabled could still serve the clan. Nearly a quarter of the town's population had a connection to the Black Lotus, while the rest lived in blissful ignorance, believing the myth that the temple produced the best scribes and accountants.

If Lai had his way, Lilian would end up here as a Cousin, sooner than later.

They turned into the alley of their destination... and skidded to a stop.

They'd lost. The Wasps were disappearing into the courtyard home. Lai poked his head out and flashed a mean gesture, followed by hand signals: *You'll never win with Lilian.*

Wen's gut twisted. Master Hu kept score of all the students, with points awarded for completed missions, duels won, and other tasks; and points deducted for failures. Thought meant to be secret, of course spies in training all snuck into his office at one time or another to see where they stood.

And in their age group, Lilian was last.

* * *

The Present

Tucking the memory away, Wen reached Lord Shi's courtyard home. Half an hour had passed since she'd escaped the barge. Outside, a guard in brown livery leaned on the stone lion by the main gate, showing no sign that anything was amiss. Of course, if clan members were still inside, he probably wouldn't know.

Wen went around to the side, and was about to scale the wall when she caught sight of Black Lotus code scrawled into the mortar, barely illuminated by the moons.

Take rear wall. Back window of main residence study unlocked.

She fiddled with her pinkie. Not knowing about the attempt to murder the imperial family and many prominent lords, Jie and the others were probably now studying the contents of Lord Shi's safe. Perhaps those contents would've uncovered the plot before anyone was put in harm's way in the first place; and if that were the case, the clan might face severe consequences. She would've sprinted around to the back if not for the occasional straggler out to view the imminent celestial event.

Jie had left faint etchings in the walls, making the insertion point easy to find. Unlike most of the other courtyard homes in the warren, no lights shined in the buildings. She followed Jie's marks to the rear, where she paused to listen for Lord Shi's chamberlain or servant. Hearing no signs of them, Wen climbed the wall and jumped down to the narrow corridor between it and the main residence.

Some of the pavestones were cracked and uneven, with weeds poking out. It was strange that a hereditary lord wouldn't pay the for the maintenance and repair and, even in less-travelled part of his courtyard home. Then again, very few lords dwelled in the warrens at all, instead living in expansive villas in the capital's northeast.

One of the window shutters hung open a crack. Indeed, as she drew closer, low, muffled sounds emanated from beyond the door. Though the words were hard to make out, the high-pitched voice belonged to Jie, and the husky one was Yangyang's.

So they were still there.

Wen needed to warn them. With Lord Shi being questioned by imperial officials, it wouldn't be more than a phase before they converged on this house. The cell sisters needed to be out before then, lest they be caught in the raid. To maintain anonymity, the clan would certainly disavow them.

CHAPTER 3

The Present

In his first week as a Black Lotus clan member, Tian had solved a murder, killed a traitor long thought dead, figured out the identity of Faceless Chang, and captured Fixer Zhang. Now they were turning over stones in a recently deceased member's story, and excitement ran up and down his spine.

Mysteries were meant to be solved, after all.

Of course, they needed Fixer Zhang to reveal her secrets, and people were complicated. Not like numbers, which always made sense. While he might be good at making connections with evidence, understanding the human heart was completely different.

At the edge of the shadows, Yangyang was signing, *Tiger's Eye*. Whatever that meant.

"Enough delaying." Jie glared at Fixer Zhang, her tone bordering on anger. In the short time they'd known each other, she'd never sounded like that. She even seemed to have forgotten about Wen, still unaccounted for after Lord Wu's moons-viewing party.

Tian's heart squeezed. Hopefully, Wen was safe after stealing Lord Shi's key.

The Tiger's Eye, Yangyang signed again, now moving into the half-elf's peripheral vision.

Jie held up the hairpin shaped like a lotus flower. "How could you have forgotten something from a week ago, that this jewelry stirred up?"

What was so special about the hairpin? And why was Jie so intense? Gone was her usual naughty grin and lightheartedness, replaced by a single-minded focus on this task.

"The *Tiger's Eye*," Yangyang said in her deep voice.

"What's the *Tiger's Eye*?" Tian asked.

Turning, Jie hissed. *Clan secret*, she signed.

Yangyang frowned. *I signaled. Tried to get your attention.*

I'm sorry. Jie bowed her head.

Meisha signed, *Lilian must've used the Tiger's Eye on Fixer Zhang.*

Tian scowled. If they'd hurry up and say what it was...

Yangyang turned to him. *It affects your mind. Now—*

How? Tian signed.

Meisha answered, *It can make you ignore pain, so you can finish a mission. Or turn you into a remorseless killing machine.*

Tian shuddered. The clan had very different ideas about the preciousness of life. He'd never let them turn him into a killing machine. He pointed at Fixer Zhang. *What about her?*

Jie signed, *It appears Lilian blocked some of Zhang's memories.*

Meisha shook her head. *How could it affect her, if she wasn't trained?*

If they spent as much time together as Fixer Zhang claims— Jie's lips twisted— *then maybe Lilian conditioned her to be receptive. It would explain a lot.*

Fixer Zhang's eyes flicked among them, her expression a mix of fear, confusion, and curiosity.

A pit formed in Tian's stomach. No matter what she'd done, she was like anyone else when facing an uncertain future.

Turning back to her, Jie held up the hairpin again. "This made you remember that Lilian was the last heir of the North."

Fixer Zhang nodded, even as her gaze shifted among them.

If she's receptive, you're the best at the Tiger's Eye, Yangyang signed to Jie. *Can you unlock her more, and trigger her to reveal what she knows?*

Tian shuddered. Unlocking and triggering sounded like something done to a dwarf lock, not a human.

A smirk formed on Jie's face. With an outstretched finger, she advanced on Fixer Zhang, who recoiled as much as the chair would allow. Jie locked her gaze. The fingers of her free hand danced in an intricate pattern. Fixer Zhang's eyes glazed over.

"She is receptive to the *Tiger's Eye*," Yangyang said.

Without looking back, Jie nodded. "Tell me what else you know about Lilian."

Fixer Zhang's face strained. Sweat clung to her brow. "Nothing." She slumped forward in the chair.

Meisha blew out a breath. *She wouldn't be able to resist Jie, so she must be telling the truth.*

Maybe this was a dead end. Nothing more to Lilian's story. Tian sighed.

"No. There has to be more." Frustration hung in Jie's voice. "Have you felt anything else out of the ordinary? Strange cravings or urges?"

"A poem." Fixer Zhang straightened. "It keeps repeating in my head."

Jie looked over her shoulder and exchanged a confused glance with the rest of them before turning back. "Recite it."

"'When three eyes open. More truths shall be revealed. Hero or traitor.'"

Jie scowled. "What does that mean?"

Fixer Zhang shook her head. "I don't know."

Tian's heart pattered. "It's a riddle!" One which begged to be answered.

Meisha touched the spot between her eyebrows. "Maybe it refers to our third eye?"

"What's that?" Tian asked.

The Yintang point, Yangyang signed. *It's where we focus when we learn to open ourselves to the Tiger's Eye.*

We need a... Whatever Meisha's twist and flick of the index finger meant, Tian had yet to learn it. He imitated it. "What's this?"

"Acupuncturist," Jie said. "Maybe acupuncture can open up that point."

Tian shuddered. Princess Kaiya received acupuncture treatments, but all those needles...

Fixer Zhang's expression lit up in recognition. "You're communicating with your hands and eyes, aren't you?"

Jie turned back to her and repeated the same complicated pattern with her fingers.

Fixer Zhang's expression went blank again.

"You never saw our sign language," Jie said.

"I never saw your sign language." Fixer Zhang's voice droned.

Tian stared, wide-eyed. "She'll forget?"

Yangyang patted him on the head. "Yes. The *Tiger's Eye* can be powerful if you are good with it, and the recipient is trained to be receptive. And Jie is the best."

"Not as good as Lilian, apparently." Jie shook her head. "We need to find an acupuncturist, and none will be open this late."

This late... Tian looked out the window, to where the Iridescent Moon neared full. Up and to its south, the White Moon was already full; and on the other side, the fully-open Blue Moon formed a triangle. Everyone said it was a perfect triangle, but the oval-shaped Blue Moon was off by a tenth of a degree.

It widened and narrowed through the year, which was why they called it the Eye of Guanyin.

The Eye of Guanyin.

Tian turned back to the others. "What if the three eyes refer to the moons?"

Everyone ran to the windows, to see if any provided a good view.

"Less than a minute away," Meisha said, craning her neck. "We'll get a better view from the second floor."

"Get up." Jie grabbed Fixer Zhang's arm and brought her to her feet, chair and all. "Up the steps."

Yelping, Fixer Zhang hobbled along. With a scowl, Jie slapped her palm into the back of the seat. A rung shattered, and the chair fell away. Fixer Zhang snarled.

Yangyang cleared a path to the steps, while Meisha took Fixer Zhang's other arm to hustle her up. On the second floor, Yangyang raced to the south window and pushed open the shutters. Jie yanked Fixer Zhang's hair, drawing her gaze to the three moons.

The Iridescent Moon reached full. Out in the city beyond, a collective *ooooh* echoed from all the people gazing at the rare event.

Fixer Zhang, however, relaxed. Her angry expression melted, and her eyes again glazed over. After a moment, she turned back. "I remember something else..."

* * *

Ten Years Ago

For seven-year-old Lilian, there was always something uncomfortably familiar when she trained the *Tiger's Eye*. A sense of déjà vu, that this was nothing new. All the focus on the *yintang* point. Her knees ached from kneeling so long on the Cave of Reflection's hard surface, and sweat trickled down her brow and into her eyes.

A candle burned low, its length indicating she'd been here for two hours. The Iridescent Moon must be waxing toward full now. Blinking several times, she looked up at Master Yan, whose fingers danced in her vision.

He was a plain-looking man, with an oval face and kind eyes. In Lianjing Township, nobody except the retired Black Lotus Fists recognized him, no matter how many times he visited.

And no matter how many times he'd tried to make her forget her four years at the temple, he'd failed. Who knew why? It always confused him. At least, that's what Jie had said, using her sharp ears to eavesdrop on the masters. Maybe he was trying again now, and not really training her ability to resist pain.

Of course, she'd been studying and memorizing all of his most secret *Tiger's Eye* hand patterns, and despite his usual finishing move to make her forget the motions, she never did.

Of course, she pretended to. It was also tempting to let him believe he'd succeeded in making her forget everything, but she couldn't imagine a life without Jie and Wen. She'd end up living in Lianjing Town, having to pretend that those two, close as sisters, meant nothing to her. And they would have to do the same.

Then again, there was always the possibility Master Yan would just have her killed. He'd ordered the deaths of more than one rebel in the North, after all.

That's why after these *Tiger's Eye* sessions, she'd fight harder, sneak harder, and learn harder.

He gave a quick bob of his head. "Very good, Lilian. You may go enjoy the moons now."

"Thank you, Master." She bowed low.

He pinched the candle, drowning the cave in blackness.

Her chest squeezed. Dark, underground places with their earthy smells always felt unsettling. She took a few deep breaths and reached out with her senses.

Master Yan might still be there, but there was no way for her to tell. He could hold his breath so long, breathe so shallowly, and move so silently, nobody would know.

Using the echo of her hum as a guide, she worked through the first part of the tunnel, until she reached a section with coffered, soundproof panel walls. Sometimes, clan trainers would follow a novice in and rearrange the walls; sometimes they would keep the path the same.

Touching the panels was out of the question: they were lined with a contact toxin that caused itching. Poor Jie always left these sessions scratching all over. Instead, Lilian sensed the lightest of breezes on her damp skin. Two twists and turns, and the muffled sounds of laughing children greeted her. One more turn, and faint light shone into the opening of the cave. Letting out a sigh of relief, she hurried out.

The fresh night air greeted her, and her shoulders relaxed. Up above, the Iridescent Moon waxed toward full. A little to its left, Guanyin's Eye was fully open, and beyond it, the White Moon formed a perfect circle.

She stepped to the side, just avoiding Lai's grab. She caught his arm and twisted. He might've fallen if he wasn't six years older and twice her size. Instead, he dropped into a low horse stance, his weight sinking like a dwarf anvil, making him immovable.

"Still with us, are you?" He seized her hair, sneering. "You're such a failure."

Years ago, she would've panicked, but she'd since grown accustomed to his bullying. He wasn't particularly smart, but he had a devious cunning, and enjoyed projecting his dominance on the younger clan members. Especially her.

Now, though, she wasn't a weak five-year-old. Four years of training had taught her many tricks. She seized his pinkie, ducked her head, and twisted. No matter his size, she was still bigger than his finger.

"Ow!" He jerked his hand back. "Bitch!"

She ducked out of the sweep of his other hand, and stepped out of reach of his follow-up. Still, he blocked the only path off the hill, intercepting her each time she tried to slip past.

"Ow!" He bolted upright, eyes wide and knees squeezed together.

Behind him, Jie was grinning, wiggling her index fingers.

Lilian laughed. Lai would be pulling his pants out of his butt once he got over the shock. She darted past him. Clasping Jie's hand, they ran down the path back toward the temple's main compound.

"Thank you," Lilian said.

"No need for thanks." Jie squeezed her hand. "That's what big sisters do."

A surge of warmth and calm settled over Lilian.

Jie grinned. "Come on, this is our first chance ever to see the three full moons! Wen is waiting on the hilltop."

They took the fork in the path and scrambled up to the summit. Several other of the younger clan members sat on the grass, staring up at the sky. Wen turned and beckoned them over, and Jie and Lilian plopped down beside her. Wen rested her head on Lilian's shoulder.

Even sitting, the hill provided a magnificent view of all the halls of the monastery. Beyond it lay the ever-changing bamboo maze which separated the secret grounds from the public temple. On the other side of a small river was Lianjing Township.

Tonight, it was only dark blobs against the black-blue sky, with every light bauble shuttered so as to provide a view of the heavens.

It was a special night, which only occurred once every eleven years. And she got to share it with her two sisters. Times like this made all the bullying and hard work worth it. Her chest squeezed.

Brushing Wen's hair away, Lilian looked up.

The Iridescent Moon was so close to full now, its soap-bubble colors swirling against the speckled stars.

Then it reached full.

Sights, scents, sounds, and sensations flashed before her. A courtyard with fluttering black banners emblazoned with a white crane. A beautiful woman, welcoming a dashing husband and his son home. Voices, all speaking in the accent of the North.

"Mei!" the beautiful woman called in a soothing voice. "My Beautiful Lotus."

Who were these people and places? They all seemed familiar, as if she belonged. Her head spun, and it was all she could do to keep from fainting.

* * *

The Present

Tian had never met Lilian, so he listened to Tang Li with rapt attention. This was more than just an account of Lilian learning the *Tiger's Eye* technique; it felt like Tang Li was reliving her own memories.

Lai seemed like a mean boy. Tian shuddered. Maybe Lai would still be at the temple when Tian started his own training. If Lilian had been a slow learner, what would he think of a ten-year-old who only knew a few Black Lotus tricks?

As soon as Tang Li mentioned Lilian brushing Wen's hair out of her face, and seeing the Iridescent Moon about to reach full, the Triad fixer swayed and nearly passed out.

Tian looked to Jie.

Shuffling, expression bunched up, she looked angry and impatient.

That wasn't how she'd been the first few days he'd known her.

It'd only been since she started questioning Tang Li.

There was something about the fixer...or maybe Lilian...that upset her.

The half-elf looked out the window at the Iridescent Moon, now waning past full. "Not enough time," she muttered.

CHAPTER 4

The Present

To think, all Tang Li ever wanted was to own a tea shop. Now she was a prisoner, sitting in Lord Shi's room, her arms bound behind her back. Up above, the Iridescent Moon had waned just past full. Her head rocked as she struggled to remain conscious.

Seeing the three moons all full had triggered more than recollections of her conversations with Lilian; it was almost as if she'd experienced Lilian's memories herself. While everyone knew about the Black Lotus Temple in Lianjing Town, which trained the best scribes and accountants in the realm, Li had never visited it herself. Still, she could see not only the octagonal tower with arching roofs at each of its eight levels, but the bamboo-grove maze and the green-tiled halls and training grounds beyond.

To the side, the Floating World Blossoms and the boy were conferring among themselves in a mixture of a strange sign language and hushed voices.

Maybe she could scream and alert the chamberlain she'd knocked out with a vase, or the old servant. No, her captors might kill her. Feigning unconsciousness, she bided her time and listened.

"If this is the *Tiger's Eye*," Yangyang was saying, "it's beyond what I've ever seen Master Yan do."

Meisha shrugged. "If he can wipe memories, surely he can plant them, too?"

"But with such clarity?" Yangyang shuddered. "I could've sworn I was listening to Lilian talk— "

"Yes," Jie said, nodding. "I remember that night of the Three Eyes, and helping her escape Lai."

Up to now, Tang Li had assumed they were a gang of thieves and rogues using the Floating World as cover, but with all the suppressed memories surfacing, she realized they were much more.

Real Black Fists.

Not just the legendary bogeymen that mothers said would steal naughty children. And she'd been drawn to Jie, somehow knowing she could unlock Lord Shi's safe. Somehow she'd also known the Blossoms in Jie's orbit could foil her employer's plan, and therefore needed to be kept away from Lord Wu's moons-viewing party.

Where was Wen? She'd made it to the party and retrieved the key, but had she foiled the plot?

"And what do you make of the Northern accents?" Meisha asked, glancing over her shoulder at Li.

As if Li knew. It was a memory within a memory.

If that wasn't confusing enough, a new revelation occurred to her: she hadn't learned how to become a fixer. Both the skills and motivation had just come to her, awoken not long after Lord Yang had bought out her contract from the Chrysanthemum Pavilion.

A new memory appeared, of a man with a face so gaunt his head could've been mistaken for a skull. Was this her recollection? Or Lilian's? No matter what, he was part of the puzzle, and she needed to know who he was if she was to differentiate between her memories and Lilian's.

Maybe her captors would know. She cleared her throat.

The rogue Blossoms, led by Jie, turned to face her.

"There's someone in Lilian's memories. H—" Her voice caught in her throat. She tried to say Boney-Faced Man again, but no words came out.

"What's wrong?" Tian approached, expression concerned. "Choking? Do you need some water?"

The courtyard seemed to flip upside down and spin around, and with her hands bound, she tipped over onto her side.

* * *

Ten Years Ago

Lilian sat up from her bedroll in the novice barracks, head feeling like it'd been squeezed in a printing press. She looked out the window at the Iridescent Moon, waned to its second crescent. Two hours had passed since all three moons shone full in the night sky.

"Are you all right?" A hand rested on her shoulder.

Her heart jumped. She turned. Wen and Jie sat on a bedroll beside her, expressions scrunched up in concern. Around them, the other novices slept.

Lilian gave a tentative nod. "Yes."

No. All those images had been overwhelming.

And suddenly familiar. Because they were more than just images. Scents, sensations, and sounds had all been a part of them. They had to have been memories.

All this time, not knowing who she was...

Mei. Her real name was Mei. The accents people spoke in suggested she was from the North. She knew from Black Lotus history lessons that the black banners with crane emblems belonged to the now-dead Yu family. Descended from the emperors of the previous dynasty, they were nobility from the North. From her memories, she was one of them.

But who?

And why had she spoken and acted like a central valley peasant when she'd come to the Black Lotus Temple? She closed her eyes and searched more newly surfaced memories.

Despite the large gaps, there was an extraordinarily thin man, whose head looked like a skull, who'd forced her to change her mannerisms and speech. She gasped.

"Are you all right?" Wen rubbed her back.

"There was a...a..." No matter how hard Lilian—no, Mei—tried to describe the man, to tell them about her origins, no words came out of her mouth. How had she fallen into his hands? What had happened to her family?

Jie applied gentle pressure on her shoulder. "Lie down. This sometimes happens after your *Tiger's Eye* sessions with Master Yan."

"That's because she's weak," Lai sneered.

Lilian looked to where his voice came from, behind her.

He wasn't there.

"Still fooled by a *Ghost Echo*?" Lai said from the side.

Lilian closed her eyes and listened. Lai's breaths, deeper than Wen and Jie's, came from the window. She turned and glared at him.

He stood outside the window, lip curled. "One of these days, Master Yan is really going to turn you into a Cousin."

With a flick of her wrist, Jie flung something. A glint of moonlight caught on the throwing star. Lai ducked down, and the star lodged into the window frame with a *thunk*.

He peeked back up. "You missed."

"I know," Jie said. "You ducked anyway."

With a snarl, he disappeared, his footsteps heading toward the older children's barracks.

"Don't mind that Turtle's Egg." Wen leaned into Lilian's shoulder.

Lilian sighed and went back to bed to ponder these new revelations.

Over the next several days, she remembered more and more. Not only was she from the North, she was related somehow to Lord Yu Qiang, a traitor they'd learned about in their history lessons. She'd searched for them in the clan's Hall of Records, and found lineages; learned that Lord Yu possessed the Yu Dynasty imperial seal and was trying to unite the North against the Emperor; but the account of the family's fall had been redacted.

If only she could confer with the others! But no matter how many times she'd tried to reveal this to Jie and Wen, she couldn't convey the information. When she tried to speak, no words would come out. When she tried to sign, her fingers would freeze up. When she tried to write, the brush would just smudge.

All of those intricate finger motions Boney Face had flashed in front of her on several occasions...

He'd used the *Tiger's Eye*.

Which meant he was connected to the clan somehow. Still, she hadn't seen him around the temple. Maybe he was in deep cover? Embedded in the North to root out possible traitors? Maybe he'd dropped her in a place where the clan was sure to find her. But if that were the case, Master Yan would know who she really was.

Unless he already knew? Perhaps she'd been young enough that they'd spared her. If only she knew how her family had died!

And Boney Face had conditioned her to act and speak like a central valley peasant.

Another face appeared in her memories. No, two faces, exactly the same. Beautiful women. They knew Boney Face somehow. They'd been working together, and they'd left her at a shrine for the clan to find.

They'd meant to trick the clan. But for what purpose?

* * *

The Present

A cool, damp cloth patted along Tang Li's forehead. Her eyes fluttered open. Her vision cleared, revealing the boy.

He spoke over his shoulder. "Lilian did this to Fixer Zhang. So who did it to Lilian?"

Boney Face, Li wanted to say, using Lilian's nickname for the gaunt man. But only a jumble of random syllables came out. It was so frustrating, not being able to convey it. Supposedly, the late Faceless Chang had used Empathy to do things like this to people, to control them.

"It had to have been before she came to the temple," Jie's voice said. "The only Black Lotus masters who were unaccounted for at the time were the Steel Orchids."

Steel Orchids! The name meant nothing to Li, but the part of her mind that was Lilian's knew the identical twins to be not just former members of the rogues, but also Faceless Chang and Gardener Ju of the Chrysanthemum Pavilion.

Li's former House, before Lord Yang bought out her contract.

Everything was coming together. These rogues used the Floating World to spy, but for whom? She opened her mouth, but again, only garbled sounds came out.

Tian turned back to her, tapping his chin. "Lilian meant for us to find out. It's like the old story of the little girl leaving breadcrumbs to find her way home. Why else would Fixer Zhang remember only when she saw the three moons?"

"What would've happened if it had been cloudy tonight?" Yangyang asked.

Li shuddered. She'd have to go another eleven years with the urge to know what was hidden in her mind.

CHAPTER 5

The Present

If Jie wasn't the best among the Black Fists at using the *Tiger's Eye*, it was only because Master Yan was still alive. Supposedly, only one of the three legendary young masters—the Beauty—had surpassed him at the technique; but after the three's deaths in a secret mission not long before Jie's birth, Master Yan had used it on the entire clan, wiping everyone's memory of their faces and actual names. All that remained was the excited chatter of their exploits, which bordered on myth.

In today's reality, they now knew Fixer Zhang was receptive to *Tiger's Eye* manipulation. Using it would be much more reliable than looking for signs of a lie. It would certainly be more palatable and faster than torture—something Tang Li would face if the Cleaners or Enforcers arrived and connected her to the safe.

That could happen any moment. It was time to quickly build some trust, and unbinding her hands would be the first step. After all, with three Fists and Tian, she wouldn't be able to escape.

"Untie her," Jie said.

"Is this 'good interrogator, bad interrogator', except you are playing both roles?" Fixer Zhang laughed through the fatigue written in her expression. She rubbed her wrists as Tian loosened the cord.

Jie smirked. "I think you want to know what Lilian left in your pretty little head as much as the rest of us."

Fixer Zhang's lips tightened.

"I thought so." Jie locked her gaze on the fixer and set her fingers into a shape.

Fixer Zhang's eyes stared through her, even though her brow furrowed.

"Why did Lilian do this to you?" Jie asked.

"I... I..."

Jie shifted her hand positions. "Answer me."

Fixer Zhang's pupils roved as she shook her head. "I can't. I want to. All I can say is, root out the mole."

Root out the Mole.

Was that referring to someone inside the cell or clan? Or the game they played as children?

* * *

Eight Years Ago

By Jie's twelfth birthday, nine-year-old Lilian and eight-year-old Wen had nearly caught up to her in size and physical maturity. Now, the Lianjing townsfolk might jokingly trick travelers and caravans into believing that the three girls really were triplets. At least when Jie covered her pointed ears, which she'd done on this winter evening as they went on the last training mission before the New Year.

Which meant this was their team's last chance to win this year. Nipping at the Wasps' heels, they'd have to score three points more than them for extra meal portions. More importantly, if Lilian didn't personally score at least two points tonight, Master Yan would probably try again to *Tiger's Eye* her into a Cousin. From the masters' chatter, he came ever closer to succeeding.

"Elder Sister," Wen whispered, gesturing with her chin to the corner of the roof tile foundry.

As advance scout with the opportunity to earn more points, Lilian stood against the wall to the building, looking around the corner.

Silent as ever, Jie and Wen hurried over.

"Status?" Jie asked.

"Wasps are making their approach from the northwest."

Jie slid past her and looked.

Using the cover of darkness, the Wasp Team, led by Dun Lai, was creeping toward the magistrate's office. Like all other magistrate offices throughout the realm, it was a freestanding building. If any of the locals had lived elsewhere before moving to Lianjing Town, they'd be surprised at how many repairs went on there, on an ongoing basis.

Which gave their own team an advantage.

"They're going to the front to pick the front door lock," Jie said.

Wen gestured to the far alley. "Then Viper Team will intercept them."

Jie nodded. Tonight, they'd allied with the Vipers, led by eleven-year-old Meisha, who always wanted to partner on night missions because of Jie's elf vision. Unlike every other night, they probably wouldn't betray each other once they'd achieved their primary objective, because Meisha didn't want to see Lilian Cousined.

Jie sniffed the air. The scents of the Viper Team percolated through on the light breeze, stronger than the Wasps, indicating they were probably in position. With her just a point or so ahead of Lai, the Vipers delaying the Wasps long enough for Jie's team to finish first should be enough to secure her win for the year. On an individual level, that would mean the best assignments in the future.

Lilian looked over and peered up at the second-floor windows. "I can't see the mark."

Of course human eyes couldn't. It was a wonder Lilian even saw the Wasp Team, the way their dark clothes blended into the shadows. But for Jie, everything appeared in shades of greys and greens. It allowed her to make out the lotus carved into the decorative shutters on the north window of the west wall's second floor. The head scribe's office: their first objective. She pointed. "That's the one."

"They moved it." Wen gestured to the south window, which had been marked last week.

Jie darted to the office. Her fingers and toes found the nooks and crannies in the mortar as she ascended to the second floor. Below, Wen and Lilian followed, though at a slower pace. Around at the front of the building, the swooshes, swishes, and light grunts indicated the Wasps had fallen into the Vipers' ambush. With Lai's skill and ruthlessness, the Wasps would still win, but all Jie's team needed was the delay.

She gave the shutter a tug.

Locked.

Which meant the office staff hadn't left the shutter unlocked like they were supposed to. Or, a locked shutter had been a mission parameter. Jie waved Wen and Lilian down. Clinging to the narrow space, her fingers starting to ache, she shifted around the corner to the north wall, to its west window.

The shutter opened. She looked down.

Wen was peering up at her, while Lilian stood guard at the corner. Jie beckoned them up, then slipped through the window.

Her vision didn't work as well in indoor darkness as outdoor darkness, but it was still possible to make out the outline of an intricately carved desk with matching chairs.

Feng Shui masters proclaimed this area to be the metal octant of a building, where the arrangement of furniture within could attract money. Of course, Feng Shui masters seemed to attract money mostly from the superstitious; including the local magistrate, who chose this room as his office.

Their second objective. For now, they were ahead.

Behind her, the two others climbed in. The scent of honeysuckle, followed by lavender, indicated Lilian arrived first. Jie gestured them over, and after closing the shutter they tiptoed across the carpet in silence, using *Seeing Ears* to make their way around the chairs. Once they came to the desk, Jie withdrew a light bauble from her pouch and cupped it so that the light only fell on the sheets of paper. The words, which were impossible to make out in the dark even with her elf vision, appeared. It looked to be a list of names.

If Lilian was better at anything, it was writing. She scribbled the list and handed it to Jie.

Jie flashed her a smile. Part of the mission was accomplished well before any of the other teams.

I have an idea, Lilian signed. *I'll forge a fake list for the others to find. You go to the second objective.*

It wasn't part of the original plan, but it was a good idea. Misinformation could lead the other teams astray, and the penalty for an inaccurate copy would cost them. It'd been pure luck the shutter to the magistrate's office had been unlocked. Jie gave a nod and beckoned Wen to follow.

They snuck through the halls to the head scribe's office. From the scents and sounds, both the Wasps and Tigers had penetrated the building, while Meisha's Vipers had likely formed a perimeter to help Jie's team escape. There wasn't much time left. The locked door yielded to Jie's deft hands, and she pushed it open.

On the desk rested a sheaf of papers, all household tax records. Their mission was to memorize as many as possible, with bonus points for finding and removing the sheet emblazoned with a forgery of the Yu Dynasty Seal. Like the heirloom, the clan's fake had been carved with Dragonscript; but instead of evoking awe, it caused disorientation so that it would be easily overlooked.

Working like a dwarf-made clock, Jie and Wen split the piles and went through the sheets, making associations to help in the memorization process.

Light footsteps in the hallway approached, no doubt either the Wasps or Tigers.

With a gesture, Jie ordered Wen to help return the items on the desk to their original spots. Of course, they could've left the papers in a mess for the next team to clean up, but that team could also decide to forgo the memorization points so that Jie's Hornets would be penalized for leaving evidence of their mission. They'd lose enough points to doom Lilian; right now, if they remembered everything they'd looked at, their mission score should both save her and push them past the Wasps for the year.

On the other side of the desk, the door opened enough to reveal the Tigers' leader, Kong. His gaze met theirs. Grinning, he opened the door all the way, revealing the rest of his team. Beyond them, the Wasps were creeping toward the magistrate's office. It looked like they'd formed a strategic alliance, to get past Meisha's Vipers.

Jie's heart lurched. Though they weren't allowed to use deadly force on each other, anyone captured would lose points. One on one, Lilian wouldn't stand a chance against any of the Tigers, let alone all three. And with three of the Wasps here, they'd be able to memorize more.

Her Hornets' only hope for winning would be reaching the safehouse first. But that meant sacrificing Lilian, dooming her to face Master Yan's *Tiger's Eye*. Jie passed the first list behind her back to Wen, then brushed code across her wrist. *Escape through the window and get to the safehouse.*

Wen looked back sidelong, brows creased. *What about you?*

Do it.

With a nod, Wen bolted to the window, unlocked the shutters, and climbed through.

"You want to be captured?" Kong snorted.

Jie smirked. "Who's going to capture me?"

Kong gestured with his hand, using their team's code. An attack pattern, but which one? The girl and boy fanned out, while Kong darted toward her. It left the window as the only line of escape, and they were almost upon her. To take the window meant condemning Lilian. Kong leaped with enough height and speed to clear the desk.

Jie swept her hands out, scattering the documents into a flurry of paper, then slid under the desk to the other side. She popped back up onto her feet and bolted to the door. She cast a quick glance over her shoulder.

Cursing, the Tigers were forced to tidy up the mess she'd made.

Grinning, Jie ran to the magistrate's office. Her smile melted when she reached the door.

Lai was holding Lilian in a chokehold near the window, his back to the door. His two Wasp teammates were copying the list Lilian had forged. At least their team would lose points, but Lilian would lose even more unless Jie rescued her.

For now, the Wasps hadn't seen her; but to reach Lai, she'd have to get past the two others. And though she could take both of them, it would warn Lai of her presence. Tiptoeing as she ran, she jumped to the desk, and used it to vault over to Lai.

"Look o—" the girl Wasp yelled.

Coming down on Lai's back, Jie wrapped her arms around his neck. When he released his hold on Lilian to protect himself, Jie twisted her hips and sent him sprawling to the ground. Lilian turned around and stared with wide eyes.

"Get out!" Jie gestured to the window.

With a nod, Lilian climbed out.

Jie rose and started to follow, but Lai wrapped her legs up in his own and scissored her to the floor. She landed on her knees, and the two others seized her arms and pinned her face-down into the carpet.

"Bitch," Lai said, straddling her back. "Why do you even help her? She's just not good enough. If she ever becomes a Fist, she'll only be good enough to fuck for information in the Floating World. She'd get one of us killed on a real mission."

Heat rose in Jie's face. Lilian was good enough, even if just barely. And there was nothing wrong with assignment to the Floating World. It was a vital part of clan operations. Selfish fools like Lai just couldn't see it.

The Tiger's leader, Kong, appeared at the door. "We didn't have much time to memorize the tax records, since we were too busy cleaning up after her mess." He glared at Jie.

Lai snarled. "Fine, let's get out of here."

Jie was going to lose points, but she had more than enough for herself and the team to both score the most points for the year. More importantly, the Wasps and Tigers would gain too few points from tax records from the scribe's office, and didn't even know they'd copied the wrong list in this room. Meisha's Vipers hadn't started off with enough points to even challenge them. Hopefully, Lilian wouldn't lose points from her temporary capture.

They went down the steps, through the vaulting audience hall, and out the front door. Meisha's Vipers had already left.

When they reached the safehouse in the warrens, they were taken one by one to meet with Master Luo. He scribbled furiously as Jie briefed him on the mission and recounted what she remembered from the tax records.

After her debriefing, he sent her to the meeting room, where Lilian, Wen, Meisha, and the other two Vipers were already kneeling. Master Pan sat at the head. He didn't look up as they entered, but gestured for them to sit. Jie's heart juddered. Her capture meant she'd lose points, but if Wen had made it back to the safehouse first with the correct information, then their Hornets' bonus points should win for the year. Her stomach was already counting the larger portions. The larger question was if Lilian had scored enough.

Lai came out last, joining the eleven other students on the floor, while Master Luo came and sat down beside Master Pan.

"Congratulations to the Vipers for winning this mission," Master Pan said. "They've scored enough to vault them to the top for the year, as well."

Gasping in unison, Jie and Wen exchanged glances. How had that happened? Meisha's Vipers had been too far behind in points before the mission began... At their side, Lilian wrung her hands.

"Lilian scored the most on this mission." Master Luo beamed.

Jie blew out a breath. At least there was that.

But Lilian had been temporarily captured. How could she have possibly scored the highest?

The other students also chattered among themselves.

"The winner for the year is Meisha. Lai comes in second, Jie third."

Meisha's eyes widened.

Turtle's Egg that he was, Lai's glare burned with hatred at Lilian.

Jie, however, could only stare. Sure, she'd been captured, but surely her team's correct copy of the magistrate's list would've been enough to keep her ahead of Lai. Still, she bowed along with everyone else in thanks to the masters for their guidance.

Master Pan looked up from his list. "You are all wondering about this turn of events."

Jie sure was. She looked sidelong at Lilian.

Sorry, Lilian mouthed.

Jie's stomach knotted. What had Lilian done?

"Each team had a mole," Master Pan said, "whose objective was to undermine their team, if it could benefit them as an individual."

Had Lilian been the mole? She refused to meet Jie's eyes.

"In this case," Master Pan continued, "Lilian received bonus points for having the only correct list. She also memorized the most documents and recovered the document with the fake imperial seal. Those extra points transferred to the Vipers, for whom she was working as the mole. She also scored bonus points for feeding her team misinformation, and getting her team leader captured. Because of this, the Hornets lost their lead, while the Vipers caught up. Jie lost her personal lead by being captured by Lai, who also lost points for failing on both objectives."

That's why Lilian had stayed back in the magistrate's office. Not to forge documents for the other teams to copy, but because she'd already given her own team the wrong copy. And to get Jie captured. Jie's heart squeezed.

But was it a betrayal, really? No, it was only a game, meant to hone their skills and make decisions based on outcomes. Jie's shoulders loosened. This result kept Lilian out of danger, and in the end, the worst that would come of it would be having the normal amount of food for the next year. And Lai becoming even more insufferable.

* * *

The Present

Studying Fixer Zhang's eyes, Jie sucked on her lower lip. The *Tiger's Eye* wasn't working on Fixer Zhang as much as it was dredging up Jie's own memories. She'd all but forgotten Lilian's betrayal that night, remembering instead that Meisha's victory had allowed her to choose her deployment. Idolizing the legendary Steel Orchids, she'd opted to enter the Floating World.

For Jie, happier memories with Lilian had since replaced her feelings of betrayal back then. Perhaps it should've been a forewarning of how their relationship would ultimately end.

Fixer Zhang was still holding back on what she knew about Lilian, either by choice or because of the *Tiger's Eye*.

In the corner, Meisha and Yangyang huddled close together.

"This is taking too long," Yangyang was whispering. "We've acquired the contents of the safe; we need to deliver them to the clan."

"What if there's something among them that triggers Tang Li's memories?" Meisha sounded hopeful. Unlike Yangyang, she'd spent time at the temple with Lilian. "Like the hairpin."

"What's left? Stock certificates, a yue ball, a gold nugget, and a sick man's souvenir. Why hasn't it happened already?"

"Maybe some other precondition has to be met?" Jie said.

The two straightened, acting as if they hadn't been questioning her authority.

"Sorry, Eldest Sister." Yangyang bowed her head. "I just think..."

Jie broke the pregnant pause. "Well?"

"Nothing." Yangyang set her first in her palm.

Jie sucked on her lower lip. Despite Yangyang's contrition, things were far from settled. Maybe Lilian's legacy would be tearing the cell apart.

CHAPTER 6:

The Present

Now that Tang Li's hands and feet were untied, it was tempting to flee. However, despite the flood of Lilian's memories coming back to her, she didn't seem to have Lilian's stealth and fighting skills. It would be impossible to escape four—well, three, since the boy didn't count—trained Black Fists.

Because that's what they were. And Lilian had been one of them, embedded in the Floating World as an imperial spy. To think, one of her employers had hoped to establish his own spy network in the Houses, never knowing that the Emperor already had one.

Now, the question was how to leave this place alive. Lord Shi's servant had probably gone to bed already, and the chamberlain hadn't appeared. Maybe she'd accidentally killed him.

Her stomach wrenched. It wasn't supposed to happen like that. Everything had gone wrong.

In here, Jie looked to be in charge, and her obsession over Lilian might be the key to getting out of this situation. Either that, or exploiting the cracks that were growing between them. And then... The trail Lilian had left in Li's mind was leading them somewhere, and as long as Jie remained in command, Li could use their reliance on her memories to go anywhere. The question was, where?

She bit her lip. She'd never had such complex thoughts in the past, beyond manipulating Hummingbirds. It was as if Lilian had become a part of her. Not only that, confused about which memories were her own and which were Lilian's, a part of her felt an affection for Jie, and also Wen.

That warred with her own sense of self-preservation. Protect her employer, and she'd be rich enough to settle down somewhere and open that teahouse. To think that she, who her scholar father had abandoned in the Trench because he thought she was too stupid, was on the cusp of achieving comfort. All that could be ruined by Lilian's presence in her mind, which prodded her to reveal everything to Jie.

And somehow, Lilian's regrets over past betrayals seized Li's heart in an iron grip, as if she'd been the real culprit.

* * *

Eight Years Ago

Lilian sat cross-legged under the chill flow of the small waterfall near the rear of the temple complex, unable to empty her mind as this training required. The guilt she felt for betraying Jie and Wen in the year's last training mission weighed on her more than the water.

She'd snuck into the magistrate's building before the mission. While there, she'd memorized all the documents in the head scribe's office, then found the sheet with the fake seal and stashed it under the magistrate's desk. She'd locked one shutter while unlocking the other, to force her team to the second objective first.

Now, guilty as she felt, it was tempered by the rush she'd experienced from successfully evaluating everyone's gain and loss in points, and maneuvering to set up her own victory. She might not be the best at bladework or stealth, but planning and deceit came easily.

Was it because of what the gaunt-faced man haunting her memories had done to her? Or the twin women? Whenever she tried to mention them, her voice would seize. She'd tried to write their descriptions down, or even use her budding painting skills to sketch them, but her hand would invariably freeze up. It was clear he'd used the *Tiger's Eye* on her, and thus had a connection to the clan.

One thing she did know: the twins could only be the Steel Orchids, who'd supposedly died in some fire in the capital. Lilian found she could talk about the fire, which had burned down someplace called the Floating World twelve years ago, but anytime she tried to reveal that the Steel Orchids still lived, she couldn't.

She let out a sigh. She might be the last heir of the North, but maybe Lai was right: all she was good for was lying on her back, gleaning secrets from sated lords.

Memories of Mama flashed in her mind. An early autumn afternoon, walking through a castle town. Father's eyes following two beautiful women in heavy make-up, wearing dresses that accentuated their breasts, hips, and slim waists. Turning her nose up, Mama jabbed him in the ribs.

"Don't be like them," she'd told Lilian.

Prostitutes. Like the ones in Lianjing's red lantern block, which Lai would often visit.

As always, her head reeled when these recollections surfaced.

Her scalp burned as someone yanked her hair and pulled her out of the waterfall.

Grabbing at the hands, she yelped.

Lai's forehead pressed up against hers. His eyes burned, and his lips were twisted into a snarl.

Her heart leaped into her throat.

"Bitch," he said. "It's your fault I lost the lead for the year. Now I won't get to choose my assignment. To lose because of you, who will never be anything more than a Floating World whore, is mortifying."

She started to respond, before he shoved her head into pool. His firm hand kept her submerged. Every instinct screamed for her to struggle, to fight for precious air.

New memories surfaced, of Boney Face dunking her head into a bucket of water. She'd fought back, as a lord's daughter should.

Lord's daughter! She wasn't just related to Lord Yu Qiang—she'd been his daughter.

Boney Face had forced her to be calm. The *Viper's Rest*, he'd called it; but based on what she'd since learned at the temple, it was just the fundamentals. He'd been trying to train her, but to what end?

Remain calm. Lai had size advantage and superior leverage, and struggling would just use up her air supply sooner. In any case, if she drowned, he'd be severely punished.

Settling her heart and mind with the *Viper's Calm* technique, she heaved her body twice and then went limp.

He pulled her up. "Oh, Heavens. Don't die on me."

Lilian held her breath. Let him think her unconscious and unable to breathe.

He rolled her on her back, tilted her head back, and brought his mouth to hers.

Disgusting!

Despite her revulsion, she forced herself into stillness as he breathed into her lungs, allowing his yang to fill her yin. He was panicking now, hands trembling. He came in for another breath.

She seized his wrist, shrimped out from under his weight, then wrapped her legs around his arm. Arching her back, she sent him head-first into the water and wrenched him into an arm bar. His scream came out as a trail of bubbles.

He flailed for a few seconds, and she disengaged with one leg and drove her heel into his temple. His body went limp. Maybe he was pretending, just like she had; maybe he wasn't. Still, if he'd inhaled water, she wouldn't have much time to resuscitate him, and she'd face even more severe punishment for killing one of the most promising students.

She flipped him over and pulled him to shore. Taking several steps back, she scanned his inert form. His chest rose and fell ever so slightly.

Good, still alive.

Maybe it would be better to run off before he woke, but this was a perfect time to deal with his bullying for good. Sitting down, Lilian hooked his heel into the crook of her elbow. With a few toe-taps to his cheek, his eyes fluttered open. He started to stand, but she torqued on his foot.

He screamed. "Bitch!"

"I am, aren't I?" She smirked. "Now, swear to never try to sabotage or bully me anymore, or you'll never walk again."

"You wouldn't," he said. "The clan would punish you if I'm not able to walk."

"You don't need to walk to be..." what did they call it? "... a Peach Bottom Boy in the Floating World."

Given the way he looked down on the prostitutes in Lianjing, and even the clan sisters embedded in the Floating World, it was probably the worst thing he could imagine. He grit his teeth through the pain, and tried to bend his knee to get closer. With more pressure, his leg straightened, and he slammed back down into the dirt.

"Fine! I swear!"

"What do you swear?" She twisted more.

"I will stop bullying you."

"And?" She applied just a little more pressure, and the joint let out a pop.

"No more trying to sabotage you."

Satisfied, Lilian relented.

He clambered to his feet, and with a last scowl at her, limped off.

She swallowed hard. She hadn't meant to do permanent damage, but that popping sound was worrisome.

Over the next several weeks, Lai moved more slowly than before, and his stealth skills suffered. No longer was he the most promising novice. Unwilling to tell anyone that it had been Lilian who'd bested him, he claimed it was a training injury, and waited too long to see doctor in Lianjing Town. Instead of receiving his first deployment, he spent the entire year regaining his strength.

* * *

The Present

Tang Li looked from Jie to Meisha to Yangyang. Li surmised from Lilian's memories that she'd never told anyone about this encounter with Lai, preferring instead to hide the true extent of her abilities. Li wasn't about to tell them now, either.

Jie's ears twitched, and she turned toward the door, knife drawn.

As if on cue, Meisha and Yangyang snapped into defensive stances. Tian followed suit, facing the door with balled fists.

Someone must be coming. And very quietly. Had Lord Yang sent his assassin? Heart pattering, Li turned to the door.

CHAPTER 7:

The Present

Against her better judgement, Wen had waited outside of the main building, overwhelmed by Fixer Zhang's revelations about Lilian. Maybe she should've entered earlier and reported on the attempted bomb attack on the imperial family and great hereditary lords, but it stirred so many memories from her youth. She'd almost forgotten about Lilian's betrayal during that New Year's Eve training mission, instead remembering the bonds of sisterhood they'd formed.

Now, though, it sounded as if Yangyang and Jie were about to have a falling out over what to do with the contents of the safe. They'd focus and work together once they learned of Lord Shi's treachery.

Wen slipped in and, peering through the dimly lit foyer, made her way to the second floor. Jie's eyes bored into hers, as did Meisha's and Yangyang's. In contrast, Tang Li's tense shoulders relaxed.

Tian dashed over and wrapped her in a hug with his little arms.

"I have news," Wen said, pulling out of his embrace and bowing. "Lord Shi planted bombs on Lord Wu's barge and the imperial barge."

Meisha and Yangyang covered their mouths. Jie's lips tightened.

Tian stared, wide-eyed, before finding his voice. "Is Princess Kaiya all right?"

Behind them, near the window, Fixer Zhang took a quick glance at the moons before turning an intent gaze on Wen. Perhaps the fixer knew more about the plot. She'd thought she'd acquired Lord Shi's key, and her ties to the Trench Triads could explain how they'd tried to keep Wen from reaching the party.

"Both barges sank; we're not sure who survived," Wen said, even while signing, *We discovered the bombs before anyone could detonate them.*

The others feigned shock, even as a slight nod of understanding passed among them.

"The clan is investigating now," Wen continued. "There's nothing else we can do."

Or was there? Fixer Zhang's gaze remained completely neutral. Forced neutrality, in all likelihood, since this kind of news would shock anyone.

She must be involved. Given all she'd revealed about Lilian, and Lords Ting, Yang, and Shi all having called on Lilian at the Chrysanthemum Pavilion, perhaps this plot ran deeper than anyone thought.

With that in mind, Wen studied Fixer Zhang with a mixture of curiosity and trepidation. It was clear Lilian had hidden a lot—perhaps some of it subconsciously. While the Black Fist side of Wen wanted to learn the truth, the sentimental part of her dreaded it.

She wiggled around a little, her body still exhausted from Lord Shi's rough treatment. At least he, the probable mastermind behind Lord Ting's death and possibly more, was finally in imperial custody.

"You slept with both of them today." Fixer Zhang's eyes fell on Wen, appraising.

Fixer Zhang had bedded both Lord Shi and his son on a regular basis in an attempt to crack the safe. Now, she was trying to find out more about the attack. Wen shrugged. "What happens in the Floating World..."

"Lord Wu's barge wasn't the Floating World," Fixer Zhang said. "You enjoy your work, don't you?"

Wen shrugged. "I'm the Corsage of the premier House of the Floating World."

"That doesn't answer my question."

"Did you enjoy the life of a Blossom?"

"It was a job, one that got me out of poverty in the Trench. But for you, it's the clan."

Wen fiddled with her pinkie.

Fixer Zhang laughed. "From what I can glean from Lilian's memories, you enjoyed the work. Her, not so much."

Disliking the work had been Lilian's proclaimed reason for betraying the clan. Wen thought back to when they'd first been chosen for the Floating World cell.

* * *

Six Years Ago

Ten-year-old Wen knelt beside Jie and Lilian, along with six others, before five of the clan elders in the Hall of Audience. With their basic training complete, they were probably about to receive their first real assignment.

Master Yan sat cross-legged in the middle, while to his right knelt Master Yin. Her reputation for sword skills preceded her. She'd been an Enforcer in the past, and later a teacher of swordsmanship—not to novices, but to full-fledged Fists. Hushed rumors spoke of her duel with Master Yan, using live blades, where they fought to a draw. Even more hushed rumors suggested they'd dueled between the sheets, as well. Her face was like carved jade: hard, but beautiful. Her eyes scrutinized them.

Wen's heart pattered. Master Yin always chose the best-looking of the newly minted Fists to go with her on a deep cover assignment.

"You nine have mastered the basics of our clan," Master Yan said, "and are now ready for your first deployment. Master Yin?"

"Stand," she said.

They all rose in unison, though Lilian was just a half-heartbeat behind.

When Master Yin rose and glided over, it was with a different kind of grace. Not the lethal dexterity of the clan, though no doubt she had it, but an elegance. She came to Wen first, and those eyes studied her.

Something deep and primal rumbled in Wen's core. It felt like being undressed, and it took all her discipline not to squirm under the scrutiny.

Master Yin broke her gaze too soon. With a nod, she turned to Jie, then looked over her shoulder to Master Yan. "Your daughter is older than the rest. Has she flowered with Heaven's Dew?"

"No." Master Yan shook his head. "Given her age, and the doctor's reading of her pulse, we think it will be within the year."

Master Yin laughed. "My predecessor said Jie's virgin price would fund clan operations for a year. With such an exotic face, I don't doubt it."

Virgin price. They were going to the Floating World, then, like Meisha had two years before. On a visit back to the temple, she'd recounted how she'd lain with men to learn their secrets. The first man she'd been with had paid enough to buy thousands of *tangyuan* sweets.

However, Lai was kneeling at the far end. It was no secret that he coped with his injury by sneaking into Lianjing Town, cutting merchants' purses, and spending their coin in the brothels. He wasn't a virgin, so how could he have a virgin price?

"But," Master Yin continued, "I also hear her fighting and stealth skills already equal seasoned operatives. Are you sure this won't be a waste of her talents?"

"I'm sure," Master Yan said. "She can sharpen the rest of the cell."

With a nod, Master Yin continued to Lilian. "She is the most beautiful of this group. Given what else I've heard, the Floating World suits her the most of any assignment."

They'd all be together.

Master Yin came to the end of the line, where Lai knelt. She afforded him a cursory glance and a nod. For his part, he trembled. Though talented in many respects, he'd never been the same since his training injury, two years before.

She walked back to the head of the room. "You are all proficient in fighting and spying. Starting now, I'm going to teach you a very different kind of skill."

That night in the girls' barracks, she lay with her head on Jie's shoulder, Lilian's head on the other, the half-elf's arms wrapped around them. None of them could sleep.

"The Floating World," Lilian murmured.

Wen intertwined her fingers with Lilian's. "Meisha says men pay to put their *jiji* inside us." How exciting it would be!

Jie joined Wen in a giggle, but Lilian remained pensive. She sighed. "I heard that, too, from both Meisha and Yangyang."

"You don't want to do it?" Wen lifted her head.

The moonlight shone on Lilian's somber expression. "Whatever the clan needs."

There was something in her tone. More than disinterest, it sounded like defeat.

"What about Lai?" Jie asked.

Lilian's lips quirked, her somber mood lifted. "This is the worst possible deployment for him."

"He likes putting his *jiji* in the Lianjing red lantern girls." Jie drew them closer.

Lillian lowered her voice. "Men will put their *jiji* in *him*!"

Wen's lips rounded. It really was the worst thing that could happen to the boy who fancied himself the second coming of the Surgeon.

The next morning, Master Yin guided the nine newly minted adepts into Lianjing Town. The townsfolk waved, assuming the group boarding the wagon bound for the capital had been contracted out as scribes or bookkeepers. Lai looked like a sulking dog, the way his shoulders slumped.

Two days later, they passed through the city walls of Huajing. It felt familiar: like Lianjing Town, only ten thousand times larger. Wen had never seen so many people in one place before.

Her heart raced as they crossed over a moat and under a gate, from which the largest red lantern she'd ever seen hung. Beyond, red banners fluttered from every building.

They'd arrived in the Floating World.

* * *

The Present

If not for her life in the Floating World, Wen mused to herself, she never would've uncovered the plot to blow up the barges with the imperial family and the realms' greatest lords on board. Instead of succeeding with his plan, Lord Shi was now in imperial custody.

She shuddered. Imperial inquisitors weren't known for the subtlety, certainly not compared to myriad questioning techniques of Black Lotus Fists. Lord Shi's last days would be painful as they tried to extract information about co-conspirators.

Sadly, his son would face the same fate. Young Lord Shi Han had proven to be a gentle soul, and probably wasn't cunning enough to be involved in the plot. Still, emperors tended to think it better to let a hundred innocents die than to let one traitor go free.

Then again, something didn't sit right with her. Something about the bombs...

CHAPTER 8

The Present

Though Wen seemed to be lost in her memories, Jie had had enough of reminiscing about her youth. Especially if Fixer Zhang was just stringing them along. So far, the recollections were just a reminder of Lilian's betrayals, which didn't bring them any closer to learning about her motives.

Maybe it was better just to leave the past in the past. Accept that Lilian had been a liar and traitor. Jie's own heart could bear that, especially if she focused on the current threat to the realm. Lord Shi, probably one of Fixer Zhang's employers, had tried to kill the Emperor's family and many of the great hereditary lords. If not for Wen, maybe the bombs aboard the barges would've exploded, plunging the realm into chaos.

Still, Lilian had left a trail, one she'd meant for Jie to find and follow. Was it for personal reasons? Or did it lead somewhere else? Perhaps all these things—from Lord Ting's murder to the Steel Orchids, from Faceless Zhang to the attempt on the imperial family—were interconnected?

"The contents of the safe," Jie said. "The stock certificates, a yue ball, a gold nugget, and some bloody sheets. What did your employer want with them?"

Fixer Zhang shrugged. "I don't ask why. I just make arrangements."

"What do you know about the bombs?"

"Nothing." Fixer Zhang's expression tightened for a split second. She knew something more.

"She looked up to her right." Tian pointed. "A lie."

Despite all the uncertainties in the situation, Jie smiled. The boy had taken to the training, and so eager was he to please that he didn't know when to reveal trade secrets, and when to keep his mahjong tiles down.

Mahjong tiles down! That was an expression Master Yin had used during those first weeks of training for the Floating World...

"The blood-stained sheets," Wen said, excitement in her voice. "Lord Shi kept them, so that must be a clue, if both the imperials and Fixer Zhang's employer wanted them."

In the corner of Jie's vision, Fixer Zhang squirmed. Wen was right.

Who had Lord Shi Plucked that he kept a sick memento of? Because that's what the sheets had to be. Jie had learned that in her first months in the capital.

* * *

Six Years Ago

In their first few weeks in the capital, fourteen-year-old Jie and the others stayed in the Black Lotus safehouse, located above an herbalist's pharmacy. Consisting of six rooms, it had hardwood floors and sliding wood doors. It smelled like Master Yin: jasmine and oiled steel. One room served as both an armory and a poison dispensary.

Fists deployed in the Floating World would stop by on occasion, and sometimes their new group would meet with the entire cell in designated locations for weapons and stealth training. Though younger than the full-fledged adepts, Jie often took the lead in drilling those skills. Still, her swordsmanship paled in comparison to Master Yin's.

The other skills they'd use in the Floating World were another story. Back at the safehouse, she watched in rapt attention as Yangyang, a curvy twenty-year-old, undressed. Though no Black Lotus member developed the same sense of modesty as the rest of the populace, and they had often seen each other naked, something about the grace with which Yangyang slid out of her clothes ignited something primal and urgent in Jie.

"You all lag behind the Floating World Seedlings," Master Yin was saying. "They learn this when they are six."

Lai snorted, even as he studied Yangyang with more than just clinical interest.

Master Yin's eyes locked on his. "You laugh?"

"No, Master." Dropping his chin, he shook his head.

She harrumphed. "Just because you've bedded a dozen Lianjing streetwalkers doesn't mean you know the first thing about the *art* of coupling. Any boy old enough to make seed can make a few thrusts."

"The way they *Called Spring* suggests otherwise." He looked up and dared glare back.

She let out a laugh. "That's what they are paid to do. That's what you will all learn to do, whether you enjoy the experience or not. Because it is when he is most sated that a Hummingbird will spill secrets just as quickly as his seed."

Jie exchanged glances with Wen and Lilian. While Wen's face brightened with excitement, Lilian's lips drew into a tight line.

With a gesture from Master Yin, Yangyang laid down. She spread her legs and lifted her knees. Wisps of hair covered her cleft.

Jie stared, fascinated.

Master Yin beckoned Lai over. "Since you are already such a master, show us Yangyang's Bud of Guanyin."

"Bud of Guanyin?" Initial excitement guttering, Lai flushed and swallowed hard.

"Of course. The Bud of Guanyin. Guanyin's Pearl. The Root of Yin. They are all names for the center of female pleasure. Surely a lovemaking master such as yourself would know."

If Lai's face could turn any redder, his head could replace one of the lanterns hanging in the Floating World streets. "I'm sorry, Master."

Master Yin snorted again. "Little Jie, show our new master how to find it."

Jie bobbed her head. Of course, the rest of them had discovered it on themselves, though Yangyang's nether regions looked plumper. Hiding her fascination, Jie bowed her head and knelt at Yangyang's side. Her hand trembled as she reached.

"Don't be shy." Yangyang laughed in her girlish pitch, not in the least mockingly.

It wasn't the first, and wouldn't be the last time someone would mistake Jie's excitement for nervousness. She started parting the folds—

"The Gates to Heaven," the master said.

With a compliant nod, Jie pulled back on the pink skin covering Guanyin's Pearl.

"In the Floating World, we call that the sepals; on either side, the petals. Yangyang's flower opens to her Jade Valley. But the rest of you..." Master Yin's hard gaze raked over them. "Most important now is your virginity. The first time you lie with a man will be the most valuable. Until then, the Flower must remain unplucked."

Unplucked, what did that mean? Jie looked first to Wen, then Lilian, but it was clearly a command. They all pressed their foreheads to the floor.

"Everything references a flower," Wen said. "What about Lai's very little *jiji*?"

Master Yin *tsk*ed. "Such vulgar language. Here, you can use stalk, stem, or stamen. In any case, it will be a rare occasion when he will use it."

A low murmur broke out, and Lai's face twisted.

"Why not?" Lilian asked, her tone suggesting she already knew the answer.

"The Floating World is where a man's dreams take flight. Some men prefer to fly with other men."

Lai's head hung.

What did that mean? Jie sucked on her lower lip, then released it. "But he doesn't have a Yin orifice."

"He has another, the same as all of us."

The girls all exchanged glances.

"He'll be known as a Peach Bottom, and Stamens will Pit him."

Ohhhhh. A feeling of guilt crept over Jie. She'd finger-jabbed him there whenever she caught him bullying Lilian.

"Any more questions?" Tone softening, Master Yin looked almost motherly with her smile.

Wen bowed her head. "If the Floating World is where a man's dreams take flight, then why do we need to learn about the center of female pleasure?"

Yangyang giggled, only to be silenced by a wave of Master Yin's hand. "Beyond knowledge being the source of power? To bring on Heaven's Dew for—"

"Is that the monthly bleeding?" Lai's head lifted and his eyes brightened. He sounded proud of himself.

"No," Master Yin said flatly. "We rarely speak of that directly in the Floating World, though among ourselves, we might call it our Best Friend. Heaven's Dew moistens the Flower."

Jie couldn't keep from squirming.

"Also, this work is hard on your body and soul. There are times you may find comfort with each other."

Jie looked sidelong at Lilian. Maybe it was like how they hugged each other across their bedrolls.

During the first few weeks with these lessons about their bodies, Master Yin also taught them to walk and move in the most inefficient ways. While stealth and quick, deceptive motions came easily, Jie found it hard to tilt her head while shuffling and bending her arms and hands at delicate angles. It came naturally to both Wen and Lilian, as well as the others. Lai would oftentimes sulk as Master Yin admonished him to find his feminine side.

Then, what she called the *Day of Choosing* arrived, where they'd put all their new skills to use. Master Yin assumed the role of the clan's shell company agent and brought them all to the Red Boat Opera House; though the only music came from unseen musicians playing stringed instruments.

Instead of actors jumping and flipping, dozens of girls and a few boys gathered in back with the agents holding their contracts. No doubt most were orphans, or had been sold by desperate parents. Now, even the youngest wore heavy make-up and elegant silk gowns as they took turns shuffling across the stage, moving just the way they'd been taught.

For today, the Houses of the Floating World would bid for Seedlings and Florets. In the case of the Black Lotus shell company, Master Yin would receive bids, but then negotiate a split instead of selling their contracts outright.

Though they wouldn't move into the Houses for another few days, Jie clasped Lilian and Wen's hands, unwilling to let go when it was their turn. They'd grown up together, and whether or not they stayed together relied on this performance. Lilian looked back, lips trembling, before a guard turned her around and pushed her through the curtains and onto the stage.

Eyes closed, Jie listened to the murmurs from the audience. Hidden among the chatter were Lilian's footsteps as they slid across the floor. They sounded so unfamiliar compared to Lilian's usual gait. It was as if she were becoming a different person already. Jie's heart clenched.

She didn't have time to panic. The guard pushed her through, and she stumbled onto the hard planks.

The room went silent.

Baubles from the ceiling bathed the stage in bright light, blinding her for a split second until she blinked away the orange afterimage.

"What is she?" a creaky voice asked in the darkened audience area.

"Half," said a woman whose voice flitted like a nightingale's.

"Half what?"

A fourth's tone sounded incredulous. "Elf?"

"Is that even possible?"

Jie peered into the dark. Though the bright light prevented her elf vision from taking full effect, she made out the shape of twenty-seven middle-aged women in fine-cut gowns. They looked to be shuffling through papers, taking notes.

The side curtains opened just enough to reveal Master Yin, who shooed her on. "Go!" she hissed.

Jie would've swallowed if her mouth wasn't so dry. She shuffled across the stage.

"She waddles like someone just Plucked her backstage," the second voice sneered.

"Madame Yin's candidates are always so graceful. This one is a black mark on her."

"It doesn't matter," a third woman said. "Men will spend their family fortunes to spend a night with a half-elf."

This must be like how cattle felt at an auction. Despite all her stealth and fighting skills, she was only good for one thing to these people. Feeling dirty and insignificant, Jie reached the other end of the stage and lunged through the gap in the curtains, into Lilian and Wen's waiting arms.

"I heard them," Lilian said.

"You did so well!" Wen squeezed her.

Master Yin snorted. "No, you didn't. But with your exotic look, I have no doubt the most prominent Houses will want you."

Over the next several days, Master Yin all but disappeared, leaving their group to their own devices. Jie, Lilian, and Wen wandered through the wondrous silk market, picking pockets.

Still, uncertainty weighed on Jie. Master Yan was keeping her mahjong tiles down, never even giving a hint of which Houses had bid on them.

Then, the day came.

Jie's heart pounded as they navigated the narrow streets to the various Houses. Each time they'd stopped at a House to deliver one in their group, her head spun. After eight years with Lilian and ten with Wen, maybe this was the end of their time together... But no, after a few hours, four of them remained without a House.

Lai, of course, would go to the Black Rose Patch. But maybe the three of them would be deployed together. Jie's heart dared to soar as they headed down the northernmost street of the Floating World.

When delivered to his new House, where a pair of middle-aged men took possession of him, Lai moped like a dog with his tail tucked between his legs. Part of Jie felt sorry for him, especially since he'd left Lilian alone for the last couple of years.

At last, they arrived at a long white wall. The red banners fluttering from its gate marked it as the Peony Garden. Behind it rose a villa larger and more elegant-looking than the rest. Red tiles covered its sloping eaves. The pink-liveried gate guards bowed, and three middle-aged women approached from the other side.

"This is one of the two most prominent Houses of the Floating World," Mistress Yin said. "Only the most beautiful, graceful girls are ever chosen."

The three looked among each other, each smiling. They'd be togeth—

"The Gardener of this House wanted all three of you, but the Chrysanthemum Pavilion offered terms on Jie I couldn't refuse. And for whatever reason, Master Yan wanted Lilian at the Chrysanthemum Pavilion, as well." Master Yin beckoned Wen.

No. Jie's heart sank to her stomach.

There's already a senior Fist embedded within, who I do not believe you've met, Master Yin signaled. *Your first objective is to identify her and make contact.*

Eyes glistening, Wen bowed. "Thank you for your guidance up to now."

So this was it. Jie took her hand and squeezed it. Lilian clasped her other.

"No crying." Master Yin's scowl punctuated her sign language. *You are Black Lotus Fists. And you will see each other often enough.*

She exchanged pleasantries with the two women from the House, then bowed. "Now come along."

Wen's shoulders shuddered as she fought back tears. Her sweaty grip clung to Jie's hand, but with a good tug from Master Yin, they slipped apart.

"Stop sniveling, girl," said one of the women, probably the so-called Gardener.

Both Lilian and Jie sniffled as Master Yin pulled them down the street.

Jie felt as if her feet were made of lead.

She pointed at the blue tiles of another long wall. "See? You're just two blocks away."

Still too far. Gathering her resolve, Jie blinked away her tears. The mansion looked almost exactly the same as the one they'd just left, though the banners read *Chrysanthemum Pavilion.* The gate guards wore sky blue instead of pink, but the cut of their uniform might have been the same.

Shan-Shan is embedded here, Master Yin traced over their arms. *She's the Corsage of the House.*

Jie exchanged glances with Lilian. Shan-Shan had left the temple six years ago, but came back once a year for the Spring Festival. She'd always been kind to the younger novices, bringing candies back from the capital. Since her last visit, she'd apparently risen to the position of premier Blossom in the Chrysanthemum Pavilion.

The Gardener and Florist emerged from the courtyard, the former favoring her left leg with a slight hobble. In a world of grace and perfection, how strange it was to see an imperfection. There had to be a story there.

Lilian suppressed a gasp. Turning her head from the newcomers, she clutched Jie's arm until Master Yin prodded her off.

Both older women greeted them with tilts of their chin, and Jie and Lilian bowed low as was expected. Indeed, Lilian seemed to be avoiding eye contact.

"Gardener Ju." Mistress Yin bowed. "Please take good care of my girls."

Rising from a bow, the Gardener favored them with a curious eye, then beckoned. "Come, Jie and Lilian. You will stay in the Seedling and Floret room. Elder Sisters Tang Li and Ju Naya will help acquaint you with our etiquette and procedures."

* * *

The Present

Studying the sheets, Jie stifled her snort at the six-year-old memories. Back then, who would've thought She and Tang Li would cross paths in a plot to kill the greatest lords of the realm?

Her fingers froze. The sheets were made of a high-quality silk, though the pattern didn't match any used by the Houses of the Floating World. Indeed, the five-clawed dragon was reserved for the imperial family. How could Lord Shi get ahold of them, let alone get a House to agree to use them for a Plucking?

Of course, there was only one known occasion when an Emperor had Plucked a Blossom...

CHAPTER 9:

The Present

For now, Tang Li had these Black Fists lost in their memories, and not thinking about her employer's schemes. She'd deflected Jie's questions first about the contents of the safe, then about the bombs. It would be better not to cross her employer, especially if he succeeded in securing the North for himself. With such a position, and his close relationship to the Emperor, he could get her released.

He could just as easily get rid of her, to avoid leaving witnesses. Therefore, she'd sell him out if it could be used as a bargaining chip to save her own life.

She marveled at this genius, that wasn't her own. Whatever Lilian had done to her with this so-called *Tiger's Eye*, it had affected her decisions: from seeking out Jie to crack the safe, to the unsuccessful attempt at waylaying Wen to prevent her from going to Lord Wu's moons-viewing party. She knew about them, even if she really hadn't understood what they were at the time.

The boy, however, was completely unknown, and the way he looked at her now was unsettling. Maybe he was like Lai had been, a Black Fist disguised as a Pistil-in-training.

Of course, Blossoms interacted with Pistils at times. They were in the same trade, after all, even if their patrons had different tastes. From what she'd gleaned from idle chatter, the training was much the same.

And under the influence of the *Tiger's Eye*, she now had both her own and Lilian's memories of that time.

* * *

From Six to Five Years Ago

Lilian found life at the Chrysanthemum Pavilion in some ways exactly the same as at the temple. At both, they studied family crests and heraldry, and since they already knew all of the sigils and symbols of the realm's noble houses, she and Jie had to feign ignorance while they supposedly learned them for the first time.

In other ways, life didn't differ much at all. As initiates in the Black Lotus, they learned toxins and poisons; here they learned herbal medicines to prevent pregnancy and disease. There, they'd cleaned the temple grounds; here, as the oldest of the Seedlings, she polished tables and chairs in the common room, mopped floors in the hallways, and performed other mundane tasks geared toward instilling discipline and an appreciation for perfection.

As time passed, they graduated to washing, just like in the temple. Of course, they weren't even allowed to touch the Blossoms' extravagant gowns—the House servants took those to launderers for professional cleaning—but the linens, bedsheets, and kerchiefs all needed to be fresh and perfect as well.

At the temple, cleaning and oiling weapons helped children familiarize themselves with tools of the trade, well before they'd actually have to use them; in the Floating World, they used very different types of toys.

Who knew there were a dozen different brushes used for painting eyebrows?

And then, there was the training.

During the day, Seedlings and Florets would practice poetry and music, tea ceremony and flower arranging. At night, Florets would sit in the corners and observe the Blossoms at work, if Hummingbirds allowed it; if not, well, every room had a spyhole or three. In this way, the Seedlings and Florets would desensitize themselves to what everyone else in the realm considered private and secret, while learning the flowery words for the basest acts.

Acts which a princess of the North shouldn't engage in. Mama would be mortified.

Yet one day, Lilian would do them. And though she'd hidden much of her physical mastery of Black Lotus stealth and fighting skills from the rest of the clan—even Jie and Wen—those techniques had taken far more effort to master compared to the techniques of the Floating World. Polishing Jade, the Dance of Dragon and Phoenix, the Clouds and Rain, all required the gentle touch of a cutpurse or lockpicker.

For her, at least.

Poor Jie didn't take to them, though Lilian suspected it was more from lack of trying. Whereas Lilian, as an Seedling, had mostly stayed out of the eyes of Hummingbirds for the first year, the older Jie had started as a Floret.

The Gardener put her in front of men's eyes from the second week, and it was then she'd first realized how exotically beautiful she was. At fourteen, she'd soon blossom with Heaven's Dew, making her eligible to receive Hummingbirds at sixteen. Even with her lack of feminine grace, within two months her virgin price had nearly surpassed the record of the rival Peony Garden's Corsage, Lusha.

As one of Lusha's apprentices, Wen reported that the diva burned with jealousy and rage. *Mongrel*, was the term she used behind closed doors. As Seedlings, Wen and Lilian had fewer privileges to leave their Houses. When their schedules aligned,

Shan-Shan would take Lilian to clan meetings, maybe a few times a week; she might only see Wen once in that time, when Zhuli was able to bring her.

Lai, poor Lai. Guilt twisted Lilian's stomach whenever she saw him. Gone was his swagger, replaced by haunted eyes and slumped shoulders. Unlike the rest of their group, he'd already started entertaining men, and he was the favorite of the notorious Lord Tong, who'd been banned from more than one House for his roughness with Blossoms.

No telling how he treated Lai. Had she never injured him, he might be leading the most vital clan operations. He'd never acknowledge her when they met, and she deserved it.

How mortifying it must be to be put in that position, forced to endure violation. She, Jie, Wen, and the others would face that, too. All for the clan. It made her shudder.

Oh, Wen. Without her constant presence, Lilian drew even closer to Jie. At night, they'd cuddle, just like they had with Wen at the temple. Unbeknownst to the other Chrysanthemum Pavilion Seedlings and Florets, they'd communicate in the clan's secret taps and traces, recounting what they'd learned.

Besides Jie, Lilian found she could confide in her mentor, Tang Li. Already twenty-six, she'd been shoveled out of the Trench by Floating World agents at age six. She enticed men with an endearing naiveté and silliness that too many Hummingbirds found attractive. The House sisters adored her honest simplicity, thinking her not the sharpest razor in the cosmetic box.

As someone who'd hidden her true skills for years, Lilian suspected it was all an act; and with the clan's subtle questioning skills, she'd confirmed Tang Li had a sharp mind, limited only by her lack of ambition. All she'd ever wanted in life was to open a teahouse.

In bits and pieces, following the step-by-step process Boney Face had used on her as a young child, Lilian trained Tang Li to be receptive to the *Tiger's Eye*. When they painted together, Lilian would draw the grounds of the Black Lotus Temple, then use the *Tiger's Eye* to make Tang Li forget. Still, try as she might, no matter with what detail Boney Face was burnt into her memory, she could never reproduce his features.

Gardener Ju, of course, was one of the twin faces Lilian saw in her memories, but the older woman showed no sign of recognizing her. She'd been a malnourished three-year-old, after all. Even so, it took a couple of weeks before she dared meet the Gardener's eye.

The first few months felt like a slog, but soon after, life fell into a rhythm. Though no one was sure of her actual birthdate, on her official twelfth birthday, a little less than a year after coming to the Chrysanthemum Pavilion, Lilian made her debut as a Floret.

One hand holding the handle of a rice wine decanter and the other cupping its base, twelve-year-old Lilian took a deep breath. While most Florets recounted their trepidation during their New Flower Viewing, this was nothing compared to the dangerous aspects of Black Lotus training.

The neckline of her simple blue dress emphasized the nape of her neck, and its slit gave only a slight view of her left calf. Meant to highlight her over the other Florets while hinting at innocence, the Gardener had forsaken her miserly tendencies when commissioning the tailor.

Lilian stepped through the kitchen doors and into the Chrysanthemum Pavilion's vaulting common room.

Booming laughter and loud chatter quieted to a low murmur, barely audible over the strumming of stringed instruments by Blossoms in simple dresses that matched hers. All eyes fell on her. Fine robes in a myriad of colors swirled.

All blood drained from her head, and it took every bit of discipline to maintain her façade of serene composure. Many of the realm's most powerful lords and richest merchants were at this very moment thinking of sleeping with her. All present today probably would someday, though one would pay a handsome sum to be the first. No doubt, beneath the impeccable manners and elegant clothes were a few ugly souls who would have tried right now, if not for Floating World conventions.

All had been handpicked by the Gardener to come tonight. She knew how to play off their egos, to get them to bid against each other. Lords had friendly rivalries with each other, while merchants loved to flaunt their wealth over the warrior class. She could usually tell who these people were from her lifetime of studying family crests and heraldic colors. Right now, they all blended into one, and their faces blurred together.

Mouth dry, she glided over to the closest group, bowed, and held up the decanter. "Wine, my lords?"

"What's your name?" one in light blue asked.

She straightened, and eyes downcast as etiquette demanded, and bowed again. "Lilian, my Lord. *Li* as in Beautiful, *Lian* as in Lotus."

"Beautiful Lotus." A man in green grinned, holding out his wine saucer. "It is an appropriate name."

Lilian poured for all of them and moved on. It didn't take Black Lotus training to feel their gazes weighing heavily on her back. To think that one day, she'd probably be required to share a bed with them.

Still, that thought wasn't nearly as distracting as the tall, broad-shouldered man in crimson livery sitting with his fellows at the next table. He radiated confidence, and indeed, even the guests at other tables hung on his every word. In her experience, men like this were usually arrogant and demanding; yet his refined features looked genial and inviting.

All her disgust from the previous table melted away, she bowed and held up the decanter. "Wine, my lords?"

His eyes met hers, and a look of confusion scrawled across his face. "You look familiar."

That face. Up close, he was handsome, with the high-bridged nose and large eyes of the North. Indeed, his companions all shared his lighter skin tone. Now that she could focus, House lessons allowed her to recognize the crimson of Yushan County, marking him as Lord Ting. Lord Yang of Cheng Fu County, and Lord Shi of Jinjing sat beside him, eyes tracking her. Black Lotus training told her more: They were three of the Circle of Four, hereditary lords who kept the North loyal to the Emperor. The fourth, Lord Tong, had been banned from the Chrysanthemum Pavilion for his particularly sharp tastes, a censure all patrons respected lest they be banned from all the Floating World Houses.

Up to now, they'd been faceless names and family crests, comrades of the traitorous Lord Yu, her father. Still, something seemed especially familiar about Lords Yang and Shi.

But not Lord Ting.

Even if she didn't recognize him, his reputation preceded him. He was their leader, the Lion of the North.

"The girl has lost her tongue." Lord Yang's bellow sounded too large for his thin build.

They probably knew what had happened to her family. To think, if they had survived, she'd be betrothed by now, and probably married within three years, to sleep with only her husband. She staggered back a step.

"Are you all right?" Despite the conventions against touching Florets, Lord Ting's large hand shot out to support her.

It was strong and warm and comforting. It sparked memories of Daddy. Lilian bowed again, if only to hide the tears that threatened.

"Lord Ting, you are scaring the poor girl." Lord Shi laughed. According to her lessons, he was thirty-six, with an eight-year-old son, Yang Lin. "She's surely never felt a man's touch before."

"My apologies, miss." Lord Ting pulled his hand back.

It felt like a sudden loss. Chin dipped, Lilian shook her head. "None needed, my Lord."

"Did I hear your name was Lilian?" he asked.

He'd overheard her at the other table. She gave a slight nod, as all Blossoms should. "Yes, my Lord."

"Please, lift your head."

Lilian hardened her resolve. She was not just a demure Floret, but also a Black Lotus Fist. Forcing back her tears, she did as commanded, but remembered to keep her eyes averted.

"Look at her." He held his hand under her chin without actually touching. If only he would; he seemed genuinely kind. "She's from the North, for sure."

Lords Yang and Shi both studied her, nodding.

"I'd surmise she has noble blood somewhere in her family tree," Lord Ting said.

More and ancient and noble than theirs.

"Perhaps a courtesan wasn't careful when entertaining a lord." Lord Yang let out his grating laugh again. "Hope it wasn't one of us, because, well... I plan to bid on her." He laughed again.

So crude. Lilian suppressed a shudder. Still, he might know what happened to Daddy, and coaxing the story out of him would be easier when he was sated.

Lord Ting flashed a scowl at his companions. "Where are you from, Miss Lilian?"

She switched to the Central Valley accent that Boney Face had forced her to learn. "I am from Fenggu Province, my Lord."

"The old capital of the Yu Dynasty," Lord Ting said. "Our ancestors came from there before relocating to the North."

Lilian buried a snort. Relocating was a generous description. The Founder of the Wang Dynasty had defeated the Yu loyalists with muskets and resettled them to the North.

"Your ancestors must've stayed behind," he continued. "It wasn't a common occurrence."

And it wasn't her circumstance. She was descended from the last Yu emperor, who'd hidden the imperial seal. Still, she smiled in agreement as a Blossom, the epitome of femininity, should.

"Lilian." Gardener Ju appeared at her side.

Lilian's soul just about jumped out of her body. Usually, the Gardener's near imperceptible limp allowed Lilian and Jie to hear her, but the Lord Ting was too much of a distraction. Lilian bowed.

"Our other guests must be thirsty," Gardener Ju said. "You mustn't keep them waiting."

"It was all my fault, Gardener." With a sincere smile, Lord Ting bowed his head.

She grinned. "You can express your repentance with a bid."

"Of course."

Oh, as kind and gentle as he seemed, please let him be her first. And surely, satisfied with her, he'd tell her about her family. Maybe he, a great Lord of the North would realize who she was, buy her contract from that first night, and then marry her.

Once she'd already served eight of the tables, other Florets followed behind her in plain dresses cut from the same bolts of cloth as her own dress. As usual with First Flower Viewings, Jie had been assigned work out of sight, lest her exotic looks steal attention away from the debutante. Oh, to be able to confide in her; but Boney Face's *Tiger Eye* prevented Lilian from doing so.

As the night wore on, the House Blossoms came out to mingle with the lords, all wearing matching blue dresses and simple makeup and hairstyles. After whetting the Hummingbirds' appetites for a girl they could not yet have, the Gardener wouldn't pass up a chance to make money. The women would all feign purity and innocence in bed tonight.

Hips sashaying, Tang Li approached Lord Ting's table. He laughed at something she said.

Her with him. Lilian's stomach twisted.

Heavens, was that jealousy? Over a man she'd just met? And not just any man, but a potential Hummingbird, whose only goal was to bed her. And here she was, entertaining silly thoughts of marriage.

Where had clan and House training in tempering emotion fled to?

She looked back to where Lord Ting held Tang Li's hand. With her charm, she'd have him coming back.

Which meant Lilian would see him more often.

But he'd also be bedding Tang Li.

The decanter shook in Lilian's hands, and her heat surged into her face.

Well, with Tang Li's unwitting training in the Tiger's Eye, there's be ways to keep the two apart. And maybe even bring her closer to Lord Yang, so the creepy man wouldn't make a bid on Lilian's Plucking.

* * *

The Present

Whenever Tang Li wanted to mention Boney Face or the Steel Orchids, their names died on her lips just like they had for Lilian whenever she wanted to reveal them.

Now, Li gasped, drawing the gaze of the Black Fists. It all made sense now, how Lord Ting had always unsettled her, and how she'd been drawn to Lord Yang. Lilian had planted those feelings toward the men in her.

A vindictive part of her wanted to bury the rest of Lilian's secrets forever.

CHAPTER 10

The Present

Wen's ears twitched. In the far distance, a chorus of horse hooves clopped. There had to be at least a dozen. Perhaps the imperial soldiers were on their way here.

Surely Jie would've heard it already with her keener ears, and calculated exactly how many.

But no, the half-elf was sucking on her lower lip, a telltale sign that she was pondering something; and it didn't look to be about the bombs or contents of the safe. In her hands, she held the sheets with the bloodstain.

"Eldest Sister," Wen said.

Jie's gaze focused. "I was just thinking about Lilian's Plucking."

Wen cocked her head. The bidding had been a complicated dance, ending with quite a surprise. How had that all played out? Lord Ting had visited the Chrysanthemum Pavilion on a regular basis, just for a chance to catch a glimpse of Lilian.

Of course, Wen, as a Seedling in a rival House, had only had second-hand information. Ah, those days. At first, they'd been miserable.

* * *

From Six to Two Years Ago

Wen's first year and a half at the Peony Garden had been the first she'd spent without regular contact—both metaphorical and physical—with Jie and Lilian. Never allowed to leave the House without a Blossom, she had to rely on the other Black Lotus plant, Zhuli, to make it to cell meetings. On a good week, she might see Jie twice and Lilian once. With that time dedicated to training in weapons, stealth, and spying, they had little time to share their more personal thoughts. It had been lonely, and though Zhuli had been supportive on a daily basis, she wasn't the sisters Wen had grown up with.

Her debut as a Floret had changed that.

The Emperor himself had honored her and the House by attending her Flower's First Viewing. It was unheard of for the Son of Heaven to come to Floating World; instead, the Chrysanthemum Pavilion and Peony Garden vied to send Blossoms to entertain His Eminence at Sun-Moon Palace.

Accompanying him was his sister's husband, Lord Lin, ruler of Linshan Province. Unlike most of the realm's hereditary lords, Lord Lin hadn't taken on lovers or visited brothels before. Now, his wife carried a potential heir to the realm, and was unable to sate his male needs. So here he was, guest of the Emperor.

And by order of the clan, Wen and Zhuli were to catch his eye.

After all, although not as egregious as the North, an independent streak ran through the people of Linshan; and the father of a possible heir, no matter how improbable their chance of ascending the Jade Throne, might try to take probability into his own hands.

Lord Lin became one of Zhuli's regular Hummingbirds, and made a substantial bid on Wen. Clan suspicions had come to naught: that fall, when Linshan Province's famed eldarwood leaves turned brilliant purple instead of red in what was considered an auspicious omen, Lord Lin's wife gave birth to a girl. They named her *Ziqiu*, Purple Autumn, and she would grow up to become one of Princess Kaiya's close confidantes.

Now, as a Floret, Wen had more freedom to leave the House. She, Jie, and Lilian were again able to spend leisure time together, despite their Houses' rivalry. It was part perplexing and part amusing that while she and Lilian became embodiments of feminine grace over those three years, Jie remained...Jie.

At eighteen, two years past a Blossom's earliest Plucking age, the half-elf had yet to flower with Heaven's Dew. In this, her Gardener stuck to the conventions of the Floating World, since Jie's price for her First Plucking continued soaring to dizzying heights.

Though not as exorbitant as Jie's, bids on both Lilian and Wen surpassed all but Lusha's virgin price. With the realm enjoying historic prosperity, too many men had too much money on their hands. As Jie often said, a male's concern over virginity, both his own and his women's, could fuel an economy.

It was that year, when Wen was thirteen and Lilian fourteen, that both flowered with Heaven's Dew, within days of each other. While such women's matters were private everywhere else in the realm, the most celebrated Florets' coming-of-age was the subject of bets in Floating World gambling dens. Even more mortifyingly, some Houses—though certainly not the elite Chrysanthemum Pavilion or Peony Garden—would auction off a Floret's first blood-stained undergarment.

Though the commoners never knew about the unrest in the North, the clan kept close watch. For now, Lord Ting, through sheer force of personality, kept the grumbling lords in check. Previously frequent whispers pining for the return of the old Yu emperor had retreated to the most private corners of the North, not even shared in the bedrooms of the Floating World. The realm was at peace.

Adhering to the adage, *More sweat in times of peace means less blood in times of war*, the Floating World cell and the rest of the clan continued its vigilance and training. At least once a month, they'd run practice missions; unsurprisingly, Jie emerged as second to Master Yin in the cell's leadership—even if she still couldn't match the master's skill with blades.

With the coming of Heaven's Dew, bids on Wen and Lilian accelerated. Lord Yang competed to be Lilian's first, but Lord Ting would always outbid him, and any other man. Over three years, his visits to the Chrysanthemum Pavilion became regular. He'd never partake of the Blossoms, instead sitting in the same chair at the same table, always asking Lilian to serve him. He'd always bring some gift, and engage in banter with her.

With a year left before she became eligible for Plucking, gambling dens were offering four-to-three odds that he'd be the first to take her to bed. Lord Yang's odds came in a distant second, having fallen to five-to-one. Though she tried not to show it, Lilian's contentment was obvious to Jie and Wen.

Lord Lin continued bidding on Wen, though not with as much enthusiasm as when he'd first met her. As a master castle designer whose province provided stone and lumber for construction, he'd been assigned by the Emperor to renovate Cloud Castle, the abandoned fortress of the Yu family.

This honor kept him away from the capital. Abandoned after Lord Yu's failed rebellion thirteen years prior, the fortifications overlooked a mountain pass into the realm of the fair-skinned Rotuvi. With the Teleri Empire finally eradicating Rotuvi's Empaths, they were looking to establish a garrison of Bovyan shocktroopers at the border. The Directori in Telesite had demanded Cloud Castle, since it lay just outside the Great Wall.

Whenever Wen and Jie discussed the logistics or speculated on the diplomatic repercussions over tea, Lilian would go silent. No amount of coaxing or cajoling could get her to share her opinion on the Yu family or their castle.

Lord Lin finished the work two weeks before Lilian's sixteenth birthday: what would be the day of her Plucking.

In the months prior, Lilian had taken herbal medicines and visited an acupuncturist on a weekly basis so that her Best Friend wouldn't come on the special day. With that out of the way, she spent those last weeks beaming, delighted that it would certainly be Lord Ting.

Because his bid was so unsurmountable.

The gambling dens had stopped taking bets on him, and offered long odds on anyone else. Rumor had it that even the Emperor had placed a bet. A new line emerged: two-to-one odds that Lord Ting would buy out Lilian's contract before any other man could be the next Hummingbird to sleep with her.

Of course, it wasn't the Chrysanthemum Pavilion who held her contract, nor even the clan's shell company which supposedly sent elite courtesans to nobles' houses. She, as well as the entire cell, belonged to the Black Lotus for life, and could never buy true freedom.

That didn't preclude the clan from planting a Blossom as a lord's wife; but none of the lords of the North could afford an elite Blossom's contract price, even if said contract were completely fictitious. Appearances had to be maintained, after all.

Still, Lilian had shared the truth with only Jie and Wen: Lord Ting was negotiating with Gardener Ju and Florist Wei to become her exclusive Hummingbird.

Would the clan allow it? As a reward for Lord Ting's loyalty, or perhaps to have a spy to ensure that loyalty? Wen and Jie both remarked that they'd never seen Lilian so flush with happiness and optimism. She was positively glowing, even more beautiful than usual.

Then, the afternoon of her Plucking, a new bid for her came in.

* * *

The Present

"Poor Lilian." Wen shook her head, recalling how it had all played out.

Jie gazed down at the sheets.

Wen bobbed her head. "I was just thinking how enamored she'd been with Lord Ting."

"That's before she found out how rough he was behind closed doors." Jie sighed, and Meisha and Yangyang all nodded in agreement.

Tang Li, however, shook her head. "I wouldn't be so sure about that..."

CHAPTER 11

The Present

When something didn't make sense, Tian couldn't help investigating and questioning until it did. Right now, something wasn't adding up, and it had nothing to do with Lilian's past with Lord Ting.

Problem was, neither Jie nor Wen seemed to be thinking about the attempt on Princess Kaiya's life.

He turned to Wen. "What did the bomb look like?"

Wen looked up, her eyes regaining focus. "It was in a barrel, marked as wine from Jinjing County."

Lord Shi's domain. Tian nodded. "How did you know it was a bomb?"

"It smelled like firepowder, and when the barrel jostled back and forth, it sounded like swishing sand and nails."

"Jostled?"

Wen's cheeks reddened. "I was holding Lord Shi's hands while lying across it."

Tian's brow furrowed. "How would that shake the barrel?"

The women, even Tang Li, covered giggles.

No matter what was so funny, the jostling hadn't caused the barrel to explode. "How would it be detonated?"

Wen shook her head. "I couldn't figure it out. There were no holes for fuses, and no place marked for a tap that could trigger a sparking mechanism."

"And if that was the way it ignited," Meisha said, "the saboteur would blow himself up, too."

"Where was it on the barge? How big was the cabin?" Tian asked.

Wen pantomimed the layout of the barge. It seemed to be a wide deck, with a one-level sterncastle taking up a third. The room looked like it was on the starboard side.

Which didn't make sense, either. He pointed to the spots in the air where Wen had drawn the barge. "If the barrel had exploded, it might've killed everyone in the room, but I don't think it could do much damage to the structure. Even if it were a larger bomb, the location above the waterline wouldn't cause a hull breach."

"Incompetent assassins?" Meisha suggested.

In the corner of Tian's eye, Tang Li's lips tightened.

She knew something. Maybe as Fixer Zhang, she'd made the arrangements for one of her many Triad or rebel employers. He turned to her. "It was a dud, wasn't it?"

All eyes turned on her, but she stared back, emotionless.

He continued, "Not only that, it was meant to be found, though not by Wen."

Wen looked from Meisha to Yangyang. "That's why we got the fake invitation to the moons-viewing party. Fixer Zhang sent the Triads to waylay us, so we wouldn't make it."

"Someone was trying to make Lord Shi look guilty." The picture was all coming together. Excitement rose in Tian's heart and came out through his voice. "And that someone was probably on the boat, so he'd have an ali…ali…."

"Alibi," Jie said.

He gave a strong nod. "Right. Alibi."

"I knew something was wrong with the picture." Wen nodded, a look of understanding blooming on her face. "It's so obvious now."

All eyes turned to Tang Li.

She licked her lips and swallowed hard. "There's something more about Lilian's story that I'm trying to understand, and it might help you now."

* * *

Two Years Ago

Sitting in the dressing niche of her new room in the Chrysanthemum Pavilion, Lilian's heart raced as she looked in the mirror. The early afternoon sun streamed in, along with a cool autumn breeze through the open windows. It was perfect weather for a perfect day.

She'd served Lord Ting food and wine for the past four years. Tonight, she'd serve him in the most intimate way.

As was custom for the morning of a Floret's Plucking, she'd bathed in water brought from Yanhu. It lay on the shores of Tear-Drop Lake, which formed when the Goddess Guanyin shed a tear that fell to the earth when it was new. Then, dressed in a robe of the purest white—not really pure, since each House usually only had one at a time, shared by all the Florets on their day of Plucking— she received a blessing from a priest of the Virility Spirit's shrine, who later consecrated her new bed.

Now, Tang Li knelt beside her, making adjustments to her dress. It was in the same style as the one from her First Flower Viewing—actually, one of the House sisters', because she'd since grown and filled out— for her last evening as an innocent Floret. It hid the not-so-innocent lacy garments that Lord Ting had sent her.

Jie stood behind her on the other side, brushing her hair. To maintain the image of innocence, Lilian would not start adopting elaborate coiffures, held in place by jeweled pins, until tomorrow. For now, she'd keep the same simple bun she had ever since coming to the Chrysanthemum Pavilion.

"You're radiant," Jie said.

"And we're fortunate for trade with the Estomari." Tang Li rose and tugged Lilian's sleeve, then nodded to the rectangular mirror standing behind the dressing table. "Because they make such perfect glass. So much better than our polished silver."

Radiant. You'd think you're a bride on her way to her wedding, Jie tapped and swiped on Lilian's back. *Not a girl exploited for her body.*

With Tang Li present, making adjustments to the dress, Lilian couldn't respond. She only smiled. It was only exploitation if she didn't want it.

And she wanted Lord Ting.

So much that she hadn't drunk the daily herbal contraceptive formula that she was supposed to have started with the arrival of her Best Friend a week ago.

She had to force herself to keep from squirming at the heat and desire swirling inside her. How would it be tonight? Would he be gentle? Or would four years of pent-up lust drive him to ravish her?

Jie's ears twitched, and Lilian followed the turn of her head. Footsteps chirped across the nightingale floor in the hall.

"*Tsk*," Tang Li said. "You'll ruin your hair."

The Gardener and Florist both appeared, the former's hobble indicating which of the Steel Orchid twins it was.

With Jie holding Lilian's hair in place, they joined Tang Li in bowing. As was the custom, the Gardener was here to go over the final, meticulous details of a Plucking. Never before had the Florist joined her; but never before had the Chrysanthemum Pavilion received such a high virgin price.

Lilian came out of her bow. "Gardener; Florist."

"Lilian," the Gardener beamed. "I have unbelievable, auspicious news!"

Her heart soared. Lord Ting must've come to terms with the House and clan shell company to make himself her sole Hummingbird. "Please." She bowed, forcing Jie to hold her hair in place yet again.

"We just received a new bid for your Plucking. It's just short of Lusha's record."

No. Lilian's posture wilted, all grace lost. Her heart hurt so much, it felt as if it might burst. How had this happened? They needed to inform Lord Ting soon, because surely he would outbid it. She barely managed to croak out, "Who?"

"The Emperor, himself."

Lilian could only gawk. At her side, Jie and Tang Li looked equally shocked. The Son of Heaven had only once visited the Floating World, and that had been for Wen's First Flower Viewing. He'd never even laid eyes on Lilian. And though it might be an unparalleled honor, it was Lord Ting she wanted. Her voice came out as whisper. "His Eminence?"

"Well, not exactly," Florist Ju said. "Lord Yang submitted the bid, with the intention of gifting your virginity to the Emperor."

Tang Li gasped. Of course she would, since Lilian had used the *Tiger's Eye* to magnify Lord Yang's limited redeeming qualities in Tang Li's eyes. He could have used such an enormous bid to buy out her contract, but instead...

"It's a great honor to our House." The Gardener rubbed her hands together. "You are to receive His Eminence at the newly restored Cloud Castle tomorrow night."

"Wait," Jie said. "How could Lord Yang even come up with such a bid?"

* * *

The Present

The way Tian drew connections had already impressed Jie and the rest of the cell; but he couldn't see how all this talk about Plucking was related to the bomb.

One thing was for sure, he resolved to never hold hands with a woman at all, let alone *pluck* her. He shuddered.

Another thing was a near certainty: Lord Shi wasn't responsible for the dud. He was being framed by—

CHAPTER 12

The Present

Tian looked like he wanted to say something when Tang Li had finished the tale, but Jie cut him off. She could hardly believe the fixer's tangled web of lies.

Jie remembered that day, and one thing stood out. It wasn't Lord Yang's bid, or that he gifted Lilian's virginity to the Emperor.

No. "Lilian couldn't have possibly been so naïve as to believe that the clan would let her keep Lord Ting's baby if she fell pregnant."

"If the baby was a girl," Wen said, "she'd end up in the Floating World."

Meisha nodded furiously. "And if he was a boy, the Emperor would use him as leverage to ensure Ting's loyalty."

Tang Li met their gazes. "Maybe she did know that would be the outcome."

Jie's heart squeezed. Lilian was the one soul she knew best, and who knew her best. Or at least, that was what Jie had believed, until Lilian's betrayal. Now, Tang Li's words carried more weight, considering Lilian's memories now lived inside her. Unless... "You're trying to distract us."

"To what end?"

Jie drew a knife. "To survive the night?"

"If I die, you'll never find out who was behind the fake bomb."

"I know who," Tian said.

Tang Li blanched, but quickly added, "But you can't possibly know Lilian's biggest secret."

"Go on." Knife outstretched, Jie froze.

Tian threw his hands up.

"I'm not completely sure." Tang Li's tone sounded genuinely apologetic. Then again, she was a fixer and a liar. "I just know there is more, and we need to keep talking about what happened."

Jie frowned. "We don't have much time."

"We never did find out how Lord Yang afforded that bid," Wen said. "If I remember correctly, his odds of winning dropped in the last week from five-to-one to twenty-to-one."

"And the gambling houses started taking bets on Lord Ting again, with odds rising from four-to-three to ten-to-nine," Meisha added. "It was a low yield for a near-certain payout."

"The winning bid was sixty-thousand *yuan*." Jie turned to Tang Li. "Enough to feed a family of ten for sixty lifetimes. Do you know how Lord Yang raised the money?"

Tang Li shook her head. "I never found out."

"I think I know." Tian was tracing lines in the air.

All eyes now looked at him.

He swallowed. "It's just a guess, but Lord Yang had bid on her before, right?"

Jie nodded. In his friendly rivalry with Lord Ting, Lord Yang had been the last to drop out...much to Lilian's relief at the time, since she'd never liked him.

"It comes down to the odds."

It was all making sense. Anger surged in Jie. "He bet on himself."

Tian nodded.

"But where did he get the money to make the bet?"

"The gambling dens." Tian drew more lines in the air. "Had Lord Ting won, they would've lost so much money."

Yangyang shook her head. "The bettors would be ready to tear the dens down and drag the owners through the streets, if that were true."

"Which is why the bid was funneled through Lord Yang," Tian said. "It's just a theory, but one that adds up. With four-to-three odds on Lord Ting and five-to-one on Lord Yang, they could still make a lot of money, and Lord Yang could win enough to submit a winning bid. I'd need to see their ledgers from that time to confirm it."

Jie frowned. She only had two days left as head of the cell, and she'd order an operation to acquire those ledgers from two years ago. "And when Lord Yang declared it was a gift for the Emperor, Lord Ting would never dare to outbid him."

"It sounded like Lord Yang liked Tang Li." Tian nodded to the fixer. "Why not use the money to buy out her contract then, instead of waiting until two years ago?"

"Timing," Wen said. "The Emperor was so pleased with the gift of Lilian's virginity, he bequeathed Lord Yang stewardship of Cloud Castle."

Jie nodded. "Lord Ting thought that he, as ruler of the county adjacent to the castle, and as the Emperor's most trusted vassal in the North, would receive it."

"So Lilian's first time was with the Emperor?" Tian asked. "The next night?"

"Not the next night," Jie said. "On the advice of Master Yan, the Cloud Castle party was a trap. One which half of the cell participated in."

* * *

Two Years Ago

After years in the Floating World, where Black Lotus cell members did little more than slip toxins into drinks, steal correspondence, and trawl for information, it'd been a long time since Jie had participated in a real operation.

Now, she, Wen, and Master Yin hid in a storage cabin on a luxurious river barge as it headed downstream toward Honggang. In the closed quarters, Wen's lavender scent mingled with the jasmine and oiled steel of Master Yin. Jie's heart raced in excitement, waiting to hear why they'd been assembled on such short notice.

Outside, night had fallen. Master Yin looked out the porthole, then stood. She beckoned them. "Our pretense has run its course."

She led them out of the cabin and onto the deck, where Lilian, Shan-Shan, Zhuli, Meisha, Yangyang, and Lai sat on benches with another six of the Floating World cell members.

Jie studied Lilian. Though her expression remained stoic, she was no doubt dying inside. She'd developed an affection for Lord Ting over the past four years, and expected to become his exclusive Blossom. It was the hope of every Blossom, to have a sole patron who was kind. Jie and Wen had been caught up in her dream, against the reality that they were Black Lotus Fists who needed to cast a wider net to collect as much intelligence as possible.

All greeted Master Yin with fists in their palms, while Jie and Wen took seats on either side of Lilian.

Master Yin gave them a nod, then spoke in a whisper so their voices wouldn't carry over to the other barges in the flotilla. "This is a test of loyalty. All of the hereditary lords of the North have been invited to the re-consecration of Cloud Castle. Do you remember its significance?"

"It was the Yu family's stronghold," Wen said.

"And a symbol of the Yu Dynasty." Jie thought back to the history of the castle. After forsaking the Mandate of Heaven, the Yu family had fled the Wang Dynasty Founder, eventually reaching Cloud Castle, just outside the Great Wall.

Master Yin nodded. "After Yu Qian's treachery and the death of his family thirteen years ago, Northerners still made pilgrimages to the castle. Therefore, the Emperor decided to abandon it, keeping a garrison on its access road to prevent anyone from entering."

Lilian's expression slipped for a split second.

Jie ignored it for the moment, picturing the map in her mind. "But now, with the Bovyan threat out of Rotuvi, we need the castle's cannon batteries to defend the pass into Cathay."

"Yes." Master Yin nodded again. "So now, the Emperor has given each of the lords of the North reason to rebel. With a small complement of imperial guards, he'll make for an inviting target."

Yangyang gasped. "Certainly His Eminence wouldn't use himself as bait?"

"Of course not. He is safely sequestered behind the walls of Sun-Moon Palace." Master Yin laughed and gestured toward the lead barge. "A decoy leads us to Cloud Castle. We also have a good idea as to who cannot be trusted."

Lilian's eyes brightened, and Jie leaned into her. If the Emperor wasn't there, it meant she wasn't going to Cloud Castle to be Plucked.

"Now," Master Yin said, "there's also a secondary mission: the Yu Dynasty imperial seal."

"Never recovered." Jie and every other clan member knew the true history, even if the imperial archives showed that the last Yu emperor surrendered the seal to the Founder.

"The descendants of Yu always claimed it was lost, but an informant confirmed Lord Yu Qian had it when he tried to start his rebellion. Lord Lin scoured the castle during his renovations, but didn't find it. Our informant says Lord Ting knows where it is."

Which was why the Emperor was testing his loyalty. Using his feelings for Lilian. Jie's stomach knotted.

At her side, Lilian's expression darkened.

"We are going into the heart of the North, and all the lords were given ample time to send couriers ahead and mobilize their soldiers." Master Yin gazed over them, pausing on each. "Twelve possible traitors. You were handpicked because of your ties to these men."

"I guess Lai will get a tour of Cloud Castle's dungeons, then?" Zhuli gave him a good-natured elbow jab.

Lai, who'd looked more alive than he had in years, wilted. No doubt he'd looked forward to an actual mission, but now he'd be Lord Tong's Peach Bottom. Did Zhuli not know how much he resented it?

At Jie's side, Lilian squirmed on the bench.

Jie sucked on her lower lip. If forced to choose between Lord Ting, and clan and country, what would Lilian decide?

"Jie will be lookout and Wen will be a runner, but both of you might be called to arms if the need arises."

After some initial logistics, planning, and weapon-checking, Master Yin bade them get some rest. When they awoke two hours later, the flotilla had docked at the city of Honggang. Located in the foothills, it was known as the Gateway to the North. The full-fledged Blossoms transferred to palanquins, while Wen, Jie, and Mistress Yin disguised themselves as porters and imperial servants.

With the Iridescent Moon waxing to full, the Emperor's decoy called for procession to stop for the night. The party occupied the nicest inns, away from the docks, on cliffs which provided a view of the river; Jie and Wen were stuck in the stables with Master Yin.

Jie didn't mind the discomfort as much as not being able to comfort Lilian. Still, she slept well, and after breakfast they continued toward Cloud Castle. Commoners stopped and knelt, foreheads to the ground, as the imperial procession passed.

At least the highway was paved, since it wound uphill. At a forced march, the trip to the Great Wall might take two hours, but the palanquins' leisurely pace stretched it to six. While such a trek during Jie's temple days might've been easy, her easygoing years in the Floating World had affected her endurance.

As the eyes, ears, and nose of the team, Jie noted an increased military presence. Not men bearing the colors of their lords, but the scent of oiled steel, gazes lingering on the imperial palanquin, and hushed whispers which perhaps only half-elf ears could detect.

There might be over a hundred threats. If all the lords' men coordinated an attack, the dozen imperial guards wouldn't stand a chance. Still, by the time they reached Chengfu Township, in a dale next to the Great Wall's gate into Rotuvi, no one had made a move. Perhaps the lords of the North were loyal; or maybe they were waiting for a more opportune moment to strike.

Their last chance of significant reinforcements disappeared when they cleared the gatehouse and its imperial garrison, and entered the mountain pass. Instead of taking the main road, the procession veered off onto another paved path, which wound up through the mountains.

Jie studied the battlements overlooking the path, where dour soldiers in imperial blue stood watch every hundred paces. With enough defenders manning the ramparts, an enemy force would take significant casualties before even reaching the main gates.

Three hundred years ago... With her free hand, she signed, *How did the Founder's siege even work?*

It didn't, Master Yin responded. *The Yu had stockpiled arms and food. They also received supplies from Rotuvi, which emerged from the Long Winter with ample harvests.*

This was all news to Jie. The histories had all extolled the Founder's genius in capturing this fort, and his magnanimity in allowing the Yu to live. The fortress was coming into view, carved into the cliff face and surrounded with stone walls. It looked as if this road was the only access point.

Wen was looking, too, and apparently thinking the same thing: *How did they get food from Rotuvi?*

Dwarf-made grain elevator, Master Yin signed. *Too small for a person to use.*

The cannon batteries came into view on the battlements. They overlooked the pass, supposedly to bombard Rotuvi troops that might dare to file through; but three hundred years ago, they would've also kept the Founder's troops from reaching the grain elevator. Though... *Back then, they didn't have cannons or firepowder.*

They had repeating crossbows, while the Founder had given those up in favor of muskets and cannons.

Jie gauged the distance from the fortress to the floor of the pass. Cannonballs couldn't reach the castle, whereas Repeaters could rain a constant barrage of bolts onto an attacker. The Founder's legendary infallibility was turning out to be more legend than fact.

The sun had already started its descent. The ravine walls blocked the view of the Iridescent Moon, but it had to be mid-afternoon, perhaps the third waxing crescent. Up ahead, the gatehouse stood open. In fact, there were no actual gates. The Emperor probably did not want a repeat of the failed siege three hundred years ago. Just how had they taken it from Lord Yu thirteen years ago? With its strategic position, it would've been impossible.

Unless someone on the inside had betrayed him.

She looked to the rear, where soldiers openly bearing the colors of the Northern counties followed.

One road in.

One road out.

CHAPTER 13

The Present

Tang Li listened as Jie recounted the journey to Cloud Castle. Lilian's memories of the trip had been of riding in the palanquin, heart squeezing with dread at times, and soaring with hope at others. Even now, Li felt as much fondness for the recently deceased Lord Ting as she did the Black Fists in this room.

What had Lilian done to her with this *Tiger's Eye*? And could it be reversed?

Because death was already unappealing, and would be even more horrifying at the hands of people for whom she had an inexplicable affection.

Horse hooves clopped in the far distance. She looked out the window toward the Iridescent Moon, now waning to its first crescent. If Wen had run here after discovering the dud, it might take imperial investigators another half an hour or so.

She'd have to stall just a little longer, then surrender to the authorities. If need be, she'd sell out her employer.

Lilian had almost betrayed the clan at Cloud Castle, because that's where the last of her lost memories came back.

* * *

Two Years Ago

Lilian had peeked out of the palanquin window at times, first in Chengfu Township, where she caught sight of the red lanterns of the brothels. It had been that very street where Mama had scolded Daddy for ogling the prostitutes.

To think, Lilian would've officially become one last night, if not for the Emperor's cruel trap. Did His Eminence not see that the lords would remain loyal as long as they were shown a modicum of respect?

Her heart squeezed. Lord Ting was the most devoted of all, holding together these lords through sheer force of will. Instead of rewarding him for his loyalty, the Emperor had given the castle to that obsequious toad, Lord Yang; and claimed her for himself.

Because even if the Son of Heaven wasn't there now, he would surely be waiting to Pluck her on her return to the capital.

If she survived today.

Maybe it would be better not to.

The next time she slid open the palanquin window was when she overheard a bearer mention their approach to Cloud Castle to a comrade. Late afternoon sun shined on the walls that ran along a ledge, its cannons pointing into the pass.

Cannons! An image came unbidden to her mind. Iron tree trunks along a wall. No, cannons. As a three-year-old, she'd thought them trees.

Cloud Castle. Daddy's castle. Stronghold of the Yu family.

She would live through today.

She'd avenge her family, and her Plucking at the Emperor's hands would provide the perfect opportunity. Blossoms who'd entertained His Eminence spoke of being stripped naked by Praise Spring Temple nuns, searched for weapons and poisons, and then wrapped in red blankets to be delivered. Unlike Lilian, none of those Blossoms knew how to kill with their bare hands.

That was later. First, survive today.

The procession came to a stop, and her palanquin lowered to the ground. Had they already passed through the gates? Surely she would've heard them open, even if they were newly oiled. The palanquin doors slid open, and a hand reached to help her out.

Jie's.

Even without looking, Lilian knew the half-elf's callouses as if they were her own. And despite her unsettled thoughts, there was something calming about them.

Are you all right? Jie tapped and swiped.

With a slight nod, Lilian looked around, squinting in the last rays of sun.

Wen was just behind Jie.

Around them, the stone-paved yard surrounded a fortress carved into the cliff face. The only wood and tile looked to be the eaves, which appeared more decorative than functional. Battlements of stone blocks encircled the ledge, and the cannons she'd seen on the approach were angled down. A small waterfall poured from the mountain above. Over time, it might've carved out the ledge from which the walls rose; but now, stone walls lined a pool. The water probably flowed into a cistern below, and then who knew where.

Most striking were the scents.

The light fragrance of chrysanthemums, now in full bloom. Smoke from a fire pit, where a pig roasted.

More memories flooded back.

Mama bleeding to death in a child's lap. Big Brother's lifeless eyes. Daddy's decapitated head.

She reeled back a step, and Jie shot out a hand to catch her.

"Are you all right?"

"Yes." No. Her hands trembled, and her breath hitched.

Jie leaned in and whispered, "You're not all right. It will be fine. Lord Ting is loyal."

If only that were Lilian's sole concern. Mama and Big Brother had died here, on a sunny autumn morning just like today. But who had killed them? She met Jie's eyes. "How did the Emperor capture this fortress from Lord Yu?"

Wen shook her head. "The masters know, but won't tell us. But I suspect—"

"Betrayal." Someone in Daddy's inner circle had turned on him. Someone who was probably here right now. Lilian searched among the twelve...no, eleven assembled lords. There were supposed to be twelve. Who was missing? She didn't recognize all of them, just Lord Yang, Lord Shi, and...

Lord Ting.

Her heart jolted.

It couldn't have been him. He was loyal to the Emperor, along with Lords Yang, Shi, and Tong. He couldn't possibly have been among Daddy's closest advisors.

Lord Tong. Of the Emperor's closest confidantes in the North, he was the only one she knew by reputation and not by face. She'd never seen him before. Lai would know. Where was Lai?

"No dallying." An imperial official, a secretary of the Ministry of Appointments from the insignias on his chest and shoulders, waved them on. Near the entrance several imperial officials hustled guests in, relieving them of their ancestral swords. A particularly large man in scarlet court robes grumbled as he surrendered his red-lacquered *dao*. It was Lord Zu, famed as one of the best swordsmen in the realm. He could hold his own against imperial guards in practice matches. There was no sign of the Emperor's decoy, nor the imperial guards with their fear-inducing breastplates.

Behind them, however, were a couple dozen soldiers in the livery of their provinces.

Taking a deep breath to calm her racing heart and trembling nerves, Lilian followed the other cell members disguised as Blossoms through the keep's gates. Where was Lai?

Light bauble lamps hung from where arches crisscrossed the vaulting ceiling. The walls and floors of the cavernous hall were smooth, and doorways on the sides led off to other rooms. While officials and Blossoms all gazed in wonder, memories were coming back to Lilian. This had been her home.

Now, though, a long table occupied the center, topped with platters of roasted meats, stir-fried vegetables, decanters of wine, and other delicacies. And knives.

A minister cleared his throat, silencing the excited murmurs, then bowed. When he straightened, he gestured back toward a doorway. Baiting. "His Eminence welcomes you. He has already retired for the afternoon. He bids you to eat and drink. Feel free to wander, but be wary: some hallways are still being reinforced."

All of the lords had undoubtedly been here before, when they served *her* father. Certainly, they knew the layout better than the minister. Still, he continued. "Porters have taken your personal effects to your rooms for the night, and when you are ready—" his eyes shifted to the Blossoms— "a page will guide you there."

Light laughter broke out. The entertainment for tonight was more than just the musicians.

"Miss Lilian," the minister said, beckoning to the hall again, letting everyone know where the decoy was. "Be ready at any time for His Eminence to call on you."

More laughter.

Her cheeks flushed hot, and she searched for Lord Ting. No doubt he would be just as horrified. There was no sign of him, nor of Lai. Jie, Wen, and Master Yin had also disappeared with the rest of the servants. According to plan, Jie would climb to the southeast tower, while Master Yin would take the kitchens as operation headquarters. Wen would be relaying information among the cell members.

"Miss Lilian."

Her heart leaped into her throat. She turned around.

Lord Ting's eyes, usually kind, glinted with an emotion she'd never seen before. Sadness? Anger? It made him look all the more dashing in his court robe. He gave a slight nod. "Come, walk with me."

"I am spoken for tonight." She bowed low, hating herself for having to lie to him. She would keep an eye on him all night, because the clan had assigned him as her target. If he made a move against the decoy, she was to neutralize him.

She raked her gaze across the room. Some of the lords leaned in and whispered among each other, ignoring their favorite Blossoms. Conspiring? Or just chatting? She flashed a hand signal to be relayed. *Send Jie down to eavesdrop.* Because while Jie, in the tower, certainly had a commanding view of the provincial soldiers in the yard, her elf ears would serve the plan best in here.

"Come." Lord Ting took her hand.

It was large and strong. A charge like lightning jolted through her. She gave token resistance before following him through two turns in hallways lined by dozens of wooden doors. He clearly knew where he was going. He came to a stop outside a door.

Her door, when she was a child.

How did she know? Her pulse roared in her ears, almost blocking out his words.

"I am so sorry." He bowed, more like a lord to his lady than a Hummingbird to his Blossom. "I've waited four years. That conniving Lord Yang. I begged him to withdraw his bid, but by then he'd already gifted you to His Eminence. This castle, which was supposed to come to me, became his. I'd hoped to buy your contract and let you be the lady of this house."

Her heart twisted. It really was her dream.

One which she could never realize as a member of the clan. And there was no way to leave it. She certainly couldn't abandon Jie and Wen. She shook her head. "It is my greatest honor to serve His Eminence. After that..."

Lord Ting shook his head. "He has insulted me, and I cannot let that stand."

No, no, no. He couldn't go down this path. Even still, she didn't reach for her bladed hairpin, the one which she'd sworn to drive through his eye if he rebelled. "There's no dishonor in this. Please, just wait."

"He has insulted all of us. He is in this castle, relatively unguarded..."

No, no, no. He was falling into the trap. She shook her head so violently, her brains might've leaked out her ears. "Please, don't say it. Don't even think it." Because then she'd have to kill him.

"Even now, eleven of us—it would've been twelve, except for that coward Lord Tong, who didn't deign to come—are ready to strike."

"What about the imperial guards? One of them is worth a dozen men. Their breastplates are imbued with magic to invoke fear."

"Imperial guards are still men." Lord Ting snorted. "Plus, our soldiers will sweep in, distracting the imperials while we take the Emperor hostage."

Just an hour ago, she'd thought of doing even worse. Now it sounded foolish. She had to talk sense into him with the logical outcome—one that wouldn't come to pass, since her cell would eliminate the threat tonight. "The imperial army will invade in retaliation."

"This plan has been in place for years, waiting for the right moment. Our own armies are ready to occupy strategic points."

How had they planned all this under the clan's nose? How had it slipped through the eyes and ears of the Floating World cell?

"It's a trap," she said. Heavens, had she betrayed the realm? She had.

He cocked his head, brow furrowed. "How do you know?"

"I overheard the imperials talking." She lied to him, yet again.

Horns blared.

He looked up. “That’s our sign. The attack is about to start. I want you to stay in this room until I come for you.” He pulled the handle, and the door opened, revealing a lit room.

It might’ve been her room in the past, but now, it had only a table and chair. On top of the table lay a broadsword and dagger. He strode in and swept them up, tucking the blades into his sash.

There was no turning back. Reaching into her sleeve, she uncorked a vial of musk toxin and dabbed some on her lips.

He spun around and walked toward the door, but she sidestepped and blocked his way.

“Kiss me.” Lifting her chin, she met his eyes before closing hers. “In case either of us dies tonight, I want you to have my first kiss.”

The space between them disappeared as first his body heat, then he himself, filled it. His powerful arms wrapped around her, turning her skeleton to jelly. He lavished kisses up her neck to her chin, each spot he touched vibrating.

Finally, his mouth came to hers, firm but gentle. She parted her lips to invite him in. Sparks raced up and down her spine as his tongue found hers. Her muscles contracted and relaxed, and she found herself on her tiptoes. His scent was intoxicating.

Not as intoxicating as her musk, though. His weight collapsed, and it took all her strength and correct body alignment to keep him from falling on top of her. Perhaps that wouldn’t be such a bad thing, except that if they were found, he’d be seen as stealing the Emperor’s prize.

Better than being seen as an outright rebel. Maybe if a clan member discovered him, they’d realize she’d used the musk toxin; Jie would surely smell it for days after. Lilian would figure out how to explain it away. She lowered him to the floor and claimed his weapons. Then she swept out of the room and closed the door behind her.

Shouts echoed through the halls, followed by the clash of steel. She dashed back through the hallway and paused at the entrance to the main hall. Inside, chaos ruled.

Still, her trained eye picked out the details with one quick glance before she ducked back: the provincial soldiers had swept in, and the imperial guards had rushed out to meet them. No doubt at least two would hang back to protect the decoy; but now, they clashed, ten of the Emperor's finest warriors to at least a hundred enemies. One stood out in his valor, his name *Ma Jun* stitched into his robes, his insignia marking him as newly minted. Officials and servants cowered under the table or against the walls.

Some of her Black Lotus comrades were caught in the fray, their eyes searching the crowd, sometimes delivering a sneak attack to a nearby enemy soldier. The assault had started so fast, they hadn't had a chance to acquire their targets. Yangyang was rising up from where she'd slashed a rebel lord's throat.

Six of the other lords, however, had broken through the imperial guard perimeter and were sprinting toward the Emperor's supposed room, broadswords in hand. All except one, who carried a musket. How had he gotten that inside?

"We need to take him alive," one lord said. "A live emperor is a bargaining chip; a dead emperor is our own death sentence."

Lilian raced back through the hallway. If memory served, it would put her right near the decoy's room. The clang of steel on steel echoed. A crack rang out—the shot of a musket.

She turned the corner.

One of the imperial guards lay in a pool of blood by the closed door, his beautiful breastplate rent. The other's arm hung limply by his side, fending off three of the lords with his curved *dao*. Of those, one was Lord Zu, who'd surrendered his red-lacquered dao; now he wielded a bulkier broadsword with ease. Two of the lords had fallen, one decapitated; the remaining one finished reloading his musket.

"Ready!" He pointed the weapon at the guard as all but Lord Zu jumped back to open a line of fire. "Stand down. You don't need to die."

Lilian drew a throwing star from her thigh and flung it in one motion. With a shout, the guard raised his sword and leaped.

Lord Zu's broadsword flashed. Her star struck the musketman just as his weapon flared, followed by a crack and then a plink.

The musket ball left a dent in the imperial guard's breastplate, but the *dao* slipped from his fingers. With his other hand, he covered his neck, where Lord Zu had hacked him. He slumped, back to the wall. The star had struck the musketman in the throat, and gurgling sounds came from his mouth as he clutched the wound.

The remaining three lords' eyes tracked the weapon from him to her.

She covered her mouth with one hand, while holding the broadsword behind her back. She shook her head and pointed back the way she'd come. "There was someone..."

"Go check it," the Lord Zu said. "We can handle the Emperor."

Nodding, the lord in emerald green stalked over and past. Lilian thrust the blade into his back. Blood soaked through his clothes as he sank to his knees. Lodged in sinew and bone, the sword wrenched from her hands.

"What?" Lord Zu turned and lumbered toward her.

Behind him, the door opened and three throwing stars whirled out, catching the remaining man in the face.

Throwing stars? With no time to think about it, Lilian spun around and ran from the enormous Lord Zu.

She turned three corners in quick succession, halted, and put her back to the wall. She wouldn't stand a chance against Lord Zu without trickery. She drew the dagger and gripped it in a sweaty palm.

The sound of his footsteps approached...then passed by. It took all her control not to blow out a breath.

In the corner of her eye, dim lantern light swept through a dark hallway to the side.

* * *

The Present

As she recounted that night, Tang Li left out Lord Ting's kiss. Instead, she told them that Lilian had seen Master Yin, still in disguise as an imperial page, beckoning him... Because somewhere in Lilian's memories, tangled in Li's brain, she knew Lilian had never revealed the entire story to the others.

"Lilian didn't mention seeing Master Yin at the time." Jie's brows knit together.

"Clearly," Tang Li said, "there was a lot she didn't tell you."

But really, Lilian didn't end up seeing Master Yin until later...

CHAPTER 14

The Present

Even as the sound of horse hooves grew louder in the warrens, Tian hung on Tang Li's words. Not because she told the story so well, but because her narrative raised new questions.

He turned to the others. "What were you doing when the fight broke out?"

Jie sucked on her lower lip and released it with a pop. "Lord Shi had just come out into the courtyard. I'd gotten the relayed message to come down from the tower, before the lords' soldiers started their attack. I'd almost reached the first floor when the horns blared."

"I was on the relay and coming back," Meisha said. "I saw Lord Shi take command of his, Lord Yang's, and Lord Ting's men, and engaged Lord Mu's men."

Yangyang nodded. "Otherwise, we would've been swarmed with enemies."

"Had Lord Shi been warned of the trap?" Tian asked.

Jie shrugged. "He claimed to have gone out for fresh air, and then rallied his troops when the other soldiers mobilized."

Something didn't add up. Tian tapped his chin. "If what Tang Li says is true about Lilian, the Northerners had planned this for a while."

"Maybe Lord Yang decided to betray them in the moment," Jie said.

"What about you?" Tian turned to Wen.

"I was looking for Master Yin, who'd left the command post."

All the girls sighed.

Something else didn't add up, namely the number of lords. "Yangyang killed one traitor, the two imperial guards at the decoy's door killed another two, Lilian killed two more, and fled from a third; someone threw stars into a seventh's face—"

"Master Yan," Jie said. "He was the decoy."

Tian nodded. "Lord Shi was in the courtyard, eight; Lord Ting had been neutralized, nine..."

"That is not what Lilian reported later." Jie shook her head. "She said Lord Ting had killed the two she had, then chased after the Lord Zu—the big one who Tang Li says Lilian fled."

"Anyway, that's nine. Two are unaccounted for."

"Shan-Shan got Lord Fu," Meisha said. "Hairpin to the base of his skull."

"Which leaves—"

"The light Lilian saw," Tang Li said.

* * *

Two Years Ago

It would've been easy to fling a throwing knife into the hooded figure's back, but something urged Lilian to follow him instead. Tiptoeing, she stayed a few paces outside the light of his bauble lamp as he took twists and turns deeper into the fortress.

Whenever he paused and held up the lamp to look back the way he came, she froze. Each time, the hood shaded all but his chin.

After a few turns, he ducked under a fallen beam, where the smooth corridors gave way to roughhewn walls. The floor remained level. The disturbances in the layer of dust suggested at least three people had come this way. She, for one, didn't remember ever seeing a place like this in her youth.

Up ahead, the cloaked man stepped over an inert form, pausing a second to roll it over.

Lai.

His eyes were closed, and his chest rose and fell ever so slightly. If the man tried to kill him, Lilian would have to intervene.

The cloaked man continued. Who was he? Who was unaccounted for?

Lilian crept over to Lai. In the darkness, without Jie's elf vision, it was impossible to tell the extent of his injuries. She patted him, and found no wetness from blood. There was a hard lump on his head, though. Hopefully, it was no more than a concuss—

A click emanated from where the cloaked man had gone. A flash illuminated the hallway. Lilian looked up to see first a cone of light silhouetting the man's form, then a rectangle, and finally a slit, before disappearing altogether.

The corridor plunged into darkness. Squinting, sliding her feet across the floor and holding her hands out, she hurried toward the spot. The scuff of her slippers over the floor echoed back, giving her an idea of her surroundings. When she arrived at the spot where cloaked man had disappeared, she felt around the wall. Her hand found a loose panel, which she pressed.

It clicked, and the wall slid open, again bathing the corridor in light. Beyond the secret door, light flooded the hallway. She blinked several times and looked at the panel—it blended in with the wall so well, she would've never seen it with her eyes alone.

A quick scan revealed another smooth hallway, this one round like a snake's tunnel, ending just six paces at another bare wall. There were no decorations, and it was impossible to tell the source of light. It shone everywhere.

What magic was this? Aksumi sorcerers must've been involved in the castle's construction; and perhaps the dwarfs had dug the tunnels when installing the grain elevator.

Up ahead, a door appeared in the wall and slid open.

The cloaked man walked out and froze. In his hand he held a fist-sized cube of jade.

A cube she'd seen before.

Back then, it was held by a thin man.

Skinny Man, she'd called him.

Memories of that day flooded back. Hiding in a musty root cellar. Being dragged out. Pig Face, slashing Big Brother Ken's throat, and then stabbing Mama in her chest.

And Skinny Man, who was the same height and width as this cloaked stranger, had delivered Daddy's head in one hand, and held the Yu Dynasty imperial seal in the other.

Her fingers trembled of their own accord, and her breaths came in quick hitches. She staggered back a step.

"Lilian." He thrusted the imperial seal behind his back. He advanced on her.

"Lord Yang." She retreated, until she was back in the roughhewn tunnel.

He lowered his hood, revealing Daddy's most trusted advisor. The one who'd betrayed and probably murdered him in his own unassailable castle. Who was probably betraying the Emperor right now.

* * *

The Present

"Lord Yang," Tian said. He'd guessed even before Tang Li had started telling the story, and was sad he hadn't said it first. "He was unaccounted for. Was he part of the plan to betray the Emperor?"

Jie's ears twitched. "Horse hooves approaching. Maybe forty."

"Imperials," Tang Li said. "Lord Shi was implicated by the bombs."

"Wait." Jie held up a hand. "At least a hundred footmen, as well."

Tian ran to the window and looked out. Mounted soldiers flashed in the gaps between the homes' walls, their banner colors impossible to make out in the light of the moons.

"Who is it?" Meisha sidled up beside him and peered through the night.

Tian shook her head. "I don't know."

"Out of the way." A gruff male voice carried through the alleys, his accent Northern. "Imperial business."

Northern accent. They weren't imperial troops, coming to raid Lord Shi's courtyard home. Had Lord Shi's own capital garrison come to secure it against imperial troops?

"It's Lord Yang's men," a female voice said not far in the distance, down below.

Tian squinted, looking to see if he could make out the Great Wall sigil of Lord Yang's Chengfu County. It was all coming together. "Lord Yang took advantage of the trap two years ago to outlast the other lords of the North. He's now trying to frame Lord Shi for the attack on the moons-viewing party."

"Wasn't he going to acquire Lord Ting's county?" Wen asked. "Maybe he conspired with the Steel Orchid in Lord Ting's murder."

Tian ran back to the bed to study the contents of the safe. He held up the stock certificates for Jinjing Lumber, which had profited from selling illegal yue. "They say they belong to Shi Mu, but the characters aren't the same as Lord Shi. I think this is a business name."

"Lord Shi's business?" Yangyang asked.

Tian swept his hand across the residence. "Considering how much money Jinjing Lumber was making, if Lord Shi was an owner, he'd have a lot nicer house."

"Lord Shi was supposed to meet with the Emperor tomorrow," Jie said. "What if he was going to present these stock certificates as proof of someone else's malfeasance? Someone like Lord Yang?"

The women looked among each other.

"This was exactly it," Tang Li said, breaking the silence. "Lord Shi was blackmailing Lord Yang, which was why Lord Yang wanted the contents of the safe. His backup plan was to frame Lord Shi for the attack on the moons-viewing party."

"What about the bloody sheet?" Tian asked. They'd made a big deal of it earlier before going off in another direction. He had to know.

Tang Li shrugged. "I don't think that was important. Lord Shi's trophy, probably."

"A trophy?" Tian cocked his head. Why would someone want to keep bloody sheets?

Wen put hands over his ears, but he struggled free.

Tang Li looked out the window and back. "In any case, those are Lord Yang's men coming to finish the job. I know you are all Black Fists, but can you stand against two hundred men?"

CHAPTER 15

The Present

If only the imperials had come before Lord Yang. Tang Li fretted, knowing that they undoubtedly had orders to kill her. All affection he might have for her aside, she was a loose thread that he'd need to cut at the neck if he was to survive his own plot.

"Make way, or die like your traitor lord," boomed a voice outside the front gate.

It was General Lu, Lord Yang's aide-de-camp. A man short in stature but giant in charisma, he was even more enormous in ambition. He'd hitched his fortunes to Lord Yang's.

"General," the gate guard said. "Lord Shi—"

Steel rasped from its scabbard, and a body tumbled to the ground in two distinct sounds. That death would be nothing compared to the one Lord Yang would deal out if he held the sword.

Jie went to the window, and Tang Li followed.

Lord Yang's men had flooded into the courtyard, the moons highlighting their orange banners.

General Lu strode at their head, a bloodied broadsword in hand. He was a handsome man, with the fine features of the North. He stopped where the chamberlain still lay unconscious on the pavestones. He prodded the prone man with his foot.

Stirring, the poor chamberlain groaned and pushed himself up into a seated position. His wide eyes fixed on the bared weapon.

"Where is Lord Shi's maid, Tang Li?"

Tang Li wrung her hands. She was trapped.

"She was here, but..." The chamberlain moaned as he shifted to a kneel. He looked to the Iridescent Moon. "Heavens, where have the last three hours gone?"

"Who else is here?"

"Just Old Yi."

General Lu turned to survey the main residence, and Jie pulled Tang Li back from the window.

The half-elf lowered her voice to a whisper: "Yangyang, Wen, and Meisha, you head back to the safehouse."

"What about you and Tian?" Wen asked. "And Tang Li?"

Yes, what about them? These Black Fists could probably walk through walls, but Tang Li had only one way out: through the courtyard. Still, new horns blaring in the distance gave hope. Their pitch suggested they belonged to imperials. She peeked back out.

General Lu jerked his hand in a tight arc. "Search."

"Yes, General," all the men answered in unison, followed by a hundred feet filing out across the pavestones.

"Imperial soldiers will come search the premises in response to the bomb," Jie said. "They should be here soon, and Lord Yang doesn't have the authority to search."

Lilian's memories reinforced what Tang Li already knew: Lord Yang only cared about authority insofar as he could get around it.

* * *

Two Years Ago

Lilian stood in the tunnel, where the door to the strange corridor had just closed, facing Lord Yang. He was Skinny Man, one of the four men who'd been there the day of her father's betrayal and murder. The second was Pig Face, most like Lord Tong whom she'd never seen, but who was said to have a round, flat nose. Fat Man and Boney Face, the gardener, were the last two.

Boney Face's gaunt, haunted look remained seared in her memory, and she had never seen anyone like him since. Fat Man, she only remembered a name. Could it be Lord Shi? He did carry a few extra *jin* around the midsection, and to her three-year-old self, that was fat.

Then again, so was Lord Ting's muscled frame.

No, it couldn't be him.

Could it?

"You shouldn't be here," Lord Yang said. "It's dangerous."

"Where is here?" She cast a quick glance around at the round corridor.

"From what I know of history, the castle was originally a dwarf fortress in ancient times, before the orcs enslaved them. That's why everything is so smooth and perfect."

Lilian ran a hand over the wall.

"Our people occupied it after the War of Ancient Gods, and it eventually fell into the hands of the Yu Dynasty. Right before the Hellstorm, they were stockpiling weapons and food in preparation for an invasion of Nothori lands. When the dynasty fell, they fled here. My ancestor was one of their vassals, and he found this secret passage."

"Where you hid the imperial seal." Lilian gestured toward the hand behind his back.

"You recognize it." He scrutinized her. "Thirteen years ago, Lord Yu Qian found it, and was going to deliver it to His Eminence to prove his loyalty. Lord Tong had other ideas. He wanted Lord Yu to use it as a symbol of legitimacy, to have the North rise up against imperial rule."

From years of learning how to detect a lie, Lilian knew from his fidget that he wasn't telling the whole truth. "How did you get ahold of it?"

"Lord Tong turned on Lord Yu. He demanded to know where the seal was. Lord Yu had told me to keep it safe, so I left it here, where I knew Lord Tong could never find it."

The licking of his lips indicated this was an outright lie, one which Lilian's own memories confirmed. "Why are you getting it now?"

"I couldn't before, because Lord Tong always had eyes on me. Then, His Eminence sealed the castle. It was only today that I had a chance to get back in. I am going to hand this to the Emperor."

Yet another lie. More likely, he was using the chaos to escape anyone's scrutiny. Time to break his composure. "Why didn't you just tell him when Lord Lin was renovating?"

"I did." His tone took an air of defensiveness. A first-year Black Lotus initiate would be able to tell it was contrived.

"Then why wait until now?"

He jabbed a finger. "You ask a lot of questions for a whore. I am a second-rank peer of the realm. Know your place."

Of course he'd resort to anger. He was bigger than her, and the shapes of a broadsword and dagger jutted out from under his cloak. It would be best to bait him.

She made her tone righteous. "I am going to tell the Emperor."

Predictably, he swung an open palm toward her cheek.

With a sweep of her hand, she brushed his attack past, caught his arm, and used his own force to launch herself. Wrapping her arms around his neck, she spun and twisted.

The leverage of her entire weight on his head sent him flipping head over heels. He landed hard on his back with an *oomph*.

Still, she'd lost her grip on his wrist as she hit the floor. He pulled his arm free and rolled on top of her. His weight just about crushed the air out of her lungs. Drawing his dagger, he raised it and started to thrust toward her head.

Another arm interposed itself between the blade and her face. Lord Yang bellowed as his arm jerked back. Heaving for air, Lillian rolled over and clambered back to her feet. She looked to see her rescuer.

Master Yin.

She held Lord Yang in a cross-arm lock, his own blade set against his throat.

"Well done, Lilian." Master Yin beamed. "That was an impressive aerial throw."

Lilian smiled. She barely caught the blur that flashed toward Master Yin.

Master Yin, however, released Lord Yang and ducked under the flash of steel. In a fluid motion, she seized his broadsword hilt and shoulder-butted him head-first into a wall. The blade slid out of his scabbard as he crumpled to the floor, and she raised it up.

It blocked the incoming sweep of a beautiful *dao* sword, the force of which sent Master Yin back a step.

Lilian covered her mouth.

The man holding the sword was Boney Face.

Master Yin gawked as well. "Who are you?"

Lilian studied his wiry frame, hidden by an older cut of stealth suit. Without a doubt, he was connected to the Black Lotus. Was he like the Steel Orchids, a former Fist thought to be dead? She started to identify him as the one who'd kidnapped her, but no words came out.

"Tiger have your tongue?" Boney Face's soft voice was the same as in her nightmares.

* * *

The Present

Tang Li considered telling the others what she could of this memory. Lilian had meant for Jie to find out about these things, after all.

There was no time to relate the whole story now, though; not with Lord Yang's men about to overrun Lord Shi's courtyard home.

At the very least, she could tell them about Boney Face. "I need to tell you something."

From where she peeked out the window, Jie turned back. "What?"

Li's mouth opened, but like Lilian's at the time, no sound came out.

CHAPTER 16

The Present

With Lord Yang's men sweeping through the east and west wings of Lord Shi's courtyard home, Jie knew there wasn't much more time. Wen, Yangyang, and Meisha could leap to the top of the outer walls and climb down, and this was a defensible position where she, Tian, and Tang Li could hold out until imperial investigators turned up—though of course, she'd need to disguise Tian, because of his banishment from the capital. From the sound of the horns, they couldn't be more than a quarter phase away.

"Go," she ordered.

Wen shook her head. "We can defend it better as a team."

"The stairs in the foyer are a bottleneck," Meisha said.

Yangyang gestured to the enormous bed. "And if we lose that position, we can retreat back to here and push that up against the door."

"Or," Tian said, "you three can hide in the library and Young Lord Shi Han's room, and attack them from the rear. When you can't hold them off any longer, you can escape through the windows."

The boy was smart. Jie looked out the window again. At least from what she could see, none of the soldiers carried bows, muskets, or repeaters.

"We'll help," Yangyang said, with Meisha nodding.

She studied them. Wen wore ill-fitting blue livery of Lord Wu; Meisha wore the brown of Lord Shi. Yangyang still wore Wen's bust binder, shawl, and skirt. "Weapons?"

"Three throwing stars and a knife," Yangyang said.

Wen withdrew a bladed hairpin and held it up.

"Nothing." Meisha shook her head. She'd had to swim in only her loincloth from the barge to the shore before Tian had given her Jinjing livery.

Jie herself was wearing a plain dress, and like Tian, only had a knife. She went to the sheets and sheared off two strips. The others watched, a look of understanding blooming in their expressions, and then joined in. She tied them around her nose and mouth, and another over her elf ears. When they were done, they all worked to move the bed closer to the door.

"Go to the other rooms," Jie said, "and Yangyang, switch to some of the kid's clothes for better mobility. I will hold them off for as long as I can on the stairs; once I fall back to this room, you attack them from the rear."

"What about me?" Tian asked.

"Protect Tang Li. Now go."

The girls set their fists into their palms and hurried out.

Outside, General Lu's tone sounded urgent. "Where is Lord Shi's dwarf safe?"

Jie peeked back out the window.

"General..." The chamberlain's head was bowed. "I can't betray my lord."

"Lord Shi is a traitor in imperial custody. I've already had to execute your gate guard for abetting him. Now, where is the safe?"

The chamberlain pointed right at Jie. She ducked back before the general's eyes followed his finger.

"Follow me." General Lu's short, rapid footsteps echoed in the courtyard.

Jie strode to the bedroom door. She opened it and stepped through, just in time to see General Lu entering the foyer.

He looked up at her and pointed. "It's Tang Li. Capture her."

Let him believe it.

His men streamed around him, running for the stairs. No doubt they expected her to flee, but instead she ran to the top of the stairs and descended four steps. The way it hugged the foyer wall to its right, the ascending men would only be able to stab and backhand.

The first clambered up, eyes filled with bloodlust. He stabbed.

She twisted out of the thrust and slashed his palmar tendons. He screamed and stared as his broadsword slipped from his fingers. With a flick of her foot, she sent it flying toward Young Lord Shi Han's room, from which Yangyang would emerge. In the same motion, she turned her leg into a hook-kick into his head, sending him back into the next soldier.

Another tried to slink around his fallen comrades; while he was preoccupied, Jie set the knife between her teeth, seized his hand, and twisted his sword free. She used it to deflect another enemy's stab into the last's leg, but then had to jump up one step to avoid one of them grabbing her foot.

"It's just a girl," General Lu shouted.

Injured men threw themselves over the bannister, to be replaced by others. She was quickly losing ground to their surge, but had managed to capture two more swords and throw them to the study door. At the top of the stairs, she turned and ran back toward Lord Shi's room.

To think, she'd stayed back to protect Tang Li, a criminal.

Because the Triad fixer had Lilian's memories, and in a perverse way, her friend still lived inside her.

* * *

The Present

Pulse racing, Tang Li stood beside Tian, still pushing Lord Shi's heavy bed closer to the door. New memories came back to her, of another desperate time where all seemed lost.

* * *

Two Years Ago

With this mysterious Boney Face and Master Yin facing off, and Lord Yang lying unconscious by the wall, Lilian climbed to her feet.

"Come now, Little Yinyin, you don't recognize me?" Boney Face settled into a Black Lotus defensive stance.

Master Yin's eyes roved over him, and her brow furrowed. "Nobody has called me that since… Your clothes. You must've been one of us, but I don't recognize you." She probed with a feint.

Boney Face didn't even move. "Come now, Little Yinyin, you didn't think I would fall—"

Master Yin surged with three slashes so blindingly fast and strong, they would've left Lilian in four pieces.

The shifts Boney Face made in his position were so subtle, he'd barely moved. Steel flashed.

Gasping, Master Yin hunched over. Her hand covered her stomach. Blood leaked out from a surgical cut.

"No!" Lilian started forward.

Without even looking away from Master Yin, he set the edge of the blade to her throat.

She froze. The precision was like the stories of Master Yan in his youth.

Now that his guard was open, Master Yin lunged with a two-handed stab.

He turned his body, letting her broadsword pass within a hairsbreadth of his gut. In the same motion, his weapon left Lilian's throat and raked across Master Yin's.

Even as her body fell, he kicked her sword in a gentle arc, which landed it in Lilian's hands.

He didn't even care that she was armed. He knelt down beside Master Yin and closed her unseeing eyes. "I'm sorry to have to do this."

With three fluid moves, he slashed across her palmar tendons, nicked her femoral artery, and stabbed her in the gut.

Lilian covered her mouth to bury a scream at the desecration. No—it was a scene manipulation, to create a false narrative.

"Little Yinyin." Shaking his head. He rolled her over and looked up. "Such a waste. You know, she was the Seedling to the Beauty in the original Chrysanthemum Pavilion. After her Plucking, the clan decided her blade skills were too valuable to waste on the Floating World, and reassigned her as an Enforcer."

The Beauty... She'd been one of the three masters struck down in their youth, along with the Surgeon and the Architect. They'd been contemporaries of the Steel Orchids. Though while the latter had gathered information in the Floating World, the former had gone on the clan's most critical missions. This man probably knew all of them. "Who are you?" she asked.

"Your elders would know me as the Surgeon."

She gasped. He was supposed to have died seventeen years ago.

He gestured to her weapon, the one he'd given her. "You have a sword in your hand. Why don't you avenge your cell leader's death?"

As if Lilian even had a chance. Master Yin was one of the best, if not *the* best, of the clan in sword fighting. She flung the broadsword to the ground behind her, lest he see it as a threat.

Who was she fooling, besides herself? She was no threat to this man.

"Wise decision." He sheathed the sword into a red-lacquered scabbard, which looked to be one of the rebel lord's. His eyes watched hers, and he held it up for her to see.

It had belonged to the large man who'd chased her. He'd surrendered it to imperial officials before entering the fortress. Lord Zu. The Surgeon was making it look as if Lord Zu had killed Master Yin.

He grinned, which made his head look like a pirate's flag. "Yes, Lord Zu. I left him by your male comrade. Lai, was it?"

How did he know so much about the cell? Did he know about the musk toxin? Lillian fiddled with the vial, using her long sleeves to hide her hand. Draw him closer, and she might have a chance of subduing him.

"When the clan comes to investigate, it will look as if Lord Zu killed Little Yinyin; that Lai stabbed him in the back, and with his dying breath, he knocked Lai out."

Would that be what the clan thought? At least Lai was still alive. "Why are you letting me live?"

"You haven't figured it out yet? Why I saved you, thirteen years ago? Certainly I left enough clues in your memory."

She'd often wondered. Was she an unwitting mole in the clan?

"Unless...were you able to see the three full moons?"

She gave a tentative nod.

"If you aren't smart enough to figure it out, maybe I chose poorly." He shook his head. "It certainly wouldn't be the first time. Let me give you a hint: coming to this castle, you should now know who you really are."

All her final lost memories had come together here. "I am the last heir of the North."

And she now knew who her enemies were.

Though why would that matter to him?

"I chose well." Grinning again, he held up a bundle of paper. "Now, here's your choice: this correspondence can clear your father's name, while confirming the treachery of the lords who died here today. In return, you will hide the Yu imperial seal for when you are ready to challenge the Emperor. And you may never reveal Lord Yang's complicity."

The first, she wanted; the second, she might not care about; and the third, well...Lord Yang was a disgusting opportunist who'd first betrayed Father and had today tried to betray the Emperor. He deserved to die. "What's my other choice? Will you kill me?"

"Of course not. Your other choice is to expose Lord Yang, but then I will take the seal and the correspondence with me, forever branding your father as an incompetent traitor."

Would he really let her live with what she'd learned? That the Surgeon still lived? No, she still had a third option: the musk toxin.

He looked back at Master Yin's body. Here was her chance to subdue him.

But no. She knew who her enemies were. When he met her gaze, she gestured behind her, to where Lord Yang started to groan. "What about him? He might know who I am."

"The musk toxin you planned to use on me: use it on him instead."

So he knew all along.

Clear Father's name. Her family name, even if no one would know she belonged to the Yu family. Let Yang go.

It was a small price to pay. She nodded. "I accept your terms."

"Good." The Surgeon went over to Lord Yang. "If you're pretending to be unconscious, just know that I have eyes and ears everywhere. If you reveal Lilian, or any of what happened today, I will make your death very, very slow."

Lord Yang didn't move; whether out of fear or unconsciousness, it was impossible to tell.

The Surgeon kicked the imperial seal up into the air, and caught it. He handed it to her.

She received it in two hands. Here it was, the symbol of her ancestors' authority over Cathay. Could she really use it to rally the North against the Empire? She looked up and met his eyes.

They locked on her, holding her in place like an Ayuri snake charmer did a cobra. "Of course, I am not one to leave things to chance." He waved his hands and fingers in front of her.

Too late, she closed her eyes. Even now, his words tugged on her.

"You will never reveal Lord Yang's complicity, nor that the Surgeon still lives."

No, she wouldn't. Couldn't.

When she opened her eyes again, she studied him. He'd tried to win her trust, to make her think the decision was her own. It was all an illusion. With his *Tiger's Eye* glaring down on her, she would've never been able to reveal him or Lord Yang, anyway.

"Put this near Lord Zu." He handed her the *dao*, and in a flash of black, he swept back through the halls.

All the tension in Lilian's body released. With a deep breath, she unrolled the correspondence and made a quick scan of the contents. She suppressed a gasp. Her father, Lord Yu, had intended to deliver the Yu Dynasty seal to the Emperor, but several of the lords had objected. Lord Zu, in particular, had written about rallying the North behind it. For his part, Lord Ting had supported her father's decision. Mention of Lord Yang suggested he'd been included in the discussion, yet there were no letters from him.

Her father, innocent and wrongly murdered in the Emperor's name.

Now, she needed to control the narrative just as the Surgeon had, part of which meant ensuring Lord Ting was safe. She tore off a strip of her dress, wrapped it around the jade seal, and placed the bundle with the correspondence into her hanging sleeve. She then dabbed the musk on Lord Yang's neck.

A new plan crystalized in her mind. Kneeling beside Master Yin, she said a quick prayer for her peaceful repose, and also for forgiveness. Master Yin had been strict, but fair; supportive but not particularly kind. Lilian uncorked her remaining musk toxin, spread it over Master Yin's lips, then stashed it into her robes.

Picking up Lord Yang's lantern, she traced her steps back. Lai still lay on the floor, Lord Zu dead atop of him. Lai held the hilt of a knife, whose blade was lodged in the back of the lord's neck. It looked just as the Surgeon had said. She placed the scabbarded sword under his limp fingers.

Lai groaned, and tried to shift under Lord Zu's weight.

Lilian knelt down beside him. "Are you all right? I'll go get help."

"No." Lai's hand closed around hers. "I can't take this life any longer. Just kill me."

Guilt knotted her stomach. All her fault. Despite the way he'd bullied her, he didn't deserve this. She pried the knife from his fingers. "I'll help you escape."

He shook his head. "Nobody ever escapes the clan. Kill me."

She couldn't tell him the Surgeon or Steel Orchids had escaped, even if she wanted to. "I won't."

"Then give me the knife, and I'll do it myself."

"How about if we scar your face? They'll have no choice but to reassign you. This is your chance." Would he betray her afterwards?

He opened and closed his mouth a few times, then nodded.

Clenching the knife, she gritted her teeth. "Alright."

Seizing her hand, he guided the edge over his throat.

Lilian gasped and applied pressure to the wound. Still, his cut was too deep and precise. His blood spurted out, and all she could do was hold his hand until the life drained out of his eyes. She had to wipe tears from hers. They'd never been friends; unlike the sisters of the cell, who'd formed a deep bond over shared experiences, he'd always kept up his guard. To think how differently things might've worked out if any number of circumstances had changed.

Rising, she returned the knife to the neck wound and wrapped Lai's fingers around the hilt. She stuffed most of the correspondence into Lord Zu's robes, but kept two letters exonerating her father. Then she ran back toward her old room, the one where she'd left Lord Ting. Bodies littered the halls; she retrieved a curved dagger from one of the fallen lords.

Her path took her by an entrance to the central hall. Inside, Lord Shi stood tall above the rest. His, Lord Ting's, and Lord Yang's soldiers had forced the rebels' surrender. The enemies knelt disarmed, hands on their heads. It didn't appear as if any of their lords had survived.

The imperial servants all knelt too, along with the cell sisters who'd returned to their guise of defenseless Blossoms. If anyone had seen their sneak attacks on the rebels, they'd find out in the coming days.

Jie and Wen weren't among them, and Lilian's stomach twisted. She searched among the dead for a dress or pointed ear.

Not seeing any sign of them, she continued toward the room.

The door stood ajar, and shadows moved within. Of all the doors in the hall, they'd found the one where she'd hidden Lord Ting. Her grip tightened around the knife hilt, and she crept nearer. She stopped at the threshold and peeked in.

* * *

The Present

Tang Li's heart pounded, and her arms and shoulders ached. At Tian's suggestion, they placed the bed in a position where the door would open only wide enough for the half-elf to slip through. The boy had been quite exacting about it; but though he stood there with his broadsword, ready to attack anyone skinny or desperate enough to squeeze through, Tian was still just a boy.

And she was no warrior or Black Fist. All the screaming and yelling made her want to curl up in a ball.

A wave of relief washed over her as Jie sidled through the space and slammed the door shut. How strange an emotion, given that the half-elf had threatened her with torture less than an hour before.

It had to be because of Lilian's thoughts and memories, still living in her. Even now, they compelled her to mention the Surgeon. "I need to tell you something. The—" Surgeon! The name died in her throat.

Jie turned to her as she came around to the other side of the bed to help push. "Go on?"

"Lilian was..." Yu Mei, daughter of Yu Qian, the... "last heir of the North." Again, her mouth refused to speak certain things. As before, the Surgeon's *Tiger's Eye* blocked her, just as it had Lilian.

Which raised a new question. Just how had Lilian told her these things?

The door shuddered as someone large slammed against it.

CHAPTER 17

The Present

From where she hid in the study, Wen listened to the sound of screaming men and clashing metal. In a close-quarters fight, Jie could hold them off—

Jie's feet scampered through the hall, followed by the tromp of boots on wood. At least sixteen men had climbed the stairs and reached the mezzanine. When their footsteps stopped and shoulders thudded against the door, Wen slipped out of the study and into the hall.

The men were all surrounding the door to Lord Shi's bedroom. Sweeping up the broadsword Jie had thrown there, Wen tiptoed over to the closest man, covered his mouth, and slashed his throat. He let out a gurgled cry.

The closest of his comrades turned around, only to receive a throwing star to the face. It had whirled right by Wen's ear.

Several more broke off from the main group and charged. The wide hallway would allow them to envelop her, so Wen backed away, taking open shots as they appeared. Two more throwing stars flashed across her vision, striking two men who could've flanked her.

Wen reached the doorway, and in the corner of her vision, Meisha burst out of Young Lord Shi's room and stabbed yet another soldier. Still, they were outnumbered.

"Flee!" Wen yelled. She turned and ran toward the study window.

Behind her, bootsteps came closer.

She leaped, turning over midair to slide chest-first over the desk and out the window. Grabbing the windowsill, she brought her knees up, dug her feet into the wall, and sprang off. With a backflip, she landed on the top of the outer wall.

A cursing soldier poked his head out the window and found her. His jaw dropped. "How did she do that?"

Further down the wall, Meisha, followed by Yangyang, landed on light feet.

Beckoning them, Wen dashed along the top of the wall, then turned along the west side. There was a line of sight to one of Lord Shi's bedroom windows, and she looked up, hoping the others were holding the attackers off.

In the courtyard, Lord Yang's archers were taking aim with flaming arrows.

Insanity! The courtyard homes were so close in the warrens. Though most were made of bricks, they had wooden supports and furnishings; if the wind picked up...

Closer now, the imperial horns blared.

Just like that night at Cloud Castle.

* * *

Two Years Ago

Horns sounded in the courtyard and carried through the halls of Cloud Castle, causing an unconscious Lord Ting to stir at Wen's feet. He was quite handsome, though certainly not as dashing when asleep. And there was only one way his slumber could be so deep.

"I think Lilian was here." She looked up and met Jie's gaze.

The half-elf sucked on her lower lip, concern etched into her features. No doubt she was thinking the same thing.

What was Lord Ting doing here? What had Lilian done, and why?

Then Jie's nose twitched, and her expression brightened. She bolted to her feet and turned to the door.

Lilian stood there, her gown stained with blood. It didn't stop Jie from rushing over and wrapping her arms around her. Lilian's tension and worry visibly melted away, and Wen couldn't help but join her sisters in a hug. Lilian shuddered as she broke into tears.

Jie leaned back and surveyed her. "Any injuries? You have blood on you."

A lot of it. Wen patted Lilian down, inspecting her, but found no cuts in her dress, nor any open wounds. She pulled back when Wen tried to lift her sleeve and examine her arm, which raised more questions than it answered.

Words dying in her throat, Lilian shook her head. Whatever she'd experienced must've been traumatic. She'd tell them when she was ready. Jie ran her fingers through Lilian's hair and pressed their foreheads together.

"Where were you?" Wen asked.

"I was trying to save the decoy by leading Lord Zu away. I lost him deeper in the castle, and was coming back here for Lord Ting."

"What do we do about him?" Wen scanned him again. "He's clearly been affected by musk toxin."

"The lips, from the scent." Jie raised an eyebrow.

Lilian's cheeks flushed red. "Maybe one of the sisters got here."

Jie sucked on her lower lip, while Wen fiddled with her pinkie. They exchanged glances. Certainly Lilian wouldn't lie to them, her two best friends.

Would she?

"It will still look suspicious," Jie said.

Very. Even now, something weighed down Lilian's sleeve.

She was never a good liar, though, and she showed no signs of a lie now. She nodded. "How did you find him among all these rooms?"

"How do we ever find things before anyone else?" Wen tapped Jie's nose.

"Let's leave him here," Lilian said. "With the door closed. Assuming a systematic search, it will take time before anyone searches this deep in the castle. And I think I know a way to delay them."

* * *

The Present

Heart pounding in his chest, Tian helped Tang Li and Jie push the bed up against the door, then started piling more furniture on top of it. The door shuddered and splintered as Lord Yang's men kicked and threw their shoulders into it. Given their average size, the frequency of their ramming, and the thickness of the door, they'd break through in a few more minutes.

Imperial horns blared again, nearer than the last time.

It would be close. Tian's palms sweated as he gripped the broadsword Jie had given him. Its weight was all wrong, so imbalanced compared to the curved *dao* he was accustomed to.

Someone yelled outside. Wen? It was hard to tell with the cacophony of sounds.

The ramming stopped. Footsteps retreated down the stairs. Had the imperials already arrived?

At his side, Jie's pretty ears twitched. She shoved them to the floor. "Cover!"

Outside, bowstrings twanged.

Arrows flew in, their heads wrapped in flaming cloth.

Jie swiped one out of the air, just before it hit Tian. Another landed in the bed, and the sheets lit. In a few seconds, the carpet was ablaze, and smoke started to fill the room. More arrows arced in through the windows.

"We'll need to jump," Jie said, pointing to the west window.

"I can't." Tang Li shook her head.

The arrows' only possible arc left a safe path, and Tian kept low as he hurried to the window.

Wen, Yangyang, and Meisha all stood on the top of the wall, just eight feet away and nine feet down. Still, the landing area was narrow for anyone who had anything larger than girls' feet. For now, they were out of the archers' line of sight.

"Hurry!" Wen waved furiously. "We'll catch you."

Jie reached his side and took hold of his wrist. She prodded him toward the window. "Go."

Resisting, Tian turned back and held out a hand. "Tang Li, first."

The poor lady was huddling in a corner, coughing, with only a narrow path between the flames. *Hold the butterfly with care...*

"Go, I'll get her once you're safe."

Using a technique little Yuna had taught him, he twisted out of Jie's grasp. He dashed back through the flames and arrows. More bells rang in the streets, their tone and pitch belonging to the fire brigade. When he reached Tang Li, she was curled into a ball.

"We can do this!" He took her wrists and pulled her to her feet.

Her eyes met his, and she shook her head. Ignoring her protests, he pulled her back toward the window. Somewhere along the way, Jie had taken her other hand.

"Over there!" a soldier yelled from the courtyard.

Tian gritted his teeth. If he was pointing at Wen and the others...

They reached the window, and he looked back toward the courtyard. A gesticulating General Lu barked some orders, and the archers began jogging to the western end of the yard.

Tang Li looked through and down. "I can't."

Jie pushed Tang Li toward the window. Every fiber of Tian's being screamed to ensure everyone was safe before he escaped, but now, he had to demonstrate. "Watch me."

He climbed out feet-first and grabbed the inside of the windowsill. He looked over his shoulder to where the women held their arms outstretched to catch him. It would be fine. He just needed to push off a little, and then gravity would do the rest. He looked back and gave Tang Li a reassuring nod.

Then he jumped, twisting in midair so as to better see how he was falling. His knees jolted as he landed, heels catching the far edge of the wall's top. Arms flailing, he started to slip, but hands caught him, keeping him from falling another ten feet.

"Thank the Heavens he lost weight," Yangyang said.

Ignoring her, Tian turned and looked back up. Jie was already prodding Tang Li out the window. The poor woman sat on the window sill, her knees bent and feet pressed against the wall.

"You can do it," Tian shouted.

An arrow whizzed by his head, followed by two more in the space between them. He turned to see some archers nocking arrows, others loosing.

"On my command," General Lu fumed. "Three teams, constant volleys!"

He looked back up, just in time to see Jie shove Tang Li.

Screaming, the woman stretched out her arms as she tumbled through the air.

Yangyang and Wen caught her, and in the same motion helped her down to the outside of the wall and followed with forward flips.

Meisha, with her long limbs, jumped and spider-climbed down between it and the neighboring wall.

She reached up and beckoned. "Hurry!"

Tian looked back to the window.

Jie was hesitating. Flames now licked the side of the building, and a constant stream of arrows filled the air between them.

"Hurry," all the women yelled. Yangyang pointed toward the head of the path between the walls, where some of Lord Yang's men were rounding the corner.

He caught a flash of Jie disappearing back into the room. Flames belched through the window. He gasped. Nobody could've survived that.

CHAPTER 18

The Present

If anyone could survive this fire, it was Jie. Not because elf blood made her fireproof—Black Lotus training had proven that not to be the case—but because she was harder to kill than a cockroach. Just before a flaming supporting beam collapsed by the window, she dashed deeper into the bedroom.

Every piece of wood cracked and blazed, leaving a narrow path, made more difficult by more falling beams. She leaped into Lord Shi's safe, contorting herself so that she'd fit, and then shut the door. If it was like the diagrams and specifications she'd seen, the safe could protect its contents from fire for six hours. If those specifications were wrong, there'd be baked half-elf for dinner.

Of course, no one would ever find her. If Lord Shi was executed for treason before Wen and the others exonerated him, the safe's combination would be lost. She had one of the two keys, too.

She felt around; an unlocking lever was there. She blew out a breath, before realizing she needed to conserve air. If she passed out, the safe would become her final resting place.

There was always the *Viper's Rest*, which would slow her body functions down, but that risked severe amnesia from which a practitioner might never recover. Back at the temple, she'd had a some close calls with even a few minutes using the technique.

Maybe that wouldn't be a bad thing. No matter how much she'd tried to banish her feelings for Lilian, and the profound sense of loss at her death, not an hour went by that her heart didn't ache. To forget all of that would be a sweet mercy.

No, she had to live and remember. Tang Li had more to tell about Lilian's betrayal.

Even with her keen hearing, no sounds from outside penetrated the safe's walls. In the utter silence, Jie thought back to the night of the Emperor's trap, after all the rebels had been captured or slain.

* * *

Two Years Ago

By the time Jie emerged from the room with Wen and Lilian, all sounds of fighting had ended in Cloud Castle. With Lilian in the lead, they returned to the central hall. The combined forces of Lords Ting, Yang, and Shi controlled the room. Rebel soldiers who hadn't fled now knelt, hands bound behind their backs.

With the exception of Master Yin and Lai, the other members of the cell huddled together in a corner, sobbing in what was undoubtedly feigned disbelief and horror. Imperial officials now scurried about, conferring with Lord Shi.

He stood over seven bodies of the rebel lords. Jie noted that some bore subtle injuries only the Black Lotus Fists could deal. Save for Lord Tong, who hadn't come to Cloud Castle, only Lord Yang, Lord Ting, and Lord Zu were unaccounted for.

An imperial official, flanked by two of the surviving imperial guards, approached Jie. Wearing a blue robe, the symbols marked him as the Emperor—though in the case, it was the decoy. He looked up, revealing Master Yan.

Jie held back a smile.

Have you seen Master Yin, he signed. *Or Lai?*

Jie gave a subtle shake of her head.

What about Lords Ting, Yang, or Zu?

No, Jie signed back.

Lord Zu was chasing me. I last saw him heading that way. Lilian tilted her head down one of the hall's exits, into a hallway.

I saw you. Well done. Take me there. Master Yan flashed a rare, approving smile. He turned to the imperial guards. "These Blossoms saw where Lord Zu went. They will take us there."

The group followed Lilian deeper into fortress, eventually coming to a fallen beam. To Jie's sensitive nose, the scent of blood hung heavy in the air. Beyond it, the walls were roughhewn. The area was unlit, and Master Yan withdrew a light bauble to guide the way.

Lai lay under Lord Zu in a pool of blood. Neither moved.

Jie swallowed her shock. Poor Lai. He'd been cruel at the temple, but life as a Peach Bottom in the Floating World had changed him. At least he'd died killing a dangerous enemy.

Master Yan knelt down and said a prayer. He paused before standing, and reached into Lord Zu's robes. He withdrew several rolled-up scrolls and tucked them into his sleeve.

Jie lifted her head as a new scent floated by. Jasmine and oiled steel, mixed with musk. Master Yin. She beckoned the others to follow.

Master Yin's body lay there, with multiple sword wounds. She must've faced off against Lord Zu. He might be one of the few people who could go toe-to-toe with her and walk away. And though he'd won, she must've injured him so grievously that Lai had been able to finish him off. The musk toxin clung to her, coming from her lips.

So Lilian hadn't lied about her not being the one who'd incapacitated Lord Ting. Jie, and probably Wen too, had been ready to lie for her. Now that wasn't necessary. Why had Master Yin opted not to kill him?

A low moan emanated from the corner, and Master Yan held up his light. It shone on a figure dressed in court robes, pushing himself up into a seated position. He shielded his eyes and blinked.

Lord Yang.

How had he ended up here?

"Your Eminence?" he said, bowing to Master Yan.

"No," Master Yan said. "What happened here?"

Lord Yang blinked a few more times. His eyes fell on Lilian and narrowed. Lilian shied back.

A very light musk scent clung to him, as well. Jie sucked on her lower lip. Master Yin must've poisoned him too.

"I saw Lord Zu pursuing Lilian, and I gave chase. Then it's all a haze. The woman touched me on the neck. That's the last thing I remember."

Just what was Master Yin doing?

"Thank you, Lord Yang," Master Yan said. He motioned to the imperial guards. "Take Lord Yang back to the main hall. I have a few more questions for these Blossoms."

The imperial guards dropped to a knee, fist to the ground. Rising, they marched off, Lord Yang in tow.

Master Yan let out a long sigh. "You have done well, Lilian, even if you didn't realize it."

In the corner of Jie's vision, Lilian covered her mouth.

"You act surprised. All these years when I was supposedly trying to alter your memories with the *Tiger's Eye*, I was conditioning you to uncover a traitor in the Floating World."

"A traitor?" Wen asked.

"Why didn't you tell us?" Jie scowled. How could he not trust them?

"The less you knew, the better. After the fire which destroyed our cell, too much slipped past our information net. The Emperor's enemies knew more than they should. I had hoped it was just the lack of experience as we reestablished the cell, but even after ten years, the leaks and misinformation continued."

The pieces were coming together. Master Yin was heading the cell. She must've conspired with the rebellious lords. Why had she tried to kill Lord Zu, but spared Lords Yang and Ting?

Master Yan continued, "Lilian subconsciously left a trail for me to follow. The trap tonight was not just for rebel lords, but for the mole inside the cell. As of now, my worst fears have been realized: it was Master Yin. We will need to make sure she didn't turn anyone else."

No. Nobody else in the cell could've done this. Jie shook her head.

"Now, I need you all to sleep." He waved his hands and fingers in an intricate motion.

Darkness encroached on the edges of Jie's vision. The last thing she saw was Master Yan catching Lilian and Wen as they crumpled to the floor.

* * *

The Present

Jie woke from dreams of love and betrayal to a darkness not even her elf vision could penetrate. Panic threatened to engulf her, but she took a deep breath.

A hot breath.

The tight confines had her balled up, and the air was stale and musty.

She was in Lord Shi's safe, with no idea how much time had passed. It was utterly, maddeningly silent.

Releasing the locking mechanism, she kicked the safe door open.

Smoky air and early-morning sunlight greeted her.

Joints aching from the position she'd been in, she started to hop out, but halted to keep from falling two stories.

The roof and floor of Lord Shi's main residence had collapsed into charred timbers and shattered tiles down below. The outer walls remained intact, though the bricks bore scorch marks.

"You're awake!" Sitting in a first-floor window, Tian clapped.

Wen, in a plain dress, rose from beside him. "Thank the Heavens. I was worried you'd never come out. Did you go into the *Viper's Rest*? Do you know who you are?"

With a shiver, Jie half-shook her head, half-nodded. "No *Viper's Rest.*"

"What's the *Viper's Rest*?" Tian asked.

"It's pretending like you're dead." Wen patted him on the head. "But you might forget you who you are. I hope you never forget who you are."

Tian shuddered. "I'll never do the *Viper's Rest*, then."

"How long I was in there?" Jie asked. "What's happened?"

"About five hours." Wen splayed her fingers. "We got away before the imperials arrived and ordered General Lu to withdraw."

"Then," Tian chirped, "we presented our evidence to Master Yan, and he told the Emperor that Lord Yang was trying to frame Lord Shi."

Jie nodded. No doubt the exoneration would save Lord Shi and his son from beheading. "And Lord Yang? Is he still alive?"

"He fled to Cloud Castle. His armies have fortified it, and they are receiving supplies from Rotuvi."

EPILOGUE

The Present

Tian always felt relaxed around Master Yan. He was one of the few people, in addition to Princess Kaiya and Peng Kai-Long, who understood him. It looked more and more like Wen, and perhaps Jie, might join that very short list.

"You've done well." Master Yan's eyes roved over all the evidence Tian had connected in the safehouse. "We'd always wondered how Lord Yang had raised the money to make his bid on Lilian's virginity."

No one ever complimented Tian. Heat rose into his cheeks. "After looking at the ledgers from the gambling dens, I'm sure of it. There's more, though."

"Go on."

"We've been taught that eighteen years ago, Lord Yu planned to unite the North against the Jade Throne, but that Lords Yang, Tong, and Shi defeated him."

"Yes." Master Yan nodded. "In reality, he was loyal. We only learned the truth two years ago in Cloud Castle, when we uncovered correspondence between Lord Yu and the other lords of the North. Lord Zu was the ringleader in betraying him. We have maintained the deception in hopes—"

"—that the real conspirators would feel either desperate or safe enough to make a move."

"Very smart. We assumed our cell in the Floating World would uncover their conspiracies, especially after Master Yin's death."

Tian shook his head. "But she wasn't a mole, and the misinformation and leaks came from the Steel Orchid and Lilian. Lord Yang was able to slip through the Floating World's net using Tang Li and the Triads to first set up Lord Ting, and then make his attempt to frame Lord Shi last night. Two years before that, he probably allied with Lord Zu at Cloud Castle, only to turn on him in the ambush. He was also at Cloud Castle when Lord Yu was slain. He has been positioning himself to be the most powerful lord in the North for almost twenty years now."

"I agree. You are very bright, Little Tian."

"There's more."

Master Yan raised an eyebrow. "Go on."

"Lord Yang was deep inside Cloud Castle on the night of the ambush. Why?"

"He said he was following Lord Zu to save Lilian, and she corroborated his story."

"But now we know she was a traitor. And we all know that Lord Zu was one of the best swordsmen in the realm. Lord Yang wouldn't have stood a chance."

"Which means he was down there for another reason."

"The Yu imperial seal." Tian paused for effect. When Master Yan didn't respond, he continued: "He was Lord Yu's trusted confidante, and was at the castle when Lord Yu was killed trying to deliver it to the Emperor. He could've hidden it at the time, which is why he spent sixty-thousand yuan to gain Cloud Castle."

"Where he is now."

* * *

The Present

Tang Li knelt on the floor of a Black Lotus safehouse, where strings connected piles of familiar items: parts from the crossbow which she'd provided Gardener Ju to kill Lord Ting. Faceless Chang's mask. Ledgers from gambling dens. And the contents of Lord Shi's safe. Supposedly, Tian had arranged their positions on the floor, making her wonder if he'd smoked yue.

A middle-aged man sat across from her. Whether she'd seen him before or not, it was impossible to tell because he was just so plain. From Lilian's memories, however, she knew him to be Master Yan, and she'd just spent the last ten hours answering his meticulously insightful questions.

"Now," he said. "You know about our clan. Why should we let you live?"

Her chest squeezed around her heart. All she ever wanted was to earn enough money to live an easy life, running a teahouse. Now, she might die without ever experiencing joy in life. "You can make me forget, right? With the *Tiger's Eye*? Like Lilian did."

"It's just as easy to kill you."

Was this it? No—if so, she wouldn't be alive now. He was offering her a way out. To prove her worth. "Lilian found the Yu Dynasty imperial seal, and I know where it is."

And she knew more, thanks to Lilian's memories.

* * *

Two Years Ago

The most common reason a Floret of the Floating World would remain unplucked after her sixteenth birthday was that she had not yet flowered with Heaven's Dew. Lilian had the most unique reason, one which had never happened in the past, nor would likely ever happen again—since before this week, Emperors had never participated in these Floating World rituals.

What the realm thought was not that far off from the truth: the reception at Cloud Castle had been so lively, the Emperor did not have time to Pluck her.

At least, that was the public reason for why she found herself in the castle of Sun-Moon Palace a full two days later. The Chrysanthemum Pavilion had to honor the contract, after all.

As with the concubines of the previous two dynasties, nuns of the Praise Moon Temple stripped Lilian bare, checked her for weapons and poisons, and then rolled her into a luxurious wool carpet. The only thing she wore was a blindfold.

Still, the Black Lotus *Seeing Ears* technique, combined with her own knowledge of the castle grounds, allowed her to track where they carried her. How ironic that her female ancestors of the Yu Dynasty had been treated this way, before the Wang Dynasty Founder's Consort had banned the harem when she ruled as Queen Regent.

The archaic safety measures wouldn't have mattered in her case: she knew many ways to kill a man, and even the blindfold could be used as a garrote.

Instead, she chose a very different kind of weapon: she opted to continue abstaining from her contraceptive herbal formulas. With her wet with Heaven's Dew, the Emperor's seed might find fertile ground. A son begotten of both dynasties would be the perfect tool to vanquish her ancestors' vanquishers.

Justified as she might be, guilt still pricked at her. She'd besmirched Master Yin's good name, when it had been the supposedly deceased Steel Orchids and the Surgeon who'd compromised the secret information coming out of the Floating World. Though Zhuli and Shan-Shan had passed Master Yan's questioning under the *Tiger's Eye* like all the other members of the

Floating World cell, they'd been reassigned to the temple. No doubt they'd remain under the elders' watchful eyes until they'd proven their loyalty ten times over.

Try as Lilian might to assuage her conscience—by rationalizing that it was the Surgeon's *Tiger's Eye* that prevented her from revealing the true culprits—she'd already chosen of her own free will to betray Master Yin's memory.

For the North.

For Lord Ting, who'd been denied the honor of Plucking her.

The nuns set her down in a pavilion on Sun-Moon Lake, nowhere near the Emperor's main residence. Perhaps the Emperor didn't want his five-year-old daughter, Princess Kaiya, to ask why he was entertaining a young woman wrapped up in a rug. Lilian had seen her playing with her friend, the son of Lord Zheng, on her way in.

With *Seeing Ears*, she listened. The waves of the lake lapped against the shore nearby, barely audible over the Emperor's excited, heavy breaths. The nuns' footsteps retreated, and they closed the doors behind them.

What should she do now? In the Floating World, a Plucking followed only a few possible scripts, none which involved being wrapped in a carpet at the Emperor's feet. Play innocent? Or seductive?

Three nights ago, she'd planned on the former for Lord Ting.

That's what she'd do now.

Within the tight confines of the rug, she wriggled to cover her chest with one arm, her Gates to Heaven with the other hand.

The Emperor's breathing came nearer, heavier and more urgent, forcing her to take a deep breath to calm her nerves. The folds of the rug loosened, then opened, and she cast her gaze down and to the side.

He gasped. Heat flared in her cheeks, unbidden.

"I've waited four years for tonight," he said, untying her blindfold.

That voice.

She looked up and met Lord Ting's gaze.

If her heart had pattered like a tentative rabbit a moment before, it now galloped like a horse. "H-how?"

"Are you disappointed?" His eyes roved over her, his expression more of wonder and fascination than of lust.

She shook her head back and forth, sending her unbound hair into a mess. "Where is the Emperor?"

"It is not my place to know." He flashed an alluring smile.

Fire erupted inside her, tempered only by a question. "But why?"

"A reward, for my loyalty. An apology, without apologizing." He knelt at her side.

She gave a nod, all shyness unfeigned. What she had wanted, to give her virginity to him, for him to find release in her, was somehow coming true.

"I have these vague memories, almost like a dream, of kissing you. It was something like this."

His lips traced a line from her belly button up, lighting her nerves like fireworks wherever his mouth touched. Her breath came out heavy, and a primal moan escaped her.

One hand cupped her breast as his lips claimed first her neck, then the angle of her jaw, and finally teased around hers. Urgent, she turned to join to him in a kiss; but he shifted each time before she could make contact. Frustrated in her need, her spine was taut as a *pipa* string.

His lips met hers as he stroked her nipple. Her breath hitched, all Floating World training forgotten.

With gentleness unexpected from his muscled bulk and larger-than-life demeanor, he eased her hand away from the Gate to her

Jade Valley. Tongue caressing hers in a leisurely circle, he explored around the Bud of Guanyin with expert fingers.

Her back arched of its own accord as he brought her to the edge of Heaven again and again, only to pause and hold her back. She ached to feel him. Her fingers and toes curled into the rug.

As she lay panting, he spread her legs. Her heart raced, her body coiling tight. He pressed against her without penetrating.

Release. Every nerve screamed for release.

She lifted her hips to take him in, only to have him move away. If only he'd stay still, if only—

The length of him filled her with an unhurried, deliberate thrust. Waves of pleasure surged up her spine. Her body bucked over and over again as all coherent thought fled.

When at last they lay entangled, languid and spent, she was able to think again. Her Plucking would be one more secret she kept from Jie and Wen, who, like the rest of the realm, would assume her first had been the Emperor.

For all her lies, both outright and by omission, whether compelled by the *Tiger's Eye* or spoken of her free will, there might be a way to tell a truth.

"My Lord." She rolled on top of him, bare skin to bare skin, wondering when he'd even disrobed. "Would you like to see what they teach us in the Chrysanthemum Pavilion?"

He met her gaze with a grin, running a finger down the angle of her jaw, coming to a rest under her chin. "I was gifted your virginity by the Emperor, himself. To partake of more..."

"For all anyone else knows, I serve the Emperor tonight." She returned his smile. "If he commands me, I dare not refuse. In the throes of passion, I shall scream *Your Eminence*, lest anyone doubt it."

His look turned stern. "Then I command you."

"Then I request a boon." She dipped her chin.

"Whatever you desire."

"A pet name. Yumei." Close enough to Yu Mei, the last heir of the North. If his seed took root in her, she'd find a way through the Surgeon's *Tiger's Eye* to tell him the whole truth.

End of Part 5

PART 6:
LAST BLOOM OF THE JADE LOTUS

PROLOGUE:

Even after his presumed death twenty years ago, Feiying still lived in the shadow of the Architect. From what he'd heard, Black Lotus Clan members still believed him to be no smarter than a Lianjing Cousin, the Surgeon only good for executing the Architect's flawless plans.

It was all a lie that Master Yan encouraged, to create larger-than-life, conveniently-dead heroes who couldn't contradict the grand stories. He certainly knew how many times Feiying had had to improvise when one of the Architect's schemes went awry.

Just like Feiying's own had. All the assets he'd acquired in Hua for his long-term plot to destroy the Black Lotus had been lost. The Steel Orchids. Fixer Zhang. And of course, Lilian. His own Bovyan Nightblades were too young, nor would Consul Haros allow their use outside of the Teleri Empire.

With these setbacks, even the boldest gambler would cut his losses.

But no. When your enemies thought you were weak, that was the best time to strike.

Killing the half-elf, who was certainly the daughter of the elf who had stolen Feiying's love, would be his first step in exacting vengeance on all those who'd wronged him.

He'd tried once before, during the uprising of the lords of the North at Cloud Castle two years earlier; but protecting Lilian's identity as last heir of the North and hiding Lord Yang's conspiracy had taken precedence.

Now Lilian was dead—but the half-elf would be returning to Cloud Castle to capture or kill Lord Yang.

And Feiying would be waiting.

CHAPTER 1

The Present

All the revelations about Lilian's past had left Jie in a pensive mood. It made it nearly impossible to concentrate on Tang Li's briefing on Lord Yang's defenses and supplies at Cloud Castle.

Jie would've rather learned about what other secrets Lilian had left hidden in Tang Li's mind. Sadly, not even Master Yan's *Tiger's Eye* technique had been able to unlock any more.

Faceless Chang's Empathy was involved, he'd surmised. Tang Li insisted there was more that she was still uncovering in her own memory—including the location of the seal of the previous Yu Dynasty.

"Time is of the essence," Master Yan said. "The Emperor has ordered us to capture Lord Yang quickly, before more lords of the North decide to join his rebellion."

Jie looked up, reorienting herself. Tian, Wen, Yangyang, and Meisha joined three Black Lotus brothers in a semicircle. In front of them, Tang Li was drawing a map, with Master Yan looking over her shoulder.

"How many soldiers does he have?" Jie asked, worried they'd already gone over this.

Tang Li pointed to the defenses on her drawing. "Cloud Castle has a standing complement of five hundred, with enough supplies to hold out for a year."

"He has ten thousand men total," Tian said. He had enough enthusiasm for all of them. "So it depends on how many of those he can pick up between the capital and the fortress."

Master Yan nodded. "His chief of staff, General Lu, has joined us. He is rallying as many of them to our side as he can, and the imperial army is marching as we speak to cut off his access to reinforcements."

Jie sucked on her lower lip. General Lu had led the assault on Lord Shi's compound, where she'd kept Tang Li prisoner. "Can we trust him?"

"We've embedded Kun in his ranks," Master Yan said, nodding to the tallest clan brother. "If General Lu turns on us..."

...He wouldn't live long. In any case, it appeared that General Lu was an opportunist. Still... "What about the Bovyan garrison in Rotuvi? They've supported the Yu family in the past."

Tian pointed to the diagram of Cloud Castle, outside the Great Wall. "They'd have to climb cliffs to reach the access road."

Jie studied the map. It was that access road which made it nearly impossible to assail the fortress by conventional means.

Tian looked to Tang Li. "Lord Yang wanted you dead to ensure you wouldn't tell the authorities about his involvement in framing Lord Shi. What would happen if you reached the castle with reinforcements ahead of the imperial armies?"

"If he suspects me," Tang Li said, "he'll kill me."

"Does he know who Jie and the others are?" Tian asked.

"Of course. He was a frequent visitor to the Floating World."

His gaze shifted from Meisha to Yangyang to Wen, before settling on Jie. "But does he know who they really are?"

Tang Li shook her head. "I didn't know who they really were until tonight."

"That doesn't mean he wouldn't," Tian said.

Tang Li shrugged. "Lord Yang wanted to establish his own spy network in the Floating World, and he thought it was his own, unique idea."

The others chuckled. The Black Lotus Clan had been in the Floating World for over two hundred years now, after all.

Jie nodded at Tian. His idea was as clear to her as if he were whispering it in her ear. She turned to Master Yan. "If this is all true, then tell the Emperor to slow their advance, and let us ride ahead. Once we are on the inside, we will kill Lord Yang."

"How will you get in?" Master Yan asked.

"Tang Li will bring us as entertainment for the soldiers," Jie said.

Tian tapped his chin. "The last thing Lord Yang saw of Meisha and Wen, they were on the barge for Lord Wu's party. He saw Yangyang disembark before the barge went out. He ordered the assault on Lord Shi's home to kill Tang Li, but if we've succeeded in cutting him off from messages, he wouldn't know the outcome."

Tang Li gave a slow nod. "All of his men who attacked Lord Shi's home are in custody."

"There were several on horseback," Jie said. "Bring the contents of the safe—"

"The Emperor has commanded that the sheets are to be delivered to the palace immediately."

Jie exchanged glances with the others. Of the items recovered from Lord Shi's safe—the sheets; Lilian's hairpin; a gold nugget; and a ball of addictive *yue* with stock certificates from the company that produced it—the blood-stained sheets were thought to be Lord Shi's sick memento from a Plucking.

Why would the Emperor want them? Had they been the sheets he'd Plucked Lilian on?

Jie searched her memories from two years ago.

* * *

Two Years Ago

At eighteen, Jie was the oldest girl still staying in the room for Seedlings and Florets. Now that Lilian had been assigned a private room, tonight would be the first in twelve years—eight at the Black Lotus Temple, four at the Chrysanthemum Pavilion—that they wouldn't be sleeping beside one another.

The night's festivities were in full swing in the common room, with none of the guests or Blossoms likely knowing of the uprising Jie had helped put down a few nights ago. Using the noise for cover, she slipped through the window and climbed the walls up to Lilian's new room. The windows had been left unshuttered, making it easy to get in.

Unlike the rooms of more seasoned Blossoms, Lilian's lacked extravagant decorations or magically-imbued paintings. She had only two of the revealing gowns suited for a full-fledged courtesan hanging on the stand of her dressing niche.

The room smelled new, with very little of Lilian's reassuring honeysuckle scent lingering in it. Jie threw herself onto the thick mattress of the rosewood bed. A real bed! It would be Lilian's first time ever sleeping in one, once she returned from her Plucking at the hands of the Emperor.

Jie's gut twisted with some intangible emotion. Was it because she'd wanted Lilian's dream of being Plucked by Lord Ting to come true? Maybe.

But there was something else. Jie stared up at the ceiling and chewed on the conflicting thoughts and emotions. Ever since Lilian's arrival at the Black Lotus Temple so many years ago, Jie had been her protector. Her big sister, her senior. Now, Lilian had crossed into womanhood, and would technically become Jie's senior in the House.

Jealousy. That was the niggling sensation Jie felt in her gut when someone was better at her than something. Lilian was not only a full-fledged Blossom now, but she'd taken the training seriously, and surpassed Jie at everything from poetry to music to seduction.

No, that wasn't it. Jie didn't even care about those things. She wasn't supposed to have stayed in the Floating World this long, anyway. What was meant to be one year to reap a windfall virgin price had already reached six. But as she drifted into sleep, she knew that the pit in her stomach was definitely jealousy.

She awoke to the door sliding open and bolted upright in the bed to find Lilian slipping in. When Lilian turned to the bed, her complexion was positively glowing. Beaming, she shut the door behind her and sashayed over. She landed with a poof in the covers and rested her head on Jie's shoulder.

Jie took in the scent of Lilian's hair. "How did it go? Was His Eminence gentle, or did he ravish you? Did it hurt?"

"A little." A smile formed on Lilian's lips. "He was tender the first time, and then—"

"More than once?" Jie stroked Lilian's hair. That wasn't a typical for a Plucking.

Pulling her closer, Lilian laughed. "How could I deny His Eminence?"

"Tell me everything."

"It was like the stories of the previous dynasty's harem. The Praise Moon nuns undressed me, searched me for weapons and poisons, then wrapped me up in a very expensive Ayuri wool carpet. They delivered me to a pagoda overlooking Sun-Moon Lake, where His Eminence was waiting. There was no art, no seduction. He just took me."

Again, Jie's stomach writhed with that emotion. Jealousy? Not that Lilian had surpassed her, but because now, something was just as important to Lilian as friendship. "Did he keep the sheets?" Many wealthy men did, after all.

"There weren't any. It all happened on the carpet."

* * *

The Present

How did Lilian really feel about Jie? So much had passed between them in the intervening two years that Jie had pushed Lilian's Plucking to the recesses of her mind. Now, though, with everything they'd learned from Tang Li, many memories were flooding back.

The Emperor had Plucked Lilian on a carpet, so the sheets from Lord Shi's safe couldn't have been from that. Just why did His Eminence want them? Jie turned to Tang Li. "What is the significance of the sheets?"

Tang Li shook her head. "All I can tell you is that they come from an inn in Yanhu."

Jie turned to Master Yan. "Lord Shi was just released from imperial custody. Can we question him?"

"He has been assigned to lead the vanguard against Lord Yang," Master Yan said. "In any case, I know the significance of the sheets, and His Eminence does not wish it revealed."

Jie sucked on her lower lip. If the Emperor had commanded secrecy, Master Yan wouldn't reveal it. It wouldn't stop clan members from trying to find out, though, since curiosity was ingrained in them. Still, it was time to focus on the issue at hand. The Emperor had travelled with Lords Ting, Tong, Yang, and Shi to Yanhu in the past. "Did Lord Yang know the sheets would be in the safe?"

Tang Li gave a tentative nod. "I would think so."

And he probably knew their significance. Jie blew out a sigh. "It will rouse any suspicion if we don't bring them."

"Does he know what they look like?" Tian's expression brightened. "What if we made a copy?"

"He probably knows," Tang Li said. "The dragon embroidered into them can only be found at that inn, and he's stayed there with the Emperor many times."

Tian's forehead scrunched up. "By imperial relay, we could get ahold of those sheets in sixteen hours."

Master Yan shook his head. "In order to get you to Cloud Castle ahead of the imperial army, we'd need you to set off within four."

"Only a handful of weavers would be authorized to make those sheets," Wen said. "Is the Yanhu inn's supplier in the capital?"

"No." Master Yan studied them all. "That weaver is even further south."

Jie searched his eyes. What she was about to suggest was treason.

CHAPTER 2

The Present

Before she'd discovered the secrets of a courtesan assassin princess locked away in her memories, all Tang Li ever wanted was to open a teahouse. Her judicious revealing of those secrets was the only thing preventing the Black Lotus Clan from killing her. Now, though, their proposed plan carried yet more risk of death.

Just a few hours ago, Lord Yang had sent men to eliminate her, with the hopes that she'd take his secrets to the grave. It was impossible to predict what he'd do when she turned up on the doorstep of his impenetrable castle.

She looked among the young women, whom she'd known for years only as Blossoms of the Floating World. All this time, they'd been spies and assassins for the Emperor. They were all willing to take the risk.

Would it work as a means of getting in? Lord Yang was nothing if logical. With his conspiracy exposed, he had no reason to kill her; indeed, she knew how to please him. And if she brought the Blossoms... well, he expected a long siege, and supposed prostitutes would keep the soldiers' morale up.

She shuddered, thinking about the profession she'd been groomed into. In this, she had not only her own memories, but

Lilian's as well. The reality of a Blossom's life, even in the Floating World, hadn't been pleasant; but for her first few assignations, it had been glorious.

* * *

Two Years Ago

The lies Lilian had told Jie, either because of the Surgeon's *Tiger's Eye* or by her own choice, were sprouting faster than bamboo after a spring rain. The guilt wrenched her to the core, but didn't keep her from adding more to the list.

The day after Lilian's supposed Plucking at the hands of the Emperor, Gardener Ju informed her that Lord Ting had paid a considerable contract price to be her second.

While it wasn't at Sun-Moon Palace on a luxurious carpet in a resplendent pagoda overlooking Sun-Moon Lake, the assignation would take place at Lord Ting's villa in the capital, for the whole night. Lilian had never visited, and looked forward to seeing where her beloved lived.

Like the afternoon he was supposed to Pluck her, which had ultimately been cancelled because of the entrapment of rebellious lords at Cloud Castle, Lilian sat at her makeup table, preparing with Tang Li and Jie's help.

"How lucky you are," Tang Li said, applying kohl to Lilian's eyelids. "Your first assignation was with the Emperor himself."

"And now the second, with a man you're fond of." Jie's voice bubbled with the same enthusiasm as when she received a new weapon, while she hemmed in the dress sleeves. The elegant gown, like the makeup, emphasized feminine sensuality. It was the opposite of a Plucking, where a Blossom appeared innocent.

“I hear he made a substantial offer to be your exclusive.” Tang Li reddened Lilian’s lips with balm.

Lilian met Jie’s eyes in the mirror. Lord Ting had been negotiating an exclusive deal with Gardener Ju since before Lilian’s Plucking, and it had been a significant amount. In everyone else’s eyes, her value had dropped, since it was assumed the Emperor had slept with her; if it were up to her, the Gardener would certainly agree.

However, their contracts were technically held by the Golden Peacock Company, a Black Lotus shell company which split profits with the Chrysanthemum Pavilion. And the Black Lotus cared less about money and more about spying on as many of the great lords and merchants as possible.

And most of the Northern lords were waiting for their chance.

For now, though, Lilian would savor her first two times with Lord Ting, and find reprieve in him during his likely frequent visits afterwards.

Satisfied with their work, Tang Li and Jie stepped back. Lilian rose and studied her reflection. Modelled on imperial court fashions, the silk gown had two pieces: a cobalt inner dress which clung to her bust, secured in part by a sky-blue sash; and a translucent white outer gown hung off her bare shoulders. Underneath it all were the lacy undergarments which Lord Ting had given her. She’d never felt so beautiful before.

When she descended the steps and glided through the common room, the Seedlings and Florets all paused in their cleaning to wonder at her. Outside in the courtyard, Lord Ting’s palanquin waited. His page and the blue-liveried porters all gawked as she stepped through the doors.

As Lilian ducked into the palanquin, she met Jie’s gaze, where the half-elf waited by the mansion’s doors. They’d known each other for twelve years, and Lilian couldn’t make out her expression. Wistfulness? Jealousy? No, certainly not jealousy.

The ride to Lord Ting's villa seemed to stretch into eternity. When she finally stepped out of the palanquin and looked to the Iridescent Moon, less than half a phase had passed. A white stone wall with elegant metal gates encircled the spacious compound. Plum trees and flowering shrubs decorated the courtyard. Beyond it, graceful tile eaves topped a white-stoned mansion. It wasn't what she'd expected of a lord from the austere North; more like the home of a first-rank noble. Maybe she'd one day be the lady of this house.

She snorted. How silly of her, thinking like a girl. A good Black Lotus operative would be looking for insertion points and escape paths, evaluating threats and assets. The question of *why* his home was more extravagant, and *how* he paid for it all, should've been at the forefront of her mind. Where had her training gone?

A chamberlain greeted her with a bow. "This way, my lady." He gestured with an open hand through the double doors.

The interior was just as well-decorated as the exterior, with scroll paintings, elegant porcelain vases, rosewood furnishing, and thick Ayuri rugs. Unlike the exterior, it felt familiar. As if she'd been here before.

Of course.

It had the same layout as a villa in Lianjing Township, next to the Black Lotus Temple. And if a replica was there, that meant the clan had modelled it on this mansion. And the clan never did anything like that without reason.

Because of the familiarity, she knew where the chamberlain was guiding her, and her heart pounded in her ears. He bowed his head and opened a set of sliding doors. "Please."

Returning his bow, she stepped through. She knelt and closed the door behind her.

Strong hands seized her and turned her around. Claiming her lips, Lord Ting backed her toward the bed. His bare, muscled chest pressed against hers. With the dexterity of a pickpocket, he undid her sash with one hand, while loosening the laces of her inner dress with his other. By the time she fell into the plush blankets, he'd stripped her naked.

The night before, he'd been gentle in the way he'd made her first time pleasurable; this evening he took her from behind with unfettered need. As his length filled her, his hands and mouth left nothing unexplored. She reveled in his urgency, in her body's ability to satiate his fire, until they both lay spent and panting.

"Yumei," he said, addressing her with the pet name she'd told him to use. He propped his head up on an elbow, and traced lazy lines near her nethers with his finger.

She smiled. It was a loophole to reveal her real name: Yu Mei, the last princess of the North. "Yes, my Lord?"

"I've been thinking about it since last night." His finger teased at her.

She fought the urge to squirm. "What is it, my Lord?"

"Remember when we first met, four years ago during your First Flower Viewing?"

"I could never forget that night." She'd been smitten with him from that moment.

He brought his hand to her cheek and turned it to him. "I said you looked familiar."

"Yes." Now she had to lead him to the connection. "That I had the look of the North."

His eyes searched hers. "You look like my past liege, Lord Yu, the last heir of the North."

Yes! The Surgeon's *Tiger's Eye* kept her from confirming her connection to Yu Qian out loud. "I see." Would he see? It was especially important, since she'd abstained from her contraceptive herbs for the last several days, at her most fertile time.

"He had a daughter, named Mei. I just thought it quite the coincidence that you asked me to call you Yumei." He chuckled.

More than a coincidence, she wanted to say, but the *Tiger's Eye* prevented it.

* * *

The Present

Tang Li marveled at all of Lilian's layered plans, many of which had been so close to fruition before her death at Jie's hands. To think, Lilian had used Li as a failsafe for that possible outcome.

Now that Li understood, she could make plans for her own survival.

When they arrived at Cloud Castle, she'd find a way to convince Lord Yang that these women were there to service the soldiers. Once inside, though, if it looked like she stood a better chance with Lord Yang than with the Black Lotus, she could betray them.

CHAPTER 3

The Present

At age ten, most great lords' sons would dream of battles. Zheng Tian might be about to take part in one. In fact, the assault on Lord Shi's townhouse might have been considered a siege, though all he'd done was push a bed up against a door to prevent invaders from getting in.

Now, he stood outside barracks and stables in the north of the capital with Jie, Wen, Yangyang, Meisha, and Tang Li. Two Black Lotus brothers were there as well, with Elder Brother Kun disguised as a cavalry officer. Lord Yang's garrison of two hundred men, most who'd participated in the attack, milled about. They'd received imperial pardons on the condition that they participate in the siege on Cloud Castle, and were now being separated and assigned to imperial units.

"We need at least twenty cavalrymen," Brother Kun called out. "Upon successful completion of this mission, your families will be rewarded twenty gold *yuan*."

All forty of the mounted soldiers stepped forward and bowed. After all, the reward could feed a large family for five months.

The question was, could the Emperor trust vassals of the traitorous Lord Yang?

"Very good." Brother Kun bowed his head and beckoned them closer. He cast a sidelong glance at Jie, and with her subtle nod, he continued. "Our assignment is to ride ahead to Cloud Castle, as if we are rejoining Lord Yang. For anyone who might be entertaining the idea of betraying the Emperor, your family's reward—and their safety—is contingent on your loyalty."

Lord Yang's men looked among themselves, and not a few muttered about the lack of faith in them.

Tian snorted. Of course, they'd just betrayed their former lord for the promise of a reward. He leaned in toward Tang Li. "Do you know if Lord Yang ever held hands with Lilian?"

She met his gaze and gave a solemn nod. "He was always jealous of Lord Ting. What Ting had, he wanted as well."

* * *

Two Years Before

For the first week of her life as a full-fledged Blossom, Lilian felt as if she were living in a dream. Lord Ting ended up paying an exorbitant amount to keep her in his villa. When he wasn't meeting with his vassals to discuss governance of his newly-expanded fiefs, he entertained her with poetry duels, moon viewing, and lovemaking.

All the servants deferred to her as if she were the lady of the house. She'd planted the seed that she was more than just a prostitute, and since she hadn't taken her herbal contraceptive, perhaps the seeds he'd planted in her would find fertile ground. If not for his meetings, which she listened in on, she would've forgotten her true identity as a Fist of the Black Lotus Clan.

When Lilian returned to her new bedroom at the Chrysanthemum Pavilion, she found Jie sitting on the edge of the bed. Her heart fluttered. If there was anything lacking about her time with Lord Ting, it was not being able to share secrets with Jie.

Lilian plopped down beside her and, using a grappling technique, tried to flip Jie onto her back. As always, it failed. With a counter, Jie ended up straddling her.

"I don't know why I even tried." Lilian burst into giggles.

Jie lowered herself and rested her cheek over Lilian's heart. "Has Lord Ting been treating you well?"

"Better than well." Lilian ran her fingers through Jie's hair. "This might have been the happiest week of my life."

Jie slid off Lilian, ending up on her side next to her. She propped herself up on an elbow. "I know Gardener Ju wants to agree to Lord Ting's terms. She's recommended as much to the Golden Peacock Company."

Lilian's heart sank. She heard the tone. "But...?"

"But I don't think the clan will agree to it." Jie ran her hand in a circle over Lilian's stomach.

Lilian interlocked her fingers with Jie's. About one week, and Lilian would know if Lord Ting's seed had taken root in her womb. Gardener Ju would insist she take an abortive, but it was ultimately the clan's decision. She just had to make them believe that Lord Ting was vital to the North, and that she, carrying his child, would be the best way to keep him loyal to the Jade Throne.

This meant deceiving Jie—the newly minted head of the Floating World cell—yet again. Lilian's gut twisted at the clash between her loyalty to her best friend and her heritage as daughter of a betrayed lord.

She could do this. Had to do this. "Lord Ting met with several of his vassals and other minor lords of the North over the week."

Jie perked up. "With so many of the rebellious lords slain, there's going to be a realignment of loyalties among the survivors."

"He was clever in the way he tested out their loyalty to the Jade Throne," Lilian lied. "They all look up to him, and will follow his lead."

"I'll send that information to the clan." Jie hopped out of the bed and headed toward the door.

"Now?" Lilian asked.

"No, I have to do some chores and run some errands. And you probably need rest."

Lilian flashed a smile. She did need a rest. Lord Ting would be arriving at dusk. It would give her a few hours before she had to prepare. When Jie slipped out, she closed her eyes and let sleep claim her.

She awoke to her door sliding open. Outside, the sun was setting. She must've been asleep for a few hours.

Gardener Ju poked her head in. She hadn't been around as much lately, leaving operations to Florist Wei. "You have a Hummingbird."

Lord Ting wasn't supposed to come until dusk! Her hand shot up to her head. Heavens, her hair must look as if a typhoon had blown it askew. If he saw her like this... "Please tell Lord Ting to give me some time."

Gardener Ju's forehead scrunched up. "It's not Lord Ting."

What? Lilian's heart leaped into her throat. "Who...who is it?"

Gardner Ju backed out. Despite her bad leg, she knelt with poetic grace and opened the door wider. It revealed a thin figure, silhouetted by the bauble lamps in the hallway.

It was highly irregular for sought-after Blossoms to receive a Hummingbird before dusk, save for First Pollinations with young lords. And their fathers wouldn't usually choose a recently-Plucked girl, instead preferring seasoned Blossoms who knew how to handle a young man's first time.

And despite this person's slight build, he was a man grown. If Lilian's heart had been in her throat, it now sank. Finger-combing her hair, she started to get out of bed, as protocol demanded.

He stepped through the door and into the brittle sunlight, revealing Lord Yang. Tang Li's regular. Despite his bluster and flamboyance, he preferred pampering behind closed doors. Tang Li usually did all the work. Now, he held up a staying hand. "No need to get up."

Lilian froze, pulse pounding, and bowed again.

Gardener Ju cleared her throat. "His lordship wished to play a game. I've told him your safe word, so I'll leave him in your capable hands." With another bow, she slid the door shut.

No sooner did Lilian rise from her bow than Lord Yang fell on her like a wolf seizing prey. Her Black Fist instincts nearly took over, but she forced herself to remain still as he pushed her down and pulled open her robe.

Leering, he pulled her wrists above her head. The Gardener's mention of the safe word said everything. Lilian had seen through the House peepholes how this type of scenario was supposed to play out: a demure Blossom was to act frightened as the Hummingbird ravished her.

As much force as he used, he wanted it to be more than an act. The pain in her arms was nothing compared to an average day at the Black Lotus Temple; still, she indulged him with a whimper. "Please, my Lord..."

"The last thing I remember from Cloud Castle is following you." He brought her wrists together and captured them in one hand. With his other, he pulled her undergarment off and held it up. "A gift from Lord Ting?"

This was the bastard who'd murdered her family and hid the Yu Dynasty seal. If not for the Surgeon's *Tiger's Eye*, she'd expose Lord Yang's traitorous intents. Instead, she turned to the side, feigning shame while really hiding the hatred that undoubtedly burned in her gaze.

"Anyway," he said, spreading her thighs and pinning them open with his knees. "I hit my head and can't remember what happened after I saw you. Tell me."

Master Yin, the Black Lotus' Floating World cell leader at the time, had knocked him out; but then had been killed by the supposedly dead Surgeon. He'd been the one to rescue her from her family's slaughter years ago, and planted her in the clan. Lord Yang apparently knew the Surgeon, though not his true identity. He either didn't remember that Lilian had taken the Yu family seal from him, or was pretending not to.

No doubt, that's what he wanted, as a symbol of legitimacy in the North. She put fear into her voice. "I was being chased by Lord Zu. I didn't see you."

"Swear it." His eyes searched hers, inviting her to lie.

For all he knew, she was just a Blossom, and not a Black Fist to whom lies came as easily as breathing. "I swear."

His lips twisted into a scowl, his expression so full of anger that her fear might not all be feigned. He took her with so much rage that she had to use her safe word.

When he finally left, not even Black Lotus training could keep her from curling up and crying. This must've been what it was like to be a Trench whore or a spoil of war from the endless battles in the Sundered Empire. Used and discarded like worthless refuse. How could she let Lord Ting see her with the marks Lord Yang had left with his teeth and nails?

And he'd never see the scars he left on her soul.

* * *

The Present

Tian was at a loss.

Tears filled Tang Li's eyes, and she hugged herself. She'd recounted that Lord Yang had held Lilian's hands at times, not because he liked her, but because he was jealous of Lord Ting.

People were too hard to understand. Tian patted Tang Li on the back, just like his mother did to him when he was sad.

Tang Li wiped her eyes. "Lord Yang always wanted to be the most powerful lord in the North. Lord Ting intimidated him, both as an individual and as a commander. He knew Lord Ting loved Lilian, so he had to possess her when he could."

Tian nodded. The things people did for ambition.

* * *

Tang Li studied Tian. She'd left out Lilian's plotting, because the boy was so smart he might've figured out even more, and she hadn't gone into so much detail with Lord Yang's depravities, since Tian's innocence made him so adorable.

She'd always had Lord Yang wrapped around her finger, and now that Lilian's recollections were surfacing in her memory, it was hard to believe what a different person he was to her. How much Lilian had had to endure.

Li couldn't help but feel viscerally some of Lilian's hatred for Lord Yang. Could she really rely on him when they arrived at Cloud Castle? If not, she'd have to hedge her bets with the Black Lotus.

CHAPTER 4

The Present

Wen sat behind the Yang cavalryman, holding on for dear life as they galloped up the road toward Cloud Castle. They'd taken a river barge to Honggang, then galloped down the road through the unsettled North. The last time she'd taken this paved road, two years ago with Master Yin and Jie, she'd pretended to be a porter, and walked by the palanquins bearing the cell sisters. A journey that had taken six hours to arrive at the Great Wall then took half an hour on horseback now.

Still, there'd been plenty of time to think. Working in an elite House in the Floating World usually meant sleeping with one man a night; at the most, she might receive three in a day. She savored sex, and with the right Hummingbird, it could even be downright titillating in a strategic way.

On the other hand, a Blossom of the lesser Houses, catering to commoners, might see up to ten men a day. Prostitutes in the brothels serving military barracks might service a dozen or more men. She suppressed a shudder. With their cover story, they'd be treated more as spoils of war. Trapped behind walls of a fortress under siege, they'd be used more than a Trench whore. For all that she enjoyed intercourse, this prospect wasn't appealing.

Looking to Meisha and Yangyang, she tried to shake the dread out of her mind. They'd all be fine. They'd be able to neutralize Lord Yang and open the gates within an hour of entering the castle.

Still, doubt niggled at her. If Lord Yang was as abusive as Lilian had related...

* * *

Two Years Ago

With nonchalant ease, Wen avoided Lilian's stab. It was even more half-hearted than usual, making it easy to catch her wrist and twist the training knife free.

"Point, Wen," Jie called from the empty theater's box above. "Let's call it for the day, early."

Around them on the stage, clan sisters saluted each other and dispersed. Some went to change back into dresses, while others took the extra time to chat.

Wen found Lilian in the corner of her vision. She'd been positively glowing after spending a week with Lord Ting. Now, a week after that, she trudged like a condemned convict on his way to the chopping block.

Her rhythms and Wen's followed a close pattern, so Wen calculated the days. Their Best Friends would be arriving any day now. Maybe that explained why Lilian was so sluggish.

That didn't seem to be it, though. Her face had a pale pallor, and she kept covering her mouth.

Wen took Lilian's hand and pulled her to the side. "Are you all right?"

"I'm fine." Lilian's hand shot up to her mouth. "I think I ate something that didn't agree with me."

"She's not fine," Jie said, coming up beside them. "She's been moping all week, and won't say why."

Lilian leaned over and dry heaved.

Wen gaped. "You're not... You've been taking your contraceptive herbs, haven't you?"

"Of course," Lilian snapped.

Jie studied her. "They're mostly effective, but on rare occasions..."

"It's not that." Lilian's lip trembled. She looked from Jie to Wen, then to the departing Sisters in their colorful day dresses. She pulled them closer. "It's Lord Yang."

"What happened?" Wen asked.

Jie clenched her fists. "He's been spending his windfall gambling earnings on her."

Wen squeezed Lilian's hand. Of course the clan wouldn't allow Lord Ting to enter into an exclusive relationship, both because of the need to collect information, and also the income a sought-after, recently Plucked Blossom could make from curious Hummingbirds.

"It's not just that," Lilian whispered, hugging herself. "He's vicious."

Jie wrapped an arm around her. "What about your safe word?"

"I've had to use it several times a night." Tears now wetted her eyes.

Even in the Houses which catered to Hummingbirds with sharp tastes, it was rare for a Blossom to need to use her safe word. And even those girls, tough as they were, didn't have as much pain tolerance as a Black Lotus Fist. Wen leaned in. "Did you tell your Gardener?"

Lilian nodded. "She says as long as he respects the safe word, there's nothing she can do about it."

That was equally strange. The Houses always protected Blossoms. Wen looked sidelong at Jie.

The half-elf's face burned. "I'm going to kill that Turtle's Egg." And from her tone, she meant it.

Taking Jie's wrist, Wen shook her head. "With the realignment of the North, the Emperor needs him more than ever to maintain stability."

Lilian bent over and threw up.

* * *

The Present

Wen shook the memory out of her head as the Great Wall came into sight. The town of Chengfu, Lord Yang's domain, was nestled into a curve in the wall, just outside the only gatehouse in three hundred *li*. Soldiers wearing Yang's colors, still distinguishable in the setting sun, blocked the road ahead.

From where she sat behind the rider, near the front of the cavalry column, Wen turned to Jie on the next horse over.

Poor Jie; she hated horses. Disguised as a young soldier because she'd been expelled from the Floating World, she gripped her rider's belt. No doubt, her gloved knuckles would be as white as her complexion beneath the helm.

Are you all right? Wen signed.

Jie gave a tentative nod. *Looks like we're coming to a stop.*

Indeed, the horses were slowing to a trot as they neared the checkpoint. Yang's garrison levelled their pikes.

At the head of the column, sitting in the saddle with much more poise, Brother Kun pressed his fist into his palm. "Soldiers of the North, we have answered our lord's call to muster. We are here to reinforce his position. What is the latest news from Cloud Castle?"

The infantry leader returned the salute. "The imperial garrison let Lord Yang, Lord Nan, and a few dozen of their men through the

Wall before news of the rebellion reached here. They've since bottled up in the gatehouse, preventing anyone else from passing. With the imperial army approaching, we'll be trapped between them and the Wall."

Wen turned to Jie, knowing what she planned.

Brute force wouldn't dislodge the defenders. It was up to their cell to get the cavalry through the Wall before it was caught between the anvil and hammer.

CHAPTER 5

The Present

On the outskirts of Chengfu, Jie hid by a wooden house, studying the closest tower of the Great Wall. Spaced three *li* from the main gatehouse in town, this one had an entrance on this side of the Wall. In her hour of listening, watching, and smelling, there looked to be no more than twenty men guarding it.

She looked back to Tian. *Any sign of them?* she signed. More as a test, since she already knew the answer.

To maintain their cover story, Wen, Yangyang, Meisha, and Tang Li had been locked in a local inn while the cavalrymen tended to their horses—though not before they'd passed on the message via clan sign language for the first three to meet at this tower.

Tian shook his head.

Jie grinned. Poor humans, with their weak noses and ears. She beckoned to the next house over.

He followed her gesture and gawked.

The sisters hid at a corner, now wearing commoners' pants and shirts instead of their dresses.

When they arrived, Jie gestured to the Wall. "Rotating patrols along the battlements, for a total of ten men. Eight men in the tower."

"And one at the light signal." Tian pointed.

"Yes." Jie nodded. There was no line of sight on that one, but beacons sat atop all the towers of the Great Wall. In an emergency, an operator who knew the secret codes would open and close the shutters, and that would be relayed from beacon to beacon along the Wall, and in the towers along the main roads throughout the realm. "Most of the imperial defenders have dug in at the main gate, since that's where Yang's men are encamped."

"I know what you're thinking," Wen said. "But there's a difference."

Jie nodded. Recapturing a beacon that had fallen into enemy hands was a training scenario they had run on more than one occasion. "The defenders are loyal to the throne."

"Does your plan limit casualties?" Wen looked up to the Wall's crenellations.

"Of course." Tian bobbed his head enthusiastically. He gestured to the battlements. "There's an eight-minute gap between patrols along the Wall. The signal operator will remain at his post, but if we can draw the remaining men in the tower down..."

Yangyang squeezed her breasts between her arms. "I am well equipped for that."

Jie swallowed her chuckle. Yangyang had tried to serve as a distraction two years before.

* * *

Two Years Ago

Jie stood behind Lilian, rubbing her back as she sat in the Chrysanthemum Pavilion's office. Earlier, at the theater after training, Lilian had been too weak for stealth. Yangyang had helped distract Old Feng, the troupe manager, so that Wen and Jie could help her slip out. Though Lilian usually turned heads for her grace, passersby gawked at her stuttering steps. Yangyang had tried to distract the Chrysanthemum Pavilion guards so that Jie could get Lilian back to her room without anyone noticing, but Gardener Ju, back again after another extended absence, had caught sight of them. She'd ordered Lilian to meet with her.

As they waited for the Gardener to arrive, Jie cursed to herself. Lilian's Best Friend was a day late, and if she really was pregnant with Lord Ting's child—or even the Emperor's—the clan would need to decide the best course of action. If the Gardener found out first, it would only complicate things.

"Are you all right?" Jie asked. "Do you think..."

The Gardener's slight but distinctive hobble across the nightingale floors was joined by a second set of footsteps. Florist Wei's scent mingled with Gardener Ju's. The door slid open, and both whisked in. Lilian and Jie bowed in unison.

Ignoring them, the Gardener plopped down in her cushioned chair across from Lilian. The Florist, abacus in hand, took up a position behind her.

"So you're pregnant," Gardener Ju said.

How could she tell? Jie sucked on her lower lip. Certainly the Gardener tracked every Blossom's monthly rhythms, but a girl could be a day off either way.

"Of course I know." The Gardener harrumphed. "I've been around brothels most of my life, and you're not the first or the fiftieth girl I've seen who ended up with a pork bun in the roaster."

Lilian uncovered her mouth. "I think so."

"You'll have to get rid of it, of course. Easier now, before its roots dig deep."

Jie cleared her throat. "What if it's His Eminence's?"

"What if it is?" The Gardener's glare fell on her. "Florist Wei?"

The abacus clicked and clacked as the Florist's fingers ran through it. She looked up, apologetic. "A pregnancy in a recently-

Plucked Blossom represents lost revenues in the hundreds of thousands of *yuan*."

The Gardener waved a dismissive hand. "In any case, it's not the Emperor's. The Wangs don't beget scions easily. My ears say that he's needed magical help for all three of his children."

Looking over her shoulder, Lilian met Jie's gaze. She looked desperate.

Gardener Ju laughed. "When the Emperor Plucked you, did a Dragonscribe draw runes on you? Did they wrap you in a Dragonweaver's sheet like the concubines from the Yu Dynasty? Or did the Dragonsingers of old march out of legend to chant while he was bedding you?"

Lilian started to speak.

Gardener Ju stayed her with a hand. "Of course not. Ting was next, and Yang was too late. It has to be Ting's. And we want Ting's money, not his whore-begotten bastard son."

Lilian sat up straight. What was going through her mind? When they'd asked her about the pregnancy, she'd avoided the question. If only Jie could see her expression. She might be able to, using the wall mirror, but looking at it would be too obvious to the Gardener and Florist.

"Gardener." Jie bowed. "If I may—"

"You may not," the Gardener said. "Why should I listen to a Seedling who can't even show obeisance correctly after six years in the Floating World?"

"My apologies." Jie attempted the bow again, but it was a motion she'd never bothered to master. "But wouldn't this be the decision of the Golden Peacock Company? It holds Lilian's contract."

The Gardener waved her hand. "We won't tell them. In any case, we haven't even heard from Golden Peacock's agent, Madame Yin, in several weeks."

Master Yin had died at Cloud Castle, and Jie had taken her place as head of the cell. The clan had already assigned a replacement as Golden Peacock's representative; certainly they would've sent word to the Houses? More importantly, the clan would want to take part in the decision-making process. Lilian would be able to control Lord Ting and keep him loyal.

Was that what Jie wanted? She squeezed Lilian's shoulder, and Lilian clasped her hand over hers. Jie bobbed her head. "Gardener, if the Golden Peacock Company finds out you made such a weighty decision without consulting them, I worry what they will think of your mutually beneficial relationship."

The Gardener studied them, eyes narrowed. Jie's unspoken threat dangled her own astronomical virgin price as a bargaining chip.

"Jie has a point," the Florist said.

"Of course you are right," the Gardener said. "Let's not be too hasty. I will make you an appointment with Doctor Fa, who can confirm whether or not you are really pregnant."

* * *

The Present

With Tian on his way back to the rogue cavalry unit, Jie and Wen scaled the Great Wall a couple hundred paces from the battlement. Jie's heart squeezed. The last time they'd climbed the Wall, on a training mission, Lilian had been with them. She'd only been eleven at the time, and Jie fourteen, well before her feelings had bloomed. Lilian's absence now bore a hole in her heart.

She reached the top and climbed through the crenels. Landing in a soundless crouch, she waited for Wen to alight behind her.

You were thinking of the last time, Wen tapped on her shoulder. *With Lilian.*

Nodding, Jie peered through the darkness, her elf vision turning the world into shades of greenish grey. Several imperial soldiers stood between the merlons, looking into the town below. Atop the platform, one manned the beacon, his head turning left and right toward the beacons on the next towers over. What a thankless job that must be, since they hadn't been used for three hundred years.
Jie and Wen stayed low as they crept along the ramparts to the tower. On the far end, a patrol from the main gatehouse approached. Motioning Wen to hold her position a couple dozen paces away from the beacon, Jie continued. When the patrol arrived and turned back, she leaned into a crenellation and imitated a peacock caw.

A scream pierced the night, jolting the men out of their complacency. Desperate raps resounded off the tower's wooden door.

"Help!" Yangyang yelled. "They're after me! The rebels!"

More than one soldier craned over to see. Higher up, the beacon keeper looked down as well. Knowing Yangyang, she would be flashing her assets. Predictably, they rushed into the tower and down the steps, leaving the hapless beacon keeper by himself.

Wen went around to bar the door to the tower's interior. Jie darted to the platform and climbed the ladder. At the top, she slunk over to the beacon keeper. With him still looking down, it was easy to sneak up on him, but impossible to reach his neck.

She moved to his left. Using a *Ghost Echo*, she threw her voice to his right. "Hey!"

When he straightened and turned, she wrapped him up in a rear naked choke. In four seconds, his struggling body went limp, and she lowered him to the ground.

With only a minute to act, Jie pulled the pins of the beacon shutters so that only the side facing the gatehouse would open. She then flipped the shutter up and down to allow the light bauble within to flash in long and short bursts.

Only clan cell leaders knew the codes, and never having had to use them, she wasn't sure if she got them right. If she did, the gatehouse would flash the message, open the gates, and let the cavalry through.

And the assassins with them.

Holding her breath, she stared at the main gatehouse. By now, Tian had mustered the rogue cavalry unit, and they'd soon be waiting outside the gates.

The gatehouse beacon answered, with the same message.

Jie blew out a sigh, and shifted her gaze to the next tower, where she'd sent Meisha and Kun to disable the beacon keeper and seal the shutters on the other end to prevent their signal from being seen by the next tower.

A few seconds later, it relayed the message, and Jie squinted in the far distance to where the next tower would continue the relay had Meisha failed.

It didn't.

This part of the plan had worked. It remained to be seen if the gatehouse commander actually believed the order.

CHAPTER 6

The Present

Tian held Tang Li's hand as he guided her out of an inn toward the horses, where the cavalry were saddling up. The plan to commandeer the beacons had worked, but would Jie, Wen, Meisha, and Yangyang make it back before they set off through the gatehouse? He looked up to the Iridescent Moon, now waxing toward its fourth gibbous. The streets were so dark, and the cell sisters had to cover two and a half *li*.

"Why are they letting you through?" one of the local Yang footmen asked Brother Kun.

"A bribe," Kun said. "The captain of their guard plans to make some money, with the assumption that a couple hundred horsemen wouldn't make a difference in a siege."

Tian tapped his chin. Of course, that wasn't true; Kun had tried to bribe them before Jie's plan to use the beacons. Still, the loyal Yang soldiers needed a plausible story as to how the cavalry made it through the gatehouse.

Jie and Wen turned the corner, just as Meisha and Yangyang arrived from the opposite direction.

Tian beamed at them, but his smile slipped when his gaze fell on Jie. She should be happy with the completion of a successful mission, but now her expression looked crestfallen. "What's wrong?"

"You were thinking about Lilian, weren't you?" Wen squeezed the half-elf's hand.

Jie let out a wistful sigh. "I was thinking about two years ago, the first month Lilian started seeing Hummingbirds."

Wen nodded. "She miscarried."

Pointing up at the castle in the distance, Jie nodded. "Lord Yang was very rough. I wonder if that's what did it."

Tian shuddered. Though he'd never met Lilian, he felt as if he knew a little of her, from the stories the sisters had been sharing the last couple of days. Still, how could anyone really know her, considering how much she hid? Was the pregnancy—wait. He looked up. "Two years ago?"

"Yes." Jie nodded. "Why?"

"Faceless Chang—Feng Rumei—was pregnant at the same time. And in the Floating World."

Tang Li gasped. "One of Lilian's memories just came back to me...."

* * *

Two Years Ago

Lilian watched in the early morning as the Floating World doctor fiddled with the lock to his clinic. Heart racing with excitement, it was tempting to go pick it for him.

"Ah, Ju Lilian! You're early." Doctor Fang now looked up from the key, which had finally turned. A man bent with age, supported by a lacquered cane inlaid with mother of pearl, he wore heavy spectacles and white silk robes. His white hair was bound in a topknot. He'd once been an imperial physician, before his son inherited the position. He walked through the door, then beckoned for her. "Come in, come in. You're first on my list."

Lilian bowed. Her hand strayed to her belly as she walked in. The heady smell of herbs greeted her, tempting her stomach into rebellion. Behind a counter was a carved rosewood herb cabinet, with two hundred long drawers. Another shelf displayed tinctures in porcelain bottles.

"Wait here." Doctor Fang motioned to the row of cushioned chairs along the wall before disappearing into a back room.

As she took a seat, two younger male assistants in white robes hurried in, bowing. A woman in her early twenties with a slight swell in her belly followed, jade bracelets jingling. Though made of high-quality silk, her dress looked to have been torn and repaired. The stitches might've been sewn by a surgeon.

Her eyes met Lilian. And what beautiful eyes! Light brown, they were easily as large as Jie's, but rounder. Though not as fair as the pale foreigners of the north, her skin tone was lighter than the locals. No doubt she was of mixed blood.

Everyone would know of such an exotic beauty if she were a Blossom, and she didn't move with the same grace.

Which probably meant... Lilian's lips rounded of their own accord. Though Doctor Fang's main clientele were Blossoms—and indeed, she'd visited every few months, and he provided the contraceptive herbs she hadn't taken—his fame in treating women's health issues had even wealthy ladies braving the shame of entering the Floating World to see him. Given this woman's unique looks, she was probably a lord's concubine, wearing a lady's old, repaired dress. Lilian bowed her head.

Despite the several empty chairs, the newcomer plopped down next to Lilian. "Hi."

So informal. Lilian nodded again. "Warmest greetings."

The woman's eyes roved back and forth in a mesmerizing fashion. "You're Ju Lilian. Got a squirt cooking?"

Lilian's hand shot up to her mouth.

"I'm sorry." The woman laughed.

The way she spoke was refreshing. Lilian bowed again. "I'm afraid you have me at a disadvantage."

"Everyone knows who you are. Your virgin price was quite the talk. My bet on Lord Yang made me a pretty copper *fen*, and my side bet that he'd offer you to the Emperor made me even more."

Lord Yang... It was all Lilian could do to keep from shuddering.

The woman laughed. "I should introduce myself. My name is Rumei."

Rumei. It was almost as common a name as Lilian. Lilian bowed her head yet again. "I am pleased to meet you. What did you mean by a squirt?"

Patting her belly, Rumei laughed. "A baby."

How strange. "Squirt, because they're small?"

"I'm from the Trench. Everything is shit. It's what we call diarrhea. If you're trying to get rid of it, you've come to the right place."

Blood drained from Lilian's cheeks. Located outside the capital's walls, the Trench was flush with illicit drugs and prostitution. Gangsters ran the place, while the imperial court turned a blind eye. The clan only collected occasional reports from activity there.

And apparently, babies were equivalent to diarrhea. Unwanted. A trouble.

But not Lilian's. Her baby would be the next heir of the North.

Through the awkward moment of silence, Rumei's eyes searched Lilian's. They were enthralling. "I'm sorry, I've got squirt mouth. I just assumed your pimp wouldn't stand for a newly broken-in whore to be with child before she could make some money."

Lilian covered her mouth. Rumei was so...coarse. But it wasn't her fault. If she was from the Trench, coarseness was all she knew. She was probably a prostitute herself, here to end her pregnancy. And when Gardener Ju had made this appointment, it was probably to trick her into the same. When Lilian found her voice again, she nodded toward the bump in Rumei's belly. "Are you here...for the same reason?"

"Oh, no." Rumei shook her head. "Or rather, originally, yes. But the seed was strong, and I came too late. Doctor Fang is also good at making sure the squirt is solid."

That was a relief. Despite wanting to smile, Lilian schooled her expression into dignified grace.

"Ju Lilian," one of the assistants called from a door.

Rumei's grin was as suggestive as a Hummingbird's. "You're up. Let's meet again sometime."

"Let's," Lilian said without meaning it. She bowed her head to Rumei, then rose and glided toward the back office.

The assistant beckoned her to a brown-upholstered chaise. "Please lie down. Doctor Fang will be with you in a moment."

Lilian did as she was told. Her gaze drifted first to the needles on a lacquered stand, then to the cushioned stool beside the chaise, and finally to the acupuncture charts on the walls. A grin tugged at her lips. The point names were poetic, much like the Blossom's techniques. And of course, where doctors used those spots to heal with needles, Fists used them to inflict pain.

The door opened, and Doctor Fang hobbled in. He took a seat on the stool. "Your wrists, please."

It was their regular ritual, his means of diagnosis—indeed, he'd predicted when she'd blossom with Heaven's Dew. Lilian extended her arms, and he pressed her pulse under his gnarled fingers.

"You are pregnant," he said. "Were you taking the herbs I gave you?"

"Yes," she lied, even as her heart soared. It was just as she hoped. If she were carrying Lord Ting's son—

"Heavens." His expression contorted. "Oh, no."

Soaring just a second ago, Lilian's heart lurched. "What's wrong?"

"The seed took root outside of your womb."

Outside of her womb? The room spun. "What does that mean?"

"Luckily, you came now." He gave her a reassuring pat. "Had you waited another two days, the seed's roots would dig so deep, there would be nothing I could do."

She blew out a breath. "So you can save the child?"

"Heavens, no." His eyes rounded. "But I can still save *you*."

"I'm sorry?"

He sighed. "The seed will never flourish. If we don't dislodge it, its heat will kill you."

No, no, no. Not her baby.

Not her.

She couldn't die, or the Yu bloodline would die with her. There'd be more chances—

"On the bright side, you won't have to worry about these accidents in the future."

All sense of hope seemed to be trickling away. "What do you mean?"

"This type damages the paths between your nest and womb. Now, relax." He took up the needles.

This couldn't be. All the happiness she'd felt with Lord Ting now felt like a dream. It was probably Lord Yang's fault, jostling her with his roughness while Lord Ting's seed was trying to find a safe place to implant.

Tears filled her eyes as he inserted the needles into her arms and legs.

* * *

The Present

From everything Tian had learned from the clan about spotting lies, Tang Li wasn't telling the entire truth about Lilian's chance meeting with Rumei in the Floating World clinic. Still, tears glistened in her eyes as he helped her onto a horse. Based on the messages passed with the gatehouse commander, the imperial garrison would let the Yang cavalry through halfway between the fourth and fifth gibbous. That left little time to reach the square.

"If your story is true," Yangyang said to Tang Li, "then Lilian was crushed."

Meisha nodded. "She seemed so happy those days."

"An act?" Wen looked to Jie. "We're learning so much more about her."

"She was fond of Lord Ting," Jie whispered. "I do believe she really wanted to bear his child."

Tian tapped his chin. What would the child's status be? "Was Lord Ting married? Did he have any other children?"

"His wife died in childbirth years before he met Lilian." Jie shook her head. "He never remarried."

It was odd for a hereditary lord not to remarry, at least one without an heir. "Who would've inherited his domain?" Tian asked.

"A cousin, who was killed during the Cloud Castle uprising. Lord Ting had little love for him."

Ting was turning out to be quite the enigmatic character. "Would he be able to marry Lilian?"

The women exchanged glances.

"It would be rare for a great lord to take a Blossom as more than a concubine," Wen said. "However, the Emperor favored him, and might've allowed it."

There might be more, though. Tian turned to Tang Li. "When you said the other day that Lilian was last heir of the North, what did you mean?"

Tang Li's mouth opened and closed. "I wish I could explain, but the *Tiger's Eye* still keeps me from saying that Lilian was..." Her mouth moved, but she couldn't say what she wanted to.

Still, the picture was becoming clearer in Tian's head. He drew lines in the air. "We don't know how. But Lilian might've been last heir of the North. She marries Lord Ting. Their child would be..."

Wen's head bobbed. "A symbol for the North."

"A threat to the Emperor," Jie said, nearly inaudibly.

CHAPTER 7

The Present

Tang Li sat on a horse behind a Yang soldier, just outside the gatehouse square. Reliving Lilian's loss had crushed her. She felt Lilian's hopelessness as if she'd experienced it herself. Lilian had endured so much hardship, and had finally found purpose, only to have her dreams dashed by cruel fate. No wonder she hated Lord Yang so much.

Li blinked away the tears and peered through the darkness up at the battlements. In her capacity as Lord Yang's courtesan, she'd passed through here several times in the past on their way to Cloud Castle. It would usually be during the day, when farmers and merchants took over the stone-paved square, and never carried the risk of imperial soldiers on the Wall showering them with crossbow bolts.

Now though, despite Tian's reassurance that it was all part of the plan, the garrison watched with wary eyes and loaded repeaters.

She looked to the others. Would they piece together that Lilian was daughter of Lord Yu, the last heir of the Yu Dynasty? Despite the general veracity of the stories she told them, she'd omitted much, either by choice or because the *Tiger's Eye* repressed it. She turned back to the Wall.

"Only the cavalry," an imperial yelled down. "Any foot soldiers who try to enter the square will be shot."

At the head of the column of horses, Black Lotus Kun gestured. The line of horses broke into a slow trot, entering the square.

Holding her breath, Li gripped her rider tighter and ducked behind his broad back. She looked to the other entrances to the square, where footmen loyal to Yang stood behind hastily-assembled barricades. From what she'd overheard, they'd decided to assault the gatehouse at dawn, using ladders to climb the walls.

It would be pure suicide. Her mind, fortified with Lilian's cunning, was already coming up with alternate solutions. Hopefully, Jie would eliminate Lord Yang before it came to that.

Up ahead, the heavy wood doors rose silently on dwarf-made gears.

They were a smaller version of the front gates to a bank in the Floating World.

The place where Lilian had had a fateful encounter.

* * *

Two Years Ago

After her miscarriage, Lilian lost all will to live. The cell sisters tried to be helpful, but since none ever wanted to fall pregnant, they couldn't empathize with her loss. They didn't know the baby had been wanted, because they didn't know her true identity. For their part, Jie and Wen never brought it up, never judged her; at the very least, they knew her true affection for Lord Ting.

And yet, preoccupied with duties in the North, he didn't call on her. And even if he had, the Surgeon's *Tiger's Eye* would have prevented her from telling him everything.

To Tang Li, however, she could confide more. Her gentle, unassuming nature provided support, and whatever secrets Lilian revealed, she could suppress with her own *Tiger's Eye* technique. Little by little, nudged by hatred for Lord Yang—Tang Li's regular Hummingbird—her motivation returned. One place she failed was trying to paint sections of the Surgeon's face, in hopes of assembling them for an older clan member to see. But no, his *Tiger's Eye* prevented her from doing even that.

In many ways, that provided a spark of motivation. He had made her his pawn. She would find a way to turn the tables on him. The frequently absent Gardener Ju gave her a month to recuperate, even as she bemoaned the growing bids from hereditary lords and wealthy merchants that she had to turn down. Each day, Lilian put one foot in front of the other. Like she had as a kidnapped three-year-old, she set her fingers in the Surgeon's unique positions for the *Tiger's Eye*.

At the end of the month, almost to the hour, she went out on an anonymous assignation to a rowhouse in the northwest corner of the Floating World. It was famous because its dwarf-made front door had survived the fire that had burned down the rest of the district twenty years before. The door, frame, and internal gears were all made of metal. While the original structure had been made of wood, the new one was made of stone, and housed a bank.

Lilian went around to the side entrance, where steps led up to a second-floor residence. Just who was she seeing? Thousands of men had used it in the years she'd lived in the Floating World, most for a single night, paying three gold *yuan* to a company which several individuals and companies held a stake in. It could be any one of the Chrysanthemum Pavilion's hundreds of regular clients, many of whom had shown interest in her.

Black Fist training took over as she looked for clues and climbed the steps. She held the sleeves of her blue gown so they wouldn't swish, and her brocade shoes swept over the treads without a sound.

Maybe she hadn't been as silent as she thought. Footsteps approached the door from the other side, and it opened she reached for the handle.

Feng Rumei stood there, features just as exotic as before. Her plain green dress did little to hide her belly. It had swelled a little more since they'd met at Doctor Fang's clinic.

It was a reminder of what Lilian had lost. Even as her gut clenched, she bowed low. "Good afternoon."

"Hello." Eyes searching hers, Feng Rumei waved a nonchalant hand, showing as much etiquette as she had the last time. Was she here with her master? Maybe he had some fetish, like wanting one lover to watch as he took another.

Lilian tilted to snatch a surreptitious glance past Feng Rumei, and listened for the sound of other activity beyond.

Three doors led out of the main room, and late afternoon sun streamed in through two windows facing out onto the main road. Paintings and calligraphy imbued with Dragonscript hung on the walls. The indentation in the embroidered silk cushion of an elegant rosewood chair suggested that was where Rumei had been sitting. The matching chairs, surrounding the oval design in the thick wool carpet, showed no sign that anyone else was here.

Perhaps her master was in the bedroom already? Lilian met Feng Rumei's gaze again and started to speak.

"Come." Rumei turned, beckoned, and waddled toward one of the side rooms.

This had to be the strangest assignation Lilian had ever heard of. She steeled herself for what she might find. Perhaps the lord was waiting there, undressed. Or perhaps he'd be restrained against some prop—something Lord Yang enjoyed, though with her bound and him delivering the punishment. She buried a shudder and took a deep breath as she followed Rumei in.

The carved, rosewood bedframe and plush silken sheets looked untouched. Nobody else was here. Lilian looked to Rumei.

With a feral grin, the woman padded over, settled on the bed, and lounged back. She patted the spot beside her.

What was this? Steps tentative, Lilian went around to the side and sat where indicated.

Pushing her down and straddling her, Rumei leaned in and claimed Lilian's lips. They were soft, supple.

Still, Lilian froze. Maybe like in the Floating World Houses, there were peepholes where an interloper could watch. She hadn't gotten enough of a sense of the entire apartment's size to know if there was space for a passage between the walls, but perhaps Rumei's master was hiding somewhere.

"We are alone," Rumei said, breaking away. Her large, brown eyes locked on Lilian's.

"What about your master?"

Rumei laughed. "I am my own master."

If she didn't have a master... "Then you—"

"Yes, I placed a bid on you."

It didn't make sense. If Rumei didn't have a master, then how was she pregnant? And if she was pregnant, why was she here, kissing Lilian?

"Oh, come now." Rumei chuckled. "Don't tell me you have never found release with another woman?"

Lilian's cheeks flushed hot. Of course, they all had in their early days in the Floating World, before the Houses had bid on them. Mistress Yin taught them how to pleasure themselves, and each other.

"There, of course you have. Now, I'm absolutely starved for sex, and I'm told that Blossoms are the best at it."

"With men." It wasn't the entire truth, but it was open-ended enough to dig deeper into Rumei's thoughts.

"Oh, a woman knows another's body better than any man can." Rumei's grin looked like that of Yanluo, Lord of the Underworld, negotiating over souls. "And you're trained to pleasure a woman, aren't you? For those lords who wish to be entertained by more than one Blossom at a time. I know."

It was true, and Lilian had been part of such jobs with House seniors on more than a few occasions. But— "Why me?"

Rumei propped her chin on her arm. "Because you fascinate me. Your history. Your inner demons. I like broken things."

What? How could she possibly know?

"About Boney Face?" Rumei raised an eyebrow. "He's an ugly shit."

What? Lilian reached for her bladed hairpin, but her hand refused to obey. "How do you know about him?"

"Since I know your secrets, can I trust you with mine?"

No, but she didn't have to know that. Lilian nodded.

"I'm half-Nothori. Some of my father's people are gifted with Empathy. I can see your thoughts. I know who you are. Who Jie and Wen are."

Lilian sucked in a sharp breath. "Do you know about—"

"The lock on your mind? Yes. You are an interesting maze of memories and thoughts, some of which you don't even know yourself."

"But you do?"

"Some of them, yes." Rumei pressed a fingertip to Lilian's brow.

Hope bloomed in Lilian's chest. "Can you unlock them?"

"What I do is different from what Boney Face did to you. While what he did is quite mundane, I don't think I can use Empathy to untangle the mess he left with—what do you call it, the *Tiger's Eye*?"

The hope guttered, but was still there. "Can you tell my friends about the Surgeon?"

"I can."

New excitement surged up Lilian's spine. "Then— "

"But I won't."

Lilian deflated like a cut pufferfish. "Why not?"

"I have use for him myself, and his value is his anonymity." Rumei yawned.

It would be tempting to reveal the woman's secret ability, but if the Surgeon could lock away memories using just the *Tiger's Eye*, there was no telling what an Empath with real magic could do. Rumei might be mind-reading right now. Lilian looked to her.

Indeed, the woman was grinning back, showing her white teeth.

"I need *someone* to know." The pleading in Lilian's voice sounded pathetic in her own ears.

"I'm someone. I want to be someone you can trust. And I want to trust you, in turn." Rumei ran a hand over Lilian's cheek.

One last chance. A plan formed in her mind. "You can see the Surgeon in my memories? Can you at least share that with Tang Li, if I promise to lock that away?"

Rumei tilted her head. "I could do that, though the Surgeon's lock on your mind will probably carry over."

"So you will do it?"

Grinning, Rumei guided Lilian's hand up her skirts. "You'll have to earn it."

* * *

The Present

With all the imperial soldiers' eyes on them, Tang Li should've been worried about passing through the gatehouse. Instead, Lilian's newly emerged memories made her think back to her own visit with Lilian to Feng Rumei's apartments. No longer Faceless Chang, Rumei had been pregnant at the time, and they'd taken tea and pastries together, chatting about their shared roots in the Trench while Lilian listened on.

But between then and the time their host and Lilian retired to a bedroom, there was a blank spot in Li's memory. The newest of Lilian's recollections explained what happened during that time: Rumei had used Empathy to implant clear images of the Surgeon, the Black Lotus Temple, and several other of Lilian's memories.

Shaking it out of her head, Li pressed closer into the cavalryman, finding comfort in an anonymous warm body.

A rigid body.

His eyes scanned the imperials on the mezzanine, his knuckles white. Though the imperials weren't aiming at them, all held repeating crossbows. Their regimental commander's jaw was locked in a grim line. Other soldiers had their hands on the winch release. If they loosed it, the gates on either side would crash down, trapping them inside.

The lead horse was nearing the exit. If the imperials were going to attack, it would be soon, before it cleared.

It passed through.

Tang Li blew out a breath. Her horse reached the other side, followed by the ones carrying Jie, Wen, Yangyang, and Meisha. But there was always a chance they would divide the cavalry in two, and Tian was riding at the rear of the column.

CHAPTER 8

The Present

Tian held his breath as his horse passed through the gatehouse. At the very rear of the column, he'd no doubt be safe: had the imperial forces intended to trap some of the Yang cavalry inside, or split them apart, they surely would've done so by now. Still, the soldiers stood high above on the mezzanine, in a far superior position.

He blew out his breath as they reached the other side and the gates closed behind him. His plan to get them through had worked.

Up ahead, finished stone blocks lay near wood framing, likely part of the construction project to connect defenses between Cloud Castle and the Great Wall. For now, if an invader from the north could make it past the fortress' batteries covering the pass, they could dash up the access road. Once the fortifications were complete, though, the castle would be truly impregnable.

At the head of column, Brother Kun raised his hand, calling for a halt. A rest, before they continued up the winding access road to Lord Yang's fort. Given how tense the soldiers were, it was a good idea.

And now, maybe he'd be able to ask more questions of Tang Li. Their conversation had been cut off by the need to pass through the gatehouse, and there were still big gaps between the time Lilian had miscarried and then plotted to kill Lord Ting and escape the clan. He had to know, and there might not be a chance after they entered the castle. Tian dismounted, only to find Jie and the others approaching.

"Good work," Meisha said to him.

Jie grinned. "I've come to expect nothing from Tian's plans."

Heat rose in his cheeks. To deflect attention from himself, he turned to Tang Li. "Somewhere along the way, Lilian taught you the skills to become a fixer."

Tang Li nodded.

* * *

The Past

With no chance of bearing a new heir to the North, Lilian gave up on her family's legacy. Lord Ting had all but disappeared from the Floating World, and she found she didn't even care. After all, she wasn't a starry-eyed little girl anymore. Her life fell into a new rhythm, as plotting revenge on Lord Yang and strategizing a way to reveal the Surgeon and Steel Orchid became the driving forces in her life.

Expecting Yang to buy out Tang Li's contract, Lilian trained her in the art of spotting talent, making anonymous connections, and organizing resources; always making her forget the lessons with the *Tiger's Eye*. Three months after the miscarriage, Yang bought Tang Li's contract. She left the Chrysanthemum Pavilion with tears and fanfare, and Lilian then had an unwitting spy in his household. She'd use whatever information she learned to seed his downfall.

As a Blossom, she spent nights on her back. Within half a year of her Plucking, she became the Chrysanthemum Pavilion's Corsage, and moved into the third-floor hearth room. As with all courtesans, her contract prices fell with each passing month; but by the time they'd levelled out, they were still the second-highest in the Floating World, behind the Peony Garden's Lusha.

If the experiences with men taught her anything, it was that they were such pathetic creatures, driven by base desires. She found that she actually enjoyed her contracts with Feng Rumei more, at least until the latter also disappeared from her life. Even with the gossip of the Floating World and the information network of the Black Lotus, Lilian never found out what happened to the exotic woman. Had she safely given birth? Had it been a boy, or a girl? Lilian's heart ached more at this loss than Lord Ting's.

Even if he bragged about the frequency of his visits, Lord Shi called on rare occasions—it turned out his famed austerity was not due to the notorious frugality of Northerners, but rather that his fiefdom didn't earn much.

It was curious that Lord Yang, with similar lands and having spent his winnings from gambling on her virgin price, could still afford a luxurious lifestyle. Using the *Tiger's Eye* on one of their tea dates, Lilian sent Tang Li digging into the lord's finances. It turned out he held a stake in Jinjing Lumber. The company provided raw *yue* sap to imperial refiners, who were under orders to create a less-addictive alternative to opium.

Lilian had Tang Li make an offhand comment about how profitable it would be to make *yue* and distribute it outside of imperial permits. Then she not only got Tang Li to steal proof of Lord Yang's ownership in the company, but also convince him that Lord Shi now had the stock certificates in his famed dwarf safe. Of course, Lilian kept them hidden in the apartments she rented in the capital. It was now a matter of waiting for an opportune time to expose him.

While plotting revenge for her family gave her purpose, she found new joy in her sisterhood with the Floating World cell. With Wen's Plucking eight months after Lilian's, they were now both

Blossoms. Meanwhile, Jie remained a Floret, and as leader of the cell, ran an efficient schedule. Still, she showed no sign of flowering with Heaven's Dew, and her virgin price had reached dizzying heights. Though the half-elf would never admit it, she was proud of the record bids, and wore her lack of feminine grace and wiles like a badge of honor. It was absolutely adorable.

It created an ironic dichotomy: while Lilian was Jie's House senior, she would always be her clan junior. It made trying to tutor Jie in the arts of a Blossom all the more difficult—and yet, Lilian couldn't deny how much she enjoyed the practice. It turned out that fingers deft in picking pockets had other talents as well. Those sessions provided a much-needed respite from nightly responsibilities for the House.

And the clan. In the immediate aftermath of the trap at Cloud Castle, the most loyal lords gained new domains or enlarged their existing ones. On the surface, all seemed settled. Still, it was the clan's duty to see what lay beneath the façade of peace and loyalty, both through assets hidden in the North, and also in the Floating World. As the months went by, a disturbing trend emerged in the cell's information network. While an idle whisper between the sheets here or a drunken murmur there meant nothing in isolation, eventually they began to add up. Resentment toward the Jade Throne again brewed in the North.

Lilian followed reports of Lord Ting's role in keeping the lords in line. Not out of personal interest—no, she'd all but lost her younger self's puppy love for him. It was more a matter of how to use that information to exact vengeance on Lord Yang. In any case, Lord Ting's affairs kept him in the North, while Lord Yang remained in the capital, currying the Emperor's favor.

Sixteen months after Lilian's Plucking, when she was on a mission with Wen, she discovered news which sent her stomach twisting.

* * *

The Present

As Tang Li recounted the year and a half, Tian marveled at how Lilian had pieced together her revenge on Lord Yang. She'd planted traitorous ideas in his head, then secured evidence of them. That had led to this attack on Cloud Castle.

Still, one unanswered question niggled at him. Everything she'd set in motion had started with sparking Tang Li's memories, first with the hairpin, and then with the three full moons. Why had she waited until then?

CHAPTER 9

The Present

As they mounted up again, Jie looked up toward Cloud Castle's batteries. The only visible section of the fortress, it would make any attack through the pass a suicide mission.

Even without having to run the pass, their cavalry column still had to make it up the winding access road to the fortress.

It'd been two years since she'd come this way, that time on foot. She'd been disguised as a porter on the procession bringing Lilian and the other cell Blossoms to the reception. Unlike then, when soldiers in imperial blue lined the battlements, the ramparts now stood empty, save for the patrol who had since run back toward the fortress. In all likelihood, Lord Yang had pulled his soldiers back to a point where they could deliver a more concentrated, sustained volley of crossbow bolts.

Probably the yard, just in front of the main gates.

With no immediate threats, Jie thought back to the time between her last time here and now.

* * *

Six Months Ago

A year and a half had passed since Lilian's miscarriage, and Jie felt nothing but relief that Lilian had returned to her old self. How foolish they'd all been, to believe that a Blossom could find love with a Hummingbird. How outrageously naïve they'd been, to think that even if Ting had reciprocated her feelings, the clan would ever allow them to be together.

Now, they sat on the thick winter quilts on Lilian's bed. A year before, she'd moved into the Corsage's place of honor in the third-floor hearth room, where a crackling fire provided heat against the winter chill. With early afternoon sun peeking through the two windows, smoke mingled with Lilian's honeysuckle scent.

Jie buffed Lilian's nails with a file, the scraping pattern mimicking clan code. *You need to practice 'Snake Entwines Its Prey.'*

Laughing, Lilian wrapped her legs around Jie's waist. Pulling her hand free, she reached behind Jie's neck and brought her down on top of her.

"I didn't mean now." With her own laugh, Jie started to sit up.

"As your senior, I say when." Lilian continued with the technique, snaking her other arm under one of Jie's. "*Entangling Dragons* will excite any Hummingbird."

It was easy enough to counter, especially since Lilian's grappling skills left much to be desired. With a reversal, Jie slipped out from between Lilian's legs and straddled her. She seized both her wrists and held her down.

Lilian's arms were so toned and shapely. She pouted in the way that sent men's hearts racing. "I was serious."

Raising an eyebrow, Jie cocked her head. Just what was the *Entangling Dragons* technique?

With Lilian maturing faster than Jie, she was now physically stronger. She shot her arms out to the sides. The motion brought

Jie downward, and Lilian tilted her head to prevent them from bashing their noses together.

"*Siren's Temptation.*" Lilian's lips tickled Jie's ear before moving down to her neck.

Wherever they touched, her skin tingled. It had never happened like that before. How strange. Jie released Lilian's wrists and ran her fingers through Lilian's hair.

Lilian continued, cupping Jie's neck and lavishing kisses up her jawline.

They'd done this so many times in practice before, but something felt different this time. Jie's pulse stuttered.

Lilian's lips were so full.

So close.

And tempting.

Then they met, like so many other times in the past.

Shudders jolted up and down Jie's spine. Her breath hitched as all coherent thought fled her. Her lips parted of their own accord. Lilian's tongue slid in, caressing Jie's.

Grinding her hips, Jie let out a primal moan.

Teeth pulling on Jie's lower lip, Lilian pushed her back, gasping for breath. "That's it. *Entangling Dragons.* You acted well enough to convince me you meant it."

She had, because it hadn't been acting. Hot with need, Jie fought the urge to lean in and kiss Lilian again, to find out if she *did* mean it.

But how would Lilian interpret it? What if she didn't feel the same way? They were best friends. Clan sisters.

For the next few days, Jie tried to wrap her head around that one kiss. What had made it so different? Of course she'd always adored Lilian. She'd been like a little sister, who Jie had protected. They'd cuddled together almost nightly for over a decade, without igniting the same sparks that had coursed through her this last time.

She obsessed over it, her heart racing whenever she caught a glance of Lilian, while also avoiding making direct eye contact.

Then, on a late morning as she finished polishing the tables of the common room, it occurred to her. She'd felt a tinge of jealousy when Lilian had fallen for Lord Ting. At the time, she'd thought it had just been because of how it affected their relationship as sisters. But what if there'd been more? Lilian was a full-fledged Blossom now. No longer a girl, but a woman.

But no, Jie had kissed several of the House Blossoms in training. This was nothing more than a silly notion.

Or was it?

At this hour, Lilian would be sleeping off her previous night with Lord Peng, but would have to rise soon if she were to make their cell training session. Jie hurried up the steps and through the hall, announcing her presence with her feet chirping on the nightingale floors. At Lilian's door, she paused and took a few breaths. This was a bad idea.

The door slid open.

Lilian stood there, hair askew. Her robe hung off a bare shoulder, exposing the curve of her neck and offering a view of her collarbone. Her large eyes were beautiful.

Jie swallowed hard.

"I know," Lilian said, smiling. "Practice."

"Yes. *Entangling Dragons*." Jie's voiced sounded husky in her own ears. Stepping into the room, she kicked the door shut. She backed Lilian to her bed so that they both tumbled into it. They rolled over, with Lilian ending up on top. When their lips met, all of Jie's nerves fired like the finale of a New Year's pyrotechnics show.

Her hands slid inside Lilian's robes, under her arms to her back, and ran over the perfect sculpting of her shoulder blades. Their tongues swirled around each other, and need bloomed inside her.

Lilian pulled back, panting. Their gazes met.

Part of Jie panicked. What were her eyes saying? Had they gone too far?

"Your entry into *Entangling Dragons* was interesting," Lilian said, her look calculating. "A reserved Hummingbird might get aroused by you taking the initiative like that."

Jie's arousal, on the other hand, guttered. She schooled her expression into calm. Practice. Lilian only saw this as practice, and any passion she'd shown was just an act. Just like any other Blossom entertaining a Hummingbird.

Thank the Heavens Jie had the perfect excuse. *Real practice soon*, she signed, placing emphasis on *real* with the sharpness of the gesture.

On her way to the silk market—where today they'd practice picking pockets, passing the loot, and returning it to the owner—she stopped by the grove of cherry trees, where folded sheets of paper were tied into knots around the branches, otherwise bared in late winter. Though most notes were written wishes, the one Jie took contained news or instructions from the clan. Still dwelling on this latest encounter with Lilian, she stuffed it into her sleeve's inner pocket.

She arrived at the market ahead of time. Ducking between two nearby buildings, she carefully unfolded the message from the clan.

Her heart sank.

It was about Lord Ting.

* * *

The Present

Jie's stomach twisted as she came out of her memories. In her jealousy, she hadn't told Lilian about the missive. Maybe it wouldn't have come as such a surprise had Jie picked the right timing for her to learn about it. Maybe she wouldn't have been so bitter toward Lord Ting.

"We're almost there," the Yang cavalryman who shared Jie's mount said.

Thank the Heavens, she'd be off the horse soon. She looked up the path, to where it opened into a yard in front of the gates...

...and suppressed a gasp. Heavy doors made of lashed timbers barred the gatehouse.

The last time she'd been here, there hadn't been gates: during the castle's renovation, the Emperor had ordered them removed, to prevent a repeat of the Founder's unsuccessful siege against the Yu Dynasty holdouts. The last clan report, from a week ago, had made no mention of gates being installed.

If they failed to capture or kill Lord Yang, he could hole up here for months. Maybe longer.

She slipped off the back of the horse and worked her way back toward the abandoned battlements.

CHAPTER 10

The Present

Wen fiddled with her pinkie as the cavalry column slowed to a halt in the open yard outside the gates to Cloud Castle. Battlements lined the right and front sides of the space, defended by soldiers bedecked in livery of the various Northern counties. To the left was a sheer cliff face that would lead to a nasty tumble into the mountain pass below. To think, this would've been Lord Ting's castle, had the conniving Lord Yang not bribed the Emperor with Lilian's virginity. How things might've turned out differently.

She looked over to see Tian helping Tang Li off of the horse. He was such a little gentleman, it filled Wen's chest with fondness. Hopefully, he wouldn't grow up to be like the entitled lords they entertained in the Floating World.

Like Lord Yang. Jealous of Lord Ting, he'd delighted in testing Lilian's tolerance for abuse.

For Lilian, who saw their work as a duty she didn't enjoy, it must've been torture.

Though the one time Wen had seen Lilian at work, it hadn't seemed so bad.

* * *

Six Months Ago

Ever since her arrival in the Floating World five years ago, Wen had always been fascinated with sex. It had all started when Master Yin had used Yangyang as a model to teach the flowery names for genitals, and had only grown with training. In the ten months since her Plucking, she realized she was different from other Blossoms. While most counted down the days until they paid off their bond, Wen exhilarated in fulfilling a different Hummingbird's fetish every night. Even if she somewhat shared the others' view that men were pathetic, they satiated her need.

Now, her heart raced as she and Lilian stepped out of a palanquin and into the snow-dusted courtyard of Lord Nan's capital villa. He'd asked for Lilian and Lusha tonight, and because of Floating World etiquette, the only way to enjoy a threesome with Blossoms from different Houses was in a third location. With his wife back home in Tieshan County, and looking to celebrate his windfall profits from *yue* sap sales to the capital, Lord Nan had summoned them here.

With rumors of a new insurrection, Wen had spiked Lusha's tea with a purgative herb that had her vomiting, and taken her place. After all, two Fists working together could gather more information than just one.

An early frost had led to a poor harvest of flowers for the clan's male intoxicant, so they had to rely on other means. Means they were well-trained in during their time in the Floating World.

Once inside, their dresses didn't stay on much longer than the fur shawls they'd worn. He took them through the sitting room and up the stairs to his bedroom, leaving a trail of lingerie along the way. Wen would never admit how much she'd enjoyed exploring Lilian's body, even if it was merely part of an act to titillate Lord Nan.

He'd taken Wen first, and at last, spent in the aftermath of their play, he lay asleep on his bed, their cheeks resting on either side of his chest. His heartbeat thumped slowly, and his chest rose and fell with his light breaths.

Wen tested his consciousness with a gentle pinch. When he didn't stir, she met Lilian's gaze across from her.

Just like old times, Lilian mouthed with a grin, brushing hair out of her face.

Pointing her chin to where Lord Nan cupped her breast, Wen signed, *Back then, we were resting on Jie's chest, and she wasn't groping me.*

Nor me. Smirking, Lilian lifted Lord Nan's hand off her ass, slipped under his arm, and rested it on the bed. She stood, her curves silhouetted by the moonlight from a window. *Light sleeper, reacts to noise.*

Wen disentangled herself and eased out of the bed. The residence didn't have nightingale floors, so it was child's play to creep to the door. At this late hour, all the servants would've retired to the smaller residence on the other side of the compound, but Wen listened just to be sure no one lingered.

Satisfied, she motioned for Lilian to follow. They both remained undressed—no sleeves or hems to swish or snag on something—but retrieved makeup cases which contained more than just cosmetics.

Just like when they'd entered, the door opened without a sound, and they slunk along the mezzanine hall overlooking the dimly lit sitting room. Two doors down, they came to what they'd identified as Lord Nan's study. The lock yielded to Lilian's deft picks, and they slipped in.

Bookshelves lined walls to the east and west, while a desk sat to the north, between two windows. Light from the Blue Moon trickled in from the shutters' seams, though certainly not enough to read by.

If Lord Nan was a light sleeper, they probably didn't have much time. Wen signed, *You check the desk, I'll take the bookshelves.*

With a nod, Lilian padded over to the desk, while Wen headed to the east wall.

Retrieving her foundation brush, Wen popped off the bristles. Light from the bauble embedded inside cast a small beam over the books. Though the titles looked to be nothing out of the ordinary for a great lord—classic literature; treatises on governance, history, and the like—they weren't arranged in any particular order.

Not only that, they were pristine, their binding showing no sign of ever having been opened. A thin layer of dust covered all. After looking back to see Lilian skimming letters, Wen crossed the room to the west wall. The organization of books appeared to be the same, except... One set of sixteen history books was aligned in chronological order, with no dust.

With his lack of intellectual depth, Lord Nan would never be mistaken for a historian. Probing the books with her fingers, Wen discovered them to be false backs, forming a safe door. Dwarf-made craftsmanship, but the clan had a similar model back home. Brush light between her teeth, she searched for an unlocking mechanism. One of the spines peeled back to expose a lock. With a few twists of her picks, it opened.

Behind six gold bars were stashed several letters. She scanned them. Most were from other lords. Some complained about imperial taxes, others bemoaned their inability to keep up with imperial saltpeter quotas. Judging from the context, it appeared that Lord Nan sat on the fence between...

Neither totally loyal to the Emperor, nor sold on insurrection. A third-rank lord prior to the Cloud Castle trap nearly a year and a half before, he'd gained Tieshan County from one of the slain rebels. In this, he was much like the other new lords, who were trying to gauge the way the winds blew.

Wen fiddled with her pinkie. Imperial impulse was to crush even the slightest hint of treason. Sometimes, she wondered if maybe extending some sweet buns would work better. For his part, reports had it that Lord Ting had worked hard to keep the other lords in line.

She looked over her shoulder toward Lilian. So enamored with Lord Ting in the past, she hadn't mentioned him lately, beyond answering questions when his name was brought up in intelligence briefings.

Lilian let out a gasp, and her brush light clattered to the desk.

"Lilian? Wen?" Lord Nan's groggy voice called from the bedroom.

Wen returned the correspondence to the safe, shut it, then closed her brush light. Lilian scooped hers up and did the same. Footsteps thumped across in the hall, and a bright line shone under the threshold. Lord Nan paused there.

Wen held her breath, and motioned Lilian to join her in a spot behind the door. If he opened it, they'd be in the blind spot, but if he came in all the way...

It rattled as he tested it, but then he continued through the hall. "Lilian? Wen?"

Using his footsteps as cover, Wen unlocked and opened the door. She peeked out to see his retreating back eight paces away, nearly to the steps leading down. He bent over at times to pick up their undergarments.

Follow me. Setting her cosmetic case between her teeth, Wen darted three steps across the hall, grabbed the railing, and went over the side. She caught the mezzanine floor, then released and landed without a sound on the thick carpet.

Lilian alighted beside her, and gestured to a cushioned chaise; out of the mezzanine's line of sight, but directly facing the steps. "We're down here, my Lord."

Lord Nan's footsteps sped up.

Lilian's didn't need to explain her plan. Wen stashed their cosmetic cases under the chaise, then sat, spreading her legs. Lilian nestled herself in between, facing her, and draped her arms around Wen's neck. Resting her chin on Lilian's shoulder, Wen cupped her ass with one hand and clung from her shoulder with the other. Wen's skin tingled where Lilian nuzzled her.

He appeared at the top of the steps, his mouth twitching into a lurid grin. "Oh, my."

"We didn't want to disturb you." Lilian drew her head back and looked over her shoulder. "But since you're awake, come join us."

Wen cast her most inviting gaze.

His manhood poked from beneath his sleeping robe. He dashed down the steps like a stallion heading to the stud farm. So predictable. They had a few seconds before he arrived.

What did you see? Wen mouthed.

Lord Ting. The Emperor wants him to marry Lord Nan's daughter. He'll be back in the capital in the next few days.

Wen searched Lilian's eyes, but whatever reaction she'd had when she first found out, she'd replaced it with a look of indifference.

Lord Nan appeared behind Lilian and reached under her arms. He cradled one of Lilian's breasts with one hand, Wen's with the other.

Wen flashed an alluring smile at him, even as she traced code across Lilian's skin. *Remember to lock his study door later.*

Letting out a moan, clearly contrived to a Blossom, Lilian gave a slight nod in acknowledgement.

Did she really have no feelings for Lord Ting?

* * *

The Present

The sound of repeating crossbows cocking brought Wen back to the present. She searched the battlements, where the Northerners were levelling their weapons. She was near the front of the column, which would make her an easy target.

Tang Li, however, had moved to the very front, and now raised her hands. "Don't shoot. Let me speak with Lord Yang."

Wen held her breath. Lord Yang had tried to have Tang Li killed back at Lord Shi's compound, but that was only because he didn't want her to fall into imperial hands and reveal he'd been behind the fake bombs at Lord Wu's moons-viewing party. Now that she was here, maybe he'd have a change of heart. The success of their mission depended on it.

Lord Yang poked his head between two men at the top of the gatehouse, his eyes raking over the cavalry assembled below.

The riders all saluted him. "My Lord!"

Beaming in their adoration, Lord Yang turned to Tang Li.

She held up the stock certificates proving his partial ownership of Jinjing Lumber. "I have retrieved the items from Lord Shi's safe, as you requested."

His eyes narrowed. "Forgeries?"

Wen squeezed her fists tight.

Tang Li unfurled the bloodied sheets.

His expression relaxed a little.

Tang Li answered in a sassy, Floating World voice: "How many impossible tasks have I accomplished for you?"

"How did you make it through the Great Wall?"

"I was able to bribe the imperials at the gatehouse."

"Oh? I have archers on the other side shooting messenger arrows over the Wall." Lord Yang pantomimed the arc of an arrow. "My commanders say the imperials wouldn't take their bribes.

Tang Li laughed. "Maybe they weren't using the right currency."

"And what did you use?"

"One of these." Tang Li gestured to Brother Kun, who backed the horse up so he was right beside Wen. He reached over and seized her arm.

Wen squealed, perhaps not all feigned.

"And there are more," Tang Li said, gesturing toward Yangyang and Meisha, still sitting on horses behind cavalrymen. "Along with supplies."

Even though this was all part of the plan, Wen shuddered. If they failed, it meant sleeping with a few dozen men a day.

Lord Yang's eyes met hers, a look of recognition blooming in his expression. It had been less than a full day since she, Meisha, and Yangyang had entertained him and Lord Shi on Lord Wu's barge. His attention shifted back to Tang Li. "How did you acquire these treats?"

Tang Li laughed flirtatiously. "I can't reveal all my secrets, can I?"

"That's not good enough. Tell me, or I will have my men shoot you."

CHAPTER 11

The Present

Tian stood a few horses behind Tang Li, and couldn't see her. He wasn't great at reading body language, but she sounded confident. He *could* see Lord Yang atop the gatehouse. With him so suspicious, her answer now might mean the difference between the success of their mission, or getting caught in a hail of crossbow bolts.

"Have I ever failed to make a backup plan?" Tang Li asked. "Some of my assets were posing as palanquin bearers. When we met at the warehouses so they could receive the balance of their payment, your capable men took them into custody. Thus, I have food, weapons, and women."

Would he believe it? Tian tapped his chin, looking up at the gatehouse.

Lord Yang's head bobbed in slow nods. "Tang Li, you are the treasure of my house. Men, let them through."

Hands loosed on reins, and shoulders relaxed. Tian blew out a breath.

Tang Li retreated back to her horse. She was shaking like a wet dog. Tian took her trembling hand and pulled her between two horses.

Though if this was all a trap and Yang's crossbowmen started shooting, the horses might panic. It sure was taking them a long time to open the gate. He looked back the way they came, wondering if he could get them to safety before they got run through by a bolt or trampled by a rampaging stallion.

He squeezed her hand.

She still trembled.

Hoping to keep her mind occupied, he asked, "Do you remember Lilian's reunion with Lord Ting?"

* * *

Six Months Ago

For a year and a half, Lilian had buried Lord Ting deep in the recesses of her mind, walling off all emotion associated with him. It was the only way she could've made it through the aftermath of her miscarriage, made easier since he'd all but disappeared from her life. The only time she heard his name was when clan reports detailed his efforts to keep the North under control, and she would speak of him like any other lord they spied on.

And, there'd been something in Jie's kiss. Even if Wen had been a much better kisser, with her it had all been an act to excite Lord Nan. With Jie, something had stirred in Lilian. Heat. Desire. Awkward enough that she'd had to explain it away as just practice. Perhaps that meant she'd finally, after all these months, gotten over Lord Ting.

Until she'd seen his letter to Lord Nan.

Now, on a cold winter evening as she sat on a wealthy merchant's lap, Lord Ting stepped through the doors of the Chrysanthemum Pavilion, bringing flurries in with him. Snowflakes clung to his heavy silk tunic, which Jie, in her role as a Floret, took from him.

The look on her face—was it surprise? No. Resignation, perhaps.

Whether it was really a hush falling over the crowd, or her pulse pounding in her ears, Lilian couldn't be sure.

"Lord Ting, Dragon of the North!" a man yelled, lifting his cup.

"Dragon of the North," rang the chorus, through a forest of raised mugs.

Lord Ting didn't acknowledge the praise. His gaze swept over the room, freezing only when it fell on her.

Her heart just about stopped.

Beyond him, Jie flashed hand signs. *Do you want a knife in his back?*

He marched through, Hummingbirds, Blossoms, and Florets alike all making way as they exchanged whispers. It felt like every eye was either on him or her.

All training in keeping calm escaped Lilian as she sat on the merchant's lap, frozen like a deer facing down the shaft of an arrow. For his part, he withdrew his hand from where it rested on her thigh, under her skirts.

Gardener Ju appeared between them, bowing. With Lilian paid for for the night, Lord Ting, peer of the realm or not, would have to choose someone else. "My Lord, you honor the Chrysanthemum Pavilion. Several of our Blossoms are avail—"

Without even acknowledging the Gardener, he placed his banking seal into her hand. Meaning she could charge him whatever she wanted. She gawked at it as he brushed by, gaze still on Lilian.

Lilian's chest squeezed tight around her heart as each step brought him closer. When he took her hand, energy jolted through her, more electrifying than Jie's kisses had been. He broke eye contact briefly to look at the merchant, who put his hands on the table.

Rising, she gave an apologetic bow of her head before letting Lord Ting guide her up the stairs. Everyone's attention weighed heavily on her back, none more so than Jie's. He started to lead her into the second-floor hall, but she tugged him toward the third floor.

He raised an eyebrow.

"I'm the Corsage of the House now," she said.

"Of course you are."

It was the first time she'd heard his voice in eighteen months. Her muscles just about turned to jelly.

When they reached her room, she started to kneel to open the door, but he swept her up into his strong arms and pushed the door open with his foot. To use a foot was considered a major breach of etiquette, but she used her own to close it behind him.

It felt safe to be cradled next to his muscular frame, but no sooner than the door shut than he set her down and tore off her outer robe. Even with the heat from the hearth, a chill ran over her. Goosebumps erupted over her exposed shoulders.

Fingers clumsy with desire, she loosened the knots of his tunic, while he unwound her sash. With a quick yank of his hand, her dress cascaded to her ankles. She pulled his robe off, revealing his sculpted chest and abdomen. He pushed her onto her bed, catching the band of her undergarment as she tumbled, and pulling it off.

Parting her legs, he settled his weight on top of her and claimed her mouth. The hardness of his muscles pressing against her contrasted with the softness of his lips and tongue. The fire blooming in her core chased away the chills prickling her skin. Wet with Heaven's Dew, she ached to feel all of him.

He filled her with his entire length, penetrating deeply with rhythmic thrusts, drawing repeated gasps out of her until her body coiled and uncoiled in waves of pleasure.

When at last they lay languid and spent, she rested her head on his chest. Of all the men she'd lain with, he was the only one who'd ever taken her to Heaven.

Each deliberate breath slowed his panting. "Heavens, that was amazing. I've needed you for so long. I thought about you every day, and came straight here from the city gates."

"I'm glad you did." She pressed closer, savoring the feel of him against her.

He tightened his arm around her. "This may all be an act to a Blossom, but I'm addicted to you."

"An act?" she asked, unable to keep the hurt from her voice. Despite what she'd told herself, she'd thought about him every day. And now, he confessed he felt the same.

He dug his chin into the top of her hair. "Lord Yang, Lord Shi, Lord Nan, all the lords of the North. They're all obsessed with you. Each has boasted to me that you love them back."

Now, hurt hung in *his* voice.

And to think Lord Yang believed she loved him, of all people. It'd be mortifying, if wasn't so comedically far from the truth. She lifted her head from Lord Ting's chest, and shook her head and met his gaze. "For them, it's an act. I've been in love with you since the first time I saw you."

"I don't deserve your love," he said.

"Don't say that."

"It's true. I've failed to protect you. I know Lord Yang hurt you in the worst way, but I was powerless to stop him."

If only he knew the true extent of her loss. If only he knew the true extent of her lethal skill, that she'd been unable to use to defend herself against that Turtle Egg's advances. Sadness welled up in her chest.

He pulled her close, stroking her hair. "There, there."

"What about Lord Nan's daughter?" The words escaped her lips before she remembered she wasn't supposed to know about it.

"I don't love her. I've never even met her. I'm going to turn down the proposal."

Lilian covered a laugh. Since when did a lord ever think about marrying for love? That was peasant talk. Still, it was reassuring. Without actually saying it, he was telling her he loved *her*.

* * *

The Present

It took half a phase before one side of Cloud Castle's front gate finally opened. What took them so long?

Still, Tian blew out a sigh of relief. Though perhaps this would only be a temporary reprieve. They still needed to capture or kill Lord Yang.

Because of the low transom, the riders dismounted and led their horses through single-file.

Tian kept his eyes on the opening as he listened to Tang Li, stopping her story when they got close. People might be hard to read, but Tang Li sounded wistful. From what she'd said so far, it seemed like Lilian and Lord Ting loved each other. Like him and Princess Kaiya, maybe.

As they passed through the gate, Tian studied the structure. The right door was made from heavy timbers lashed together. Blocks of stone were stacked up behind it. The left side was also lashed planks, though instead of just being braced against the entrance like the right, it had six brass hinges.

On the other side, it looked like they'd fortified the movable door with more stone blocks. No wonder it took them so long to open.

The paved yard stretched ninety-two feet from the gate to the far wall, and forty-three feet from the edge of the ledge to a fortress carved into the cliff face. Stone battlements ran along the edge, with cannons angled down into the pass.

A small waterfall, only a few feet wide, tumbled down from the mountain above and into a twenty-foot-diameter pool. Based on what he'd read about Cloud Castle, there was a cistern underneath.

"Captain," Lord Yang called from the top of the gatehouse. He pointed at Wen, Yangyang, and Meisha. "The girls must be tired from their harrowing ride. Let them freshen up. Take them to the hot springs. When they're done, bring them to my chambers."

Tian had to fight his grin. Lord Yang was inviting vipers into his den. Of the three plans, this would be the safest.

The captain took Wen's arm, firmly but not ungently, and led the three women in. The way his eyes roved over them made Tian's stomach churn. Still, once the three of them were alone with Lord Yang, they should be able to end the rebellion quickly.

"What about the horses?" one of Yang's men asked. "They're useless behind castle walls, and we'd have to feed them."

"Stable them for now." Lord Yang pointed to the far end of the fortress. "We can always use them for food."

Poor horses. Tian shuddered.

A hand seized his shoulder and whipped him around.

Lord Nan.

Tian had met him with his daughter a few weeks before his banishment.

"You," the lord said. "I recognize you."

Tian looked past him to the gatehouse. Lord Yang was gazing at Tang Li, but now his attention shifted to Tian.

Lord Nan seized Tian's wrist. Holding it up, he marched a few steps toward the gatehouse. "Lord Yang, this is Lord Zheng's son."

CHAPTER 12

Present

With Lord Yang approaching, and Tian's cover blown, Tang Li trembled. This had all been a mistake. Lord Yang was a suspicious man, and the cover story had been too unbelievable.

And it would end in disaster, unless she could think of something now.

Instead, her mind was flooded again with Lilian's memories.

* * *

Two Months Ago

Lilian was a day late.

And she was never late. So much that Gardener Ju had already removed her from the House schedule for three days.

Now, Lilian sat in Doctor Fang's office. Sweat clung to her brow, and probably not just from the late summer heat. She couldn't possibly be pregnant. The miscarriage had left her barren.

But if she were...

Who had she slept with when she would theoretically have been the most fertile?

Only Lord Ting. Each month since he'd returned to the capital, he'd paid the Chrysanthemum Pavilion to have her stay at his villa for a week. Just like he had right after her Plucking. It had made her wonder how he could afford it. She'd searched his records and correspondence while he'd slept, and discovered he'd invested in Jinjing Lumber—the same as Lords Nan and Yang.

"Lilian." One of the assistants beckoned her to office.

"Is the formula for your cramps not working this month?" Doctor Fang smiled as she entered and bowed. Then, his expression startled. "Do— Oh! Let me feel your pulse."

Could he tell she was pregnant, just from looking at her? She extended her hands.

He pressed his fingers on her wrists, his brow growing even more wrinkles. He shook his head. "This...this isn't possible."

"What isn't, Doctor?"

He looked at a list of herbs she was taking, then met her gaze. "Your regular formula prevents disease, but since your miscarriage, I didn't think it was necessary to strain your health with contraceptives."

Hope stirred in her heart. "Am I—?"

"Pregnant." He bowed his head low. "I am sorry I overlooked this. If we act now, I can make—"

"No!" Lilian shook her head. Then, eyes widening, she bowed. "I'm sorry, Doctor. Please. Please don't. Not yet."

He cocked his head. "You want to keep him?"

"Him?"

He nodded. "Your pulse says it is a boy."

A boy. An heir to the North, with blood from Yu and Ting bloodlines. Her heart thumped hard against her chest.

His legitimacy would be validated by the Yu imperial seal. She'd hidden it in Cloud Castle. Hopefully, Lord Yang hadn't uncovered it.

She met the doctor's eyes. "Please, keep this a secret for now."

"Your Gardener—"

"Please, no." Lilian shook her head. Formerly one of the clan's Steel Orchids, Gardener Ju seemed to be more concerned with making money than involving herself in the fate of the Empire. Still, she knew of the Surgeon, so her ultimate goal was unknown. Better she didn't learn of this pregnancy. Lilian set a purse on the table.

The doctor stared at it, and pushed it back across the table toward her. "No need. May the Heavens punish me if I reveal your secret."

She bowed low. "Thank you."

Unable to contain her excitement, she just about skipped through the doors. Outside, she hailed a rickshaw driver to take her to Lord Ting's villa. The *Tiger's Eye* still blocked her from revealing her lineage, but at the very least she could tell him she carried his child. And in order to secure the boy's legitimacy, she'd have to wed Lord Ting. He'd turned down Lord Nan's daughter, but he still wouldn't be able to marry a Blossom. Not unless he bought out her non-existent contract. Ultimately, it would be up to the clan to decide. Surely they'd allow it? Lord Ting was favored by the Emperor, and she could claim to control him better if they were married.

No, it would be better to hedge her bets. She lowered her hand as the rickshaw approached, and turned toward the Chrysanthemum Pavilion. The best way to convince the clan would be to go through Jie. And this meant deceiving her. Lilian's heart clenched. Whether through half-truths, lies of omission, or outright falsehoods, she'd tricked the one who trusted her the most on too many occasions.

But this was necessary. For her unborn child. A block away from home, she ducked into an alley. Drawing her bladed hairpin with a shaking hand, she settled her nerves enough to make a shallow cut into a vein on her inner thigh. She used her undergarment to staunch the large dot of blood. It wasn't much, but herbs always kept her Best Friend light. It should be enough to trick Jie's keen sense of smell.

When Lilian arrived at the House, she took a seat on a stone bench under one of the cherry trees, and sent one of the Seedlings to find Jie. With several deep breaths, she calmed her mind. Could she mention the pregnancy?

Wearing a plain blue dress, Jie approached with her usual confident gait, flashing her always devious grin.

Lilian's heart leapt into her throat. Even with Lord Ting back in her life, the kisses she and Jie shared had left something unspoken hanging between them. The half-elf was more than just a clan sister and best friend now. And Lilian was about to betray her.

"How may this humble Floret assist the House Corsage?" Jie bowed more with lethal dexterity than feminine grace.

"Come, sit." Lilian patted the spot beside her on the bench, while flashing clan signals. *Eldest Sister, Lord Ting has been feeling unappreciated for his work in keeping the North pacified.*

"Thank you, Elder Sister." Jie sat, their hips just a hair's breadth away. *What do you recommend?*

"Please braid my hair." Lilian turned at an angle, giving easy access to her head. *Twenty-four-phase vigilance.*

Jie's fingers felt soothing as they worked the tangles out.

Lilian closed her eyes to savor the sensation, and leaned closer.

Jie's breath tickled as she whispered, "You're the perfect candidate for that."

With a slight nod, Lilian traced symbols on Jie's leg. *If we make it look like my contract is a gift from the Emperor, it would help secure his loyalty.*

"You don't seem happy about it."

Lilian had tried to keep her facial expressions neutral, but if she made it seem like she didn't actually want this, the clan would be reassured of *her* loyalty. *He's been rougher lately. I think he's frustrated.*

"That's no excuse." Jie's hands froze, and there was venom in her voice. "Did he hurt you?"

"No. No. Maybe a little."

"Maybe we should assign someone else, then." Jie resumed her braiding.

If it's to look like a gift from the Emperor, it will have to be me. Don't worry, I can endure it.

I can't. Jie lowered her hands and leaned into Lilian.

Part of Lilian wanted to confess her lies right there and then. *We risk losing Ting, and therefore the* North.

Jie sighed. *I'll send word to the clan.*

But if they didn't agree to that, she'd be pregnant with an unrecognized bastard boy. The clan would take him, and raise him to be a Fist. And if his experience at the temple were anything like hers, it would be a hard life. If he were handsome, they might assign him to be a Pistil in the Floating World.

No, she couldn't let that happen.

* * *

The Present

Tang Li couldn't let it happen.

Let what happen?

She blinked her eyes several times to clear away the memories.

Flanked by six guards, Lord Yang strode toward them, jaw set into a tight line.

Her mind cleared. It would be safer just to sell the Black Lotus Fists out. That was the logical decision.

No. Some part of her wouldn't let her do it. She bowed to Lord Yang, "My Lord, he was on the highway when we passed through. He claimed he could swing a sword, so we let him join."

Lord Yang studied the boy for a few moments before nodding. He turned to Lord Nan. "What was his name again?"

"Zheng Tian," Lord Nan said. "Lord Zheng wanted to betroth him to my daughter, but then he was banished from the capital."

Li had heard both about the betrothal and the banishment. Maybe Tian was better off as a Black Fist.

"He's a good-looking boy. Though if he's blindly loyal to the Emperor like his father, he might turn on us."

"No, my Lord." Tian shuffled on his feet. "I am banished. My sword is yours."

Lord Yang studied him a little longer, then gestured to Lord Nan. "A marriage to your daughter will give you a claim to his province in the future. He is your charge for now. Take him along with you."

"Yes, my Lord." Lord Nan bowed. Dismissed, he headed toward the fortress with Tian in tow.

Tian looked over his shoulder, eyes meeting Tang Li's. *Will you be all right?* he mouthed.

She nodded, her attention drawn away only when Lord Yang cleared his throat.

He flashed a victorious grin. "Well, my dear, I am happy we were able to reunite. You've done well."

Tension loosened in her shoulders. This would be over soon. Once he joined Wen and the others in bed, they'd neutralize him. Li could then recover the Yu Dynasty seal to fulfil her deal with the Black Lotus, and get on with her life.

One of his guards, whose face was covered by a scarf from the nose down, leaned and whispered something to Lord Yang.

Lord Yang's gaze bore down on Li. He pointed. "I don't recognize him."

Li followed his gesture to a group of soldiers, Black Lotus Brother Kun among them. Oh, no. Well, if anything, she was a good liar. "Kun. He's a Huayuan provincial cavalry lieutenant, but I've used him for tasks before."

"Oh?" Lord Yang beckoned. "Lieutenant Kun."

Bowing his head, Kun jogged over.

Never did Tang Li imagine they'd be able to get Kun so close. Kun could end this right now. The six guards would be no match for him—and indeed, the two other male Black Fists were flanking. Her nerves settled.

"My Lord," Kun said, bowing again. When he rose, a knife flashed in his hand.

A sword swept through the air. Kun's body crumpled to the ground. His head rolled free, sightless eyes staring into space. Covering her mouth, Tang Li screamed. Yang yelped.

Something whizzed by her ear, and would've hit Yang had he not been jerked out of the way. Scarf Face flung a knife to the side, while spinning and chopping with his sword.

One of the Black Fists dropped to his knees, red oozing between his fingers over his neck. The other lay face down in a growing pool of blood.

Recovering his composure, Lord Yang turned to Scarf Face. "Why did you do that?"

"Imperial assassins," Scarf Face said, flicking his blade clean and sheathing it.

Tang Li studied him. What parts of his face were visible were thin-skinned, like paper. And his eyes...

Boney Face.

Also known as the Surgeon.

In the recesses of her mind, Lilian's memories and fears surfaced. He'd posed as Lord Yu's gardener at this very castle. He'd returned in the ambush two years ago, and had threatened Yang in such a way that they clearly knew each other.

"There are three more," the Surgeon said.

Oh, no.

Shoulders hunching up, Lord Yang looked around like a lost child. "Where?"

Scarf Face snorted. "Stop sniveling, act like a lord."

Frowning, Lord Yang straightened. For a proud man, he tolerated a lot from the Surgeon. "Where?"

"The three girls."

Tang Li's heart sunk.

"It can't be." Lord Yang shook his head. "They're Floating World Blossoms."

The Surgeon chuffed. "You were the one who wanted to bribe Blossoms for information about your peers. Emperors well before our time thought of it first."

Lord Yang's face jerked to her.

Heart thumping hard, Tang Li shook her head. "I didn't know."

"I didn't ask if you did." He advanced a step.

Tang Li retreated. "I swear."

"Don't worry about them," the Surgeon said. "I've already mixed a toxin into their bath water. It will make them quite pliant. I'm more concerned about the half-elf skulking around."

CHAPTER 13

The Present

As the only half-elf in the realm, and perhaps the only living one in the world, Jie was immediately recognizable as the disgraced Floret of the now-destroyed Chrysanthemum Pavilion. Lord Yang had bid on her virginity, no less.

Thus, her role in the plan was to find a secondary insertion point.

With Lord Yang's men massing near the gatehouse, the battlements that lined the access road were abandoned. She picked a spot that was shaded in the late afternoon sun, and whose line of sight was shielded by the bend in the path.

Climbing the ten-foot rock base proved easy, given all the foot and handholds. The wall above rose another ten feet, and she used climbing claws to dig into the mortar between the cut stone blocks. She gained the top, pausing between crenellations to make sure another patrol hadn't come this way.

Satisfied, she dropped down to the paved battlements and crept toward the fortress. It didn't look as if the defenders would send men this way, but if they did, she'd jump back between the crenellations to let them pass.

In the yard before the gatehouse, the cavalry was working its way single-file through the open door. On the walkway ahead,

Yang's crossbowmen were lowering their weapons and heading back to the inside of the fortress. Three sentries remained.

Now, it was time to wait for nightfall.

She jumped back in between crenellations. And instead of thinking about the plan, she found herself lost in recent memories of another time she'd been hiding.

* * *

A Month Ago

Heart pattering, Jie ducked into an alley near the wish trees in the Floating World. Now early afternoon, less than a day had passed since she'd sent the request to have Lilian gifted to Lord Ting, and she held the response in her hands.

It was such a fast response.

And Jie wasn't sure she wanted to read it. Of course she hoped for the best for Lilian, and despite what she'd said about Lord Ting getting rough, she'd seemed so happy since his return to the capital. On the other hand, if Lilian moved in with him, Jie wouldn't have as many chances to see her. Not to mention, there was so much that was left unspoken and unresolved between them. Just the one week out of each month where Lilian stayed with Lord Ting left a hole in Jie's heart.

Jie shook the silly thoughts out of her head. Clan first. Country second.

Self last.

With trembling fingers, she unfolded it and read the coded language.

Request for Lilian's reassignment is denied. She has the patronage of all the lords of the North.

Jie sighed, mostly in relief. It was better this way, especially if Lord Ting was becoming abusive. She folded the missive up and continued on her way to the cell's meeting.

Today they'd broken into two teams of thirteen, each tasked with finding and stealing the other side's kerchief in the silk market, and returning it to the designated spot without getting tagged. All while maintaining proper decorum for a Floating World Blossom.

As she neared the giant lantern hanging above the Floating World's main gate, the scent of lavender wafted on the air. Jie turned.

Hiding in the shadow of a teahouse was the cell's newest member, Yuna. Jie had rescued the then-precocious two-year-old from the Trench six years ago, just before Jie, Wen, and Lilian had been deployed to the Floating World. They'd seen her on annual trips back to the temple, where her skills had advanced in leaps and bounds. Now she'd grown into a little beauty just in the last half-year. Master Yan had tasked Jie with grooming her to eventually take over as cell leader, but for now, she was under Wen's tutelage at the Peony Garden.

Where's Wen? Jie signed. As a Seedling, Yuna wasn't supposed to be out without one of her House Blossoms.

She sent me ahead. Yuna hurried over.

"Recite the words from last time."

"Black, seven, knife, water, man, sky, poison, hair, horse, needle, red, knife."

Jie nodded. All were correct, which was unusual. For all of Yuna's admirable skills, verbal memory wasn't one of them.

They continued to their team's rendezvous point outside the silk market, where Lilian was walking with Mai. As always, Jie's heart floated at the sight of her.

Hidden in their greetings were instructions for how they would locate the other team's kerchief and use decoys and relays to bring it back to their destination. As Blossom and Floret from the same House, Lilian and Jie ducked under the tent covering the market together. Now close, the coppery smell of blood mingled in with Lilian's usual honeysuckle scent. Not from a wound, but rather from her Best Friend. Like the last two days, the low saturation of the odor indicated it was lighter than usual this month.

"This is a pretty color." Jie gestured toward a jade bracelet, while signing, *The clan disagreed with the suggestion.*

Lilian's lips pressed into a tight line, and she nodded. "It's not what I was looking for."

"I'm sure we'll find a better option." Would they?

The game took an hour, with their team losing. Lilian had been distracted, and she'd never really excelled with this particular skillset, anyway. The other team, with Meisha leading, had done a better job of passing the captured banner unseen and setting decoys.

When they returned to the Chrysanthemum Pavilion, Jie followed Lilian as she went to her room and threw herself onto her bed. She stared at the ceiling.

Jie stood at the bedside. "Are you all right?"

Lilian turned her head and their gazes met. She scooted over, an unspoken invitation to join her.

Staring at the tempting spot on the bed, Jie swallowed hard. For fifteen years, they'd lain together as best friends, sisters. Since Lilian had become a full-fledged Blossom almost two years ago, it had been less frequent, and usually when one of them needed comforting. In the last several months, after they shared a passionate kiss, it'd been an excuse to practice Floating World techniques.

Or rather, they'd used practice as the excuse. At least that's what Jie had hoped. Surely there was something more? Surely whatever feelings Lilian had once harbored for Lord Ting were no more? Tentatively, Jie slid onto the bed.

Their eyes locked on each other. In someone physically perfect, Lilian's eyes were still the most beautiful part of her. Her honeysuckle scent was intoxicating. Jie's pulse raced.

"I'm glad the clan disagreed," Lilian said. "With the way he's become, having to spend every night with Lord Ting would be unbearable."

Relief washed over Jie, replaced by excitement as Lilian leaned in with a kiss. Her lips felt soft, her tongue tantalizing.

Jie loosened the frog clasps at the collar and shoulder of Lilian's gown. Its top settled at her waist, revealing the curve from her arms to her shoulder to her neck, and the soft basin formed by her collarbones. With her long, delicate fingers, Lilian worked Jie's dress off. Heat coursed from wherever they touched bare skin, but as always, Jie burrowed beneath the blankets and crossed her arms over her chest. Her body was so thin and flat compared to Lilian's full curves.

With a reassuring smile, Lilian gently eased Jie's arms open. She sunk down and ran her tongue over a nipple. A jolt ran up Jie's spine, and her back arched of its own accord. Lilian's fingers walked down Jie's belly, pushing off her undergarments to reach the apex of her thighs.

Several minutes after reaching Heaven for a fourth time, Jie could finally form a lucid thought. While they had practiced similar techniques over and over in the past, something was different this time. Even with no words passing between them, it left no doubt that Lilian really meant it. Really felt it.

Jie's heart swelled. Panting, she slid her hand up Lilian's thigh, hiking her skirts up along the way. Her fingers found the thick cloth of period underwear.

Lilian stopped her hand. "My Best Friend," she whispered.

Jie pouted. Best Friend or not, she wanted to take Lilian to Heaven, to help her feel what Jie felt herself. Still, she withdrew her hand...and froze.

"What's this?" She touched the yellow-purple splotches on Lilian's inner thighs. "Did Lord Ting do this to you?"

Squeezing her knees together, Lilian turned her head to the side and cast her gaze down.

That bastard! If Jie had been floating in the Heavens moments ago, she'd now crashed down to earth. "I'm going to kill him."

Lilian looked up, shaking her head. "It's not that bad, really. He doesn't mean to do it. It's just... angry sex. And sometimes, it leaves a mark. It'll fade away."

How could she defend him? Jie searched Lilian's eyes.

"It's all right," Lilian said, even if her tone didn't sound convincing. "I'll tell him to be gentler, and he'll listen. He's not a bad man."

He'd better listen. Because loyal lord or not, if he hurt Lilian again, there'd be a reckoning at Jie's hands.

* * *

The Present

With the peaks casting dark shadows as the sun set, it was time for Jie to move. Still, she couldn't help but think of how things had turned out. She opened her hands to find her knuckles white.

If only she'd interceded on Lilian's behalf, at the first sign of Lord Ting's cruelty, maybe Lilian would have never turned against the clan.

Now, it was time to take vengeance on Lord Yang for her, just as she'd taken vengeance on the Peony Garden for entrapping Jie.

She slipped down and crept along the ramparts, closer to the side lining the anterior yard. All four sentries stood between the crenels, watching the last of the cavalry move through the front gate. It was just a matter of getting past the first, who might see her in his peripheral vision.

Scooping up a pebble, she tossed it so it landed on the far side of him. When he turned his head, she slipped in behind and continued on her way. At the end of the walkway, she came to a tower carved into the cliff face. The door was open, so she peeked in.

Stairs wound up one level, and from the sounds and smells, there were more soldiers up there. One door clearly led out to the battlements between the courtyard and anterior yard. The second, she opened to reveal a set of steps going down to the interior courtyard.

In wafted the coppery scent of blood.

Jie crept down the steps and scanned the courtyard. Yang's men were dragging three bodies away, one headless. Still, they were all familiar.

Kun and the other two brothers.

Tang Li must've betrayed them.

Tian, Wen, Yangyang, and Meisha were nowhere to be seen, but they were probably in danger.

CHAPTER 14

The Present

Tang Li's arm hurt from where Lord Yang's fingers dug in, dragging her down the hall of Cloud Castle.

"You betrayed me," he snarled. "Bringing assassins to kill me."

She shook her head. "I swear, my Lord—"

He yanked open a door and dragged her in.

Sharp instruments lay neatly arranged on a table. Chains and ropes hung from the ceiling. A sturdy saltire cross with manacles rested against a wall in front of her.

A torture chamber. Heartbeat in her ears drowning out all other sound, she struggled against his grip, to no avail. He yanked her to the cross and locked the manacles around her wrists and ankles. They rattled as she pulled against them.

"Calm down." He slapped her.

She took a deep breath, her gaze falling again on the table with implements of torture. Beside the flaying blade was...a feathered whip? And next to a hot poker were paddles.

"Welcome to Lord Tong's playroom." Lord Yang grinned. "He paid me a pretty sum to have it installed here, so that he could use it on peasant girls and boys during his visits."

Lord Tong's reputation for sadism and ignoring safe words had gotten him banned from the Floating World. She spat. "Another traitor."

"Lord Tong?" Lord Yang grinned. "No. Well, yes. He betrayed Lord Yu."

Lilian's father. Tang Li yanked at the manacles again.

"But no, Tong's the Emperor's lapdog. You, of all people, know I'd planned to frame him for treason."

"What do you want from me?"

He lifted her skirts. "What have I always wanted from you?"

It was no big deal, she'd slept with him enough over the years. Enjoyed it, even, thanks to Lilian's *Tiger's Eye* influencing her. If it would keep her alive... She flashed an alluring smile. "Sex."

He shook his head. "Honesty. And you haven't been honest with me. Now I don't know who I can share my deepest thoughts with."

"I didn't betray you. I can still be your ear. And your lover."

"Oh, we will get to sex." He grinned. "Just not yet. I'm saving my energy for the three assassins. And my own assassin, well, he's going to get some information out of you first." With a grin, he turned on his heel and left.

Tang Li yanked at the bonds until her wrists and ankles were raw and chafed. At last, she blew out a long breath and thought about the past.

Lilian's past.

* * *

Two Months Ago

Torn between friendship and duty, Lilian knotted her skirts between her knees and scaled down the wall of the Chrysanthemum

Pavilion. It was her last night off, and she needed to put her plan into action now.

Still, her heart ached. Jie was in love with her, and a little part of Lilian felt the same. It felt awful having to trick her best friend into believing the bruises on her thigh had come from Lord Ting, and not from the shallow cuts she'd used to draw blood. It felt even worse having to manipulate Jie's feelings, so much that Lilian hated herself in this moment. Her foot slipped.

She caught herself before plummeting to a possible death and probable miscarriage two stories down. She took a deep breath. There was no choice. More than sisterhood, she had to do this for her unborn child, lest he grow up as a pawn of the Black Lotus Clan.

She'd rolled around in her bed and left all the clothes she'd worn for the last three days under the covers. Hopefully it held enough of her scent to trick Jie's nose. Now, she crept through the alleys and, stealing a cloak from a drunken reveler at a food stand outside of the recently-opened Yue Heaven, slipped out of the Floating World.

A rickshaw took her toward Lord Ting's villa, as she originally planned yesterday afternoon. Though this time, she had a concerning and mysterious message, given to her by a little pickpocket in the Silk Market earlier in the day. Calming her shaking fingers, she unfolded it and reread it in the light of the moon.

Kill Lord Ting. Will pay 60,000 gold yuan. Meet behind the Long Life Noodles tonight, third waxing gibbous.

Sixty thousand. Not only would that feed a family of ten for sixty years, it was probably no coincidence that it had been her virgin price. And that it was Lord Ting? Whoever it was knew he was her patron. Or, it could be the clan, testing her. She looked up to where the moon waxed halfway between the first and second gibbous. Training taught her to scout out a location well before an arranged meeting time.

When Lilian arrived a block away, she paid the rickshaw driver and kept to the shadows. The very few passersby took no notice of her, and if she'd gained a tail, she didn't see it. Long Life Noodles was closed, though light spilled out of the windows in the residence above.

Knife in hand, she looked around the corner into the alley.

Also deserted.

She went to the rear of Long Life Noodles.

A finger-sized tube with her name on it rested against the wall. She opened it, finding paper wrapped around a glass vial. The texture as she unrolled it was the same as the first message.

Pour this in his tea on the Sixth Day of the Eighth Month. If you agree, leave message under the lucky cat figurine in the Jade Teahouse. Pick up messages at the cherry blossom grove, third tree, second lowest branch, same paper as this.

Her heart seized. This was a real hit, on the father of her child. Not only that, it was for a very specific date. Who was the prospective employer? Perhaps the clan, testing her loyalty? But then, they wouldn't want Lord Ting dead, since he was vital to maintaining peace in the North.

The toxin would provide a clue. She popped the vial open. A pungent smell wafted out: pokeberry extract, mixed with Dead Man's root.

She snorted. Whoever it was, they weren't sophisticated. Not only would the taste and smell be evident, this one vial wouldn't be enough to kill someone Lord Ting's size.

Still, if someone wanted Lord Ting dead, it might ultimately fit into her larger goal of escaping the clan.

A near-hopeless endeavor, since nobody escaped the Black Lotus. The only way out was to get *Tiger-Eyed* into a Cousin in Lianjing, or die.

Except for Gardener Ju and the Surgeon. Both had faked their deaths: Gardener Ju through the fire that had left the Floating

World a smoldering ash pile two decades before; the Surgeon, supposedly killed by Altivorcs during a secret operation in Vyara City.

The key was to fake her death, and now Lord Ting's, while framing Lord Yang and killing Gardener Ju.

She pondered how she might accomplish it on another rickshaw ride, which delivered her to Lord Ting's villa with the Iridescent Moon waxing to its second gibbous. Gawking, the two guards bowed.

"Come in, my lady," one said, opening the gate.

Butterflies swarmed in Lilian's belly. Any other visitor, arriving unannounced, would usually have to wait for the chamberlain to approve their entry; at this hour, they might even be turned away. She, of course, recognized them from her many trips here, though they weren't senior enough to guard Lord Ting when he travelled through the city. In this, they might be part of her burgeoning plan.

She flashed them an alluring smile, then continued through the courtyard with a sashay of her hips, the weight of their leers on her ass.

One ran past her and into the main residence. Before she reached the door, Lord Ting emerged, beaming, with the guard on his heels.

"Yumei! You shouldn't be travelling alone at night." He took her hands in his.

"My Lord." She bowed. "I have to tell you something in confidence."

He dismissed the guard with a tilt of his head, then guided her into the foyer. "I've already told the chamberlain to prepare some wine."

"I cannot drink." She waved her hand back and forth. "Please, can we speak somewhere in private?"

His eyes searched hers, then gestured to his study, down the hall from the sitting area.

She headed to the room, one foot in front of the other as her heart pounded in her ears. Would he agree to her plan? Or was he too loyal to the Emperor? Head bowed, she knelt and opened the door, allowing the man to enter first as etiquette demanded.

Waiting outside the door, he took her hand and raised her to her feet. He bowed. "My lady."

What did this mean? Turning her head to hold his gaze, she entered the room.

He followed her in, closed the door behind him, and pulled a chair out for her. It was as if he'd studied the cultural norms of the fair-skinned.

She settled on the edge of the seat and bowed her head. When she spoke, she kept her voice low. "My Lord, I have news."

"You are carrying my child."

Lilian looked up. "How did you know?"

"I asked a midwife about women's rhythms, and after conversations with your Gardener, I surmised when you were most likely to conceive. I've been having you here during that week every month, but it's taken so long, I was worried you were barren. That's why I always gave you that juice. It comes from Twins Island in the Sundered Empire, famous for fertility potions."

She kept her expression impassive, even as she considered his words. He'd been trying to plant his seed in her for several months now, without even telling her. Could she hold it against him, considering she'd never told him about their prior pregnancy? But why? The bigger concern was that Gardener Ju, as a former clan member, would probably be able to surmise what he was trying to do, if not why.

"You're not saying anything," he said, voice trembling.

"Why did you do it?" she asked.

"Because a pregnant Blossom can't make money for her House. Surely your Gardener would sell me your contract."

He was so naïve in his heroism, making him all the more adorable. She shook her head. "What if she doesn't? Every one of the lords of the North wants to bed me. They still will, even if I'm pregnant."

"I want you," he said, "because I love you. They want you because I love you, and..."

"And?"

"It's just a suspicion." He leaned in closer and lowered his voice. "You resemble my late liege lord, Yu Qian. We've always thought his entire family was slain, including his daughter, Mei, when many of his other vassals betrayed him."

She covered her mouth. Had he figured it out? This was exactly what she was going to try to tell him tonight, with an elaborate scheme to help him connect the dots, since the Surgeon's *Tiger's Eye* prevented her from saying it outright.

Excitement rose in his voice. "When you asked me to call you Yumei, it made me think. You must be close in age to her, and it was too much of a coincidence. I sent one of my men to the Central Valley to check your birth registry. He thinks it was forged."

She tried to say *yes*, tried to nod, but the *Tiger's Eye* prevented it.

"However, Lords Yang, Shi, and Tong might've figured it out, too."

Of course, they knew she'd survived. Lord Yang had been there when Lord Tong had given her to the Surgeon at the time. Though from her meeting with the Surgeon in Cloud Castle, it seemed like he had never intended to reveal her identity to them; had they really figured out she was Yu Mei, daughter of their lord Yu Qian? Maybe one of them was behind the hit? She sucked in a sharp breath, thinking back to her assignations. In the months that Lord Ting had been gone, Yang and Shi had tried to see her during her fertile time, never knowing about her miscarriage and subsequent infertility. Lord Tong, of course, had been banned from the Floating World, and she only knew what he had looked like fifteen years ago.

Though if these lords knew, surely the clan masters would? And through them, Jie would as well?

"So were you like them," she said, feigning anger in her voice, "trying to impregnate me based on some wild speculation, so you could make some claim about past dynasties?"

He looked like a wet dog, the way he shook his head. "No. I was trying to protect you from them. But if you did fall pregnant... Tell me, what do you remember of your childhood?"

The *Tiger's Eye* prevented her from revealing all of her memories, but she'd come here to convince him of her plan. Could she trust him to keep everything secret? Because if not, they were as good as dead. "I trust you will never repeat this to anyone else: some of my earliest memories were training to be a Black Fist."

It was hard to tell if his mouth or eyes were wider. That clearly hadn't been what he was expecting. Then, his lips tightened. "This isn't a joke."

She rose from the chair. "I'm not joking. I can tell you the placement of every piece of furniture in your house, from the two-inch change in position of the left chair in your sitting room, to the number of petals in the flowers on your family altar."

He gawked again. "You wouldn't have to be a Black Fist to do that."

Imitating his voice with the *Mockingbird's Deception*, she threw her voice to his side with a *Ghost Echo*. "Not everyone can do this."

He turned to the origin of her *Ghost Echo*, then back to her, shaking his head. He lunged at her, hands going toward her throat.

She sidestepped, seized one of his hands, and then twisted it so that he buckled to his knees.

"I...I don't believe it," he said through gritted teeth.

"Do you need more proof? Shall I climb to the rooftop, as I have several times in the past?" She released him.

He stood, wringing out his hand. “I mean, I do believe it. I just always thought Black Fists were myths to keep naughty children in line.”

“You must never reveal that you know this, or who I really am, because others like me will kill you.”

He licked his lips. “I’d planned to ask the Emperor to let me take you as my wife.”

“The Black Fists will never allow it, and they will recommend the Emperor deny your request.”

“Why? What does it matter to them?”

“I belong to them. I am their tool. If they ordered me to kill you, I would obey.”

His shoulders slumped. “You’d kill me?”

“Because if I didn’t, they’d send someone else to. And, in fact, someone does want to kill you.” She passed the two messages to him.

His eyes roved over them. “Where did this come from?”

“I’m trying to find out.” She went over to his desk and popped open the secret drawer.

He held out a staying hand. “What are you doing?”

She pulled out records and correspondence she’d dug up in the past. “My first suspicion is that it has to do with Jinjing Lumber. You and Lord Yang are making illegal *yue*, and then laundering the proceeds through inflated reports from other sources of income.”

“It was Lord Yang’s idea.”

It was Lilian’s idea, fed to him through Tang Li, to set up Lord Yang. Now, though, the father of her unborn son was involved. “Why did you go along with it?”

“The North is poor, and keeping the lords in line requires money.” He let out a long sigh. “And, it was the only way I could protect you from Lord Yang during your fertile time.”

There was apology in his tone, as well there should be, considering how *yue* destroyed lives and livelihoods. Then again, imperial policy had done the same to the people of the North. Her people. "I have a solution. The question is, are you willing to give up everything for me, to disappear for a long time?"

His eyes searched hers for a moment before he nodded. "Yes."

He truly did love her.

"Then I have a plan that will both keep you alive, and also reveal the traitors involved in the betrayal of—" her father— "Lord Yu. The ringleaders escaped punishment at Cloud Castle."

He nodded. "What do you need me to do?"

To help her leave a trail. "First, I need you to sign over your share of Jinjing Lumber to Shi Mu."

"Lord Shi?" He cocked his head. "He has nothing to do with this."

"Different *Mu*. It's a company which holds a share of Jinjing Holdings, which in turn holds part of Jinjing Lumber." And was also Lord Yang's means of entrapping Lord Shi, but the Surgeon's *Tiger's Eye* prevented her from saying it.

He shook his head in confusion.

She suppressed a chuckle. For all his dashing valor, he didn't have a sense for business. She said, "We must get your name disassociated from Jinjing Lumber."

His head bobbed in slow nods. He was so adorable, her heart squeezed.

If her plan worked, they'd both escape together.

* * *

The Present

Tang Li woke, her shoulders and hips sore from sleeping bound to the cross. Had she been dreaming? Or were these Lilian's actual memories?

If so, then the hit on Lord Ting had been a ruse.

And a part of her needed to tell Jie.

CHAPTER 15

Present

After two years since Wen's last visit to Cloud Castle, she'd almost forgotten about the majesty of the vaulting halls and smooth corridors carved into the mountainside. All constructed by dwarves in antiquity. Now, she learned, it also had caves with natural pools of hot water.

The air was wonderfully warm and damp. Standing on tiptoes on a rock formation, balancing so she wouldn't slip on the slick surface, she looked up a vent.

"Come on, silly," Meisha said. "When's the last time you got to soak in hot springs?"

Beneath her casual words, however, she was signing. Wen turned away from the vent.

Meisha and Yangyang sat naked on rocks, scrubbing out the sweat, dirt, and grim from travel. Their dirty dresses lay folded on a nearby stone. A guard had quite enjoyed searching them for weapons, but they'd passed all but their bladed hairpins to Kun and Tian, who'd leave them hidden in designated spots.

"The Yu family was living large back in the day." Yangyang laughed, even as she signed, *This is easy.*

Too easy. Yangyang frowned. "I wouldn't have minded being a Yu Dynasty concubine, if this was what life was like."

"Lord Yang wants a foursome before he shares us with his men," Wen said. *And if Kun hasn't taken care of him first, that's when we'll strike.*

Yangyang nodded. "Maybe a fivesome, with Tang Li."

Meisha rose and strutted over to the pool. Dipping a toe into the water, she tested the temperature. She grinned and sank in.

We get to be clean and *relaxed when we kill him*, Yangyang signed as she stood and joined Meisha in the pool.

Sitting where the others had just washed, Wen chuckled and started to scrub away her travel grime. Her hair was a tangled mess, and dirt washed through it as she poured a basin of water over her head. She was brushing wet locks out of her face, when she realized it.

Yangyang and Meisha were quiet.

Wen wiped water from her eyes and found them both in the pool, asleep. She lifted Meisha's eyelid. The dilated pupil and blue tinge in the whites suggested dreamflower intoxication.

Their cover story hadn't worked. And of course, Lord Yang had worked with the Steel Orchid, and dreamflower was easy to get ahold of.

"They've been quiet for a few minutes," a muffled voice said from the other side of the door.

"Let's check."

Shit. Wen ran to the thermal vent. Careful with her footing, she climbed the rock underneath, then leaped up. The walls of the vent were slick with moisture, but her fingers found crevices and she pulled herself up into it. She pressed against the sides with her hands and feet.

The door opened.

Wen froze. If someone checked the vent, she'd have to fight.

Four men shuffled in.

"It worked," one of them said.

"Where's the third?" Lord Yang demanded. "You were supposed to stand guard."

"I did, my Lord."

Arms and legs aching, Wen held her breath. It wouldn't be the first time she'd fought naked and unarmed, but against four men...

"Then where is she?" Anger rose in Lord Yang's voice.

"I will search."

"You'd better find her. You two, take these to the playroom." Lord Yang turned on his heel and stomped out.

Playroom. Lord Yang had always been pretty plain in his tastes, at least with her. Not with Lilian, though.

Water sloshed as the men lifted Yangyang and Meisha out of the pool. No doubt, their hands lingered where they shouldn't.

One of them laughed. "If you find her, maybe you'll get to do this."

Yangyang let out an unconscious yelp.

Anger burned in Wen's face, but she waited as two sets of footsteps left. The third was moving around the room. Squirming as quietly as she could, she inverted, lowered herself to the opening, and hazarded a glance.

With his back to her, the same solider who'd brought them here was rummaging through their clothes.

Taking advantage of his diverted attention, she flipped and landed in a crouch, keeping the rock formation between them. She crept closer, ready to draw his knife and—

She stubbed her toe on the uneven floor.

The man spun around, knife ready to slash. Then his eyes locked on her chest.

In that split second, she surged in, seized his knife hand, and twisted it up and over so that it lodged in the middle of his throat. It was a clean cut, missing the major arteries and veins, but severing his windpipe. He collapsed to his knees, clutching his throat wide-eyed as his chest heaved in a futile attempt to draw in air.

Yangyang and Meisha couldn't be so far away. As fast as she could, she stripped the man of his tunic and sash and put them on. The knife she thrust into the sash, and binding her hair into a topknot, she inserted all three hairpins into it.

After dragging the body over to the pool and dumping it in, she dashed out into the empty hallway. The damp footprints faded well before the hall split two ways. Which way could they have gone? Despair welled in Wen's chest.

"How come we have to carry grain, and you get to carry naked women?" A man's laugh echoed down the corridor to the left.

Wen hurried in that direction. At another intersection, she bowed her head at a man carrying a sack, and continued at a brisk walk the way he came. A few moments later, she caught up to the two soldiers with her friends draped over their shoulders.

"I want to carry yours." One paused and nodded at Yangyang.

"Fine. She was getting heavy, anyway."

"At least she was soft!" the first laughed, reaching over and groping Yangyang's breast.

With them switching off, it would be the perfect chance to neutralize them. Still, Meisha and Yangyang would likely be out for another hour, and there was no way Wen could carry both. The playroom might be the safest place for them.

When they resumed, she followed, until at last they came to a door. They went in, and though it would be safer to wait for them to come out and face them one at a time, Wen couldn't bear the thought of them molesting her friends. She slunk in behind them.

Tang Li, still dressed, was manacled to a saltire cross. Her lip trembled as she watched the soldiers lay Meisha and Yangyang on tables.

Wen gestured to the men, and mouthed, *Distract them*.

Tang Li's eyes widened for a split second, but then she gave a slight nod. Wen ducked behind a column and peeked back.

"Don't touch them!" Tang Li said.

Turning, the first soldier nudged the second. Both leered at her.

"What are you going to do about it?" the second said, running a finger up the inside of Yangyang's thigh.

"What's the fun when she's asleep?"

"You're right. Lucky me that you're awake." The first headed over, and the second joined him.

Close together, backs to Wen, they made for easy targets. She slashed one's throat while driving the hairpin into the subclavian artery of the other.

"Are you all right?" Wen asked, looking for a key to the manacles.

"Yes. But just in case I don't make it out alive, I need you tell Jie something about Lilian."

* * *

One week ago

With two days to go before she executed her plan, Lilian slipped the last update under the lucky cat at the Jade Teahouse. Through her correspondence with her anonymous employer—she dropped messages off here, and he left his in the cherry tree grove—she'd explained how crude the poison was, and outlined a better plan to kill Lord Ting. He'd put her in touch with Su, a minor lord in Lord Ting's domain, who'd likely take over when Ting died. Su's participation in the hit was her employer's only condition.

She'd staked the Jade Teahouse out several times, and confirmed that it was only Su picking up her messages. Unless it was an act, he didn't appear smart enough to be her anonymous employer, and even following his trail, she'd yet to figure out who was.

She was fairly certain it was Lord Yang trying to kill Lord Ting, most likely to solidify his position as the most powerful lord of the North. She had yet to determine the significance of the date, and nothing on Lord Ting's schedule provided hints. Maybe her employer didn't want him attending Lord Wu's moons-viewing party?

Otherwise, everything was going smoothly. If her experience with the Surgeon at Cloud Castle had taught her anything, it was how to create scenes and establish narratives. She'd used some of her savings to purchase a large amount of alcohol and firecrackers, and had them packed into one of the Chrysanthemum Pavilion's storehouses. During her visits to Lord Ting's villa, she'd practiced assembling the repeater quickly, and shooting from the sitting room mezzanine to a target in the corner.

Every day, she practiced the *Viper's Calm* to the edge of the *Viper's Rest*, slowing her breath to one inhalation and one heartbeat for a count of three hundred.

Despite Doctor Fang's admonishment to abstain from intercourse for her baby's health, Lilian had to keep up the pretense that life went on as usual. She continued receiving Hummingbirds. On the side, she bedded four of Lord Ting's men. She convinced each she was madly in love with them in order to turn them against their lord, as part of her plan.

For Lord Ting's part, he followed the doctor's orders and refused to penetrate her. Still, he had stayed with her at the Chrysanthemum Pavilion as many nights as he could to prevent others from doing so. Those nights, she'd pleasured him in other ways, but also had him make it sound as rough as possible. She screamed her safe word enough times that Jie's keen ears certainly heard it. When they'd met this morning, Jie had believed the act enough to request reassignment for Lilian, not knowing that by the time she got the answer, Lilian would be dead or disappeared.

During meetings with Tang Li, Lilian used the *Tiger's Eye* to plant more memories and triggers in her mind, and specifically those tied to the lotus hairpin. She also included the location of the Yu Dynasty seal as a failsafe.

As another part of her plot, she arranged for Lord Shi, currently busy in the North, to sneak into the capital for a free night of pleasure in his courtyard home—she used *yinghua* flower toxin to coax him into opening his dwarf safe, where she hid her hairpin and stock certificates in some blood-stained sheets. The contact toxin would make him forget all about it. She included the safe's combination in a painting she gave to Tang Li, in the event Jie couldn't hear the dial.

Now, message dropped off, she headed to the cell meeting in the opera house. The late morning sun warmed her pinned-up hair. The streets were quiet, as was typical for this hour in the Floating World, but up ahead, one of Lord Ting's guards stood near the opening to the north-south alley between the red-roofed shrine of the Money God and the orange-tiled shrine of the Fox Spirit.

Lin. One of the guards she'd seduced into joining in on her plan. Back to the wall, he held a knife, looking ready to rush into the alley. Just what was he up to?

Click. The telltale sound of a crossbow echoed in the alley.

Click. Click. Click. Lin darted in.

A man screamed.

Picking up her skirts, Lilian dashed over to the opening and peeked into the alley.

"Bitch!"

Foot bent at an awkward angle, Lin was straddling what looked to be a girl, pushing a knife down on her. She gripped his wrist, but he had a weight and strength advantage. At the far end of the alley,

Chen advanced on them, repeater in hand. Though he wore a mask, his body language was memorable.

Lilian's heart leaped into her throat. Just what was happening? What kind of men had she hired? She looked again.

The dress. It was what Jie had been wearing this morning. Pointed ears.

"Hey!" Lilian yelled.

Lin looked up.

She reached into her sleeve and flung a throwing spike.

It lodged into his eye, snapping his head back in a spray of blood.

At the far end of the alley, Chen skidded to a stop. His expression twisted in confusion.

Scowling, Lilian waved him away.

He cocked his head for a moment, but then ran off.

Just why had they attacked Jie? Retrieving the four crossbow bolts, Lilian hurried over to the prone half-elf and knelt. "Are you all right, my sweet?"

Jie's eyes fluttered open. Gawking, she shrimped out from under Lin. Blood soaked into her dress, but it appeared to be his.

"You saved me." Jie nodded, her tone filled with disbelief. "That might be the best throw you've ever made."

Was that supposed to be a compliment? Lilian nodded back. Of course, she'd always held back, never revealing the extent of her skill. "I never imagined you would need me to save you."

"How did you find me?"

"Coincidence." Luck, really. Lilian offered her hand. "I was on my way to the gathering when I saw this man waiting on the street, with that knife."

Jie took Lilian's hand and scrambled to her feet. She leaned over Lin's body before looking up. "He knew who I was and where I would be."

"Impossible." Lilian shook her head. She hadn't told any of Lord Ting's traitorous men who Jie was. They never came to the Chrysanthemum Pavilion, and wouldn't know her from there. "The only ones who know our identities are other clan members."

"He was waiting. He lulled me into complacency by acting like a drunk merely picking a target of opportunity."

Why would he do that? Chen was in on it, too, so Lilian needed to track him down and question him. "That means the crossbowman..."

"Knows about me, as well." Jie nodded. "And now also you, if they didn't already."

If only Jie knew just how well Chen knew her. Lilian covered a feigned gasp with one hand, while holding out four crossbow bolts. "We—" well, she— "need to track the crossbowman down."

"We also need to warn the others, and get word to the clan to bring a Cleaner to take care of this mess." Jie wrung her hands. As head of the cell, she felt a responsibility to the sisters.

That made it even harder to betray her. But for now, Lilian needed to track down Chen and find out why he and Lin had ambushed Jie. And do something about the body. "I'll inform the clan." Lilian studied Lin's corpse and feigned a shudder. Then she yanked her throwing spike out of his face.

"Before you go," Jie said, "let me see what instructions they left for us." She unfolded a message from the clan, obvious from the sixteen folds which would tear in the hands of anyone who didn't know how to unfold it.

Lilian rested her chin on Jie's shoulder. Together, they read.

Chatter in the North of a hit on Lord Ting. He is key to stability there. He must be protected.

Lilian had led Jie to believe she wanted reassignment out of the Floating World, but this news would mean the clan would never agree. Just as she'd hoped, as a backup plan in the event her first plan failed. "I didn't expect any other outcome."

"I'll think of something." Jie turned and leaned in. Their foreheads touched, sending warmth through Lilian.

"Now," Jie said, "we need to hurry. I'll continue to the meeting. You go to the safehouse and bring more assets back to the silk market in an hour."

"As you command, Elder Sister." Lilian saluted with a fist in her palm. Of course, the last thing she needed for her plan to work was for other clan members to get involved. She turned and ran; but when she got to the end of the alley, she waited for Jie to depart and then crept back to the body. She ripped Lin's shirt off and stuffed it into the eye socket so that his blood wouldn't make a mess.

Then, she hurried to Chen's hangout, near Yue Heaven. Predictably, he was there with the three remaining traitors, ordering his favorite roasted meat from a street vendor.

She grabbed him took them all into an alley. "Why did you attack that girl?"

Chen turned, expression scrawled with confusion. "You told us to!"

What? There was a story behind this. "When?"

"Last night!" Zhang said, his scar crinkling in his forehead. "You said she'd get in the way of our other plans."

This wasn't possible. She'd been with Lord Ting last night, and before that...there was a blank spot. "What time?"

"Waxing half."

Right around dinner time. She'd eaten at the Chrysanthemum Pavilion, went to her room to prepare for Lord Ting, and then... nothing. Her next memory was Lord Ting arriving, at the waxing third gibbous. She'd stood on the second-floor mezzanine, lining her shot up on his favorite table, then beckoned him up to join her. In between, three hours were missing.

Which meant she'd been musk-toxined or *Tiger-Eyed.*

The former would've left her hungover, meaning it had to be the latter.

The Surgeon? Who else had this level of skill, except maybe her and Master Yan? Surely he was talented enough to kill Jie himself. Unless he didn't want to reveal himself, and wanted to stage it as an assault. He was a master at manipulating crime scenes and creating narratives, after all.

Now, though, one of her turncoats was dead. Would her plan still work?

* * *

The Present

With Yangyang and Meisha now covered with blankets, Wen finished picking the manacles, stunned at the revelation that Lilian's plan had been so elaborate. She'd been a traitor to the clan, but never intended to kill Ting. The whole part about her henchmen thinking she'd ordered them to kill Jie didn't seem to make sense, though.

Freed from the restraints, Tang Li shook out her arms and legs. "There's more."

"Tell Jie yourself," Wen said. "Right now, I am going to retrieve my weapons from where Kun and the others left them."

"They're dead. Killed by...killed by..." Tang Li's lips moved in no clear pattern, and no sound came out.

"Lord Yang discovered them?"

Tang Li gave a half nod, half shake of her head. "His guard. Very dangerous."

"All right." Wen studied the instruments on the table. Once they woke, Meisha and Yangyang could use some of them as weapons. In the meantime, her best chance was to take the traitor lord by surprise. “You stay here, and watch after them. I’m going to go hunt Lord Yang.”

Shaking her head, Tang Li grabbed Wen by the shoulder. “The guard is very dangerous.”

Dangerous enough to kill Kun and the others. Still, Wen needed to scout, and perhaps connect with Tian and Jie. “I’ll be fine.”

CHAPTER 16

The Present

Tang Li cursed Lilian's *Tiger's Eye*. She'd so wanted to tell Wen about the Surgeon, but like before, she couldn't say it.

"Bar the door." Wen slipped out of her grasp and headed out.

With a sigh, Tang Li looked to Yangyang and Meisha. Wen predicted they'd be unconscious for another hour, and hopefully, the Surgeon was too busy hunting Jie to come back before they awoke.

She lowered the bar, even if she doubted that would keep him out.

Then, more of Lilian's memories came back to her, no doubt planted during their last meeting.

* * *

One Week Ago

The Surgeon's interference and the ambush on Jie had created new uncertainties in Lilian's plan. Now, even if they didn't know who was behind the attack, the cell would be on high alert.

With little time to spare before someone stumbled on the body, Lilian brought her three henchmen to the back of a closed gambling den. She picked the lock as they looked on, gawping. No matter, since they wouldn't live past tomorrow night to tell anyone. Inside, they rolled up a rug and then took back alleys to the scene of the attack. Lin's body still lay there, his blood thankfully absorbed in the cloth she'd stuffed into his eye socket.

It was time to set the scene to confuse Jie's sharp senses.

"Drag him to the middle of the alley," she said.

Grumbling, they did as they were told and wrapped him up in the rug. What little blood had spilled onto the pavestones, she cleaned with a solvent. They took the body through the back gate of the Chrysanthemum Pavilion and left it in a rarely-used storage building. The three crossbow bolts she'd retrieved, she took to her room and hid in a secret compartment under the rug.

Then, she ran as fast as she could to the silk market. As of now, Jie believed the entire cell were possible targets; Lilian had to turn this inconvenience around and make it work in favor of her plan. As she ran into sisters, she signed, *No help coming.*

Part of her felt awful having to scare some of the people dearest to her.

Though if they were scared, none, even down to the youngest Seedling, showed it. Then again, that youngest Seedling was Yuna, a fierce and brilliant girl.

The Peony Garden's Corsage, Lusha, snorted near the middle of the market. The sound was distinct in its derisiveness, her typical prelude to an insult. "Uncultured half-breed."

Half-breed? Could that be...

"Come to the Peony Garden tonight for a poetry duel, if you dare. There will be many guests on hand to celebrate Young Lord Peng Kai-Zhi's First Pollinating. His father has contracted me for ten thousand *yuan*."

The throng erupted in chatter. The reception was supposed to be epic. Lord Peng Xian had paid for the Floating World's most prominent Blossoms to attend, including Lilian. That, on top of an ungodly ten thousand *yuan* for a First Pollination.

Then, Lilian's heart sank as Jie's voice replied, "And to think, my virginity is already worth over ten times his son's."

Goading Lusha was never a good thing. Lilian braced for a retort...

Which never came.

"As for your challenge," Jie said, "I'll be there."

What? No! With the Peony Garden an exact replica of the Chrysanthemum Pavilion, Lilian had planned a dry run of tomorrow's staged hit tonight. If Jie was there, she might realize what was happening.

For now, though, Jie was here, appearing among the crowds with her alluring grin. She bowed. "I couldn't find the color you wanted."

What? Had she not just accepted a poetry duel from a master poet? Oh, right, she was pretending that she'd been looking for something in the market. Lilian beckoned. "Then we must hasten back for lessons."

As they headed back to the Floating World, Jie passed a message to the cell sisters. *Resume regular activities. Maintain vigilance. Watch for light atop the Lotus Shrine.*

Despite her outwardly flippant demeanor, the order showed Jie was concerned about a real threat to the cell; the light would be a signal for everyone to meet at the safe house.

And with the Surgeon lurking around, Lilian might have to use that light.

As they walked, Jie turned to her. "The Peony Garden might've been involved in the attack this morning. Lusha's guard had eaten the same thing as Masked Crossbowman."

Was that what she thought? Maybe it was better to let Jie believe it, so she wouldn't connect the attack back to Lilian's own plot. Though now, Jie was risking bids on her virgin price with a sure loss to Lusha in a poetry duel. And it was tempting fate to have Jie poking around the Peony Garden while Lilian was doing a dry run. Well, she would just have to find a way to keep Jie from going. She gave a tentative nod.

Once across the moat, Jie whispered, "Why no clan support?"

Because the last thing Lilian needed was more clan members on high alert around the entertainment district. "Only one brother was at the safehouse," she lied. "The Emperor stayed an extra day at the summer villa, so all extra hands are there to protect him. The only ones left in the city are in critical areas."

Of course, Lilian hadn't gone to the safehouse, because she'd been busy disposing of Lin's body. The Emperor was most likely following his original itinerary, which would put him back in the capital in two days—so Jie wouldn't learn about Lilian's lie until it was too late.

Jie said, "We need to dispose of the body before anyone finds it."

"We do?" Lilian's pulse picked up a pace. Jie's keen nose might detect the solvent used to clean up Lin's blood.

"Come on. It will cause quite the stir, and the local authorities won't know what to make of his fatal wound." Jie grinned. "It was a great throw."

"You already said so." Lilian faked a smile. Maybe it would've been better to leave the body there. "But I don't mind you repeating it."

Jie leaned in and rested her head on Lilian's shoulder. "It was a great shot."

Lilian squeezed her hand, hoping to delay Jie just a few more minutes.

By the time they reached the opening to the alley, there was no activity. Jie turned the corner...and froze.

Lilian's jaw clenched. Had she sniffed the solvent? Or was it just surprise?

She turned to Lilian. "You said there was no Cleaner?"

Maybe she had detected the solvent. Lilian gave a tentative nod. "If not us, then who?"

"Masked Crossbowman or his friends." Jie knelt over the spot where Lin had fallen and set her hand on the pavestones. "He was quite dead, so he couldn't have walked off by himself. That means—"

"They—" well, Lilian— "didn't want his body found, either." After all, the last thing they needed was imperial investigators swarming the Floating World.

Eyes on the pavestones, Jie went deeper, right to the spot where Chen and the others had dragged the corpse.

"What are you doing?" Lilian asked, even if it was obvious.

"A trail."

Lilian knelt, pretending to look for clues she knew only half-elf senses could detect. "Where?"

Sniffing the air in the cutest way, Jie pointed. "They covered the wound; otherwise there'd be a blood trail, or a sign that they'd cleaned up afterwards."

It was time to lead her astray. Lilian looked up the shrine walls on either side, each rising nearly fifteen feet. "They somehow lifted him up and over?"

Jie pop-vaulted to the top and looked over the side of each wall, then came down and sniffed again.

"Any clues?" Lilian asked, knowing there were none.

Shaking her head, Jie sniffed around. "For now, our only lead is the guard at the Peony Garden."

Lilian's head rose and fell in slow bobs. How had she made that connection? "What do we do now?"

"I need your help with improvised poetry."

"Whatever for?" Lilian asked, pretending as if she hadn't overheard the conversation.

Jie grinned. "I am going with you to the Peony Garden's soirée tonight. I accepted a poetry duel with Lusha."

"You did what?" Lilian feigned surprise. "She's the most celebrated poet in the Floating World in a generation."

"Then you can't tell the Gardener or Florist that's why I'm going with you."

Oh, Lilian was going to tell, all right. Not only did Lilian not want Jie poking around the dry run, but the Surgeon was also on the loose, out for the half-elf's head. Claiming a trip to the privy, Lilian instead went to Gardener Ju.

"Lilian," the Gardener called before Lilian even reached the open door to the office. The Gardener always wanted to keep all the House girls in awe of her, and used her Black Lotus skills to learn each person's footstep patterns, habits, and quirks. She'd never shown signs of knowing Jie's and Lilian's affiliation with the clan, but perhaps she was hiding it.

Though the Surgeon's *Tiger's Eye* had always prevented Lilian from telling the others about the Gardener's true identity, part of the escape plan would either leave her dead, or expose her past life as one of the clan's celebrated Steel Orchids.

Lilian entered and bowed.

Going over financial records with Florist Wei, the Gardener sat at her desk. Her eyes flicked up. "What brings you here at this hour?"

"It's Jie," Lilian said. "She plans on going to Lord Peng Kai-Zhi's First Pollination tonight."

"Oh?" Grinning, the Gardener rubbed her hands together. "She'll certainly catch the eye of the wealthiest men in the realm. Maybe push her virgin price higher."

Lilian shook her head. "Not if she loses her poetry duel to Lusha."

Florist Wei covered her gasp.

The Gardener's smile twisted into a snarl. "Florist, go summon Jie, now. Lilian, you wait here."

"Please Gardener, don't tell Jie I told you. She really wanted to go."

When the Florist returned with Jie, the Gardner fixed her with a stare. "I heard from Gardener Yang at the Lily Pond that you plan on engaging Lusha in a poetry duel tonight."

Jie bowed her head. "It would be my honor to—"

"Absolutely not." Shaking her head, the Gardener leaped up and slapped her palm on the desk. She glared from Jie to Lilian and back again.

Florist Wei stood behind her with a sympathetic gaze. She was the motherly figure that the Gardener was supposed to be, the carrot to the Gardener's stick. She folded her hands into the long sleeves of her green dress.

Jie bowed her head. "Please, Gardener. I can't back down. I'd lose face."

"Not as much as when Lusha humiliates you." The Gardener's eyes narrowed. "You've been here for six years, and still have less grace and propriety than a second-year Seedling."

It was true. Though the rest of the House just assumed Jie was awkward, Lilian knew Jie didn't care about the sex trade. After her Plucking, she'd likely leave the Floating World to make use of her considerable stealth and fighting skills.

Now, though, she bowed low. Even if the motion was contrite, no doubt Jie was hiding anger.

The Gardener rounded her desk, subtly limping from an old injury to her left leg. She harrumphed. "You'd be worthless, if not for your exotic face and pointed ears."

Behind her, the Florist gave a subtle shake of her head.

The Gardener's ire shifted to Lilian. "And you: not only allowing her, but trying to hide it."

"I'm sorry." Lilian bowed low. For someone with very little kindness, at least the Gardener had decided not to reveal Lilian's complicity.

The Gardener turned back to Jie, jaw set in a tight line. "Many wealthy patrons will be there tonight, including three of your highest bidders. If you lose badly, they'll be well within their rights to rescind their bids. That would be bad for our House, and bad for your contract holder."

Statements like this were evidence that the Gardener didn't know who they really were. After all, the Black Lotus Clan didn't have contracts with their Fists; and while one of the clan masters had once said Jie's virgin price would fund operations for a year, they no doubt valued her in other ways.

Jie bowed lower. "I'm sorry, Gardener. I wasn't thinking of the consequences."

"It's time you learned," the Gardener said. "Once you finish your afternoon chores, you will be confined to Lilian's room tonight, with a guard posted outside the door. His overtime pay will come from your bond."

"As you command, Gardener." Jie held her bow, no doubt grinning ear to ear. And Lilian knew why: even though her room was on the third floor, Jie could climb down the walls blindfolded. And since she thought the Peony Garden was involved in this morning's plot, she would find a way to get out.

Well, in this, Lilian had a solution: a newer dwarf lock, once which maybe even Jie couldn't pick. She'd also recommend the Gardener post a guard in back.

When the Gardener dismissed them, they left.

Lilian flashed hand signals. *Is there anything I can do to convince you not to go?*

Of course not. Jie grinned, following Lilian back to her room.

While Lilian prepared for the soirée at the Peony Garden, Jie decoded a poem she'd received from one of her contacts in the silk market. The gist, made unclear by the ambiguity necessitated by poetic form, was that Lord Shi had dropped an exorbitant amount of money in the Houses.

Though Jie didn't know what to make of it, Lilian knew well from Tang Li's infiltration of both Lord Yang's and Lord Shi's households: Lord Yang was funneling profits from illegal *yue* to pay for information from several Blossoms, using one of Lord Shi's disloyal vassals to avoid it being tracked back to him. Tang Li revealed that in this, Lord Yang thought himself quite ingenious, never knowing that the Black Lotus Clan had operated in the Floating World for generations.

Before she left for the Peony Garden, Lilian bolted her window with a dwarf-made lock. Hopefully that would keep Jie out of trouble.

CHAPTER 17

One Week Ago

On her way back from a visit to Wen's room in the Peony Garden, Lilian stood on the second-floor mezzanine, lining up her shot. She'd snuck two of Lord Ting's traitorous guards in: Chen, as one of Lord Ting's vassals in crimson livery; and Zhang, dressed as a wealthy merchant—if someone asked him about the scar on his head, she'd told him to say it was a childhood accident. Zhang now sat where Lord Ting normally did in the Chrysanthemum Pavilion.

Almost every variable and contingency had been accounted for. Satisfied her plan would work, she descended to mingle with the guests. Wearing formal court robes, Young Lord Peng Kai-Zhi sat near the stage. At just sixteen, this was likely the first time he'd ever had a scantily-clad woman sitting his lap. It was probably why he was glowing red, though that might also be the alcohol. Lords, officials, and Blossoms took turns bowing, with all the men toasting him and the women paying homage to Lusha. Arrogant bitch that she was, she beamed at all the attention; small consolation, perhaps, since Jie's virgin price had far surpassed hers.

Besides Lilian, Wen was the only other Black Lotus member at the reception. Little Yuna was already in bed in the Seedling and

Floret room. Would the Surgeon be lurking in some shadow? Lilian remained vigilant, evaluating everyone in the room.

Out of the corner of her eye, she caught Lord Yang. Soon, upon her plan's successful completion, he'd be the most wanted man in the realm. She'd finally have revenge for him betraying her family.

Still, he hadn't been on the guest list. That he was here now, during her dry run, added more evidence that he was the one behind the hit. Though, given his association with the Surgeon, why hadn't he contracted him? Or maybe he had, and the Surgeon subcontracted to her, for whatever reason.

Eyebrows clashing together, Lord Yang strode toward Chen.

She buried an expletive. Would Lord Yang recognize Chen as one of Lord Ting's many faceless guards? Surely he would realize he wasn't really a minor vassal.

Lilian picked up her skirts and stepped into Lord Yang's path. "My Lord, thank you for your visit the other day."

Lord Yang's determined scowl melted, replaced by a feral grin. "Lilian!" He placed a hand on her hip.

Such a hateful man. She tried not to shudder, even as guilt twisted in her gut. She'd *Tiger-Eyed* Tang Li into feeling attraction for this man with no redeeming qualities.

"Are you contracted for tonight?" His eyes locked on her cleavage. "Lord Ting has been keeping you to himself so much these days."

Floating World training taught a Blossom to expose more when a prospective Hummingbird ogled them, but Lilian pulled her outer gown tighter about her shoulders. She bowed and lied. "Yes, I am meeting with him later."

He looked around. "Where is Lord Ting? I saw one of his men here..."

Lord Ting was at his villa, making last preparations, but Lilian lied again. "I'm not sure. I would assume he is around here, if his men are."

"You!" a voice boomed near the middle of the room. It was Deputy Xun of the Ministry of War, and patron of the Chrysanthemum Pavilion. "You're the half-elf Floret from the Chrysanthemum Pavilion! Jie, was it?"

Jie? Lilian's heart leaped into her throat. How foolish she'd been thinking a lock and several guards could contain the resourceful half-elf. Just how had she gotten out, though?

"It's Ju Jie!" someone said.

"I bid thirty thousand *yuan* on her virginity."

"She's almost too awkward for a Blossom, but that face!"

Lilian bowed to Lord Yang. "Excuse me. I must see to my Floret." She turned and slipped through the crowds toward the voices.

So small, Jie was hard to pick out in the mass of milling bodies.

"So, you are the Chrysanthemum Pavilion's famous half-elf."

"Yes, Master," Jie answered, fear trembling in her voice.

Lilian turned toward the exchange, to find Minister Li of the imperial treasury near the west wall of the common room. His large body obscured Jie, his body language exuding possession and dominance. It had intimidated more than one Blossom into an encounter she didn't enjoy. Anger welling in her, Lilian pushed her way toward them.

Despite the taboo against men touching Florets, Minister Li was lifting her chin with a finger. "What is your virgin price up to? I would like to make a bid."

"I'm sorry," Jie said. "Only my Gardener and Florist know. You will have to speak with them."

Though her voice wavered, it was all an act. It would take more than a pudgy brute to scare Jie. It didn't slow Lilian's urgency to reach them.

"I'd like to speak to *you*," Minister Li said.

Ewww. Lillian threaded between two more guests and seized Jie's hand.

Jie's hands swam in the motion of a joint manipulation.

Lilian responded with an escape. "Minister Li, thank you for finding my Little Sister."

Jie's eyes locked on Lilian's hand, then swept up her sleeve to her eyes.

"Come along now, Little Jie." Lilian used a gentle tone, even as she swept and tapped Jie's hand. *What are you doing here*?

"Thank you for your interest, Master." Jie bowed, while tapping back, *Scouting*.

Minister Li stared at the both of them. His mouth moved, but no words coming out.

"Come, Little Jie." Lilian pulled Jie toward the entrance. *Too big a risk. We need to get you out before Lusha sees you.*

"Look what—I mean, *who* we have here!" Lusha's voice carried over the crowd. "I didn't see Little Ju Jie from the Chrysanthemum Pavilion. Lilian said you had later declined the invitation. Come, pay respects to Young Lord Peng."

The din of conversation gave way to hushed whispers. Guests looked from Lusha to Jie. A path between them opened up as the crowd parted.

Unabashedly grinning, Lusha beckoned.

"I'm sorry, Miss Lusha." Lilian bowed. "My Little Sister is dizzy from all the guests. I was going to take her out for some fresh air."

Dressed in a blue gown with a white inner dress, the Peony Garden's Gardener stepped into their path. She motioned toward the entrance. "Oh, it is much too cold outside. We don't want you freezing."

It wasn't cold on this late summer night at all. The House guards in their pink livery blocked the entrance and the doors to the veranda. This was a trap, set up with the meeting in the silk market this morning.

The Gardener's grin suggested she'd planned it all. "I will assign one of our men to escort you to the conservatory. Plenty of fresh air, with all the open windows. Over here, Shixian." She hooked her hands into the crook of a handsome young man's elbow and pulled him through the guests.

Shixian's eyes locked on Jie, hungry. Were they planning on taking Jie by force? They'd be in for a surprise.

Though, even with House rivalries, conventions protected Floating World girls from rape.

Shixian approached, his robes and body language marking him as a military officer. He was a tall, striking man with a strong jaw and a high-bridged nose.

Jie retreated a step, tapping a message into Lilian's arm. *He's the one from this morning.*

What? That'd been Chen, who was nowhere to be seen right now. Lilian's brow furrowed as she mouthed, *Are you sure?*

Jie's eyes took in Shixian before shifting beyond him. Lilian followed her gaze.

Wen was shaking her head ever so slightly, though her expression betrayed concern. She signed, *Not a House guard. Get out.*

Brushing her hair behind her ears, Jie signaled with a combination of finger motions and eye expressions. *I will handle. Maintain line of sight.*

Lilian's pulse raced. Jie knew it was a trap, but she was misreading it as a continuation of this morning's attack, and not the Peony Garden's attempt to humiliate her.

Shixian reached them and bowed. "Miss Jie."

"Mister Shixian." Jie bowed back, but didn't reach for any hidden weapons. Indeed, she wore a smile, the one usually reserved for Lilian.

Lilian's stomach knotted.

He extended a hand toward the exit, and Jie followed, looking more intrigued than alert. If Lilian didn't know any better, she'd say Jie found him attractive. She'd never expressed interest in anyone before; probably because the men they met in the Floating World weren't the most appealing specimens in the realm.

They strolled through the common room archway, across a hall, and under another arch. Lilian followed, but two of the House guards barred her way into the conservatory. No matter how much she turned, it was impossible to see what was happening. She could get past these guards, either with violent or stealthy measures, but that would give away her true identity.

And therefore ruin her plan for tomorrow.

Her unborn baby, or Jie? She could only save one.

No, there was no real dilemma. Jie was secretly proud of her virgin price, and wouldn't make any foolish decisions, not even for a dashing, handsome man. And if he tried to force himself on her, well, he'd be in for a surprise.

She waited by the door, focusing on the sounds.

Her heart froze.

Jie was moaning.

The sound, Lilian knew well from their many times *practicing*.

A combination of jealousy and concern all spurred Lilian into action. She started forward.

When both guards reached for her, she crossed her arms and seized their wrists. She stepped back and pulled them into each other. She whirled around them and darted into the room.

And skidded to a stop. Other guests pushed in behind her.

With his back to Lilian, Shixian held Jie in the corner, locked in a passionate kiss. He was standing, robe hiked up to reveal his pumping, bare buttocks. Her legs were wrapped around him.

Oh Heavens, no. Jie had just forfeited her astronomical virgin price. What was she thinking?

"Sir!" Lilian barked, "Unhand my Little Sister."

Jie broke the kiss and looked over his shoulder, confusion written in her expression. Then it cleared. She pushed Shixian away, and her skirts—dropped down to cover her legs.

Lilian glanced at the gathering crowd. There were too many witnesses to rewrite this narrative.

The Peony Garden Gardener and Lusha pushed through the chattering masses and passed to either side of Lilian. They exchanged knowing grins.

Rage burned in Lilian's face. They'd planned this, to protect Lusha's record virgin price.

"You've broken the rules of the Floating World, girl." The Gardener made a show of jabbing a finger at Jie. "A Blossom may not entertain a Hummingbird in another House without the Gardener's permission."

"I thought... I thought..." Mouth agape, Shixian shook his head. "I wasn't a Hummingbird."

Jie nodded. "No. He...he wasn't. He was..."

Lusha held up Jie's undergarment and brought a hand to her chest. "Heavens, are you saying you gave in to passion?"

Lilian's fists tightened. No, Jie would never—

Jie could only shake her head.

"So much for your virgin price." Lusha cast a victorious, cruel smile.

Jie glared at Shixian, the accusation in her eyes sharp enough to kill.

He waved his hand back and forth as he took a step back. "I am so sorry. I didn't know."

"Liar." Her voice rose. "You used a kerchief embroidered with Artistic Magic."

Lilian's blood boiled. They'd used magic to lower Jie's guard.

He shook his head. "I know nothing about—"

"This?" The Gardener held up a kerchief. There was nothing special about it. "It looks quite plain."

Lilian snatched the undergarment from Lusha, shoved Shixian out of the way, and came to Jie's side. Maybe she'd expected her tear-filled eyes, given what had just happened to her, but Jie looked more calculating than anything. Lilian draped an arm over her, pulled her close, and positioned herself to shield Jie from prying eyes.

Wen, too, shuffled to their side.

"Are you all right?" Lilian asked.

Jie gave nodded, signing, *I thought the Peony Garden had hired assassins. I was wrong the whole time.*

Anger still blazing, Lilian looked over her shoulder.

Gardener Dan was doing nothing to prevent more visitors from coming in to share in Jie's disgrace, while Lusha wore a triumphant smirk. Both of these bitches would pay for doing this. As for Shixian, he looked even more distraught than Jie. Maybe he had been tricked into this, as well? No matter, he was now on Lilian's vengeance list.

"You worthless whore!" Gardener Ju's voice rose above the excited conversation.

The room fell silent, and onlookers made way for Gardener Ju. She stopped before Gardener Dan and bowed repeatedly. "My apologies, Gardener, for my Floret's indiscretion." She turned back and glared.

Wen shrank back.

Fighting not to cower as well, Lilian kept between Jie and Gardener Ju. "Gardener, I—"

The Gardener jabbed a crooked finger at Jie. "That harlot couldn't keep her thighs closed. She's lost us a hundred and fifty thousand *yuan*."

Gasps broke out around them. Everyone knew the bid had broken Lusha's record, but the amount had been speculation, known only to the Gardener, Florist, and the highest bidders. The figure was staggering, twice Lusha's, and enough to feed a village for a decade. Half of it would've gone to the clan, via its shell company.

Cowed, Jie and Lilian followed the Gardener and several House guards back to the Chrysanthemum Pavilion. Already, the news had spread, and onlookers all pointed and whispered among themselves. Tears glistened in Jie's eyes.

Lilian berated herself, even as she kept an eye out for the Surgeon. She should've found a way to keep Jie away from the Peony Garden. It was her fault.

She didn't have much time to think about it when the Gardener ordered the guards to cast Jie into the very storehouse where Lilian had stashed the alcohol and firecrackers. It was far more than the House would use for two New Year's Festivals, and confined there for the whole night, Jie would surely get suspicious.

At least they hadn't chosen the storehouse with Lin's body, which would've been a dead giveaway.

Lilian tried to check in on Jie a few times that night, only to be turned away by the House guards. How lonely she must be, haunted by dark thoughts. And with the guards rotating all night, there would be no making it past them.

At last, Lilian gave up. If one good thing came out of this, it was that she was able to prepare without worrying about Jie figuring things out. She covered the head of one of the crossbow bolts with spongewood soaked in a red dye. Once it struck Lord Ting, he was to bite into a poison capsule, which would make him appear dead.

Then, knowing anticipation would keep her awake, she drank dreamflower pollen and went to bed for the last time in the Chrysanthemum Pavilion.

Tomorrow was the day she'd escape the clan.

* * *

The Present

Sometimes, it was hard for Tang Li to tell where she ended and Lilian began. Tears filled her eyes as Lilian's memories and regrets flooded over her. If not so concerned with her own escape from the clan, Lilian would've been able to protect Jie better.

Concerned mostly with self-preservation, Tang Li tended to caution. Now, though, she was filled with the determination to protect the cell sisters.

She walked over and brushed the hair out of Yangyang's pretty face, and adjusted the folded blankets under Meisha's head.

Yes, no matter what happened, she would protect these two tonight, or die trying. She'd—

The door to the playroom rattled up against the bar.

Tang Li's heart jumped into her throat. Surely that wooden bar would hold out against a few men trying to get in?

Knuckles rapped at various heights on the door, until the pitch changed at the bar. The door thumped with a resonant thud, and the bar splintered in the middle.

How was that even possible?

The door swung open, revealing the gaunt face of the Surgeon.

CHAPTER 18

The Present

Tang Li dashed behind a column as the Surgeon slipped into the room and closed the door behind him.

He padded over to the cross. "Tang Li. There's no use hiding, I already saw you. Lord Yang said you were bound. How did you get out?" The manacles jingled.

With him by the cross, she was closer to the door. If she ran fast enough... But what about Yangyang and Meisha?

"I guess picking locks would be a handy skill, given your other identity. Right, Fixer Zhang?" He turned around the column.

How had he gotten there? His voice had just come from the cross. Tang Li backed up until she hit the wall.

"You are not Black Lotus, are you?" He studied her.

"What if I were?"

"I once thought so, considering your skill at allocating assets. But the last time I saw you with Lilian, I figured it out."

The last time she met Lilian. That'd been the day of the hit on Lord Ting. Tang Li closed her eyes and thought back to how that had all turned out—but instead of her own memories, they were Lilian's.

"I do believe Lilian learned the deeper tricks of the *Tiger's Eye* from me, without me realizing it. And indeed, she might be even better."

* * *

One Week Ago

Lilian woke to the Gardener summoning the entire House together. Mid-morning sun streamed in through the windows, and outside, servants were cleaning the outer walls, as she'd requested for Lord Ting's special night in the House. The water was part of her plan.

Donning a dressing gown, she left her room and looked over the mezzanine balcony.

Down below, Jie knelt at the edge of the common room stage. Arms outstretched, she balanced trays laden with rice wine-filled cups.

Rage boiled Lilian's blood. It was cruel and humiliating, and for any girl other than the Black Lotus cell sisters, it would be tortuous.

Lilian ran down the steps and joined the gathered Seedlings, Florets, and other Blossoms.

From the base of the stage, Gardener Ju poked Jie in the chest, probably hoping some of the rice wine would spill. "I've sent word to the Golden Peacock Company to see what they want to do with you. You'll still fetch an ungodly amount, from all the Hummingbirds who've eyed you over the years."

Lilian tried to catch Jie's attention, to at least give her encouragement. Around her, the other girls did the same.

"Now," Gardener Ju said, "Lord Ting has reserved the entire House for him and Lilian tonight. He wants it empty, so the rest of you have the night off..."

All part of Lilian's plan. She'd used all her savings and some of the down payment for the hit to reserve the entire House. It would only be her, the Gardener, Lord Ting, and her handpicked guards.

"...all except Jie. You will serve dinner to Lord Ting and Lilian tonight." The Gardener gestured to the corner of the stage.

What? Lilian's heart sunk. Jie couldn't be here tonight. It would ruin everything.

"Maybe he will be your first Hummingbird."

No, no, no. If Jie were here, she'd foil the plan. Not to mention, it went against Floating World conventions for a girl, no matter her age, to see a man before her first period. Lilian knelt and pressed her forehead to the floor in the most contrite position possible. "Little Sister Jie has not yet flowered with Heaven's Dew. She can't receive Hummingbirds yet."

"Gardener!" All the girls joined in, even Florist Wei.

In the silence, broken only by the sobs of some of the Seedlings, the Gardener's hard glare sent shudders through them. Lilian, though, refused to wilt.

The Gardener harrumphed. "Little Jie has lived in the House long enough without earning her keep. Now that the blossom has been plucked, it doesn't matter. Youth is a commodity with diminishing returns, and the fact you've not blossomed with Heaven's Dew makes you even more unique for the Floating World. It will allow us to set an even higher contract price for your regular assignations, and schedule a few a day."

A few a day? There was a certain pride in belonging to an elite House of the Floating World, as well as countless conventions. One of which was that a Blossom in the top two Houses would typically only entertain one Hummingbird a day, three at most. This was too much. It set a precedent that they could never go back from.

Jie dared look up. "Gardener—"

"Silence! Who gave you permission to speak, selfish little slut?" The Gardener turned to the Florist. "Send out invitations to all who have bid on her."

Sniffles and sobs grew louder.

Lilian's heart was breaking for all these girls who'd never undergone Black Lotus training. She pressed her forehead to the ground again. "Gardener, please."

The Gardener's hand smacked on the stage, silencing the room. "Don't think that just because you are the Chrysanthemum House's Corsage I won't turn you out. I'll make sure no Floating World House will take you in. Golden Peacock Company will contract you to some back-alley whorehouse in the Trench, where you'll service fifty lowlifes a day."

If only it were so easy. The Black Lotus Clan needed eyes and ears in the Floating World, not the Trench. Time to take a stand, for all Floating World girls now and in the future. Even if it would ruin her meticulous plan for tonight. It was time to expose the Gardener as one of the famed, and supposedly dead Steel Orchids. She stepped forward, finally ready to reveal her true skills as a Black Fist.

The Gardener backed up a step, her path of retreat blocked by stage. Her left leg buckled; that would be Lilian's first target with a sweep kick, followed by a bladed hairpin to the throat. The room went silent.

"I'll do it, willingly," Jie said, shooting Lilian a warning glance. She mouthed, *The other girls.*

Sighing, Lilian relaxed, took two steps back and knelt. To think, she'd almost sacrificed her hopes for her unborn child. "I am sorry, Gardener."

"I'm glad that is settled." The Gardener's voice cracked, though she straightened and squared her shoulders. She pointed to the corner of the room. "Tonight is an important night. For now, you are going to scrub his favorite table clean and polish every wood surface until I can see your pretty little reflection in them."

Lilian suppressed a sigh of relief. With Jie busy for the next couple of hours, she'd have time to make changes to her plan, just in case she couldn't' find a way to get Jie out of the House tonight.

After the Gardener dismissed the girls and everyone dispersed, Lilian returned to her room. Uncovering her secret storage space, she doused one of the crossbow bolts in musk toxin. It was the first bolt to go into the magazine. If Jie was there tonight, Lilian would entice her into catching it.

Satisfied, she went out to her last meeting with Tang Li. Now an accomplished fixer, she'd saved about half of what she needed to realize her dream: to open a teahouse. Quite fond of her, Lilian would give her unknowing confidante a portion of the blood money.

As she strolled through the near-deserted streets of the Floating World, a stare weighed on her back. Try as she might, she couldn't make her tail. None of the clan, save for Jie and Master Yan, were that good. Maybe the other Steel Orchid? She was unaccounted for. And of course, there was the Surgeon.

If it was him, what did he want, besides targeting Jie?

She turned into the Nine-Tail Fox Shrine.

As planned, Tang Li knelt on a cushion before the altar, with her back to the entrance, wearing a white dress with red leaves. The woman praying beside her had an air of familiarity. Maybe an asset Lilian had introduced to Tang Li in the past?

No, Feng Rumei's voice spoke in Lilian's head. *Don't be shy, come join us.*

Feng Rumei! It'd been a year and a half since they'd last met. The exotic Empath had disappeared not long before she was about to give birth. Lilian shuffled over and knelt beside Tang Li.

Go on, I know your business with your Fixer Zhang.

Of course she would. Making a show of throwing a coin in the donation box, Lilian passed a folded sheet of paper to Tang Li. As per her correspondence with her anonymous employer, it designated Fixer Zhang as the one to hold the seal to the bank account with the bounty once she'd received proof of Lord Ting's death. Tang Li's commission would bring her closer to her dreams.

Would Lilian's mission succeed? There were too many variables that had just been introduced, including Jie's assignment to stay at the Chrysanthemum Pavilion tonight, and the Surgeon. What if he planted other orders in her?

Remember this? Rumei's voice spoke.

Two memories returned to Lilian, the first of her time as a three-year-old, being conditioned by the Surgeon. He'd taught her to bite the tip of her tongue and dig her thumbnail into her index fingertips. The second was her subconsciously doing those motions when Master Yan had tried to use the *Tiger's Eye* on her.

Lilian's eyes widened, and she turned to look past Tang Li at Feng Rumei.

Rumei winked. *I'll be watching to see the outcome of your plan. If you need safe haven, I'm sure Faceless Chang of the Red Dragons in the Trench would welcome you with open arms.*

No doubt to service fifty men a day. Suppressing a shudder, Lilian rose and bowed. Then she headed back to the Chrysanthemum Pavilion to prepare for the big night.

Halfway there, a hand pulled her into an alley and covered her mouth.

Her heart leaped into her throat, and she stared wide-eyed at the Surgeon.

CHAPTER 19

One Week Ago

Heart racing, Lilian took a deep breath to calm herself as the Surgeon locked his gaze and drew circles in the air with his fingers. She recognized the pattern: it was meant to coerce the truth out of her. She bit the tip of her tongue and dug her thumbnails into her index fingers, just as he'd taught and made her forget.

"Tell me, what were you doing with Fixer Zhang?"

She had to make him believe the plan would go on. "She is my go-between for the hit on Lord Ting."

"Who was the woman with her?"

"She was pregnant when I was. We sometimes had tea with Tang Li." All true.

The Surgeon's eyes narrowed, but then he formed new finger patterns—this time, the ones he and Master Yan used to plant an order. "Tonight, you will spare Gardener Ju, and kill the half-elf instead."

Forcing herself to appear *Tiger-Eyed*, Lilian flashed the acknowledging hand signal.

He waved his hands in front of her again, the pattern to make her forget.

She closed her eyes and made a show of wobbling on her feet. When she opened her eyes, he was gone. She blinked several times to make it appear as if she were coming out of the *Tiger's Eye*.

Pretending that nothing was amiss, she returned to her home for one last day.

Jie was just about finished with her chores, and Lilian acknowledged her with a smile as she passed. How would she be feeling right now, after she'd lost so much and been publicly humiliated?

Lillian would miss her. So much had been left unsaid between them, their intimacy laughed off under the guise of practice. Lilian wasn't sure how she felt, besides that electricity felt whenever they kissed.

Now, though, with the Surgeon targeting Jie for some unknown reason, and the possibility of her ruining the hit, it was again time to manipulate her emotions again. She flashed an alluring smile. "Come join me when you're done, and I'll show you what Lord Ting likes."

Jie's eyes widened for a split second before she nodded. It was late afternoon by the time she finished, came up, and she threw herself into Lilian's bed.

Settling behind her, Lilian tried several times to cuddle and provide comfort, only to be rebuffed. Finally, she got up and went to her makeup table to prepare for tonight. This was their last time together, and Jie was wasting it by bottling up.

The silent treatment allowed doubts to creep over Lilian. Maybe this was too risky, staging a hit. Su had to be the only survivor, so as to report back to her employer...but what if one of Lord Ting's guards killed him? Or if Su took matters into his own hands?

At last, Jie propped her head up and broke the silence. "What were you thinking, challenging the Gardener?"

"Those are your first words?" Lilian lowered her brush. Was that what she was thinking about, and not about Shixian's rape? "I would ask you the same. Don't make this about me. Why did you even go last night? I told you it was dangerous. What if the Peony Garden really wanted to kill you? You never listen."

"I was worried that all our sisters were compromised. I had to hope it was just me."

It was everything Lilian loved in Jie. Her selflessness. Her dedication to the cell sisters. Lilian would miss that. Still, to maintain her own act, she set her lips in a tight line.. "You should have left it to Wen. She would have figured it out. You always take it upon yourself."

Jie sighed. "I don't want anyone else to get hurt."

Oh, how Lilian would miss her. "At some point, you have to trust the rest of us."

Jie shook her head. "I could never forgive myself if Wen had gotten caught."

"She wouldn't have. She's not as stealthy as you, but she's still good." The three of them had been together so long. Lilian fought off tears by glaring. "Did you ever think that maybe you taking charge of everything has prevented the clan from seeing worth in the rest of us? Maybe that has kept many of us stuck spreading our legs in the Floating World."

Hanging her head, Jie blinked several times.

A part of Lilian died at what she was doing. She rose and went over to her bed, then sat down in the arc formed by Jie's bent form. "Oh, my sweet. I'm so sorry."

Were those tears trickling down Jie's cheek?

Lilian climbed over her to the other side of the bed, then curled up against Jie's back. She pressed her cheek against Jie's.

"I wanted to give myself to him." Jie pressed back into her. "But I wasn't going to. I couldn't, not with so much money at stake."

Though it must've hurt Jie's pride to have forfeited her virgin price, at least her first time had been with someone she wanted to sleep with. In that, they were alike, even if Jie would never know.

Lilian stroked her hair. "I know. Our bodies aren't our own. No matter how much it is drilled into us at the temple, and here in the House, a little piece of me dies every time."

"Clearly, the Peony Garden had ill intentions, but they hadn't planned to go so far as to have me murdered."

Lilian nodded, recognizing Jie's desire to change the subject to things she could control. Their cheeks brushing each other. "Which means someone else is targeting you."

"And maybe not just me."

Lilian held her breath. This line of thinking threatened to put the cell on high alert. Though maybe she could use that to her advantage. "What if there's a traitor? A mole?"

"No." Jie closed her eyes. "We're like the Steel Orchids. I trust each and every one of them with my life."

Oh, if only Jie knew that one of the Steel Orchids lived in this very House. Part of Lilian wanted her to figure everything out. "You have a blind spot with us."

Jie sucked on her lower lip, which she always did when pondering, and held it for a long while. "You're right. We need to contact the clan, to implement an objective evaluation."

"When?"

"Now." Jie started to rise.

Lilian held her down. That was the last thing she needed now, but she could use the idea to her advantage. "I'll go. There's still time before Lord Ting arrives."

"Masked Crossbowman saw you, too. It's too dangerous."

If Jie had figured out that Lilian was working with Chen, she could figure out the plan. "Trust me. Trust my skill."

Their gazes met, and Lilian's heart stirred. She loved this girl. Whether as a friend or something more, she couldn't tell. And if Lilian executed her plan correctly, this was the last she'd ever see her. She took in Jie's eyes and lithe form, the point of her ears and the lip she always sucked. This was it. Cupping Jie's cheeks, Lilian leaned in with a deep kiss.

Jie reached around to the small of Lilian's back and the nape of her neck, drawing her closer.

Every nerve lit up, and heat blossomed in her. If she didn't break the kiss now, she never would. She pulled back, Jie sticking to her.

"I'll be all right," Lilian said.

The look in Jie's eyes...so much sadness. Just like Mother, when she took in her dying breath.

Lilian turned away. Slipping off her robe, she went to her secret compartment for her stealth suit.

"I wore your stealth suit yesterday, and got it dirty going up the chimney. It's under Little Wen's bed in the Peony Garden."

"So that's how you got out." Shaking her head, Lilian giggled. She'd hoped to keep the stealth suit in her escape. Instead, she went to her wardrobe for a dark shirt and pair of pants. Once she'd put them on, she twirled. "How do I look?"

"Like a pig." Jie grinned.

Lilian did her best imitation of a snuffling pig. With one last look at her sweet, beautiful, talented, beloved Jie, she opened her window shutters and climbed out.

Clinging to the shadows, she descended, ran out the back gate, and sprinted the block to the Peony Garden. The sun hung low on the horizon, and the Iridescent Moon waxed to its fifth crescent. Half a phase to go. The operation was timed to end before Blossoms retired to their rooms with Hummingbirds. She slipped in through the rear, climbed to Wen's room, and crawled through the window.

When she landed in a crouch, a blade pressed to her throat.

Lilian froze, and held her hands up.

"Lilian?" Wen asked. The blade left her neck.

Standing, Lilian turned and wrapped her other best friend in a hug. Whereas Lilian's feelings for Jie were more ambiguous, Wen was just a sister. Practice came naturally with Jie, but it'd been awkward performing with Wen for Lord Nan.

Even so, Lilian would miss her just as much.

Wen pushed out of the embrace. She was wearing her stealth suit. "I found out where Masked Crossbowman ate!"

"Where?" Lilian had wanted to use Wen to draw Jie out of the Chrysanthemum Pavilion and to safety, and this might provide an opportunity.

"There's a stand outside Yue Heaven." Wen pointed in the general direction. "There were four armed men there, whispering about a hit. I just got back here, and was going to get Jie."

Lilian suppressed a sigh of relief. Thankfully, she'd found out too late to do anything about it, and this would work perfectly with her plan. "I think they know who we are, and are targeting us. I'm going to go use myself as bait. Go get Jie as backup."

Wen hooked Lilian's elbow. "Are you sure?"

Lilian nodded. This was working perfectly.

"What?" Wen asked.

"Hmm?"

"Why are you looking at me like that?"

Because Lilian would miss her. She reached out and brushed out a tangle in Wen's hair. "Because you were less than perfect. There, I've fixed it."

Wen flushed red and took Lilian's hand. "Be careful."

"I will." With one last look at Wen, Lilian descended, then ducked into an alley.

When Wen passed on her way to the Chrysanthemum Pavilion, Lilian followed at a distance. Staying downwind so that Jie wouldn't smell her, she hid in an alley with line of sight on the rear gate, and waited.

From the conversation up front, Lord Ting had already cleared the gates with his three guards and Su, and had entered the common room. Soon, the guards would leave parts of the repeating crossbow for her.

It wasn't long before Wen and Jie dashed out in opposite directions, Jie headed toward Yue Heaven. Just where was Wen going?

Probably Jie, in her stubbornness, had sent Wen to safety, figuring she could handle all four men on her own. She probably could. And by the time Jie ran there and back, she'd be too late.

Lilian slipped back into House from the rear, stopping by the storehouse with Lin's body to retrieve the magazine. She checked it just to be sure: one with musk toxin for Jie, one with coma poison for Lord Ting, one for Gardener Ju, one each for the guards, plus five more, just in case. She'd spare Su, so he could report back to Fixer Zhang, who'd release the funds.

Skirting around the common room and sticking to the safe spots in the nightingale floors, she collected the crossbow parts, assembling it as she went. Save for Lord Ting conversing with Su, and Gardener Ju skulking around somewhere, the Chrysanthemum Pavilion was empty, just as she'd arranged.

The route, which she'd timed several times over the last days, ended at the spot with a good line of sight on Lord Ting's favorite table. She balanced the stock on the bannister and took aim with the repeater.

He was sitting there, handsome as always. This was the right thing to do. Soon, very soon, they'd be free of court intrigue and clan machinations. Free to raise their unborn child.

Bowing repeatedly for Lilian's lateness, the Gardener came to pour more wine.

Lilian's heart squeezed.

No, not the Gardener.

Florist Wei.

* * *

The Present

Tang Li opened her eyes to find the Surgeon close to her, waving his fingers in a mesmerizing pattern. Though the last thing she remembered about Lilian was their meeting at the Nine-Tail Fox Shrine, she somehow knew... She bit the tip of her lip and dug her thumbnails into her index fingertips.

Then she flashed the hand signal indicating he held her in his *Tiger's Eye*. Would he believe it worked?

"Are you in there, Lilian?" the Surgeon asked. "You died before you fulfilled my plans for you."

Was part of Lilian in her? It would explain some of her decisions lately. Though how had it come to pass? Tang Li shook her head, and spoke in a droning voice. "Lilian is gone forever."

The Surgeon let out a sigh, and looked down at his feet.

Here was her chance.

He looked up and met her gaze.

Following Lilian's childhood memories from when he'd kidnapped her, Tang Li set her fingers into the *Tiger's Eye* pattern for planting memories.

"Bitch!" The Surgeon drew a knife.

Li switched to a new pattern.

Flashing the subconscious response, the Surgeon relaxed, the knife returning to his sheath.

"Why do you want to kill the half-elf?" she asked.

"Vengeance on her father."

He knew her father? "Who is it?"

His lips sealed, and he stared off blankly. He'd buried this information deep in the maze of his psyche, and Li didn't have enough skill with the *Tiger's Eye* to navigate those twisted corridors.

She could, however, remove the threat to Jie. She repeated the planting memory pattern, and he acknowledged it with a hand signal.

CHAPTER 20

The Present

Using all the sleight-of-hand tricks the cell had taught him, Tian planted the sisters' weapons in the designated spots as he followed Lord Nan on a circuitous route. He had to split his attention between doing that and listening to the lord explaining their supplies of food and arms.

Complicating his endeavors was his pure awe at the subterranean fortress. It was even grander than the way it was described in the histories.

"Now, Young Lord Zheng," Lord Nan said. "We will retire for the night. The imperial army should arrive sometime tomorrow, and we will need to be rested."

"Yes, my Lord." Tian set his fist into his palm and bowed his head.

As they walked down an abandoned corridor, Tian's hands sweat. The traitor's back was to him, an inviting target.

Hold the dragonfly with care, Princess Kaiya's voice spoke in his head. *For even their fleeting lives have value.*

Could he kill this man, whose only crime was loyalty to his own lord? Who wanted nothing more than prosperity for his region, which the Emperor exploited?

There was an intersection up ahead. It would be better to wait, to make sure there were no sentries there.

A shadow flashed in front of them.

A squawk escaped Lord Nan's mouth as his hands moved to his neck. Blood sprayed.

Tian buried his gasp.

"Are you all right?" Wen asked. She wore a Yang uniform, and held a bloody knife.

He gave a tentative nod. "Where are the others?"

"Safe, for now."

"Hey! What's going on here?" yelled a voice.

Tian turned to see six of Yang's men drawing their swords.

I'll find Lord Yang. You go defend the others. Second right, fourth left, first left, third right, seventh right, down, third right, second left, fourth door. Wen bolted into a run. "Traitors! You'll never catch me!"

No doubt, she meant for him to go the other way. He dashed through the halls, following her directions, pushing past soldiers who joined the chase.

At last, he arrived in a torture chamber.

Tang Li was there, tending to the two cell sisters.

His cell sisters. Something funny fluttered in his stomach. Around these girls, there was a sense of belonging he never felt anywhere else. He'd defend them, or die trying.

The jingling of weapons grew louder in the hall.

Tang Li smiled at him. "Before we die, let me tell you more of Lilian's story."

* * *

One Week Ago

Lilian's hands sweat as she took her finger from the repeater. What was Florist Wei doing here? She was supposed to have gone to the theater tonight, while Gardener Ju remained behind.

For Lilian's plan to work, she needed a female body, burned beyond recognition. It was supposed to be the Steel Orchid, not the Florist. Lilian had taken careful measures to ensure that only a handful of traitors would die tonight, but now... It was time to call off the plan. There might be another way.

How would her employer retaliate? If it was really Lord Yang, he'd probably go skulking back in the shadows until the next opportunity arose. But he also had plenty of proof that Lilian had planned to assassinate Lord Ting, and correctly suspected her as being daughter of Lord Yu. And, once Jie returned, possibly with the rest of the cell, they'd figure out Lilian had betrayed them.

"They said she had a surprise for me," Lord Ting said, even though he knew the plan, "but I've been waiting for an hour. Where is she?"

The Florist bowed low. "My apologies, my Lord."

The doors to the common room flung open. Jie rushed in, twisting between the chairs and tables.

Florist Wei, or her unborn child.

He'd be a symbol of hope for the North, whose people were crushed by the greed of imperial policy.

Tears in her eyes, Lilian took the first shot at Lord Ting, cocked, and took the second shot at Florist Wei.

Jie covered the distance in a blink of an eye, dodging past Su. She leaped with an outstretched hand...

...and swiped the bolt out of the air.

She slid face-first across the table, smashing dishes and overturning food.

The second bolt flew true, lodging into Florist Wei's chest. Her scream was cut short by a gurgle..

Jie popped into a flip, and landed in a crouch in front of Lord Ting.

Lilian backed into the shadows. Any second now...

Legs buckling, body swaying, Jie fell to her knees.

In that split second, Lilian's heart soared. Her plan had succeeded, save for having to sacrifice Florist Wei instead of killing Gardener Ju. She lined up for the shot on Lord Ting's stomach and squeezed the trigger. Hopefully he'd remember to bite into the poison capsule.

Her blunted bolt zinged through the air.

Click. Another crossbow bolt shot out from the far archway to the veranda.

It seemed to fly in slow motion, an impossible arcing shot headed straight toward Lord Ting, yet there was nothing Lilian could do to stop it.

Jie's eyes remained locked on Lilian's harmless shot. The musk toxin hadn't knocked her out. Her hand reached for the bolt. She'd be able to catch—

The other bolt slammed into Lord Ting's back, knocking his body forward while whipping his head back. He slumped over. Her bolt zipped past the sweep of Jie's hand, glancing of Ting's shoulder. She fell face-first to the table.

No, no, no. Lilian buried her scream and shifted her aim to the archway, but no one was there.

Still, Lilian had a good idea who it was: the erstwhile Steel Orchid, Gardener Ju.

"Great shot!" Su yelled, turning to her and lifting his fist.

His words buzzed in her ears as she rushed along the mezzanine, not caring about the chirping nightingale floors. She ran down the steps, and was about to dash across the common room to try to save Lord Ting.

She froze before entering the common room, and squinted.

Lord Ting didn't move, not even his chest rising and falling with life-giving breath. Blood trickled down the side of his mouth.

No, no, no. Lilian's heart squeezed so tight, she couldn't breathe herself. The father of her child, the only one worthy of uniting the North, dead. The Florist, too, by Lilian's own hand.

Her plan had utterly failed, because of her employer's backup. Tears blurred Lilian's vision. It would be better just to die now. The triggers she'd set in Tang Li's mind would still exact vengeance for her.

"Is the half-elf unconscious?" One of the guards, Chen, strode toward Jie.

"You saw her catch the bolt?" Su said. "She's dangerous. We should kill her."

"I want to have some fun with her first." Chen was reaching for the hem of Jie's pants.

No, not that. For Jie, Lilian needed to be strong. Taking a deep breath, she wiped the tears from her eyes, squared her shoulders and strode in with an air of triumph. They had to believe everything had transpired as she'd planned. She levelled the crossbow at Chen. "Step back, Chen. Touch her, and I empty this magazine into you."

Chen stepped back, hands in the air.

Su turned to her. "She's a witness."

"I have plans for her. And If we leave too many bodies, it will raise questions. Now, do as we planned." Keeping the crossbow pointed at Chen, Lilian came over to Jie and checked on her.

Unconscious, but unharmed. Lord Ting, on the other hand, was definitely dead.

Lilian fought back the tears. Part of the failed plan was a quick death for all of these men except Su; they'd still die, but she'd castrate Chen first.

And no matter what, Jie had to live. The question was, could they both survive?

"She's more than she appears," Su said. "We can't leave her alive."

"Mister Su." Lilian glared at him. "Your master wanted spies in the Floating World. I can convince Jie to join me. She's an invaluable asset."

Su muttered something under his voice.

Lowering the crossbow, Lilian gestured to the guards. "Now, as we planned, get the alcohol and firecrackers from the storeroom. And some rope. Blankets from the bedrooms."

The men exchanged glances, but then went to follow her orders.

Satisfied, she set the crossbow down, but kept it within reach. Gently, trying not to look at Lord Ting's body, Lilian eased Jie off the table and set her into a chair. She picked the food and shattered porcelain shards out of her hair and clothes.

When Su came back with rope, he boxed Lilian away from the crossbow.

Shit. Feigning nonchalance, Lilian bound Jie's hands behind her back, through the rungs of the chair; she tied her ankles together instead of to the chair legs. She kept the tension loose, to make it easier for Jie to break free when the time came.

Because Lilian had taken the possibility of Jie's interference into account. With her skill, she'd be able to escape what was going to happen.

Lilian just needed to maintain the narrative to escape, herself.

CHAPTER 21

One Week Ago

Lilian had been so careless in her grief, she'd allowed Su to take control of the crossbow. Her original plan had been to shoot the three traitorous guards here, while letting Su live to report back to her anonymous employer. Once he'd left the House, she would've given Lord Ting the antidote, lit the fire, and escaped. The backup plan in the event Jie arrived was to leave her an open path through the bath wing.

Now, Lord Ting was dead, and Su in possession of the crossbow. She had to improvise.

Taking into account the final stage of her plan: the timing, in order to draw crowds out to create cover. She'd have to finish within half a phase, or else Blossoms and Hummingbirds would be too preoccupied to venture out.

She hurried to the Gardener's office and scribbled a note to Jie.

My Sweet. I am happy you found this, because it means that you survived. However, you also fell into my last trap. While you followed Ting's men, my trail has gotten colder. You were always too impulsive. Goodbye, my sweet. I've always loved you.

She folded it up and wrote Jie's name on the outside.

When she returned, she made a quick scan. The men were still moving cases of fireworks and alcohol to the designated spots.

Flammable materials blocked all exits save for the archway to the bath wing.

And now Chen, an expert shot, had the crossbow.

She gave the message to Scar Head Zhang. "When you leave, go to the silk market. Leave this message under the jade trinket vendor's table. Three down, two over from the entrance."

"What is it?"

"It has to do with our payment."

With a nod, Zhang stuffed it into his sleeve.

Coming up behind Jie, Lilian popped open a vial of scented salts and retreated several steps.

Jie stirred. Her wrists pulled against the bonds. "Wen! What did you do with Lilian?"

After all these years, Jie still underestimated Lilian. A laugh escaped her. "Nothing."

Jie froze.

"Not Little Wen. She worships the ground you walk on." Lilian came around and sat in Jie's lap, facing her. This would give her no pleasure, having to hurt Jie like this; but Su and Chen had to believe the narrative. Sighing, she cupped her cheek. "I told you you had a blind spot."

"Why?" Jie asked, shaking her head. "Why did you do this?"

"I told you." Lilian had set this up over the last several months, and for now, Jie had to believe it. "I wanted out of this life. I'd held out hope that you'd be able to convince Master Yan to reassign me, but here's the truth: I played the Little Sister you adored for too long, and the clan thinks—thought—all I'm good for is sating Lord Ting's desires."

"I can convince Master Yan. I swear."

Lilian shook her head. "This was my last chance to get out."

"The clan will hunt you down," Jie said. There was no malice in her tone, only affection.

Despite the betrayal. Lilian's chest squeezed, and it took all her willpower to maintain a façade of nonchalant victory. She gestured to Lin's body near the hearth. It was supposed to be mistaken for Lord Ting, because nobody would mistake his large frame for Lilian. "Not if they think I am dead."

Jie gasped. "You stored him in that cellar."

Along with the musk-coated bolt, but she didn't have to know that part. Lilian nodded.

"That's where the stench came from. You used a ruse, thinking I would kill him when he attacked."

It was time to spin another lie. "No. You were always a threat to the plan, and I'd originally planned on removing you altogether." Sighing, she pointed at Chen, crossbow strapped to his shoulder, carrying a crate of alcohol. "I couldn't bring myself to do it, and trusted your blind spot."

"She already killed one of your comrades," Jie yelled to Chen. "What's to keep her from sacrificing you next?"

Chen halted. "Lin ran his mouth too much. We were going to kill him anyway. Less ways to split the reward."

Little did he know that in the original plan, Jie was right: he would've died here, too.

Jie squirmed beneath her. "How did you even get the body here?"

Lilian pointed toward the others. "With help, of course, while you were warning the other girls."

"You never went to the safehouse to warn the clan."

She was putting it all together. Of course she would. Lilian smiled. "No. I needed the clan *not* to get further involved."

Jie's gaze shifted to the crates near the hearth. "The White Lightning and firecrackers. You are going to set the House on fire."

"Inspired by the training accident twenty years ago. I made sure all the girls and staff would be gone, and the distance from the mansion to the courtyard will keep the flames from spreading to the rest of the Floating World. The Gardener even agreed to douse the compound walls because I said they were too dirty for Lord Ting's visit."

Jie tilted her head toward the Florist. "What about her?"

Lilian's biggest regret. Still, nobody could know. She shook her head and kept her tone flippant, even as she ran a hand over Jie's cheek. "An unfortunate casualty, but her body is more likely to be mistaken for mine than the other one."

Jie's jaw tightened.

"I was worried you might figure it all out when the Gardener confined you to that specific storehouse."

"I was too busy crying over what that man did to me. Did you plan that, too?"

"No!" Lilian's heart sank. Despite the cruelty she was showing now, it hurt to think Jie would believe she could go that far. "Of course not. I never wanted you going to the Peony Garden at all, because then you'd find out they had nothing to do with Masked Crossbowman. I even told the Gardener to keep a guard at the door and below the window, and used a dwarf lock, which you somehow picked. I never imagined they would do that to you. Before I leave the Floating World forever, I will poison the Peony Garden's Gardener, ruin Lusha's face, and castrate your rapist."

Jie shook her head. "Your plan was worthy of the Architect, except that you left me alive."

Always part of the backup plan. Lilian brushed her cheek. She leaned in and whispered, "Don't you see? I never even wanted you here. When I left earlier, it was to trick Wen into getting you as far away as possible."

"So I wouldn't foil your assassination?"

Is that what she thought? Lilian's chest ached. "So I wouldn't have to make you choose between me and the clan."

"But you knew I'd come back. The crossbow bolt was meant for me to catch."

"A good plan always takes into account unlikely factors. Like this one." If only Lilian had taken into account the possibility of her employer hiring another assassin. His own backup plan. Now, it was time to mislead Su, even if a small part of her hoped Jie would agree. "Join me. We can start our own clan. A sisterhood. The ones who contracted me to kill Lord Ting will pay well for our skills. Please."

"I can't just betray the clan that adopted me."

"You have thirty seconds to decide." Lilian squeezed Jie tight. Of course she'd refuse. With one hand, she used one of the Surgeon's secret *Tiger's Eye* techniques to plant a suggestion in Jie's mind; with the other, she traced *bath house* in clade code on Jie's shoulder. "Please."

"Are you sure this is what you want to do? No one will ever have to know you were involved in this plot."

That Jie would keep that from the clan came as a surprise, and made Lilian feel even worse. "Then I'll just be spreading my legs at some other House."

"I understand." Jie brought her heels up to the edge of the seat.

Lilian slid deeper into Jie's lap. Jie pressed her cheek against hers.

Oh, this was Jie's set-up. Lilian braced for the first move, even as she pretended to be lulled.

The chair bucked. Jie fell backward, Lilian on top of her. The chair broke apart under their weight. Lilian protected her head as she went into a back roll. She ended up on her back. Jie stood over her, ankles tied and hands still bound behind her back.

Flipping to her side, Lilian scissor-kicked Jie's legs, missing as the half-elf vaulted up. The way she drew her knees to her chest and swung her bound arms out was a thing of beauty.

Lilian spun up with feet first, bent over, and landed in a defensive crouch. Around them, the men watched with wide eyes.

For her narrative to work, she needed to put on a show, and get the men in position for Jie to kill them. She launched a flurry of punches. "You tricked me!"

Even with all four limbs bound, Jie jumped back and landed on the table. Lilian slowed down her attacks to give Jie time to pick up a porcelain shard and saw through the rope around her ankles. She slid off, putting the table between them.

Lord Ting's men now closed with kitchen knives and cleavers. Lilian leaped onto the table, motioning Zhang and Su back so that they could deliver their respective messages.

Idiot that he was, Su paid no heed. He and Bei started around either side of the table.

Lilian needed to make sure he survived, or else the payment wouldn't be guaranteed. Then, she lost her balance as Jie threw the table up onto its side. Su and Bei rounded either side.

Shit, shit, shit. Even with Jie's hands still bound, Su was as good as dead.

At least Zhang was still alive to leave the message in the silk market.

Lilian took one last look at Lord Ting. The father of her child was dead because of her failure to foresee a second assassin. Heart squeezing, she turned and ran toward the exit, motioning for Chen and Zhang to light the trail of firepowder to the makeshift bomb by the hearth.

Snatching up a cloak she'd left near the door, she pulled the hood over her head and dashed out of the House. The gate guards started toward her, but she gestured them back. They needed to be back near the outer walls if they were to survive the explosion.

She slipped between their reaching hands, and swept up Lord Ting's *dao* set on a table inside the wall. She cleared the outer gate and arrived in the street. Chattering passersby afforded her curious glances.

The explosion rocked the Chrysanthemum Pavilion, flames blowing the first-floor shutters open. People on the streets dropped to the ground, covering their heads.

Lilian didn't look back. Instead, she broke into a run. Jie would be emerging from the baths soon, where she'd pick up Chen's tangy marinade scent.

Run. But to where? Her original plan had been for her and Lord Ting to use the confusion to escape the Floating World, then take back alleys to Songyuan Quays. They'd chartered a barge to take them all the way to Honggang in the North.

Now, Lord Ting was dead. With Su dead too, she might not even be able to claim the bounty. It was just her, and since Jie knew she'd survived, the clan would hunt her. She'd be living on the run, and when her belly swelled, she wouldn't be able to flee much longer. They'd catch her, for sure.

Her shoulders slumped. What did she have to live for anymore?

Vengeance.

Not for her family: Lord Yang's fate was sealed by the clues left in Tang Li's mind.

But for Jie.

Lusha.

Gardener Dan.

Shixian.

They'd all hurt Jie, and in a small way, had led to the failure of her plot tonight: had all gone as planned, Jie would've spent the night with the other House girls at the Red Boat Opera.

She caught sight of the Black Lotus Shrine. The light at the top of its spire shone, signaling the cell to retreat to the safehouse. None of the sisters would be able to stop her.

With her last bit of resolve, she ran to the Peony Garden.

* * *

The Present

During Tang Li's story, Tian pushed some tables and the heavy cross in front of the door. Now out of breath, he drew his sword.

The door thudded up against the makeshift barricade, sending the pile back a few inches. It wouldn't hold that long.

Another judder, and a few more inches opened up. Tian angled himself and stabbed at the closest attacker.

Then the door burst open, and men pushed in.

It was him, a ten-year-old boy, against dozens; his only chance was to use the door as a bottleneck.

A sword chopped down.

Side-stepping, Tian slashed across the man's midsection, opening up his gut. With the backstroke, he caught the second soldier trying to leap over his fallen comrade.

Still, there were just too many.

CHAPTER 22

The Present

Standing at entrance to the vaulting grand hall, Jie peeked in.

With several of his men in tow, Lord Yang was stomping down the middle. "Where is Lord Nan? Lord Gen? Lord Xun? Lord Fan?"

Jie smirked. She'd killed Lords Gen and Xun already, and used a Mockingbird's Deception to imitate their voices, giving their men conflicting orders. Now they were in disarray.

She scanned the entirety of the room, and counted thirty soldiers. To kill Yang with so many men around him, she'd have to get close enough with a throwing star.

Her gaze paused on another side entrance.

Sword in hand, Wen nodded and signed, *Nan, Fan, dead.*

Jie sucked on her lower lip. Though their plan and two backups hadn't worked, all of Lord Yang's allies were in dead, their soldiers leaderless. *Kun? Li? Meng? Yangyang? Wen? Meisha? Tian? Tang Li?*

Men dead, Wen signed, shaking her head. *Yangyang, Meisha unconscious. Tian and Tang Li defending.*

Three brothers, dead. Jie's chest tightened. Well, there were two of them, against over thirty men. She signed, *How many throwing stars do you have?*

None. Wen shook her head.

I have three. You create diversion, I'll take Yang. It might be a suicide mission, but—

Click, click, click. Thwip, thwip, thwip. Jie turned just in time to see three bolts darting toward her. Just like how Lilian's betrayal started.

She ducked back into the passage, and the bolts smashed into the walls nearby.

"Assassin!" the crossbowman yelled.

"Two! Girls!"

Shit.

Swords rasped from scabbards, tunics swished, and footsteps pattered toward her. She hazarded a glance out to see a group of five surging in Wen's direction, and another fifteen men running toward her.

And all Jie had was a knife. So unfair. She turned to run, only to find another six soldiers bearing down on her from the other side.

She ducked beneath the first slash, sidestepped the other, and sunk her knife into a third's liver. She grabbed his arm and pulled it into the direction of another hack. When the weapon slipped from his hands, she caught it.

Still, the onslaught pushed her into a corner. Swords in hand, several men encircled her, while spearmen formed up behind her.

* * *

Wen gauged the distance to Lord Yang. Five men bore down on her, but if she got past them, only thirteen guarded Lord Yang. Of course, there was also a soldier with a repeater, who could unleash the rest of his magazine in the time it took her to close the twenty feet.

She charged, and for a split second, her five attackers paused. Then they swarmed in. She slipped through thrusts and chops, and countered with quick stabs of her sword or the fling of a hairpin. Two men went down, and she was through, but now the remaining three were in pursuit, while more of Yang's guards formed up in front of him.

Click, whoosh.

She pulled up short as a crossbow bolt flew through where she would've been had she not stopped.

Click, swish.

She sidestepped the thrust of one of her pursuers, caught his wrist, and pulled him into the bolt's path. He cried out, and she plucked his sword away. She continued on a path to Lord Yang that kept the two others between her and the crossbowman.

"Kill her!" Lord Yang yelled.

With a communal shout, his guards rushed toward her. With them converging from one direction and the first group surging in from the other, she was surrounded in seconds.

There were too many.

She'd die tonight, having failed her mission. She looked to Lord Yang, who stood alone. Maybe there was a chance; if she could just slip between two of the men encircling her and dash, maybe she could reach him before—

A guard, face covered from the nose down with a scarf, came up beside Lord Yang, moving with lethal dexterity.

Hope guttered in Wen's chest as she dodged a stab.

"Yes." Lord Yang raised his fist, his voice triumphant. "Kill h—"

His scream pierced the air.

Everyone froze. Wen joined the others in craning their heads to see what happened.

"Traitor!" a man yelled.

"Kill the traitor!"

The guard who'd taken his place at Yang's side flicked blood off his sword and fled.

Many of his erstwhile comrades chased after him, revealing Lord Yang's headless body.

* * *

The dagger hilt felt slick in Tang Li's sweaty palm as she prepared to enter the fray. Tian had slain or incapacitated four men, who lay near the door, but now they'd pushed the boy back and started to flank.

She blinked away tears. This was finally it. An ignoble end to a street rat turned Blossom turned fixer. There'd be no teahouse in her future.

Muted horns blared.

Everyone froze and exchanged glances.

The horns sounded again, louder this time.

"Pull back!"

"Pull back!"

A chorus of voices echoed the same order.

The glaring soldiers backed out, then turn and ran.

"What happened?" Li let out a sigh of relief as Yang's men retreated.

"I'm not sure. It sounded like they gave up." Tian shook his head, but then stared at her. "You did something, didn't you?"

He was such a smart boy. Li grinned.

Tian's lips rounded. "But—"

Yangyang groaned and stirred.

Li looked down at her. "Are you all right?"

"No, I feel like the last time a Hummingbird drank me under the table." Yangyang held her head.

"Me too," Meisha said, sitting up. The blanket slid to reveal her slender form.

When she did nothing to cover up, Tang Li looked sidelong at Tian. More for the boy's innocence than Meisha's modesty, she wrapped the blanket around Meisha's chest.

The door swung open.

Tian turned, sword raised, but then relaxed.

Jie and Wen came in, blood splattered over their clothes.

Li's heart soared, even as she scanned them to make sure the blood wasn't theirs.

"It's over," Jie said. "One of Yang's men killed him."

Li smiled to herself. When she'd held the Surgeon with his own *Tiger's Eye* technique, she'd tricked his eyes into seeing Lord Yang as Jie. Of course, she wouldn't reveal to the Black Lotus that she knew the *Tiger's Eye*.

With an affection for Jie that probably came from Lilian's memories, she took the half-elf's hands. "Let me tell you the rest of Lilian's story."

* * *

One Week Ago

It was small consolation that in the aftermath of Lilian's botched fake hit on Lord Ting, everything else was falling into place. Because of the fire at the Chrysanthemum Pavilion, guests and Blossoms were streaming out of the Peony Garden to watch when Lilian arrived.

Slipping in through the rear gates, Lilian snuck in through the kitchens, then made a quick loop over the joists and joints of the second-floor mezzanine to scout. Gardener Dan stood at the front door, bowing to Hummingbirds as they left. On the second and third floors, it sounded like only one Blossom remained with a man—and as fate would have it, it was Lusha in the Corsage's room.

At least something was going right in this otherwise dreadful night. Lilian ducked into Wen's room. Stripping away the cloak, she searched among the poisons in the secret compartment beneath the rug. Most were intoxicants, affecting memory and lowering inhibitions, but like all Blossoms, she had a vial of powdered *yue* bark toxin.

Lilian slipped it into a pouch and took three of Wen's throwing stars. Using one of Wen's sashes, she tied Lord Ting's sword to her back, then crept down to the first floor and waited for the last people to leave. Despite the loss of business, Gardener Dan was grinning. Of course: with the Chrysanthemum Pavilion as her main rival for the wealthiest and most prestigious clients, she saw the fire as an opportunity.

One which she wouldn't live to enjoy.

Lilian darted out and seized the Gardener in a crook-wrist lock.

"Ow, ow, ow!" The Gardener gave up struggling, as any movement would send pain flaring through her wrist. "What are you doing here?"

"You're going to do something for me." With a foot, Lilian lowered the bar over the front door. Maintaining the joint lock, she guided the Gardener to the kitchen. She pointed with her chin at a kettle on a counter. "Pour two cups of tea."

"Why?"

Lilian squeezed tighter.

Jolting to her tiptoes, the Gardener yelped. "Okay, okay."

Loosening the lock, Lilian claimed a knife and set it to the Gardener's throat, ready to avoid a splash of hot water if she got any bright ideas.

Stiff as the corpse that she would soon be, the Gardener picked up the kettle and poured the tea into two cups. Steam billowed off it. "Why am I doing this?"

"We are going to have a talk." Lilian prodded the Gardener. It was time to establish a new narrative. "Now, carry those cups to your room."

"What do you want?" the Gardener demanded. "It this about the half-elf whore?"

Lilian dug the blunt end of the knife into the Gardener's throat, eliciting a shriek.

"Okay, I'm going." She picked up the teacups.

Lilian kept close, her sensitivity from years of grappling training preparing her against a possible attack from the Gardener. But no, she wouldn't try anything. Hope was such a dangerous tool. Right now, the Gardener hoped there was a way out of this, that she could satisfy Lilian's demands.

It was slow going as Lilian balanced the teacup and nudged the Gardener along, but at last, they arrived in the Gardener's room. The intricately carved furniture and paintings from famous artists had been bought on the backs of the Blossoms. Lusha's manufactured moans echoed in the hearth.

"Set them on your bedside table." Lilian uncorked the vial with a flick of her thumb. She turned the Gardener around and, blocking the view of the cups, dumped the powder in. She took a cup in each hand and passed the poisoned one to the Gardener. "Now drink, and we will talk."

The Gardener sniffed the tea, but the tea aroma would mask the scent of *yue* bark powder. "I'm not thirsty."

"Drink it."

The Gardener's tone grew desperate. "I won't be able to sleep. I have a small bladder—"

With Lusha's gasps echoing from the hearth as a backdrop, Lilian advanced on the Gardener with the knife.

"Fine." The Gardener brought the cup to her lips. Her throat bobbed as she gulped the liquid down. Just one sip would do it. "Now, what did you want to talk about?"

Lilian gestured to the bed. "Sit."

Brow furrowed, the Gardener did as she was told, wobbling as she did. "Fine, I'm sitting."

Lilian nodded. "Now, you will tell me where I can find Shixian."

"He's just a cavalry officer for the Huayuan Provincial Army." Gardener Dan wet her lips.

This, Lilian knew, but there'd been a telltale sign of a lie. "He's more to you, isn't he? A Hummingbird?"

Gardener Dan shook her head, with no sign of a lie.

"You're originally from Huayuan. Family, then?"

Gardener Dan's eyes widened for a split second, but she continued shaking her head.

"I see the resemblance now. Where can I find him?"

"It's not his fault." The Gardener shook her head. "I told him the half-elf was a gift for his promotion."

That would explain his reaction that night. Still, it didn't exonerate him. He'd still done the deed. "Where is he?" Lilian took a step forward, flipping the knife over in her fingers.

"Oh, you're so good," Shixian's muffled voice echoed in the hearth.

The Gardener sniffled.

Lilian smirked. The Heavens may have turned their back on her earlier, but now, they were making things too easy. "Thank you, Gardener Dan. You've been a worthy rival for many years. But now, you're probably feeling a little lightheaded. That's your brain shutting down."

"Huh?"

"I want your last thought to be of what you did to Jie. You will die knowing why I punished you and Shixian."

"It's not Shixian's fault." The Gardener's voice cracked.

"I won't kill him. I'm just going to make sure he won't sire ancestors to set offerings at your family altar."

"It...it was just...business." Gardener Dan collapsed onto her bed, eyes fluttering.

Lilian tucked her in.

Then, she crept up to Lusha's room and slid open the door.

Shixian lay on the bed, bound spread-eagle to the posts. Lusha straddled him, head thrown back in fake ecstasy as she rocked over his hips. Lilian had planned to quickly subdue Shixian before turning on Lusha, but this was just too easy.

With the thick carpet muffling her footfalls, Lilian tiptoed in, climbed onto the bed, and set the blade to Lusha's throat.

Lusha froze.

"What? What's wrong?" Shixian craned his neck. When his eyes met Lilian's, he gasped. "What are you doing here?"

"To join in on the fun. I see you like rope play." Lilian reached with a leg and picked up an unused length of cord between her toes. "Lusha, be a dear and tie that around one of your wrists."

"Lilian?" With a trembling hand, Lusha took the cord. She set it between her teeth and tied one of her hands.

"Now, wrists together."

"What are you going to do to me?"

"You should be asking what I will do to you if you don't listen." Lilian turned the knife and drew a line under Lusha's chin.

Lusha screamed. "All right, please. Please don't hurt me." She put her hands together, then whimpered while Lilian wound the cord around and then between her wrists.

"Now, hands above your head." Part of Lilian balked at the idea of what she was about to do. Did they really deserve this?

No, but when Jie found them, she'd know Lilian had done it for her.

Tying the cord around the knife handle, Lilian threw it over one of the rafters. Leaping off the bed, she caught it on the other end and tugged.

Squealing as the line pulled her, Lusha picked herself off of Shixian and tiptoed back to the edge of the bed.

Lilian came around. She let some slack out and pushed Lusha off. When she landed, Lilian pulled her to her tiptoes, then tied the end to the bedpost.

Taking no pleasure in vengeance, Lilian drew the blade over Lusha's face, while her victim screamed. Tears mixed in with the blood.

"Stop!" Shixian yelled, yanking at his bonds. "Please, stop."

Lilian turned to him. "Lusha and the Gardener plotted, but it was you who used magic to rape my sister."

"I didn't know!" He shook his head. "The Gardener told me she'd paid for it. That it was a gift. I didn't know about the virgin price. I swear. I—"

Lilian took hold of his manhood and cut it off.

He shrieked. Lusha's screams reached a crescendo, so loud that Lilian cut a strip of cloth from the bedding and stuffed it in her mouth.

Tears filled Lilian's eyes. Vengeance or not, this was just too cruel. What had she become?

A shadow flitted through the window. Lilian flung a throwing star at it, but whoever it was executed a beautiful handspring, twisted midair, and landed in a defensive crouch.

Jie. She held a knife in her right hand.

How did she find them? No matter how much Lilian had hid her true abilities, she couldn't match Jie in a knife fight. Switching to a side stance, she drew Lord Ting's sword. It was heavy, requiring both hands. "How—?"

"Don't you remember? You told me you'd come here to punish them."

Lilian laughed. "I guess you're not the only one with a blind spot."

"No." Jie's eyes darted left and right. "You planned everything so well, I'm surprised you didn't predict the possibility of a final confrontation."

"Who says I didn't?" Lilian said, even though she hadn't.

"Because I suspect I would already be dead." Jie lunged with a stab.

Gauging the timing, Lilian swept the sword toward where the knife would be.

Jie pulled up short. "You are full of surprises."

Blade extended. "I've always held back. Just like you taught me."

"You always let the other sisters win, then." Jie kept just out of range. "To hide your true ability."

Lilian lowered her weapon. "I'm not going back."

Jie shook her head. "The clan wouldn't take you back, after what you've done. I have no choice but to bring you in for questioning."

"Or let me go."

"You know I can't do that." Jie surged forward.

Lilian swept the sword in an arc, but Jie dodged and countered with a slash. In the ensuing flurry of slashes, Lilian held back as her blade bit into Jie's flank.

Jie jumped to the light bauble lamp. She removed the marble and crushed it underfoot, plunging the room into darkness. Then, she surged to Lilian's flank. Lilian turned and chopped.

Like a ghost, Jie came from the other side, capturing Lilian's wrist and then wrapping her up in her legs. The sword twisted out of her hands, and before Lilian knew it, her elbow buckled with pain. Jie must've used a *Ghost Echo* to throw her voice, and then jumped into an inverted arm bar. In the dark, her elf vision gave her an advantage. Now, her weight hung from Lilian's shoulder, threatening to throw her off-balance.

Doing her best to bend her elbow, Lilian reached across and grabbed her own wrist. Faced with relentless pressure, she thrust her shoulder down.

Jie slammed into the floor with an oomph, and her grip slackened.

Now free, Lilian popped up and sprinted to the door. She threw it open, allowing light to pour in from the common room. If only she could retrieve Lord Ting's sword...but no. Too risky, no time. She bounded across the hall and flipped over the mezzanine balustrade. Her feet landed on the second-floor railing, and she ran across it to a column, which she slid down.

She reached the front doors and unbarred them, then looked up to find Jie still on the third floor. Would this be the last time she ever saw her darling friend's face? If only their parting had been earlier, in her room.

But no, her plan had turned sideways when she hadn't taken into account the second crossbowman. With a sigh, she dashed through the front doors...

And skidded to a halt.

Outside, shadows moved around the courtyard. At first glance, over twenty, moving with silence and skill.

The rest of the cell.

If they didn't know she'd betrayed them, maybe...

No—if they were here, they probably knew.

This was it.

It was time to write a new narrative and set up her failsafe plan.

She turned and ran back in, closed the doors, and then barred them. She spun around to find Jie waiting, dagger in hand.

"What is it?" Jie pointed her dagger at the doors.

"The clan sisters."

Jie closed her eyes for a moment, then opened them. "They are spreading out to block every route of escape. You can't beat us all.

Just tell me who hired you to kill Lord Ting, so the clan won't torture it out of you."

Would Jie really let the clan torture her? Lilian closed the distance between them, shaking her head. "Oh, Jie. I don't know. Whoever it was knew that Lord Ting was my patron, and left a message offering me enough money to buy out my contract. I went to the meeting place, only to find another message with a vial and instructions to poison Ting. It was a crude mixture, one which he would've noticed before he drank enough to kill him. I left a message saying as much, and told my new employer to leave it to me. We've been corresponding ever since."

"And you did all this? Not knowing who your employer was?" Jie asked. "It could've been the clan, testing you!"

That had only been a consideration for about one day. Lilian shrugged. "I decided months ago that I was through with the clan, one way or the other."

"Where are you exchanging messages?"

All of this would help Jie uncover the truth. "I drop my messages off under the lucky cat figurine at the Jade Teahouse, and pick up messages from the same grove of trees the clan uses."

The cell sisters appeared on the mezzanine and archways in perfect synchronization. It was a testament to Jie's training regimen.

Lilian's heart filled with pride.

"What's happening?" Wen asked, expression contorted into confusion.

Lilian searched her eyes, wishing she could assuage her worry. But what could she say?

Yuna started to climb over the handrail.

Jie signaled them back with a hand.

Just the two of them. Tears threatened. All these years they'd been together. Lilian smiled. "Let this be our last dance."

Jie blinked away her own tears. "There has to be another way. The *Viper's Rest*, maybe."

Shaking her head, Lilian surged forward with her knife. Jie gave up ground, avoiding and throwing half-hearted counters.

Too half-hearted. Jie had to at least try to make Lilian's plan believable. "Come on!" Lilian slashed in a zigzag, with deadly precision.

"Jie!" Little Wen threw a shortsword over.

Lilian swept it out of the air, but Jie pulled it from the scabbard. Now armed with a sword in one hand and a dagger in another, Jie should've been overwhelming.

"Dead." Lilian stabbed Jie in the chest with the scabbard, then hit her ribs with the backstroke. "Dead. Come on, honor me with a good fight. I'm not going to hold back anymore."

Jie just gawked.

Anger welled in Lilian's chest. The only way to get Jie to fight was to use deadly force. Scabbard in one hand and knife in the other, Lilian surged forward with a barrage of cuts and stabs.

Jie moved like poetry. Together, their techniques blended in a beautiful flurry. It was as if they were two bodies, merged into one. Like the duel of their tongues, or the entangling of their bodies when they made love under the guise of practice. Lilian hazarded a glance up to see the sisters looking on with teary wonderment.

Pain bit into her wrist, and her fingers went slack around the knife. It'd severed her palmar tendons. Lilian swung with the scabbard, but Jie's blade cut through it. The broken edge flew through the air and scraped over Lilian's cheek.

She stumbled forward, careening into Jie. They both fell to the ground, Lilian on top. She lifted herself up. Jie appeared as a blur through her tears, as did all the sisters on the mezzanine. This was it. "They're all watching."

"It doesn't matter." Jie shook her head. "These aren't fatal wounds."

No, they weren't. Lilian could still survive this. Was it worth it? Lord Ting was dead, and the clan would learn of her treachery. Even if they allowed her to live, they'd raise her unborn child to become their tool. She smeared blood from her ruined wrist over her neck.

Jie started to throw the knife away.

Lilian caught her wrist with her good hand. There was another way. They locked gazes. Keeping close so the others couldn't see her hands, she moved her fingers in one of the Surgeon's secret *Tiger's Eye* patterns, followed by sign language: *Stab to the center of the throat; you will see a fatal wound.*

There were no major arteries or veins there. As long as Jie didn't stab too deep...

Jie's eyes glazed over for a split second, before her hand formed the subconscious signal of acknowledgement.

If this didn't work, this would be the last thing Lilian ever saw. Even if it did work, she might forget who she was forever. "Set me free," she said.

Jie stabbed.

The knife point headed straight toward the middle of Lilian's throat. At the last second, Lilian backed up a fraction just to make sure the weapon didn't sever her trachea.

The tip sliced through flesh, and pain seared through Lilian.

With a heaving breath, she put herself into the *Viper's Rest.*

* * *

The Present

Tang Li took a deep breath and met Jie's gaze.

Tears welled in the half-elf's eyes, and she shook her head. "I drove my knife through her neck. I saw the blood."

"You saw what she wanted you to see."

"What did she hope to accomplish? To wake up buried in a coffin, with no idea who she is?" Jie seized the collar of Tang Li's dress. "Why didn't you tell me this before? We need to send word to the temple before she runs out of air."

"I didn't remember until now," Tang Li said. "I'm not even sure how I could possibly know it, since all this happened after my last meeting with her."

Jie stalked out of the room, Wen on her heels.

"Where are you going?" Tian yelled at her back, before turning back to Tang Li.

"A clan courier station. I'm sure of it." Meisha held the back of her arm to forehead and groaned.

An urge tugged at Tang Li's mind. "I need to go home."

CHAPTER 23

The Present

Ever since she'd fulfilled her contract that Lord Yang had bought from the Chrysanthemum Pavilion, Tang Li had rented a secondary wing in a merchant family's courtyard home. Located inside the capital's walls, but close to the Trench, it had a private entrance in the rear that made for anonymous coming and going. The family never spoke more than a greeting to her.

Now, four days after Lord Yang's death at Cloud Castle, she finally made it home. She unlocked the gate, passed through to the tiny courtyard, and entered her house.

Even though nothing was out of place, something felt wrong.

She crept through the entry hall and peeked into the sitting room.

Her heart just about stopped.

Sitting in a chair with his back to her, a man with silver streaked through his hair leaned over the tea table. He was shuffling through her papers.

She'd acquired a knife in Cloud Castle, and her hand strayed to it now.

"This is quite good," the man said, holding up a painting.

The voice. She retreated a step, even as her eyes fell on Lilian's illustration of the training grounds of the Black Lotus Temple.

He looked over his shoulder, revealing the plainest face imaginable.

Master Yan.

"I remember this night, eleven years ago. Well, I certainly remember the one last week, since it kept us quite busy." Smiling, he held up another painting of the three full moons.

Lilian's failsafe, just in case Li wasn't able to see the celestial event. It would've triggered all the same memories.

"But this, this is like some of the experimental art the fair-skinned Estomari dabble in." Smirking, he gestured to a collage of four portraits—it'd been Lilian's attempt to get past the *Tiger's Eye* and depict the Surgeon. Sadly, it looked nothing like him.

Li opened her mouth to explain, but again, the Tiger had her tongue.

"I'm not quite sure what to make of this one." He held up a strange rune.

A new memory flooded back to her.

* * *

A Week Ago

Through her information network, Tang Li intercepted the request she'd been waiting for. The Golden Peacock Company—a Black Lotus shell company that usually acted as a front for its Fists embedded in the Floating World—needed a five-foot-long box shipped to the Golden Link Bakery in Lianjing.

The Golden Link Bakery also being a Black Lotus front.

How Li knew the Black Lotus Clan existed, she wasn't sure; she just knew that if she were in charge there, she would've established their own shipping company to move assets and Fists about the realm, and make money doing it.

In any case, given the size of the box, they were undoubtedly transporting Lilian's body back, never knowing she was in recuperating in the *Viper's Rest.*

How she knew, well... It had to be yet another one of the strange insights that made her such a good fixer.

And for whatever reason, Li was compelled to subcontract to Red Dragon Shipping, a semi-legitimate business of the Red Dragon Triads in the Trench. Legitimate, in that they were legally incorporated through the Ministry of Trade; not so legitimate in that they bribed officials to turn a blind eye to illegal *yue* shipments from the North.

The caravan consisted of six horse-drawn carriages carrying trade wares, all guarded by triads. One bore Lilian's box, along with one bereaved half-elf who spent the entire trip crying over said box. Li and Feng Rumei rode at the front of the next carriage, wearing leather armor and helms to hide their identities.

"Just a precaution," Rumei had said. "Because I can make her see us with different faces."

When the caravan stopped for a break, Jie finally left the box alone—and only because Rumei had used Empathy to plant a suggestion that she needed to relieve herself. Wiping tears out of her eyes, the half-elf disappeared into the woods.

"Come on." Rumei hopped off the carriage and trotted to the next.

Li followed. Inside, they opened the top of the box.

Lilian lay there, a peaceful expression on her pale face. She looked very dead.

"She's really alive?" Li asked.

Eyes closed, Rumei put her hand on Lilian's forehead and nodded. "Cold as death, but still alive."

"Why are you doing this?" Li wondered why Rumei was even here.

Rumei set her hand on Tang Li's forehead. "I love her."

Like the late Lord Ting. Like Jie. And like Li, too, perhaps.

Rumei's hand felt cold.

A surge of Lilian's memories flowed into Li's mind, and she staggered on her feet.

"Now," Rumei said, unfolding a sheet of paper. "You will forget this happened until you see this symbol."

What? Tang Li tried to turn away, but felt compelled to look at the paper.

* * *

The Present

Tang Li came out of the memory, heaving for air.

Master Yan studied her. "What recollection did that spark?"

There was no point in lying, since he had surely received word from Jie's courier about Lilian in the *Viper's Rest*. "It explained how I knew Lilian's last memories."

He nodded. "The most advanced techniques of the *Tiger's Eye* are powerful, but I think this goes beyond that. I suspect it has to do with Faceless Chang."

"Yes."

"Interesting bedfellows, you two. Though like my daughter, you all shared an affection for Lilian."

"Yes."

"Now, did you bring what I asked for?" He held out a palm.

With a bob of her head, she withdrew and unwrapped the Yu Dynasty seal. It'd been right where Lilian had hid it two years ago, deep in Cloud Castle. She set it in his hand.

He held it up to the bauble lamp and studied it, then turned to her. "Well, Fixer Zhang, I have one more task of you: my disciples left the Trench a mess. We need someone to fill the vacuum left by

Faceless Chang's death. You will become the new Faceless Chang." He set his fingers in the *Tiger's Eye* command.

Tang Li bit the tip of her tongue and dug her thumbnails into her index fingertips. Then, she flashed the hand signal for acknowledgement.

For now, she'd do it. The cleaning of the Trench—her own birthplace—would be a profitable endeavor, after all.

It would leave her a few steps closer to opening her own teahouse.

* * *

The Present

Feiying hated the frigid weather on the western edge of the Arkothi plateau; yet it was here, near the border city of Fronteros, that his patron implemented his forward-thinking ideas.

Among them, the training grounds where Feiying taught the stealth and fighting skills of the Black Lotus Clan. His students: Bovyans who were too small to serve as shocktroopers. Now, a month after killing the half-elf at Cloud Castle, Feiying waited in his patron's study. He'd snuck past all the staff and guards in Fronteros' palace, and had waited for an hour.

At last, the door finally opened.

Haros Bovyanthas, Consul of the Teleri Empire's Directori and Warden of the Western Marches, skidded to a halt. His hand strayed to his arming sword.

"Your Eminence," Feiying said, the Arkothi words tasting strange in his mouth after the months back in his homeland.

"Feiying." Haros' posture relaxed. "Where have you been all this time?"

"Cathay."

Haros studied him. "Did you finally get your revenge on your rival?"

"Yes." Feiying couldn't suppress his grin. At long last, the half-elf spawn was dead, and her father would mourn the loss. "Of course, I was looking out for your interests, as well. I've sown more seeds for the weakening of Cathay. They will be ripe for your plucking in ten years."

EPILOGUE

The Present

It'd been three days since the rebellion had died with Lord Yang, and Jie had finally reached the Black Lotus Temple with Wen and Tian. With no riders to take them, they'd jogged the entire way.

The courier relays would've arrived in a day. Surely Master Yan would've exhumed Lilian's coffin. Even in the *Viper's Rest*, she'd need fresh air. Probably more, since she was pregnant.

Now at the Black Lotus Temple, they left Tian behind in the main hall. Though fatigued to the core, Jie sprinted with Wen through the training grounds, asking anyone and everyone where Master Yan was.

When at last they found him, he was in the garden pruning *yinghua* flower vines.

"Master," Jie asked through heaving breaths. "Where is Lilian? Has she awoken from the Viper's Rest?"

He turned and smiled. "Yes."

A wave of relief washed over Jie, and she exchanged hopeful glances with Wen. "Does she remember who she is?"

"That's a little more complicated. Walk with me."

Complicated? With another glance at Wen, they followed him back the way they'd come.

Jie's pulse raced. Surely she would've seen Lilian had they passed her. If not, she certainly would've picked up her honeysuckle scent.

Her heart sank as they made their way through the bamboo maze between the training grounds and the public temple. It just about stopped when they came to the bridge to Lianjing town.

Master Yan pointed to a store off the highway.

Lilian.

Jie's heart soared.

Standing in a storefront, Lilian was bowing to a passing caravan.

Which meant she'd been Cousined.

Jie looked to Wen, whose brow furrowed in consternation.

"When she woke," Master Yan said, "of course she didn't remember who she was. I've used the most advanced *Tiger's Eye* techniques to ensure she never does. As far as anyone is concerned, the Yu Dynasty died with her father, Yu Qian."

Tears filled Jie's eyes. "Will I ever be allowed to talk to her?"

"Of course. You'll be here at the temple, training initiates. Including Little Tian. He has much catching up to do."

It was too cruel. To see Lilian on a near-daily basis, but never be able to tell her how she felt. The childhood they'd shared together. The affection between them. Jie's heart squeezed so hard, she couldn't draw her breath.

At her side, Wen was sobbing.

"I'm sorry, but that's the way it has to be." Master Yan sighed. "But if you desire, I can make you forget all about her, or that you were ever assigned to the Floating World."

* * *

Three Years Later

Li Mei wished she knew why her parents had given her such a generic name. It was one of the few things she recalled when she awoke hysterical in a doctor's office in Lianjing town, three years ago. She didn't remember her mother or father, or where she'd been born and raised.

Her last memory had been of receiving news of her husband. Along with the famous Lord Yang, he'd being slain in a skirmish with the fair-skinned barbarians to the north, who'd destroyed Cloud Castle by igniting its firepowder stores.

In her grief, she'd apparently tried to take her life by slashing her wrist and stabbing herself in the throat. Now, she worked an abacus, the four fingers on her right hand barely movable from the self-inflicted wound to her wrist tendons. Her neck, too, bore a scar; the doctor said it was a miracle she could still speak.

The greater miracle, her two-year-old son, played in the street with the other children. Thank the Heavens she'd lived, because it turned out she'd been pregnant.

Despite being a widow, life was good. She had incredible reflexes, a sharp memory, and an eye for detail; she'd found success in arranging trade deals. As the town beauty, more than one young man had asked for her damaged hand in marriage. She'd refused them all.

Because none stirred her heart like the half-elf girl, Jie.

She walked by now, as she did almost every day, with her friend Tian. She waved and smiled at Li Mei.

Oh, that smile!

Li Mei's heart fluttered.

The two were both temple wards learning to be scribes and accountants. It'd been amusing to watch their banter over the last two years: though she was older, he'd recently surpassed her in size and maturity.

As tempting as it would be to invite her for a cup of tea, it seemed Jie only had an eye for Tian. He, in turn, seemed in love with the memory of some girl from his past.

Part of Li Mei wanted to smack them over the heads and make them realize the blessings they had here and now, with each other.

The End

Jie's adventures continue in Songs of Insurrection, Book 1 of the Dragon Songs Saga.

APPENDICES

Provinces of Cathay

Province	Ruling Family	Resources
Dongmen	Zheng	grain, stone, guns
Fenggu	Han	Timber, rice, grain
Huayuan	Wang	Livestock, rice, wheat, lumber, firepowder, guns, precious metals
Jiangzhou	Liu	Timber, wheat, silk
Linshan	Lin	Wheat, millet, timber, porcelain
Nanling	Peng	livestock, steel, stone, gems, crossbows
Ximen	Zhao	Fishing, rice
Yutou	Liang	Fishing, rice, iron, copper, fish paste
Zhenjing	Wu	Ships, rice, fish

Twelve Counties of the North

County	Ruling Family	Resources
Changchun	Chang	Wheat, saltpeter
Chengfu	Yang	lumber, copper
Gulin	Su	Saltpeter, stone
Hongzhou	Heng	Fish, stone
Jinjing	Shi	Wheat, lumber
Lushan	Zu	Copper, bronze
Shashan	Zhang	Sand, quartz, stone
Tieshan	Nan	Iron, stone, saltpeter
Tonggang	Chu	Copper, stone, saltpeter
Xuejiang	Fan	Ice, saltpeter
Yindong	Zha	Silver, stone
Yushan	Ting	Jade, saltpeter

Time

As measured by the phases of the Iridescent Moon:
Full = Midnight

1st Waning Gibbons = 1:00 AM

2nd Waning Gibbons =2:00 AM

Mid-Waning Gibbons = 3:00 AM

4th Waning Gibbons = 4:00 AM

5th Waning Gibbons = 5:00 AM

Waning Half = 6:00 AM

1st Waning Crescent = 7:00 AM

2nd Waning Crescent = 8:00 AM

Mid-Waning Crescent = 9:00 AM

4th Waning Crescent = 10:00 AM

5th Waning Crescent = 11: 00 AM

New = Noon

1st Waxing Crescent = 1:00 PM

2nd Waxing Crescent = 2:00 PM

Mid-Waxing Crescent = 3:00 PM

4th Waxing Crescent = 4:00 PM

5th Waxing Crescent = 5:00 PM

Waxing Half = 6:00 PM

1st Waxing Gibbons = 7:00 PM

2nd Waxing Gibbons =8:00 PM

Mid-Waxing Gibbons = 9:00 PM

4th Waxing Gibbons = 10:00 PM

5th Waxing Gibbons = 11:00 PM

Celestial Bodies

White Moon: Known as Renyue in Cathay, and represents the God of the Seas. Its orbital period is thirty days.

Iridescent Moon: Known in Cathay as Caiyue, it is the manifestation of the God of Magic. It appeared at the end of the war between elves and orcs. It never moves from its spot in the sky. Its orbital period is one day, and can be used to keep time.

Blue Moon: Known in Cathay as Guanyin's Eye, it is the manifestation of the Goddess of Fertility. Its phases go from wide open to winking.

Tivar's Star: A red star, a manifestation of the God of Conquest. During the Year of the Second Sun, it approached the world, causing the Blue Moon to go dim.

Hunter Kor: A constellation, always in pursuit of the White Stag

Lycea the Betrayer: A star, avatar of the Goddess of Betrayals

White Stag: A constellation, always hiding from Hunter Kor

Fortuna: A constellation of the Goddess of Luck

Human Ethnicities

Aksumi: Dark-skinned with dark eyes and coarse hair. On Earth, they would be considered North Africans. They can use Sorcery.

Ayuri: Bronze-toned skin with dark hair and eyes. On Earth, they would be considered South Asians. They can use Martial Magic.

Arkothi: Olive-skinned with blond to dark hair and light-colored eyes. On Earth, they would be considered Eastern Mediteraneans. They can use Rune Magic.

Bovyan: The descendants of the Sun God's begotten son, they are cursed to be all male and live only to thirty-three years of age. They are much taller and larger than the average human. Their other physical characteristics are determined by their mother's race. They have no magical ability.

Cathayi: Honey-toned skin with dark hair and eyes. High-set cheekbones and almond-shaped eyes. On Earth, they would be considered East Asians. They can use Artistic Magic.

Eldaeri: Olive-skinned with brown hair. With features and small frames, they are shorter in stature than the average human. In a previous age, they fled the orc domination of the continent and mingled with elves. They have no magical ability.

Estomari: Olive-skinned with varying eye and hair color. They are famous for their fine arts. On Earth, they would be considered Western Mediterraneans. They can use Divining Magic.

Kanin: Ruddy-skinned with dark hair. On Earth, they would be considered Native Americans. They can use Shamanic Magic.

Levanthi: Dark-bronze skin and dark hair. On Earth, they would be considered Persians. They can use Divine Magic.

Nothori: fair-skinned and fair-haired. On Earth, they would be considered Northern Europeans. They can use Empathic Magic.

ACKNOWLEDGEMENTS

First, I would like to thank my wife and family for the patience they have afforded me as I pursued my childhood dream of fiction writing.

A huge thanks to my sister Laura for her spectacular job with the maps and covers.

And finally, an even huger thanks to the readers of The Dragon Songs Saga who contacted me, wanting to know more about Tian. You are the reason this book happened. Of particular note are Brittany Timmins, Samantha Mikals, and Ticiana Marques, who bombarded me with messages about the characters.

And, no thanks could be complete without mentioning my long-time crit partners, JC Nelson and Kelly Walker.

ABOUT THE AUTHOR

JC Kang's unhealthy obsession with Fantasy and Sci-Fi began at an early age when his brother introduced him to The Chronicles of Narnia, Star Trek, and Star Wars. As an adult, he combines his geek roots with his professional experiences as a Chinese Medicine doctor, martial arts instructor, and technical writer to pen epic fantasy stories.

www.ingramcontent.com/pod-product-compliance
Lightning Source LLC
Chambersburg PA
CBHW030345310726
48979CB00001B/191

* 9 7 8 1 9 7 0 0 6 7 0 3 3 *